Greenwood Riven

V.L. Purvis-Smith

Acknowledgements

When the European War raged and Pearl Harbor was attacked, people reacted to forces over which they had little control, constrained by discrimination patterns peculiar to their communities. Thank you to the individuals, institutions, and organizations who helped me imagine how people grappled with those challenges in fictional Greenwood county, a farming community on Colorado's High Plains.

Among the individuals who contributed knowledge of events during that era are Fred Arguello, Jesus Beruman, Ann Purvis Bogner, Pauline Cardenas, Joyce Coville, Alice and John Deatherage, Shirley Sakai Gunning, Dorothy Reyher Keding, Allen and Rose Maruyama, Minoru Mochizuki, Robert Moriguchi, Tayeko Namura, Kathryn and Robert Reyher, Robert H. Rawlings, Iola Woods, and Tencha Avila, specifically, her play *No Number Home* that portrays the fear and conflict engulfing a colonia when a son goes AWOL.

Institutions and organizations include the Amache Preservation Society and Museum, Granada, Colorado; the site of Camp Amache, a National Historic Landmark; the Denver University Amache Research Project; the Denver Public Library's Genealogy, African American and Western History Resources; the Pioneer Historical Society of Bent County, Las Animas, Colorado; the Lamar Public Library, Lamar, Colorado; the Trinidad History Museum, Trinidad, Colorado; the Presbyterian Historical Society, Philadelphia, Pennsylvania; the Henry Ford Museum, Dearborn, Michigan; the Union Pacific Railroad Museum, Council Bluffs, Iowa; the Lester F. Larsen Tractor Test and Power Museum, Lincoln, Nebraska; the

Japanese American National Museum, Los Angeles, California; and local newspapers of the period.

I am especially grateful to Lighthouse Writers Workshop, Denver, Colorado, and faculty member Douglas Kurtz who graciously mixed challenge and encouragement appropriate to my needs.

Innumerable friends and family members supported and urged me to bring this book to completion including my husband, Terry Purvis-Smith; my son and daughter-in-law, Steven and Kelly Adams-Smith; my daughter and son-in-law, Julie and Guillaume Fouque; grandchildren André, Ben, Melanie and Sophie; sister-in-law and brother-in-law Pat and Frank Eichenlaub; and friends Nancy and Dan Hofmann.

Contents

June 1939

Martha McLennan Lundgren

She slid the knife blade into loose, damp earth and tracked the dandelion's root. Clutching its leaves and flowers, she eased it from the soil and peeked over her shoulder at the playpen under the guise of tossing the weed into the bucket.

Anna's chin rested on the topmost rail, her pout radiating a two-year-old's injured pride at being confined. Her heaving shoulders kept time with each residual sob, but Martha couldn't pull dandelions and prevent Anna's likely dash for the irrigation ditch that ran full.

Martha's subterfuge led to scratches from thorns on an overgrown rose bush and an errant dandelion. She busied herself with the next one, threw it toward the bucket, escaped the thorns, and glanced at Anna.

Resigned, Anna had plopped on her bottom and was tugging at blades of grass through the playpen bars, protected in shadows cast by the line of cottonwood trees separating front yard from lane. Martha leaned back on her heels.

She looked north for the dust trail marking the Case tractor's progress. Each decrease in the angle of sunlight had lengthened the slivers of shade cast by the still-short corn, and she no longer had

1

to squint against the glare. The muscles of her face and shoulders softened, along with the contours of the high plains.

Art drove the tractor near the fence by the county road, which meant the cultivator had turned under acres of weeds since she last checked, but she hadn't finished half the yard. She turned back to dandelions.

She heard a vehicle's triple honk, the signature greeting of her younger brother ever since he got his '35 Ford pickup as a high school graduation gift last month. Anna squealed, anticipating a visit from her favorite uncle. Leave it to Alex to disrupt the equilibrium with her daughter, but the truck, its ordinarily shiny black surface covered with dust, passed the lane. Boys crammed into the cab and back waved and shouted. She lost sight of them in the cloud of dirt and gravel kicked up by the tires. Spurned a second time, Anna stood and shook the playpen's rails.

Determined to snatch more time for weeding, Martha wiped sweat from her forehead and licked the scratches on her arm to stop the stinging. She tucked wayward strands of her wavy black hair into the bandana and saw Anna's blue ball rolling by the bucket. Martha resisted the invitation.

With another triple honk, Alex passed Art. He must be headed to the canal that ran along the north side of the place she and Art rented from Papa. A quick dip in the swift current of mountain snow runoff would refresh the boys before their softball game. But Alex shouldn't exploit his popularity with his chums on account of his new truck.

Anna cooed with delight, and Martha involuntarily turned. A small stack of grass rested in the playpen between Anna's legs, and she gripped a dandelion flower. It dangled on its long stem; she maneuvered it toward her mouth. Martha laughed, stood, and rescued the flower. She brushed the yellow pollen off Anna's cheek and wiped blades of grass from her lips.

Martha scanned the cornfield and spotted Art driving toward the house alongside the fence. The canal's ridge was visible on the horizon a half-mile away. The black pickup sped toward him, coming back down the road. She tightened her grip on the squirming Anna and watched Art jump off the tractor, crawl through the barbed-wire fence, hop over the irrigation ditch, and vault into the truck bed. The pickup turned and raced toward the canal.

She tucked Anna under her arm and sprinted into the house for her medical bag. Within minutes she wedged Anna's box that Art had built between the seat back and dashboard in the cab of their battered Chevy pickup parked by the back porch. She set Anna and the medical bag in the box and drove to the end of the lane. Alex's truck rushed toward her.

She shifted into neutral by the mailbox. Alex slowed. Art and Luis Marquez sat on their knees in back, hunched over something.

Art lifted his head, dripping wet, and screamed, "It's Frank Ogawa! Goin' ta the hospital. Get the others!"

Martha yelled for Alex to stop so she could trade places with Art, but Alex took off.

Alex should have come to her first. He knew she was in the front yard. Perhaps the shock of whatever happened made him seek help from Art, who was closer, but if Frank's injuries were so critical he had to be taken to the hospital, she should be with him. She considered chasing them down, but they'd be in town before she caught up, and Frank would be in Doc Claffey's hands.

Toshiro Miyoshi

She slipped the truck into gear and sped to the canal, turning just short of the bridge onto rutted tracks that ran beside the water, and the whole lot of abandoned boys clambered in, some still pulling on their clothes. As she'd suspected, most of the church softball team.

Ken Himuru took Anna from her box, tossed it with the medical bag into the back, and jumped into the front seat after Maurice Giffard. "Drop me off at Mr. Miyoshi's. I can't explain clearly to the Ogawas in Japanese what's happened to Frank, but I'll tell Mr. Miyoshi. He'll take me and translate."

Martha gave Ken credit for having a plan, but the haste with which the usually taciturn Ken removed Anna and ordered Martha to Mr. Miyoshi's betrayed his panic. He wasn't taking into account that Mr. Miyoshi would be nearly as upset as Frank's parents, Mrs. Ogawa being his sister-in-law. Ever since his wife and daughter died in childbirth nine years back, he'd nearly adopted the Ogawa children.

"Ken, be considerate of Mr. Miyoshi. The Ogawas are his only family."

"Mr. Miyoshi thinks of us all as nieces and nephews, Mrs. Lundgren. He'll understand."

Martha didn't argue. That Mr. Miyoshi would understand was beside the point. Ken didn't know Mr. Miyoshi as well as she did and should break the news gently. Her friendship with Mr. Miyoshi began when she was an infant. In the early years he sharecropped for Papa and now rented from Papa, too. He, Papa, and Art shared everything — equipment, failure, and success.

She turned into Mr. Miyoshi's lane, just south of theirs. Ken reached across Maurice and pressed the horn in a series of blasts, clearly disregarding her advice to ease the shock.

Mr. Miyoshi emerged from his barn, and, as the Lundgren pickup rolled to a stop, Ken jumped out. He handed Anna to Max Lambert, who had jumped out of the truck bed. Martha pushed her door open to follow Ken so she could hear the report about Frank's accident, but Maurice's pallid complexion stopped her.

"Maurice!" she yelled.

He didn't respond. Max started to climb into the cab with Anna.

"Max, wait," she said. "Give Maurice air."

Maurice toppled forward; his forehead rested on the dashboard.

Martha shouted to Hugh Ufford to hand her the medical bag. Alex's friend since first grade reacted immediately because Martha was as much his bossy big sister as she was Alex's.

She readied the smelling salts, eased Maurice's head and shoulders back, and waved the salts under his nose. Ken approached Mr. Miyoshi, who listened for a moment before disappearing into the barn where he kept his Studebaker.

Martha turned to Hugh. "Tell me what's happened, now."

Hugh opened his mouth, but Max, juggling Anna in his arms, sobbed from the other side of the truck. "We don't know! Frank an' Jimmie had their clothes off before we got ta the canal."

Martha watched Anna's mouth pucker, prelude to a howl, balanced the unsteady Maurice against the back of the seat, and ran around the front of the truck to rescue her.

Judging Max to be the most immediate source of information, she said, "Continue."

She needn't have wasted her breath. He jabbered on. "The two of 'em jumped out of the truck as soon as Alex stopped, an' Frank dove off the side of the bridge. The rest of us undressed pretty quick, but then we heard Jimmie screamin' he couldn't find Frank. We all jumped in but the water was movin' fast, an' it was deep. Luis Marquez found Frank underwater, stuck in what some thought were the branches of a tree that washed down, but the water was too muddy for me ta tell. The current started washin' Luis an' Frank away, an' we all grabbed hands with Ken holdin' onta the pilin's under the bridge. Alex left; I thought he went for you, you bein' a nurse an' all. We were tryin' ta pull 'em out when Alex came back with Mr. Lundgren. I don't know if Frank was breathin' or not. Maybe he hit his head, or got stuck. We don't know. We just don't know!"

The telling overwhelmed Max, and his sobs choked off his speech.

Mr. Miyoshi pulled alongside her. She reached through the Studebaker's open window and touched his arm. "Will you be all right?"

"Yes, but it is difficult. You should be with Frank."

"I agree. By comparison, a crying baby and a fainting boy are minor problems anyone can solve. Please, hurry to the Ogawas."

"I'm not a cry baby, Mrs. Lundgren, I'm not," Max protested.

"Max, I was referring to Anna. You're very brave for what you're going through."

From his description, it was possible that, in those early minutes of the emergency, Alex had decided Art's physical strength was more important than her nurse's training. That she could understand, but Alex should have stopped at the mailbox for her.

The ordeal was more than the boys could handle, judging by Max's sobs and Maurice's fainting spell. As the youngest, Jimmie Ichikawa sat frozen in the back corner of the truck bed. Completely uncharacteristic of the boy known as the perpetual motion machine.

"I'm driving everyone home."

They responded with a chorus of protests that they go directly to the hospital.

"No, your parents'll take you."

Reverend Murray Macgill

After she dropped off the last boy, Maurice, at his house in town, she laid a sleepy Anna in the box. The way to the hospital took Martha by the drugstore where her younger sister, Alex's twin, worked at the soda fountain. Louise emerged as Martha drove by. Martha honked, and she strolled over.

Annoyed by Louise's unhurried response, Martha quickly described Frank's accident and concluded with, "So, come with me. I'll stop at Josie's where you can keep Anna while I run to the hospital. Josie and Earl'll want to know about Frank. He's probably in Earl's history class and Boy Scout Troup, and Josie taught him at Eagle View. And you should call Papa. Hopefully, he hasn't already left for the ballgame. Even though Art's with Alex at the hospital, Alex is sure to be frantic."

The tragedy captured Louise's attention. Frank was only two years behind her and Alex. She answered with uncharacteristic solicitude. "Sure, I'll help."

Before Martha could thank her, Louise added, "Of course, there won't be a ballgame."

Martha didn't respond to the obvious.

She relayed the afternoon's events as Josie, their older sister, served supper. When Martha finished, Josie carried the full plates to the refrigerator.

"What are you doing?" asked Earl.

"We're going to the hospital," Josie said. "I taught Frank, his sister Suzie, and most of the boys on the church team at Eagle View and in Sunday school. Now they're in your classes."

"Josie, there's not enough space in that tiny hospital for a crowd, and I'm hungry."

Even Louise stared at him. She snapped, "Earl, they might not do it this way where you're from in Montana, but here in Greenwood, when calamity touches so many, everyone goes. Folks'll notice who's come and who hasn't. As one of Frank's teachers, you have to be there."

Martha and Josie nodded their agreement.

Earl threw up his hands. "But we'll ride with you, Martha. No need to clog up the street with extra vehicles."

Martha crossed the highway that ran through Greenwood and joined a caravan winding toward the hospital. She fell in line between the Lamberts and the Uffords. Mr. Miyoshi's Studebaker was parked in front, and vehicles belonging to families of boys on the team were pulling into the church's gravel lot across from the hospital.

Martha, Josie and Earl followed Maurice and his parents, Edith and Claude Giffard, into the building. Martha and Josie exchanged their surprise with raised eyebrows because Claude rarely left his business at the lumberyard, not even for ballgames. Edith tended to get emotional at the slightest provocation and avoided the hospital. But Edith seemed rather subdued, and Martha didn't speak so as not to unsettle her.

The Ogawas occupied the alcove, the area customarily reserved for the family in crisis. Martha bowed her head to Mr. and Mrs. Ogawa, both of whom returned the greeting. Mr. Miyoshi's hand rested on Mr. Ogawa's shoulder.

Their three other children sat at their feet, a group that included Marguerite Marquez. Marguerite's arms encircled Suzie Ogawa, who sobbed against Marguerite's chest.

Martha followed Josie and Earl down the corridor, puzzled that Marguerite would be so familiar with Suzie, and in these circumstances. She grabbed Josie's hand and drew her close. "Why is Marguerite here?"

"Surely you remember Suzie and she were school chums in fifth grade," Josie whispered. "When I promoted Marguerite from fifth to seventh, both were unhappy about the separation. From what we just saw, though, they're still close."

Perhaps the Ogawas accepted the Spanish girl on account of her school achievements; Marguerite wasn't an ordinary field hand.

Other families lined the hallway and generated an unnerving silence. Martha spotted Art and Alex in a cluster near the operating room door that included Luis and Elena Marquez, Marguerite's older brother and sister.

Luis slid down the wall and squatted on his haunches, elbows on his knees. He held his head in his hands. Elena rested her hand on his shoulder; next to Luis on the other side Alex replicated Luis's pose. Martha, Josie, and Earl joined them.

Art shook his head, indicating the outcome was in doubt. Martha's anger flared. She didn't fault Alex. He was only eighteen and he'd panicked, but Art should have had the presence of mind to exchange places with her in the truck bed. Perhaps if she had been standing by the mailbox with medical bag in hand, Alex would have stopped long enough for the transfer.

Marguerite joined Elena and Luis, more appropriate than with Suzie Ogawa. And it was right they be with Alex. Last year, the two boys witnessed Luis's father's death. José Marquez, the McLennan's hired hand, climbed up the front of the McLennan hay wagon and it splintered. He fell. The horses bolted and dragged the wheels over his body. Unable to save José, now the boys shared the anguish of Frank's accident.

Martha prepared herself for a long wait, but the front door banged open as prelude to Jimmie Ichikawa's entrance. Disapproving sighs ruptured the silence.

"I found Rev. Macgill at the ball field!" Jimmie shouted. "He's right behind me."

The sighs changed to murmurs of approval. News of Rev. Macgill's imminent arrival also calmed Martha. Many of the Japanese children attended the church, and Rev. Macgill was popular with the young folks. Besides, he announced all the games, and the boys involved with Frank's accident played on the church team.

Rev. Macgill knelt in front of Mr. and Mrs. Ogawa and took their hands in his. Perhaps he spoke; Martha couldn't tell. Then he worked his way toward Alex and Luis, a handshake here, a squeeze on the arm there.

Papa had slipped in behind Rev. Macgill. He must have been preparing the ball field when Jimmie delivered his news. Papa stayed by the door, removed his hat, and scanned the room until he located his family. When he did, Martha signaled with a shake of her head, duplicating the one Art gave her. Papa responded with a sigh that expanded his broad chest.

Tears filled her eyes. She wasn't that different from Maurice; both needed their papas to bear the tragedy's weight.

Rev. Macgill stopped in front of Luis, who stood to greet him. Rev. Macgill refused Luis's hand, embracing him, instead. The slight Luis, engulfed in Rev. Macgill's massive arms and held against his big belly, nearly disappeared. Now the fatherless Luis had a man to lean on. Rev. Macgill frequently led services at the Spanish church across the railroad tracks that the Marquez family attended; sometimes,

Alex sang in their choir. Alex stood, and Rev. Macgill pulled him into the protective circle.

Ken Himuru's family arrived — his white mother, Japanese father, and sister. In spite of Ken's earlier, intrusive behavior, Martha admired his efforts to overcome his reserve and pursue his objective of taking Mr. Miyoshi to translate the news about Frank's accident to his parents. Ken's sister, Lily, moved between groups as Rev. Macgill had. When she reached Luis, she delivered what sounded like the Ogawas' formal thank you for finding their son in the murky water.

Martha stood opposite the operating room door, so she was the first to see Doc Claffey emerge. Because she had worked in his office during breaks in her nurses' training, she recognized his neutral expression, the mask that concealed dreadful news.

"Broken neck. Nothing we could do," he whispered as he passed by.

Relief tempered her sorrow because she included herself in the "we," as part of his team. Nothing she could have done. Still, she should have been standing by the mailbox with bag in hand, and Art should have made Alex stop.

Art put his hand on her shoulder, and she answered his unspoken inquiry with bowed head. She hesitated before slipping her arm through his.

Rev. Macgill followed Doc to the alcove. Everyone understood the choreography. As they exited, the family clusters cast sympathetic glances toward the Ogawas. Martha was the last to reach the front door. She turned and watched Mr. Miyoshi, Rev. Macgill, and Doc support the grieving family on their walk down the corridor to view the body.

March and April 1941

Elena Marquez

"Push. Harder! Again!"

Martha pretended to make an effort but maintained the foolhardy belief that she had power to stop premature labor. She didn't remember having such intense contractions with Anna. She withdrew and imagined herself curled under the boughs of the spruce tree in the Home Place front yard. She rested on a bed of crushed fallen needles whose odor mingled with that of moist dirt. In this, her childhood haunt, a breeze moved. The air entered the cups of her ears, brushed gently against the skin and explored each ridge of cartilage.

The ache in the small of her back throbbed; she screamed simultaneously with the sharp cramp in her abdomen. Light from the yellow bulb dangling above the gurney penetrated the twilight of her daydream, and she yanked her head to the side. Her knees snapped shut. She heard Doc curse and let her legs flop open.

Before she registered the meaning of his words, "I'm inserting forceps," she winced. Cold metal touched the labia. She shrieked as it absorbed the heat of her labor and burned into the vagina.

She escaped the pain by fixing her attention on the incongruity of Elena Marquez stumbling through the door with her mop and bucket. Elena raised her head, and Martha saw her own fear reflected in Elena's black, iridescent eyes. Elena's lips moved. Martha strained to hear, but the sound disappeared into the walls and ceiling.

Martha focused on Elena's eyes and started to fall into pooled depths of distress and sympathy, but Elena's scream arrested Martha's descent. Elena released the mop and bucket and brought her hands to her cheeks. "*Dios mio!* He will kill her, and the baby!"

No one moved to silence Elena. Perhaps she was an apparition, visible and audible only to Martha. Martha's gaze shifted to Elena's open mouth, and her fall resumed into its dark recess.

Carrie Lundgren

Three days later, exhausted, Martha held Carrie to her breast and caressed the pink lips, willing them open. Carrie licked drops of milk oozing from the nipple and savored the taste.

She reminded Martha of a newborn calf, but when Martha squirted milk into its face, it sucked the teat into its mouth and butted the udder. Carrie's random movements bore no resemblance to those of a resolute calf. Only after innumerable swipes did Carrie take the nipple. Asleep, she lay placidly; awake, she intermittently jerked her head, which was covered in dark, curling hair, and her stiff arms flailed until Martha corralled them.

Martha cupped Carrie's head in her hand and tried to steady it against her breast, but Carrie's strained neck muscles resisted guidance. Even when Carrie found the nipple, Martha couldn't straighten Carrie's taut legs to prevent the knees from poking her abdomen.

Carrie swallowed and gagged. Her mouth clamped shut. Yet, again, Carrie would wake in an hour, ravenous and agitated.

Art arrived well after sundown, looking as exhausted as Martha felt. For several weeks he, Papa, and Alex had farmed their places and Mr. Miyoshi's, ever since Art had found Mr. Miyoshi collapsed by the tractor in the middle of a field. Thankfully, Art got him to town before the appendix ruptured. Mr. Miyoshi spent ten days in the hospital and would recover soon enough, but cows needed milking and hogs had to be fed.

Alex did Mr. Miyoshi's morning chores, and Art finished the evening ones at both farms before he visited the hospital. Neither she nor Art resented helping. Mr. Miyoshi did the same, and more, for them, and, before that, for Papa and Mama, as a sharecropper.

Art took off his hat and ducked through the door out of habit, even though he had clearance. Martha smiled as she always did when she bothered to notice the contrast between his white forehead and sun-browned cheeks.

"What? Are ya laughin' at me, woman?"

He leaned over, lightly brushed her lips with his, and took Carrie from her arms, a series of gestures executed so smoothly they were completed before Martha reacted to anything more than the kiss. The grace of her tall, gangly husband still charmed her. Their baby lay almost hidden in his bony hands. Cradled. Safe. Martha's body ached to feel the same comfort.

He watched her watching his hands. When she looked into his light-blue eyes, she caught her breath. The compassion reminded her of Elena's when the forceps entered her body. Martha's tears, at the surface since Carrie's birth, ran down her cheeks.

"You probably know I blacked out when she was born. She's not quite right."

The speaking of it made it real. Martha had barely allowed herself to think it, even though she knew from how folks glanced at Carrie.

An expected response would be to hover over the bassinet and coo. Instead, a curious peek and a surprised, "She's tiny, but so beautiful!"

In a soft voice he said, "Martha, Doc thinks if Carrie survives, we should put 'er in the Children's Home in Denver. He thinks we won't be able ta handle 'er. He thinks it'll be better fer us all, 'specially Anna."

His tone was matter-of-fact, and her comprehension lagged behind, as it had when Doc made his announcement about the forceps.

She roused herself. "Put her away? How do parents not keep their baby? How would that be better for Anna? What would she think when she's old enough to know we gave away her little sister?"

The idea was so foreign Martha's questions would have continued had Art not interrupted. "Anna might not remember there was a little sister, leastwise, not this little sister. Doc says there's no reason we can't have other children. Doc says…"

"Doc thinks! Doc says! Doc doesn't know. No one does. Besides, it's his fault. He wants to hide Carrie. She's evidence he could have killed us both with the forceps, just as Elena Marquez said!"

"Elena Marquez?"

Martha rose to a sitting position. Her bottom ached. She grabbed the bedrails and half-lifted herself but didn't dare pivot back. If she let go, she would land on her rear and fall against the pillows. The muscles in her arms quivered from holding her weight. She cried out, anticipating the pain.

With characteristic fluidity, Art was out of the chair, baby in one arm, the other serving as a lever against her back to ease her down while taking off the pressure. His sudden movement was sure to wake Carrie, and Martha anticipated her cry, dreading the struggle that awaited them with the next feeding. She felt tingling in her breasts, and the milk started to come, but the only sounds she heard were her own sobs.

Emma Miyoshi

Martha sat outside the hospital door on a wooden chair, grateful for the warmth of a late-afternoon sun. She held Carrie, all bundled up against a brisk April breeze, but Cora Jane Collins, recently graduated from the same nursing school as Martha, insisted they come in. The women reached a compromise. Cora Jane slipped a pillow under Martha's bottom and held Carrie just inside the door.

Because Martha was looking for Art in their green pickup, she didn't pay attention to the gray Chevy coupe that parked in front of the hospital until Art emerged from the driver's side. Then she recognized the vehicle. Mr. Miyoshi had purchased it new last year and drove it on special occasions; otherwise, it stayed in his barn. His coupe and their '33 Chevy truck that Papa bought at Peter Collins's foreclosure sale in '35 shared nothing other than the manufacturer's name and four wheels.

Circumstances in Cora Jane's life overlapped those in Martha's. Not only did Papa buy the pickup two years after Mama died; he bought the Collins farm. Martha now lived in the house where Cora Jane grew up. Both she and Cora Jane enrolled in nursing school after devastating loss — Martha's, of her mother; Cora Jane's, of her family's farm. Any money left from the sale had most certainly gone to Cora Jane's education and the purchase of her parents' Country Store.

When Art reached the hospital steps, he ducked his head and grinned. "I'll tell ya 'bout the coupe after I get ya in."

Martha sank into the soft upholstery, Cora Jane handed over Carrie, and Martha said, "This is the most comfortable I've felt in over a week. You surely didn't ask to borrow this."

"Ya know me better 'n that. Yer father offered 'is Chrysler yesterday, an' I was gonna drive it, but last night, when Miyoshi and me was eatin' supper…"

"Mr. Miyoshi came for supper?"

"Well, not 'xactly. He's feelin' lots better. The past week he's been at our house fer breakfast a few times 'cause he's gettin' started with repairs on the stalls in our barn. It's light work he can handle while he builds strength. I've eaten supper there, now an' then."

"With Anna?"

"Sometimes. Other times, she's been with yer family at the Home Place. Thing is, Miyoshi still has leftover food. All the Japanese wives cooked fer him when he came home from the hospital. Ya know how they are when we combine at one a their places. If there's six men, they cook fer sixty. Maybe not that extreme, but the table's covered with food — chicken, beef, pork, rice, bread, all kinds a potatoes, vegetables, an' not just one pie er cake but a couple a each. Miyoshi's 'frigerator an' his cellar're still like that table, so we been tryin' ta make a dent in it."

"Sounds like quite the sacrifice."

Martha pictured the abundance and was delighted Anna had participated in some of the meals so as to be better acquainted with Mr. Miyoshi.

"Anyhow, when I finished our chores an' his last night an' we was doin' our best ta take care a all that food, he offered his coupe ta bring ya home. I said I'd be takin' yer father's Chrysler, but he persisted. Ya know how he is when he's determined 'bout somethin.'"

Martha nodded and lifted the blanket covering Carrie's face. She slept peacefully, and everything about her looked like a normal, beautiful baby girl, just a very small one.

"Finally Miyoshi reached 'cross the table, put his hand on mine, an' said he wanted ta tell me 'bout his wife an' baby. I don't know what surprised me more, that he had a child or that he would tell me, well, such a private story."

"Art, we've talked about this, although not recently."

"Must a been when we first married, 'fore I was familiar with 'im. I forget details when they're not attached ta folks I know."

"I'm sure I told you his wife came from Japan with Mrs. Ogawa. They were sisters, and the families in Japan arranged the marriages. Mr. Ogawa went to Japan for his wife, but Mr. Miyoshi's was what they call a picture marriage. He met her when the ship docked in Seattle. As I remember, their mother eventually came to this country and lives with Mrs. Ogawa's brother in California."

"I'll be," said Art. "Min an' Lucy Himuru are exceptional, him marryin' a white, American woman."

"Well, yes, I suppose so, but no one I know talks openly about the Himurus' unusual marriage, and Min and Lucy seem to move comfortably between Japanese and American families. The children, Ken and Lily, don't seem to have trouble. But with Mr. Miyoshi, I know the story about his wife and baby because I was there, not for the birth but shortly after. I was nearly fifteen, and Mama and I went to help, the year before she died. Instead of me telling it, though, I'd like to hear Mr. Miyoshi's version."

"What I'm 'bout ta say isn't quite his words. He was more, delicate. They'd been married fer a while 'fore his wife got pregnant, an' the baby came early, like Carrie. She was born at home, an' Miyoshi shook his head an' said, 'Blood, so much blood.' I suppose she hemorrhaged. Don't know why the baby didn't survive, but I wasn't gonna ask. Just listened. He made it sound like yesterday. His sorrow is, ya know how folks say, like an open wound. We sat together, quiet. Then he said some Japanese words, *shi* somethin' er 'nother."

"*Shikata ga nai*. He uses the expression when things go terribly wrong but can't be avoided. Then he says one must go on with life."

"Don't know 'bout that, but it's hard fer a man ta tell that kind a private story. Course I wasn't gonna refuse his coupe!"

"I feel especially close to him because Mama and I arrived even before the Japanese women, after the baby was born, on account of living across the road. We helped the midwife clean up. Mrs. Miyoshi, her name was Miyoko, died several hours later at the hospital, and the baby, Emma, died the next day."

"Strange how ya work side by side with a man an' not know his sorrow."

Husband and wife rode in silence, respecting Mr. Miyoshi's grief, before Martha heard herself speaking thoughts she hadn't intended to say aloud.

"When he mentions Emma, he pairs her name with *Kodakara*. I think it means his treasure. A treasure that can't be replaced. Art, Carrie is our *Kodakara*. We can't put her away."

His silence led her to believe he agreed even as she wondered at his concentration on the familiar road. Carrie's muscles tensed, and Martha shifted position.

Anna Lundgren

When they walked in the kitchen door, Anna was helping Louise in the dining room by setting spoons in their proper place. When Anna saw Martha with the baby, she took Louise's hand as though seeking protection, or perhaps guidance.

"Let me put the baby down and hang up my coat, honey," Martha said. "I want to give you the biggest hug ever."

She walked through the dining room and into the living room, put the bundled Carrie on the sofa, and slipped off her coat. Anna followed through the archway, but she didn't come to Martha; she headed toward the bundle. Art moved to intercept her. Martha signaled him to stop. She had so wanted Anna to meet Carrie in the hospital, but Doc forbade a visit, given Carrie's fragile "condition," as he called it.

Four-year-old Anna slowed and approached the sofa on tiptoe. Martha took Art's hand, and they walked over to stand beside their uncharacteristically shy daughter.

"Do you want to see your sister?" Martha asked.

A solemn nod of the blond curls.

"Come, sit by her while I take away the blankets."

Martha knelt stiffly by the sofa. Art lifted Anna onto it and took his place beside her. Louise watched from the archway. Carrie didn't stir as Martha gently pulled the blankets away from her head.

Without being prompted to talk softly, Anna murmured, "Mama, my baby's pretty, the way you are."

"Thank you, Anna," Martha whispered.

Anna's was the first comment about the resemblance, and it moved Martha. Perhaps others thought it unseemly to compare an ill newborn to the mother. She wondered if Carrie's hair would remain as dark as hers. She'd noted the first time she held her that Carrie's face was distinctly heart-shaped, so like her own, so unlike Art's and Anna's square jaws.

Anna reached to touch Carrie's hair, but Art obstructed her hand.

Again, Martha stopped him with a whispered, "It's all right."

Anna's fingertip rested lightly on a dark curl, then Carrie's forehead. Martha glanced at Art, expecting his usual indulgent smile when Anna surprised everyone with her precocious ways. Instead, he frowned and lifted Anna off the sofa.

"Let's let Carrie sleep," he said brusquely. "Anna, when Carrie's asleep she's very cuddly an' beautiful, but when her diaper gets wet, she wakes up an' cries. If that happens, come fer me or yer mama."

He saw Louise standing in the archway and snapped, "Can't ya get supper on the table 'fore she wakes up?"

Startled by Art's gruffness, Louise whirled and hurried through the swinging door to the kitchen.

Martha didn't know what to make of Art's behavior. She wanted to take his hand, but Papa and Alex came in from the back porch, and Art moved to hold the swinging door for Louise. Alex took the pot of pork stew from her, and that freed her hands for the bread plate and coffee pot.

The only traits Louise shared with her twin brother were superficial physical ones — their dark brown hair and eyes and Mama's tall, slim build. But Alex's hair curled and Louise's hung straight, her continual complaint.

"Uncle Alex, come see my pretty baby," Anna said.

He'd been her buddy the past month, after Doc told Martha she risked another miscarriage if she didn't stay in bed. Alex took Anna into the fields to plow, with her all bundled up and sitting between his legs on the Case tractor's broad metal seat. He must have taught her every song he knew. When the fields were muddy, he played Tinkertoys with her in the living room at the Home Place and told her stories. He drove her into town for treats at the soda fountain on weekends when her Aunt Louise was there, who conjured specialties just for her.

"Uncle Alex already saw Carrie in the hospital," Art sharply observed, and his long strides brought him back to Martha's side.

This time, Martha successfully captured his hand.

He took a deep breath and said more calmly, "Everyone's hungry. Let's eat."

Martha hesitated, even though she was in sympathy with Art's impatience.

"But Josie and Earl aren't here yet," she said.

Papa reacted to signs of a dispute by putting on his public face, that of the Robert McLennan people knew as successful farmer and Greenwood County commissioner, albeit a recently defeated one. By the time he passed through the dining room and reached her in the living room, his smile and good will dominated the gathering. Art was four inches taller, but Papa seemed larger. He shook Art's hand.

"Want to tell you again, Art, how much Miyoshi and I appreciate all your work since he went under the knife with that appendix problem, given everything you've had on your mind."

He gathered his daughter in his arms and said, "You've been out of circulation a while, Sis. Sunday's Easter, and Josie's at choir practice. It's Thursday night."

Of his four children, he nicknamed only Martha, her special connection to Papa. "Sis" probably had its origin in Josie's baby talk, her name for the sister just one year younger than she. The twins, who came along five years later, also called Martha "Sis." Mama stuck with "Martha."

Papa added, "We offered to bring Earl out with us, but he doesn't let Josie drive alone these days, even though she can't be five months along and it's only four blocks from their house to the church."

Martha kissed Papa on the cheek, and he whispered in her ear, "And I can't tell you how proud I am of you, Sis, for handling everything so well this past month. I know it's been hard."

She gave him another squeeze and extricated herself. She couldn't answer his sympathetic words without crying, so she turned on Alex with, "Why aren't you at choir practice?"

"Gee whiz, Sis! Sang my solo last week, Palm Sunday. Didn't figure I needed ta be there tonight. We've rehearsed for months, and the songs don't change that much from year ta year."

Martha rolled her eyes at Papa, who shrugged in response, as though he had given up on a son who did the minimum. However, Alex's nonchalant answer might be his way of saying he chose Carrie's homecoming over choir practice.

"Well, I'm glad you're spending the evening with us," she said.

Alex smiled and took his seat, which confirmed her guess. They settled into their accustomed places, and Papa said grace, thanking God for Martha's safe return, for the new life entrusted to the family, and for the affection and loyalty that carried them through good times and bad. A simple prayer spoken from his heart, as his always were, and Martha heard no out-of-the-ordinary sentiments. It was as appropriate for the arrival of a healthy child after a difficult birth as for Carrie.

"Thank you, Papa," she mumbled.

"Oh!" Louise said. "I forgot the sweet peas from the Eagle View Women's Club."

She retrieved the flowers from the top of Mama's piano in the living room and placed them in the center of the table, which completed the transformation of supper into a celebration.

Martha took several bites of Louise's pork stew, which was so tasty Martha said it was the first real food she had eaten in weeks, and Carrie whined. Martha excused herself and took Carrie into the bedroom. After sunset the breeze had turned cold, and Martha could feel the draught seeping in around the windows. No one had thought to open the door and let in heat from the living room furnace.

Perhaps because she was cold, tired, and hungry, nursing went worse than usual. When Carrie fell asleep, Martha tucked her into the bassinet by the bed, pleased that Louise had arranged it for Carrie's homecoming, an unexpected show of tenderness.

Martha emerged to discover Papa and Alex had gone home, and she heard Louise reading Anna her bedtime story in her small room next to the kitchen. Art must be outside finishing the chores, much later than usual.

She sat on the sofa to wait for Louise but fell asleep. She woke when Art roused her with a whimpering Carrie in his arms. Someone had put a blanket over Martha, and, other than the light coming from the bedroom, the house was dark.

"I already changed 'er," Art said. "She's been doin' this off an' on fer the last thirty minutes. Wanted ya ta get more sleep, but she's at 'er limit. Why don't ya feed 'er out here, where it's warmer?"

Still groggy, Martha mumbled, "Thanks for helping me get some rest. Will you hold her while I run to the outhouse?"

She walked into the kitchen and switched on the light. Someone had cleaned up. She hadn't heard a thing. She saw a small crock bowl of pork stew on the warm coal stove and stole two more bites, planning to finish later.

The cold air on the screened back porch jolted her fully awake. She grabbed her jacket off its hook, stepped into the yard and, out of habit, looked north for the Big Dipper. Millions of stars blinked and sparkled. She stopped under the dome of sky that arched over the disc of flat plains beneath it and traced the Milky Way from horizon to horizon.

The magnificence of the night sky usually lifted her spirits, but its vastness weighed down so heavily she could scarcely breathe. The silhouette of an owl gliding overhead moved between her and the stars. She took a step, then another, and ran toward the outhouse. Her fingertips touched the frost and left their imprint on the wooden latch.

April and May 1941

Dr. John Claffey

"What's her weight, Doc?" Art asked.

"Going down, and she doesn't have it to lose. Four pounds, eight ounces. Three weeks ago, at birth, four pounds, twelve ounces."

Martha and Art moaned. She maneuvered Carrie's shirt onto a stiffened arm and asked, "What do you recommend?"

Martha caught the end of a glance between the men as though Doc were saying, "You know what I recommend."

She resented their alliance. Hers had been the closer relationship with Doc. When she worked for him during her nursing studies, he explained complicated procedures and included her in examinations of patients with unusual diagnoses or injuries. Why exclude her from discussions about Carrie?

To resurrect their frank conversations, she said, "Art's told me you recommend we put Carrie in the Children's Home. He's also probably told you I don't agree and think we need to give it another month, at least. I'm only asking what you recommend about overcoming her difficulties with nursing. A lot of effort with little success, as her decreasing weight shows."

"A month? Martha, are you saying you think Carrie'll get well in a month?"

"Not at all. I know Carrie's isn't a temporary illness. I'm not simple-minded. I'm only saying we'll know better in a month whether we can deal with her at home. And do you have ideas about a diagnosis?"

Art's nervous cough signaled his reentry into the conversation. "Martha, look what this is doin'. Ya don't get sleep. Ya spend all yer time with Carrie, an' I'm busy, so Anna's at the Home Place most days. Not that Anna minds, but I sure miss 'er. Thank the Good Lord we have Luis Marquez as hired hand now, an' Louise's home from business school ta help, but if Louise isn't cookin' meals fer us, Josie is, an' Earl isn't gonna put up with that much longer, what with Josie expectin'. Carrie's a strain on the whole family. I'm not much help 'cause I don't know 'bout takin' care of a baby with 'er problems. Ya got more confidence on account a yer nursin', but ya don't really know. It's too hit er miss."

Art's lecture raised so many objections she tried to sort out where to begin her rebuttal, but he wasn't finished.

"What's more, we're all gettin' attached ta 'er. I'll grant she's beautiful, an' somethin' 'bout 'er, well, draws people. But she ain't well. Ain't it better we give 'er up 'fore somethin' happens?"

Martha shot back, "You mean, before she dies? You think nurses at a children's home will take better care of her, or they just won't be as torn up, if she dies?"

Doc and Art exchanged another look. Martha regretted her outburst. What she spoke in anger and intended as sarcasm confirmed their opinion she was overly emotional and, therefore, should be excluded from decisions about Carrie.

Before she could redeem herself, Doc said, "It also could be the case she'll survive infancy and become increasingly hard to care for. Shouldn't she be with her own kind, in that event?"

Such a suggestion didn't deserve an answer. "With her own kind," he'd said, as though Carrie wasn't human.

The force of their alliance beat her down. If Mama were still alive, if Josie were with her, she'd oppose them.

Instead, she'd win them over to her position of giving it more time. As for Art, she'd restore familiar routines. As for Doc, she'd behave as though nothing was out of the ordinary between them. And when family was around, she would participate in conversations instead of withdrawing to rest.

Then again, after a month of lying prone before Carrie's birth, and in these first weeks of Carrie's life, Martha's isolation could have affected her in ways she didn't recognize. She recoiled at the idea of visiting the home in Denver, but Carrie was ill. It wasn't like Martha not to consider feasible treatments, and handling Carrie might get more demanding.

Mrs. DeFries was of such help before Mama died. If she were invited for a visit, she might have practical nursing suggestions and would help Martha weigh the merits of visiting the home. More importantly, her visit might placate both men.

"Doc," she said, matching his condescending manner. "For the time being, what suggestions do you have about feeding Carrie?"

Not until they were driving home did she realize Doc hadn't given a diagnosis. She should have pressed him.

Art Lundgren

Early on a Saturday morning several weeks later, Martha and Art climbed into the cab of the pickup.

"I know yer still 'gainst the idea, but I'm glad yer open ta seein' the home," he said as he steered around puddles from the overnight showers.

Perhaps he drove slowly because he'd washed the truck yesterday and wanted to avoid splashing mud or was afraid to get stuck in the slippery clay soil underlying the gravel. Her body tensed from habit as they eased up the incline to the highway.

When she drove and a vehicle approached from the left, a full stop meant she stalled before making the turn from the slope. She couldn't get the hang of sliding her right foot off the brake and onto the gas pedal while letting out the clutch with her left before the truck began to roll backward. Josie didn't have a problem; neither did Louise. Martha's solution was to let the stalled vehicle coast back down, restart the engine and make another go at it, hoping she could ease onto the road without hesitation.

Mud and incline — Art wasn't fazed. He kept talking as he made the right turn onto the highway, but his voice was softer, more cautious.

"I was wonderin' what ya meant, that day in the hospital, when ya said it was all Doc's fault. An' the part 'bout Elena Marquez in the operatin' room. I thought we could talk now 'cause yer seemin' more like yerself. Ya know Elena lost 'er job on account of it."

Martha didn't know. Yes, Elena walked in where she didn't belong and certainly her cry and the crashing mop and bucket upset Doc at a delicate moment in the delivery. But to fire her?

Martha had the window rolled partway down and didn't want to talk. She breathed in the cool, fresh air. She heard birds singing in the bushes along the river as the truck approached the bridge, and the rising sun turned the cloud remnants a soft pink.

"Martha?"

"Not just yet. Maybe after we get through town."

She wanted to hold on to the delicious feeling that everything was normal, including her. The aroma of the lilac bushes when they drove down their lane not ten minutes ago lingered in her nostrils, and Maude's brilliant red and yellow tulips at the Moulton place splashed color into her springtime of otherwise endless hours inside, encouraging Carrie to eat. Primarily, though, she'd had a whole night's sleep because they'd left Carrie in town with Josie after supper.

Martha rolled the window all the way down and took a deeper breath: the rank smell of standing water in the rushes by the river below and the faint odor of manure from the back of the truck replaced the lilacs' scent. No matter! The smells translated into lush hay and corn.

She shifted her weight, and her dress caught in the cracked seat cover. At least Art had wiped off Tip's muddy paw prints. In spite of Martha's objections, he allowed their collie-shepherd mix to ride in the cab instead of making her jump in the back. Not only were the paw prints distasteful, but Tip's long hair, matted with mud from jumping in and out of irrigation ditches, brushed streaks of dirt everywhere. A closer inspection revealed Art had done his best to clean them off, too.

She tried to see how much water flowed in the riverbed below. With the snow runoff and last night's rain, it was at least twice the amount from last month when they brought Carrie home. What a difference from the dry channel of several years past, during the dirt storms.

"I wonder how much snow will still be on the mountains west of Denver."

She wasn't aware she speculated aloud until Art answered, "Hard ta tell."

He slowed as they entered town and made the curve west, passed Ralph's Market and the drug store, and pulled up to the stop sign.

Theirs was the single vehicle on the road at that hour; still, Art stopped. She wouldn't have. She glanced at the marquis on the movie theater out of habit. *Comrade X* with Clark Gable and Hedy Lamarr.

The early morning drive cleared her head. She should take breaks like this now and again. A quick trip to Collins's Country Store would be enough.

She thanked God for her family. Just as Alex had been drawn to Anna from her infancy, Louise was drawn to Carrie, to everyone's surprise, not least Louise's. Impatient and curt with everyone else, she handled Carrie's tense body with a touch as soft as Art's. Louise protected Carrie from sudden movements and loud noises so as not to alarm her and set off spasms. When the jerking overcame Carrie, Louise cradled her tightly enough to give a sense of security without the confinement that made Carrie stiffen. Louise was the one to point out that when Carrie's movements were too constricted she showed signs of pain.

And Josie was as attentive to Carrie as she was to Anna. Anyone who knew Josie would conclude she was simply being herself and doing everything well, including caring for an infant. Martha hoped Josie wasn't overly concerned something might go wrong with her baby. Surely Earl was so protective of Josie on account of that fear. He rarely looked at Carrie, and he never held her.

Josie went all out with supper last night — fried chicken, mashed potatoes and gravy, creamed corn. Martha brought fresh asparagus that grew wild along the irrigation ditches and her Black Cake with its coffee-flavored frosting, which she could make blindfolded. It was a mystery Josie didn't have success with it. How many times had they watched Mama scoop flour out of the bin by hand and mix it with a pinch of this and that?

In any case, Louise would be helping Josie later in the afternoon, when she finished work at the soda fountain, only because Josie was pregnant and might be tired if she had a difficult night with Carrie. Otherwise, there wasn't much about children of any age that fazed Josie. In five years with fifth and sixth graders, she'd learned to handle most anything.

No teacher could have taken better care of Bennie Ogawa after his brother, Frank, died in '39. Afterward, Josie described Bennie bursting into tears in Sunday school whenever he felt on the spot. The other children responded as that age would, with teasing and ridicule, but Josie said she encouraged them to put themselves in Bennie's shoes and give him time.

Martha wasn't sure how Josie worked arithmetic into Sunday school lessons, but that's how she got Bennie's mind on something else. He was proud of his extraordinary gift for it, and Martha was proud of Josie. How unreasonable that the school board members made a teacher as dedicated and talented as Josie "retire" the moment she married. They were worse than Doc, who acted like women who bore children couldn't think straight.

With a start, she heard Art say, "Hey, woman. We're well outta town. Can we talk now?"

Maybe her musings about family and Frank Ogawa's accident connected with Art's questions about Doc and Elena. She'd figure it out as she talked.

"I was remembering Frank Ogawa's accident. It might have to do with what you asked. What's happened with Carrie probably isn't Doc's fault, just as he couldn't save Frank. He did everything he could. If he hadn't used forceps, both Carrie and I could have died."

"I'm grateful we'll never know."

"Well, I am too."

For several miles, they silently absorbed the impact of such an outcome.

"As for Elena Marquez, at the time, I thought I imagined her. It was so odd. She burst in with a mop and bucket. Completely out of place. She made a mistake, and it looked to me she knew she didn't belong, but when she saw Doc insert the forceps, she was terrified. She screamed and dropped the mop and bucket. At least, I think she screamed, and I think I saw the things fall, but I didn't hear them hit before everything went black."

"What does that have ta do with Frank Ogawa?"

Now that she had begun, words came fast. "Just that horrible, unexpected things happen, and you want to know why. Many times folks swim in the canal, and nobody gets hurt. So you ask 'What made it a tragedy for Frank?' You look for who, or what, to blame. But with Carrie, and with Frank, and with José Marquez when the horses spooked and he fell, what good is it to find fault? Alex still blames himself for José's death. And for Frank's, to a certain extent. As Mr. Miyoshi says, '*Shikata ga nai.*' It can't be helped. You have to go on with life."

Martha paused for breath, and Art didn't comment. "However, when the Ogawas moved to California, maybe thinking they'd leave their grief behind, you know they didn't. The grief went with them. And because they left, Susie and Bennie Ogawa lost their best friends, not just their big brother. Don't know what it did to Chris Ogawa, him only a year younger than Frank. Same with Josie and me. If anything happens to her…"

The thought of losing Josie was too awful to consider. She'd lost Mama; she couldn't lose Josie, too.

"It's hard for children to make new friends when they carry grief like that. And here, without his friend Bennie, Jimmie Ichikawa doesn't have his same bounce and optimism, now that he's running with those boys who are always in trouble."

"Martha, I don't get what yer sayin.'"

She was prattling like Max Lambert, when he blurted out his account of Frank's accident that day. She didn't want to cry, but she felt the tears coming. She slid closer to Art and put her hand on his arm to calm herself.

"I'm not sure. I have to see the home first. But if we decide to put Carrie there, we might be like the Ogawas, thinking we're leaving the grief and hardship behind but only adding to it."

Art slowed the truck, pulled onto the shoulder of the road, and shifted into neutral as the truck rolled to a stop. He put on the emergency brake, and Martha anticipated he would walk over by the barrow pit to relieve himself. Instead, he turned off the engine, put both hands on the steering wheel, straightened his arms and pushed back. He stared straight ahead. When he spoke, his voice was thin, hard.

"Martha, I love ya, but it's like ya been livin' only in yer own head. Trouble is, ya think everyone sees an' feels what ya do. Once ya got somethin' figured out, that's the way it is. Yer done, but ya haven't actually talked ta anyone 'bout it, maybe the other day with Mrs. DeFries but not with me."

Martha cringed. She hadn't meant to exclude Art from Mrs. DeFries's visit, but what did he care about rearranging the dresser top to hold the items she needed for changing Carrie? Or how Mrs. DeFries starting cutting small squares of soft cloth for her to wipe off her nipples after nursing before Martha told her they were using bottles now? Anna had been so easy Martha was lazy about keeping the nipples clean, but with Carrie, wiping them would have helped with the chapping. Or how Mrs. DeFries rigged up the cheesecloth bag with starch to pat Carrie down and sooth her prickly heat? And Mrs. DeFries agreed they should visit the home, so there was nothing to discuss concerning Mrs. DeFries.

He'd never spoken that harshly to her. She sat very still, hardly daring to breathe. She didn't have anything figured out, not this time. She considered herself outspoken, and he told her often how he appreciated that about her. Was he saying she wasn't outspoken enough?

Absent her response, he moved back to the Ogawa topic. "I heard the Ogawas had an opportunity out in California, but maybe they ran because Frank's death hurt too much. I don't know, an' so what if they ran? Ya gotta put distance 'tween you an' what gives ya that much pain. It'd be plain stupid ta hang 'round somethin' hurtin' ya that bad. Or maybe yer fearful, fearful ya won't be able ta do what's bein' asked of ya."

Something about Carrie must be changing the way they acted toward one another. Was he afraid of Carrie? But he was so capable. From the first, in the hospital, he calmed Carrie and seemed more comfortable with her than she did. She never doubted his ability to handle what life threw his way, but did he feel weak?

She thought his pursuit of the idea of the Children's Home was to relieve her of so much work. Or perhaps to protect Carrie's fragile health. Or all of them from grief, if Carrie died. But maybe Art was just protecting himself.

Perhaps she was doing exactly what he accused her of, keeping her thoughts and questions to herself. But what could she say? If she speculated about his fears aloud, wouldn't that sound accusatory?

She hadn't heard the vehicle pull up behind them. She jumped when the deep voice came through Art's open window.

"Ya okay, Art? Got a problem with yer truck?"

The crinkles on the round face peering in Art's window pressed into a bemused smile. Sheriff Burleigh wasn't known for friendly chitchat or for being reasonable, but he managed both with Art. The truck was pretty banged up. Peter Collins had driven it hard, and he sold it at the foreclosure without doing any repair work. But for Papa's tinkering, and now Art's, it would've stopped completely by now.

Art chuckled. "Thanks, Burleigh, but I think she'll start. Just takin' a break."

"I'll wait till ya get goin'."

The everyday-like exchange between Art and Howard Burleigh reassured her. She waited until Art shifted into third and rested her hand lightly on his. He didn't pull it away, and he didn't press his point about how she kept her thoughts private. But he didn't say anything, either.

By eleven o'clock, they agreed they were hungry. Art turned down a lane and stopped under one of the biggest cottonwoods she'd ever seen. The farmhouse was off in the distance, so they weren't bothering anyone, and they were invisible from the highway. She retrieved the picnic basket from the back, and Art walked around the truck with two bottles of pop he'd bought from the filling station in the last town. They sat together on the running board and balanced their ham sandwiches on their knees.

"Guess ya got me figured out by now. Ya usually do."

"I'm not sure."

"Well, it ain't hard. Who the hell knows why the Ogawas hightailed it? But I can tell ya why I think my daddy did. Afraid as he could be. He couldn't get work, nowhere. Not Kansas, not Colorado. All the 'no' he got, every day a his damned life, just piled up on 'im. He ran ta liquor, but even a bottle couldn't take him far enough away."

Martha tried to swallow a bite of sandwich, and Art took a swig of his pop.

"Ma had one picture — them on their weddin' day in thirteen. So young, ya wouldn't recognize 'em. Her lookin' up at 'im, eyes full a love, a little smile on her face. Him grinnin' straight at the camera like he was gonna take on whatever came his way."

Martha knew the general story of Art's past, but not these details. She couldn't guess where the sad memories were leading him.

"I swear I never saw those expressions. Ma's face was, well, blank most a the time, an' Daddy's grin turned dumb, like whatever anyone said would be fine with 'im. He'd been beaten down so often he had nothin' left in 'im ta talk back."

Art finished his pop and turned to face her. "I'm afraid, Martha, afraid Carrie's our first turn a bad luck, an' I'll start down the road my daddy traveled."

Martha couldn't quite grasp his meaning. "If Carrie's the start on our road to defeat, what will be at the end of that road?"

"That I'll leave ya, an' the girls, like my daddy left Ma an' me."

Martha laid her hand on Art's leg, wanting to protest he was nothing like his father, but she had never met Mattie or Carl Lundgren. She was a freshman when Carl left, Art a junior. She did know Carl heard they were building roads in the mountains, and he went up there, thinking he might get a job. Art said he drank, but she hadn't known it was that debilitating. Months passed, and Mattie and Art heard nothing. Mattie moved back to Kansas to help her sister take care of her children — six or eight of them.

Art didn't go because he figured his chances were better in Colorado. Even though times were hard in '31, he could finish high school. He doubted he would get an education in Kansas as an older boy in a family with so many mouths to feed.

For several months, he lived with Rev. and Mrs. Macgill. Once he'd compared himself to a drowning cat, saying they pulled him out of the water. Then his friend, Eddie Mattson, invited Art to work on their ranch that summer. Art stayed on for a couple years.

Even now, Art received letters from Mattie, written in a childlike scrawl, in response to his occasional notes. Perhaps the writing was his mother's, or maybe she dictated to a niece or nephew. Martha suspected the latter. Several times she suggested they drive to Kansas for a visit, but he always found excuses not to leave the farm.

Martha could think of all kinds of reasons why their road wouldn't end where Carl and Mattie's had, but she wasn't sure Art would believe her. Instead, she said, "I understand why we have to visit the home. It's a safety valve, isn't it?"

The Matron

They didn't locate it until after two o'clock. From the front porch they could see the whole sweep of mountains, all the way from Pike's Peak in the south to Long's Peak in the north.

"Well, there's yer answer," Art said.

Martha thought he referred to the home's suitability because, from the outside, the two-story house with the "Administration" sign by the front door looked almost homey. Two tall lilac bushes with their blooms just opening stood on either side of the wide steps and perfumed the air. The porch extended the length of the house and was deep enough on the left end to accommodate both wooden bench swings that faced each other. Martha and Art had a similar swing that he'd anchored to a two-by-four running between the cottonwoods by their back porch.

Or maybe he meant the answer to her earlier question about snow. All the peaks were white above timberline. She smiled up at him, appreciative of his attentiveness, even to casual comments made hours ago. He took her hand and rang the doorbell.

While they waited, Martha surveyed the expansive grounds — several large brick buildings, and a barn with pens at the back that she guessed provided vocational training for the older children.

A girl about eleven years old opened the door and greeted them with a sweet smile. "Good afternoon. May I help you?"

"Hello there, young lady. We're here ta see the home, an' the administrator, if he's available," Art explained.

The girl frowned and asked, "You're not here about an adoption?"

"No, we're not," Art said.

The abrupt answer caught Martha's attention. Usually he was more cordial with strangers, especially children.

"Just a moment, please."

She left the door open and them standing on the porch.

In response to Martha's puzzled look, he replied, "We don't need ta explain our business ta a child."

Martha nodded in agreement, and they stood quietly. She felt awkward holding hands and let go. She was about to walk to the end of the porch for a better view of the mountains when a matronly woman appeared.

"May I help you?"

She had the biggest breasts Martha had ever seen. The enormous protruding mounds reached their maximum extension just above her waist. Perhaps her white blouse, buttoned as it was all the way to her neck, highlighted the expanse of her chest. With some effort Martha kept her eyes fixed on the woman's face, which was extraordinarily kind, although her yellow teeth detracted from her smile.

Art explained they had a crippled baby and their doctor recommended the home.

A crippled baby. Martha didn't think of Carrie in those terms. She almost missed Art's more specific description.

"Doc thinks she might have spastic paralysis."

Hot tears filled Martha's eyes. She rested her hand against the doorframe to steady herself but quickly withdrew it to brush off the sharp chips of peeling paint. This conversation should not be happening on the front porch of a facility she had never visited with a grotesque woman she had just met. She should have heard the diagnosis privately, in Doc's office. Contrary to what Doc and Art thought, she hadn't lost her brains in childbirth! Martha was so angry her heart pounded.

The housemother asked, "Is she feebleminded?"

Martha forced herself to maintain a calm outward appearance and pretended she, too, possessed all the relevant information.

"She's too young ta tell," Art responded.

"Well, come in, but I must tell you we cater to orphans and neglected children, even though we're also known as a home for dependent children. Our babies aren't here long before adoption, but it's harder to find homes these last ten years. You know, first the hard times, and now conscription and the European War. Families aren't secure."

As they entered the nursery, Martha was nearly overcome again, this time by the smell of disinfectant. It recalled her nursing-school days, but the odor was much stronger. They walked down a wide hallway with one row of cribs to their right and another to their left. A child occupied each crib, some seated, some standing, some napping, a total of eight.

Martha heard the door bang open behind her, and the matron shouted, "Here comes your mama!"

Martha whirled and saw two girls entering, scarcely older than the one who greeted them. The standing toddlers jabbered, jumped up and down and shook the sides of their cribs. The younger ones crawled to the edges of their mattresses and babbled noisily. The commotion woke the sleeping children, but when Martha sought out the matron's face, anticipating displeasure, the woman beamed.

"This is the happiest time of day, when the older girls come to play with the babies. Isn't it adorable?"

Adorable? All Martha could envision was Carrie's reaction to the uproar. Her head would bob, her arms and legs would flail, and it would take quite a while to, as Art put it, get her organized again.

She craned her neck to see around the woman's bulk in order to gauge Art's reaction. The color had drained from his cheeks. His downcast eyes fixed on the floor. She, too, looked down and noticed circular spots, some as large as saucers, where the linoleum was worn through to the boards.

They approached double doors at the end of the corridor, and he asked, "Are there little ones?"

"Oh," said the woman. "They're through here, but they're napping, and I don't want to disturb them. We feed and change them every couple hours. We really don't have the staff, but we do what we can. I've been told there should be one staff member for two or three babies, but we tend up to four, sometimes more."

She chuckled and took hold of his arm. She drew him close.

"You know how it is. The bosses haven't figured out that with more children, they need more help."

The jovial woman seemed to care for her charges, but Carrie had to be fed frequently, and each feeding required prolonged, quiet attention so she wouldn't aspirate. The home didn't have time for Carrie. Martha bit her lip hard and successfully held back the tears.

"I'd take you to see our administrator, but he isn't here this afternoon. Maybe you could come back another day?"

Art regained enough poise to say, "Ya've been quite helpful. Thank ya. We'll show ourselves out."

Martha stopped on the porch to steady herself before grabbing the rail and walking down the stairs. She took deep breaths of the lilac-scented air. Art got as far as the curb by the truck before he doubled over, gagging.

She drove to Colorado Springs, where they stopped for a hamburger and cup of coffee. She wasn't hungry, but she ate to stave off exhaustion. Other than necessary exchanges of information, they didn't speak.

Art said he felt well enough to drive. The sun was setting behind Pike's Peak as they left town, and ordinarily they would pull over and enjoy it, but both just wanted to get home.

In the dark, headed east from Pueblo, Martha gathered courage to ask what she hoped was a neutral question.

"Was the home what you expected?"

"Ya know it wasn't."

He gasped. Not until he stopped the truck, rested his head on the steering wheel, and his shoulders heaved did she realize the gasps were sobs. He turned and laid his head in her lap. He gripped her knee so hard it hurt. For some time the ragged breathing continued; she caressed his neck and shoulders. Finally he sat up and held her.

"We can't leave our baby in that stockyard. I'll help all I can. I wish yer mama wasn't gone."

And Martha cried. Tears enough between them to salve years of sorrow.

May 1941

Fran Reeve

For the Mother's Day service, Martha was back in the choir. They moved into the corridor leading to the front of the sanctuary and heard the first notes of the processional, "For the Beauty of the Earth," one of Mama's favorites. On Mother's Day the year she died, they sang it as a duet — Anna McLennan's soprano blending with Martha's alto. Martha sang verse four with gusto.

> *For the joy of human love,*
> *Brother, sister, parent, child,*
> *Friends on earth and friends above,*
> *For all gentle thoughts and mild;*
> *Lord of all, to thee we raise*
> *This our hymn of grateful praise.*

The words confirmed she and Art had made the right decision to keep Carrie at home. Nowhere else would Carrie be enfolded in the joy of human love as with family. Mama would approve. Martha hoped she wouldn't embarrass herself with sentimental tears.

In unison, the choir sat on the pew that ran the length of the front wall. Martha settled in by tucking her music into the polished mahogany rack attached to the half-partition separating them from the rest of the chancel. The placement of her folder, the order of worship, hymns, where everyone sat — she knew it all, having been a choir member since fall of her freshman year.

Anna caught her attention from the second row to Martha's left, seated primly on the cushioned, theater-style seat next to Art in her new blue hat with ruffles. Martha almost laughed aloud that Anna put on such airs at her age, particularly since she had to balance herself on the front edge so the seat didn't fold and capture her.

Josie and Earl sat with Carrie in the row along the back of the church for a quick exit if unfamiliar noises agitated her. When Martha said she was ready to rejoin the choir, Josie informed everyone she was stopping. Josie claimed she hadn't ever enjoyed singing, confirmed that she couldn't follow the alto part during Martha's absence. Josie much preferred teaching Sunday school. Martha protested they'd always sung together, but Josie prevailed.

Earl glanced anxiously at Josie. Martha scowled. Granted, Josie had miscarried last summer, almost a year to the day from when Martha lost her second baby, but if Earl was concerned about anyone, it should be Carrie. A six-pound infant wasn't a burden for the strong, athletic Josie.

Martha searched for Papa at the entrance, where she expected to see him handing out bulletins to latecomers before he slipped out for a smoke, but he was already gone. She checked again to see how Carrie had done with the sounds of organ, piano, and choir. All seemed peaceful.

When Martha looked toward Louise seated at the piano, Louise executed a series of acrobatics with her eyebrows and pointed her chin toward the congregation. Martha followed the imaginary line and saw nothing unusual. She caught Louise's eye and shrugged her shoulders.

Louise repeated the series of expressions to such an exaggerated degree that Martha checked if anyone noticed before she more deliberately followed the direction implied by Louise's chin. Martha spotted Papa seated about fifteen rows back on the right, at the end next to the folding doors that ordinarily shut off the adjoining foyer but were open to accommodate the overflow Mother's Day crowd. Not his customary place, but no reason for Louise's grimaces. When Martha looked at her again, Louise emphatically nodded in Papa's direction.

Martha obliged in time to see Papa turn toward the woman seated on his right. Martha couldn't identify her because she was facing Papa, and her yellow hat with its broad brim hid her profile. Martha stared as Robert McLennan — Papa was surely the most handsome widower in the county — gazed at the woman and patted the hand she rested on his arm.

From the time that Martha was Anna's age and Papa looked at her like that, she'd believed two things: he loved her completely, and his dark-blue eyes penetrated to her most protected secrets. Accordingly, she was always forthright with Papa. When he watched Mama that way, she couldn't guess what feelings he evoked in Anna, his wife.

Then Papa smiled at the woman, a smile that for Martha meant a blessing of trust and confidence. What blessing did it impart today? Mama died nearly eight years ago. Martha had assumed Papa would remarry, but as time passed his status as widower became fixed, at least in her mind.

She stifled a gasp when the woman turned toward Rev. Macgill, who moved from his chair to speak from behind the pulpit. Frances Reeve, the high-school English teacher who arrived before school started last fall, originally from Oklahoma and more recently from a nearby district. The gossip from Josie and Earl before Thanksgiving was that every boy in her classes had a crush on her, but she was an excellent teacher. She must be at least ten years younger than Papa.

Martha had seen Miss Reeve once, when Louise pointed her out the Saturday before Christmas in the drugstore. Martha moved toward her to introduce herself, but Miss Reeve hadn't noticed and hurried out the door. Martha's impression of the stylish, attractive woman in the black coat with gray scarf and matching wool hat was favorable, but Martha hadn't thought about her since.

Even at a remove of fifteen rows, Miss Reeve's auburn hair and startling green eyes, accentuated as they were by the yellow hat, drew attention. Papa's wavy blond hair, which barely showed gray at his temples, and his sun-browned complexion contrasted with Miss Reeve's coloring in a way that highlighted the handsomeness of them both.

When Martha looked back at Louise, the contortions on Louise's face made Martha cover her smile with the back of her hand — rolling eyes, turned-down corners of her mouth, Louise's inverted way of showing approval. Martha agreed. Papa could have made a much less attractive choice, given the eligible widows in Greenwood.

How odd for Miss Reeve to show up at church with him on Mother's Day. Not that Martha begrudged Papa his happiness, but if they had been seen together publically before, why hadn't anyone mentioned it? Why hadn't he said anything? Were Louise's elaborate efforts to draw Martha's attention to them because she was also seeing them together for the first time? Or was Louise doing Martha the courtesy of bringing her up to date about old news? Would Miss Reeve come to the Home Place for Sunday dinner after church?

Martha looked toward Art. Her puzzled expression elicited a mouthed, "What?" Martha mimicked Louise's eyebrow-and-chin technique, hoping he had the sense to wait until everyone stood for the next hymn before he turned to investigate.

She leaned forward slightly to catch Alex's attention from where he sat to her left with the other tenors. He studied the music for the solo he would be singing later in the service. Annoyed, she looked to her right to see if Mrs. Macgill, organist and choir director, made note of Alex's last-minute preparation. Martha questioned, yet again, why Mrs. Macgill allowed him to continue in the choir. Mrs. Macgill chastised anyone who attended practice erratically, except Alex, and he was the worst offender. Someday he would learn his charm and good looks carried him only so far.

Martha thought of Alex and Papa as opposites when it came to responsible behavior, but Papa might be as haphazard as Alex in regard to personal matters. Courting a woman secretly and making it public on Mother's Day, in church?

Martha tried to catch Art's attention. Had he seen Papa and Miss Reeve? But Anna occupied Art with her stream of whispered questions and comments.

Alex McLennan

As Martha hurried to position the vase of purple and yellow iris picked from her garden in the center of the dining room table at the Home Place, Louise was asking Josie if they should set a cover for Miss Reeve. Martha listened for Josie's answer to learn what it revealed about Papa's romance. Meanwhile, Rowdy's deep bark signaled the turn of Papa's beige Chrysler into the lane.

"I don't think so," Josie answered. "If he comes in, sees the extra setting and she isn't with him, he might be self-conscious. Let's let him take the lead."

From Josie's comment, Martha couldn't infer if Papa's interest in Miss Reeve was news or not, but apparently this was the first time he might bring her to the house because no one knew the protocol.

Martha offered her opinion. "He's already taken the lead by holding her hand in church. That's a public announcement. If she has come with him, we should show some hospitality by having…"

The slam of the screen door on the porch made the decision. If Robert McLennan had entered at that moment, he would see his three daughters frozen in an awkward tableau. Art prodded them by clearing his throat.

Anna rescued the moment. She ran toward her grandpa as he entered and sang out, "Happy Mother's Day!" Upon hearing the spontaneous chorus of nervous laughter from the adults, she buried her head between his legs in embarrassment.

He swooped her up and gave her a big hug. "Happy Mother's Day to you, too, pumpkin."

Louise brought out the roast surrounded on its platter by carrots, potatoes, and onions. The day would proceed as usual. Dinner, conversation, some shared activity for the men. Clearing and washing the dishes for the women.

A visitor wouldn't notice that the full platter didn't match the place settings. Nor would he see the hairline cracks in its glaze from years of sitting in the oven, keeping food warm for whoever was in the barn finishing chores. It was Mama's platter, and ever since her death, they only used it on Mother's Day. If Papa didn't talk to Anna about it, Martha would, as a memorial to Mama. She silently rehearsed the words.

Honey, this platter was your Grandma Anna's. Look at all those tiny cracks. Many were already there when she was a little girl, your age. This platter came with her mama, your great-grandmother, all the way to Colorado from North Carolina, after the Civil War.

Anna would understand neither the geography nor the history, but she needed reminding of the platter's connection to her, through her Grandma Anna.

Everyone took their seats, and Josie said, "I want to point out Earl made the green beans."

"So, yer puttin' yerself on the level of the Creator Himself, are ya, Earl?" Art teased. "First, ya make a baby, an' now green beans?"

Bless her heart, Martha thought as she watched Josie's face turn beet-red. She's so modest. But Josie joined in the laughter. Even Earl smiled.

The conversation continued with gentle banter after Papa said grace and while he sliced the roast. No one mentioned Miss Reeve. The longer her name went unsaid, the stronger the silent consensus grew that if the topic were to come up, Papa would be the one to introduce it.

Normally, Alex would be in the middle of every tease, but he was silent.

"What's wrong, Alex?" Martha asked. "Feeling left out because no one wished you 'Happy Mother's Day'? By the way, your solo was nearly perfect. I saw women wiping tears from their eyes, and some of the men. Imagine what you could accomplish if you practiced."

Instead of the repartee she expected, Alex looked up from his plate with a hurt expression.

Martha was about to mumble an apology for her backhanded compliment, but he answered, "Sis, today's the first time ya took Carrie out in public, right? A special day for the Lundgrens, an' don't folks usually crowd around ta see a new baby?"

"I suppose so. What are you getting at?"

She had been in the choir room before and after church, so when she met up with everyone outside, Art was holding Carrie, and the crowd had thinned.

Instead of answering, Alex directed his next question to Josie. "When ya were holdin' 'er, did anyone ask ta see 'er?"

Earl squirmed uncomfortably, presumably because Alex's question bordered on interrogation and put Josie in an awkward position.

"No. I mean, yes. What I mean is, none of the women did, as you would expect, but I assume that if either Art or Martha had been holding her, they would have stopped for a peek. Jimmie Ichikawa spoke to me, as he always does, and he asked to see Carrie."

"How'd he react?"

"When I pulled the blanket away from Carrie's face, he stared and said, 'Why, she's beautiful!' I had the impression he was surprised."

"I'm proud of Jimmie," said Alex, "even though he was prob'ly bein' more curious than polite. Everyone's heard Carrie's crippled. They won't welcome 'er as they would a normal baby."

Alex's bitterness had several implications. He seemed to echo Doc's opinion that Carrie wasn't quite human because she was crippled, but he might be taking offense that people shied away from her.

Martha noticed Anna looking up at Alex from her chair next to him. Anna hung on his every word, so of course she would question this sour mood of her typically cheerful hero.

"Alex, let's talk about this after Anna's left the table," Martha said.

Alex looked down at Anna and flashed a smile. "Anna, sit on my lap. I'm gonna tell ya somethin' very important. Ya know I love ya, an' I love your little sister. It might be, Anna, that Carrie won't ever sit at the table an' eat with us. She might never run, or even walk, but that's because she's special. She's so special that all of us have ta take care of her, includin' all the children an' grownups at church. I'm just upset some of the grownups didn't help today. Maybe we have to teach 'em how."

"Shall I be a teacher like Auntie Josie?"

Alex laughed. "Prob'ly neither of us will be as good a teacher as Auntie Josie, but yes, Anna."

With his usual animated expression, Alex sat Anna back on her chair.

Martha smiled at him and said softly, "Happy Mother's Day, Alex."

Alex's carefree attitude was so annoying, but he had gifts of observation and candor. She couldn't wait to ask him what he thought of Papa and Miss Reeve.

She heard Carrie whimpering in the bassinet and went to the kitchen to prepare a bottle. She waited for it to warm, removed it from the pan of water, and tested the temperature by flicking droplets of its contents onto the inside of her wrist. She cringed as they landed like so many ant stings. She would miss even more of the dinner conversation while she cooled the liquid.

Louise and Josie were surely aware of the courtship, but why their uncertainty about whether to set a place for Miss Reeve? Or were her sisters behaving as Art and Doc did when they wouldn't include her in conversations about Carrie? Did they think they were protecting her by keeping Papa's love interest a secret during her confinement before Carrie's birth and this past, impossible month when she and Art were learning how to handle Carrie and making the decision to keep her home? But this was wonderful news, so why the silence? Was there something to hide?

Excluding her extended no courtesy. She needed her family to be frank so she could count on their full support in light of Alex's disturbing observations about folks shunning Carrie. She didn't intend to keep Carrie cloistered.

When she returned, the conversation had moved to Rev. Macgill's sermon.

Art was saying, "But both Niebuhr brothers were pacifists durin' the World War, weren't they?"

Papa chuckled. "Mac doesn't pull his punches, does he, to bring up something as controversial as a dispute between famous brothers on Mother's Day? I'll bet Al Ivarson's beside himself that Mac harps on arguments about pacifism and war. Al's so against any talk of war. He's convinced war is Roosevelt's plot to make himself a dictator. Mac's clever, though. Doesn't take a position when he's standing in the pulpit. A newcomer wouldn't know if he supports the pacifist brother or the one who thinks we should take on Hitler."

Martha, relieved Papa spoke lightheartedly about Al, said, "So, Papa, you're not so much interested in whether we should take on Hitler as you're delighted the sermon got under Al's skin?"

Papa's smile disappeared. "I don't want to carry a grudge, but the man annoys me. I can accept he defeated me in the last election, but only because the Republicans made a clean sweep of the state. If it had been a fair fight between the two of us, I don't think he'd have won. He's just plain ignorant."

Martha's eyebrows must have shot up at his vehemence because Papa quickly looked down at his plate. "Sorry. Otto Lambert scolds me when I talk like this. Says I reflect poorly on him. Says if he'd have known I was such a sore loser, he wouldn't have stepped aside for me in thirty-eight and let me run as commissioner when he moved into this district, and he's only half teasing. Otto sets a high moral standard. That man's a true pacifist. A Quaker who won't fight in any war, regardless of who's president."

Spontaneous nods around the table, even one from Earl, indicated everyone's respect for Otto Lambert.

"Al, he's another story," Papa continued. "If a Republican president wanted war, Al's hat would be first in the ring. There I go again. I'll stop about Al, but I'd tend more toward the pacifist side if it weren't Al's position."

Martha and Josie rolled their eyes at one another. Papa was aware his jabs at Al Ivarson were unseemly, but he couldn't let go of his animosity.

Not convinced he was finished with Al and trying to steer him in another direction, Martha asked, "Papa, if you'd tend toward pacifism, does that mean you're still under the influence of that professor from Colorado University who spoke months ago at the parish house?"

"I saw you two share that look of yours," Papa said. "Clearly, you agree with Otto that I'm out of place expressing my resentment about Al. But as for the professor and Mac's sermon, both of them caution against drawing a simple line between whether to prepare for war or not. The professor's head of the journalism department and made a good case that we have to be very careful about propaganda, about appeals to our emotions that play on our desire to protect democracy. We could be drawn in without carefully considering the consequences."

Earl drew his breath to enter the conversation, and Martha saw Josie's back straighten, tensing in anticipation Earl would say something irritating, which he did more often than not.

"Back to the Niebuhr brothers," Earl said. "Yes, during the World War they believed it's inconsistent for Christians to fight, to meet force with force, but I admire the older brother, Reinhold, who isn't hesitant to admit he thinks differently now. He says we have to stand up to Hitler, even if it means war. That puts me in an awkward position because I also have sympathy for Al, that following the president's recommendations to build up our defense gives him dictatorial power."

They all stared at their empty plates. Earl was usually less direct when he expressed his views, and he'd managed to reintroduce Al.

Papa gave a considered response that subtracted both Al and Roosevelt from the discussion. "I think Mac's point isn't so much about whether or not to go to war. He's trying to help us think through how our beliefs influence our decisions. The Niebuhrs are an example of how good men disagree."

Louise, who seldom entered family debates, said, "Although I couldn't figure out at first why he preached that sermon on Mother's Day, about such strong disagreements between brothers, I think it fit the occasion. What mother isn't thinking about the European War and what it means for her children? What it already means for all those suffering families? And you can't ignore conscription. One of the few times I bought the newspaper was when the selective service list appeared with the names of my two brothers-in-law. Also, many of my school chums are thinking about going to Wichita or California to build airplanes."

Louise's surprisingly observant comments stopped the conversation again. It was one thing to talk about differences between the Niebuhr brothers, men they didn't know, and another thing entirely to think about one's friends working in defense plants and family members going into the service. Alex was too young to register, Papa too old, but not Art and Earl. Thankfully, their lottery numbers put them toward the middle of the list.

Martha watched Louise closely because these rare moments when Louise spoke signaled she was about to take significant action, or already had. Martha attributed Louise's indirect manner to the fact that she was unfortunately placed in the family: too young to share the same interests as Josie and Martha; at an even more tender age when Mama died; and she didn't have close girlfriends as Martha and Josie did.

Unless you counted Eleanor Moulton, but Eleanor was only Louise's friend of convenience. Everyone, including Louise, knew the so-called friendship was to place Eleanor in closer proximity to Alex, whom she had been passionate about since — forever. Eleanor dropped so many hints about her attraction that it was laughable. Then again, at that same age her older brother, Walter Moulton, nearly made a spectacle about his attachment to Martha.

When Martha and Josie had decisions to make, they spoke openly; Louise slid hints about her intentions into tangentially related conversations. In any case, Louise surely wasn't going to spend her life at the soda fountain, where she'd been helping out since graduating from business school last month. Perhaps her plans to leave home were already percolating. One had to tread carefully and be as indirect with Louise as she was in broaching a sensitive topic.

Martha was about to ask what Louise thought of girls working in the defense plants, but Louise started clearing the table. "Who's ready for dessert?"

Josie pushed her chair back to help, but Earl motioned her to sit. "I'll clear."

Martha handed Carrie to Josie and followed Earl into the kitchen. He methodically arranged the pots and dirty dishes waiting at the sink before going to the dining room for more. Admittedly, his orderly approach made sense.

She removed the peach pie from the top of the coal stove, where it had been warming since she'd prepared Carrie's bottle. She set it on a trivet on the oilcloth covering the kitchen table and served the pieces onto dessert plates.

Robert McLennan

Now that she was with the whole family after her several months of absence, their temperamental differences seemed especially striking, and the various combinations of Mama's and Papa's physical traits in their children made them hardly seem related. Martha had black hair like Mama's but wavier than Papa's blond hair and less curly than Alex's. Her eyes were an even darker blue than Papa's. Josie had Mama's long-limbed build and Papa's blue eyes and blond hair, but it was straight like Louise's. The twins shared Josie's and Mama's physiques but had brown hair and eyes. No one inherited Mama's black eyes.

The men were just as varied. Art was taller than Alex but weighed about the same, which accentuated his gangly appearance. Of them all, though, Art was the most agile. Earl was only an inch taller than Josie and looked every bit the high-school history and English teacher — thin, stooping, his sandy hair already balding, glasses, not physically robust like Art, Alex, or Papa but forceful in defense of his principles and politics. Papa was stocky, not fat, just muscular, and as opinionated as Earl, but in his years as a church officer and county commissioner, Papa had acquired a repertoire of humor and tact Earl had yet to learn. Papa's arguments with Earl were like chess games in which Papa controlled the moves and Earl conceded in frustration.

Martha was the shortest of her sisters, sturdy, with round hips and breasts, the feminine equivalent of her father's build. Temperamentally, she was also most like him. She held well-defined opinions that she didn't hesitate to defend. She had helped him with his successful campaign for county commissioner and still faulted herself for not being more active last fall. If she hadn't been on the sidelines for so much of her pregnancy with Carrie, maybe he wouldn't have lost to Al Ivarson. But Papa was probably right that the statewide Republican sweep would have brought Al into office, regardless.

However, the Fran Reeve question made Martha feel distant from Papa and hesitant to ask him the simplest question: when had he started courting Miss Reeve? She wanted to tell him she was happy for him, impressed by his good taste, and that delay for so many years after Mama died was apparently worth it.

Earl helped her carry the dessert plates to the dining room. She'd canned so many peaches from the western slope last summer she still had a handful of jars on the cellar shelf. However, she'd read in the paper that the home demonstration clubs should increase their canning to three hundred quarts of fruits and vegetables to make more food available to the soldiers, and Papa continually reminded them that greater farm production goals were meant to avoid the rationing they'd suffered during the World War.

Thinking about all those quarts wore her out, as if she could be any more tired. She'd have to give full attention to planting the rest of the garden. On her last trip to the dining room, Martha brought the crock pitcher filled with fresh cream to pour over the warmed slices of pie, so thick it poured out in lumps.

Her father looked inquiringly at his plate and said in a voice that started as a tease but concluded sounding somewhat disappointed. "What? None of your mama's Black Cake on Mother's Day?"

Before Martha could answer, he said, "I want everyone to know I'll not marry as long as Alex and Louise are at home. This place is theirs, until they have their own families and livelihoods. And Fran agrees."

What seemed like a full minute passed before Martha gathered her shattered thoughts. Marriage? She had only seen Papa and Miss Reeve, uh, Fran, together for the first time that morning.

And what an impossible stipulation! So unlike Papa, not to talk over something that affected all the family. What if Louise and Alex were to remain at home for some time? Wouldn't Fran grow to resent them? For that matter, wouldn't delaying his marriage make him increasingly bitter toward Alex and Louise, the longer they stayed?

On the other hand, wouldn't the twins feel they were denying Papa his happiness unless they left? They might make ill-advised decisions in order to get away. Did Louise already know Papa's position, and had that prompted her to attach the oblique comment referencing airplane construction to the conversation about Rev. Macgill's sermon?

If Martha were one of the twins, she wouldn't tolerate Papa's ultimatum. Instead of letting all his children meet Fran and get acquainted on a friendly basis, his announcement put a wedge between her and his children. It wasn't fair to her, and surely it strained her bond with Papa.

Perhaps this wasn't the first time since Mama's death that Papa had made this declaration to a woman. If so, no wonder he hadn't remarried. Who would wait around indefinitely?

Papa's intention to protect Louise and Alex had the opposite effect; he undermined their welfare, and Fran's, by keeping his own counsel. This must be what Art felt like when he accused her yesterday of working out everything in her own head and reaching decisions without talking to anyone.

When she surveyed the expressions on faces around the table, they were all somber, but no one looked as devastated as she felt. If

Papa had consulted with the others and she spoke up, she would be the only one in disagreement.

But she had to say something. "Papa, your decision puts Alex and Louise in an unfortunate position, and it certainly is awkward for Fran."

"Martha, I don't need to explain my reasons, except to say I intend to protect the twins' interests. Fran agrees. Please don't question me."

Humiliated, Martha pushed back her chair, prepared to leave the room. If Papa had ever rebuked her publicly like this, she was too young to remember. And he'd called her "Martha," not "Sis."

But leaving seemed childish. She didn't move, and she didn't take her eyes off her hands folded in her lap.

No one else spoke. They must have had an indication this was coming, or, at the very least, known that Papa's courtship with Fran Reeve had progressed to the point of conversations about marriage.

That must be why Fran hadn't come to dinner; she and Papa decided she shouldn't be present for his announcement. Martha wouldn't leave the room, but neither would she express any regret for contradicting Papa.

Josie, who was clearing the dessert plates, interrupted her thoughts. "Sis, you haven't touched your pie. Why so quiet? The men are going outside for a game of horseshoes. Let's clean up and join them. It's such a beautiful afternoon."

"Josie?"

Martha couldn't continue. Josie acted as though she didn't interpret Papa's announcement as cataclysmic, nor had she noticed how he'd humiliated her sister. And Martha hadn't heard talk about horseshoes.

"Yes?"

Rather than asking her point blank what she thought about Papa and Fran, in her confusion Martha said, "Never mind. I––I'll finish clearing. Louise and I can clean up. You go outside. Will you keep an eye on Anna? And will you help me set Carrie's bassinette on the porch? I'd like her to get some fresh air, too."

Martha washed and Louise dried. Martha had intended to ask Louise about her defense plants comment, but she was absorbed by Papa's announcement and rebuke. Shaken that she hadn't heard any of the conversation following Papa's scolding, she wondered what else she had missed these last months besides Papa's courtship. It may have started before Christmas and was the reason Louise pointed Fran out in the drugstore that Saturday. That must be the case, given it was Louise, who, with a conspiratorial grin, had drawn her attention to Papa and Fran in church.

Martha couldn't gather her jumbled thoughts. Papa's reprimand. Louise's oblique airplane comment. Alex's observation that folks would shun Carrie.

Carrie was a beautiful baby, and even more defenseless than a normal infant. Everyone should welcome her, which led Martha to believe that Alex reached his peace too quickly with their callous disregard by vowing to "help" them love Carrie. Why would she want to help any of them?

She was also unnerved by her inability to enter the discussion about Rev. Macgill's sermon beyond teasing Papa about Al. She had failed to keep up with the increasing threat of war, a threat so real her husband and brother-in-law were registered for the selective service.

Papa's concern to keep the farm for Alex was absurd, in light of the fact that Alex would register as soon as he turned twenty-one in January. Did Papa intend to make Fran wait until his old age to marry, until the uncertainties of international politics were clarified?

Speaking of international politics, she hadn't answered dear Muriel's last two letters, the one from the Hawaiian Islands and the one about her arrival in the Philippine Islands. Martha hadn't thought about Muriel Giffard for weeks, perhaps because Muriel's experiences as a Navy nurse in those exotic places seemed like a fairy tale, remote from their afternoons in high school at the Giffard lumberyard doing their homework and the trials they shared in nursing school. Martha hadn't known what to write, and, if she had, she didn't have time. But just now, Muriel seemed so close, closer than Louise putting dishes away in the cupboard beside her. She must answer Muriel. But she was exhausted.

Martha's only clear thoughts were that neither she nor Papa had told Anna the story of Mama's platter, and he hadn't expressed an opinion about their decision to keep Carrie at home.

Al Ivarson

Martha was still awake when Art crept into bed, obviously trying to keep the springs from creaking, an impossible task even for someone as coordinated as he.

"I need to talk to you about today," she whispered.

In the dark, Art's exasperated sigh sounded louder than the squeaky springs.

"Yer not sleepin'? What's the good a me feedin' Carrie so ya can get ta bed early? Who's gonna get up with 'er in the middle a the night? Now we'll both be wore out."

"Art, I so appreciate your help, but there's something more critical than my sleep tonight. Remember how you scolded me for keeping my thoughts to myself? A strange trait for a family that talks all the time, but Louise does it, and today Papa did it."

"Martha, I'm so blamed tired."

"Please, it's important. I was dumbstruck when Papa said he wouldn't marry Fran until Louise and Alex left home. I didn't even know he was courting her! Did you?"

"Don't know. I guess. I know they went ta the Fireman's Ball."

"Oh, that would have been about the time Doc sent me to bed in February. Do you think no one mentioned it because they thought it would upset me?"

"Martha, I didn't hear mention a the ball till recently, an' so much's been happenin'. Miyoshi's ruptured 'pendix an' needin' ta help 'im. Frettin' 'bout the selective service lists. Then, too, I was worried sick 'bout ya on account a the troubles with bein' pregnant an' all the scarlet fever an' measles goin' 'round."

Art was right. So much happening around the time Papa would have started courting Fran, if that's when it began. Maybe no one left her out on purpose. Still, it was a noteworthy piece of news to omit.

Art turned toward her. "And ya were so upset 'bout not gettin' ta go ta *Gone with the Wind* with yer Eagle View club. It was all outta kilter. I guess yer fit 'bout it made me careful what I told ya."

"Art, I didn't throw a fit. I was disappointed, yes, but eventually I saw the wisdom in staying close to home."

"Well, ya were more emotional than I'd seen 'bout somethin' so insignificant. I took it ta be on account a the problems with Carrie."

She turned on her side and snuggled into the curvature of his body.

"There's another thing," he said. "Remember how worried I was 'bout yer father and Al Ivarson — that dust up they had at the stock meetin' when they was talkin,' yellin' was more like it, 'bout whether ta help the British? Al was so mad at George Moulton fer sayin' how there was worse things that might happen ta his boys than ta die in a good fight. Al wouldn't stop, 'bout how everyone knows Roosevelt's gettin' ready fer war and Al'll have none of it. Robert insisted he calm down an' respect other men's opinions. Called 'im a fool. Said he always was one an' always would be. We nearly had ta separate 'em. Robert needs ta get hold a hisself. Election was six months ago."

It was Martha's turn to sigh. "Thanks, dear. Yes, a lot is happening, for all of us. I don't know what to do about Papa and Al, but I think I'll take the girls to town tomorrow and ask Josie and Louise about the business with Fran. I could stay for the Book Review Club meeting. Other than church today, I haven't been anywhere in a long time."

"But Al did tell a funny joke after Robert called 'im a fool. Al was prob'ly tryin' ta calm things down by introducin' some humor. He said when the pilgrims arrived the Injuns was runnin' the country with no taxes, no debt, no relief, no third term, an' the women did the work. An' white men thought they could improve on a system like that."

Martha didn't answer. Papa was right; Al was a fool and the joke tasteless. But she suspected anything Al Ivarson said would make Papa angry.

She also wanted to talk to Art about handling reactions to Carrie, but they needed sleep. Perhaps she should reconsider Alex's suggestion to help folks by explaining Carrie's difficulties and showing them how to treat her. If they were to make silly noises in her face as they did with other babies and she started one of her spasms, they'd be afraid of her. Surely they would welcome Carrie, if they knew how.

Martha was worn out, with Carrie, the trip to Denver, and Papa's announcement about Fran, and she worried that she hadn't heard the conversation about horseshoes. As she reminded herself to talk to Louise about airplanes, a giant replica of Mama's blue-and-white platter with its hairline cracks drifted across her mind's eye.

May 1941

Edith Giffard

Martha heard the bedsprings squeak and reached for the alarm — five twenty. The first morning Carrie hadn't wakened them. Art slipped on his pants.

"Good morning," she murmured.

"Well, mornin' sleepy head. How'd the night go?"

"She woke once, at two. Ate and went right back to sleep. I feel wonderful!"

"In that case, I'm comin' back ta bed."

Martha assumed he was teasing, but he let his pants drop. She drew a quick breath and her skin tingled from the middle of her abdomen around her buttocks, a sensation she hadn't felt for some time. She threw the sheet back.

He crawled in beside her, and Carrie whimpered. They groaned and rolled to their respective edges of the creaky bed.

"Remember, today I'm talking with Louise and Josie about Papa's 'I'll not marry' decree and might stay for the Book Club meeting."

She wanted his thoughts about introducing folks to Carrie, but he walked into the living room and brought Carrie from her bassinette. He laid her on the bed.

"I'm glad yer gonna spend time with yer sisters an' friends, but bring the truck back by three. I need ta haul fenceposts fer Al."

He stepped back but didn't take his eyes off Carrie.

"She's a prettier partner fer ya than I am. Hmm… Been lookin' fer a nickname an' just found it. Partner. She's that already, fer us both. Guess she won't leave our sides, the way Anna will, the way Anna already does."

Martha examined his face for regret or resentment but saw only tenderness. She picked Carrie up and noticed a frown that passed quickly. Surely simply lifting her from the bed wouldn't cause pain.

"It's nice of you to help the Ivarsons."

"We're neighbors, whether Democrat er Republican. Robert an' Al should remember that."

And he was out the door.

After Martha fed Carrie, she telephoned the Home Place to suggest meeting Louise at the drugstore, but no one answered — still outside doing chores. Martha wasn't eager to discuss family matters publically, in the balcony over the soda fountain, but she wanted the conversation about Papa and Fran with both her sisters, today.

Martha called Josie at six forty-five, before Art came in for breakfast. Earl didn't answer until the fifth ring.

"Knew it had to be a McLennan," he grumbled. "No one else calls this early."

Martha chose to make light of waking him. "Earl, enjoy sleeping in while you can. Won't be long before that baby will have you up at five. Is Josie nearby?"

Absent Earl's response, Martha guessed she wasn't because it took a while for her to answer. "I was in the bathroom. What's wrong?"

"Nothing. I want to meet up with you this morning, and Louise."

"Why so mysterious?"

"Don't mean to be. I'm just behind on news, not only about family. Could I pick you up around ten, and we can have coffee at the soda fountain?"

"I'd like that. You also noticed Louise's odd comments yesterday about building airplanes?"

"Yes, that and Papa's intentions regarding Fran."

"Hmm… We have more to talk about than a cup of coffee's worth. Why don't you stay in town for dinner, before the Book Club meeting at one? Is there a chance you'd attend? Edith Giffard's hosting, and you could catch up with her about Muriel."

Martha hesitated. She had second thoughts upon learning the meeting was at the Giffards'.

"I haven't written Muriel for months, and I don't know what book you're discussing."

"Doesn't matter, with Edith doing the review. The book's *Embezzled Heaven* by a refugee from Austria, Franz Werfel. We're several months behind the Book of the Month Club schedule. I'm certain Edith has done a thorough study of it, and his life, and will talk the entire time, just as I'm certain her house will be a mess, but Mrs. Hayes is bringing refreshments."

Martha wasn't familiar with the author or the book and decided she didn't want to spend time in the chaos of Edith's home with the women of the club, who all had indoor bathrooms and preoccupied themselves with nothing more substantial than fancy desserts.

"Depending on how Carrie's doing, dinner with you, but I'll forego club this month."

Enoch Gwynn

Accompanied by Josie, Martha parked in front of the mortuary, down the street from the drugstore. Enoch Gwynn emerged, waved, and turned toward the corner. Martha and Josie walked the other direction with the girls. As Josie opened the glass door of the store, Martha heard Enoch call her name.

Josie entered with Anna; Enoch scurried toward Martha. "So good to see you out yesterday. What a crowd we had at church! May I see the baby?"

Enoch never lacked for words, which Martha attributed to his profession. He probably filled the silence by babbling away at corpses in his kind and high-pitched voice.

When he looked at Carrie, he paused. "Why, she's beautiful."

Jimmie Ichikawa's comment and that of others, word for word. Time to test Alex's proposed tactic of helping folks get acquainted with Carrie.

"Thank you. Of course, as her mother I think so, too. Even though she has more than an infant's usual difficulty with coordination when she's awake, we're learning how to hold her so she stays relaxed. It helps not to make sudden movements or loud noises."

Enoch cautiously moved his hand toward Carrie's face. He caressed her forehead with the tip of his index finger, as Anna had, and was silent. When he spoke, his voice was soft, his cadence slow.

"She's so tiny, a miniature of you."

Her explanation about Carrie apparently put him at ease, and he continued in the same slow, quiet manner, so unlike him. He didn't take his eyes off Carrie.

"Martha, I need your help. There's been an accident. A man and boy, who appears to be about five years old. Killed on Collins Curve earlier today. Sheriff Burleigh determined the man's identity, a Mr. Maher, and he's going out south to notify the family, who might live near your uncle Malcolm. I'm cautious, though, because Burleigh isn't the best messenger to carry harsh news to a young widow, particularly since we don't know their circumstances. Would you go with him? I know you can handle it, with your training and temperament."

He looked up, and for an instant Martha saw a depth of sorrow in his eyes she had never noticed, not even at the time of Mama's death. It disappeared as quickly as Carrie's grimace had, so ephemeral she doubted having seen it. Enoch's pleasant demeanor hid a sadness that must more accurately represent him. He resumed his high-pitched chatter.

"But I see you and your daughters are here to enjoy a soda pop with your sisters. Please forgive my intrusion. I'll be on my way."

With a polite efficiency that matched his, Martha responded, "Enoch, thank you for your confidence in my capabilities. I want to say yes to your request, but give me a moment to arrange for Josie and Louise to take the girls."

She re-entered the world of daughters, sisters, and the impending conversation about a father on the precipice of making a romantic mistake before the full weight of accepting the task struck her. Given her circumstances, she couldn't function as a capable nurse, although her desire to take on Enoch's mission was as strong as wanting the conversation about Papa.

She turned back to tell Enoch no, but Louise called out. "Martha, why were you and Mr. Gwynn talking so earnestly? I've always thought he was sweet on you."

What a silly thing to say. Enoch was much older and didn't hold a candle to Art. Instead of pursuing Enoch, Martha responded to Louise. Josie left Anna looking at knick-knacks with a stern warning not to touch and joined the conversation. Martha summarized the details and, rather than telling them she'd said yes, asked their opinion.

Neither hesitated. Of course Martha should assist. Josie offered to take the girls.

Louise summarized what neither Josie nor Martha said aloud. It was irresponsible to send someone as crude as Burleigh on an assignment requiring finesse. Only last week he'd burst into the honky-tonk joint frequented by workers at the Caddoa dam construction site and, without warning, smashed two slot machines with a baseball bat. Granted, the machines were illegal. Still, Louise couldn't forgive herself if she let a man like that loose on a woman with these problems.

Louise's account of Burleigh and the honky-tonk bar sounded more realistic than Art's summary of the incident from the article in the paper. Conceivably, Louise was an eyewitness, given that she played piano up and down the Valley, in who knew what kinds of venues.

"Mr. Gwynn's right to ask," Louise said. "You have the suitable experience, along with Millie Swanson and Mrs. DeFries. But Mrs. DeFries's services as a practical nurse are always in demand. At the moment, she could be anywhere, and Millie's probably at one of the rural schools completing her county nurse visits for the school term. This requires immediate attention."

Josie added, "I don't mind missing the Book Club. Louise can take me and the girls to your place in your truck where I'll have everything I need, can't you, Louise?"

"Yes, and Alex or Papa will drive me back to town. But Earl isn't going to like it, you with both girls. He'll say it's too strenuous, given your 'condition.' Art can take Anna with him."

"That won't work," Martha said. "Art's at the Ivarsons' helping dig postholes to fence in their north pasture."

Josie chewed on her lip as she did when working on a problem and said, "Anna's more help than bother, a four-year-old going on fourteen. If you're not back before Earl's home from school, he'll think I lingered at the club meeting. He doesn't need to know."

She winked at her sisters, and the three broke out laughing, which prompted Carrie to flail arms and legs.

Martha soothed Carrie and said, "We'll have two happy husbands. You'll be home in time for supper, and Art'll have the truck when he needs it."

They had handled Enoch's request with dispatch, typical of her family. Surely the three sisters could come up with a plan to deal with Papa and his declaration about delayed matrimony. She must have imagined her isolation yesterday during Sunday dinner at the Home Place.

Vera Olmstead

At the end of an hour's drive, some of it on dead-end dirt roads that led into pastures, Sheriff Burleigh turned up the lane to a one-room house.

"This here's the only other place it could be, if Hank understood Maher right when he left his pickup an' took the car out a the lot fer a spin. Said he was movin' his family from out south ta Greeley an' wouldn't need a truck no more."

The house looked abandoned. The ripped screens hanging on the two front windows twisted as though captured in their attempt to escape, and the few remaining flecks of white paint clung to the weathered wood, seemingly worn out from hanging on so long in the face of persistent wind and sun. A lone juniper and windmill stood, determined, at the far end of a dilapidated barn.

However, the sound of automobile tires grinding on gravel brought a thin, barefoot young woman with a hoe in her hands from behind the house. Her ragged feedcloth dress hung from her bony shoulders.

Burleigh made no move to get out of the Buick. "This is a surprise. The husband an' son were better kept."

Martha emerged warily from her side, speaking slowly, reassuringly. "Hello, Mrs. Maher. My name's Martha Lundgren. My uncle, Malcolm McLennan, lives down the road from you, on the other side of the arroyo."

"Whada ya want from me?" Mrs. Maher answered in a surprisingly deep voice, given her small frame.

"Uh, nothing. I, uh, we, Sheriff Burleigh and I, have something to tell you. Can we go inside and talk?"

Burleigh took this as his cue and opened his door. Mrs. Maher raised the hoe. Martha backtracked. Maybe having the law in her driveway threatened the girl.

"Would you prefer the sheriff wait here while you and I talk?"

Mrs. Maher turned toward the back door, which Martha took as assent. She trailed about ten feet behind as they walked through the dust. Martha still had on her hat and gloves from her trip to town, ridiculously formal, so she removed them. She thought Mrs. Maher spoke when she passed the lean-to near the door.

"Beg pardon; I didn't hear," Martha said.

"Wasn't talkin' ta ya," Mrs. Maher growled.

They entered the dark room. An unlit kerosene lamp sat on the warped wooden tabletop. The interior looked swept clean. Other than the table and coal stove, the only furnishings were an icebox, three chairs, and a bed. A teddy bear rested on it, along with a child's ball. The stove was cold. A shelf on the wall held several plates, some silverware, three glasses, and a tin cup. Martha surmised Mrs. Maher hadn't eaten breakfast. She motioned for Martha to sit.

"Mrs. Maher, as I said, my name's Martha, Martha Lundgren. What's yours?"

"Vera."

"Have you and your family lived here long?"

Uncle Malcolm hadn't mentioned new neighbors, but she saw him infrequently. Besides, social life wasn't something he noticed.

"Since sometime 'round Christmas."

Martha abandoned the chitchat because it was obviously as strange for Vera to have an unknown woman in her home as it was for Martha to be there. She leaned forward, closer to Vera, who was sitting across from her, placed her hat and gloves on the table, and rested her hands on the smooth, worn wood.

"Vera, I'm sorry for not stating my business sooner, but what I have to say is very difficult."

Martha searched Vera's impassive face in the dim light.

"Early this morning, Sheriff Burleigh was called to the site of an automobile accident at what we call Collins Curve, up near the town of Greenwood."

Vera's body stiffened, but her expression didn't change.

"The vehicle skidded off the road and landed upside-down in the barrow pit. Your husband and son were killed."

Vera's face remained immobile, and Martha debated whether, if Vera hadn't understood, she should rephrase. But Vera raised her hands to cover her face. Martha still couldn't decipher her reaction. After prolonged silence, Martha stood, picked up her chair, walked around the table, and sat next to Vera. She gathered Vera in her arms, and Vera's body softened against hers.

"I'm Vera Olmstead. Freddie's my son, but that man, Maher, ain't my husband. Don't even think his name's Maher."

Vera drew away. Martha noted the purple bruises on her forearm.

"Yer sure Maher's dead?"

"Well, yes. I didn't see the body but the mortician told me he was."

"He did this ta me."

She pointed to the bruises.

"An' this."

She turned her head and pulled back strands of hair that partially covered more bruises on her swollen left cheek.

"An' this."

She drew her dress well above her knees and showed Martha raised red welts on her thighs.

"From 'is belt. Yesterday. Just ta be sure I didn't leave till he got back, he said."

Now Martha was inclined to cover her eyes, but she didn't.

"Tell me."

In a monotone, Vera concisely narrated a story Martha could scarcely absorb. Five years ago, during a dirt storm, Maher appeared at her family's farmhouse in Oklahoma. A drifter. Her mother served him food, and he went on his way.

Late that night, he came back. Wind muffled the sound when he shattered her bedroom window. He gagged her with the damp towel she had tied over her nose and mouth to sift the dirt-filled air and dragged her out the window. A shard of glass tore away flesh on his arm and her leg.

"This here's the scar."

She stood, turned, and lifted her dress again to reveal a scar running about four inches down the back of her upper leg.

He stole what they needed along the way, she said, and Martha could imagine they looked like any of the hundreds adrift on the countryside during the dry years.

Freddie was born twelve months later, somewhere in Arizona. Eventually they wandered into Colorado and lived in abandoned farmhouses, like this one. Vera saw no possibility of escape, until last Christmas. Maher took Freddie to Greenwood's drugstore to pick out a present. Maher often took Freddie with him. Sometimes they were gone for days, but this time he brought Vera along. He went back later and stole the gift, the teddy bear. Vera nodded toward it on the bed.

And Vera was silent.

Martha waited. Perhaps this was Vera's way of mourning her boy. Vera picked up where she left off, as though she hadn't paused. She said that in the store she saw a familiar face, her schoolteacher from home, Miss Reeve.

Martha opened her mouth to exclaim — something — she didn't know what, and closed it again. She leaned in, closer to Vera, who evidently interpreted Martha's movement as empathy. Vera rested her head on Martha's shoulder.

She said she passed Miss Reeve in the aisle, pulled at her coat sleeve and whispered, "Miss Reeve, I'm Vera Olmstead. Ya know me from home. Get word ta my family I'm kidnapped an' here, near this town."

Maher rounded the corner, and Vera slipped by Miss Reeve.

Martha steadied herself by gripping the wooden table. Fran Reeve? The carefree woman in church whose hand Papa caressed and whom he graced with his smile? How could she behave that way, knowing a girl desperately needed her help?

Vera droned on. In February, her younger, and only, sister, Ida, appeared.

"Ida an' I look like twins, so when Maher saw 'er at the train station by chance, he knew we was related. She told him she was 'spectin' Miss Reeve 'cause the woman she lived with an' worked fer in the town near our farm wrote Miss Reeve ta tell 'er she was comin'. Everyone remembers Miss Reeve 'cause, well, 'cause she's so beautiful. Ida went an' told Maher all that."

So Fran Reeve had ignored both Vera's plea in the drugstore before Christmas and the letter informing her of Ida's arrival? But Fran must have been in contact with someone in Oklahoma after encountering Vera, or Ida wouldn't have known to make the trip.

"Maher told Ida he was my neighbor and would bring 'er ta me. That I lived a long way from town. No need ta wait fer Miss Reeve. Maher's like that, was like that. A smooth talker."

"And your parents?"

"Ida said they left our dried-up farm when she moved ta town. They were goin' west, but she never heard from 'em."

According to Vera, the two girls plotted several times to escape with Freddie. Once they got as far as the highway, which Martha estimated was five miles from the house, but Maher always found and beat them. Eventually he locked Ida in the lean-to and threatened to kill her if Vera ran away again.

Martha couldn't fill the gaps in Vera's story. Miss Reeve, Fran, had been in touch with people in Oklahoma, who were perhaps teachers in town or her own family, and they had notified Ida about Vera's location. But why hadn't Fran searched for Vera?

Ida, as a young girl would, took it in her head to come to Greenwood for Vera. Someone wrote Fran telling her Ida was on her way. Why hadn't Fran been at the train station when Ida arrived? When Ida didn't return to Oklahoma or write, why hadn't someone come looking for her?

Vera's story was so extraordinary Martha had difficulty imagining Fran as a participant. What could explain Fran's failure to play an active role in the girls' rescue?

But aloud, Martha asked, "And the story about moving to Greeley that he told Hank, the Chevy dealer, when he left the truck and took a new automobile for a drive?"

"He ain't said nothin' 'bout movin' when he left with Freddie…"

Vera's voice trailed off and she took some moments to regain it. Perhaps her relief that Maher was gone hadn't overpowered the fact of Freddie's death, after all.

"When he left, he was drivin' the pickup he stole last year in Albuquerque. Must a though he'd get rid a it an' steal the automobile. Maher's smart. Never gets caught… Until now, by that there Collins Curve."

And by his mention of a "family" out south, unless he left that clue on purpose. If he hadn't returned, the girls surely would have died, terrified to disobey him by leaving the premises.

Ida Olmstead

Martha stood. "Let's get Ida."

"How?"

"A crowbar, your hoe. Anything to pry open the door. Lean-to's so rickety it shouldn't be hard, with Sheriff Burleigh to help us."

"An' now there ain't no Maher ta kill 'er, er me, if we let 'er out."

A gunshot brought Vera to her feet. Maybe Burleigh had discovered yet another miscreant on the property and shot him, or had been shot. They ran out to find him staring at what appeared to be Vera's double, a girl emerging from the lean-to.

"Heard bangin' in there. Shot off the lock. Who's she?" he said.

Did Burleigh ever consider the consequences before he acted? What if an errant bullet had struck Ida?

Vera went to Ida; Martha passed along her information to Burleigh. In turn, he described what he'd seen by poking around the place because the discrepancy between what he assumed was Maher's social position and the farmhouse prompted some "investigatin'."

He had found a cabinet in the feed room of the barn, cabinet and room secured by padlocks, which he broke off with a crowbar from his Buick.

"Why didn't you use your crowbar on the shed? You nearly shot Ida!" Martha shouted.

Burleigh ignored her and continued. The cabinet contained a stash of items, including cans of vegetables and fruit, tools, decks of cards, soap, beauty products, knick-knacks, some small Navajo rugs, and, wrapped in one rug, a cache of Indian jewelry, along with several crates of clothes.

"Guess he stole it all ta resell it," said Burleigh. "What a scoundrel! Leavin' that nice pickup with Hank at the Motor Company, along with 'is name, an' takin' a new vehicle an' wreckin' it on Collins Curve. Said him an' 'is family was movin', but I doubt he intended ta come back here. Oh, there's also a skinny cow."

"I don't think he was coming back, either. Vera says his name probably wasn't Maher."

Enough about Maher. The immediate problem was what to do with two dirty, distressed girls who had gone through, to speak bluntly, hell. Probably Ida hadn't eaten since Maher had left yesterday, and Martha had smelled the foul odor of an un-emptied chamber pot coming from the shed.

"Sheriff, I have to get these girls cleaned up so we can take them to town. They don't seem to have family, so we need to figure out where they'll stay. Why don't you drive over to Uncle Malcolm's and see if he can take the cow while I give them a bath? Is there a washtub in the barn?"

"Don't remember seein' one."

"Can't we at least bring them some cans of that food?"

Suddenly, all Martha wanted was to be home. What Enoch presented as a difficult task had turned into an impossible one. The cruelty she witnessed was beyond anything in her experience. The ill and suffering folks she saw in her nurse's training and in Doc's office were usually surrounded by family, as far as she could recall. The embrace of loved ones who mourned with the bereaved tempered the shock of senseless accidents, like the one that killed José Marquez in their hayfield, or Frank Ogawa's death after diving into the canal. Who gave these girls solace?

And Fran Reeve, a woman she had yet to meet officially, was in a position to help, and she had not. Papa intended to marry Fran, maybe, someday. The delay was well advised, but not for Papa's reasons.

Overwhelmed, Martha started with practical matters. Building a fire in the stove and heating water for a bath would take too long. Besides, there was no tub, but the windmill and juniper hinted at water nearby.

Maybe the cow gave milk, and Vera's hoe hinted there might be a garden. If no milk and no garden, Burleigh would probably shoot holes in some cans of food and make the girls suck out the contents.

They were sitting on the back step, embracing one another, rocking back and forth. Vera caressed Ida's hair.

Martha started her own "investigation." She found a full horse tank in the little corral. A splash in it would take care of baths, for now.

Burleigh walked out of the barn with two cans of corn and pulled a wicked-looking knife from his pocket. He sliced open the lids and handed her the cans without comment.

"Thank you, Sheriff. Now go on and find Uncle Malcolm so I can bathe them."

When she reached the back step, Vera and Ida were gnawing on carrots, evidently from Vera's skimpy garden. Martha offered the corn, which they eagerly accepted. Carrots and corn devoured, Vera retrieved the tin cup. She walked to the barn, and Martha kept Ida company.

Martha introduced herself, but Ida stared right through her. Vera returned with milk in the cup.

"Don't know what we'd a done without that cow," she observed in her flat, raspy voice.

She agreed to Martha's suggestion about a horse-tank dip but refused to wear the flour-sack dresses again.

Ida spoke, in a voice as gentle and soft as Vera's was harsh. "I brought a suitcase. Where do you suppose he put that?"

Martha described the stash in the barn, so they looked there first. No suitcase. Maher must have sold it and the contents. She and Vera examined the several crates. One contained a man's suit, overalls, dress shirts and work shirts, some slacks, and sweaters. Women's clothes rested in another. Nice dresses, everything a bit large for the girls, but some would do. There were slips, panties, even several pairs of hosiery and garter belts. The third and fourth crates held an assortment of shoes, the fifth, women's hats and gloves.

Martha made mental note to tell Burleigh that the men's clothing was slightly worn, even the hats, and all were the same size. Perhaps disguises for Maher, as circumstances required. The women's clothes were new and in multiple sizes, intended for sale.

The girls searched through the crates. Still no sign of Ida's clothes. She selected a black-and-white checked dress, black leather pumps, dusty-rose gloves, and a straw hat to match.

"Ida, your choices are lovely," Martha said.

Ida didn't answer and retreated to a corner.

Vera took longer, fingering each item. She commented in her neutral manner, "He had all this an' made me wear an ole flour sack."

She chose spectator shoes and a navy, deep-kick pleated skirt, a white blouse and navy accessories. Martha was also impressed with Vera's good taste and urged her and Ida to take several of the housedresses, sporty oxfords, and some anklets.

How could Maher have cultivated such refined tastes but treated the girls so brutally? Art never would have assembled such a stylish assortment. How peculiar. How…evil.

New wardrobes in hand, they walked to the horse tank. Vera and Ida slipped off the flour-sack dresses and Martha made note: no underwear, and, judging from the bulge in Ida's abdomen, she was pregnant. The magnitude of Maher's depravity nauseated her.

When Burleigh returned, he nodded with approval at the girls' transformation. "Let's get 'em ta town. I'll send someone back fer the evidence."

"Sheriff Burleigh, if the county sells the stolen items, shouldn't Vera and Ida receive the proceeds?"

"Them's legal matters. Up ta Judge Arnold ta decide."

If left to Burleigh, Martha doubted the girls would get anything. She'd be sure to inquire further.

Vera disappeared into the house, emerged with the teddy bear and ball, and said, "I'm ready."

May 1941

Parker Hayes

When they reached town, Burleigh parked in front of the mortuary and said he wanted the girls to identify the bodies. He seemed oblivious that Vera was a mother whose son had just been killed.

Martha softened his directive. "Vera, you can spend time with Freddie, if you want."

"Well, that, too," Burleigh countered. "But I want the identification first fer Miss Reeve. Then you can spend time with your son, miss. I don't want no more confusion 'bout gals from Oklahoma."

Martha looked sideways at Burleigh. "You've known about Vera and Ida? Why didn't you do something sooner?"

He heaved his bulk out the driver's door. "It's complicated legal business."

Another phony answer. If she understood Burleigh correctly, at least two people knew about "gals from Oklahoma," he and Fran Reeve. Why hadn't they taken steps to locate them? How had Maher's subterfuge continued long enough for him to draw Ida into his lair, too? If Fran had met that train, she could have protected Ida, at

85

least. From holding Fran responsible, Martha easily blamed her for fomenting as yet unknown disasters in the McLennan family.

Vera's deep voice broke through Martha's reverie. "Mrs. Lundgren? Are we goin' in now? The sheriff's waitin' at the door."

Martha assumed the girls would follow Burleigh, an assumption they obviously didn't share as they still sat in the back seat. Burleigh wasn't their companion; Martha was, and she would have to see it through.

She turned to give them a reassuring smile before opening her door but stopped when she saw Ida rocking back and forth.

"I can't," Ida said, twisting her fingers together in the dusty-rose gloves. "I can't see him again. Don't make me. Don't make me. Don't make me."

Vera scooted over and put her arm around Ida's shoulders. "You don't have ta, honey. I'll do it."

Ida leaned away and, with her eyes shut, continued to mouth the words, "Don't make me. Don't make me."

Martha hurried around to Ida's door and slid in beside her. She peered around Ida to encourage Vera. "Go with the sheriff and identify Maher. You can come back later to see Freddie. We have to get Ida away from here. I'll stay with her."

The wait in the hot car lasted longer than Martha expected.

When Vera returned with Burleigh, she explained, "It might a been someone who jus' looked like 'im. I made 'em take off his shirt so I could see the scar on his arm from when he pulled me outta the broken window."

Burleigh nodded in grim approval. "We have ta stop by Miss Reeve's now, so she can identify this Vera. What's the matter with her?"

He jerked his thumb toward Ida.

"I'm not sure," Martha answered. "When she thought she would have to see Maher, she began to repeat, 'Don't make me,' and she hasn't stopped. She won't respond to anything I say. Why all this identification? We have to get the girls settled somewhere."

"Already told ya. Complicated."

Burleigh turned north at the corner and drove several blocks before turning west and stopping in front of the largest house on the block, a two-story red brick with a wide screened porch on the front and west sides and white columns interspersed along the white railing. Parker Hayes's home. Fran must rent rooms from him.

"Sheriff, after you take care of your business with Miss Reeve, we need to stop at Mrs. DeFries's. I don't know where you intend for the girls to stay, but given Ida's condition, they should probably be with Mrs. DeFries while decisions are made."

She assumed Burleigh intended to install the girls at the hotel and the bill would be paid from county welfare funds until after the funerals. Then the two would be sent back to Oklahoma. But that wouldn't do. Ida's condition suggested she needed more supervision than Vera could give. Martha hadn't told Burleigh Ida was pregnant. Perhaps Ida didn't even know.

Burleigh grunted. Now more familiar with the nuances of his monosyllables, Martha assumed he agreed. He evidently hadn't thought past his need to put together whatever pieces of the crime puzzle Fran could supply.

Ida continued her murmuring, and Martha rested her hand over Ida's to stop the finger-twisting. Vera sat stiffly in the front seat with Burleigh.

Suddenly Vera called out, "There she is. There's Miss Reeve."

Fran walked — rather, strode — along the sidewalk toward them on their side of the street, approaching the Hayes home from the opposite direction. She turned toward the house, and Burleigh honked the Buick's horn. She looked back, recognized the sheriff's car, smiled, and waved. Burleigh yelled across Vera for her to stop.

Vera called out the window, "Miss Reeve, I'm Vera Olmstead, the girl in the drugstore."

Fran did not move.

Burleigh got out, leaned over the top of the vehicle, and said, "It's confusin.' That other girl I told ya I sent back ta Oklahoma? Evidently another Vera. If ya remember, ya weren't sure 'bout the last name, or the town where ya taught her. And now we got a third girl. Please get in the car. We'll go ta the jail an' straighten things out."

Another Vera? The situation sounded less like complicated legal business and more like someone covering his tracks.

Fran seemed frozen in place, nor did she answer. Was she shocked? Indifferent? And from Burleigh's few words, Fran sounded more involved than Martha supposed.

Fran finally spoke. A smooth voice that complemented her physical appearance. Confident. Measured. If Fran were a singer, she would probably be a contralto.

"Sheriff, I hardly know how to answer. To say this is a shock doesn't express it because you assured me months ago you found Vera and sent her home. Wouldn't my apartment be a more comfortable setting for the conversation we need to have?"

Now Burleigh hesitated. Probably he preferred his home territory, his office at the jail; then again, he would have to transport all four women in the hot car, which meant more delay.

"Why, thank ya, Miss Reeve," he answered.

Fran's composure either intimidated him or brought out the better man.

Martha helped Ida out and saw the damp imprint on the seat. Incontinent. Ida was in worse shape than Martha thought. She guided the murmuring girl to the sidewalk. Fran reached out to greet her, but Martha motioned her away. She drew back.

"I'm Martha Lundgren, a nurse. Ida's not well. I went out south with Sheriff Burleigh this morning, where we found the girls."

Fran moved toward Vera, and Martha surmised Fran hadn't connected a Lundgren to Robert McLennan, her maybe-someday-husband. Martha guided Ida to the shade of the elm tree and watched Fran embrace Vera. Martha checked the wet spot on the back of Ida's dress. The black and white pattern hid it well but couldn't mask the smell.

Martha saw Parker Hayes walking toward the house from the other direction. It must be five thirty. Mr. Hayes was a man of habit whom no one accused of keeping "banker's hours," although he was the bank's president. Mr. Hayes's reputation as a hard worker even commanded the respect of the farmers. Mrs. Hayes approached the group from the front steps of the porch, turning the gathering into a convention.

How would Burleigh handle his "complicated legal business" and Mr. and Mrs. Hayes? Martha had only a smattering of information, not much to contribute, so she stayed under the elm with Ida, who had even less to say. Martha saw the third Hayes, sixteen-year-old Charlie, amble around the corner from the high school, the same direction Fran had come from.

"Afternoon, folks," Burleigh said. "Mrs. Hayes, Mr. Hayes."

He shook Mr. Hayes's hand and tipped his Stetson to Mrs. Hayes. "Mr. Hayes, given yer standin' in this town, I feel I can, an' prob'ly should, trust ya with the story I'm 'bout ta tell."

Typical Burleigh. Legal business too complicated for Martha was readily available to Parker Hayes. Burleigh always knew whom to flatter. He seemed to forget his objective had been to confirm something with Fran, and Martha could tell from Mr. Hayes's curt nod he wasn't eager to be privy to the sheriff's business.

Evidently interpreting Mr. Hayes's nod as agreement, Burleigh hurried into his tale, unaware of Charlie's approach from behind.

"Last winter Miss Reeve brought me disturbin' information that a girl from Oklahoma, a former student, was kidnapped an' in this area. We had only the first name, Vera, an' we didn't know which a Miss Reeve's schools this Vera was from."

Burleigh cleared his throat and drew in his belly, which had the salutary effect of making him seem taller.

"My office did some investigatin' by contactin' the sheriffs' offices in the places where Miss Reeve has taught 'bout girls missin' with the name a 'Vera.' Didn't turn up nothin'. Two months later, when I picked up a fella stealin' tools from the dam site, I found a young woman in his shack. Said she was from Oklahoma, an' I recognized the town as one where Miss Reeve lived. Her name was Vera, same as the name I had from Miss Reeve. I sent her home an' told Miss Reeve I took care of it."

So Fran had attempted to track Vera down, through Burleigh. Perhaps the calls he made to other sheriffs' offices had prompted Ida's ill-advised quest.

"Today I find another Vera from Oklahoma kidnapped south a town by another thief who had her younger sister locked in a lean-to. Ida. She's standin' over there. These clothes they're wearin' are from what he stole. This business 'bout two 'Veras' is quite the coincidence. I only need Miss Reeve ta confirm this is the Vera we been lookin' for, which, I admit, I should a done the first time, so we can send these girls home. That'll end it."

End it? Burleigh showed no awareness of the girls' suffering. A solved case was all he needed. Burleigh's brusqueness had disappeared, and the way he ingratiated himself in front of Mr. and Mrs. Hayes was pitiful.

In spite of their habitual poise, they seemed shaken by Burleigh's story, a rough one, roughly told. Charlie's mouth dropped open, and he stared first at Ida, then at Vera, then at Ida again, probably gauging whether he and Ida were close to the same age.

Fran and Martha instinctively moved to protect the dignity of the girls, Fran by taking Vera's hand and Martha by taking Ida's and moving her further from the group, closer to the flowerbed in front of the house. Ida didn't resist and seemed unaware the conversation was about her.

Vera addressed Fran in her flat voice, without accusation. "You didn't meet Ida at the train station, when she came for me."

Martha could see Fran's face clearly; it reflected a range of emotion — puzzled, kind, worried, puzzled again.

She put her arms around Vera. "No, honey, I didn't. How would I know to meet Ida at the train station?"

Vera rested her head on Fran's shoulder. "They wrote ya a letter she was comin' fer me. The people she lived with. They wrote ya a letter. But ya didn't meet her. Maher saw her at the station an' picked her up. He beat her an' did terrible things ta 'er."

Before Fran could answer, Mrs. Hayes broke into the now-jagged chronology of events. "Charles, Parker, let's go inside and let the sheriff handle this. The girls have been through enough today."

She put her hand on Charlie's shoulder and steered him toward the front porch. Mrs. Hayes clearly intended to protect his innocence; hers wasn't a concern for the girls who bore the consequences of Maher's cruelty.

Because of Mrs. Hayes's indifference, Martha's opinion of the entire family plummeted, almost as low as her opinion of Burleigh. She faulted both herself and Fran for not insisting they have the conversation in private, in Fran's apartment. There was never a need to involve the Hayes family, unless it was for Burleigh to brag about solving a mystery.

But Mr. Hayes didn't comply with his wife's order. "You and Charlie go ahead. I have several questions for Sheriff Burleigh."

No one spoke while Mrs. Hayes ushered her son up the steps.

After the screen door slammed, Mr. Hayes said, "Burleigh, what's going to happen to these girls, and why did their folks send one child to rescue another?"

Ida knelt by the bed of iris. Her repetition of "Don't make me" was replaced by "Pretty flowers, pretty flowers." Thank the Good Lord she was still somewhat aware of her surroundings.

Burleigh wasn't one to have meaningful answers, so Martha called out, "Sheriff, please take us to Mrs. DeFries's where we can get the girls settled and medical care for Ida."

Fran reacted first.

"I'm coming with you. I'm partly responsible for this horror going on so long, and this time I'll see it through properly."

"Sheriff," Mr. Hayes added, "you might not know off-hand just how much the county can contribute to this kind of situation, but if there's financial need, please come to me."

Having other adults sympathize with the girls' plight brought Martha immediate relief. The word "horror" came as close as any to describing it. They weren't cases needing solving but children needing attention.

Martha's opinion of Mr. Hayes rebounded, if not of Mrs. Hayes. From Papa's stories about farmers during the hard years, she knew Mr. Hayes extended loans to desperate families in last-ditch attempts to save them from foreclosure, and, no doubt, to businessmen in similar straits. Mr. Hayes had heard and seen enough trouble over the past decade not to run from it, not the way Mrs. Hayes had.

Charlie didn't need his mama's protection. He needed his father's example. Charlie was the same age as Jimmie Ichikawa, who had witnessed Frank Ogawa's accident in '39, and nearly Martha's age when Mama died in '33, old enough to learn about life's cruel turns.

Luis Marquez

Burleigh dropped Martha off around seven o'clock, hours after she thought she'd be home. She hadn't eaten since breakfast and struggled to open the Buick's heavy door. He wasn't one to bother with the courtesy of helping a lady. She pushed herself out and the door slammed shut, pulled by its own weight.

Art emerged from the barn. He hurried toward her, the furrow between his eyebrows growing deeper with each stride. Perhaps he thought she had returned earlier and only now realized how late she was. She straightened her shoulders and smiled to cover the signs of her exhaustion. She wanted to direct his sympathies toward Vera and Ida, not herself.

Art's first words were, "Where's yer hat?"

She might hide fatigue but not the wrinkled and stained dress, the mussed-up hair, and missing hat. She hadn't seen it or her gloves after she placed them on the table at Maher's, and the memory recalled the smooth, warm wood pressing against her fingertips and Burleigh shooting the lock off the shed door. Martha turned her head toward the car, the first time she'd cried that day.

She half bent and called to Burleigh through the open window, "Thanks for the lift."

He leaned over from behind the steering wheel, grumbled, "Evenin', Art," and started rolling up the window before Art answered, evidently as eager to leave as Martha was to have him go. Art raised his hand in half a wave. He watched Burleigh back the car, turn, and drive down the lane, so he didn't see Martha wipe away her tears.

She turned to Art and rested her head against his chest. She inhaled deeply to replace the smell of Ida's urine with the smell of him. He started to push her away.

"I'm all sweaty. Ya never want ta touch me after I been workin' in the barn."

"I know, but right now your smell's why I want to stay close."

Blunt remarks about body odor embarrassed her, and she laughed to cover her discomfort. Art's hands still rested on her shoulders.

"Ya all right? Yer a lot later than Josie said ya'd be."

"No, I'm not all right. I've seen and heard things today I never thought were possible. I'll tell you later. How are the girls?"

"Don't really know," Art answered. "Earl picked up Josie hours ago. He's put out she was here all day, least that's what Elena said when I last talked ta 'er."

"Josie's gone? Elena Marquez is here?"

"Yep."

"Why?"

Art drew the deep breath that indicated he was about to launch into a painstaking summary of the events bringing them to this moment. Martha was too worn out to insist on the abridged version.

"The ditch rider came by ta let Alex an' Robert know there'd be an extra run a water, if they wanted it. He couldn't find me 'cause I was at the Ivarsons', diggin' the holes fer the fenceposts, so Alex, Luis, an' Robert set the water on both places, which was too much work fer 'em with Anna, too. It was Luis's idea ta get Elena fer Anna."

So they didn't burden Josie with both girls, after all.

"I didn't know 'bout it till late this afternoon, after Earl came out from town fer Josie. Elena took Carrie, too."

Martha followed the general outline of the logistics, and by the time Art concluded his recitation, she exerted her remaining energy for a lecture that began with, "What were you thinking? Elena hasn't met Carrie. She doesn't know how to handle her. And Anna might see Elena from time to time at the Home Place, but how well acquainted could they be?"

Martha didn't wait for an answer. She hurried toward the house, expecting to find Carrie in spasms and Anna in tears. Art followed on her heels.

She smelled coffee brewing and hamburgers frying when she stepped through the screen door onto the porch. They entered the kitchen together. Elena was walking to the stove from the kitchen table where Anna pushed red and black checkers around the board. Carrie slept in her bassinette, clearly visible through the door into Anna's narrow bedroom.

Anna glanced up long enough to declare, "Hi, Mama. I'm playing checkers! Elena's here, and she's fixing us a nice hot meal."

Elena smiled at Martha and Art, as though it were the most ordinary thing for her to be standing in their kitchen, but her large black eyes overshadowed the smile. Instead of tumbling into their pools of unknown depth, as she had the day Carrie was born, Martha relaxed into billows of soft, dark feathers. Their caress soothed her jagged nerves. Her girls were safe.

The sudden reversal of feeling in the familiar surroundings affected her sense of balance. She steadied herself by leaning against the sink before she headed over to hug Anna.

"Thank you, Elena. How clever of you to tuck the bassinette into Anna's bedroom, near the kitchen for convenience. Carrie's close enough to sense everyone's presence but sufficiently removed to muffle any sudden noises that might startle her."

Elena nodded by way of accepting the compliment and said, "I am so glad you are home after a difficult day. You seem very tired.

Your sister, Mrs. Bates, and Anna showed me how to look after Carrie."

Anna snuggled against Martha. "I helped Elena, Mama."

"And Mrs. Bates told me about the tragedy at Collins Curve. How is the mother doing?"

The musicality of Elena's voice captured Martha's attention more than the content of her words. Martha marveled at the contrast between the sound of it in her kitchen with the welcome smells of supper and Vera's hoarse speech in Maher's desolate, one-room house, struck by the disjunction between Vera's lethargy and Elena's vitality.

Six weeks ago, Elena had screamed at the sight of Doc's forceps, "He will kill her!"

A self-sacrificing and protective gesture. And Martha never reciprocated. But what could she have done? Doc would have fired Elena, anyway. Nothing would have have dissuaded that man, but she didn't even make an effort. At least Elena tried to stop Doc from doing irreparable harm, which resulted in considerable personal loss.

And three years ago, after José Marquez fell under the wagon wheels and Doc came out of the operating room to tell them he was dead, Elena moaned and sobbed; today, Martha was with Vera for over six hours, and Vera didn't shed one tear. Perhaps Vera's injuries were too deep, her scars too coarse, for tears to make their way to the surface, even after learning about the death of her son.

Papa said Alex was hysterical after José Marquez died. Alex was just seventeen, not that much younger than Vera. Alex wept through the night, insisting he could have saved José if he held a tighter grip on the horses even though Papa repeatedly assured Alex that he didn't have the strength when they spooked like that. If anyone was at fault, he was for not noticing the rotted wood.

Was Alex still trying to make amends by assisting Rev. Macgill at the Spanish church where the Marquez family attended? And did Frank Ogawa's accident in the canal the next summer multiply his regret, that he failed Frank as he had José?

As for Vera, Maher saw to it that she couldn't protect Ida or save Freddie, but she did exploit the opportunity for escape when she clutched at Fran's coat sleeve in the drugstore. To survive she planted carrots, coaxed milk from an emaciated cow, and locked her heart away.

Art prodded, "Martha, I'd like to hear, too, how it went today."

Martha laid her right hand against the side of her face to support the weight of her head, a hand that also felt abnormally heavy. Art and Elena deserved to know, but should she relate such a story in front of Anna?

"I'm giving you the short version and will fill in details later. As I talk, you'll understand. I only ask you to react calmly so as not to alarm the youngest in the room."

She gave the outline of what she saw and heard, careful to use words like "abduction" instead of "kidnap" and "scoundrel" to disguise "robber," a word Anna would definitely know. Nor would Anna recognize "violation" in the sense she used it.

Art's response was to drawl, "Well, I'm not sure I wanna hear the details in the grownup version. I get the general picture. What's gonna happen ta those girls?"

"We'll have a better idea after they spend several days with Mrs. DeFries. Fran'll find out if they still have ties in Oklahoma. I'm glad she was with me. Fran can handle young people in difficult circumstances, and she's forthright without being obnoxious. Now that I'm acquainted with her, I'm baffled she would agree to Papa's condition about postponing their marriage. She's a strong-minded woman."

"It's only till Alex an' Louise're settled," Art said.

Martha nearly shouted, "Do you know how long some folks take to settle? Years and years! Papa's putting a heavy burden on them, and on Fran, to make her wait. Besides, Alex is so irresponsible. He enrolls at the junior college, drops out, enrolls again. He says he hates farming, but he's not making progress on anything else."

Having Elena in their kitchen seemed natural, not like having a guest at all, so not until Anna transferred her concentration from the checkerboard to her mama's face did Martha realized she had disclosed more McLennan family business than was appropriate. But she wouldn't apologize.

Martha lowered her voice and said, "Elena, maybe you have similar feelings about Luis — brothers can be helpful and loving sometimes and very irritating at others."

Elena, seemingly as composed as Martha was trying to be, answered, "I do know about brothers. At least Alex is younger than you are. Since our father died, Luis thinks because he is the oldest, and the brother, he is now head of our family, but he is much stricter than our father was. We tease him that he is as harsh with us as our uncle Zeke is with our cousins."

Elena's comments seemed lighthearted until she sighed, "Our mother lets him treat us this way. Just because he is the only Spanish boy we know to graduate from high school, she thinks he is very smart, but Marguerite is smarter."

"Yes, Josie, uh, Mrs. Bates, has always said Marguerite is one of the best students she's had."

Hopefully some of Luis's sense of responsibility would rub off on his friend, Alex, now that the two worked side by side. Luis was surely more undone by his father's death than Alex. And Luis pulled Frank out of the canal. But unlike for Alex, the ordeals seemed to have "made a man" out of Luis.

Elena served the plate of hamburgers and a bowl of warmed, home-canned corn with slabs of the butter Martha churned last week melting over the top. "Please, sit down. Fresh strawberries are washed and sliced in the refrigerator. You can have them with cream for dessert."

A horn sounded in the driveway — three short beeps.

Although everyone knew who gave the signal, Elena explained, "Luis and Alex are here to take me home. I must go."

At the door she blew Anna a kiss. "I enjoyed the evening. Good night."

She slipped out before either Art or Martha considered how they should thank her.

May 1941

Muriel Giffard

When Martha woke, both girls still slept and Art was outside, an opportunity to answer Muriel Giffard's recent letters. Until the past few days, Martha scarcely had energy to survive daily demands, and news about home folks had seemed pedestrian given Muriel's circumstances. Martha crept into the dining room and pulled her writing materials from the bureau drawer.

> *May 1941*
>
> *Dear Muriel,*
>
> *I have read and reread your letters about your arrival in Manila and the stop at the Hawaiian Islands. The profusion of flowers and their fragrance when your ship docked at Honolulu sound positively intoxicating. It all seems so exotic that I have not known how to answer.*

The words sounded stilted, but if she began again, she would be all morning on the first sentences.

> *You describe playing tennis in Manila and sipping cocktails by the pool at the Officers' Club. I am relieved to hear everyone*

*there sees little threat of war with the Japanese, occupied as
they are in China.*

Martha hesitated. She needn't repeat details Muriel already knew.

*Perhaps your mother has written about Carrie's birth, now
six weeks past. She arrived early and the delivery was difficult.
Doc says she has spastic paralysis, but we will not know its
severity until she matures. Doc thought we should put her in the
Children's Home in Denver, but visiting there convinced Art and
me that we can give her a better life with us.*

Again she paused, doubtful that even their long friendship could
bridge their differing circumstances.

*I have not been myself these past months, partly on account
of irregular sleep, but you and I suffered that in nursing school
and it did not affect me this way. Perhaps the difficult pregnancy
isolated me, and I am still consumed by the time Carrie requires.
(Art insisted we name her after my grandmother, even though
I suggested his mother's name, Matilda. I thought "Mattie"
winsome enough.)*
*I find myself at the kitchen sink or in the garden, unaware of
time passing. My thoughts drift. I enter and leave conversations
to feed Carrie and miss important details, which is normal. But I
also leave them mentally, even when I am physically present.*

She might be giving the impression of verging on a breakdown,
but her intent was to communicate her rationale for the next piece of
news — her shock about Papa and Fran.

So when Papa announced on Mother's Day that he and his friend, Fran Reeve, the new high school English teacher, will not marry until Alex and Louise are settled, I was completely taken aback.

Marriage! I did not even know he was courting her and was quite upset no one told me. Perhaps someone did mention it, and I failed to pay attention.

I surely would have remembered if Papa hinted at a romantic involvement. You know how close we are. I can only conclude he did not take me into his confidence because he questioned the value of my opinion or my ability to keep his affairs private. It does occur to me as I write that perhaps he was respecting my difficulties with the pregnancy and Carrie, but his discovery of a woman with Fran's qualities would have been welcome news!

When I took issue with his plan (who knows when Alex and Louise will be settled?), he chastised me publically and said not to question him. I was mortified and will not bring up the topic with him again, even though I think he is making a mistake. I agree he should guard Alex and Louise's interests, but he could protect them in ways that would not postpone his happiness.

I thank the Good Lord I have Art. When he and I talk, solutions emerge to what seem insurmountable problems. I only wish I could still talk with Papa in a forthright manner.

However, I lived through something yesterday that, while it set me spinning, restored some of my self-regard. It also made me long for you because neither Art nor Papa understands as you do. The incident was as foreign to me as imagining your poolside cocktails at the Officers' Club, but it was grim. It also put me in direct contact with Fran, Papa's fiancée. (I suppose I can call her his fiancée as they have discussed marriage.)

Martha wrote the specifics about Vera and Ida, including Fran's part, and observed,

Although the ordeal left me exhausted, I woke this morning with renewed energy, as though making a contribution to someone else's welfare was a necessary tonic. Perhaps I will feel more like myself if I work several mornings a week in Doc's office. I will not hide that I envy your placement in the arena of world affairs. Doc's office is hardly equivalent, but I can be of some help.

When I returned last night, Elena Marquez was here with Carrie and Anna. She had prepared supper and was so pleasant. She has been working in the fields since Doc fired her from the hospital on account of her unseemly conduct in the operating room. She mistakenly entered to clean it when Carrie was born. (She screamed only because she was trying to protect me from the forceps, which must have been a gruesome sight to the uninitiated.)

Her talents indicate she deserves more than the drudgery of thinning beets, evident in the ease with which she handled Carrie, still a difficult task. How unfortunate she did not return to high school after her father's death. (You remember José Marquez and how he fell under the wagon wheels. Elena is José's older daughter.)

You might wonder that I would trust Carrie and Anna to a Spanish girl, but Luis, her older brother, works for Papa in a very responsible manner. You also might recall how enthused Josie was about the capacities of one Marguerite Marquez, the girl she promoted from fifth to seventh grade. Marguerite is

*Luis and Elena's younger sister. Perhaps Josie and I could share
the expense if Elena worked for us both several days a week
after Josie's baby is born, expected early in September.*

Martha hurried to complete the letter with other bits of news
— the numbers of army convoys on the highway, how quickly
the boomtown at the dam site had grown to accommodate all the
construction families moving in, and the subsequent increases in
rural school enrollments.

She sealed the letter, taken by the idea Elena could help her and Josie
with children and housework. She would pay her part from the money
she earned at Doc's office, if Art agreed and Doc would have her.

Elizabeth DeFries

After breakfast, Martha rushed through her chores, anxious to
visit Vera and Ida. She arranged two baby quilts in the box Art built
for Anna four years ago, snuggled Carrie inside, and lifted Anna into
the pickup.

"Stay seated, Anna," she cautioned, "and don't touch the door
handle or roll down the window."

"Mama, you don't need to say that every time."

She eased the truck up the incline and onto the highway without
stalling, and she and Anna counted all the vehicles in the army
convoy going the opposite direction. She ran Muriel's letter into the
post office, taken aback by the number of boys lined up to talk with
the Marines recruiter sitting at a desk in the lobby. She skipped down
the marble steps, climbed into the truck, and drove to Mrs. DeFries's.

If only Fran was along, but she would have left for school an hour
ago. Martha wanted her to meet Carrie and Anna, and she wanted

a complete account of Fran's involvement in the Olmstead girls' tangled mess.

Martha reached Mrs. DeFries's, waited for Anna to step onto the grass, and extricated Carrie from the comforters. Carrie was wide awake, and Martha couldn't tell if her mouth twisted into a smile or a grimace during the awkwardness of getting her out of the box.

Martha cooed and grinned down at her, and, when they reached Mrs. DeFries's front door, Anna said, "Mama, let me talk to Carrie, too."

Martha knelt and balanced Carrie on her knees. If it had been a smile, perhaps Carrie would do it again for Anna.

"Very softly, very slowly, very gently, Anna."

Anna's words came out as a little song. "Carrie, Carrie, I love you. Carrie, Carrie, yes I do."

Anna hummed her little ditty and said, "Mama, she smiled at me!"

Carrie might not be feebleminded! "Maybe. Let's keep it a surprise for your papa until he notices. She's too young for us to be sure. For now, it's our special secret."

No one answered Martha's knock.

"Let's walk around back, Anna. I have new friends for you to meet, and they're probably having coffee and little cakes in Mrs. DeFries's garden."

The garden was empty, and they trudged back, deflated.

"Mama, I wanted a little cake."

"I was looking forward to one, also."

She loaded the girls into the truck and debated whether to go by the mortuary in the event Mrs. DeFries was there with the Olmstead sisters, but then Mrs. DeFries's worn black Model-A pulled up to the curb. She motioned to Martha.

Martha approached the driver's side of a vehicle as sturdy as Mrs. DeFries herself in her black lace-up shoes. Vera sat with her head in her hands. No sign of Ida.

"Martha, we have sad news," Mrs. DeFries said. "Ida wandered out of the house last night. The deputy sheriff discovered her around two a.m. babbling on the curb in her nightdress in front of the bank. He thought she was a drunk streetwalker and put her in jail. Sheriff Burleigh discovered her early this morning and brought her back to us. Vera and I were still asleep."

Appalled, Martha asked, "Where is she now?"

"I took her to Doc first thing, and he and I agree she needs to be at the Colorado State Hospital, just for a short while, we hope. Of course, you probably realized she's pregnant."

Vera threw up her hands and climbed out of the car.

In a subdued voice, Mrs. DeFries said, "Vera's quite upset by Ida's pregnancy, and Ida's general condition, as you can imagine. Doc called ahead to the hospital, and, as Greenwood's ambulance driver, Enoch took Ida to Pueblo. When he returns to the mortuary this afternoon, I'll help Vera complete the arrangements."

Mrs. DeFries lowered her voice further. "I think Vera needs to be there, too. No child can go through what she has without a severe reaction."

The overnight developments distressed Martha more than she could say. Jail in a nightdress? And the state mental hospital? Would there be no end to the indignities Ida and Vera were to suffer from their treatment at Maher's hands?

Martha walked around the car and embraced Vera where she stood on the grass. Vera accepted the gesture as she had the day before and rested her warm, sun-browned cheek against Martha's. Martha caressed her hair.

Mrs. DeFries asked whether Martha wanted to accompany them to the church for the meeting with Rev. Macgill about the funerals, but Martha heard Carrie's cries coming from the now-open window of the truck's cab.

Anna's shout followed immediately. "Mama, Carrie's crying and needs you! Her diaper's wet!"

Martha foresaw another drawn-out day if she were to go with Mrs. DeFries. She wouldn't impose again on Josie, even if Earl hadn't made a fuss.

"I can't," she said. "I need to be with my girls. I'm sorry, but please tell Rev. Macgill Freddie's funeral should be separated from Maher's, for Vera's sake. I can sing at Freddie's service, and perhaps Alex will, too. I'll persuade our entire family to come, to be there with Vera."

Mrs. DeFries touched Martha's arm. "You've done more than enough, Martha. You know that, don't you?"

But Martha was thinking if she were part of the planning, she would propose nothing happen at the church for Maher. Let Rev. Macgill do something at the graveside without any participants. Better yet, just dump him in the ground. Martha could taste her bitterness, and she clenched her fists.

She should go by the mortuary to view his body and replace the monster he had become with the mere mortal he was, but Enoch was on his way to Pueblo with Ida in the hearse that doubled as Greenwood's ambulance.

Please, Heavenly Father, she prayed, let the people Vera and Ida meet at the hospital be like Enoch, Fran, and Mrs. DeFries, even Parker Hayes, folks who will guard their welfare.

Martha stopped the truck at the end of the street for another army convoy. She rested a hand on Carrie's tummy and rocked her from side to side. The motion soothed them both. In the face of devastating developments for Vera and Ida, Martha held on to her hope about Carrie's mental capacity and the thought that, as soon as work slowed on the farm in the fall, she would help in Doc's office.

Vaguely aware of Anna's invitation to count the vehicles, she answered, "Go ahead, honey. You do it."

"One, two, three…"

After "ten," Anna assigned arbitrary numbers.

"…Thirty-nine, ten-teen, twelve. Fifteen! Mama, I counted them all!"

Her total represented half the convoy's length.

Martha gave Anna an indulgent smile because she had succeeded in assigning each vehicle a number. Sometimes even grownups calculated fragments and failed to see the whole.

July 1941

Jimmy Stewart

Art and Martha walked into the drugstore laughing with a like-minded group.

"Whew! That was some smell," Art said to no one in particular.

"I hope I'm not carrying it on my clothes," another voice chimed in. "I wonder who the pranksters are."

"What's going on? Why aren't you at the Saturday matinee?" Louise asked of Martha from the soda fountain counter.

Martha wiped her eyes. "Can't you smell it?"

"Smell what?"

"That's a relief. Someone threw a skunk sac into the lobby. The odor overpowered everyone. My eyes still burn. We left at once, even Gil and Sheila."

"Gil and Sheila?"

"The characters played by Jimmy Stewart and Lana Turner in *Ziegfeld Girl*. I'll always wonder how it ended because no one can go inside that theater anytime soon."

More people drifted in, and Louise said, "I better put on my apron because they'll have a hard time keeping up with orders."

"Why aren't you at Giffard's lumberyard?" asked Martha.

"I worked this morning. Claude, uh, Mr. Giffard, gave me the afternoon off to get ready for the dance tonight. Oh, Papa and Fran are upstairs. You should join them."

"We got the time," Art said, "thanks ta those rascals, whoever they are."

When they reached the top of the stairs, Fran called, "Come over to our table. Movie finished already?"

To Martha and Art's surprise, they had Anna.

Fran stood and extended her hand. "It's always good to see you, Art, Martha."

Papa didn't take his eyes off Fran, and Martha shared his admiration.

He said, "I know you're wondering why Anna's here. We went to see how Josie's getting along and ended up rescuing Anna. Earl might be good with high-school students but not with a little one who's four. He had cards with letters of the alphabet laid out on the dining room table and wanted Anna to pick the one matching the word he called out."

"What do you mean, Papa?"

"She was frustrated because when, for example, he said 'apple,' she was to select the 'A.' But he hadn't taught her the words that matched the letters, which she does know. I've seen to it, and we were going to surprise you."

"Why didn't you or Josie help him?" Martha asked.

"She was busy with Carrie in the kitchen, and I hesitate to make suggestions when it comes to Earl on account of his pride. When we offered to take Anna, he seemed disappointed. Maybe we should have left her and let him figure it out, but doggone it, he's a grown man. My granddaughter's well-being is more important."

Louise came for their order, and Papa said, "Why aren't you at the lumberyard?"

"I already told Martha. Surely you see how busy we are. What do you want?"

They told her, and Louise hurried to the next table.

"Why's Louise so impatient? I asked a civil question."

"Of course you did, Papa. Mr. Giffard gave her the afternoon off to prepare for the Fourth of July dance tonight, but, as you can see, she's pitching in to help with the unexpected crowd."

Martha described the melee with the skunk sac and directed the conversation back to him, thinking Fran might be interested to hear more details about Papa's past. "We always give Josie credit for being a great teacher, which she deserves, but her talents aren't wholly her own. You wouldn't have been out of line to make a suggestion. You came from Canada to Colorado to teach, for how many years?"

"Well, I taught at Pinion four years. Then Malcolm and I bought our first sheep, and when your mama and I married, we rented the Home Place."

"How old was Malcolm when you left Canada?" Fran asked.

"Seventeen."

Fran rested her hand on Robert's arm.

"That means you were only twenty, Robert. How did you manage?"

Fran's breathy demeanor resembled that of an infatuated schoolgirl, not the poised woman who'd just greeted them, and Art squirmed. But Art hadn't seen Fran and Papa gaze at one another like this, as they did when Martha first spotted them in church together.

Papa didn't answer immediately. Instead, he rested his hand on hers and smiled, as he had that Sunday, seemingly unaware of them. It was Martha's turn to look away in embarrassment.

He hadn't forgotten Fran's question, though. "We were much worse off in Canada, and I was a far better father to Malcolm than our own ever was. Yes, I'll take some credit for Josie's success in the classroom."

He proceeded to describe several of the games he had played with Josie and Martha when they were children, how he took them outside and taught them about clouds and barometers, how they collected insects in the field and sorted them in jars with their scientific names pasted on the outside.

He played similar games with Anna, reciting nursery rhymes and patiently answering her questions. Anna loved being with her grandpa.

Fran obviously loved being with him, too.

Papa's deft change of subject from the difficulties of his childhood to the pleasure he took in teaching didn't escape Martha. All she remembered from Papa's bitter accounts of Canada was that his stepmother and her son cheated him and Uncle Malcolm out of their rightful share when their father died. He had rarely referred to it since Mama's death, and then only briefly. The haste with which he changed topics confirmed it wasn't a subject to explore, at least not in Fran's presence.

Papa was saying, "In any case, Josie and Earl's was a thoughtful offer, to take the girls this afternoon so you could go to the matinee. Even with Elena helping you, it's a busy summer. Art, you haven't even made it to a softball game. Maybe Josie and Earl'll propose taking the girls tonight for the Fourth of July dance, since they haven't had Carrie more than an hour. I doubt Earl will want Josie flying around a dance floor, and he can complete his alphabet project with Anna."

Inspired by the romantic moment between Papa and Fran, Martha said, "Art, I'd love to go. We haven't been to a dance for at least a year."

They had been so busy cutting hay last week in the heat, and Josie's suggestion she keep the girls during the matinee had promised several hours in an air-conditioned theater. She felt cheated, having seen only part of the movie. Anyway, the dance would be a lot more fun.

"Now that's an idea I'd get behind," Art answered. "I assume Louise is playin' with the band?"

"Probably, which is why Mr. Giffard let her go early," Martha answered.

Fran said, "I thought she only played in church."

"She does sacred pieces well, but the formality constrains her," said Martha.

Art followed with, "You should see 'er let loose at a dance. She plays without the music sheets."

Martha didn't want to prevail on Earl and Josie again in the same day, so she teased her father, "You'll volunteer Earl and Josie to take care of your granddaughters, but not yourself?"

Even under his dark tan, she could see him blush, which, in turn, made Martha regret her lighthearted jab. As much as he protested he'd choose his granddaughters' interests every time, without a doubt he preferred taking Fran to the dance. She should do everything possible to encourage the romance and sabotage his ill-advised plan to delay marriage. Otherwise, he could be an old man before his wedding day.

"So what was the movie about?" asked Papa, again changing the subject.

"Jimmy Stewart was gonna lose 'is girlfriend, Lana Turner," Art answered. "Hard to tell from the little we saw what was gonna happen with Judy Garland an' Hedy Lamarr."

"That's a powerful trio of actresses," said Fran.

Papa focused on Jimmy Stewart. "And to think he's in the army now. I heard about a Colorado boy seeing him in a mess hall. Said he's so tall his legs don't fit under the table. Had to sit all crooked. Bet he has trouble with army cots, too."

Martha easily pictured Jimmy Stewart in an army mess hall across from a Colorado boy just like Alex. She had a special fondness for Jimmy Stewart. He and Art moved their tall, thin frames with the same agility. To think, the actor's face had filled a movie screen not thirty feet from her only minutes ago when in reality he was sitting at tables in army mess halls.

She imagined Art sleeping uncomfortably, alone, on army cots. Last fall with the conscription, he registered at age twenty-six. If his number came up, the fact that Papa was on the draft board made it more likely he'd be called because Papa would bend over backward to be impartial. She involuntarily slipped her arm through Art's, as though he might be torn from her side any moment. He looked somewhat taken aback by her boldness.

In an increasingly unpredictable world, she wanted to treasure Art every moment, and she wanted Papa to marry Fran sooner than later. She had to go to the dance, even if it was frivolous. Either Josie or Elena could handle the girls.

Eleanor Moulton

Folks still clattered up the steps to the balcony, chuckling about the stink in the movie theater. Martha heard Alex's laugh and saw him at the top of the stairs with Hugh Ufford. They joined Eleanor Moulton, who sat alone. She beamed at her former classmates. Poor Eleanor. Anyone could see she how wild she was about Alex and that he didn't share her passion, although he occasionally took her to a dance or movie.

Earlier, Martha had seen Alex and Hugh enter the theater with Luis and Elena, before the brother and sister went up to the balcony, the Mexican section. For the first time, Martha was struck by the irony that they were sent to the theater balcony and forbidden from the one at the soda fountain.

Martha walked over and sat in the fourth chair, next to Alex. "Excuse me for interrupting, but do you know if Elena is free to stay with the girls tonight so Art and I can go to the dance?"

"Sis, how would I know?"

"No need to be prickly. It's just that I saw her and Luis go into the movie theater with you, so I thought you might be aware of their plans."

Evidently mollified by her explanation, he said, "I don't think they had anything in mind for tonight, but, Sis, ya can't assume she's gonna say yes just because somethin' nice's come up for ya. She's already helpin' ya out quite a bit."

"Alex, I'm not assuming anything."

Alex's criticism stung. Papa had suggested Elena work several days a week for her and Art, and, really, they couldn't have kept their heads above water without her, what with Carrie, the expanded garden, and all the farm work. Martha would feel less awkward if they were paying Elena, not Papa, but he claimed it was worth it to have more of Art's time. With that and Luis as his hired hand, he stayed well ahead of the grasshoppers, weeds, and runs of water. He was even raising more pigs, for the army, he said.

Alex was the one making assumptions. He must think she would take advantage of Elena. Not at all. She would pay Elena tonight, the amount, she didn't know, nor could she guess what Papa's arrangement was with Elena.

"Alex, when Elena helped that day I was delayed by the situation with Vera and Ida out south, I had the impression she was volunteering her time because the circumstances were so, unique. But Art and I'll pay for tonight."

"Do ya even know where she lives? After all the years the Marquez family's worked for us?"

"I assume they still live in town, south of the tracks."

"But not in the same house ya visited when Mr. Marquez died. They couldn't afford the rent an' moved ta the Spanish colonia near the haymill, where they worked in the fields till Elena got the job at the hospital. This winter, with her workin' there, they could rent a nicer place in town again. They might have ta move back ta the colonia, though, since Elena's left the hospital. Ya don't have 'er for enough hours durin' the week ta make up for what she's lost."

"Alex, I appreciate the fact she lost her job on account of what happened the day Carrie was born."

"Doc didn't show 'er any leniency, which was very unfair."

"I agree. Although I passed out almost the moment she came into the room, I think she was trying to protect me when she screamed."

"Ya shoulda stood up for 'er. Ya know Doc better than most."

"Alex, at the time, I thought I was hallucinating. It wasn't until well after that I learned Elena lost her job. Besides, Doc's a stubborn man. I doubt I could have influenced his decision."

Alex looked at her long enough to make her uncomfortable. He seemed to be weighing whether to believe her that she couldn't have helped Elena or to blame her that she hadn't tried.

The tension left his face, and he seemed to accept her defense. "I'll ask if she can help ya tonight, an' I expect she will. I'll let 'er know you'll pay. I can drop 'er off, but you'll have ta take 'er home."

Martha stood and patted his shoulder, relieved Alex wouldn't hold a grudge against her for Doc's intolerance. Alex was basically generous. He would be helping his friend earn extra money, and his sister would enjoy an evening out with her husband.

Alex called out, confirming his willingness to let bygones be bygones. "Sis, wasn't that swell, at the movie just now? Can't remember somethin' that excitin' happenin' in this town. Trouble is, they'll catch the ones that did it, an' I'm afraid Jimmie Ichikawa played a part. I saw 'im, Paul Kelly, and the boys they run with dash outta the theater, an' I doubt they were there for *Ziegfeld Girl*. If I noticed, others did, too."

Martha hoped it wasn't true. Rev. Macgill kept Jimmie active on the softball team and had him lead some of the church programs for young people. Still, Louise had mentioned Paul Kelly was in trouble for minor theft at the lumberyard. If Bennie Ogawa were still around, Jimmie wouldn't be, as Art said, "runnin'" with the Kelly crowd.

Millie Swanson

She walked back to the table puzzling over what to pay Elena. Cherry pickers got one cent per pound, beet workers were paid by the ton, and when they hoed, by the acre. Josie earned around eight hundred a year when she taught, and Martha and Art cleared almost nine hundred in '40, a very good return. She was aware the men tearing up the Santa Fe tracks to reroute the trains around the dam earned around sixty cents an hour because Alex inquired about it before he decided to stay at the junior college. Rural high-school girls who lived in town during the term were given room and board in exchange for their labor. But none of those arrangements applied to Elena. Martha needed Art's opinion.

At Papa and Fran's table, the conversation was also about finances.

"They say discontinuing the County Health Unit is to save money," Papa said, "but the state pays half the cost, so it's not the five hundred a month savings they claim. If they keep the public health nurse, which they might, they'll pay all her salary and save only fifty to seventy-five dollars."

In a panic, Martha asked, "What are you talking about? Why is there any question about keeping Millie Swanson as the public health nurse?"

"I'd tell you to cool down, but then I'd need to take my own advice. Al Ivarson and his cronies are chipping away at the programs Otto Lambert, Claude Giffard, and I supported when we were commissioners. These so-called commissioners have dissolved the Health Unit. Just like that."

"What? With all Millie does? And the clinic for crippled children? The..."

"I know the list, probably better than you. We're also losing the sanitarian and health director. This will cause big problems. We can't afford to be without a sanitarian to inspect what's going on at the boomtown by the dam. It takes only one or two poorly built privies in the wrong place and we'll have typhoid. The Army Corps of Engineers is on a tight schedule, and the major's falling behind on account of it being so hard to obtain steel and such, now that he's competing with ship, tank, and airplane builders. He has to have healthy labor. He's probably already contacted the governor. And if the State Board steps in, you can bet it'll levy the county for the costs. So where does county government end up? Looking foolish, that's where."

Papa's disquisition barely registered. Martha focused entirely on losing Millie.

"I don't understand. Imagine what it would have been like without Millie monitoring scarlet fever and measles at the schools. She quarantined some families and closed the Pinion School for a week. Teachers and parents won't tolerate losing her."

The epidemics also might have been a factor in allowing Maher to go undetected because they had hit the families out south so hard. Folks had been too involved in their own affairs to take notice of a light in the abandoned house, if they had been out at all.

Fran joined the conversation. "At our last meeting of the American Association of University Women before summer, in

April, Millie wouldn't accept any committee assignments for the fall because she said she might not be here. Her fiancé's working at Douglas Aircraft in California, and if he stays out there, she'll move. I wonder if she had some inkling the commissioners would take this step."

Josie had talked to Martha at length about the April AAUW meeting but hadn't mentioned anything about Millie's plans to relocate. Josie was so taken with the Latin American theme — waitresses in costumes of full, colorful skirts; nut cups in the shape of sombreros, and the food and entertainment also along the Spanish theme.

Josie even borrowed the sheet music for one of the songs, "No Hablas Mas" by Ernesto Lecuona, and asked Louise to play the Cuban piece for Martha on Mama's upright piano housed in Martha's living room. The recital took place after Martha came home with Carrie.

Why hadn't Josie mentioned Millie's possible relocation and her fiancé? That news took precedence over songs and nut cups. Had Martha known, she would have made it a point to visit Millie. She began as the county nurse before Anna was born, when Martha still worked in Doc's office. Martha always thought they would be friends, but Millie's work and Martha's babies filled their respective lives. Their cordial relationship didn't realize its promise, and now Martha felt the impending loss more intensely than if a friendship had existed. Her regret strengthened her resolve to capture and enjoy every moment with the people she loved.

"I'm very sorry she might be leaving."

With equally heartfelt words, she addressed Art. "Let's go dancing. I've arranged for Elena to stay with the girls."

Louise set down four glasses of iced tea, along with Anna's sundae, and rushed off to serve other customers.

The Intruder

In spite of her earlier exertions at the soda fountain, Louise went full-throttle at the piano in the dance pavilion, bouncing up and down the length of the bench. The other musicians played adequately, but Louise spiffed up their performance. She and the bandleader seemed to compete over who could out-do the other, band or Louise. Martha judged that the cascade of notes coming from the piano put Louise ahead.

Music fed Louise, and Martha couldn't understand why she chose business school instead of a career in music. If Martha had talent like hers, she wouldn't waste it. But Louise protested music wasn't her work; it was her fun. She refused, as she said, to study it to death.

The dancers fed off the energetic contest. Breathless and hot, Martha excused herself. She walked onto the dock at the small lake nearby and took in the night sky. Such a contrast to the April evening they brought Carrie home, when the pinpoints of silver stars strained to shine through the black night's crushing weight; tonight the fuzzy balls of light sparkled against the soft fabric of heaven. Martha traced the pattern of the Big Dipper, the enduring constellation that had oriented sailors, soldiers, sheepherders, and farmers for millennia.

Martha's lofty thoughts quickly descended when she realized that, as a woman alone, she spoiled the fun for several couples sharing the dock. She turned toward the pavilion. The band was taking a break, and Martha had to weave her way through the many twosomes strolling on the grass by the lake. She decided the long way around would get her back to Art more quickly. She walked along the edge of the grass until the crowd thinned before she turned up beside the west side of the pavilion, intending to enter from the back.

She turned the corner in the building's shadow, and a couple stood arguing in the shaft of light cast through the open door, the identity of the woman unmistakable. Fran's auburn hair glistened.

"How dare you come here? This is my home. You'll ruin everything. You have to leave; you must leave."

She punctuated her ultimatum with a slap across the face of a gaunt man who stood with his back to Martha.

The force of Fran's anger reached through the darkness, and Martha flinched. But the man stood firm. Not angry. Helpless.

He extended both hands, palms up, and spoke with a soft, resonant voice.

"But everything's changed. I come ta tell ya how everything's changed."

Fran whirled and, with her determined stride, quickly put distance between herself and the man. She didn't turn her head as she walked into the pavilion, and when Martha looked back to where the man had stood, he was gone.

Martha fell against the wall. Naturally, Fran would have other suitors. Martha had to alert Papa. He would lose Fran if he kept to his plan of a protracted engagement. But he had categorically refused to discuss the matter on Mother's Day.

She wanted to hate the gaunt man, Papa's rival, but she couldn't. The pleading tone of voice, the way he matched Fran's willpower by absorbing her blow, the invitation implied by his extended arms, all conveyed the character of a man with strength born of suffering.

Because Martha couldn't hate him, she was scared. Perhaps Fran wouldn't sustain her animosity, either.

But she should trust Fran's determination and the forceful slap. The way Fran looked at Papa, in church and today at the soda fountain, gave witness to her loyalty. Martha wouldn't speak of the incident. Fran handled it. That was that.

September 1941

Josie Bates

Starting the first of the month, Martha telephoned Josie every morning, hoping the baby would come soon and relieve the anxiety of waiting. Then again, just because Carrie had problems didn't mean Josie's baby would, and her pregnancy had gone smoothly, save for Earl's endless stewing.

Today, Martha was going to the Ladies Missionary Society and didn't telephone. She would stop by Josie's and urge her to attend on the spur of the moment so she couldn't consult Earl, who would undoubtedly nix the outing.

Carrie was born in Martha's eighth month; after Josie passed that mark with no mishap, her disposition lightened. Perhaps she harbored her fears as far back as February, when Doc sent Martha to bed.

Earl hadn't relaxed at all, perhaps with reason. It was the case that Josie had miscarried once.

Anna strained to reach Josie's doorbell. Martha boosted her by resting Anna's bottom on her knee. "You're inches away, honey. Don't give up."

"How much is an inch?"

Martha started to compose a hasty answer, but she reminded herself of Mrs. Bro's advice. Josie had given her Mrs. Bro's book, *When Children Ask*, for Christmas, and the author wrote that just as parents don't starve their children's hungry tummies, they mustn't starve their curiosity. With Carrie still shifted to one arm, she showed Anna the measure from her knuckle to the end of her own thumb.

"How many of those, Mama, until I reach it?"

Martha measured, and they determined she lacked four.

"When, Mama, when will I be tall enough?"

Martha had yet to discover why this was such a significant milestone. "It's hard to say, but perhaps you're growing part of an inch a month. Christmas comes in four months, so maybe you'll reach it then, maybe a little later. We'll measure your progress every time."

Through the pane of glass, she saw Josie waddling through the living room. By the time Josie reached the door, Martha was laughing out loud. "It's funny to see you walking so awkwardly. You're the graceful one."

"Careful," countered Josie. "I'm still taller."

Anna ran over to shuffle through "her" alphabet cards on the table.

"What are these, Auntie Josie?" She pointed to a stack of what looked like campaign buttons next to the cards. Josie wasn't one to let used items accumulate, but she couldn't bear to waste anything. Martha hoped the buttons weren't for Anna. They had too many of Josie's discards.

"I'll tell you if you can name the letter on each of them."

"It's a V," shouted Anna. "On every single one!"

"Whom do you think they're for?"

"For me?"

"One is for you. And the others?"

"For Carrie, Mama, and Papa. What are they?"

"They're 'Victory Buttons,' Anna. The V is for 'Victory.' Everybody's wearing them to show how much we want the British to win the European war. It's a victory when people win."

To Martha she said, "Earl's collected them from the bank and newspaper office. They're hard to come by. Mr. Hallet at the newspaper has reordered several times."

Anna brought the blue-and-white buttons to Martha, who observed, "They're very attractive. But what are these marks on the bottom?"

"The three dots and the dash? They're Morse Code for V," answered Josie. "Haven't you heard how people in the occupied countries sometimes either tap or clap out three short sounds, the dots, and prolong the sound representing the dash? They also hum the first notes of Beethoven's Fifth Symphony, which duplicates the rhythm. It's said all the tapping, clapping, and humming drives the Gestapo crazy. Want to try it, Anna?"

Josie and Martha hummed the Beethoven sound of resistance several times while Josie clapped the V Code, and Anna joined them.

"Anna, shall Auntie Josie pin your Victory button on your sweater?" Martha asked.

Anna's answer was a vigorous, affirmative nod with, "And pin Carrie's on her blanket! And yours, too, Mama! Put it on your sweater so everyone can see."

Martha let Josie pin on Carrie's button but declined Josie's offer to attach hers. Anna ran back to her cards.

"I came by to kidnap you for the Missionary Society meeting," Martha said, "and I'm not sure it's polite to wear a Victory button in that setting. Some families are very sensitive about any association of our country with war. Won't you come? The speaker is Dr. Salisbury from the Ganado Mission in Arizona."

"Martha, this isn't fair. You know how interested I am in the Ganado School."

Martha pressed her advantage. "And I'm excited to hear about their nursing school, the only one in the country for Indians. They let in qualified girls from any tribe, not just the Navajo from the reservation. You look fine. All you need is your hat and gloves. Let's leave now so I can stop by the post office to buy our defense stamp for the week. I'll get your sweater while you tidy up."

Josie walked over to the chair where her purse lay, seemingly preparing to leave. Instead, she pulled out her wallet and handed Martha a dollar.

"Sis, I know you mean well, but this afternoon Jimmie Ichikawa's coming by for help on his essay for Judge Arnold. I really don't have enough energy for the Missionary Society and Jimmie. By late afternoon I'm so tired I could go to bed for the night. But take this dollar for the school. I've heard Dr. Salisbury is a persuasive speaker and always asks for support."

"I miss doing things with you, just the two of us. The meeting won't be but an hour. We wouldn't have to stay for refreshments."

Carrie whimpered and Martha shifted her to the other arm.

"Sis, come, sit next to me on the sofa. I need to get off my feet, and you'd be more comfortable with Carrie."

They sat and Martha rested Carrie on her lap. Josie caressed Carrie's hair. "I have a confession to make. When you and Art married, I lost my best friend. That's not to say I don't appreciate Art, but things changed between you and me."

"Josie, why didn't you ever say anything?"

"What would I have said? That I'm jealous of your husband?" Martha looked askance at her.

"What? Am I being too frank?" Josie asked.

"No, not at all. Maybe I'm jealous of Earl, and that's why I've not given him half a chance."

"Oh?"

"Everything, well, almost everything he does, irritates me, but maybe it's because you have another best friend!"

Josie laughed so heartily that Carrie jerked. Martha cooed and rocked her, and Carrie smiled her crooked grin.

"Sorry, Carrie," said Josie. "Martha, Earl isn't a tactful man. He can irritate me, too. But it's especially difficult for him around the family. On almost every issue he's at odds with someone, and he tries so hard to be pleasant. He really does."

"Well, this casts a completely different light on things, to realize I'm jealous and he's trying to be pleasant. I don't expect him to change his opinions, but I can be less antagonistic."

"I'm not asking you to alter your behavior. Earl would be mortified to know we've talked about him."

"I'll be subtle. He won't suspect. I just don't need to let him annoy me so. Sorry. I shouldn't have said that."

"Don't apologize for something that's obvious. You've been especially impatient with him recently."

"Josie, no, I…"

"No use denying it. I'm not angry. I'm just saying I noticed, and I gave you a lot of latitude because of the strain you and Art were under."

Martha felt the tears coming. Quietly, almost to herself, she said, "Is that why you've been so good about helping with the girls, because you're worried about me?"

"Well, of course. You don't think I'm normally that nice, do you?"

Josie lifted the pillow she used for her naps on the couch, feigning a hit on Martha's head. Martha reflexively ducked.

"You missed," she taunted.

"I don't think so," said Josie. "I'm glad you're feeling more like yourself, although you're going way overboard with all the canning. Why do you do it?"

"Lots of reasons. First, it's economical. Second, Mama did it. Third, they're saying it'll make a big difference in the amount of food available for Europe and our soldiers. Fourth, I enjoy gardening, and what would I do with all that food if I didn't can it? Fifth, it gives me bragging rights. You want me to go on?"

"No! I've heard enough to make me feel like a slacker."

"You're far from that. But what's this about Jimmie and Judge Arnold?"

"Do you remember the skunk sac incident at the theater?"

"Who could forget? Art and I were there that afternoon, you'll remember."

"Jimmie was one of boys who hatched the plan to toss it into the lobby. As punishment, Judge Arnold's requiring they each write an essay on 'The Life and Habits of the Skunk' that Joe, the theater owner, will have to approve."

Martha checked to see if Josie said it with a straight face, which she had, but then Josie realized how funny it sounded. Both sisters broke out laughing.

Still giggling, Martha observed, "Well, actually that's a suitable punishment, if all the boys take it as seriously as Jimmie. Has Joe gotten rid of the stink?"

"Jimmie says he has. Incense didn't work. It only sweetened the smell, which I can't quite imagine. Cinnamon did it. I don't know how, but the theater is open and folks are going."

"And so am I — going, that is, to the meeting."

Martha reached out to give her sister a hug and Josie leaned over her big belly to kiss Martha on the cheek. Josie took advantage of the proximity to the now-sleeping Carrie to blow her a kiss, too.

Before she walked out the door, Martha said, "Josie, Burleigh told me Judge Arnold would decide about the disposition of Maher's cache of stolen items. I don't know if that's happened, but surely enough time has passed. If the judge is as practical with that as he's been with Jimmie and the other boys, maybe he'll see that Vera and Ida get some of the money. It's only fair, don't you think?"

Earl Bates

The next morning Martha called at nine. No answer. She tried again at nine thirty. Nothing.

Perhaps something had gone horribly wrong and everyone knew but was afraid to tell her. From Josie's comment yesterday about giving her latitude and Art's observation months ago about how emotional she was during her pregnancy, Martha knew her unpredictability had been a concern, at least to the two of them.

But now, five months after Carrie's birth, surely her family wouldn't purposefully exclude her about something as important as Josie's baby. She walked onto the back porch and saw Anna was busy "baking" mud pies on the warm cement surface that covered the root cellar. Anna's arms and hands were caked with dirt, but somehow her dress had escaped disaster. Still, it would take forever to clean her up for a ride into town.

Tip napped in front of the barn door. Art must be inside. Martha hurried across the lane and entered. Her eyes adjusted to the dark interior, and she called for him. Silence.

She heard hammering from the direction of the chicken coop and headed there.

"What are you working on?"

"I'm replacin' rotted-out boards in this wall, but I been thinkin'. Why don't we buy some fall-hatched pullets an' make the coop bigger? By next spring they might be layin', an' you know what's bein' said. The more eggs for defense, the better."

"Pullets are cheaper than dairy cattle."

"What're ya talkin' 'bout?"

"That the British killed most of their cattle because they couldn't feed them, which is why they need dairy products, as well as eggs. And the army needs eggs. Everyone needs eggs. Expanded production is a good idea."

Anna walked up to the chicken fence, afraid to come in because sometimes the cranky hens chased her. Her dress hadn't been spared a mud bath, after all.

Martha described her suspicions about Josie, and Art answered, "I'm worried 'bout the baby. Things can go wrong pretty quick. Why don't ya make a trip into town? I'm finished here. I'll clean up Anna an' watch Carrie."

Martha hadn't talked about worries when it came to Josie's baby, perhaps on account of her suspicion that dwelling on possible mishaps made them come true.

"I had no idea you were anxious about it."

"Didn't want ta dwell on it. Don't ferget a dollar fer the stamp."

"But I bought one yesterday, our quota for the week."

"I know, but if Josie's had the baby, maybe we should buy a second ta honor it an' those families in occupied countries. The thought a what they're goin' through…"

Martha squeezed Art's hand to show agreement, but she didn't trust herself to speak, moved as she was by her husband's empathy — the extravagance of two dollars, along with what she gave Maude Moulton for the Red Cross quota. And the Ganado school. And relief for China …

When Martha reached town, she decided to swing by the hospital first. She saw Earl and Josie's Ford parked in front. She pulled in behind and was nearly out of the truck before it stopped. She dashed in the front door, startled to find Cora Jane at the reception desk. If Josie was in labor, why wasn't Cora Jane with her?

Cora Jane greeted her with a wide grin. "You have an excellent sense of timing, Martha. I'll not say more other than the baby was born about thirty minutes ago. Do you want to wash up and join the happy family?"

Martha felt muscles relax that must have been tense for months.

When she entered the room, it was different than she anticipated. Instead of the baby resting in Josie's arms, Earl held it. No matter. Earl was all coos and clucks; Josie looked tired but happy, content, proud. Just as a healthy mother would.

"Sis, come and meet Robert Earl Bates," Earl said, as if it were the most natural thing that his sister-in-law had appeared, unannounced, in the first hour of his son's life.

Happy tears streamed down Martha's face. She didn't know if she cried because Earl called her "Sis"; because she wasn't prepared for a nephew, realizing now she assumed all along she would have a niece, either of which was fine; pleased because they named him after Papa; or relieved because Josie was fine and so was the baby. She must have floated across the room to meet little Robert because she arrived by Earl's side without being conscious of walking the distance.

A slight hesitation, and Earl handed Martha his son. Another surprise. Martha hadn't thought Earl would readily relinquish his precious package, certainly not to her.

Martha looked up at Earl's face as she received the baby and saw he was crying, too. With that, she forgave Earl his bossy ways and was very grateful Josie had a husband who cared so deeply. Martha could even forgive him for being a Republican. She felt honored to be the first in the family to hold little Robert.

"Hello, nephew," she whispered.

He slept, and, in spite of his blotchy newborn's complexion, she declared him the most handsome boy ever born.

"We'll call him 'Robbie,' so as not to confuse the two Roberts," said Josie.

Martha handed him back to his father and went to her sister. She sat on the side of the bed and took Josie in her arms. They laughed and they cried, and they laughed and cried some more.

"I'll hear all the details later, when you've rested," Martha said. "I thank the Good Lord it all went so well."

Elsie Lambert

Martha headed to the post office, marveling at how freely she moved, as though her dread about Josie's baby and delivery had been a layer of wet, heavy wool she'd worn all these past months. The weight had simply dissolved.

She stopped first at Ralph's Market. To celebrate, she would buy Anna the Wheaties she begged for every visit to the store, along with several cans of Gerbers for Carrie. She checked her purse and found four dimes, in addition to the dollar for the defense stamp. More than enough. And she would buy something colorful at Gambles to hang on the sling-chair Art had rigged up for Carrie. Carrie couldn't coordinate her hands to reach for the toy, but she would notice it.

Sheriff Burleigh brushed past Martha on his way out the market door. She mustered a quick "Good morning," to which he replied with a grunt that was less cordial than usual.

Ralph stood by the cash register, the fingers of his right hand tapping the counter, those of his left combing through his thin brown hair.

"Morning, Ralph. You look worried. Something wrong?"

"Yes and no. Probably more yes than no."

His fingers kept tapping.

"What should I make of that?" asked Martha.

"Guess it won't do any more harm than's been done to tell you. I caught a Mex'can boy stealing a candy bar. Young, maybe six or seven. Normally I'd give him a talking-to, even though he probably wouldn't understand English, and let him go. This morning, Burleigh happened to be in the store and saw it all. I have a broom closet in the back, and he said to lock the boy in there, to teach him a lesson. Otherwise, 'People like them don't learn a damn thing,' according to Burleigh. Excuse me."

The "damn" didn't offend Martha; "people like them" did. The same outcast group to which Doc consigned Carrie. She didn't trust herself to react calmly and remained silent.

"Said I wouldn't do it," Ralph continued. "Boy's too young for that kind of punishment. Burleigh jerked him from me and half dragged, half carried him to the closet. Practically threw him in and demanded I get the key. Locked the door and gave me the key. Said I better not let the boy out till he comes back, or I'll answer to him. It's not right, but what am I to do?"

Ralph's description of a child in a locked closet recalled Ida's imprisonment in the lean-to. With absolute clarity about what should be done, Martha's words tumbled out. "Well, Burleigh didn't threaten me. Give me the key. Tell Burleigh your customers were furious to hear a boy banging around in the closet and you had no choice but to let him go. Or tell him I overpowered you."

Martha paused at the thought of pinning Ralph to the floor and hoped he hadn't visualized the absurdity of it. She switched to a more realistic scenario. "Besides, Ralph, Burleigh might get tangled up in something and not even come back today. Then what would you do? You'd have on your conscience that you kept a child locked in a dark closet for eight, ten hours! Probably the boy took the candy bar because he was hungry. Imagine the state he'll be in by then! What will people say, Ralph? It won't be good for business; you can be sure of that."

Martha was nearly screaming, and Elsie Lambert walked in. Martha turned on her. "Elsie, when your Max did wrong as a child, did you lock him in a closet all day? Did you?"

Elsie looked from Martha to Ralph. "Seems there's a disagreement."

They launched into the story politely enough, alternating lines. By the time they finished, Elsie was as irate as Martha.

"Give me the key, Ralph," Elsie said. "Prisoners at the jail get better treatment. They have light, they can go to the toilet, and they get dinner. And you tell Burleigh that your customers said they would spread the scandal about his cruelty over the whole county if you didn't give them the key. He's too much a politician for that argument not to stick."

Elsie's indisputable position fueled her own anger. "This is unconscionable. Our Friends churches from up and down the Valley gather clothing for migrant workers, and here's a boy in my own town who needs something even more basic: food. He deserves mercy, not brute force. I'll tell the pathetic tale in any case."

She commanded the respect due an older woman, and her point about prisoners in jail getting better treatment would convince anyone that Ralph couldn't be faulted for giving over the key. Besides, Otto Lambert, Elsie's husband and a former county commissioner, was respected throughout the county. Maybe as Quakers they were silent in church, but both Martha and Ralph knew the Lamberts would speak widely about the violent treatment of the boy.

Even then, Ralph pled, "When you talk about this, don't include my role in the boy's escape. I don't want trouble from Burleigh."

Conceivably the explosive sheriff might storm in with his baseball bat and knock cans off shelves, or worse. He outweighed Ralph by a good thirty pounds. And he had a gun. Still, she was disgusted.

"Ralph, think about it. If Burleigh really wanted the boy locked up all day, he would have taken the key after he secured the door. Instead, he left it with you, probably knowing you would let the boy out after a suitable time. But Burleigh acted hastily, as he always does, and couldn't back off without looking like an idiot, excuse me for saying so. Don't worry. Elsie and I'll support you. Let's get the boy."

When Elsie unlocked the door, the three adults looked down on a thin, trembling child cowering in the corner. As Martha could have anticipated, he had wet his pants.

Martha knelt down. "*Buenas dias, muchacho.*"

She held out her hand. The boy cautiously put his hand in hers, and she helped him to his feet.

"*Donde esta su casa?*" she asked.

Asking where he lived was the wrong question. Panic registered on the boy's face, and Martha surmised he dreaded the punishment awaiting him at home nearly as much as what he had already gone through.

Ralph could simply let him go, but what about the wet pants and shoes? With her dollar forty, she could buy him a new pair of pants at Penney's in the next block, and maybe John, the manager, would throw in some shoes. But how would the boy explain new clothes to his family? And what would she be teaching him? That if you steal a candy bar you'll get new clothes?

"What should we do?" Martha asked Elsie.

"I'll wait here. You go to the welfare office, or to Father Moore. Neither of us speak enough Spanish to handle it, and there'll be folks at either place who can help."

Marguerite Marquez

Martha's choice was the welfare office, not the Catholic Church. She had heard that Father Moore didn't let any Mexicans in on Sundays after the Spanish side was full, even when the other side had plenty of open pews.

And Elena told Alex she had seen a little girl, a neighbor of theirs, wandering up and down in front of the church one Sunday without her older sister. When Elena asked the child where her sister was, she pointed to the church. The child said Father Moore told her to wait outside because she had forgotten her headscarf, but he ordered the older sister inside.

If he barred respectable adults and a small girl from church, who knew what he did with Mexican thieves, regardless of age?

Marguerite, Elena's younger sister, stood inside the door of the welfare building. She was considerably taller than Elena, and Martha hadn't remembered she was so attractive. But the last time she saw Marguerite would have been the night Frank Ogawa died. Girls that age could change a lot in two years.

"Hello, Marguerite."

"Hello, Mrs. Lundgren. Why are you here?"

"I was about to ask you the same thing, and on a school day?"

"I'm part of the vocational program, and we work several hours a week in businesses or county offices. I'm assigned here."

Martha told the little boy's story, which Marguerite relayed to someone down the hall. When she emerged, she explained that she was to go with Martha and see what she could do informally in order to minimize difficulties for the boy and his family.

But did Marguerite have the requisite maturity? Then again, she was smart, she spoke Spanish, and if she couldn't deal with it, she could call on folks to help.

Mary Claffey

For the second time Martha had handed off responsibility for children in desperate straits. She could excuse herself from Ida's life because she couldn't give Ida what she needed and from the boy's problems because she couldn't speak his language. But at what point could she no longer be excused? She surely had loftier duties than buying more defense stamps or chickens to lay more eggs, or rescuing one girl from a lean-to or one boy from a broom closet.

She had medical training and wasn't using it. She sacrificed for that training and asked her family to sacrifice for it, and she'd never intended to set it aside. She could be more useful than with these sporadic, Good Samaritan gestures.

Even though she had Elena's help several mornings a week, she had drifted through the summer, working beside Art, Papa, and Mr. Miyoshi on the farms, taking care of her girls, canning her three hundred quarts, and had yet to approach Doc about assisting in his office or Josie about sharing Elena's time and the cost. Now that summer was almost over and she was free of her anxiety about Josie, she resolved not to delay.

She stopped at Doc Claffey's office. Mrs. Claffey sat at the reception desk.

"Martha, it's so good to see you, but I hope you're well. As much as I enjoy folks coming by, I always greet them with a measure of caution, given they've come here."

"I'm fine, perfectly fine, more than fine. Don't you know that Josie had her baby this morning?"

"No! How's she doing? And the baby?"

Because Mrs. Claffey didn't know, Martha assumed Doc had gone directly on another call after Josie's delivery.

"She's wonderful. And so is her son. Robert Earl Bates."

"A distinguished name for a little tyke. He has a lot to live up to, with that father and grandfather!"

"Yes, I suppose so."

Martha had been in town much longer than she and Art anticipated, and she still had to buy the stamp. Mrs. Claffey could chitchat forever, so Martha directed the conversation toward her purpose.

"When will Doc be back?"

"In two days."

"Two days!"

"Yes, he left for Denver yesterday."

"Then who delivered Josie's baby?"

"Oh, Dr. McFarland. An old friend of ours. Retired. Lives in Pueblo. Been helping out when Doc's in Denver at the army induction center. We're expecting Doc will be ordered there full-time, with so many boys entering the service, so we're planning on moving."

Doc Claffey was such a local fixture. She couldn't imagine the community without him, or Mrs. Claffey. "I didn't know Doc was spending so much time in Denver. What plans do you have for the office?"

"We're hoping Dr. McFarland will come out of retirement and work full time because the doctors we know who haven't been snatched up for defense are already doing double time in their communities to fill in for those who've left. We're stumped about a nurse-receptionist, though. Why did you stop by?"

"I — I was hoping to talk to Doc about helping out several mornings a week. My nursing skills are a bit rusty, I'm afraid, but…"

"Martha, don't you see? You're part of the answer! I'll let both doctors know of your interest. I'm sure Dr. McFarland will contact you right away."

Robbie Bates

Martha walked into the kitchen, and Anna ran to her. "Does Auntie Josie have a baby?"

"Yes! A healthy boy named Robert Earl Bates. We're to call him 'Robbie.'"

Art was putting leftovers on the table for dinner. He beamed. "Well, ain't Earl the diplomat, ta name him Robert Earl instead a Earl Robert."

"Yes. Earl has more to him than I give him credit for."

She had planned to use the leftovers for supper. She surveyed the fresh melon from the Ichikawas' vegetable stand, the cold fried chicken, and potato salad. They could have a picnic.

"Let's spread a blanket in the front yard and eat outside. There might not be many warm days left."

"Seems like a lot a work, just fer dinner. I got ta get back out. It's one a the few days this month fields ain't too muddy."

"I have so much news, most of it very good, that if we were to make this a picnic it would seem like a party, very appropriate for today. Besides, you and I can talk better if we're outside where Anna can play. In the long run, it'll save you time."

During the meal, Martha described Anna's new cousin, and they made a toast to him with their milk glasses.

"We'll all go to town tonight for a quick visit. I'm sure Cora Jane, er, Miss Collins, will let you see him," Martha assured Anna, who ran off in search of ladybugs.

Martha told Art the story of the boy and the candy bar. She cautioned she was keeping the Wheaties and Carrie's toy a secret until the next morning, when Anna would be expecting her usual porridge or scrambled eggs.

"Art, you're not as upset about the boy as I thought you'd be."

"Burleigh's always quick ta act, but that's what folks like 'bout 'im. He didn't take Greenwood ta the state championships when he was quarterback because he's timid. Doesn't put up with tomfoolery. Someone has a problem; he takes care of it."

"Surely you don't support his actions?"

"I guess what yer sayin' is extreme, even fer him. Do ya suppose it's all this talk 'bout sabotage? They claim they've found German spies in other parts a the state. Adds to his load. And with all the riff-raff that's come in on account a the dam, that hasn't made his job any easier. More drunks an' thieves than usual, from what I read in the paper. I'm not sayin' the workers are drunks an' thieves. I'm just sayin' a boomtown attracts that kind. You know 'bout the attempted robbery at the lumberyard from Louise, much more serious than what the boy Paul Kelly tried there this summer. This time robbers nearly got away with the safe. That's just one example. Another is the chicken thief."

"Chicken thief?"

"Yep. Uffords lost several, an' last week Al Ivarson took a shot at someone takin' brown Leghorn fryers out a his yard. The thief let go a the fryers an' got away by crawlin' through the tall grass along the ditch bank. Al called Burleigh, an' it was eleven o'clock at night, but Burleigh came right out. A course, Al is one a the commissioners, but I think Burleigh would come fer anyone. Good people know they can depend on 'im. All I'm sayin' is Burleigh has his hands full. Maybe it's gettin' ta 'im."

Martha reconsidered Burleigh and his thorough "investigatin'" at the Maher place the day Freddie died. Maher, or whatever his name, was an extreme case, and not all of Burleigh's problems were that vile. She appreciated that he took his job seriously, but maybe he gave everything equal weight and lumped together a boy stealing a candy bar with a criminal like Maher.

This was a good time to introduce working in Doc's office, relaxed as they were in the shade, Carrie resting comfortably in the crook of Art's arm. Anna had moved from collecting ladybugs to chasing butterflies and was at the far end of the lawn.

"Art, here's another thing."

She explained the Claffey's circumstances, her thoughts about working in Doc's office several mornings a week, and her proposal to increase Elena's hours above what Papa paid.

As was his habit when pondering something involved, Art picked a long blade of grass with his free hand and chewed on the tender end, in lieu of a toothpick or cigarette. He didn't smoke when he held Carrie.

Martha waited, but had second thoughts. She should tell him more about why working as a nurse was so important to her, but in as few words as possible. She, too, wanted him to get into the fields. Rain was forecast, and they'd already lost the morning.

"Art, this isn't something we have to decide today. I've been thinking about it all summer. I have a specialized form of training that's needed right now. I'm withholding something of value. You just said how the European war's putting pressure on Burleigh, and now it's changing the Claffeys' lives, which means Greenwood will have a new doctor with no one to help him."

She didn't tell him she was thinking about including Josie in the arrangements, which would help with their cost for Elena. That could come later, after she talked to Josie, who also had a profession she loved. With so many male teachers being drafted, sooner or later the school board would have to change their restrictive policy of not letting married women teach. Martha didn't want Art to interpret what she was about to say as overly pessimistic, but he needed to know how strongly she felt.

"Art, I'm not usually bleak about things, but I think war is coming for the United States, unlike Representative Chenoweth who's voted against every national defense effort since becoming a member of Congress. For some women it's enough to pay more taxes, buy defense stamps, and can a quart of green vegetables for every day of the non-growing season. For me, it's not."

"No one could mistake ya fer anyone's daughter but Robert McLennan's. Don't let Earl hear yer criticism a Chenoweth, though. It would spoil his celebration right now."

"But even Earl hands out Victory Buttons, Art."

Art took the blade of grass from his mouth. "Yer Robert's daughter in other ways. Ya care 'bout more than just yerselves an' yer own family, which is sayin' a lot, on account a how much you care 'bout yer family. I respect that. I wonder if it comes from yer church upbringin', or if it's just part of yer family's way."

"I don't know what to say."

"No need. I have ta think 'bout what yer suggestin'. It'll put a load on me on account a how I rely on ya. Don't know how long we'll have Alex an' Luis because they'll register come January, them turnin' twenty-one an' all. If they're called, they'll go. They're not married, an' with Robert bein' on the draft board, he'll want ta be clear he don't have favorites."

"Yes, I know."

Art said he'd think about it. She translated that to mean he'd come around. She'd write Muriel tonight.

October 1941

Mama's Black Cake

Fran proposed a barn dance the first weekend in October to honor the birth of Papa's namesake, but Papa didn't want to call attention to himself. He acquiesced when Josie suggested they call it an ice cream social.

By mid-morning of the big day, Martha finished her Black Cake and set up the ice cream freezer in the dirt by the cellar where saltwater runoff wouldn't kill the grass. She and Anna turned the crank until Anna's "help" interfered. The three beeps of Alex's horn signaled a welcome interruption.

"Which would ya rather have, a strong arm for the freezer or distraction for Anna? We've already made three batches over at the Home Place."

Martha noted the usual accompaniment in the cab — Elena and Luis — and relief turned to annoyance. "Alex, on Monday Elena will have Robbie for the first time, in addition to both girls. Plus, I was hoping she could come tonight when Carrie tired of the excitement. Elena and I talked about it. You're overworking her."

"She'll just be here till noon helpin' get the barn ready. She wanted ta come."

Elena's partial wave indicated affirmation.

Martha turned back to the freezer but resented Alex's intrusion on her plans with Elena. Too often, Alex involved her, and Luis, beyond their place as hired help.

Over her shoulder, Martha said, "To answer your question, I'm sure Anna would find whatever you're proposing more interesting than what's going on here, if you don't mind."

"Wouldn't have asked if I minded."

Anna agreed enthusiastically to help "get the barn ready for Robbie's dance," having no idea what that meant. Luis lifted her into the cab, and she scrambled onto Elena's lap.

"We'll be back for the piano before noon, I expect," Alex called out the window.

Moving Mama's piano from the Lundgren living room to the barn couldn't possibly be good for it, but Martha hadn't protested. Everyone wanted Louise to play along with the fiddlers.

She gave up on the freezer with a final quarter turn of the crank and lifted the metal canister from the icy water. She carried it to the kitchen sink, careful to wipe away the salt before lifting off the lid.

Cook gets first taste, she assured herself. The soft peach ice cream was so tasty she scooped out a bowl for herself, allowing an extra spoonful or two for Carrie, just up from her nap.

Art found them sharing the ice cream, and when Carrie squealed with each bite he said, "Sounds too good ta resist. Gotta keep ya company. Next ta yer Black Cake, fresh peach ice cream's my favorite dessert."

"I've also made the cake, but I suppose it'd be obvious if someone snuck a piece."

As she spoke Martha moved toward the swinging door to the dining room and retrieved the cake plate from the top of the buffet. She sat it on the kitchen table. "Then again, in all the excitement tonight, who'll notice?"

Dolores Ruiz

Puffy clouds drifted across the otherwise clear sky throughout the afternoon, and the air stayed dry and warm, without a breeze, a contrast to the cool, wet weather all through September. Martha helped at the Home Place from dinnertime through supper, after it became clear that the installation of Fran's decorative plans for the barn required an army.

The family surveyed the barn's transformation in awe. Fran's artistry didn't live up to Edith Giffard's, but it came close. Carrie, entranced by the colored Christmas lights strung overhead, didn't take her eyes off them, nor did Robbie, the guest of honor.

Vehicles started pulling into the McLennan lane when the western horizon was still brushed with orange and the eastern sky turned indigo on its way to black. Soon the barn vibrated with dancers and music. As usual, Louise was the star without being conscious of it. The fiddlers followed her lead, and Martha kept their glasses filled with iced tea, afraid old Mr. Ufford would otherwise collapse any moment.

With Elsie's help, Josie and Earl shielded Robbie and Carrie from some of the hubbub by staying on the fringe, near tables laden with cakes, pies, and ice cream.

Around ten o'clock Elsie signaled that Elena had arrived, an hour later than expected. Martha made her way through the crowd and took a wide-awake but calm Carrie from Elsie's arms. Martha watched Luis back Alex's truck all the way up to the road, between the parked vehicles that lined both sides of the lane. Alex must have agreed to lend his pickup for Elena's transportation. At least he had the good sense not to invite the Marquez brother and sister to the dance.

Elena emerged from the shadows. Illuminated by the light coming out the barn doors, she couldn't hide her red, swollen face. When Martha noticed, the tears reappeared. Martha steered Elena into the relative quiet between vehicles.

"Elena, what's happened?"

Elena took many deep breaths before she spoke. "Dolores will have a baby. I would not say anything, but today..."

Elena's cousin, Dolores, had been in Josie's fifth/sixth-grade classroom with Susie Ogawa and Marguerite, Elena's sister. Josie had taken the trio of bright girls under her wing, and they set the standard for the others, even surpassing the accomplishments of older children.

Josie promoted only Marguerite directly into seventh, but Susie and Dolores were hardly less bright. The year of Dolores's graduation from eighth grade, Josie was beside herself that Dolores wasn't going to high school and mourned her loss of opportunity.

"Yes?"

Dolores's pregnancy was certainly a tragedy because she couldn't be more than sixteen and wasn't married, as far as Martha knew.

"Several weeks ago, when Uncle Zeke learned of it, he demanded the name of the father. He assumed it was a local boy and that Dolores behaved badly. For days Dolores refused. He was violent with her, which upset us very much."

Elena pulled a hankie from her sweater sleeve to wipe her nose.

"Uncle Zeke is traditional. He insists an eighth-grade education is more than girls need, but I think he also wanted to keep her close, to protect her because she is pretty."

By contrast, when José Marquez died, Elena's only alternative was to leave for the fields after her sophomore year; Zeke Ruiz had no excuse for withdrawing his daughter from school.

"Finally Dolores broke down and told him. The father is a friend of a man who came to work in the beet fields. He forced himself."

Elena looked directly into Martha's eyes, which she did infrequently, and Martha saw the hatred. Martha knew that hatred intimately and continued to harbor it for the dead man, Maher. Perhaps because Elena knew Ida and Vera's story, she sensed Martha wouldn't shrink from the horror of Dolores's suffering.

Martha could scarcely contain her fury, not just at the man who'd ravaged such a precious child but also at Zeke, her father. His was the first desecration, by violating his daughter's intelligence. Were it not for him, Dolores might not have been in the fields and exposed to such a man.

Elena held Martha's gaze and continued, "When she told Uncle Zeke the father's identity, he immediately went to Sheriff Burleigh, who learned the monster was in Albuquerque. I heard only this afternoon that the sheriff drove there and brought him back as far as Raton, where they met Uncle Zeke and Dolores this morning. They all went to a judge, and Dolores was forced to marry. Dolores and her new husband, Joe Roybal, rode back with Uncle Zeke, and the sheriff followed."

A father and the law, men who should have protected Dolores, debased her further, Burleigh by not locking up Roybal and Zeke Ruiz by forcing his daughter to marry her assailant.

Martha supported herself by leaning against the fender of the nearest vehicle. She swallowed the bile rising in her throat and asked a random question to keep her thoughts moving forward.

"I suppose Zeke took her to Raton on account of the wait for physical examinations before marrying in Colorado?"

"Yes. Otherwise, Aunt Pauline and my mother were planning on taking the bus to Santa Fe on Monday with Dolores and leaving her with their sister. Dolores would have the baby there, and she would stay to raise it. We would lose Dolores, but she might have a tolerable life. Uncle Zeke knew the plan. Now she will never escape."

Elena began to sob, quietly, hatred overcome by grief. Two men passed them in the shadows. Martha moved Elena toward the house to protect her privacy.

Cradling the now-restless Carrie in one arm, she said, "I'm taking you home so you can be with your family tonight."

Martha felt Carrie's body tense and anticipated her spasms, but Elena's heartache overshadowed the need to ease Carrie's immediate discomfort, or to fulfill her own responsibilities at the dance.

"No!" Elena said. "It is sad there, worse than death. I must rest my thoughts in the silence of your home. I want to be with Carrie because she heals my heart."

Martha handed Carrie to her. When she held a tranquil Carrie close and Carrie looked up at her, she still felt an eerie connection to eternal innocence and wisdom, the way folks do with newborns. Carrie was one of God's few creatures who would never, could never, hurt anyone, whose squeals of pleasure expressed unsullied joy. Martha knew the truth of Elena's longing to be with Carrie as surely as she knew the truth of Elena's hatred of the man who attacked Dolores.

Art appeared with Anna asleep in his arms. "She was curled up on Fran's lap. A big day fer a little girl."

"Last time I saw her, she was dancing, after a fashion, with Papa. Will you drive Elena and the girls to our place? She'll stay with them until we also reach the point of collapse."

Zeke Ruiz

Martha sought out Josie and corralled Elsie Lambert on the way back. The three huddled in the shadows at the north end of the barn, an ill-advised location. They heard raucous laughter and watched the Moulton brothers, Walter and Edgar, stagger past.

Elsie murmured, "Martha, I sometimes wish you and Walter had married, if only because it would have spared my Addie. Why she put up such a struggle to win him from you, I'll never understand."

"Elsie, I would have stopped seeing him even if Art hadn't come along…"

Nothing she said would convince Elsie that Walter ever held any interest for her.

After the brothers disappeared, the women scurried across the lane, onto the porch of the Home Place, where Elsie spat out the words, "Burleigh's gone way too far. Whatever entered his mind?"

Josie ran out the screen door and vomited on the gravel path. Without comment, Martha retrieved the rake, Elsie filled the pitcher that sat by the pump on the porch, and they eliminated the signs of Josie's distress.

They resolved to call Rev. Macgill to discuss Dolores's plight. He might know her parents, Pauline and Zeke Ruiz, through Pauline's sister, Aneda Marquez, Elena's mother and a stalwart member of the Spanish church even before José's accidental death.

Martha would enlist Papa to attend, and Elsie assured them Otto would come, assuming Rev. Macgill consented to Martha's request for a meeting before church. If anything were to be done about Zeke and Burleigh, it would take men with Papa's and Otto's standing, and Rev. Macgill's, to see it through.

Zeke Ruiz was rumored to be a Penitente, or closely associated with them. If so, he clearly didn't practice the charity the Catholic fraternity claimed to promulgate; he imposed only its severe judgment on his daughter. In effect, he flagellated Dolores when Joe Roybal should take the punishing blows.

Hank Philson

When Art struggled out of bed to do the chores, Martha relayed a tale nearly unbelievable in the light of day.

"As soon as ya feed an' dress the girls, bring 'em ta me in the barn an' head over ta the Home Place. If Alex an' Louise aren't already awake, get 'em up an' tell 'em ta hightail it over here ta help. We got Robert's cow on account a the party in their barn. I'll meet ya in town fer church."

No one was awake when Martha walked into Papa's kitchen. She stoked the fire and made coffee. No one emerged when the aroma penetrated to the bedrooms, so Martha knocked on each of their doors. The novelty of her presence woke them from their foggy sleep.

Martha didn't sugarcoat the story. Alex's face turned white, then an angry red. Louise was somber, Papa furious.

"It's not our place to interfere with Zeke and the way he runs his family," Papa said, "but it's high time we took action about Burleigh. Sure, I'll come to the meeting with Mac."

Martha telephoned and Rev. Macgill agreed to talk. Leaving before Martha poured their coffee, Alex and Louise drove off in the Lundgren's truck to help Art.

Martha sipped hers while Papa dressed. The familiar morning smells in her childhood home momentarily pulled Martha back to a sense of normalcy, save for Papa's bloodshot eyes.

They climbed into the Chrysler, and Martha said, "A wonderful party last night, Papa."

"Maybe too wonderful," he answered grimly. "Al and I can be civil over a shot of whiskey. Make that several. Good thing we have a Quaker like Otto Lambert to keep us sober under usual circumstances."

"I'm glad you let your hair down, Papa. You've been working very hard."

"Want to be one of the first to hear the gossip?"

"What gossip?"

"Al's beside himself. Confided to me Fred Warner's being investigated for embezzlement of county funds."

"No! It's a marvel, first, that Al confided in you and second, that the district by the dam has a commissioner under investigation. What a contrast between Fred and the high-minded Otto who represented them before the Lamberts moved here, to Eagle View."

"It's just a rumor, but the fact Al's upset enough to tell me says there's truth to it. Al's not smart, but he's honest."

"As you are, Papa. I mean, honest. Unlike Al, you're smart, too."

"Well, that's a relief to hear!"

Papa was smart, maybe even when it came to his insistence about delaying his marriage, given the stranger at the pavilion.

She said, "If anyone should be investigated I'd think it should be the third commissioner, Hank Philson. I've never trusted him."

"Just because he's a used-car dealer?"

Martha playfully punched him on the arm. "Regardless of what he sells, he's a shyster."

Papa parked in front of the church next to Josie and Earl's Ford. "At least they had a good night's sleep on account of taking the guest of honor home to bed at a decent hour."

"We'll see. Robbie might have celebrated late into the night."

The Spanish-Americans

No one looked especially fresh when Martha surveyed those gathered, which, to her surprise, included Earl. After "good morning" formalities, Rev. Macgill invited them to take their seats.

Josie made a point of sitting by Martha and whispered, "Earl's as upset about Dolores as I am, probably because I still talk about her lost opportunities."

Rev. Macgill was saying, "Martha told me the details on the telephone. I don't think we can do much about the marriage because Zeke Ruiz approved, maybe even pressed for it. The scandal of his daughter having a bastard child would be unthinkable. This is simply a shotgun wedding, albeit an especially tragic one."

Several in the group squirmed to hear Rev. Macgill use the word "bastard" in mixed company, and everyone muttered their displeasure that he thought their hands were tied. He continued without apology for his crude language, and Martha thought the word probably best conveyed Zeke's raw emotion about his daughter's predicament. An ignorant man protecting his family from humiliation might sacrifice a daughter.

"Concerning Burleigh, last month Martha came to me about the incident with the boy he locked in the market closet, which, now with his being an accomplice in Dolores's tragedy, is part of a pattern of his disrespect for Spanish-Americans. Perhaps you've noticed the weekly report in the paper about men arrested for drunkenness usually lists a disproportionate number of Spanish surnames."

The group was silent, but Martha noticed Elsie and Otto nodded their agreement. On her part, the connections Rev. Macgill made between the boy, Dolores, weekend drunks, and the Spanish people confused her.

Rev. Macgill waited for comments; no one spoke.

"I feel horrible about Dolores," he said, "but she's a casualty of many factors, some in the Spanish-American community and some in ours. And we won't get rid of Burleigh. For the old-timers, he still carries the aura of the quarterback who led Greenwood to the state championships, and I don't think this group of county commissioners will stand up to him. Of the three, there's not one man with the moral strength to do it."

Martha was surprised Rev. Macgill spoke so openly about his lack of confidence in Al, a member of the church; usually he was more circumspect, but only McLennans and Lamberts were present, and save for Earl, they shared the sentiment. Also, he might have heard the rumor about Fred Warner and embezzlement, and she wasn't surprised Rev. Macgill had a low opinion of Hank Philson.

"Are you concluding we can't help Dolores?" Martha asked.

"I haven't said that. I'm only describing our limitations."

In the midst of more grumbling and protestation, Martha left the room in disgust. There had to be some recourse for Dolores. Martha hadn't thought Rev. Macgill would acquiesce to Zeke's cruelty. She and Elsie had broadcast the story about Burleigh's rough handling of the boy, and surely they could do something similar about his outrageous treatment of Dolores. Then again, if they raised a hullaballoo, they'd violate Dolores all over again with their lack of discretion.

Burleigh's only responsibility should have been to pick up Roybal and bring him back to jail. What pushed Burleigh to use brute force and smash slot machines with baseball bats, shoot locks off sheds, throw children into closets, and force girls to marry men who ravaged them?

She would challenge him to his face.

Howard Burleigh

He was at the jail sorting out drunks from Saturday night. A cursory glance confirmed Rev. Macgill's observation. Most of them were Mexican, but she was sure the majority of weekend drunks were white, judging by the number of them hanging around the barn dance last night. She couldn't imagine Burleigh would throw Walter Moulton into a cell, another Greenwood football hero.

"Mornin', Martha," he said. "What're ya doin' here on a Sunday mornin'?"

Confronting the man seated behind the desk wasn't like the encounter with the devil Martha had envisioned. The devil wouldn't look that haggard.

"Why'd you do it?"

"Do what?"

"Force Dolores Ruiz to marry Joe Roybal. That's his name, isn't it?"

Burleigh slid a pile of papers to the side of his desk and didn't bother to look up.

"That's not how it was. Zeke Ruiz came ta me. We forced *him* ta marry *her* an' take responsibility fer what he done. After you an' me saw that hellhole a Maher's, why're ya even askin'? We gotta make men do the decent thing."

"Look at me when I'm talking to you," said Martha, and she placed both her hands on his desk.

She leaned toward him. Burleigh lifted his head and stiffened, but Martha didn't retreat.

"Do I have your attention?"

She didn't mean to sound that sarcastic and moderated her tone. "I doubt marriage to a child he's violated will cause Joe Roybal to accept responsibility, but you've chained her to the man who tortured her. It's as if you handcuffed the chicken thief to Al Ivarson."

Martha reconsidered. Being handcuffed to Al might be suitable punishment.

She quickly added, "Or, if Maher survived the accident at Collins Curve, you might as well have handcuffed him to Ida. He wouldn't have objected."

Burleigh stood. Martha wouldn't let him intimidate her with his size and drew herself to her full height.

"Don't talk back ta me, Martha Lundgren. I could arrest ya fer comin' inta my office like this, but I won't. What's done is done."

"You would arrest me but not Joe Roybal?"

"I did pick him up in Albuquerque, but released him in Raton, after the judge married 'em."

"So marriage is a punishment?"

Burleigh wearily passed his hand over the stubble on his chin, and Martha saw the melancholy expression similar to the one in Enoch Gwynn's eyes the day he'd asked her to help deliver news to a woman they assumed would be Maher's widow. Their sorrow must originate in the bottomless depths of cruelty and grief they handled on a regular basis.

"Sheriff Burleigh, you don't have to handle every criminal act with brute force. There are degrees of punishment; circumstances differ. You should have brought Joe Roybal back and put him in jail for trial."

He sneered, "Then why don't ya run fer sheriff if ya think there's better ways a doin' the job? A woman sheriff fer Greenwood. Now that's funny."

He snorted, and she clenched her fists.

He said, "I doubt a jury's gonna convict a Mex'can man fer what he done ta a Mex'can girl, but *I* made him face it."

Burleigh sat and shuffled the papers on his desk as though she had disappeared. There was no getting through to him. For him, and evidently Zeke Ruiz, it was more important to force a man to take responsibility than to consider Dolores. By herself, Martha wouldn't convince them otherwise.

She drove back to the church in time to practice with the choir and wondered if the group in Rev. Macgill's study had come to any resolution. At the very least, she hoped they formed a delegation to talk with Burleigh about his excesses. As Elsie said, Burleigh was susceptible to political pressure. The more upstanding citizens, such as the McLennans and Lamberts, who disagreed with his methods to his face, the better.

She wouldn't have thought it possible to absorb one more shock, but at the end of the service Rev. Macgill announced that, after more than a decade in Greenwood, he would be leaving before Halloween. He was in the reserves and had been called to duty as a chaplain. The family would be moving to an army base in California.

Without his counsel, who could help Dolores face her grim future? Who would help any of them with life's calamities?

Anna McLennan

Two Saturdays later, Martha and Josie surveyed the rectangular space that accommodated overflow crowds from the church sanctuary. For the Macgills' going-away party, the chairs had disappeared and two long tables arranged to form a V occupied the center of the area. Red, white, and blue streamers ran down the center of the white tablecloths with vases of carnations in the same colors placed at intervals. The coffee service was laid at one point of the V and the tea service at its opposite. Filling the remaining surface were cakes and pies, paper nut cups of mints and salted peanuts, and platters of cookies.

Ribbons in the patriotic colors hung above another table placed against the rear wall and framed a large sketch of an American flag waving in the breeze. Outlines in the foreground suggested armaments of war. Cards and several gifts, presumably from each of the church's organizations, lay strewn on the tabletop.

After Mama's funeral, the Women's Study Group had arranged two tables lengthwise in the middle of the same area, but the white cloths bore nothing colorful, only the tea and coffee service at opposing ends and platters of the same foods. The table against the rear wall that day was piled with cards, too, arranged around a vase of white and pale-pink roses.

Martha grabbed Josie's hand and held it tightly.

Josie didn't withdraw and said, "I suppose you're as upset as I am upon hearing Rev. Macgill's report about Burleigh just now. If Elsie had been here, she would have objected, but I couldn't think what to say."

No, Martha hadn't been particularly upset. She could have predicted Burleigh's reaction to Papa, Otto, Earl, and Rev. Macgill. They urged him to moderate his reactions in cases like Dolores's, but, as he had with Martha, Burleigh argued his point. Unlike Earl, a teacher, and Rev. Macgill, a minister, he usually had to move fast. Folks expected them to be deliberate and take time, even years, to do their work. Farmers like Otto and Papa, the same. Couldn't hurry nature. High school students and seeds took months to grow into harvest, but Burleigh couldn't be hogtied. He had to make quick decisions, and that's what he'd done with the "Ruiz business."

Rev. Macgill concluded that, until Burleigh's haste and excess got him into trouble with more white citizens of the county, he wasn't going to change. Maybe he wasn't even capable of change.

Martha had grabbed Josie's hand because she was distressed by the sad memories of Mama's funeral. She didn't mention them, though, and fastened onto the topic of men leaving for service.

"Well, Rev. Macgill probably realized any plan about Burleigh would be pointless because he won't be around to enforce it. As for Art and Earl, surely they won't select Art on account of his family and the farm, given the 'Food for Freedom' efforts. And maybe because Earl has a new baby, he won't be sent."

"Sis, lower your voice. Guests are starting to arrive."

Josie quickly looked around the room to see if any of the other women were watching, but she didn't let go of Martha's hand.

Edith and Claude Giffard approached, and Josie commented, "Edith, as usual, you've designed a lovely arrangement, and the sketch of the flag on the wall is stunning."

Edith beamed at the compliment, let go of Claude's arm, and threw her arms around both sisters. Josie blushed at Edith's effusive thank-you, and Claude looked away uncomfortably.

"Martha, have you a recent letter from Muriel?" Edith asked. "She's …"

Martha was vaguely aware that Edith went on and on with news that Martha already knew from her own correspondence with Muriel.

The Giffards finally walked over to the Ivarsons, but the intensity of Martha's grief about Mama hadn't diminished. "Josie, I've lost Muriel Giffard, Doc, and now the Macgills to defense. Muriel's on the other side of the world. It's only a matter of time before Louise takes advantage of opportunities opening for young women. Her work as accountant at Giffard's Lumberyard can't be that interesting. She could end up in Washington, DC, California, or any point between. And Alex is sure to go."

That war might pull their family so far apart elicited a sigh from them both, and Martha continued, "Circumstances beyond Papa's control are going to allow for an earlier marriage than he anticipated. He's more committed to Louise and Alex's interests in the farm than they can be, given world affairs."

Josie gently extricated her hand. "Sis, your grip's so tight you're cutting off the circulation in my fingers."

She put her arm around Martha's shoulders and held her, an unusual demonstration of affection for the reserved Josie, given the setting. Their physical proximity allowed Josie to speak softly. "I'm upset the Macgills are going, too. Everyone is, but Rev. Macgill's well-suited to be an army chaplain and is obviously looking forward to what he sees as a new adventure."

Josie started to withdraw her arm, but Martha prevented her by reaching up and laying her hand on Josie's. She was desperate for the reassurance of Josie's touch.

"Sis, you're more distraught than the Macgills' departure warrants. Surely it isn't Papa's decision to delay his marriage that's upsetting you so, although you and I still haven't had a serious conversation about it. But now isn't the time."

"Josie, the conversation about Papa and Fran isn't difficult. He doesn't seem to have discussed it with anyone, at least not with me. Has he talked about it with you?"

"No, and I don't expect him to."

She successfully pulled away, but Martha forged ahead. "He announced he'd wait until Alex and Louise were settled as though it were an imperial decree, and only several months after he started courting her, as I understand it. That's so unlike him, not to talk it over. It's obvious he loves Fran. If he delays marriage indefinitely, she won't wait around forever."

"Sis, I said, another time."

Not everyone might leave on account of defense. Perhaps not the gaunt man at the dance pavilion, and Papa's excuses for delaying his marriage — Alex and Louise's circumstances — might dissolve as quickly as the Macgills' departure had materialized. Then Papa would be ready to marry but Fran's determination to keep the stranger out of her life might not hold. Papa had to reverse himself, and soon.

"We must take our places to serve," Josie continued, "but I will say this. As well as Earl and I are getting acquainted with Fran through the high school, we don't know anything intimate about her past. She might have been disappointed in love, and more than once, so she's content to wait. Also, while she's very fond of Papa, she's taught for over a decade and made a considerable commitment to her profession. She won't abandon it lightly, and Papa shouldn't assume she will. They have a lot to sort out."

Josie walked toward her end of the serving table to pour the coffee. Martha followed.

"Sis, what are you doing? Take your place at the tea service."

Martha had to finish the conversation. Fran's commitment to her profession paled in comparison to the possible impact of a renewed relationship with the man at the pavilion who was so determined to win back her affection. But Martha would give no hint of that to Josie out of loyalty to Fran.

Instead, she said, "What about Louise and Alex? Doesn't this pressure them to make choices about their futures that shouldn't be rushed?"

Josie stopped and turned to Martha. "I don't see it that way. Papa's decision is loving and sensible. You've just pointed out you and I have professions and husbands. We're secure. Alex's future is uncertain. He might have to go at any time after his twenty-first birthday, but, then again, he might not be called right away. Where would Alex live and what would he do if Papa married before he's called? Louise has that position at the lumberyard and says she's moving to town, but you and I know how unpredictable she is."

Martha opened her mouth to enumerate her list of objections, but Josie, in the stern voice of an older sister and woman used to commanding the attention of distracted children, said "Martha, take your place, now. We've carried on this conversation longer than is polite."

Finally aware of the number of guests milling around and waiting to be served, Martha self-consciously turned to the opposite point of the V where she was to pour. She and Josie saw Papa's situation so differently, and she couldn't disclose that Fran had another suitor lurking in the background.

After seeing Fran slap that pathetic man, Martha was torn between her admiration and her fear that elements of Fran's past might intrude in unexpected ways. Josie recognized they knew little of Fran's history, which led Josie to a different conclusion: delay was desirable. Martha dwelt on her fear Papa might lose Fran, but maybe Josie was right that if he married in haste, Fran would bring him grief.

She had only two more empty cups on the table before her but many more people in her line when Maude Moulton walked up with a tray of clean ones. Martha smiled her thanks and retreated into her thoughts. They took a distinct turn. Josie's comment about Fran's commitment to her profession confirmed Josie's own professional enthusiasm. She hadn't hesitated when Martha proposed Elena care for the children three days a week and had immediately speculated she might be called to substitute, on account of the increasing shortage of male teachers because of conscription. With Elena's help, Josie was free.

The endless numbers of bridge clubs and women's organizations wouldn't have satisfied Josie, even though Martha reckoned there were over eighty of them in the county. Josie was a McLennan and would want to be more useful than women like Edith Giffard and Mrs. Hayes, who devoted themselves to so many of the groups.

However, did Earl value Josie's professional capabilities as Art did hers? She couldn't imagine Earl saying he admired Josie's concerns beyond those of his family, as Art had.

Not that Martha didn't feel useful on the farm. Farming and nursing had a closer connection than most folks thought. Roosevelt's people estimated forty-five percent in the country were undernourished. "Food for Freedom" wasn't an empty slogan.

But as grateful as Martha was every day for her nurse's training because it equipped her to be a good mother for Carrie, she was eager to exercise her skills more widely. She couldn't be a navy nurse as Muriel was, nor could she and Art relocate as the Macgills were, but they were useful in Greenwood, both of them on the farm and she in Doc's office.

Maude interrupted Martha's thoughts. "Mrs. Macgill has asked for tea. Pour a cup for her and another for me. I'll take it to her."

Maude didn't need to be so officious. The same words out of anyone else's mouth would be simple statements, but Maude acted as though she were lady-in-waiting and Mrs. Macgill the queen. Martha wondered if Maude had any idea her sons routinely made drunken spectacles of themselves.

Martha's thoughts careened in yet another direction to speculate about the gifts on the table. She couldn't bear to dwell on the Macgills' actual departure.

They'd asked folks not to buy them going-away presents. Too much to pack, given how hurried the move was, and the money would be better spent on any of the numerous campaigns for funds.

Still, the Ladies Missionary Society purchased a kit of toilet preparations and a coin purse for Mrs. Macgill; Martha knew from Art the Men's Club was giving Rev. Macgill a billfold. Perhaps there was money left over from the donations for the gifts to tuck into the purse and billfold. Probably the young people bought pen sets for the daughters to encourage correspondence.

The Macgills' departure tore a sizeable hole in Greenwood. Mrs. Macgill had started the Valley orchestra and directed the church choir and community Women's Chorus. The two younger daughters were also talented musicians and the oldest an able athlete on the girls' basketball team — all key participants in school activities.

Rev. Macgill announced the softball games. He played minor roles in the high school class plays and major ones in the Valley theater group. He was a dynamic member of most of the men's organizations and crucial in maintaining all the church groups and the Spanish church, not to mention his around-the-clock availability for emergencies.

Most families depended on Rev. Macgill's counsel at one time or other, but surely the McLennan family would grieve his departure more than most. Save for decisions that concerned farming, Papa didn't make a significant one without talking to "Mac," unless, perhaps, his decision not to marry until Alex and Louise were settled. Rev. Macgill wouldn't counsel something so impractical.

Martha drifted further into the treacherous territory of her grief about Mama and the Macgills' departure. Rev. Macgill had sat with them through several long nights by Mama's bedside when she was dying, and Art might not have stayed in Greenwood had Rev. Macgill not invited him to live with them when Art's father abandoned the family. Martha was sure Art had conversations with Rev. Macgill about Carrie, and she didn't doubt they talked over her plan to work in Doc's office.

Art stood before her, waiting for a cup of tea. She made herself smile. "You never drink hot tea!"

"Ain't too late ta start a bad habit. Besides, who can resist such a good-lookin' hostess?"

He bent down as she handed him the cup and whispered in her ear, "I'm checkin' on how yer doin'. Yer smilin' but not talkin'. Fer Martha Lundgren, that's unsociable. Probably none a the others noticed on account a jockeyin' ta have one last word with the Macgills. But I did."

Martha was grateful for Art's attentiveness, but his tenderness threatened her carefully constructed barrier of mental distractions. "I'm afraid if I talk I'll break down and spoil the party. It's better I go through the motions and keep my sorrow about their departure to myself."

October and November 1941

Llewellyn Thompson

Cloudy, cool days slowed the frenetic pace of harvest and calmed Martha's agitation about the Macgills' departure and Dolores's ordeal. Rainy weather meant some farmers lost the hay cut and lying wet in their fields, but Art managed to get theirs in the stack. He decided not to go elk hunting with Papa because there already was too much snow in the mountains, and he helped Al Ivarson unload his feeder lambs and establish them in repaired pens.

In Art's spare time, he shot rabbits. Mr. Miyoshi said it was pointless, but Art persisted. With the disruption of fur shipments from Europe, a pound of pelts brought sixty cents, as opposed to the twenty-cent price last year. Ladies' hats still needed trim; more to the point, twenty-seven rabbits devoured as much hay as one cow. Unchecked, batches of new bunnies would eat even more crops come spring.

But Martha suspected Art stayed close to home on account of her three mornings a week with Dr. McFarland, to be sure the arrangement worked. She left Carrie and Anna at Josie's, where Elena met them. Martha picked them up at noon, along with Robbie, and drove everyone back to the farm where Josie collected Robbie and Elena late in the day.

Josie picked up where she'd left off the past winter, which included her many club meetings and occasional substitute teaching. Several male teachers had left for the army, and the board had no choice but to call on her.

Alex, social as ever, was hardly around. On weekends, he went to football games, dances, and church socials, and during the week he always found something to take him out of the house in the evenings — roller-skating, movies; he even learned to play bridge! His sisters suspected some young lady prompted that interest.

Martha loved having the three cousins together, but perhaps Papa enjoyed them most because he could drive across the road when he came in from the fields and play with them all. Those interludes surely helped him adjust to Alex's scarcity and Louise's move to town, where she had taken rooms to be closer to her work at the lumberyard.

One afternoon when Josie came for Elena and Robbie, he was snuggled in Papa's arms, sound asleep in the overstuffed chair next to the piano.

"They've been napping for the past half hour," Martha whispered to Josie from where they stood in the dining room, peeking through the archway.

Papa, not taking his eyes off Robbie's face, answered quietly, "He is, but I'm cataloging each expression that passes over my grandson's face. What's the news from Eagle View School, Josie? Martha said you taught there today."

Josie walked in and sat on the sofa. "Tonight the teachers are having a party for the Spanish-American parents, and the party for the Americans is tomorrow night. Oh, you'll be interested in this. I hear that at the County Council meeting of parents and teachers, everyone complained about not having a school nurse since Millie Swanson left in August. They protested to the commissioners, who finally promised to hire one by the first of the year."

Papa looked up. "Well, I can't imagine why the County Council folks would complain. The commissioners have functioned as the Health Unit since they dissolved the real one. By now they should have enough confidence in their medical judgment that one of them could be the nurse."

He inquired of Martha, "Don't you think Al would do? He's delivered enough lambs he's surely qualified to treat scarlet fever, and polio. He and the others are so skilled that the State Board of Health forced them to chlorinate two wells by the dam construction site and condemn two others, after they claimed they had everything under control."

Martha sympathized fully with Papa, but not with this childish sarcasm. It was nearly a year since he'd lost the election. He should rise above his resentment and be grateful a public health nurse would be back in place soon.

"I don't know how all this foolishness will end," he said. "Al surely can't undo everything Otto and I worked for. We even left the county coffers with a surplus of over eight thousand dollars."

Robbie squirmed and poked his fists toward the ceiling. He awoke without a cry and studied Papa's face.

"Guess it's your turn to examine me. You're a smart boy. I can tell you agree."

Martha and Josie rolled their eyes at one another, and Josie retrieved her son. "You'll have to compete with his father for his political allegiance, you know."

"Hmm… Sis, what's the news from Dr. McFarland?"

Martha, ready to move beyond snide remarks about Al, said, "He's nice. Gentle with patients. Go by and introduce yourself. He's still getting acquainted, and he'd be grateful to meet someone who isn't sick, injured, or having a baby. Especially not injured. We're seeing a number of wounds from the dam site, even though they have a small emergency treatment building there, as you know from your several visits. The site's so massive, with hundreds of men and all that equipment, I'm certain we hear about only a fraction of the accidents. Today they brought in a man with a fractured kneecap who fell from a twenty-foot ladder. Yesterday a worker lost a finger."

Papa grimaced. "Don't know I'd be comfortable meeting the new doc at the office, with all that gore."

"He doesn't have the, what can I call it, the fire Doc has, but he's a good physician. Folks will probably adjust quickly to his mild manner. It's a sacrifice for him to be here because his wife isn't well, so she won't be moving down from Pueblo. Their children are grown. His youngest son finished air training and sailed for the Philippine Islands recently."

"Oh?"

"I should write Muriel and tell her to watch for him."

"How many American soldiers are in the Philippine Islands now?" Papa asked. "You surely don't think she'll meet this particular one. Besides, she's a navy nurse."

Martha laughed. "I'll bring you up to date, Papa. Muriel has a beau. He's a co-pilot on the four-motored B-17s. Listen to me, as though I know about airplanes. That's how she describes them. Anyway, pilots might run across one another."

"We're being too lighthearted, talking about defense as if the purpose is for boys to meet girls. I hope war doesn't come to us in the Pacific. It's terrible in Europe. What awful cost for the Russians, and the Germans."

"Papa, I've not thought about him for some time, but what do you hear of Llewellyn Thompson?" Josie asked.

"A mutual acquaintance, who calls him 'Wally,' said his parents don't know if he left Moscow when the embassy staff relocated with the move of the Russian government. I'm worried, given the German advance, that he might not have gotten away. I sure do admire him."

"I overheard Elsie Lambert talking about him with someone in the market," Martha said. "He must be the only local hero she can commend because he's a diplomat, not a soldier. Otherwise, her principled stance against war doesn't permit her to enter many discussions without offending someone."

Martha walked toward the kitchen to start supper. She hesitated at the door when she heard Papa talking to Elena, who sat at the dining table holding Carrie.

"And what's the news from your family?" he asked.

Was he tactfully inquiring about Dolores? Out of politeness, she and Josie never inquired and only heard news if Elena offered.

According to her recent report, Joe Roybal kept his distance. Apparently Dolores's brother, Rudy, and Luis visited several times daily in the first week and successfully communicated that Roy would answer to them if he roughed her up in any way.

Consequently, Roy took another room and rarely visited his new wife, an arrangement Rudy kept from their father, Zeke. However, he and Luis fully informed their mothers, Pauline and Aneda. Zeke had forbidden Pauline from having anything to do with their daughter, which was unthinkable. Thank the Good Lord Dolores had her brother, her cousin, Luis, and a discreet aunt in Aneda Marquez.

"Not much news," Elena said. "Most of my family works in the sugar beet fields, and it is too muddy for harvest. One day, though, my cousin pulled a beet with a root sixty-three inches long. They showed it to Mr. Hallet at the newspaper, and he took a picture. Usually the roots break off. Possibly the whole thing came out because the ground is soft from the rain."

Papa whistled. "Sixty-three inches! That's barely a foot short of two yards."

No one had paid attention to Anna, concentrated as she was on her Mickey Mouse coloring book at the dining table. She lifted her head. "The beet had short feet but it filled two yards?"

Everyone laughed, but Anna ignored them. Used to being patronized, she said, "Grandpa, I already know an inch is this."

She held up her thumb in the manner Martha had shown her weeks ago and gave him her raised-eyebrow-I'm-waiting-for-an-answer look.

Papa started to explain, then thought better of it. "Sis, where's your yardstick? Anna and I'll go outside to consider this matter."

Martha assumed the lesson on measurement and homonyms would take some time. She and Josie probably took to Mrs. Bro's book on account of Papa raising them according to a similar precept: take children's questions seriously. Josie left with Elena and Robbie, and Martha put Carrie in her sling chair while she fixed supper.

Papa's comments about Llewellyn Thompson were troubling. It was all well and good to collect "Bundles for Britain" last winter when the clothes and shoes went to anonymous folks. But she easily imaged Mr. Thompson facing down Hitler's soldiers if they reached the outskirts of Moscow.

Papa followed Mr. Thompson's career closely, from when he was a diplomat in Ceylon and Geneva and now in Russia. Was it already more than a year since the McLennan family had marveled together at how long he took to get there, from San Francisco to Tokyo by ship and the weeklong train trip on the Trans-Siberian railroad?

His aunt, a librarian, hosted a gathering before he left for Russia. When Martha shook his hand, he looked at her intently, not a glance most men give when meeting a woman, but in the eye, and asked what she had done after graduation. He congratulated her on completing nurses' training, even before learning she was Robert McLennan's daughter. To think, a person she'd touched faced the threat of German invasion.

War loomed as an unrestrained, palpable force, as it did that afternoon in the balcony at the drugstore, when she was so desperate to go to the Fourth of July dance. But she was foolish to draw the comparison between Art on the farm and Jimmy Stewart in the army, as though she would never dance with Art again if they didn't go that very night.

Perhaps she also exaggerated the danger Mr. Thompson faced in Moscow. Threats faced by people across oceans did not affect her. Then again, men she knew would be called. Rev. Macgill was gone. So was Doc. How difficult to react in proportion to the sense of danger hovering just beyond her grasp.

She wanted to remain calm, as Elsie Lambert did. Regardless of how alarming the news, Elsie maintained her position against war. The Lamberts didn't even buy defense stamps and bonds; instead, they sent money to Quaker hostels in the Midwest for relocated European refugees. Elsie said many of them were Jewish. Quakers were certainly broadminded.

Martha was still ashamed to remember her demeanor at the Macgills' farewell party when she was so preoccupied by their departure, Mama's death, and worried about Papa and Fran. She didn't even commend Rev. Macgill on serving his country. Josie and Art were right to chastise her for not being cordial.

Papa and Fran. She hadn't seen Fran for several weeks, other than to pass at church, whereas Josie's friendship with Fran was comfortable on account of them being members of AAUW and the Book Review Club.

Martha wasn't envious of their companionability, and she didn't miss the club. Too little program and too much gossip on the part of otherwise idle women who put on airs of having great sums of money.

She didn't think highly of folks with money, especially after reading the editorial from *The Pueblo Times* about folks apparently doubling and tripling their wealth on account of the European war. If she understood, they were the objects of proposed congressional action to limit war profits. The rich cashed in while the ninety-nine percent without hope of measureable profit carried additional responsibility for defense with the enactment of the new tax bill. She ardently agreed that the rich shouldn't be allowed to pile up millions while farmers and other laborers paid their share in taxes and war bonds.

Art's entrance from the porch startled her so, she let out a soft cry.

"Ain't Halloween yet. Wasn't tryin' ta scare ya."

She managed a chuckle. "I had so many thoughts running around in my head I was miles away."

Short of going to club meetings, Martha did want to know Fran better, and she hadn't heard anything about Vera and Ida for some time. After she cleaned up supper and tucked in the girls, Martha telephoned.

"Martha, what a lovely surprise."

Beyond inquiring about Vera and Ida and learning they were doing as well as could be expected, Martha hadn't thought what to say.

"Uh…" Perhaps talk about Halloween and school. "I imagine you're busy these days, with homecoming, Halloween parties, and your classes."

Fran politely described her activities and asked, "How is everything with the Lundgrens? Robert tells me you're enjoying your new schedule at the doctor's office."

The stilted conversation disappointed Martha. They had no common interests, as Josie and Fran did. To become better acquainted, she'd need Papa. The Halloween party at Eagle View. She'd invite them, and the obligatory small talk would have served as prelude to an acceptable reason for disrupting Fran's evening.

"Yes, it's good to be of help to Dr. McFarland as he gets acquainted. I don't know that you've heard about our annual Halloween party at Eagle View School. It's gained quite a reputation on account of the elaborate costumes folks think up, and I was wondering…"

"Oh, yes, Josie regaled me this week with stories about the various outfits the two of you devised over the years."

Encouraged, Martha infused more enthusiasm into her invitation. "Would you help convince Papa to come? If the two of you attend with us, Art won't grumble so about it. And you would meet more families in our rural district, in addition to the ones who so enjoyed you at Papa and Robbie's party."

They concluded Fran would persuade Robert to go as Anthony to her Cleopatra. Martha was realistic. Art would risk no more than the staid farmer costume — overalls and a checkered shirt.

"I'm so glad you called and proposed this."

The conversation reinforced Martha's opinion of Fran as energetic, intelligent, and forthright. Martha should have invited her and Papa for a special occasion sooner, without the rest of the family. Perhaps Martha had unwittingly hesitated to draw closer to Fran on account of the scene between her and the man at the dance pavilion. The Halloween party would remedy that error.

Ellis Ufford

Martha easily outfitted herself and the girls as the farmer's family. She and Anna wore print dresses with full skirts and matching hair bows. Martha pinned a similar bow in Carrie's dark, curly hair. They went to the schoolhouse in Papa's Chrysler, but the parking area in front was already full. He dropped them off and went across the highway to the lot in front of Collins Country store.

All the scary decorations and costumes intimidated Anna, so she stayed in her grandfather's arms. When it was announced that Robert McLennan and Fran Reeve won for the best costumes, Anna declined to accompany them onstage. She held on to Martha's leg.

The square dancing was to start, and Art caught Martha by the waist with one arm and handed Carrie to Fran with the other. Fran coddled Carrie in her arms, seemingly pleased to be given the responsibility, and Anna scampered back to her grandfather.

Fran shooed Martha toward the center of the gymnasium and said, "Don't worry. I'll take her to one of the classrooms where it's quiet."

Hugh's father, Ellis Ufford, called the dances, and his grandfather, old Mr. Ufford, fiddle in hand, sat behind Ellis on stage. Hugh and Alex hadn't materialized, nor had Louise. Her music must be in demand elsewhere, and Halloween costumes were out of the boys' ken.

When Art and Martha stepped into the center, Ellis yelled Art's name and something Martha didn't make out.

Art threw back his head and laughed, "Hang on, darlin.'"

The squares of four couples formed, and they smoothly executed the patterns.

After a short break, Ellis shouted, "You warmed up yet, Art Lundgren?"

Three different couples quickly joined them, and all the other sets moved to the side. Parents gathered their children to watch.

"Art, what's going on?"

"Ellis challenged my dancin'. It's gonna be very fast an' complicated, but I'll guide ya. The others know what ta do. Ya'll be fine."

Martha heard the first notes of old Mr. Ufford's fiddle, but from then on it was a blur of familiar "allemande left," "do-si-do," and "swing your partner" mingled with calls she couldn't decipher until she heard "lead your honey to a big soft chair." She ended up in Art's arms with Ellis's final holler, still on her feet, to the applause of the crowd.

Art twirled her. "I told ya, ya could do it!"

Ellis walked by and grumbled, "Art, next time I'll get the better of you!"

"Why's he upset?" Martha asked.

"He's not. Ellis an' I have this contest. He dreams up complications ta throw me off, but he never has. Guess we ain't done it since dances at the Pinion School."

"Well, you have quite the reputation, because folks at Eagle View seem to know about it."

Art was the best dancer in the place, not just in Martha's eyes. They'd met at homecoming Martha's junior year. He was a year older than Josie and best friends with Eddie Mattson, Josie's beau until Mama died, before she left for teacher's college. Eddie was the first to call her "Josie," and the name stuck, except with Mama, who always used her full name, Josephine.

Martha couldn't remember which girl Art escorted that night. She was there with Walter Moulton, her off-and-on beau throughout high school and a classmate of Josie and Eddie's, so she and Walter spent the evening with Josie's crowd. She danced with Art only once because every girl in the gymnasium wanted a turn with him.

Mama died that summer, and she and Art didn't start courting until after Martha's first year in nursing school. The two always agreed, though, they fell for each other during that dance.

The men slapped Art on the back and congratulated him on his agility; Martha accepted compliments from the women, until she saw Fran hurrying toward her, guided through the crowd by Papa.

"Something's wrong with Carrie," Fran said.

Martha brushed her lips against Carrie's flushed forehead and felt its dry heat. "Papa, please get the car. We have to take Carrie home."

Doctor Angus McFarland

Throughout the night, Martha used cold compresses, and by morning Carrie's body wasn't as hot. Still, she lay listless when Martha put her down and didn't even respond to Anna's cajoling. Carrie had no appetite. By Sunday night she slept less fitfully but still had a temperature. Mid-day Monday Martha decided to take her in to Dr. McFarland.

Art helped load the girls into the truck and resolved at the last minute to go with them. "This temperchure an' her refusin' ta eat er drink is worryin' me."

"I'm glad you're coming, even though it's probably nothing more than a cold."

As they drove out the lane, Maude Moulton turned in. Art rolled down his window.

"Hello, folks," she said. "Just coming by for the Red Cross roll call. Our county quota has doubled this year to over twelve hundred dollars, and I'm encouraging everyone to dig deeper."

She took a breath, and Art said, "Mornin', Maude. We're on our way ta Doc with Carrie. Can't talk now. Why don't ya come back later?"

He drove on and left Maude with her mouth open.

"That's the only way to handle her," Martha said. "Just keep moving, or she'll talk all day. I wish you hadn't suggested she come back. I've already taken care of one donation for the Red Cross and, what with defense stamps and new taxes, this family can't dig any deeper."

Martha shifted Anna to the other side of her lap and said, "Honey, I need to take the quilt off Carrie because she'll get too hot, and that will make the fever worse."

"I'll help, Mama. When will Carrie get well?"

In her mind, Martha modified Anna's question to "When will Carrie get well from this particular illness?"

Carrie would never be "well."

"We don't know, punkin," Art answered. "We're takin' her ta Doc McFarland so as he can help 'er."

Martha turned her head toward the window to hide her anxiety. Art's eyes fixed on the road, as though all their lives depended on him driving in a straight line. Neither parent spoke, and Anna remained silent with her hand resting on the edge of the baby car box. Martha wasn't conscious of inhaling and exhaling until she noticed that her own breathing, Art's, and Carrie's were synchronized shallow gasps for air.

"Doesn't seem to be pneumonia," Dr. McFarland said.

Carrie lay limp on the examining table.

"But she's very weak. Perhaps her fragile constitution reacts this way to a cold any of us would shake off. Hard to say if it's influenza. She can't tell us if she's aching or has a sore throat, but it's red. I'd say take her to the hospital; however, I think you could do better with her at home. She'll be in familiar surroundings and get more rest. And she'll have you, Martha, as her nurse, the best care around."

Art gave Dr. McFarland a slight nod, which Martha interpreted as agreement with the compliment. She was as gratified to see Art had confidence in her as she was by Dr. McFarland's judgment Carrie should be at home.

"What else should I be doing?" she asked.

"I certainly don't expect you to work in the office until this clears up. By the way, thank you for your telephone call this morning saying you wouldn't be in. Continue giving her little sips now and then as she'll manage. Water, broth, strained fruit juices only, until she starts to regain strength. And continue with the cold compresses, to keep the fever down. If she has trouble breathing, hold her upright so she can rest comfortably. You could try a croup tent. If you're worried, telephone, and I'll come to you. Don't bring her out again."

"Maybe she could sleep in 'er sling chair," Art said. "I could rig it up in 'er little crib. That'd keep 'er head up."

Both Dr. McFarland and Martha answered, "Yes."

"And keep her isolated," Dr. McFarland added. "As weak as she is, she shouldn't be exposed to anything else, and isolation would prevent whatever this is from spreading, especially to Anna."

He looked like Santa Claus — round face, rosy cheeks, and twinkling smile, but without the beard and bulging stomach. Just now he wasn't smiling. "She's not sick because of anything you've done or failed to do. She's just not strong, so when she's ill, she has a harder time of it."

Martha saw why folks fell in love with him. Clearly, he wanted to help. Her next question had already formulated itself in her mind. Why? Why did Carrie have to bear an additional burden of illness? But no physician could give a satisfactory answer. Questions of "Why?" were better addressed to a theologian, and Rev. Macgill was gone.

Rowdy

Anna was in bed for less than an hour when they heard the dogs howl; the strays prowled close by, and the noise woke her. She came into the living room, rubbing her eyes and crying. "Papa, are the wolves going to eat us?"

Martha was as startled as Anna to hear the dogs. The pack had begun roaming the farms about two weeks prior, but Martha thought they staked out their territory further east. One family estimated they killed fifty sheep by frightening them into running and piling on one another until they suffocated.

She neglected to answer Anna and tied on the smock that hung over their bedroom door, the room now dedicated to Carrie. She stood by the crib and scrutinized her sleeping baby. Carrie's breathing was still shallow, but even. The howls hadn't bothered her. Martha would get Anna settled and bring in the hot plate with the teakettle and rubber hose for a croup tent. Carrie wasn't coughing, but perhaps moist air would ease her breathing.

Art asked Martha from the doorway to retrieve his rifle from the wardrobe and also neglected to answer Anna's question. When Anna saw the gun, she wailed. Martha slipped off the smock and enveloped Anna in her arms.

"Honey, those aren't wolves; they're dogs like Tip. But their owners don't take care of them so they're looking for friends. They play together at night."

"But their games are deadly," muttered Art under his breath. "Punkin, I'm gonna lock Tip in the barn so she doesn't go with 'em. They play too rough. I'm takin' my gun ta Grandpa's so we can scare 'em away from the sheep that are visitin' his fields. Stray dogs upset sheep."

"Will Rowdy play with the stray dogs?" asked Anna.

No one trifled with Rowdy, Papa's rugged mix of several breeds that combined to make him a diligent, and large, watchdog. Anna gave him a wide berth.

Rowdy accepted the annual visit of the sheepdogs when the herder moved the flock onto Papa's corn stubble in the fall and allowed them to go about their herding, and they let him guard the place. But he wouldn't be tolerant of the strays. Martha imagined Rowdy and the sheepdogs, faced by external threat, becoming allies. She winced, visualizing the canine battle.

"No, honey. Rowdy won't play with the strays," she answered. "He won't let them on Grandpa's land. The sheepdogs won't play with them, either. They'll protect the sheep. That's why Papa's going to help Grandpa and is taking his gun. By firing the gun in the air, they'll try to scare the pack away before Rowdy and the sheepdogs fight them."

Martha's objective was to convey a mild sense of danger without causing Anna distress. Another occasion to be grateful to Mrs. Bro's truthful, practical manner. Neither she nor Josie would have relied so on such books if Mama were still alive.

Martha must have succeeded because Anna yawned and asked, "Why are the blankets and pillow on the sofa?"

"That's where Papa will sleep tonight, so the bed won't squeak and wake Carrie."

"Tuck me in again, Mama."

Anna seemed convinced that between her papa, grandpa, Rowdy, the sheepdogs, and the gun, no danger threatened her.

But instead of going toward her room, she ran to the door of Martha and Art's bedroom and, in a stage whisper, said, "Don't worry, Carrie. Rowdy will protect us."

To Martha she said, "I'm ready now."

Martha lay in bed reading. Carrie's breathing seemed regular, so she didn't set up the croup tent. Another hour passed before Art returned.

"We didn't 'complish much," he said. "The pack moved off, but I'm afraid they'll be back. What should I do with Tip? I locked 'er in the barn, but every time she hears those durn dogs she barks an' scares Ginger an' Beulah."

"Bring her inside. I'll spread a towel on the kitchen floor for her."

Martha intended to stay awake until three o'clock, when she and Art agreed he would take over, but she couldn't. She woke when Tip nuzzled her hand. She could hear the strays howling and the whistles of a passing troop train. The sounds mingled in a terrifying dirge. Her panic forced her to full wakefulness, and she leaned close to the crib, listening for the rhythm of Carrie's breathing. She heard nothing. She switched on the overhead light. She jiggled Carrie, who didn't stir. The body was still warm.

Martha lifted it and held it close. She sat on the bed and rocked back and forth.

"I'm so sorry I couldn't protect you. I'm so sorry."

She knew Carrie was dead, but she couldn't stop rocking and talking and singing.

Art knocked on the bedroom door at the agreed-upon time. Martha still sat on the edge of the bed, Tip at her feet, swaying from side to side with Carrie's body in her arms.

She sang "Away in a Manger," one of the series of lullabies she had been going through for some time. Art put on the protective smock and sat next to her, apparently thinking she comforted their ill daughter. When Martha started "Jesus Loves Me," he slipped his arm around her and looked down at Carrie.

Only then did Martha react to his presence. She turned her head and buried it in his chest; their baby's body rested between them.

Reverend Henry Behm

When they returned from the mortuary and walked into the cozy kitchen, Martha noted the calendar was still turned to October. She tossed her coat on Anna's bed and walked around the table to flip the page, but stopped before pushing the nail back into the wall. Securing the calendar to November would surrender autumn to winter and Carrie's life to the past.

Martha laid the calendar on the table, sat down, and rested her head on her arms. What evidence of Carrie's life resisted time's advance? Carrie died before she could speak a word or draw a picture. Even if she had lived several years, what word could she have spoken; what picture could she have drawn? Other than her baby clothes and a few photographs, Carrie left nothing tangible. Would Martha only remember that Carrie died the night the dogs howled? That she sang for hours to a body? She couldn't cherish those memories.

Doc and Art were right. Anna might forget she had a little sister.

A familiar sound interrupted her thoughts, but she failed to interpret it. Art was making a pot of coffee and didn't respond, either.

Anna reacted. "Someone's knocking at the front door."

"Everyone comes ta the kitchen porch," said Art.

"Apparently not everyone," observed Martha as the knocking resumed.

She stood, but vertigo forced her to rest her hand momentarily on the table before she could walk through the dining room. When she opened the living room door, she found herself nose to nose with a man dressed quite formally for a Tuesday morning. He was but inches taller than she, and Martha estimated she outweighed him. He smiled self-consciously because he seemed to have just stepped back onto the stoop from peeking in the living room window to confirm they were home.

Art, who arrived at the door behind Martha, spoke first. "Rev. Behm, come in. We're not used ta arrivals at the livin' room door."

Rev. Behm looked down at the cement block he stood on, barren of a doormat, and at the living room rug he would be stepping onto.

"Shall I remove my shoes? Or go to the back porch and enter properly?"

He answered his own question. "I'll begin my visit in the manner to which you are accustomed."

He spun around and resolutely walked across the brown grass to the lane.

As Art and Martha hurried to meet him at the back door, Art commented, "I thought he was headed back ta Colorado Springs yesterday after preachin' Sunday. That's why I suggested gettin' Rev. Jenkins fer Carrie's funeral."

Rev. Behm was one of several ministers doing the preaching until the new man arrived, and Martha hadn't met him. In spite of herself, Martha smiled, amused that she and Art scurried to grant their visitor entry after having already greeted him.

"He's an odd little man," she said, "but likeable. I wonder what he has to say."

If Rev. Behm had resembled Rev. Macgill in any way, Martha would have opened her door out of politeness but made no effort to establish rapport. No minister could replace Rev. Macgill and presume to assuage her grief. However, this prim little man presumed nothing, not even entry through the front door.

Rev. Behm listened to Art describe Carrie's death. Because he listened to Art, Martha told him the story of Carrie's birth. He listened to Art's story of the visit to the Children's Home and their decision not to put her there. He listened to Anna's directions about how to play with Carrie so as not to excite her and send her into spasms.

"I regret I'll not have the pleasure of meeting Carrie," he said, "but now I know something of how special she was for each of you. I expect that, over the next several weeks, you'll hear many comments from your friends and family that she was extraordinary for them, too."

Martha disagreed. "Other than our family, and Elena, no one really knew her. Why would they make such comments?"

"Enoch Gwynn telephoned right after you left the mortuary and invited me to come by for a visit before I left town. Very hospitable of him as someone who knows the community well. He mentioned Carrie's death and seemed quite moved by it. Described her as beautiful when tranquil, but that when active her face was somewhat contorted and conveyed an impression of pain. That made him uncomfortable, and he wanted to turn away, but when she squealed with delight, this perception changed. He said she was a capsule of life's contradictions, combining as she did her difficulties and pain with her beauty and unqualified expressions of joy."

Rev. Behm spoke eloquently, but Martha hoped that someday Enoch would tell her himself. She nodded by way of accepting Rev. Behm's defense of his opinion.

He pursued his point. "Perhaps you don't realize Carrie's profound effect. Parents of children with spastic paralysis don't usually involve them the way your family has, so the public isn't routinely exposed to children with her physical abnormalities."

Rev. Behm's frank manner appealed to Martha, and she answered by offering Elena's comment about how holding Carrie "healed her heart."

Art, with an unusually quiet Anna in his lap, said, "Ya never told me Elena felt like that 'bout Carrie."

Martha's eyes filled with tears. "I didn't mean to withhold it. She said it the night of the barn dance, when we were so worried about Dolores."

Martha was pleased Rev. Behm had come to call, even though they conversed about such intimate feelings. She doubted she, or Art, would have much to say without him present, exhausted as they were by their grief.

She imagined a dollhouse-like kitchen with the two of them as static figures sitting at the table, legs and arms askew. Rev. Behm animated the bereft, stiff bodies, which was important because family and neighbors would arrive soon, as the news spread. The Eagle View Club representatives would probably appear first with food and offers to tidy the house. Martha wanted to be in a position to receive them.

She smelled the coffee and offered it.

"Thank you. Yes," he said. "When I leave, I'm driving home, to Colorado Springs, and it'll fortify me. I must get back to my church."

She anticipated Rev. Behm's next comment would concern Elena and Dolores and why she'd mentioned them. She prepared to explain the connections of the Marquez and Ruiz families to the McLennans and the Spanish church.

Instead, he asked, "Do you have a Bible? Sometimes our human words fall short of expressing profound feeling, and I find God's Word can say for us what we cannot."

Art produced their Bible and Rev. Behm read a rather lengthy passage from Isaiah. At first, Martha didn't pay attention as he droned on, but familiar words penetrated her numbness, words she had sung.

"He was despised and rejected of men, a man of sorrows and acquainted with grief."

The alto "Air" from Handel's *Messiah*. She listened more closely.

"He hath no form nor comeliness; and when we shall see him, there is no beauty that we should desire him…. We did esteem him stricken."

Enoch's description of Carrie: difficult to look at, seemingly in pain. Stricken.

Rev. Behm continued, "He was afflicted, yet he opened not his mouth. Neither was any deceit in his mouth."

Elena's reaction to Carrie, as well as her own feelings about Carrie's innocence: "Holding her heals my heart."

"As a sheep before her shearers is dumb."

Would that not have been Carrie, had they deposited her in the Children's Home? Unable to voice objection?

Rev. Behm concluded, "The mountains shall depart, and the hills be removed; but my kindness shall not depart from thee."

Her hands rested on the table, and Art covered one of them with his. She opened her eyes and saw the tears in his. It seemed the effort to control his emotions inhibited his speech.

Martha addressed Rev. Behm. "For the past seven months I've asked 'why.' Why was Carrie born early? Perhaps I didn't take proper care during the pregnancy and harmed her. All along I've thought she suffered; I do think she was often in pain. Why was she given the additional burden of this illness? Did I take her out too often and expose her to something she was too fragile to resist? When she died, I wasn't even awake. I thought she was improving."

Martha was crying but she made herself talk through the tears. "The part you just read, about the Lord's kindness never departing, implies there isn't an answer to 'why.' What I mean is, when we ask 'why,' the answer we are given is that He knows suffering and helplessness, and throughout such suffering, He doesn't abandon us. Wasn't there another phrase about kindness?"

Rev. Behm found it and read, "… with everlasting kindness will I have mercy on thee, saith the Lord thy Redeemer."

"Everlasting kindness," Martha repeated, almost through her teeth, which tinged her voice with anger. "That's quite a contrast to the world we live in."

He watched her closely but didn't speak.

"Rev. Behm, do you believe the Lord's kindness is everlasting, or that cruelty, suffering, and death define the permanent condition of our lives?"

She was grieving Carrie, but dwelling on the suffering and death of her child seemed selfish with so much misery in Europe and China.

So she said, "I couldn't help but remember various phrases from Handel's *Messiah* as you read, one being 'Why do the nations so furiously rage together?' That brought to mind the alto and tenor duet Alex and I sang one Easter."

And she sang, "O death, where is thy sting?"

"I'm not sure what you're getting at," Rev. Behm said.

"The nations rage furiously and no 'King of kings' or "Lord of lords' delivers them. Handel's wrong about that and about death not stinging. It stings a lot, for a long time. Mama's death eight years ago still hurts, and Carrie's will for decades to come."

He offered, "My son died, stillborn. The sting of his death lingers. I can't answer to your satisfaction, but I do believe divine kindness and love are everlasting, not cruelty and suffering. I take God's kindness to mean both mercy and justice, and I attempt to live accordingly, showing mercy and justice to my fellow man."

At least he tried to be honest. For a man with an unassuming physical presence, he conveyed surprising personal confidence, and she was grateful for his tribute to Carrie. Her quarrel wasn't with him; it was with God.

She replied, "Maybe it takes a lifetime to discover the answer to 'why.'"

The Bundle

Rev. Jenkins conducted the funeral. She and Art appreciated the turnout, and the comments, cards, and letters confirmed Rev. Behm's observations about Carrie's influence.

Martha wrapped the correspondence with Carrie's clothes and several photographs in Carrie's yellow baby quilt, made by Mama for Josie and her, and put the bundle under the bed. She pinned on a note describing Carrie's brief life, addressed to those who would never know her. Perhaps Anna would cherish the bundle someday and not forget she had a baby sister named Carrie.

November 1941

Freddie

Martha left Dr. McFarland's office early and stopped at the Beauty Shoppe for a finger wave to spiff up for the Pinion School Thanksgiving Dinner. She and Art had attended every year since their wedding, one of the few times they drove out south to see the Mattsons and Uncle Malcolm, if he remembered to come.

She was late picking up Elena and the cousins. Josie answered the door.

"You look, you look…" Josie said.

She didn't complete her sentence before Anna chimed in, "Like a million-dollar baby!"

Anna responded enthusiastically, but she didn't move from where she and Elena played with Robbie, who lay on his baby blanket spread on the red-and-black Oriental rug. Carrie used to occupy Anna like that. Had Robbie replaced Carrie in Anna's affections so soon?

Josie hugged Martha and said softly, "I was going to say, you look as if you're feeling better. That style flatters you. I'm jealous. My straight hair holds it for five minutes; yours will last a week."

Martha held her hands stiffly at her sides and didn't return the embrace. Josie stepped back.

"I thought a wave would perk me up. So far, it isn't working. I'm slogging through quicksand just to do the most basic chores. Please, don't tell me it'll take time. Everyone tells me that."

"It's only because we want to help. We just don't know how."

Josie deserved more for her consoling efforts. Martha's voice softened. "And I don't know, either, how anyone can help. Sometimes I feel lost and need direction to find my way, but I have no idea what the destination is. Other times I'm impatient and want to scream at everyone to stop bothering with silliness and get busy with what's important. But I don't know what that is, either, because nothing's important to me right now. So who can help? I'm too confused and worn out to know what I need."

Martha flopped into Josie's overstuffed chair and squealed in pain. She reached between the seat cushion and back and pulled out the knitting needle that had jabbed her bottom.

"Thanks! This is one way to get my mind off my problems!"

Josie and Anna rushed over. Martha accepted their hugs and all three laughed. Elena looked bewildered.

"Elena, I'm all right. It just startled me. After being so melodramatic, I deserve a poke in the behind."

Moved beyond her emotional impasse, she chattered, "Did you know that with the metal shortage, Ethel now sorts through the dust and hair after she sweeps the Beauty Shoppe to save out the bobby pins? She says the price for them has tripled. Who would have thought defense would take metal away from bobby pins?"

Josie didn't answer. Perhaps the trivia seemed odd in light of the preceding maudlin conversation. Martha changed the subject.

"Didn't expect to see you here. Thought you were teaching today."

"Just ran home for a minute to see the kiddies. I'm headed back to the school. I'll be honest. Since Carrie died, I've not wanted to leave Robbie's side. Life is so…"

"Fleeting? Precious? Short? Fragile?" Martha's interruption sounded mocking, but she hadn't intended it that way.

"All that, and more," Josie answered, apparently not taking offense.

Martha was thinking of Carrie's life and death when she inserted the words into Josie's sentence, but remembering Carrie's body in her child-sized coffin also called to mind Freddie in his. A healthy son instantly killed in an automobile crash, and Vera, the mother, hadn't cried. But at the funeral Vera ever so deliberately replaced the teddy bear in Freddie's arms with the ball. She said she didn't want Freddie standing before God in heaven with a bear that his daddy stole, as much as he loved it. She wanted him playing "kick," as they called their game, and laughing.

Freddie's skin was smooth. No scratches. No signs of injury. Doc said he died from internal bleeding, so his little boy's body simply looked asleep. As Carrie's had. As though they would wake any moment and smile.

Art and she would pass the turn to Maher's shack when they drove to Pinion School. She hadn't been out south since the day Freddie died on Collins Curve. Was that how she would mark time now, from the death of one child to the next?

Julia Mattson

The Saturday of the Thanksgiving dinner was cold but sunny. Martha wedged her Black Cake plate between her feet on the floor of the pickup and held a warm apple pie on her lap. She was tired of showing up with the cake at every event but didn't want to disappoint those who looked forward to it. Maybe if she added an apple pie she could wean folks from it.

"Martha, Ellis Ufford'll be there, an' ya know what he'll want," Art said.

Anna, cradling her doll that now accompanied her everywhere, asked, "What will Mr. Ufford want, Papa?"

Martha answered, instead, her spirits lifted by the memory of the exhilarating square dance. "He and your papa play a game."

But the recollection of Fran pointing out Carrie's flushed cheeks overcame the sound of the crowd's applause and her pride in Art's virtuosity. She owed Anna the full explanation, but the liveliness disappeared from her voice.

"Mr. Ufford invents square dances to trick Papa. He hasn't yet, so he keeps making up new ones."

"Whada ya think?" Art asked. "Shall we accept his challenge?"

"We?"

"Yer the only one I'd dance with, the best partner I got."

Art's voice cracked. After that morning, when he came back to bed, when he laid Carrie down and first called her that, Carrie was his only "partner."

"Papa, I thought Carrie was your partner."

Art couldn't talk.

Martha answered for him, again. "Yes, Anna, Papa will always have Carrie as his partner in his memory. Folks also use the word 'partner' to refer to the man or woman they dance with."

Martha reached around Anna's head and rested her hand on Art's shoulder.

"Art, I hope Ellis won't feel he can't issue his challenge on account of Carrie."

Art cleared his throat. "I brought it up 'cause I'm afraid I won't be able ta dance. My feelin's 'bout Carrie pop up unexpected, an' they're so strong they knock me right over."

"Art, I hadn't realized."

Anna touched his leg and said, "I'll help you up if you fall down, Papa."

Art's laughter filled the cab. "You two women sure do a good job a takin' care a me. See, it's been like this, bouncin' 'tween extremes. One minute I'm so sad I can't locomote, an' the next I'm giddy as a schoolgirl."

Art's admission alarmed Martha. She relied on his even-tempered disposition, and now they were both capsizing.

"We'll have to help each other," she said. "I go through ups and downs, too. You probably think I stay at 'down,' but just now, when you reminded me about Ellis, I felt happy at the prospect of another of his challenges."

Anna gave up following the conversation and had her own with the doll.

"How 'bout we see what we're feelin' later, if he brings it up."

He was simple enough to decipher. She wasn't, although she was trying to be more expressive, ever since Art pointed out how she kept her thoughts to herself, that day, on the drive to the Children's Home.

She was a little disappointed but said, "That sounds fine."

They drove into the schoolyard behind the Mattsons, and Julia was out and waiting before Art stopped. She ran over and opened the door for Martha. Martha last saw her at Carrie's funeral, but they didn't have opportunity to speak.

"Julia, thank you for coming to Carrie's service. Knowing you were there was a comfort for both of us, as was the kind note from Eddie and Bertha."

Martha's words sounded like a mandatory form of politeness, but she sincerely meant them. Eddie was like a brother to Art, and Julia a second mother, maybe more so than his own had been. Martha thought of Julia as her second mother, too.

Julia took Martha in her arms. Both were short with soft curves and full breasts. Their eye color also matched. The one contrast was

Julia's thick blond braid, now turning gray, wrapped in circles at the back of her neck.

Martha added, "We always look forward to Pinion's Thanksgiving and seeing you and Gust."

Gust gave Art a hearty embrace; the day would be good medicine.

"As we look forward to seeing you. I'm glad to hear Bertha sent a note. She's a very sweet girl. I wish we saw them more often, but it's as hard for us to get away and make the drive to Colorado Springs as it is for them to come down for a visit."

Julia spotted Anna shyly waiting in the cab. She peeked in and said, "Hello. You've grown a lot since I saw you last. Do you want to come inside and play with the other children?"

Anna crawled across the seat to avoid the cake on the floor and let Julia lift her out. They followed Martha and the pie, Art circling around to grab the cake as he listened to Gust's crop and livestock report.

The schoolroom was a whirl of activity. Martha filled a plate for Anna, but lost track of her whereabouts except when she saw her playing follow-the-leader with a group of children. Martha watched Art carry his plate from one group of men to another, and she tried to concentrate on the chatter of the women around her, to no avail. She prepared a plate for herself but set it down half eaten. The food had no taste.

Malcolm McLennan

When it came time for dessert, Martha moved behind the table to help serve. She was ready when the first person came forward and found herself looking into Uncle Malcolm's pale-blue eyes, set off dramatically by his tanned cheeks. She hurried around the table to hug him.

"Uncle Malcolm! How is it I didn't see you until now?"
"Just came in," he answered in his gentle voice. "Thought you might be here, and didn't want ta miss a piece of your mother's Black Cake."

Involuntarily, the volume of Martha's voice lowered to match Uncle Malcolm's as if something louder would scare him off. "Then it was worth the effort, if only for you. Art and I so appreciated that you came to Carrie's funeral."

He held up a paper bag with something inside. "Made this for 'er, but didn't get up ta Greenwood before…"

He looked sadly at the bag. "Brought it ta the funeral, but seemed strange ta give it ta you then, on account of being too late…"

Martha had learned to allow Uncle Malcolm time to say what he had on his mind. She was aware that Julia stepped into the place she abandoned. Most of his neighbors knew that if Malcolm McLennan appeared at a public function, it was for a purpose significant enough to draw him out of his hermit-like existence. They protected him, until the thing was accomplished.

He drew a deep breath. "But wasn't right ta bring it back, either. So, here it is, for you an' Art ta remember Carrie. Wanted ta know her. Robert said she was the most beautiful baby he ever saw, just tiny."

From the time Martha was Anna's age, she had noted Uncle Malcolm's odd way of phrasing things. He rarely used personal pronouns.

"Thank you," and she clutched the bag to her chest. "I wish you could have held her, Uncle Malcolm. Folks said she brought them peace. I always thought she'd be with us today, for the Pinion Thanksgiving, and you would meet her. She seemed to be doing fine, then…"

"Not in our nature ta anticipate death. Comes of its own will."

Yes. That's how it happened. Martha stood on her tiptoes and kissed his cheek.

He touched the place as though the kiss made a permanent imprint, not unwelcome, and said, "The skinny cow, the one from that barn? She's doin' fine."

He turned and walked out the door, without his cake.

Later, as everyone packed to leave, Julia called Martha over behind the pot-bellied stove, by the windows. "Martha, I need to tell you something."

Julia rushed headlong into her tale. "Oscar and I had two children."

She momentarily lost her nerve but squared her shoulders. She whispered, and Martha strained to hear.

"Our first died of scarlet fever when he was three. Eddie was a baby. Martha, if people tell you time heals, particularly with the loss of a child, they aren't telling the truth. I live each day for Gust and Eddie's sake, and I haven't fallen into the hole at the center that Oscar left, but it's still there. I've learned to circle it so as not to slide in. Sometimes the path around is wide and interesting and I lose sight of that pit, but other times the way is narrow and I have to watch my step."

Martha had no trouble envisioning the void Julia described, and it opened so wide the center of the one-room school seemed to disappear. Martha balanced on the edge with Julia, whose hand she grabbed to steady herself.

Julia, seemingly unaware of Martha's grip, said, "This might not be making sense, but that's how I see it. You'll probably find a way to survive that's different."

The void expanded, and the stove almost toppled in. Martha steadied herself against the windowsill with her other hand. Julia still whispered.

"I do know the path around was wide when Art lived with us. I won't say he filled the hole. Nothing fills it, but life was sweeter when we had more than three. Four's the right number for us."

"Does Art know?" Martha asked in a low voice.

"I doubt Gust told him. Gust made me throw away everything that reminded him of Oscar, so Art wouldn't even have seen a picture. But I kept one, and the little hat Oscar always wore. Martha, I'm loving this, saying his name aloud."

Julia's sudden laugh startled Martha, and the hole rapidly shrank.

"I keep the picture and hat in my underwear drawer, so Gust won't find them."

Martha was speechless. She would never have suspected Julia, a cheery, kind woman, carried such a potent secret.

She was ashamed she was behaving as though she was the only mother crushed by the sorrow of losing a child. How many women did she converse with during any one month who concealed such grief?

"Martha?"

Martha hadn't heard the question.

"I shouldn't have spoken about these things. I've done you more harm than good. I'm sorry."

"Julia, no, no. You misinterpret my silence. You touch me deeply, and I'm not adept at putting strong emotions into words. Please believe me. I'll use what you've said many times in the days and weeks to come. It's just, I had no idea. I had no idea."

Julia didn't seem convinced. Martha had nothing else to say and was relieved Anna ran over to tell her Art waited outside.

They pulled out of the schoolyard and drove several miles before Martha asked him how he thought the dinner went.

"Fine, but I'm disappointed in Ellis. When the dancin' started, he coulda asked."

"Maybe he didn't want to put you on the spot, or wasn't sure how to bring it up. Anyway, it would have been unseemly for us to dance, so soon after the funeral."

Art ignored Martha's conclusion. "What's so hard 'bout askin'? Ya just say it."

As with Julia, Martha was uncertain how to answer. Art was irritated, but exactly why, she didn't know.

Anna broke into the conversation with, "I like Thanksgiving. I have a new friend. His name is Ernie. We played hide-and-seek."

Martha patted Anna's knee. "I'm glad, honey. I saw you playing. It looked like lots of fun."

A spectacular sunset played out to their left as they drove north. Wispy clouds in the west turned golden, pink, and fuchsia before fading to a dull gray. After the long silence, Martha decided to take a chance and "just say it," as Art clearly preferred.

"I'm sorry about Ellis. Sounds as though you might have danced."

"No, I would a liked ta been *asked*. Why is it everyone shies away from me? I don't have anthrax. My daughter died. Ya say, 'I'm sorry, Art, fer yer loss.' Then ya go on. I tried ta join in conversations, but when I did, the talk stopped. Just stopped, an' they drifted away, one by one. How long will I have ta put up with that 'fore men treat me like I'm normal again?"

Martha hadn't felt "normal" since Doc sent her to bed before Carrie's birth, although she had done everything in her power to carry the baby a full nine months. She had failed. And even when she knew things weren't right with Carrie, she tried to make a happy life for her in the embrace of a loving family. She did better after Alex's Mother's Day observation that people had to be helped to feel comfortable around Carrie, even though the effort drained her.

The night the dogs howled and Carrie died, she was up against forces beyond her capacity to defeat because when she'd last checked, Carrie's breathing was almost normal.

But she moved forward with her work on the farm and with Dr. McFarland. She would not fall into the hole created by Carrie's death. She would not. Maybe coping with a daughter's physical abnormality and grieving were similar. The one afflicted had to make the effort.

"Art, folks might be thinking they're showing respect by letting us alone. Perhaps we have to take the first step to talk so they know we're ready."

His response was a weary, "That's what I did. I'm tired. Maybe things'll look brighter in the mornin.'"

Martha said, "Oh, I almost forgot. Did you see Uncle Malcolm come in?"

"Nope, missed 'im."

"He was only there long enough to give me this."

Martha handed the brown bag to Anna. "Why don't you open it, honey? Uncle Malcolm gave it to us to help remember Carrie."

Anna laid her doll on the seat and shook the bag. A square picture frame fell out.

"Careful!" Martha cautioned. "Let's turn it over and look at the picture."

She and Anna exhaled an appreciative "Oh" in unison.

Art didn't take his eyes off the road and asked, "What is it?"

Martha examined the picture without answering.

"Well, what's the mystery?"

"Art, it's hard to describe. Seems to be a collection of dried prairie flowers, their petals, actually. Some very small. They're arranged to resemble a snowflake — complex, fragile, and vibrant. Very unusual. He would have spent hours collecting the flowers and composing this. And the frame appears to be hand-carved. It's also quite delicate, a sort of filigree design."

Martha continued to study it. "I'd call it a symphony exclusively for Carrie. He never met her, but it's a perfect tribute. Small, delicate, striking. A bouquet that will last for some time, lacking only the fragrance of the living plants, covered as they are with glass. Perhaps because I'm seeing it in the dim light of dusk, it has an almost ethereal quality."

"Let me hold it, Mama."

Martha sat the snowflake on Anna's lap, and Anna clutched it to her chest.

"Let's hang it in my bedroom, where Elena put Carrie's crib for her naps."

"Well, that's a good idea. Let's think about it," said Martha.

Martha preferred to display it in a more public place, perhaps the dining room.

"I'd pull over ta look," Art said, "but it's gettin' too dark ta see anything. I'll study it when we get home. Malcolm's so gentle, like an injured animal that comes out a hidin' from time ta time, peeks around, then scuttles back inta the sage."

"Yes," Martha said absently. "Oh, there's something else in the bag, Anna."

Anna wasn't interested. She clutched the picture tighter.

The items were Martha's hat and gloves, the ones she'd left on Vera's wooden table six months ago.

Martha's impulse was to throw them out the window and leave them lying in the desolation between Pinion School and

Greenwood, to vanish in the wind and dust. She wanted no souvenirs from that day.

But Uncle Malcolm had saved them for her. They came back in tandem with the nearly indescribable tenderness of the flower-petal snowflake, perhaps cleansed by their sojourn in his hermit's cabin, reminders that Maher hadn't destroyed Vera and Ida, even though he had come very close.

November 1941

The Sage Café

As Art crawled out of bed Tuesday morning, he said, "Don't fix breakfast fer me. After I do chores I'm goin' ta town an' test yer theory by eatin' at the Sage Café. Farmers an' town men stop by there of a winter's mornin'. We'll see if they talk ta a grievin' man. Wish me luck."

"Good luck," said a somewhat amazed Martha.

Art never ate breakfast at the Sage Café. Doing so was something of a joke because "eating at the Sage" was synonymous with gossiping and lollygagging. But maybe Art needed frivolous companionship.

She cleaned away her breakfast, woke Anna, and sat with her while she ate her Wheaties. They started a game of checkers, but Anna wasn't interested, and Martha saw a long morning ahead. She hadn't the gumption to tackle inside chores she had put off for months.

Uncle Malcolm's snowflake sat on the dining room table, there being disagreement about where it should hang. It was simply too beautiful to stay tucked away in Anna's room; however, Anna's distress each time Martha and Art suggested other locations put off a decision. The picture obviously meant a great deal to her, but Martha wasn't ready to give in.

"Honey, let's you and I cut out snowflakes from newspapers. We can hang them on your bedroom wall."

"Oh, let's do! And Carrie's snowflake can hang in the middle!"

Evidently no substitutes for Uncle Malcolm's masterpiece would do, but Martha grabbed a pile of old newspapers off the porch and they went to work at the dining room table. For the next half hour they cut snowflakes. Martha wearied of scissors, but not Anna. She had abandoned the effort to make a snowflake that matched Uncle Malcolm's craft and cut paper scraps into ever-smaller pieces.

Aimless, Martha returned to the kitchen to scrub the floor, but she only got as far as taking out the mop. She sat, staring at nothing in particular.

Art returned around 9:30. The weather hadn't warmed much since early morning, so when he opened the kitchen door a cold draught blew in. The fresh air revived Martha, somewhat. If she had stepped outside earlier, she might have shaken off her lethargy.

"It's cozy in here," he said. "You want all the gossip?"

"Sure, why not? Sit down and I'll make fresh coffee."

Art threw up his hands. "No! No more coffee! I'm drownin' in coffee. In fact, let me run ta the outhouse first."

Anna came into the kitchen from the dining room, paper fragments glued to her tangled curls by static electricity.

"Where's Papa?"

"Running to the outhouse."

"Let me see."

Martha lifted her so she could look out the window over the sink. He rounded the cellar's cement cap in several long strides.

"Papa runs fast."

She wiggled out of Martha's arms and went back to her scissors. Martha sat at the table with the dregs of tepid coffee from the enamel pot that had a permanent resting place on the coal stove.

When Art re-entered, he immediately started his story. "Fer the first time, I heard somethin' juicy 'bout the commissioners 'fore Robert. Well, actually I heard the beginnin' a the story 'fore him an' Doc walked inta the Sage."

"Papa was at the Sage? And Dr. McFarland?"

Art grinned. "I bet there's a lot we don't know 'bout them two."

Martha giggled, enjoying the role of collaborator. Papa had been tight-lipped about Fran and, now, come to find out, about his forays at the Sage Café. Did he hide other escapades? If so, she hoped they were of a benefit similar to the one with Fran and as harmless as mornings at the Sage. She was equally pleased to hear about his budding friendship with Dr. McFarland.

"This time the commissioners got all the Chamber a Commerce bent outta shape, an' Parker Hayes gave the commissioners what fer."

Martha had a hard time picturing Mr. Hayes being anything but dignified and measured, but she didn't interrupt.

"Story is, Al Ivarson tangled with the Farm Security Administration men. Told 'em they couldn't enlarge their office in the Welfare Buildin'. Then said if they did they'd have ta pay rent. When the FSA men announced they would move ta 'nother town where they wouldn't have ta pay rent 'cause their whole purpose is ta lend money ta farmers who can't get loans anywhere else, all hell broke loose."

Art talked fast, but she thought she followed the story.

"That's where Parker Hayes comes in. He told Al it's an economic benefit ta have the FSA office in Greenwood an' Al should back off. Al denied the whole thing but the FSA men said they had five witnesses that Al wanted ta charge 'em rent. So, what do ya think a that?"

Martha was more tickled with Art's excitement than she was concerned about the commissioners, but she said, "What's going to happen, do you think?"

"It's already happened. Hayes got 'em together, an' they hashed it all out. The FSA is stayin', expandin' their office an' won't pay a cent fer rent."

He leaned forward and rested his arms on the table. "I have more. Ruth an' Alice Jennings set a jar on their counter ta collect money so as our newspaper can be sent ta all our service boys free. Isn't that swell? They serve good food plus clever ideas ta help other folks. I hope ya don't mind I put a dime in the jar, an' my name'll be in the paper next week as a contributor."

Art concluded his recital by tipping his chair onto its back legs, something he never did because it cut into the linoleum and Art liked to keep things nice. Martha worked hard to suppress a smile. He acted like a kid after school who plopped down at the table and filled the family in about all the events of the day.

"Art, you know how you asked me to wish you luck when you left this morning? Sounds like you had more than luck."

Art banged the front legs of his chair back on the floor, slid it back from the table, rose, and gave Martha a peck of a kiss on her hair.

"It was a good idea ya had, makin' the effort ta get out. Everyone was so excited 'bout Al an' Parker Hayes they didn't bother with that silent respect fer grief that means no one talks ta me. Maybe after this mornin', they'll be past it."

He opened the door into the dining room and blew Anna a kiss. Martha took her cup to the sink to rinse it and, through the window, watched him yank his overalls off the hook on the porch and pull them on. She envied his vigor.

Art popped his head back in the door. "Don't fix a big dinner, neither. I'm stuffed with Ruth's eggs, bacon, an' pancakes. Next time, let's all go together. Oh, if Anna plays outside be sure she's dressed fer the cold. Hasn't warmed any."

Alex walked in not five minutes later. Martha still stood at the sink. She hadn't heard his pickup pull into the driveway.

"I'm workin' in the barn today," he said. "Ya think Anna wants ta come an' play with the kittens?"

"Let's ask her. I'm sure the answer will be yes. She can cut paper into scraps only so small."

The draught caused by opening the swinging door into the dining room blew fingernail-sized bits of newspaper all around.

Anna cried out, "It's snowing inside! Isn't it beautiful, Mama?"

Martha covered her face with her hands, gave Alex a sideways look and decided not to chastise either of them over spilled milk, or, rather, a paper blizzard. But she couldn't bring herself to agree it was beautiful.

"Yes, Anna, it's beautiful!" Alex shouted.

He swooped her into his arms and they spun around, stirring up the paper bits until both were dizzy.

Martha bundled Anna, Alex all the while insisting she needn't be clothed in so many layers because they'd be in the barn. Martha relented when it came to Anna's scarf and gloves. She was too tired to insist and left them on a kitchen chair.

The Void

She stood looking onto the porch from the sink window for some time after Alex and Anna left. Their departure drained the last energy from the house. The sound of Art's excited telling of the town news, gone. Alex's enthusiasm about his plan for Anna and the kittens, gone. Anna's resolute clip-clipping of her papers, barely audible but persistent in Martha's awareness for most of the morning, gone.

She didn't dare turn and walk across the kitchen floor for fear she would disappear into the vacuum. She didn't remember, when Julia described the hole at the center of her life, the one she carefully picked her way around, feeling the terror of it, the panic of being sucked in if she lost her footing.

Alone in her kitchen, it seemed the immensity of the night sky when they brought Carrie home had collapsed into the space behind her. Its weight began to haul her toward its center. She gripped the edge of the sink.

But the memory of Julia's description of it expanding and shrinking gave the void shape. Martha slowly turned. Startled, she saw that the red-and-white-checkered oilcloth on the kitchen table hadn't disappeared. She smelled the coffee grounds scorching on the bottom of the pot. The black coal stove still dominated the kitchen, and the stovepipe thrust up, through the wall and into the channel that used to be a chimney.

Martha slid along the wall opposite the stove and ventured into the dining room. It, too, presented itself with familiar visual arrangements and colors — the dining table and floor covered with bits of paper. Uncle Malcolm's picture resting on the table.

She lowered herself into the easy chair by the radio cabinet and turned it on, but the static was so annoying she switched it off. She walked into the bedroom and sat on the edge of the mattress, reassured by the squeak of the springs. She leaned over and pulled out Carrie's bundle of pictures and clothes. She lay down, rested the parcel on her chest, and flipped the edge of Mama's yellow-and-white comforter covering their bed up and over the length of her entire body.

In her dream, Art's voice called from a great distance, but she was immobile, unable to answer or walk toward him. He called with greater urgency, but she was too worn out to overcome the distance separating them. In the magic of the dream, he traversed the space in a single step and grabbed her arm. Only as he shook it harder, until his grip seemed it would break the bone, was she able to fill her lungs with the air she needed to speak. Her "Yes?" was barely audible.

He slid his arm under her shoulders and forced her to sit upright.

"Martha, wake up! Wake up!"

She could hear the desperation in his voice and wanted to reassure him she was awake but simply couldn't speak.

Only when he moved Carrie to the center of the bed and turned Martha so her feet were on the floor did she wake sufficiently to ask, "Why did you put Carrie behind me? I can't reach her."

For the first time in his life, Art slapped a woman, on her left check, and it stung. Martha blinked her eyes to see through the tears.

She shook her head, not so much to allay the pain as to clear her thoughts, grateful for the physical discomfort that displaced the emotional lethargy.

"Art, I dreamed you were here but I couldn't wake up. Hold me. Hold me. Am I awake? Are you here?"

Art pulled Martha to a standing position and held her. The separation of her body from the surface of the bed convinced her she was out of the dream and really in Art's arms.

"When everyone left and I was in the house alone for the first time since Carrie's birth, I was terrified."

At the mention of Carrie's name, Art's head turned toward the bundle lying in the center of the bed. Martha reached for it. Art stopped her.

"Art, I'm all right. I've kept a few photos of Carrie and some of her clothes, wrapped in her quilt, along with a note, so I won't forget her smell, her size, her face, what it was like to hold her. Too few people will remember her as time passes; I want always to have more than a vague recollection."

Art studied Martha's face, and, seemingly convinced she was herself again, said, "Eddie Mattson tol' me once that when he was young, maybe eight er so, he saw 'is ma take a packet outta her dresser drawer. She didn't know he was there, in the doorway. He was practicin' his 'Injun walk,' as he called it; he's still pretty good at sneakin' up on people."

So Art knew.

"Somethin' 'bout the way she handled the bundle spoke ta its value, an' several days later he slipped inta the bedroom an' opened it. He saw a hat an' the picture of a child — a little boy. He couldn't figure out why they would be so precious fer his ma ta be that secretive. He secured the stash, hopin' he put it back 'xactly as he found it, an' he asked Gust."

Martha drew in a quick breath of air. "He asked Gust?"

"Ya know 'bout Oscar, doncha?"

"Julia told me at the Thanksgiving dinner."

"Eddie said it was the only time he ever saw 'is father cry. Gust told 'im it was Oscar's picture, 'is big brother. Gust knows 'bout the picture an' the hat in the drawer. Oscar died an' it broke 'is heart, Gust said. He tol' Eddie never ta talk 'bout Oscar again, an' that 'is ma knew never to say 'is name, neither. He ordered Eddie not ta tell 'is ma he'd seen the stash, an' they ain't talked 'bout it since, so far as I know."

Both Martha and Art were silent, Martha thinking that keeping up the pretense of a secret bundle surely amplified grief.

Art pulled her down next to him on the edge of the bed. "So I know why Gust didn't say nothin' 'bout Carrie. He just went on with conversation at Thanksgivin' dinner like she hadn't lived. You know he didn't come ta Carrie's funeral. But I understand, so I go along."

It saddened Martha that Gust didn't know the price Julia paid for her silence and how tenderly his family, and Art, protected his heartache.

"Martha, don't hide Carrie's bundle. Keep it, an' don't hide it from Anna, neither. From time ta time, show 'er an' tell 'er 'bout 'er sister. And when yer feelin' as low as ya are today, tell me."

She nodded her assent and reached for his hand, shaken by the force of the void. Was her deep sleep a sign she had begun her fall into it? What if Art hadn't woken her in time?

When Art asked, "Where's Anna?" she nearly jumped off the bed, she was so startled by the intrusion into her thoughts.

She forced herself to answer in what she thought was a normal tone of voice. "She's with Alex, playing with the kittens while he works in the barn."

"Just saw 'im pull out the lane from the Home Place. Looked like he was headed ta town. Couldn't tell if she was with 'im. Ya suppose he left 'er with Robert?"

Martha thought she had regained her equilibrium, but not enough to formulate a sensible answer. She asked a question of her own. "What time is it?"

"Somewhere 'tween two thirty an' three, I 'spect."

"Alex came for her this morning, just after you went out. I'll go pick her up. I needed some time, but not this much."

The cold, bracing wind cleared the last of the fog from Martha's thoughts. If she ever had those sensations again, she wouldn't stay in the house. She'd get out, into the fresh air.

Neither Anna nor Papa were in the barn, the garage, or the house. She even checked the small bunkhouse behind the garage that had fallen into disrepair after Alex took it into his head to "live" there for the several years he wanted to be away from all his sisters. It wasn't like Papa, or Alex, for that matter, not to give her details about their plans with Anna, so she was left to suppose they'd fed her dinner and Anna was with one of them. The only activity she saw in the fields was the sheepherder moving the flock to the corn stubble up by the canal.

Papa probably had business at Mr. Miyoshi's and had taken Anna with him. She always enjoyed wandering on the gravel pathways that wound through his garden.

Estevan

By four thirty, Papa still hadn't brought Anna home. Martha called Louise at the lumberyard. "Hi. Alex took Anna to play with the kittens late this morning and hasn't brought her back. Do you know where they are?"

Louise didn't reply.

"Louise, if you're busy, telephone back."

"No, I'm not busy. I'm trying to remember. Papa stopped by here at noon, and I think he said Alex and he were going to Milt Hartwell's office to talk about, whatever it is they discuss with him. I can't imagine they'd take Anna for County Agent business — wheat allotments, that sort of thing."

Martha found Art in the barn, struggling to mend a gunnysack from the pile beside him. He balanced on the milk stool.

"Art, what're you doing? I mean, I see what you're doing, but why?"

"Milt Hartwell says we should mend the gunnysacks we have from this year fer hopper bait. Next year sacks'll be hard ta get on account a the European war, an' hoppers'll be bad, judgin' by the amount a eggs they laid this season. Seems like everything'll be hard ta come by 'cause of defense — tires, parts fer equipment. Ya name it."

"I can help with the mending. But now that you mention Milt, Louise says Alex and Papa were going to see him this afternoon. She didn't think they'd take Anna along, but that's where I suppose she is."

Art looked up from his mending. "No, I don't think they'd take 'er neither, least wise, not without talkin' ta us first. Martha, somethin's wrong."

They walked out of the barn together and saw Alex's pickup stop at the Home Place mailbox before he drove into the lane. In the dusk, he had the lights on. Martha and Art climbed into their truck. Alex was almost in the house by the time they parked.

"Hi, Sis," Alex called out. "Did Anna tell ya 'bout the kittens? She wants the black an' white one."

When Papa walked into the house ten minutes later, they had sorted out that Martha was probably sleeping when Alex dropped Anna off, just before dinner, maybe around twelve thirty or one o'clock. He had called in at the kitchen door. He thought he'd heard Martha answer.

He'd left Anna standing in the kitchen, still in her coat. They speculated she had wandered back outside, maybe to the outhouse, maybe to the barn looking for Art. That was four hours ago, and she hadn't eaten since breakfast.

Martha screamed at Alex. "You're always in such a rush and never pay attention. Never, never drop her off without confirming Art or I are there, without actually seeing us."

The tirade would have continued had Papa not stopped her. "Martha, this isn't the time for blame. It's dark. You yourself said she doesn't have her scarf or gloves, and the temperature's already dropped below freezing. I suggest we enlist Miyoshi's help. She might have wandered that way because she enjoys his Japanese things, and he loves telling her about them."

They all considered Papa's theory, but he said, "Then, again, Miyoshi would have telephoned or brought her home if she had made it as far as his place, so maybe she never reached it."

Papa mapped out a plan. "Art and Martha, if Miyoshi doesn't know anything, call folks. Tell them Anna's lost and they should bring flashlights. We can spread people out on your place, mine and Miyoshi's. She can't have wandered further than that. Alex, find Luis and Elena. They know every inch of our farms and can help us. What else should we do?"

"Just that when Elena comes," Art said, "bring 'er ta Martha, Alex. Between 'em they can figure out where Anna mighta gone from what she's been interested in seein' or doin'."

After Papa silenced her for upbraiding Alex, Martha sat immobile. She marveled that the three men set out strategy in such a calculated manner, as if discussing the layout of next year's crops. She clenched and unclenched her fists as though flexing her muscles would control the quivering inside. To a degree, it worked.

Then she thought of another possibility. Someone had snatched Anna, someone like Maher. Before she spoke it aloud, she shoved the thought aside. To say it would make it dangerously real. She concentrated on the conversation around her.

"Tip's not been around all afternoon, neither," Art said. "Didn't think much 'bout it because she disappears sometimes. But maybe 'er an' Anna both bein' gone ain't no coincidence."

Papa added, "Other than everyone being careful to not rush through the fields in their vehicles for fear of running her over, what else is there before we separate? I'll look around here again, although I can't imagine she crossed the road alone, unless she was so taken with the kittens she came back. You need to check your barn, too.

She's probably cold, hungry, and tired. She might have curled up somewhere to sleep. And I'll call Burleigh."

Burleigh. Maybe Papa had also thought of kidnapping. But to Martha, he only said, "You should stay at your house with Elena, where folks can report."

The men moved to tackle their assignments, but Martha remained frozen in place. Art came back from the kitchen door and helped her stand.

"You have ta be strong," he hissed in her ear. "For the daughter who's still alive."

They climbed into their pickup. Martha shivered, even though she wore her coat and scarf. From sitting in Papa's warm kitchen, she shouldn't be that cold, but she couldn't stop shaking.

"Art, Papa cautioned everyone not to tear through the fields, but I picture Anna curled up in a ditch somewhere, hopefully with Tip, staying warm. With the miles and miles of irrigation ditches on the farms, how will we find her?"

What Martha didn't say was, How will we find her if she's miles and miles away, trussed up in the back seat of a stranger's car?

"If Tip's with 'er, Tip'll sound the alarm at an approachin' vehicle, an' we'll see 'em," Art said.

By the time Elena and Luis arrived with Alex, two teams were searching with Mr. Miyoshi, four on Art and Martha's place, and two on the Home Place. Over thirty people.

Louise came out from town with Earl, and the two of them were assigned to a team on the Home Place, even though no one in the family thought Anna would cross the road. The one time she had ventured that far without telling anyone, she was four and looking for Alex. Art spanked her. Her only spanking. And she had been reminded many times since not to cross it, a painful experience for them all.

At one point Martha heard Art talking to Sheriff Burleigh out by the porch, and she was surprised at her relief. Burleigh wasn't without skills, quick thinking and tenacity among them. If Anna had been taken, he wouldn't rest until he found her. He'd pursued Dolores Ruiz's attacker, as ill-advised as the outcome was. If Burleigh found Anna, she and Art would be there to stop his overreach.

She wasn't prepared, though, for Burleigh to come into the house, nor did she expect him to be so polite. He removed his Stetson. "Martha, Elena. A hard night fer everyone, but let's us talk 'bout what ya've done with Anna since…" Burleigh coughed. "…Since the baby's funeral."

Elena and Martha stared at him.

"Here's what I'm thinkin'. Yer little girl is lookin' fer 'er baby sister, maybe. Little ones don't get the whole idea 'bout dyin', ya know? Has she talked 'bout lookin' fer 'er sister, an', if she has, where do ya suppose she'd look?"

However Martha expected him to begin his investigation, it wasn't with this. But it made some sense. After trying to come up with an answer, Martha and Elena concluded Anna hadn't mentioned anything along the lines Burleigh suggested. His next series of questions had to do with the places she played, or wanted to play, but the various teams were already looking there.

Then Burleigh asked, "Do ya make anything a Tip bein' gone, too?"

The two women shook their heads and all three sat at the kitchen table, thinking.

Martha heard the pack of strays howling in the distance. They hadn't been an immediate threat since the night Carrie died. But if Anna and Tip were out in the fields somewhere…

Martha didn't let herself imagine anything more and simply said, "They're getting an early start tonight."

"Damn dogs," mumbled Burleigh. "'Scuse me, but they're causin' more trouble than a bunch a drunks."

Elena sat upright. "Anna has talked often these past several weeks about the stray dogs and how they are only playing. She says they are looking for friends. At other times she says, 'Papa locked Tip in the barn so she could not play with her friends.'"

Martha added, "Anna played with a little boy at the Pinion Thanksgiving Dinner all afternoon and announced to us afterward that she had a friend. Maybe that's her way of missing Carrie and trying to replace her."

"And?" Burleigh said.

Neither spoke, so he asked, "Where does this line a thinkin' take us?"

Martha said what she thought was the obvious. "Just that she misses Carrie's companionship more than I realized. So it might be especially important for her to find a friend for Tip, out of a sympathy she's not felt before."

"Where are there other dogs," Burleigh asked, "besides the strays an' Rowdy?"

From his own experience, Burleigh knew Rowdy wasn't a potential friend. When he visited the Home Place, Papa had to secure Rowdy before Burleigh could get out of his Buick.

Elena and Martha answered in unison, "The sheepdogs."

"But she'd have to cross the road," Martha added, convinced Anna wouldn't do it.

"It's a place ta start," said Burleigh. "But keep thinkin' if this leads nowhere."

Why had Burleigh spent so much time with her and Elena? Surely it occurred to him, too, that Anna had been taken. He should be patrolling the roads. Contacting neighboring police departments. The search should have started hours ago. They wasted precious time while the distance between them and Anna grew. Still, Martha didn't allow herself to mention it. She prayed that someone like Maher wouldn't kidnap a girl as young as Anna.

Art, Martha, and Elena rode in the Lundgren's pickup; Burleigh and Papa followed in the sheriff's vehicle. Art drove along the ruts between the corn stubble, barely creeping. Martha and Elena leaned forward, scanning the ground illuminated by the headlights, ready to yell if they spotted a little girl tucked in a cornrow.

Art looked in the rearview mirror from time to time and watched the sheriff's Buick bounce along. He grumbled that it was no wonder the county had to replace the tires so often. His comment was just enough to shake Martha's determination not to speak her worst fear.

She screamed, "No, the sheriff's tires wear out because he cavorts all around the country on pointless trips, to New Mexico for Dolores's rapist, everywhere, until it comes to our daughter. Anna's been taken! He doesn't know what he's doing! He should have started a statewide search! She would never cross the county road to the Home Place, never!"

She dropped her forehead to her hands on the dashboard and sobbed. She felt Elena's hand rubbing her shoulder, but it brought no consolation. And Art didn't stop the truck. They didn't believe her. Why was everyone so dense? Then again, Burleigh had surely alerted others. Maybe his deputy was pursuing the man who had Anna in his car at this very moment. She lifted her head.

Before the headlights reached as far the sheepherder's wagon, the pickup encountered the three sheepdogs, who attempted to herd away the slowly moving vehicle as they would a cow or horse. Suddenly, they withdrew into the darkness and Tip appeared, followed by the herder, who carried a large sheepskin bundle.

Elena jumped from the truck before it stopped. The sheepskin quivered and out popped Anna's head. Martha's foot slipped on the running board, and she tumbled out, onto her hands and knees. No one noticed. Art had Anna in his arms when she reached them.

In the confusion of tears and hugs, Elena pieced together the sheepherder's story from his Spanish telling of it. Toward dusk his dogs raised quite a fuss, and he, Estevan, followed them to the spot along the irrigation ditch that attracted their interest. There he encountered Tip, who was guarding something with a determination that matched the sheepdogs' intent to drive her away. The "something" was Anna, huddled in the tall, dry grass. Estevan quieted the dogs, which calmed Tip, and he retrieved Anna.

He described a child no longer able to walk, cold, and hungry. He took Anna to his wagon, wrapped her in the sheepskin, and fed her coffee, bacon, and biscuits. She revived soon enough, and he was taking her to the Home Place when they met him in the field.

Anna snuggled in Martha's arms as they bounced along the cornrows. Before she fell asleep, she said, "Tip didn't like the sheepdogs at first, but they're friends now."

When Martha carried Anna into the kitchen, she roused herself. "Mama, why won't you let me have Carrie's snowflake on the wall in my bedroom?"

Martha choked back her tears. "Papa'll hang it over your bed in the morning."

Elena turned down Anna's covers and slipped out while Art and Martha tucked her in.

Alex and Louise tiptoed into the house.

Martha blocked Alex before he reached Anna's door. "Don't ever come in contact with my daughter again."

Her voice was soft, but the venom unmistakable.

Impasse

Martha carried a full egg bucket across the lane and sat it gingerly by the cellar door. She turned at the sound of Papa's voice coming from the porch.

"What do you do with all those eggs?"

"Store them in the cellar, crate them and, on my way to Dr. McFarland's tomorrow morning, I'll take them to Safeway. They send them to Pueblo for grading and give us a check. I also save some for the Collinses to sell at the Country Store."

"You'll need a second bucket when your new layers produce. You have time for a cup of coffee?"

He rarely dropped by for coffee. Said hers was too strong. This was not a friendly invitation; it was a directive.

"Of course. I didn't hear you drive in. Where's your truck?"

"Had Alex drop me by your mailbox. Went to the kitchen first. Where's your truck?"

"At Mr. Miyoshi's. He's cleaning out his barn. Art and Anna are collecting his scrap iron for the Boy Scouts and will come here next."

"If you think your truck can carry the weight, they can search for scrap in my barn, too."

Papa never missed a chance to good-naturedly ridicule their dilapidated form of transportation. He was, in fact, rather proud that the Old Truck, once his, was still on the road.

"I'll mention it. Pot's on the stove. Pour two cups. I'll be right there, after I carry these eggs down."

Papa delivered one more attempt at light-hearted banter. "Don't trip. It'd be a real mess to clean broken eggs off those cement steps."

Martha read the signs. He set a congenial tone but wanted to discuss a serious matter. Someone had already "tripped." Otherwise, he'd get right to the point, not wait for the egg deposit, and not bother with the ceremonial cup of coffee.

The small-talk phase was short, and he omitted comments about her strong coffee. He hadn't taken a sip before he said, "We were all upset about Anna. Even Al. He was part of the search, you know."

Given Papa's animosity toward Al, that Papa gave him public credit was remarkable.

"I hadn't known," she said.

He seemed satisfied she understood that the search for Anna pulled together such disparate people. Martha recognized this tactic, too. By getting her concurrence in stages, she would accept his conclusion about the topic he circled but hadn't yet disclosed. Even someone as vile as Al Ivarson would agree. Whatever his point, Martha determined she wouldn't submit in silence as she had on Mother's Day when he refused to discuss his decision about delaying marriage.

"Papa, Anna could have died. If you're saying everyone recognized that could have been the outcome, I agree everyone was upset."

"But she didn't die. Estevan found her. He fed her. He was bringing her to us."

"Yes, and Elena, Art, Anna, and I are taking him a gift, a wool scarf, and thanking him again. Elena says anything more would insult him because he was doing what anyone would in that circumstance."

Papa seemed to consider the next gambit. "I had Alex drop me off and head back to the wagon wheel he's working on because I wasn't sure you'd allow him in the yard on account of how you've laid down the law he's not to see Anna again."

It was Martha's move. If Papa was concerned about keeping her and Alex separated, he could have driven himself over. Why the elaborate arrangement for the ride, and was he going to walk home? Perhaps that's why he wanted to know where their truck was. She decided not to mince words.

"Yes, I'm angry at Alex, and I told him to stay away from Anna."

Papa leaned forward, having arrived at the purpose of his visit. "And how do you intend to enforce that? Not come over to the Home Place? Forbid Alex from driving into your lane or from helping Art? Stop going to church?"

So the ruse of having Alex drop him off at the mailbox was to show the impracticality of her edict. But he should allow that, even before they found Anna, Martha was tired, upset. Were it not for Art's slap, she might still be paralyzed in the twilight between wakefulness and sleep. If Papa would listen…

He didn't stop. "Those are just the logistical problems. What about Anna? You're not the only one to lose Carrie. Anna's lost her sister. Seven months might not be long in your life, but Carrie's seven months on this earth was a long time for Anna. And now you're taking Alex from her, too, probably her best friend."

Anna's search for friends for Tip prompted the quest that put her in danger, and now Papa accused her of denying Anna her most cherished friendship. Martha erupted. "His carelessness threatened my daughter's life. I have a responsibility to protect her. Why aren't you on my side? Can't you see the risk? You, of all people, know he's not dependable."

She'd gone too far. Her attack on Alex would push Papa to defend him.

Papa straightened his shoulders, but his words were measured. "Martha, Alex and you are my Anna. I love you both. Alex is horrified at what happened. He swears when he called in the door he heard your voice. How many times in even one week does this scene play itself out? I'm not saying he heard you, but I can imagine he thought he did. He would never knowingly leave Anna alone."

Martha noticed her physical reaction before her thoughts took shape. The blood in her fingers pricked like crystals of ice pumped from a frozen place in her chest. To think, she might be at fault, fallen as she had into that deep sleep. Alex's shout from the kitchen wouldn't have penetrated. Still, he should have located her before he left Anna standing there, alone.

Martha reoriented herself to Papa's voice. He had surely noticed her stiffen when she recognized how she, as well as Alex, was at fault. But he continued. "Alex didn't sleep at all that night. I know because I didn't sleep much, myself."

Because Papa's softer tone didn't shatter her rigid torso, she didn't fortify her defenses. She let herself realize she was also asleep when Carrie died. And Mama. Because she thought Carrie was recovering, she let down her guard, as she had when she thought Anna was safe with Alex. When Mama died, she was just too exhausted. She had failed her mother and both daughters.

"And I'm worried about you," Papa said, "cutting yourself off from your only brother, who loves you very much. I think you love him, too. Consider carefully before you break a bond that strong. If you want Alex supervised when he's with Anna, you can make proper arrangements, but this business of severing ties is no good — not for you, not for him, and most certainly not for Anna."

If he hadn't lectured, if he had shown more sympathy, if he had understood her harrowing experience of nearly losing two daughters within a month, Martha might have considered his appeal. Moreover, Papa insinuated she didn't love her brother as much as he loved her.

All she could say was, "Carrie's seven months was a lifetime for me, too, Papa. I won't lose another child."

Instead of walking around the table to hold his daughter, Papa answered, "I think you're exaggerating the danger with Alex."

The bang of the screen door announced Anna and Art's return. Papa rose from his chair. "Before you two get your coats off, will you give me a ride home?"

Martha remained at the table. She had tried to speak up for herself, and Papa hadn't listened. He allowed that Carrie's death took its toll on Anna, but not that it nearly paralyzed her, his daughter.

She made some allowance because for as long as she could remember she'd understood how the threat of family discord recalled the pain of his childhood in Canada. The household rule was that quarrels be solved by bedtime, reinforced by the devastating effect of family strife on Uncle Malcolm. Reflexively, Papa's children patched up their disagreements, even though none of them knew the details of what happened to the two brothers.

Attack

That Sunday afternoon, Anna sat beside Martha on the piano bench while Martha played "Away in a Manger." She loved late winter afternoons at the piano because the light shown through the west-facing windows unimpeded by the leafless cottonwoods and elms.

The rays swept over the sheet music, not that Martha needed it for the familiar tune.

"Let's sing together, honey. I think you know the words. The teachers at Eagle View School want me to help with the Christmas program, so I'm practicing. You can come, too, and sing with the other children."

Their voices joined, "The stars in the sky looked down where He lay/The little Lord Jesus, asleep on the hay."

The same words she had sung the night she held Carrie's body, with the hope that the lullaby would carry her daughter's soul into the sky where she would be cradled by the stars that guarded the Baby Jesus.

But the night she stood in the yard when they brought Carrie home those brittle pinpoints of light blinked impassively across the expanse of the firmament. Perhaps the universe was even hostile, because when Carrie died, it echoed the whistles of the troop trains and howls of stray dogs on the prowl. However, the lullaby portrayed creation as being of a different character, one that watched over the divine child.

She and Anna continued, and Martha paid closer attention. For the first time, she noticed the Baby Jesus's abrupt relocation from manger to sky.

The cattle are lowing, the poor Baby wakes,
But little Lord Jesus, no crying He makes.
I love Thee, Lord Jesus, look down from the sky
And stay by my cradle 'til morning is nigh.

The soothing tune was so counter to the wrenching image of the lyrics. In the space of a breath, the serene baby in the manger whom even the stars attend joins them to become every child's guardian.

She marveled that she hadn't noticed the Baby Jesus's sudden displacement to the heavens in all the times she had sung the song; or perhaps the words were meant to represent the lurch from cradle to heaven when children die. They're here, in your arms, and they're gone.

Heavenly bodies, magnificent and impenetrable, evidently don't register human sorrow until joined by the infant/adult Jesus. Men might use stars as a compass, but, of themselves, they offer no comfort, contrary to the lullaby's portrayal of stars guarding the manger.

Anna didn't know the next verse and interrupted. "Can we sing 'Jingle Bells'?"

Determined to hold on to her child, Martha involuntarily put her arm around Anna's shoulder and played the "Jingle Bells" melody with her left hand.

They started with the chorus, Martha thinking she might have a talk with Rev. Behm. She'd first heard him preach that morning and thought his lack of pretention winsome and his sincerity genuine. She was glad he would become their new minister after Christmas.

Something about his amusing physical quirks, stemming in part from his small stature, endeared him. Everyone in the choir chuckled about the short stool he introduced behind the pulpit, but theirs was a good-natured acceptance that without it he would be dwarfed. He seemed to accept his deficiencies, compensate for them, and get on with the job. She didn't think she would feel foolish telling him about the ominous void that manifested itself in the wake of Carrie's death.

Art came into the living room but penetrated the space only several steps beyond the arch. "Martha, Anna. Get yer coats an' come with me."

The quiet urgency in his voice unsettled Martha, but neither she nor Anna moved.

"Alex just stopped by the barn," Art said. "He tol' me there's terrible news an' we should all be together at the Home Place."

Martha slid off the bench. "If Alex is there, I can't go. This morning at church was painful, sitting in the choir pew with him, in front of everyone. I still can't talk to him. Hopefully, no one noticed we weren't speaking."

As if to herself, she added, "And I'm still smarting from Papa's scolding."

Art, who was already walking back through the dining room, turned. "Martha, from Alex's tone, what we're 'bout ta hear might make yer disagreement not that important."

Martha bristled. Art sounded like Papa. Neither of them took seriously her grief about Carrie's death and her near loss of Anna. Before she could speak, Art made his way through the swinging door into the kitchen, and Anna scampered after him.

Art was helping Anna with her coat when Martha entered. "You haven't discussed with me whether I want Anna to see him. I'll answer, in any case. I agree with Papa that it's not fair to Anna to keep her from Alex, and you'll be there, but I'm staying here. I'm not ready to talk to him, or Papa, either."

She was at a loss to interpret Art's look.

He bit his lip. "Suit yerself, but I don't like ya bein' here alone. At least turn on the radio."

Martha assumed Art didn't want her to be alone on account of her deep sleep the afternoon Anna wandered off. But at the moment, she wasn't sleepy. She was hungry. Art and Anna would be eating Sunday evening pancakes with Papa and Alex. That was Papa's ritual, and he always mixed enough batter for anyone who dropped in.

After they left, she made herself a cup of fresh coffee and a sandwich from the leftover ham. She finished eating, cleaned up the kitchen, and went back to the living room. No use turning on the radio, with the static. She sat down with the *Ladies Home Journal* Josie had given her that morning at church.

By seven thirty Art and Anna still hadn't returned. She looked out the living room window and saw five or six cars in the lane by the McLennan home, including Earl and Josie's.

The phone rang. It was Josie. "Martha, don't you know? The Japanese attacked Pearl Harbor. Thousands are dead. I'm coming to get you."

And she hung up.

Martha scarcely knew what Josie meant. It wasn't plausible that the Japanese came halfway across the Pacific to attack Pearl Harbor.

With trembling fingers, she struggled to button her coat. The news caused some of the trembling, but that she let personal affairs blind her to something of such magnitude shook her to the core.

She walked outside to wait for Josie. To the south, she saw the headlights of two vehicles pulling into Mr. Miyoshi's lane.

Treachery

Mr. Miyoshi knocked at the kitchen door early Monday morning. Art was still in the barn doing chores and Anna in her pajamas.

"Please, come in," Martha said. "Even if you've had breakfast, you can join us for coffee."

She wanted to ask him about the attack. Perhaps he had information from his Japanese newspapers that could explain it.

He answered with uncharacteristic formality. "Thank you, but I cannot. I have many families to visit. I am here to apologize for the treacherous attack on America by the country of my birth."

Mr. Miyoshi's head was down, his hat in his hands, and the apology so carefully worded that she sensed he dared not deviate from the text. Rather than saying anything that might throw him off course, Martha simply touched his arm; he flinched. He looked up, and she saw his tears.

"I am sorry. I am so sorry," he said.

He backed away, bowing as he went, turned, and hurried toward the barn.

Wordless, Martha stood in the open door. Anna reached for her mother's hand. "Why's Mr. Miyoshi crying?"

Martha picked her up and pressed Anna's head to her shoulder. She answered with the first thought she snatched from a multitude of possibilities.

"He's very sad about the attack on Pearl Harbor in the Hawaiian Islands, the one we heard about on the radio at Grandpa's last night."

Her voice muffled in Martha's shoulder, Anna said, "He didn't say 'sad.' He said 'sorry.' Did Mr. Miyoshi do something wrong?"

Martha stumbled into, "You're right. His words said he was sorry. But I think his tears spoke louder and said he was sad. You heard his words; I listened to his tears."

Anna lifted her head from Martha's shoulder, seemingly intrigued with the vocal capability of tears but not losing sight of her question. "Mama, what did Mr. Miyoshi do that was wrong?"

"Maybe he thinks he has to apologize for the bad thing the Japanese soldiers did. Mr. Miyoshi was born in Japan, but he hasn't lived there for a long time."

"Is that why he's crying, because he has to say he's sorry for what someone else did?"

"Perhaps, or he's sad so many Americans died in the attack."

"I'm cold, Mama. Let's shut the door."

Relieved that the chilly air stopped Anna's questions, Martha said, "Yes, and run get anklets for your feet, and a sweater."

Art's first words when he came into the kitchen were, "What do ya make a Miyoshi?"

Anna chimed in, "He's sorry for the bad thing the Japanese soldiers did."

Both Martha and Art took a moment to consider Anna's response.

"I think that about sums it up," Martha said.

Anna occupied herself with her scrambled eggs, and Art observed, "I'm worried 'bout the whole thing with Miyoshi. Many Americans won't see any difference 'tween 'im an' the Japanese soldiers."

Martha's concern for Mr. Miyoshi and their other Japanese neighbors took shape as a lump in her throat. They finished breakfast in silence.

Defense

By noon, Martha and Dr. McFarland had finished with patients. He suggested she leave. "In times like these, we should be with our families. Probably that's why so few came to the office today; everyone's staying close to home."

"Will you head back to Pueblo this afternoon, to be with your wife?"

"No. I've been asked to attend the defense council meeting tonight, in light of the fact that there's no county Health Unit."

"That's generous of you. I'm sure you'd rather be home. What have you heard about the Philippine Islands and your son?"

"Nothing, but it's only a matter of time before the Japanese attack American bases there. Compared to Pearl Harbor, the Philippine Islands are located in their back yard. Surely they're learning from Hitler's disastrous Russian invasion not to extend themselves too far."

"Perhaps," Martha answered, doubtful anyone could anticipate the battle plans of a nation, especially after yesterday's attack.

His several comments generated a cascade of thoughts — the McFarlands sacrificed the companionship of retirement so he could help his friend, Doc, who had been called back to service; he dispassionately evaluated what might happen in the Philippine Islands, in spite of the obvious danger to his son; military action threatened Muriel at the Canocao Naval Hospital in Manila; and, at home, decisions taken at the defense council meeting would have any number of consequences. Cataclysmic changes awaited them all.

She longed to retreat into the relative simplicity of her grief about Carrie, her ferocious desire to protect Anna, and her fury at Alex, but if she hadn't been nursing that anger, she would have followed Art's suggestion to turn on the radio and immediately joined the others.

She didn't think she was self-absorbed. Her ideal was Dr. McFarland — self-sacrificing, informed, balancing family and community concerns — but she wasn't behaving like that at all.

She walked out on the front porch of the house where the doctor's office was located and saw Art, Elena, and Anna by the truck, but she told herself not to reach any premature conclusions. She must accustom herself to unexpected deviations from routine.

"We caught a ride inta town with Alex," Art explained. "He, Luis, an' Hugh are enlistin'. After we take Elena home, I wanna shop fer another truck. Robert thinks it'll get harder ta buy any vehicle, just like we've been cautioned 'bout farm equipment. The Old Truck might not last much longer, but we'll hang on ta it until it gives out. If ya keep workin' in town, ya can drive the New Truck, as long as the old one keeps runnin.' Whada ya think? It could be our Christmas."

Martha didn't follow Art's line of reasoning. All she heard was the news about Alex, Luis, and Hugh.

"They're enlisting? All three of them? Today? How soon will they go? Do you think it's wise? Shouldn't they consider this more carefully and not get caught up in the panic? Isn't this another instance of Alex reacting without thinking, and he's pulling Luis and Hugh along with him?"

Art raised his eyebrows. "Panic? I'd call it patriotism. All three a 'em'll be called ta serve, anyway. Alex turns twenty-one next month. The sooner them an' boys like 'em enlist, the sooner they can be trained an' sent. If I was in Alex's shoes, I'd be enlistin', too."

Martha turned to Elena. "What do you think?"

"I am worried about Luis, but also about my cousins from New Mexico who are already on the Philippine Islands. They will need help. I agree, Mr. Lundgren, that the sooner Alex and Luis go, perhaps the shorter the fight will be. Also, Luis wants to learn many new things, perhaps how to fly airplanes or shoot big guns. This is his personality, to work hard and overcome difficulty. We praise Marguerite for how smart she is, but Luis is the first in our family to graduate from high school. He looks for adventure and is excited about going."

All the McLennans were proud of Luis, the first Spanish boy ever to graduate from Greenwood. What a loss if…

Elena's comments were the second within the space of twenty minutes about war and the Philippine Islands, amplifying Martha's dread about Muriel's safety. She leaned against the truck. Assured by its solid, smooth surface, she could grant Elena's point that boys like Alex, Luis, and Hugh were needed to protect Muriel and the other Americans there, but at what cost?

"Art, tell me again about the truck."

He repeated his logic, but Martha was still absorbed in her thoughts. They had struggled so long, making do with the Old Truck, Martha hadn't imagined having anything else. Now, in the space of an afternoon, they might spend most of their savings, and they hadn't even worked up to it. She shook her head in disbelief.

"There'll be so many things come up we can't imagine," Art said, "that we gotta be ready fer the things we can. Don't say no 'fore we've talked it over."

"You misinterpret me. I'm not disagreeing about the truck. I shook my head to clear my thinking. I'm lagging behind you because I wasn't at Papa's last night when everyone was probably talking about the possibilities you hint at. How much do you suppose we'll have to spend?"

"I'd know if ya'd asked me that question a week ago, but with the attack… Last year Gust bought a '39 Ford truck with four new tires fer two twenty-five. I mention the tires on account a the short supply a rubber. We'll want good tires, an' they'll add ta the expense."

"I know about the scarcity of rubber," she snapped.

Carrie had consumed her attention in life and death, but Martha wasn't completely ignorant.

"Um…" Art regained his train of thought. "Gust's new truck was in good shape. We can bet the cost'll be more now, if we can find one. That's why we have ta do it soon, 'fore prices jump."

"If Alex is enlisting, we could offer to buy his truck. Papa already has his Chrysler and the pickup. What does he need with an extra vehicle? In any case, we should shop around to get an idea of prices and what's available."

"Glad ta hear ya talkin' this way. I been pullin' ya along fer awhile, an' it's good ta have a regular conversation."

Elena quietly inserted herself. "I do not think Alex will sell his truck. He is very proud of it. If he leaves for the service, he might want to know he has something of value to come home to."

Martha considered Elena's comment––not just the substance, but that she spoke up for Alex.

"Elena, thanks fer yer opinion," Art answered. "The attack affects us married folks different. Ya probably know better how Alex would react. Do ya think we should at least ask 'im, in case he'd like the extra cash, if he goes away?"

Elena answered without hesitation. "No. You, Mr. Lundgren, could say you are thinking about buying a new truck and ask his opinion. He would be pleased if you asked his advice, but right now he is very upset by the…"

She paused, as though weighing her words. "By the argument with you, Mrs. Lundgren. I think he would be insulted if you asked to buy his truck, with this bad feeling between you."

Martha drew back. Until this moment, Elena hadn't offered her thoughts about matters concerning the private business of the McLennans. She was a respectful, silent observer, but obviously saw a great deal. It wasn't proper for Elena to presume to speak for Alex, and Martha's dispute with her brother shouldn't be part of a conversation about purchasing a truck. She would be more circumspect around Elena.

They dropped Elena off and drove back over the tracks to Hank's Motor Company.

Tactics

On their way home, after checking at the newspaper office for any new want ads, they reviewed their position.

"Hank has the truck I want, the blue one," Art said.

"I wouldn't have thought so. You barely looked at it."

Anna laid her head on Martha's lap and curled her legs up on the seat, worn out from the late hour last night at Papa's.

"That's right. If Hank thinks I care, he'll give me a hard time. A man's gotta be careful dealin' with Hank er he'll take advantage.

Trouble is, I can't wait 'round an' drop by casual-like later in the week. Truck won't be there. I gotta make the offer today. I'll telephone when we get home."

"Yes, be very careful in business dealings with Hank, but if you make an offer, he'll know it's the one you want."

"But I won't act eager, er he'll have the upper hand."

"I don't have patience for this kind of maneuvering. If I set a price, that's the one I expect. I'll trust you, though, because I think you can get the better of him."

"I didn't know ya had such a good opinion a me!"

The prospect of a new truck lifted Martha's spirits. "The blue one's my favorite, too. At least the outside seemed to be in good shape. What if the motor isn't, though?"

"Didn't ya recognize the truck? It's Max Lambert's. Ya know 'ow the Lamberts coddle their 'quipment. Max might be younger'n Alex, but he's a better mechanic. I don't even need ta drive it ta know it's a good buy. Trouble is, the fact it's with Hank means Max's leavin'. Can't imagine he's enlistin', on account a the Lamberts bein' such pacifists, but if he's sellin' 'is truck he must be goin' somewhere."

"Elsie and I never talked about what Max'd do if we entered the war. But if they lost him to the army, they'd be inconsolable. They've already lost Addie to Walter, even though she only lives in town. She's repudiated everything they believe, as far as I can tell."

"Ya don't know that, just 'cause she married a Moulton."

"Addie rarely visits them, that I do know, and it's a shame Elsie hardly ever sees Harriet, her granddaughter. Art, if the truck you want is Max's, I'd hate to think we'd be adding to Otto and Elsie's heartache by buying it. They'd see it regularly, which would multiply their grief."

"If Max has flown the coop an' joined the army, I'd think they'd be pleased ta know 'is truck is in good hands."

"Art, are you being sincere or making up reasons for us to buy that truck?"

"Otto an' Elsie know better'n most we need a new vehicle, an' that it's a good buy. They ain't gonna hold it 'gainst us."

"I'm just thinking about Elena's reasoning about why Alex wouldn't want to sell. But we turn around and buy Max's truck, and whatever the reason he's let go of it, it's bound to be emotional."

"Martha, if we tie ourselves in knots worryin' 'bout every little thing, we'll never find a truck. Difference 'tween Alex an' Max is this: Max handed his truck over ta Hank. It's gonna be sold, one way er 'nother, an' we might as well be the ones buyin' it."

"That's a good point. And hopefully Elsie and Otto won't begrudge us, but I need to talk to you about something else."

"What?"

He stopped the Old Truck by the porch door; Anna was sound asleep and neither parent moved.

"Art, I let my grief and pride blind me to the importance of your invitation to go to Papa's last night."

Art turned and rested his arm on the back of the seat. "I'm glad yer bringin' it up. I didn't know what ta do. Didn't wanna force ya on account a how uncomfortable you'd be with Alex, but I did think ya'd take my advice an' turn on the radio. I also worried if ya turned it on an' weren't with the rest a us when ya heard whatever bad news Alex was warning us 'bout, ya'd have 'nother a those, those spells. If Josie hadn't called, I was 'bout ready ta come fer ya. Martha, ya got ta settle this thing with 'im, 'specially if he leaves."

Art called her deep sleep a "spell." Meaning she wasn't herself. Meaning he, too, must think Anna's disappearance was partly her fault because if she had been herself, she would have heard Alex announce Anna's return.

If he had stopped there, without saying she had to settle it with Alex, she would have admitted she had indulged in a kind of luxury, a luxury of grief since Carrie died. But Art was just like Papa, more concerned that she get past her anger with Alex than with Carrie's death and Anna's disappearance. Grief was a bigger problem than anger. Josie said they all wanted to help, but they weren't, not Josie, not Papa, not Art, and certainly not Alex.

A gulf widened between her and Art, like the void that lurked behind her in the kitchen the morning Anna disappeared. She laid her hand on Art's arm, as though physical connection could hold her world together. She returned to the topic of the attack.

"I understand that, given Pearl Harbor, I, we, have to make room for more than just our own concerns and prepare for demands we can't imagine."

She winced when she recognized her tactic was similar to Papa's. Agree in stages so you and the other person overcome your differences.

"I don't have any argument with ya," he said. "The unexpected's why I'm proposin' ta buy the truck, when we still 'ave a chance at a decent one."

The thing about that tactic was, it worked to solve disputes, but she still felt alone in her grief. "So I have a proposal. There's a meeting tonight to organize for local defense. Dr. McFarland's been asked to attend. I'd like to go, just to listen. I think it will pull me out of this, this hole I'm in about losing Carrie. Going to the meeting is my version of your breakfast at the Sage Café. I'd be part of a larger picture and know more about what the attack means for us."

"Yer makin' sense."

"I'm sure Papa'll be going. I'll swallow my pride and ask to ride with him. Maybe doing this together will restore some of his confidence in me."

And your confidence in me, she silently added.

"Swallow yer pride?"

"Yes, he also thinks I'm being too hard on Alex. But I'm not ready to talk to Alex, not yet."

Rapprochement

Papa started the Chrysler. Neither he nor Martha spoke. She couldn't endure it if he pressed her to make up with Alex before the army took him.

She went on the offensive. "What do you think'll happen tonight?"

"I'm not sure. These meetings all over the country are supposed to get folks organized, but so much has changed in only twenty-four hours. Thousands lost in the Hawaiian Islands. Thousands more enlisting, Alex included. You and Art buying a truck. Everyone's shocked and outraged, if those words even begin to describe the state the country's in. Some could miss the point that we have to pull together, and they'll make the meeting about Roosevelt. That could lead to fireworks."

The matter-of-fact answer was reminiscent of their conversations during his political campaigns. Maybe they could avoid the brother-sister rift.

"Fireworks?"

"Well, take Al and me," he answered. "We represent two ends of the pole when it comes to Roosevelt and defense. Actually, sometimes I can't tell what end of the pole he's at, or maybe we're just on different poles."

Papa chuckled. "Could be he's not even hanging on to a pole. I'll use that sometime to irritate him."

Surely his answer didn't mean he'd dwell on Al at the expense of rising to the challenges before them. She was about to tell him so, but he backtracked.

"Maybe it's because Al doesn't hear so well, which we all know started in the trenches of the World War. Could be getting worse. That would explain why he sometimes says things completely unrelated to the topic at hand."

As though a sympathetic comment about Al was one too many, he said, "Still, he drives me to distraction."

"Papa, what do your differences with Al have to do with my question about the meeting?"

"I imagine he'll be chairman, and he's so emotional about Roosevelt I don't know what we can expect."

So, Papa's fixation on Al did pertain to her question about the meeting, and it kept the topic of Alex at bay.

"Al'll do anything to undermine the New Deal," he said, "from endangering the health of children by eliminating school lunches and Millie Swanson's position to interfering with work at the dam site because he's dissolved the Health Unit. He calls Roosevelt a dictator about increasing industrial capacity for defense, a consistent position for him to take, but does an about face when it comes to conscription."

"How's that?"

"Conscription means preparing for war as much as anything Roosevelt's done, but Al supports conscription, I guess because he's a veteran. He's the heart of Greenwood's Veterans of Foreign Wars and must think army life is good for boys, discipline and all that. That's my point — I don't know what he thinks, or if he thinks. Roosevelt's Civilian Conservation Corps has been teaching boys to read and giving them food, discipline, and jobs for years, as the army does, and the CCC's not had to do with war, so why hasn't Al supported it? Folks even say the boys who've been in the CCC are the kinds who otherwise wouldn't have passed the literacy and physical tests for the army. So, the CCC prepared them, but Al's violently, and that's not too strong a word, against it. He's against a program that helps boys and wasn't connected to defense, but he supports conscription."

Only then did Martha remember Art's story about the stock meeting where men separated Al and Papa on account of their differences about defense preparations. His fear about potential fireworks wasn't idle speculation.

"Hard to follow anything to do with Al. As a veteran, you'd think he'd want the best for the boys. That would mean we shouldn't send them off without ships, tanks, and munitions, and that takes us back to increasing industrial capacity for defense. Of course, everyone hoped selective service wouldn't mean more than a year's worth of training and the boys'd return home. Al might not have believed they'd be sent to fight. But now…"

The burden of the attack silenced them.

Martha's recent conversations with Papa, with anyone, for that matter, were usually narrow affairs about farm and family. Even though Papa's topic was Al Ivarson, talk about conscription and the CCC got her mind on matters of national importance, an exhilarating relief.

But Papa wasn't finished with Al. "Lindberg's one of his heroes. Al was as convinced as Lindberg we could avoid this war. Even after the attack, Lindberg probably wants to talk nice to the Japanese, just as he's wanted us to talk to Hitler."

"Wasn't Lindberg only saying it's Europe's war and we should stay out? Surely the attack has changed his opinion."

"See how riled up I am? Going on about Al when we have to pull together? Maybe you'll handle it better."

"In what way?"

"By controlling yourself, not speaking out of turn, understanding folks'll say things when they're scared they wouldn't if they were thinking straight."

Why would he think she'd do better? He'd made clear she bungled the affair with Alex.

"Papa, I have every confidence you'll handle yourself well. Speaking of folks being scared and upset, Mr. Miyoshi stopped by our house this morning. He kept saying 'I'm sorry.'"

"Yes, he spoke with Alex and me, too, before Alex left to enlist."

"What do you make of it?"

"Miyoshi demonstrated great courage to apologize for this brazen assault. He had absolutely nothing to do with it; still, he went to every neighbor, hat in hand. Maybe some will think of his visits as a defensive maneuver, to deflect suspicion from the Japanese who live around Greenwood, but he's sincerely distressed by Japan's treachery. I can't picture myself doing what he did today."

His words stung. Unlike Mr. Miyoshi, who wasn't at fault, she was partly responsible for Anna's disappearance and refused to apologize.

"Papa, Anna said much the same thing, that Mr. Miyoshi cried because he didn't do anything wrong but had to say he was sorry for the Japanese soldiers."

"Miyoshi cried? By the time he got to us, there weren't tears, just profound regret. This is very hard on him."

They crossed the bridge into town, and she said, "To reassure you, I don't intend to say anything at the meeting. I'm there to learn."

"Sis, I'm glad we're doing this together."

Given how he disapproved of the way she had treated Alex, his affectionate remark meant a great deal, but she answered matter-of-factly. "I'm glad, too. Going to a public gathering reminds me of our old days campaigning."

Hostilities

Parking places were scarce even four and five blocks from the school, but Papa found an opening in front of Josie and Earl's. He turned off the motor, and Earl walked down the front steps, spotted the Chrysler, and waved. A barely audible puff of air escaped Papa's lips.

"What?" Martha asked.

"Here comes Al's Republican heir. My son-in-law has political aspirations, I'm sure. But he's smarter than Al. And he can hear. What'll we do, Sis, if Earl ever decides to run for county commissioner? I can't see myself campaigning for him. How 'bout you?"

Martha couldn't imagine her brother-in-law entering politics and blurted out, "Don't know I'd have the time. I'd be too busy on your campaign for reelection."

Papa laughed and patted her arm. "That's the spirit."

The three walked to the school together. She forgot Papa's speculation about Earl's ambitions as quickly as she did most things concerning Earl. The moment of generosity with his newborn son had been an exception, not a new beginning between them.

A crowd as somber and silent as their trio streamed into the gymnasium. It seemed Papa overstated his warning that people would be riled up.

After they entered the double doors, they headed to the bleachers on the right. The upper rows were already filled, so they walked the length of the gym and sat on the first row near the stage. Although punctuality for Papa meant arriving at least ten minutes early, even he hadn't anticipated such a crowd.

Before the meeting started, Arne DeFries walked down the steps of the stage and whispered something to Papa, who stood and followed him. Papa took a seat next to Al Ivarson.

"Earl, what's happening?" Martha asked.

"Arne evidently wants Robert to join the group at the table on stage."

Martha wanted more than a statement of the obvious and was about to say so, but Earl continued, "Robert might have lost the election; however, he's not lost the respect of the community. Everyone knows it isn't his fault Republicans did so well in Colorado last year, and the new commissioners haven't won much confidence so far. But I suppose you know that."

She wasn't prepared for Earl's frank opinion about the county's political life or his favorable estimation of Papa. He almost rekindled her affection from their exchange over the newborn Robbie. And Papa had just said Earl was smart. She must keep reminding herself Earl had more to him than his rigid, opinionated behavior disclosed.

"Normally you'd think Al would be chairman," he said, "since it's a countywide meeting, but Al's hearing's so bad he doesn't do well in a setting like this. Arne's conducting it as mayor and wants as much help near him as he can get. Robert'll inspire confidence from this crowd, just because he's on stage, and he'll be an asset to Arne, who doesn't maintain his composure."

Papa's timing was off concerning Earl's political aspirations. Earl's appraisal of Al's hearing difficulties and Arne's weaknesses hinted that Earl was party to discussions about how they should handle the meeting.

She hadn't been in a gathering where Papa played a public role for a good while, and she was anxious on account of his worries he wouldn't handle himself well. His proximity to Al, the man he'd railed about for the last fifteen minutes, surely wouldn't help.

Martha agreed with Earl about Mayor Arne DeFries. Easily
flustered, he was the opposite of his sister-in-law, Elizabeth DeFries,
who remained calm in crisis. Maybe it was her discipline as a nurse,
or the influence of her husband, Arne's brother. He'd reputedly had
a more composed temperament, but he'd died from influenza in the
last days of the World War.

Still, she applauded Mayor DeFries's shrewd decision to have
both Robert McLennan and Al Ivarson on stage. Two rivals seated
next to each other communicated that adversity brings folks together.

The mayor turned the first part of the meeting over to Sheriff
Burleigh. He started off with, "We're all wonderin', now that our boys
at Pearl Harbor have been so viciously attacked, will the Japs do
somethin' treacherous here?"

Martha gasped. That was Burleigh, putting it the worst possible
way, but she heard a number of folks mumble their agreement.

"I'm here ta tell ya tonight that I have a telegram in my hands
from the FBI, just like every sheriff in every town in our great, strong
country does, sayin' I can arrest any Jap alien suspected a bein' a
public danger, if I go through the FBI."

Martha sat upright. Whatever she and Art feared for Mr. Miyoshi
and the others wasn't this. Not so soon. Not so openly hostile. Not
from a public official.

Burleigh thundered, "I'm assurin' ya tonight, that if ya suspect
any Jap, tell me an' I'll handle it. I'm contactin' the Denver Police
Department ta come train our Valley men so our folks are protected,
our water is protected, the dam construction site is protected, an' our
electricity is protected."

He drew a straight line from Pearl Harbor to Mr. Miyoshi, as
though Mr. Miyoshi was already plotting to blow up the dam! She
scanned the faces of the crowd of perhaps three hundred in the

gymnasium and satisfied herself that neither Mr. Miyoshi nor his friends were present to hear this assault on their integrity.

Burleigh lowered his voice. "The mayor also has a telegram. His is from the guvnor's office an' instructs us 'bout other measures."

Martha swallowed several times to drive the pounding of her heart from her throat back to its proper place in her chest. To her amazement, applause erupted when Burleigh took his seat at the table. Thankfully, the vehicles in Mr. Miyoshi's driveway the night before and his early morning apology signaled his people already knew to devise strategies for self-protection.

A voice behind her yelled above the applause, "Send the Japs back; send the Japs back."

Several others took up the chant.

Martha jumped to her feet and shouted, "Mayor DeFries, Mayor DeFries, may I speak?"

Those nearest her grew quiet, and Arne DeFries heard Martha above the chanting that was spreading throughout the gymnasium.

"Martha, Martha Lundgren. You wish to speak?"

"Yes, thank you, Mayor DeFries."

The crowd grew quiet.

In a strong, clear voice she said, "I want to make clear which Japanese Sheriff Burleigh is referring to. Many of our Japanese neighbors have lived next to us for several decades. Their children, who go to our churches and schools and play on our basketball, football, and softball teams, are Americans. I assume, Sheriff, that the Japanese you're referring to are folks we don't know who are behaving suspiciously, whom we have reason to suspect. Is that correct?"

Burleigh looked in Martha's direction and frowned, seemingly irritated that her call to be recognized had silenced the applause. He remained seated and grumbled, "Sure, that's what I meant."

A voice behind her hissed, "No, he meant any Jap is a threat."

Martha looked toward Papa. He slowly passed his index finger over his lips. She took the motion as an indication to stop.

"Thank you, Sheriff," she said, "for making clear that our Japanese neighbors are not the threat you're referring to."

Out of the corner of her eye, she saw Lucy Himuru slide off a bleacher near the doors. It was the case that Martha hadn't caught sight of any Japanese in the audience, but Lucy was married to one. Lucy probably reached the same conclusion Martha did: many in the crowd saw them as enemies. Lucy was right to leave, for her own safety and to report to the others.

Earl patted Martha's arm. She didn't know if the gesture was a sign of support or a signal she should restrain herself. She kept her eyes on Papa's face but couldn't interpret his expression.

Al evidently hadn't heard the exchange between Martha and Burleigh and stood as though to take charge. "Now we'll hear from Mayor DeFries, who'll inform us 'bout the steps our state an' county'll take in the next weeks an' months ta protect us from the Jap threat."

His intrusion rescinded Arne's authority. Arne lacked Howard Burleigh's flamboyance and proceeded to read through the material he had in hand, pausing from time to time for questions. He described putting extra guards at the dam construction site, at reservoirs, even some major headgates. City wells would be locked and fenced, power plant employees armed, and on and on. Walter Moulton worked at the power plant, and he, a drunk, would have a gun. Not reassuring.

But the flood of information seemed to soothe the crowd, and everyone listened intently. A number of committees had to be established: fire, police, public works, education, among others. One was a medical committee, which must be the reason Dr. McFarland was asked to attend. He also had a seat at the table, on the other side of Al. Without a county nurse or Health Unit, the committee responsibilities would fall to him.

The crowd departed quietly, as it had arrived. Martha, Earl, and Papa didn't talk, either. Only when Papa pulled away from the curb did he comment. "I was proud of you tonight, for defending our Japanese friends. But you have to be careful. First, if I had been running the meeting, I wouldn't have let you speak. Second, I wouldn't have opened the meeting to questions about the material from the governor's office. They can come later, when folks aren't so stunned."

"Why's that?"

"DeFries could have lost control. The only reason he didn't when he called on you is because you're a woman and it shocked him, and the others, that you would stand up in the middle of a crowd getting all worked up and challenge a popular figure like Burleigh. In this case, Al's poor hearing served us well because he got the meeting back on track."

But she was the first to restore order by standing up for Mr. Miyoshi. Al had little to do with quieting the crowd.

"Martha, now you're publically identified as sympathetic to the Japanese. Judging by how quickly folks picked up the chant of a few rabble-rousers, no man could have said what you did and reached his car afterward without someone stopping him, probably physically."

"Papa, you're frightening me."

However, Martha saw how easily Burleigh stirred up the meeting, and she was afraid Papa was right.

"Please, please be careful. Promise me you'll be more judicious. Involve yourself in some kind of patriotic effort to allay suspicion. You're not going to change the minds of folks frightened by every Oriental-looking face they see, but you can be an example for those who know it's outrageous to suspect Miyoshi and the others."

"Papa, I agree I should be more careful, but I'm already working at Dr. McFarland's office. That's community minded. I don't have to go overboard just to satisfy hateful people."

Papa reached toward her in the dark cab of the truck. She took his hand.

"Martha, your stubbornness, your bold nature, and your honesty are just the qualities that might get us through these times, but you have to choose carefully when to act. Tonight wasn't the time. I'm serious about more public involvement."

Papa's warning sobered her, but she was convinced she did the right thing. Actually, she wasn't tough enough on Burleigh. "I'll try to choose my moments more carefully."

They passed the decorated fir tree in the park and drove down Main Street. Colored Christmas lights and evergreen boughs that draped across the street between the lampposts created a tunnel for the length of two blocks, insufficient to transport them from the grim mood at the gymnasium into joyous anticipation of the holidays.

"I haven't been to town at night since they turned on the lights," Martha said. "They look out of place."

"Oh?"

"With all the changes in the last twenty-four hours, I must have assumed Christmas was cancelled. But of course that was silly."

"Maybe Christmas'll be more significant than usual, with Alex enlisting and all."

She stiffened and let go of his hand. "Yes, that could be."

She'd kept the topic of Alex at bay all evening, but she heard the sadness in his voice, and he had complimented her courage and outspokenness at the meeting.

They crossed the bridge leading over the river and out of town.

"I was overly harsh with Alex," she said. "I'll talk to him."

She wasn't promising an apology, just indicating she was ready to talk. She expected Papa to be relieved.

"Martha, I don't think he's ready. He's been like a second father to Anna, as far as his feelings for her go. When you banished him from her life, well, it's not much of a stretch to compare it with how he felt after the Marquez accident, even the tragedy of Frank Ogawa's death. You're always saying you think Alex is irresponsible, but, if anything, he feels too responsible — for not stopping the wagon before it ran over Marquez, for taking the boys to swim in the canal that afternoon, and for Anna."

She knew exactly how Alex felt about José Marquez and Frank because that's how she felt about Mama, in spite of Mrs. DeFries's assurances that Martha had done all she could. And about falling asleep when Carrie was dying and when Anna disappeared.

Papa was saying, "Surely you know the one he feels most responsible for is Anna. Thinking he nearly caused her death laid him low, with Anna's disappearance coming so soon after Carrie died. Now that he can't see Anna…I don't think I'm wrong when I say he's relieved to enlist, to get away from home, and it's not a private matter. Everyone knows you blame him. It breaks my heart it's like this between the two of you…"

So she'd deeply wounded both Alex and Papa. What did he mean by "everyone knows"? Certainly the whole family, and Fran, but how many in the gymnasium tonight knew about the rupture in the McLennan clan? Probably enough to make her sound like a hypocrite for defending her Japanese neighbors, folks resembling the enemy, while blaming Alex, the darling of Greenwood, for Anna's disappearance.

"Papa, I'm sorry. I'm so sorry."

War

"I'm glad he prepared me," Martha informed Art when she entered the living room.

"Fer what?"

He turned off the radio.

"How badly folks behave when they're scared, but Papa couldn't prepare me for how fast it's all moving."

"How's that?"

"The mayor had a telegram from the governor's office describing in detail how everything's to be organized, just one day after the attack."

"Now I wish I'd a been there."

"Nothing was decided. The meeting simply informed everyone. There'll be another in a couple days to get organized, who's on what committee and all. In general, though, I think folks left reassured, even though the preparations assume an attack here. Yesterday the world fell apart, and today people heard how they can hold it together. I'm not one to say how effective the plans are, but they give ways to cooperate and keep busy."

"Martha, ya might be encouraged, but I'm not, from what I'm hearin' on the radio. War's officially declared on Japan, an' they're attackin' the Philippine Islands."

She sank onto the sofa; he left the easy chair and joined her.

"Dr. McFarland thought that would happen," she said. "I'm sure Muriel's affected, but all of it is so far away. The Philippine Islands and her. I'm at a greater loss to imagine what she might be going through now than I was this summer. Tell me more."

"Other than sayin' our boys an' the Filipino troops're fightin' back, they don't give details."

"What must this uncertainty be doing to Edith and Claude Giffard? They'll be sick with worry about Muriel. Edith's nervous as it is. I must go by and see her."

"Ya keep sayin' that but ya don't go. Why? Ya barely even speak ta 'em at church."

"I feel awkward around Edith. She's…I don't know. She and I are quite different. And Claude's so quiet. How Muriel could be part of that family, I've never figured out. Muriel and I hardly needed to talk to understand one another. But now that she's on the other side of the world and her life is so different from mine, I no longer know the person I'm writing…"

"That's kinda how I feel 'bout my ma, an' she's only in Kansas."

Martha thought Art was making a light-hearted attempt to lift her spirits, but when she looked at him, the sadness in his expression said otherwise. They each had drifted far from the childhoods represented by Muriel and his mama, and the attack called attention to the distance by drawing a distinct line between past and present.

But those parts of their lives were irretrievable, so she asked, "Did you talk to Hank about the truck? Did you talk to Alex?"

"Yep, an' yep. Alex don't have ideas 'bout a truck but said he'd listen 'round, which tells me he ain't interested in sellin' an' that he don't know nothin' 'bout Max. He's sure lost his spunk. Hank called back an' wants twenty-five dollars more'n I'm willin' ta spend. I told 'im I'd stop by in the mornin' an' we'll talk. It'll be a process a negotiatin' ta somewhere in the middle a the difference 'tween us, but you an' I're so lucky ta find a decent truck the first day a lookin' that I'm not gonna let a couple a dollars spoil the deal, 'specially now war's declared."

Martha rested her head on Art's shoulder. "There's something I haven't told you about the meeting."

When she finished describing the chanting, how her question to Burleigh ended it, and her father's cautionary words, Art sat straight up on the sofa and faced her.

"Arne DeFries should've stopped 'em. He was responsible fer keepin' order. Martha, ya got to think 'fore ya act. I hope we hear 'bout plenty others in that gym who felt the way ya did an' that folks won't hold it against ya, against the family. Ya might even a made it worse fer the Japanese."

"Why do you say that?"

"Those folks, the ones who started the chant, don't listen ta reason. An' whoever whispered that Burleigh was referrin' ta Japanese like Miyoshi is angry an' afraid enough he'll use more extreme means ta protect 'imself than just reportin' somethin' out a the ordinary ta Burleigh. What I'm sayin' is ya might a stoked a fire, not put it out. Miyoshi knows how scared folks are, an' how mean they can be. Why else would he make the effort ta 'pologize fer the attack, even ta us who know 'im?"

As an afterthought, Art added, "There must be quiet ways ta help Miyoshi, an' the others."

"But Art, unless more clear-headed folks speak up, the hatred will grow. You have to pull it out before it takes hold."

"We been on a roller coaster a feelins this past month, with Carrie dyin' an' Anna lost. I'm not myself half the time, an' I don't mind sayin' so. One breakfast at the Sage isn't gonna cure me. I'm not sayin' what ya did tonight was wrong, but now everyone's shocked out a their usual selves like we've been. Lots a folks might act strange. I'm askin' ya ta be extra careful."

Art's confession of weakness captured Martha's attention more than his, and Papa's, words of caution had. She scooted back under his arm.

"I need your reminder that when someone breaks a leg they don't enter a race until it's mended. My damaged heart isn't healed, either, and I shouldn't pretend it is by going full steam ahead. I'll be more cautious."

She felt Art's arm tighten around her and knew her sentiments reassured him, a good time to introduce another disturbing discovery of the evening.

"You said Alex has lost his spunk. I might be to blame. I've hurt him deeply. Papa doesn't think he's even ready to speak to me. I'll feel awful if we don't straighten it out before he goes, but I don't know what to do."

Art drew air into his chest. An inaudible sigh of relief that she was ready to talk to Alex? An admission he, too, was at a loss? They whispered her name together. "Elena."

"Yes," Martha said. "She might have a suggestion for how to approach Alex. She gave the right advice about his truck, but I hesitate to draw her into further into our family affairs."

After a long silence, she asked, "Shall we put up a Christmas tree this year? It was so strange to drive under the colorful lights on Main Street after the meeting. Christmas, the birth of the Prince of Peace, and December 1941, treachery and death."

December 1941

Lily Himuru

The second of Art's work boots dropped on the porch floor, and he called out, "I smelled stew all the way from the barn."

"You couldn't have, not after shoveling manure!" Martha countered from the kitchen.

Anna skipped to the door, but backed away from him and said, "Papa, you stink."

"Let me pull off these overalls. Truth be told, I'm not quite finished. Who wants ta come out after dinner an' help?"

Anna and Martha crinkled their noses. "You have any other jobs we can assist with?"

Art leaned against the doorframe. "Yep, ya can drive back ta town with me as soon as I finish cleanin' the barn an' get our new truck. Hank an' I agreed on a price. Just gotta stop by the bank fer the money."

"Want to stay in town for supper with Josie and Earl?" Martha asked. "Josie invited us to listen to Roosevelt's talk tonight about the war. If we have time after we buy the truck, we can do a little Christmas shopping beforehand."

"This is so topsy-turvy," Art answered. "Like ya said last night. Buyin' a new truck, Christmas, an' the president talkin' ta us 'bout

261

war. All jumbled up. I'd like ta go ta the next defense meetin' tomorrow with Robert, if ya don't mind."

"Not at all. You can better represent a calm Lundgren family, ready to fight for freedom."

Art pumped the handle to wash his hands in the porch basin. Martha and Anna set the table and served the stew and fresh cornbread. Art didn't come right in, and when Martha looked out the window she saw him in the lane in his slippers with Mr. Miyoshi and Lily Himuru.

Martha walked to the back door and yelled, "Lily, we haven't seen you for so long! Mr. Miyoshi, Lily, please come in. We're about to eat dinner, and there's plenty to go around."

They entered the kitchen, and Anna ran to hug Lily.

Lily held up a hand to stop her. "Anna, I'm so glad to see you, but I've been very sick. I think I'm well now, but let's not take a chance you'll catch it. Here, I'm blowing you a kiss rather than sharing influenza."

Anna held out her hands, and Martha noted with relief that Lily pantomimed the blow. So many were coming down with flu this year.

Anna giggled and caught the "kiss." Lily was Anna's favorite Sunday school teacher, but she left for college in September. Lily made even simple things lots of fun.

"Mrs. Lundgren, Mr. Lundgren," she said, "I was so sad to hear about Carrie. I'm sorry I wasn't here for her funeral."

The solicitous remark caught Martha unprepared, and she glanced at Art. The same expression passed over his face that she suspected was visible on hers. They should have anticipated Lily's kindness, but neither could speak.

When she had control of herself, Martha said, "Thank you, Lily. Anna, please take Mr. Miyoshi's hat and coat. Mr. Miyoshi, I'm sure you'll stay so we can catch up with Lily."

She was expecting him to protest they couldn't, but he readily handed over the hat and slid off the coat.

"I already invited 'em," Art said, taking Lily's things. "They've come ta talk somethin' over, an' when they realized we were sittin' down ta eat, they said they'd stay. I think the smell a the stew convinced 'em."

Anna took Mr. Miyoshi's things and laid them on her bed next to Lily's. She ran back and expectantly held up her arms to Mr. Miyoshi, who lifted her and held her close until she squirmed to be put down.

"There's been too little affection this week, hasn't there?" said Martha, and she briefly rested her hand on his shoulder; this time he didn't flinch.

After Art said grace, Lily launched into the purpose of their visit. "My brother Ken called this morning from Fort Collins. He's been working on a project with one of his professors, and they finished yesterday. His usual ride left Saturday, though, for Christmas vacation. Ken was taking the bus, as I did from Denver on Sunday right after church, before, before…the news was widely spread, so I didn't have any problems. Or perhaps I was left alone because I'm a Japanese girl…"

Martha put down her spoon, fearing what was to come next.

"However, at the bus station Ken wasn't allowed to buy a ticket. He went to the train station, and they also refused. He has no way to get home. We're afraid that if Mom and Dad drive up for him, they'll be stopped, a white woman and a Japanese man…"

The probable outcome didn't need explanation.

"But we don't think Mom should go alone, either. The numbers and length of convoys on the roads are staggering. Dad and I definitely can't travel without the threat of being detained. We're hearing that people of Japanese ancestry aren't allowed more than a short distance from their homes. We don't know what to do, but we're anxious to have my brother home. I came to ask Mr. Miyoshi's advice, and Mom and Dad are talking to the Lamberts."

Of course Lucy Himuru would go to Elsie. What with their friendship and the Lamberts' position against war, she'd be sympathetic to Ken's predicament.

If the Lamberts couldn't assist, certainly Martha and Art would. This was one of those quiet ways to help that Art wondered about last night. A nod from him across the table confirmed they were in agreement.

Even if the authorities detained Art for a reason neither could anticipate, surely he could come up with a plausible explanation for being on the roads. Then again, if his effort became widely known around Greenwood, it might confirm the Lundgrens were Japanese sympathizers. However, the family's reputation would surely neutralize criticism over time. More worrisome, Art and Ken could be attacked on the return trip by hoodlums with the same hateful attitude she saw last night. But what were the chances of that?

Save for Anna, no one had touched the stew.

"Well," Art said, "it just so happens I'm goin' ta town an' pickin' up a truck that's in excellent condition. I was lookin' fer a way ta give it a test drive. Max Lambert's truck. He left it with Hank. I suppose he's enlisted."

Art bit his lip, having abandoned his attempt to lighten the mood between his first sentence and his last.

Lily stared at him. "You're buying Max's truck? Then he must be gone, but I'm certain he wouldn't enlist. He's a more determined pacifist than Mr. Lambert. But why would he leave now?"

Each of them silently considered possible answers to Lily's questions. The mantle clock in the living room struck the half hour and stirred Mr. Miyoshi to speak.

"Perhaps we will know when your mother returns from her visit to the Lamberts. But I am certain of one thing. Max's sudden departure must be difficult for them, and we should not add to their burden by asking them to bring Ken home."

"Then it's settled," Art said. "I'll go fer Ken an' ask Alex ta come along. He'll wanna be part a this on account a his friendship with Ken. He an' Hugh Ufford are loadin' some a Robert's scrap iron this afternoon. I don't think he'll object ta bein' pulled away. Two white men with one Japanese man in a truck won't likely be bothered, maybe stopped, but not bothered, if we tell 'em he's our hired hand. We'll pick 'im up at his boardin' house. Alex knows where that is. He's visited there."

Mr. Miyoshi protested, "We did not come to ask you to make the drive. We came for suggestions. We know from Lucy's report of the meeting last night that people are very angry at us. We want your honest opinion."

"Martha's described ta me what happened at the defense meetin'. It ain't safe fer any a ya ta be on the roads. Miyoshi, I think ya already understood the danger Monday mornin', er ya wouldn't a come ta us an' apologized fer the attack."

Mr. Miyoshi bowed his head. "I apologized because I am ashamed of the treachery of Japan, not because I am afraid. I am ashamed to be Japanese. I want to change my face so I do not look Japanese. So I can be Japanese like the Lamberts are German but are seen as Americans."

Taken aback by Mr. Miyoshi's bitterness, Martha looked at her folded hands on her lap and Art cleared his throat.

Lily said, "But you were the biggest promoter of the Japanese school. You…"

"I built the school when I thought it was important for American-born children to know the language and customs of their parents. But now…"

Martha chose the awkward pause to give her interpretation of what happened at the meeting, mostly to deflect attention from Mr. Miyoshi because his bitterness upset her. His ancestry was such a proud part of him; he was rash to talk of discarding it. If he tore out his beautiful garden, destroyed his bathhouse and threw away the Japanese objects in his home, what of himself would he have left?

She finished by saying, "I wanted to give my version of Burleigh's presentation and the despicable chants because I'm ashamed of the behavior I saw on Monday night and for the way Ken's being treated. Mr. Miyoshi, you might want to disassociate yourself from the Japanese, but I'm not proud to be white today. I'm afraid it will get worse. Art's is a good plan. The risk to him and Alex is minimal, if they're together."

She wanted to believe what she said about the risk, and no one took issue with her. She picked up her spoon, only to notice her stew was completely cold.

"Please, hand me your bowls so I can stir dinner back in the pot and serve it warm. Everyone needs to eat. It's going to be a long day."

Max's Truck

By the time they got the money out of the bank and handled all their business with Hank, it was past three o'clock. Martha telephoned the Himurus from Josie's to let them know Art and Alex were setting out.

"I'm relieved you called," Lily said. "My father's in town looking for you."

Out Josie's dining room window, Martha could see Art and Alex climbing into Max's Truck.

"Lily, wait. Josie, run, catch Art."

Josie complied, and Martha idly noticed Josie had regained her speed and grace from before her pregnancy. Martha's schoolgirl feelings of envy and pride in her big sister crept back, from when Josie won all the medals in the girls' track events and played on the basketball team.

"Go on, Lily."

"Ken called to say that when he went back to the boarding house, it was locked. He remembered the landlady planned to drive to Nebraska to be with her sister for Christmas but didn't know she was just waiting for him to leave."

Martha could see Art and Alex coming up the porch steps. She was as anxious for them to get going as they were and urged Lily to finish.

"We described to Ken what happened at the defense meeting and why Mr. Lundgren's coming for him. It'll be hours until Mr. Lundgren gets there, and Ken can't hang around with his suitcase and not call attention to himself. He'll search for somewhere safe to wait. Please tell Mr. Lundgren to call us collect when he arrives so we can direct him to Ken."

Martha relayed the message to Art.

"Imagine if ya hadn't talked ta 'er before we drove off. Then where'd we be?"

"I'd expect you to call from Fort Collins when he wasn't at the boarding house, and we'd figure it out."

Martha didn't feel as confident as she sounded. She qualified her answer. "But this is a warning something might go wrong. Here we have a young Japanese student wandering around town carrying a suitcase. Well, half Japanese, but no one will make that distinction. The sooner you pick him up and get back safely, the better. Don't worry about Anna and me because I'll stay at Josie's. I don't want to be at home by myself for the next twelve hours."

He quickly kissed her forehead and said, "Let's hope this works."

A Nice Friend

By four, Robbie still hadn't woken from his nap. Martha decided to go shopping without Josie. She had the ten dollars Art gave her for family gifts and hoped the additional ten that he withdrew from the bank for the trip to Fort Collins would be sufficient.

"Go ahead," Josie said. "I'm hesitant to take Robbie out this late, anyway. It's getting cold, and I don't want him to catch the flu. I'll have supper ready. Remember, Earl likes to eat at six, particularly since Roosevelt's on the radio tonight."

At six precisely, no doubt. The rhythms of Josie's life were so different from hers. Farm meals were served whenever folks got in from the fields and chores. And Martha was tempted to remind Josie cold weather didn't cause the flu. Scientists said it was something smaller than bacteria, something they called a "virus," but she wasn't in the habit of contradicting her older sister.

Martha and Anna bundled up and walked the several blocks downtown. Their first stop was the "Give-a-Doll" window at the newspaper office. Still fifteen days until Christmas Eve and the display was already half full. Anna could only see the dolls at the bottom, and Martha picked her up to inspect them all.

"Look at the one in the green coat, Mama! And the one with the red bonnet!"

Anna took Martha's face in her mittened hands and turned it toward each doll.

Within minutes she had drawn attention to many of them, enamored with one, then another. Determining Anna's favorite wouldn't be easy.

"Who are the dolls for, Mama?"

"They're for little girls whose mamas and papas don't have enough money to buy them one for Christmas."

"Why don't the little girls ask Santa Claus, and why are the dolls in the window?"

Indeed, why not just ask Santa?

"We don't know whether Santa will be delayed this year by the war, so parents are helping him."

Now she'd given Anna something to worry about. Was Santa clever enough to evade the fighting? But perhaps the poorly thought-through answer was sufficient, and realistic. Even someone as young as Anna should know this wasn't a normal Christmas.

"Dolls are in the window so folks contributing them can see which ones are already there and can buy the kind they want."

Martha started to ask Anna which she liked best, but Anna pursued the explanation's logic. "Are we going to buy a doll for a little girl and put it in the window for folks to see?"

Martha had stopped for Anna's benefit; it hadn't occurred to her to donate a doll, which Martha took as another example that her vistas, which had narrowed a year ago with the difficult pregnancy, were still bound by her own concerns. How long before she engaged the wider world?

"I hadn't thought about it, honey," Martha confessed. "I was just enjoying the dolls. What would you like to do?"

"Let's buy one different from all the others," Anna answered, excited by the prospect.

Martha caught Anna's spirit, and the errand that loomed as a chore without Art and Josie transformed into an adventure in generosity.

"We'll see what we can find," Martha replied, with liveliness not equal to Anna's, but sufficient.

Santa Claus hadn't gotten the help Martha expected from the doll window; maybe Gambles would oblige. They moved down the sidewalk with other shoppers, some grimly determined to celebrate in spite of war, others looking a bit sheepish that they enjoyed the evening.

Mother and daughter entered the gaily decorated store with a handful of jovial women. The contrast between the warm interior and the crisp weather outside prompted Anna to shed coat, scarf, and mittens at once, even as she looked critically at the fifteen or so dolls on display.

"It makes a difference if we're choosing a doll for a girl your age or a younger child, don't you think?"

"Yes, Mama," Anna answered impatiently, as though Martha had asked a simple-minded question.

Anna scanned the selection again and offered her judgment. "There aren't many baby dolls in the newspaper office window. I like this one in the yellow blanket, for a little girl. Most of these are for big girls like me, who can button and unbutton. Not the one in the red dress with the black trim. She's making a sassy face."

That was helpful. Martha was drawn to it because of the gorgeous dress and hadn't even noticed the doll's expression. "And for big girls, which ones in particular?"

"The one on the end because she looks like she would be a nice friend, and the one in the middle because she's so happy. A poor girl might be sad, and a happy doll would help her laugh."

"So of the three, the baby doll and the two others, which should we buy for the window?"

Martha hoped Anna wouldn't choose the "nice friend" to give away. She wanted it for Anna, given how friends were so in the forefront of Anna's thoughts the past several weeks, friends for her and friends for Tip. Or the "happy doll." Perhaps Anna's selection of that one indicated she suffered her own bouts of sadness, now that Carrie was gone.

"The baby doll with the yellow blanket, like Carrie's, for the window," Anna said. "It's soft and cuddly, and there aren't enough baby dolls there for little girls."

How had Art put it at Thanksgiving? That some things laid him low? Anna's casual reference to Carrie's blanket had that effect. Martha cleared her throat to test whether she had voice to reply.

Anna anxiously inquired, "Mama, are you getting the flu?"

"No, no. That's a very good choice. You have excellent reasons for that one. Will you look at the baby toys for something Robbie might like?"

While Anna ran off to find the baby toys, Martha wasted no time grabbing the "nice friend" and baby doll off the shelf. She asked Irene, the clerk, to hold the "friend" behind the counter and took the baby doll that Irene wrapped in tissue paper.

It was barely in her hand when Anna ran up holding a red rubber ball.

"I found it! Robbie's Christmas present! We can play ball!"

Robbie might reach for the ball but was scarcely able to hold it, much less approximate a game of catch. Still, rubber balls would soon be in short supply, if they could be found at all.

"Anna, you're right. That's a perfect gift for a baby boy."

She paid for the ball and handed Anna the package.

"We have to hide it so Robbie won't find it," Anna said. "So he'll be surprised."

Irene and Martha burst out laughing, both picturing a four-month-old in search of gifts. Anna ducked behind Martha's dress in embarrassment.

Irene came from behind the counter and knelt by Anna, a surprisingly graceful maneuver for such a large woman.

"Honey, that's just my happy laugh, picturin' how surprised Robbie'll be. Give me a big Christmas hug, sweetie."

Anna didn't withdraw from Irene; rather, she threw her arms around the substantial shoulders and laughed with her, sounds Martha wished she could bottle for the uncertain months ahead.

"Where's Art?" Irene asked. "Usually you do your Christmas shopping together. He's one of the few men I know who not only help their wives but seem to enjoy it."

"Yes, a shame he's missing out," Martha said to buy time while she thought of an answer. An outright lie wouldn't do because Anna had been party to the conversations about Ken.

"He's out for a drive with Alex. We bought a new truck today, and I suppose even Christmas shopping can't compete with it!"

"Oh, that's good news, not only that you found a truck in running order but that he's with Alex. Your family is such an example for Greenwood that I hate you've been having differences over…"

Irene paused and nodded toward Anna. As was Irene's routine, she watched Martha carefully to measure the reaction.

Against her will, Martha frowned. If Irene knew about her and Alex, everyone did. Irene was a well of information, or misinformation, depending on whether it was your story she told or someone else's. Rarely were subjects of the stories able to track the numerous links in the chain of reporters who, usually inadvertently, served as Irene's sources.

In this case, Irene's version was inaccurate. The whole family wasn't at odds, just Martha and Alex. And perhaps Papa. According to him, the falling-out broke his heart, but Josie hadn't spoken of it, nor had Louise.

Problem was, if the accused corrected Irene, he wasn't believable because obviously he was trying to cast himself in a more favorable light. But if nothing was said, Irene amplified her own version of events.

"Yes," Martha answered, as offhandedly as she could manage. "The Christmas spirit has a way of healing wounds."

Better to keep Irene's attention on the overly exaggerated family feud than reveal the real objective of Art and Alex's "drive." Martha couldn't imagine the convoluted twists and turns Irene would invent to dramatize Ken's rescue.

They stepped into the cold air, and Martha wiped the beads of sweat from her forehead.

"Mama, it's cold. Why are you sweating?"

Another partial truth was in order. "I didn't take off my coat the way you did. It was warm in there."

Martha quickly moved to the next order of business. "When we put the baby doll in the newspaper office window, I want to ask Mr. Hallet if he knows how I can get *Berlin Diary* for Uncle Earl."

Anna stopped. "Uncle Earl's a teacher, Mama. It's a lot of work to have a dairy farm. Have you asked if he wants one?"

Martha's spontaneous chuckle came out more like a cackle and startled Anna.

"It's all right, honey. Just as Irene said, grown-ups like to laugh at Christmas. You're correct. I can't imagine Uncle Earl as a dairy farmer, either. He'd never be cleaning out manure the way Papa was this morning, would he? Uncle Earl's much too particular to be a dairy farmer."

She knew for a fact Earl had yet to change Robbie's diaper.

"Honey, *Berlin Diary*, not dairy, is the name of a book, and Uncle Earl does like books, wouldn't you agree? But we have to keep it secret, as we're doing with Robbie's ball."

"Uncle Earl always carries books. I like books, too, Mama. But I don't have many, and some of the pages in my *Little Black Sambo* are torn. May I have another book?"

"We usually get books for you from the library so the stories are fresh. But I'll mention to the family you're old enough for more books, and maybe somebody will buy you one for Christmas."

Anna clasped her hands in delight.

December 1941

Franklin Delano Roosevelt

Anna twirled around Josie's living room in her pajamas. "Isn't it fun spending the night at Robbie's?"

Her contentment mirrored Martha's. Their shopping adventure, although a short segment of an otherwise trying day, allowed Martha to immerse herself in the pleasure of Anna's company, a welcome break from thoughts of war.

"Where are your nightgown and toothbrush, Mama?"

Martha lifted Anna and twirled with her. "I didn't bring them. We'll go home when your papa returns with Ken and Uncle Alex, but they'll be late so it's like spending the night."

Earl looked up from his newspaper and smiled. "Guess I've lost claim to my own house. It's Robbie's place now."

Martha opened her mouth to reciprocate his friendly comment, but he added, "Too bad Art will miss Roosevelt. And you should have planned on staying all night. They might not be back until dawn. You haven't taken into account the increased numbers of army convoys clogging the roads."

Martha was going to protest that they had taken those factors into account, but Earl turned back to his newspaper.

As if on second thought, he lowered it. "I can't understand why Art agreed to this. He needn't have, just as you didn't need to speak last night at the defense meeting. Both circumstances called for more measured responses."

He evidently agreed Burleigh's incendiary remarks and Ken's situation required action, just something less. Was Earl concerned that his in-laws would adversely affect his political aspirations, or did his comments arise from his contrary nature? Whatever the case, it wasn't worth the mental expenditure of effort to decide.

Martha got as far as formulating what she thought would be, as he advocated, a "measured response" to his objections, but he didn't allow for any response at all because, again, he buried his face in the newspaper.

Earl spoke more respectfully to Art and Papa. In fact, the two sons-in-law frequently carried on lengthy, cordial conversations. And sometimes Earl was deferential toward Papa, in spite of their conflicting politics.

Stymied, Martha said, "I'll read Anna her nighttime story. Let's sit at the table, honey."

Anything to escape Earl's arrogance and not cause friction between her sister and husband. He bounced between tolerable and imperious most unpredictably.

When Josie extended the invitation earlier that morning, Martha had eagerly anticipated the evening. The two couples rarely spent time together, but now the foursome was a threesome, and Earl's criticisms increased her apprehension. Clearly, Art had to help retrieve Ken, but Ken might be picked up by the town's equivalent of Burleigh or attacked by hate-mongers. Also, Art was driving an untested vehicle hundreds of miles through the night to an undisclosed location.

Earl turned on the radio. Martha reacted spontaneously. "The sound is so clear on your new radio! Our old Philco is all static."

Earl nodded, and his apparent smugness forced her to concede his point about measured responses. Less enthusiasm about the radio's sound quality would have dampened his self-satisfaction. Not that Martha resented Earl's new radio, or Josie's electric stove, for that matter. Earl's continual exercise of his superiority simply got on her nerves.

Martha forgot Earl the moment Roosevelt spoke. The president said that an hour into the Pearl Harbor attack the Japanese envoy delivered a diplomatic message to the secretary of state implying Japan still sought cooperation in the Pacific — the treachery!

Roosevelt traced how Japan repeated the pattern of Hitler and Mussolini, gangsters who sneak up in the dark and strike without warning — deceptive, dishonorable, perpetrators of dastardly crimes. Martha readily drew a comparison with Maher, after he received food from the Olmstead family and snuck back under the cover of dust, wind, and night to abduct their daughter.

Mr. Miyoshi was undoubtedly listening to Roosevelt and feeling even more ashamed of Japan and his ancestry. If Earl understood Mr. Miyoshi's unbearable position of being dumped into the same category as the "gangster," Imperial Japan, Earl would know Art's trip was, indeed, a measured response. He wasn't rescuing dozens of Japanese, only one young man who was being treated like a criminal, forbidden free movement that only last week wasn't questioned.

The president's news of the fighting was all bad. The Philippine Islands, attacked. Wake, Guam, and Midway probably lost, and the destruction at Pearl Harbor so enormous as to threaten the United States' ability to hold firm in the Pacific.

Clearly Muriel was in danger in Manila, with little hope of rescue anytime soon. What Martha told Art last night about the distance she felt from Muriel, sincerely felt in the moment, wasn't true now. Muriel was so close in Martha's mind she could see the tiny mole just to the side of Muriel's right nostril and smell the powder she liberally applied with a large, cream-colored puff at the back of her neck. Muriel, a woman of habit, probably had that very same powder in her boudoir at this moment.

The void opened around her, and Martha felt herself sliding. Unprepared, she was inclined to flee the room, but she gripped the arms of the dining room chair in which she was seated, the one Josie pulled in front of the radio for her.

She concentrated on the president's words. As a reminder, he said that in the eighteen months since the fall of France, the United States had been preparing with the manufacture of a steady stream of tanks and planes.

Thank goodness for the industrial preparations that upset folks like Al Ivarson.

But, Roosevelt said, much more was needed. The list was daunting, and he cast giving all one has to fight for the existence of the nation as a privilege, not a sacrifice. Just as it is a privilege for any man, old or young, to be in the army or navy, it is a privilege for each industrialist or wage earner, the farmer or shopkeeper, the trainman or doctor, to work longer and harder at the task for which he is best fitted.

That surely discredited Earl's "measured response" theory. There was nothing measured about the all-out fight Roosevelt urged.

She had several months' momentum of working at what she was fitted to do — nursing. Art and she did what they were fitted for in other ways, too — the additional chickens, defense stamps and scrap iron, the copious amounts of fruit and vegetables she canned last summer.

Of course, none of it was equivalent to Alex's enlistment, or the danger Muriel faced in the Philippine Islands, or Llewellyn Thompson's trials, regardless of whether he evacuated to Kuibyshev or remained at the embassy in Moscow.

Martha would work longer and harder, as the president suggested. She would start by volunteering for the medical committee to help Dr. McFarland in his single-handed effort to take on what should be the responsibilities of a fully functioning Health Unit — if he would welcome her assistance. How foolhardy for Al Ivarson, Hank Philson, and Fred Warner to dissolve the Unit, now that it was needed for defense! Surely other opportunities would arise, and she would volunteer for them, too, which would satisfy Papa's concern that she be seen working for patriotic causes.

Roosevelt concluded by saying that the nation must resort to force for the purpose of building toward ultimate good, not simply to destroy immediate evil. The objective was to win the war and to win the peace that followed.

What lofty goals! Reflective of an immeasurably broader perspective than the vindictiveness of the rabble-rousers at the defense meeting whose only goal was revenge against the Japanese.

But did his words convey sufficient moral purpose to change the hearts of folks like the Lamberts? Or would they continue to hold to their Quaker belief that resorting to force to fight evil was just as evil as the aggression of the perpetrator? But if, as Roosevelt reasoned, defeat of the enemy wasn't the goal of the war, rather, if the goal was to build toward an ultimate good, how could they object? Elsie hadn't hesitated to meet evil with moral force for good that day at the market when Burleigh so wrongly confined the boy in the closet.

Martha was sure the Lamberts would be pleased when they learned from Lucy Himuru that Max's Truck was the vehicle that rescued Ken from his de facto imprisonment in Fort Collins. But it was odd no one knew why Max's Truck was available for sale. In the excitement following the attack, she and Art assumed Max had enlisted. But now she agreed with Lily. The army was so counter to his beliefs that enlistment couldn't be the reason for his sudden departure. And it was sudden or he would have made known that he wanted to sell and not done business with Hank. It was common knowledge that Hank watched out only for himself.

But Roosevelt's stirring appeal overtook Martha's thoughts. What noble aspirations! How could those opposed to war object any longer? As Roosevelt himself said, it was always an illusion the United States could isolate itself from the rest of humanity.

Earl turned off the radio and growled, "Despicable — a reasonable armament was called for the last several years, but now he uses a tragedy of this enormity to justify a complete transformation of our industrial economy. There'll be no stopping him."

Martha was stunned by Earl's vehemence and his misrepresentation of Roosevelt. Surely Josie would correct him, but she calmly put down her knitting and said, "Martha, let's put the kiddies to bed, shall we?"

The incongruity of Josie's words with the intensity of Roosevelt's speech, Earl's anger, and Martha's own mental state rendered her mute. Martha nodded a dumb assent and followed Josie to the bedroom.

When they reached their destination, Josie whispered, "Thanks for not contradicting Earl. I thought the speech marvelous, as I'm sure you did. Ever since I've known Earl, he's been so riled up at Roosevelt that even though we're at war he might not come around. Sometimes, when I'm upset by his outbursts, I have to talk to Papa to straighten out my thoughts."

Martha would rather be at the Home Place discussing the speech with Papa, too. Perhaps Fran was there, and her company was so much more enjoyable than Earl's. Then again, there was the problem with Alex…

But Martha wouldn't dream of going to Papa behind Art's back, and she was sorry Josie had gone behind Earl's. Probably that's how Papa reached his conclusion about Earl's political aspirations, by reading between the lines of what Josie reported, but Papa should encourage Josie to work things out herself.

"Earl especially admires Senator Burton Wheeler," Josie said, "less on account of them both being from Montana than for Wheeler insisting for this last while that the country do nothing to bring us closer to war, such as assisting England, not with lend-lease, not with anything. Even though Wheeler's a Democrat, Earl wanted to name Robbie 'Burton Earl Bates'!"

The prospect of that outcome moved Martha to speak. "I wonder how Papa would have reacted to that! And Burt Bates isn't a particularly attractive name. How do you stand it?"

"What? The differences in our political views?"

The "it" Martha referred to was Earl's highhanded attitude, but Martha didn't correct Josie. She suspected Josie's conversations with Papa weren't so much for political clarity as for confirmation of her intelligence and maturity. Surely living with the condescending Earl wore a woman down. Such a shame that Josie and Eddie Mattson parted ways after high school.

"When it comes to discussing politics," Josie explained, "I've learned to find something Earl and I are likely to agree on so we can have conversations instead of fights. Actually, that was Papa's suggestion."

Martha, surprised Josie hadn't identified that particular tactic of Papa's herself, asked, "Josie, are you advising me to talk with Earl about Roosevelt's speech? How on earth will I know where we'll be likely to agree?"

"I'm not advising one thing or another. I'm just saying, if you want to talk to him, that approach works. When we go out, follow my lead."

If Josie had implemented a strategy to deal with her husband, perhaps she, former track star and basketball player, hadn't lost as much backbone as Martha thought.

The conversation never took place. When the sisters emerged from the bedroom, Earl was correcting school papers that he spread all over the dining table.

He looked up briefly. "I have to finish these. Christmas vacation coming up."

A master at the art of diversion.

He continued, "I do agree with Roosevelt on several points. We have to be vigilant about rumors, particularly ones that claim complete disaster. They're most likely perpetrated by saboteurs on account of their demoralizing power. And we shouldn't expect much information about battles, ships, troop movements, and the like, which would compromise our positions. I'm glad he explained that. Also, his phrase, 'the ethics of patriotism,' about how newspapers and radio stations should restrain themselves, is well chosen."

Earl turned back to his work; Martha and Josie's nods of agreement went unseen.

Josie asked him, "Want some hot cocoa?"

He shook his head. Not so much as a "no, thank you."

Martha put her arm around Josie's waist, and they went through the swinging door to the kitchen.

Martha giggled, "Earl did our work for us. You've schooled him well on finding points of agreement."

Still, Martha was disturbed that her sister involved Papa in her marital discord, and that Papa participated.

Claudia Giffard

Martha expected they would discuss Roosevelt's talk, but Josie asked for help with a project. For the next half hour the two experimented with making miniature popcorn Christmas trees decorated with cranberries for the AAUW Christmas luncheon.

In exasperation, Martha scooted back from the table. Struggling with the trees was completely at odds with Roosevelt's call for increased effort. At least Art was contributing, although rather bizarrely, in his rescue of a half-Japanese boy from misguided patriots.

"I'm making another cup of hot cocoa," she said. "Look at my lumps of popcorn; yours actually resemble trees. Who comes up with these projects?"

"These are Bess Arnold's idea, and aren't that difficult, probably because she's a teacher in the lower grades and knows students get frustrated if something doesn't work immediately. AAUW ladies have the same short fuse."

"Want more cocoa?"

Martha measured the powder and sugar. Her interest was more to enjoy the ease of not scorching milk over the well-regulated heat of the electric burner than drinking the beverage.

"No, thanks." Josie continued the superficial chatter. "The hardest favors I've made were the sombrero nut cups. Edith Giffard's idea. She's so artistic, but what can you expect from someone who weaves her own blanket from local wool?"

"What?"

From popcorn trees to sombrero nut cups and weaving wool blankets? How much more absurd was the evening to become? Edith's daughter, Muriel, was likely being shot at as they spoke!

"Edith belongs to the Extension Club, and some had the idea to weave blankets from their own wool, so last spring Edith asked Freda Ivarson to sell her some. Freda mentioned to me she didn't see the point. You know how practical Freda is. She asked Edith why she just didn't buy a blanket at JC Penney's if she needed one, but Edith persisted. Freda said if Edith was fool enough to waste time like that, she'd just give her the wool."

Martha broke in with, "Josie, under usual circumstances, I'd be interested in this conversation, well, somewhat interested, but we're at war! This is silliness. Popcorn trees? Sombrero nut cups? Blanket weaving?"

When Josie looked up, Martha saw her tears.

"Martha, I'm barely hanging on. How many thousands of tanks and planes will we need to meet the demands of modern warfare, as Roosevelt phrased it? I can't conceive of all the killing. Look at us after losing Carrie. After almost losing Anna. Multiply the loss suffered by mothers and aunts into the thousands. No, the millions! How will the world bear all the grief? The enormity of it! At least I can solve the problem of popcorn trees."

"Oh Josie, Josie."

Josie rarely lost her composure. Martha wrapped her arms around her sister's heaving shoulders. Her only indication of distress had been her invitation to leave the room before Martha could contradict Earl about Roosevelt's speech. And perhaps her mention of the conversations with Papa to straighten out her thoughts. Josie's activities in the women's clubs must betray a deep need for companionship that Earl didn't provide.

"Martha, I don't know what I would have done without you tonight."

"You'd have made popcorn trees for the AAUW Christmas luncheon to calm yourself," Martha assured her, "as you're doing."

Just as I went Christmas shopping with my daughter, she almost said aloud.

"Josie, you're right. We'll lose our minds if we only think about war. And it strikes me I'm cruel to be so critical of Edith. Maybe the blanket weaving indicates she's been worried about Muriel for some time. Muriel always said her mother had her head in the clouds, and that was difficult for Muriel. You remember how embarrassed she was to bring friends to her home."

"Embarrassed" was hardly a sufficient description of Muriel's discomfort around her parents. Perhaps Martha avoided visiting the Giffards because to befriend Muriel's mother was to be disloyal to Muriel. Edith was a disaster. Scatterbrained, undisciplined, unpredictable. By the time Muriel was a sophomore in high school, she did the cooking, or the family wouldn't have eaten regular meals.

Martha also had a great deal of sympathy for Muriel's little brother, Maurice, because his twin sister and playmate, Claudia, died when he was seven.

Claudia's death. Rheumatic fever. Edith wouldn't have had the skills to oversee her seven-year-old daughter during the long months of recovery. Of course. Another grieving mother.

And judging by how Edith lavished attention on Muriel and Maurice, she loved her children desperately. Unfortunately, her excessive affection was another source of discomfort for Muriel, and their father was hardly around. Only when Martha learned the meaning of "taciturn" did she have a way of understanding Claude Giffard, and Papa seemed to respect him when they were commissioners together. Still, Claude's penchant for avoiding his family, especially his wife, was inexcusable. That Louise managed to work well with him at the lumberyard was a puzzle.

"I've been slow to understand Edith's artistic temperament," Martha said, "and she's probably doing what comforts her. In spite of her flighty manner and terrible housekeeping, I must visit. With the fighting in the Philippine Islands, she'll be worried sick about Muriel."

"Surely Muriel's safe enough," said Josie. "The Japanese wouldn't attack the hospital, would they? Isn't Muriel's somewhat protected, located as it is on a naval base? And it's not that women are actually in the thick of battle."

"I don't know. I just don't know."

But Josie's observations reassured her, somewhat.

They cleaned up the Christmas tree project and returned to the living room, passing quietly by the dining room table where Earl was engrossed with his papers. Josie sat in her armchair and knitted; Martha slipped off her shoes and picked up a *Saturday Evening Post* from the top of the magazine pile. She curled up on the sofa and flipped through half the publication before realizing she hadn't read a word. Now that Roosevelt's speech was over, the evening became an interminable wait for news from Art.

The jangle of the phone on the wall by the kitchen door startled her awake.

After Earl said "hello," he didn't speak further into the receiver. Instead, he called through the arch separating the dining area from the living room.

"Collect for you, Martha."

Martha hurried over and he whispered, "You're fortunate he was able to get a call through, what with the heavy volume on account of war."

But Art did get through. No need to raise the specter of failure.

"Yes, I accept the call," she answered the operator.

Art reported quickly. They'd reached Fort Collins a half hour ago; they'd located Ken at St. Andrew's church after confirming with the Himurus where he'd be; they'd stopped at an all-night diner for hamburgers; Ken, who hadn't eaten since breakfast, waited for his meal in the truck with his head down; and they were heading home. Ken planned to travel hunched over in the middle of the seat, making it appear that only two white men were in the truck. Art didn't know how long the return would take, what with all the convoys. Would she please telephone the Himurus?

"You sound so tired," she said. "Should you stop somewhere for the night? You could stay with Eddie and Bertha Mattson in Colorado Springs."

Yes, he was very tired, but no, they all wanted to get home. He and Alex were sharing the driving. The truck was comfortable. And she was to leave Earl money for the collect call because he didn't want Earl to feel any obligation about the effort to get Ken home.

Although cordial, the conversations she observed between sons-in-law must have enough substance for Art to have an idea about where Earl would stand on money matters. For her part, Martha wasn't about to expose herself to more criticism by presuming Earl would cover the cost of the call.

"I've already thought to leave money," Martha said. "Please be careful."

Mama's Quilt

Martha slept on the sofa, covered by the red-and-white quilt Josie inherited from Mama. A soft knock woke her. She leapt up and saw Alex's face through the pane of glass, illuminated by the porch light. Odd that Alex came to the door, not Art, given the rift between sister and brother.

"Where's Art? What time is it?"

"He's in the truck. We gotta get 'im home. He's real sick. It's around four."

"What's wrong?"

"Don't know. Says he's got the chills, an' he aches all over."

"You take Ken in Max's Truck. I'm not comfortable with it yet. I'll drive Art home."

Martha didn't take Anna out of Robbie's tiny bedroom for fear of disturbing him, left a note of explanation for Josie and some change for the call on the kitchen table, and grabbed her coat.

Art stumbled out the door of the vehicle and was too wobbly to walk to the Old Truck unassisted; Ken supported him on one side and Alex on the other. Martha walked ahead of them on the sidewalk.

"Sis, ya can't get him inta the house by yourself. We'll follow ya. Then I'll take Ken ta his place."

The chill of the old Chevrolet was such a contrast to the cozy cab where Art had spent the last thirteen hours that he started shivering and complaining of the cold before Martha reached the end of the block. She made a U-turn, Alex and Ken following, pulled up in front of Josie's, ran inside, and grabbed Mama's quilt. On her way back to the truck she noticed lights in Walter and Addie Moulton's living room next door. So much for keeping Ken's rescue under wraps.

She tucked the quilt around Art. His teeth chattered, and he rested his head back. Whatever the diagnosis, Alex was right — Art was very sick.

Addie Lambert Moulton

The fever didn't break for two days. Art required Martha's constant attention, and they didn't want to expose Anna, so she stayed in town with Josie.

Friday afternoon, Martha telephoned Anna for their daily conversation.

Anna concluded, "Mama, Mama, don't hang up the telephone! Auntie Josie has to talk to you. Mama? Are you still there?"

"Yes, honey. I understand. I won't hang up."

"Mama, she's coming. Don't hang up."

"Anna, I'm not hanging up, but don't you hang up, either. Both receivers have to stay off the hook."

Anna had a habit of slamming the receiver down as soon as she was finished speaking regardless if someone was waiting a turn, and it was so difficult to get back on the line these days.

A breathless Josie said, "I asked Elena to change her plans. She was to leave at noon, but I need her to stay. Robbie's been fussy all morning, so I haven't finished preparations for the meal Earl and I are hosting tonight for several of the teachers. Let me catch my breath."

Josie certainly sounded harried, and if the day were as hectic as she claimed, Martha had no doubt Elena would agree to Josie's request out of the goodness of her heart.

"I asked her before I remembered she was to help her mother prepare for the Christmas program at the Spanish church. She's been talking about it all week."

"Josie, should I make other arrangements for Anna?"

"No, no! Anna's a delight and keeps Robbie entertained. I just wanted you to know Alex stopped by and went on at great length about how we take advantage of Elena, and wouldn't it be easier if he could take Anna and Robbie for several hours."

It would be hard to determine whether the overly dramatic Alex was rubbing in Martha's unreasonable prohibition about him being with Anna or sincerely protecting Elena's interests.

"Josie, I want to get this thing between Alex and me settled, but Papa doesn't think he's ready to talk. If the opportunity arises, could you reinforce my willingness, in subtle or not so subtle ways?"

"Oh, Martha, I'm glad to hear it and will do all I can. One more thing. Addie Moulton stopped by, as if I needed an interruption, and quizzed me about Max's Truck being in front of our house so early Wednesday morning. I decided it best to tell the truth. Who knows what tales she'd dream up, otherwise? I don't think she'd heard Max had gone. Isn't that odd, that she wouldn't know the whereabouts of her own brother? She was quite upset."

"Not so odd. She isn't in close contact with her family. I have to run. The Himurus just drove in. Lucy and Ken have been doing our chores the past few days."

They had insisted on helping, convinced the all-night drive made Art sick. No amount of explaining persuaded them he would have come down with the flu, regardless.

December 1941

Family

"Hi, Grandpa. Stay in the lines, Mama. You're almost done with your red parts."

He glanced at the sheet of paper lying on the kitchen table. "Red and black? Striking colors, but I can't make out the picture."

"It's just a squiggly design. Didn't I color my black parts beautifully?"

He sat next to Anna, picked up a green crayon, and pretended to place his mark. There proceeded a tug of war that ended in laughter.

"Pumpkin, here's your crayon. I wouldn't draw on your picture. I'm here to talk to your mama."

He turned to his daughter, and the humor disappeared. "Martha, it's Fran. I think she has what Art does. Wasn't at church this morning. Went by her place this afternoon and left her in bed just now, covered with every blanket at her disposal. This is sure a mess."

"Oh, Papa, I'm sorry. It's a bad influenza this year."

"That's what I hear. I can't stay with her. Wouldn't look right. She has plenty of friends, but none would help the way you do. Will you tend her? I've already dropped her school papers off with Earl. He teaches both English and history classes and will finish some of the grading. I'll give the rest to the other English teacher. Most of

Fran's students are sick, so they won't care when she returns their assignments."

"Of course I'll help. It couldn't come at a worse time for her."

Or for me, Martha almost said aloud. A string of difficult nights with a restless Art, and she had yet to do any Christmas baking, although she could take along her pile of mending and some of the ironing.

Of course folks would think it improper for him to nurse her, but given the amount of time they spent together, they were already closer than most married folks. Illness was another argument for marriage, what with Louise living in town and Alex enlisting.

"Yes," said Papa. "She's put so much into the school program, and she'll miss the Christmas parties. She's already decorated her place for the AAUW meeting Saturday. Looks real nice. Such a shame."

Both were silent, knowing how much Fran enjoyed the social events she would have to forego.

"Needless to say," he said, "I'll stay with Art and Anna."

Martha grinned. "Oh? And of what help will that be?"

"Alex and I know how to keep a home, thank you. I'll sleep on your sofa, just as I slept on ours those final weeks your mother…"

Martha filled the pause quickly to rescue him from the awkward comparison of the two women's illnesses. "I know all you do at the house. But Alex'll be called soon. Wouldn't you prefer being with him right now?"

"I'd prefer Fran wasn't sick. It's not like I won't be seeing him. I'm sure he'll come here for meals, if you approve, that is. I'd also prefer for Louise to drop in more often."

Approval was another opportunity to demonstrate her willingness to make up with Alex, and maybe Josie had communicated to him that she was ready to talk. Alex had been such an integral part of her daily routines that she never realized how much she accomplished without Anna underfoot.

She agreed about wanting to see Louise more frequently. Her absence meant Martha ran by several times a week to do a proper job of straightening the kitchen and dusting, unbeknownst to Papa. As loudly as Papa protested how he and Alex did housework, things had a way of unraveling with their lick-and-a-promise method. Both twins were absent from her life, and everything was out of kilter.

Martha went to the bedroom and described Fran's condition to a much improved but easily tired Art.

"Ya have ta help Fran. I couldn't a taken care a myself this past week."

"I should leave right now, from the way Papa describes her condition. He'll stay here with you and Anna, and Alex will drop in from time to time, I'm sure."

Art said, "Do what's necessary," and turned on his side.

She pulled her overnight case from under the bed, but even the noise of her packing didn't keep Art awake.

The more she thought about Louise's scarcity, the more irritated she became. Louise had no right to absent herself from family responsibilities, even if she had moved into town and was undoubtedly working hard at the lumberyard, given the holiday hours. Possibly Louise was also busy with her music at various Christmas dances and all the farewell galas for so many boys leaving for the service.

On Martha's way out, Papa said, "You didn't react when I suggested Alex might come over for meals. Have you smoothed things over?"

Martha gripped the doorknob and kept her eyes on her hand. She barely recognized herself in the hysterical woman of that terrifying evening Anna wandered off. Unbidden, Earl's "measured response" advice repeated itself. Instead of lashing out at Alex, she should have tamped down the fear and grief that clouded her admiration of his energy, his vocal talents, his affection for his nieces and nephew, and his eagerness to be of help, demonstrated most recently by going to Fort Collins for Ken.

"We haven't talked yet. Papa, I understood how badly I hurt him when you pointed out how responsible he feels for Anna's disappearance, even more than for José and Frank. Tell him I've invited him to come by, if he wants."

This signal of her willingness to make amends didn't place any obligation on Alex. She hadn't yet solicited suggestions from Elena about how to approach him, but maybe the accumulation of small steps would overcome the breach.

"I don't know what else to do, Papa. How would you handle this, given he still doesn't seem ready to talk and I probably don't have much time before he goes?"

"I'm not sure, but I'm pleased you're trying. I'll keep my ears open." He gave her the kind of bear hug he hadn't in a long time.

Anna slid off her chair and ran around the table to join in. Papa swooped her up.

"Mama, are you going to nurse Auntie Fran?"

"Yes, I am. Grandpa and Uncle Alex will help you take care of Papa while I'm gone."

Martha was the one to come up with "Auntie Fran" for how Anna should address her. Everyone agreed "Miss Reeve" was too formal. When she and Papa married, Anna could easily drop the "Auntie" for "Grandma," even though Fran in no way resembled a typical grandma.

Martha drove the Old Truck down the lane toward the county road, preoccupied with imagining what life would be like for Papa with Alex in the service. A heavy workload, and, worse, loneliness. Papa and Fran should be making wedding plans.

Alex's departure surely would be like that of other boys. They were summoned, their names appeared in the paper, and in short order they were at the train station ready for the ride to Denver and their physical. If they passed, they could be sent that night to training camp. No reason Alex wouldn't pass. He was both healthy and literate. She hoped he wouldn't leave before the first of the year, though.

He hadn't expressed himself about Carrie since the funeral, but her death and Anna's lonely sojourn in the cold fields surely affected him as deeply as they had Josie, which Martha only understood when Josie compared the two events with her dread about millions of boys dying on account of war, after Roosevelt's speech. And Louise was discovered sobbing behind the hearse after Carrie's funeral, the one who everyone recognized as the most adept at soothing Carrie.

Martha's regret over failing to appreciate the depth of her family's grief about Carrie nearly overwhelmed her. Just look at Uncle Malcolm's snowflake, and he never even met Carrie!

The hostility between Alex and her had the effect of, as Papa reported, breaking his heart. It bothered Josie. She said as much when she agreed to drop hints to Alex that Martha was ready to talk. The talk behind closed doors was surely about her lack of discretion, her loss of emotional control, her self-centeredness. Even Irene at Gambles knew about it.

But she wasn't so self-absorbed that she would send her brother off to war without trying to restore their bond. She almost pulled into the lane at the Home Place, determined to make amends with him right then. Surely he would see how sincerely sorry she was to have hurt him, but the windows were dark. Sunday evening. Alex was at church with his friends.

Martha had no idea what Louise knew about Alex's feelings, other than the fact that Louise witnessed Martha's outburst. Martha and Louise only passed at choir practice and church.

Where was Louise spending her time? Did she have a beau? If Fran started feeling better in the next several days, Martha would visit Louise at Giffard's Lumberyard and invite her for coffee and a sandwich at the Sage. What a nice Christmas surprise!

And that would give her a chance to talk to Claude Giffard about Muriel without having to visit Edith. At least the lumberyard was orderly. With the house, one couldn't predict the chaos. But that was her self-centeredness taking over again. She must visit Edith, undoubtedly in worse shape than ever, threatened as she was by the loss of Muriel.

Profession

Distracted by her planning, Martha arrived across the street from the Hayes home in what seemed only minutes. Fran stood in the doorway of her apartment wrapped in a burgundy robe. Given the cold night and Papa's description of her condition, her front porch was the last place she should be. Martha prepared to jump out of the truck, but Fran lifted her hand, apparently waving to someone.

The someone was a man folding his tall, bony frame into the passenger side of an automobile parked in front of the house. Silhouetted by the hall light behind her, Fran blew him a kiss. Martha was certain he was the one Fran slapped at the Fourth of July dance. The vehicle started, and Fran disappeared behind the door.

Martha sat paralyzed with her hands on the steering wheel of the still-running pickup. The automobile with the man inside pulled away. The lights in Fran's apartment went dark.

What transpired to change the unambiguous summer slap into a winter kiss? Her feelings for Fran did a summersault from affection and admiration to revulsion. She felt sick. She opened the door and leaned out over the running board. The nausea passed. She was inclined to drive away, but what would she tell Papa? That she left because Fran blew kisses to another man? A more measured response was in order.

Martha turned off the motor and collected herself by resorting to a mental checklist, as she would with any patient.

For one thing, Fran probably wasn't feigning illness to remove Papa from the scene that evening. His description of Fran's condition was too similar to Art's when he came down with the flu. Fran might not even have expected the man's visit, given she was in her robe. Then, again, the robe signaled a certain level of intimacy…

But what had the two resolved that would lead to a tender farewell taking great effort, given Fran's probable weakness?

She wouldn't leave Fran tonight because her training required her to give succor regardless of the morals of the patient. In the past, she'd treated drunks and thieves, though not any murderers, at least, not that she was aware of, and she would care for Fran, despite Fran's infidelity, because Fran was sick.

She let herself in the door, overnight case in one hand, medical bag in the other. She'd return for the basket of mending and ironing.

She found Fran collapsed on the floor of her bedroom, still in the satin burgundy robe. Martha ran out on the porch and rang the Hayes's doorbell. Mrs. Hayes answered. She was a delicate woman, but to Martha's surprise, she agreed to assist. They struggled to get Fran into bed.

The first twelve hours were more difficult than with Art, perhaps due to Fran's collapse after standing at the door in the cold. Fran's tossing and groaning didn't allow Martha any rest, and Fran threw off the cold compresses as soon as Martha laid them on. Martha alternated between pleading and forcibly holding them in place.

By morning, Fran's fever was so high and Martha so exhausted she called Dr. McFarland. He came right over but saw no need to move Fran to the hospital. Her symptoms were similar to those of too many others he'd visited in the past week.

Martha telephoned Papa to report.

"Martha, I can't see her."

"No need. I understand you're busy with work at both places. Besides, she's sleeping less fretfully, and you wouldn't want to wake her."

Left unsaid was that she could catnap when Fran rested, which would be more difficult with Papa around.

"No, it's not because I'm busy. It's because I can't bear to see her so ill. I went through too much with your mother…"

"Papa, Fran's not sick the way Mama was. Fran has the flu, nothing like Mama's Bright's disease. Most folks recover from the worst part in less than a week, as Art has."

Papa didn't come back with the rejoinder uppermost in Martha's mind: Carrie hadn't recovered.

While Martha offered him assurance, her thinking went in another direction entirely. She was horrified to realize she hoped Fran wouldn't survive. Her death would solve so many problems.

It would be an unspeakably hard, but honorable, grief for Papa. However, if he learned Fran was unfaithful, or if he lost Fran to another man, Martha couldn't anticipate his reaction. He suffered a broken heart because two of his children had an argument; Fran's treachery was immeasurably worse.

Dr. McFarland came again late in the afternoon.

Fran grabbed his hand and cried out, "Jake, I'm sorry. So sorry. I didn't know. Please forgive me. Please, please forgive me."

"Yes, yes. It's all right, child. It's all right," he said, absently.

Fran strained to lift her head off the pillow and protested, "No, you don't understand. All these years, the sadness, the loneliness. I'm so sorry, so sorry…"

He laid the cold compress Martha handed him on Fran's forehead, but Fran kept murmuring, "Jake, Jake."

"I wonder who this Jake fellow is," he mumbled.

Even though the comment didn't require a response, Martha said, "Perhaps it's a dream."

But Martha knew the answer. Dr. McFarland's build was similar enough to the man's she had now seen in Fran's company twice that probably Fran thought "Jake" sat by her.

The regret in Fran's voice was striking. Whatever happened between her and "Jake" caused significant damage. If Fran were capable of hurting one man so deeply, what awaited Papa? Or, if reunion was finally taking place between Fran and "Jake," where did that leave Papa, a man who, only that day, explicitly compared his alarm about Fran's illness to his anguish over his wife's death?

Papa, with his unsuspecting vulnerability, was like the ships sitting in Pearl Harbor. She had to warn him, but of what she didn't know. She must learn more about "Jake" and what prompted Fran's ardent apology.

Dr. McFarland's voice startled her. "Martha, you have another hard night ahead. I'm sending her to the hospital."

No, in Fran's weakened state, she might disclose more details.

"Let me call my sister," Martha said.

"She has a little one. We don't want to expose her to this."

"I'm thinking of my other sister, Louise, who works at Giffard's. She's not married, so exposure of another family isn't in the picture. I'll give her a call."

Louise didn't answer. She could be anywhere, but she'd return to her rooms sooner or later to sleep before work the next day.

"Dr. McFarland, I'll reach her eventually. It'll be fine."

"Martha, you absolutely cannot stay alone for another night. You've been taking care of your ill husband for the past week. And now this. If I knew more women qualified to assist, I'd telephone someone."

She wasn't prepared for his stern response. Martha thought for several moments.

"Lily, Lily Himuru. I'll try her if I don't reach my sister. Lily's already had the flu, and she would come."

Martha gave Lily's name only to forestall Dr. McFarland. Although she preferred Lily's company to Louise's, she resolved to go to great lengths to avoid calling Lily to prevent her involvement in an enterprise that might reveal sensitive information concerning the McLennan family.

"That's a short list. However, I'll trust that if neither is available, you'll find someone. You understand my concern, don't you? I have an obligation to protect your health."

His demeanor changed and his rosy smile appeared. "I need you back at work. Greenwood can't afford to have one of its two nurses ill, with this flu epidemic. I can't call on staff members at the VA hospital. They have their hands full enough as it is."

His smile vanished. "They're preparing for patients to be transferred in from hospitals on the West Coast to make room for wounded men."

This was the first Martha heard of it. Perhaps the news wasn't public yet, and Dr. McFarland was taking her into his confidence. It made sense that mental patients in the veterans' hospitals would be moved away from the coast to make room. Another instance of how quickly everything could change.

Martha searched his face to verify his sincerity about her importance to him, to Greenwood. She thought of herself as only a part-time assistant, certainly not indispensable as Mrs. Claffey had been for Doc. But Dr. McFarland's insistence she guard her health increased her confidence. Moreover, he spoke to her as one professional to another, unlike Doc's patronizing manner.

If Art agreed, Dr. McFarland might welcome her offer to serve on the medical committee announced at the defense meeting. The decision to return to nursing had been the correct one.

Immediately, she was devastated by the wicked hope for Fran's death. She compromised herself professionally, and conniving to extract more information about "Jake" made her lapse worse. She disgraced herself by putting her own interests above the needs of her patient and disregarded her own health in the process.

Deep lines of exhaustion radiated from the dark circles under Dr. McFarland's eyes. She rested her hand on his arm.

"Doctor, please don't worry. I'll have someone with me tonight. And you need rest, too."

Louise McLennan

She planned to give Louise until eight o'clock before she tried Lily. At seven fifty, Louise answered.

"Sis, don't you remember? Stores stay open until eight thirty for shoppers now that Christmas is less than two weeks away. But it was slow tonight so Mr. Giffard sent me home early. Besides, his wife came to help, although she's not of much assistance. She's a wreck, worrying about Muriel, not that he's in any better shape."

Martha winced, pricked by her guilt at not visiting Edith, but she heard Fran groaning. Rather than sympathizing about the Giffard's troubles, Martha explained Fran's condition and Dr. McFarland's concerns.

To Martha's surprise, Louise answered unequivocally, "Certainly I'll help. I hold Fran in high regard."

But in rapid succession, Louise set out her demands. "Is her cupboard stocked? I haven't had supper yet. And I'll want plenty of coffee."

"Actually, no, it isn't. She must eat with Papa most of the time. And I finished her can of coffee this afternoon. I haven't had supper, either. Will you go by Josie's and see what she has to spare?"

When Louise arrived, Martha was ravenous. She had toast and coffee for breakfast and the sandwich Mrs. Hayes brought by for lunch. The meat loaf and potatoes Josie sent over tasted like a banquet.

After cleaning up their late supper in the tiny nook of a kitchen, the sisters examined the large table that was fully extended from the dining area through the archway into the living room. Its centerpiece of popcorn Christmas trees and the cotton fringe surrounding a faux mirror lake rested on a white linen cloth. Red taper candles in silver holders sat at both ends of the table, and the several tiny ice skaters positioned on the mirror wore colorful winter costumes. Both agreed the arrangement would captivate even the most critical club members.

Evergreen boughs laced with lights and red ribbons draped over the bay window. Louise plugged in the lights.

"Louise, should you take such liberties?"

"Why not? No one else'll be here to appreciate them."

Perhaps thirty more of the tiny trees rested on the green velvet covering the semicircular bench beneath the window. A narrow red ribbon banner emerging from the base of each tree carried a name. The calligraphy was cramped and small, but skillfully done.

Louise commented, somewhat disdainfully, "I saw Edith, um, Mrs. Giffard, working on those ribbons the other day. She was using a magnifying glass, if you can believe it. I think she made those costumes for the skaters, too. Why anyone would waste time on something like this, I have no idea."

Louise evidently had yet to land on whether to call the Giffards "Mrs." and "Mr." or by their first names, a sure sign she was maturing. The choice would be easier if Louise married. Marriage conferred overnight permission to use given names, although that liberty felt awkward at first.

Martha came to Edith's defense, in spite of agreeing with Louise. "She's an artist and probably gets a great deal of satisfaction out of creating something beautiful. I'm sure all the AAUW members will 'oh' and 'ah' over it. That would please anyone, I'd think, to have the approval of friends, and it probably takes her mind off Muriel. Maybe some people look at your music in the same way, that your time could be better spent."

Louise ignored Martha's thinly veiled criticism about her neglect of the family and asked, "So Fran was to host the AAUW Christmas party this Saturday?"

"Yes, the trees are favors Josie helped make. I tried to shape some, and they're harder than they look. Fran's also missing the Christmas program and parties she's worked on at school. She's a talented woman…"

Louise picked up one of the trees and examined the writing on the banner. "But what?"

"We shouldn't be handling the party favors, and what do you mean, 'But what?'"

Louise set the tree back in place. "You're being prissy. Sounds as if you hold Fran in high regard, too, but… So I'm asking, 'But what?'"

Martha was too tired to answer, even if she wanted to. Louise was so much work, and Martha wasn't about to disclose the recent revelation about Fran's indiscretion.

"But nothing. I need sleep."

"You really should stop by the Giffards'. They're worried sick about Muriel."

Martha snapped back, "Yes, I am, too, but when have I had a moment since the attack? Do you know about the trip to Fort Collins to pick up Ken? Do you know how sick Art's been?"

"I'm just saying…"

"You're never around or you'd know about Ken because Alex would have told you. After all, you, Ken, and Alex were all in the same class."

Martha didn't intend to sound that accusatory. She lowered the pitch of her voice and spoke slowly.

"I'll show you what to do with Fran."

"Fine, but don't assume Alex would tell me any news just because we're in the same place at the same time. The way it is with you and Josie, it's not like that between him and me."

Louise didn't seem to speak with regret. She wasn't close to Martha or Josie, either. She seemed so alone.

They agreed she would wake Martha at two o'clock, unless there was a change for the worse.

Wounded

Louise shook Martha's shoulder with a surprisingly light touch.

"Martha, I think the fever broke. Her gown's all wet from perspiration. Martha?"

"I hear you. What time is it?"

"It's three o'clock. I wanted to let you sleep, but now that there's a change, I thought you should know. If you can handle the rest of the night, I'm going home."

Typical Louise, not offering an iota more than had been asked.

"Let me check her, first."

Martha switched on the table lamp by Fran's bed.

"Oh, it's you, Martha. I thought you were here. But didn't I just see Louise, too?"

"Yes, she's helping out. We'll change these damp sheets and get you into a fresh gown, then she's going home."

Fran's eyes closed.

"Louise, heat some water on the stove. We'll give her a sponge bath when we change her gown."

"You're in Parker Hayes's home, for Pete's sake. There's running hot water. I'll get a basin ready, and a cloth."

Louise had a way of making Martha feel ridiculous. She tried to sound off-handed. "Old habits die hard. Since you won't have to wait for the water to heat, guess you'll be home that much sooner."

When they opened Fran's gown, they saw the thick scar that ran from her left armpit and across the top of her left breast.

Louise let out a low whistle and whispered, "God Almighty. Fran grew up on a farm, didn't she? Must have been some kind of accident. Surely Papa knows about this."

They started to turn her, a familiar process for Louise, who, as a twelve-year-old, helped Martha day and night with Mama's care. No wonder Louise was so good with Carrie. Louise's acerbic exterior must protect a sensitive heart.

Fran, with eyes still closed, tried to pull the covers over her body.

"We're turning you to remove these damp sheets and sponge off your back." Martha said. "You'll rest more comfortably in a dry, clean gown."

Fran had no strength to resist, and Martha couldn't tell if she was fully awake. The scar on her back ran diagonally from below the right shoulder blade to her waist.

"These were serious injuries," Martha commented.

"What do you suppose caused them? How long would it take to recover from something like this?"

"You never recover," Fran answered, quietly.

Louise and Martha looked at one another across Fran's body.

Martha was the first to regain her composure. She managed, "I'm sorry for your injuries and that we didn't know to protect your privacy."

Had Jake done this? If he approached Fran at all, it should be on hands and knees! But if he were a violent man, why hadn't he reacted forcefully when Fran slapped him? And why would Fran have apologized so fervently in her delirium to a cruel man in the person of Dr. McFarland?

"It's our secret, our secret." Fran pled. "Please don't tell anyone, not anyone."

She went limp in their arms.

Louise mouthed the words. "Papa doesn't know."

Martha agreed and was mortified she had assumed more intimacy between Papa and Fran than was evidently the case.

The extent of Fran's injuries, in addition to her abject apology to "Jake" in the person of Dr. McFarland, elicited Martha's sympathy. However, so much about Fran Reeve remained hidden. Perhaps Alex and Louise's interests weren't ever the issue; Papa used them to protect himself, or Fran. Not that he knew about Jake or the scars, specifically, but maybe he sensed Fran's history was contaminated and chose to be cautious.

The more pieces Martha assembled, the less she understood the puzzle, certainly not adequately enough to disclose anything to Papa. She was in a delicate position, in the crosshairs of competing allegiances. Which one required protection? Fran or Papa?

Louise responded to Fran's plea with, "We'll not say anything to anyone, Fran."

How uncharacteristically genuine of Louise.

Martha remained silent and busied herself by gently wiping Fran's back. She brushed softly over the scar. Neither sister spoke as they dressed her and gathered up the damp sheets.

Meanwhile, Martha tried to organize her mental disarray. She was sympathetic toward Fran for more reasons than the abject apology to "Jake" and the scars. Fran was a lovely woman; she was friendly but not overly so. Martha appreciated her reserve, which gave the impression of self-assurance and authenticity.

Fran spoke her mind, but not the way Earl did. Fran respected other viewpoints, whereas Earl argued folks down. No wonder Fran was such a popular teacher, although her physical attractiveness played a role, certainly with the high school boys.

Whatever their source, Fran's wounds had their origin in violence, a horrible accident or inflicted injuries, a supposition reinforced by Fran's statement that one never recovered from them and her plea that Martha and Louise not reveal them.

Louise interrupted Martha's interior debate. "I'm going. I'll take the sheets and launder them. You've done more than enough."

A new twist from Louise, offering more than was asked.

"Louise, I do appreciate your help. And I'm thankful you were here when we saw…what we saw. Earlier, I was desperately exhausted, and if I was snippy, I didn't mean it."

"Thanks. But I meant what I said to Fran. I'll not divulge her secret, and I hope you won't, either. I'm sure there's an explanation. She'll tell us when she's ready."

Martha gave a noncommittal shrug but inwardly agreed, as much as she didn't want to be the keeper of Fran's secrets.

"Oh, about Ken Himuru," Martha said and summarized the events.

"I don't believe this. Ken! He was our valedictorian. And a Boy Scout, for God's sake! He and Alex joined DeMolay together. No white boy could be more American. What's wrong with folks?"

Concluding that Louise wasn't aware of the antagonism being heaped on the Japanese around Greenwood, Martha briefly described Mr. Miyoshi's visit the morning after the Pearl Harbor attack and the scene at the defense meeting.

"From what I'm hearing," Martha added, "Colorado Japanese are so worried about being blamed, they wrote a statement of loyalty to Governor Carr. I read about it in the paper when Art was sick. But Louise, please don't take the Lord's name in vain."

"Martha, you insult me almost every time you speak. Usually I let it go, but stop treating me the way you do Alex, as though we're still children."

Louise might as well have slapped Martha across the face. The shock of Louise's firm voice and her criticism disarmed any protest Martha could think to make. Still, she tried.

"Louise, I…"

"I have to go if I want to catch a couple hours' sleep. Don't forget the Giffards."

The balance between them had shifted. Her younger sister had left the family nest in more than a physical sense. What little authority Martha and Josie maintained over her, they no longer had. If Louise hadn't had a similar conversation with Josie in which she exerted her independence, she would soon.

And Louise couldn't be clearer about her perspective regarding the animosity between Martha and Alex. In Louise's eyes, Martha's outburst about his carelessness with Anna disclosed flaws in Martha, not him.

December 1941

Gossip

At noon, Fran had toast and coffee in bed. Martha telephoned Art.

"Lucky ya caught me. Just grabbin' a bite a dinner."

"Tell Papa the patient's much improved. Why doesn't he eat supper here? He can pick something up from the Sage. Ruth and Alice'll know what to send."

"Does that mean yer comin' home?"

She wasn't coming home until she saw how Fran behaved around Papa, given "Jake's" recent visit and the disclosure of the scars.

"If she has a good night, I'll leave first thing in the morning, after I take a bath. Hot running water spoils a woman. Are you feeling better?"

"Still shaky. How long 'fore I get over this?"

"I'd expect several weeks. This influenza is worse than last year when Josie nursed Louise for just two days."

"I'm disappointed I didn't get ta the defense council meetin'. Ya heard Robert was appointed chairman a the education committee, I imagine. Prob'ly a good thing neither a us was there or we'd a spoiled his chances. Not only is word goin' 'round 'bout how ya spoke up at

309

the first meetin', but most folks know 'bout Alex an' me pickin' up Ken. Amazes me how fast gossip travels."

"No, I hadn't heard about Papa. I've only talked to Dr. McFarland and Louise. He didn't say anything about the meeting, and Louise doesn't keep track of Papa, or any of us, for that matter. The appointment's a well-deserved vote of confidence, but he'll be very busy with it and the draft board. Maybe he won't be so antagonistic toward Al, now that he's back in circulation. What, specifically, are folks saying about us?"

"Nothin' serious. The ones who talk ta me are generally approvin', but they're neighbors an' friends who think along the same lines I do 'bout the Japanese families 'round Greenwood. Don't know what others say."

"It's a relief that folks we know aren't against us. Addie Moulton probably started the gossip about Ken. Their light was on when you picked me up, and she asked Josie about Max's Truck. Josie thought it best to tell her the truth, or she'd make up something outlandish. Curious thing, though. She didn't know anything about Max or his truck. Give Anna a kiss for me. See you in the morning."

She wasn't much for talking on the telephone, and Josie was coming by soon for the AAUW party decorations. The luncheon meeting was moved to her house, and she was frantically cleaning and decorating, even though her spotless home needed no extra attention.

Martha gathered up the party items to put on the porch. She gingerly placed the popcorn trees in the box, cushioning them in the tissue paper Fran probably intended for wrapping presents. The tiny ice-skaters required more meticulous wrapping.

The tedious job gave her time to think about Louise's criticism. It hurt, but Martha much preferred the confident, less petulant little sister. Besides, Louise was right. Martha did treat the twins as if they were still thirteen. Getting Louise away from the Home Place was healthy, and the same could be true for Alex, if his departure for the service didn't entail so much peril.

Ernest Hemingway

Mid-afternoon Fran called for Martha, who was well into Fran's copy of *For Whom the Bell Tolls*, untouched ironing and mending in the laundry basket at her feet. Anna was right. They needed more books in the house; then, again, when would she have the time? Reluctantly, she went in to Fran, who motioned her to sit in the chair by the night table and, even in the dim light in the darkened room, noticed what she held in her hand.

"I'm glad you've had a chance to do some reading. I feel guilty for keeping you from your family. What do you think of the story?"

"Are you asking me as an English teacher or as a woman?"

"What difference would it make?"

"If you're asking as a teacher, I'd discuss an interesting passage or describe my favorite character. If you're asking as a woman, I'd tell you how upsetting the book is."

"I'm asking as a woman, then."

"The brutes that war makes of men, and, of women, although I have some admiration for the female character named Pilar. And the violence Maria suffered at the hands of her captors. If I'd read it when it was published last year, before Vera and Ida, before the Pearl Harbor attack, it would have been a compelling story but only that, a story. Reading it now… It's about people I know. Vera and Ida, but also Muriel Giffard, my friend. She's a Navy nurse in Manila. Horrible things might be happening to her as we speak, as they did to Maria. And in several months Alex will be a soldier, perhaps in the midst of battle where he'll see and do the unthinkable."

Fran's answer seemed not to be directed at Martha, rather at some point beyond the doorway. "We think calamity that vast is far from us, or that we can keep it at a distance, a story of someone else's life, in another country, which are reasons we stayed out of this war so long. But it came to us, anyway. Vera and Ida came to us, anyway."

Fran turned her face toward the wall. Martha thought Fran had fallen asleep, so she turned toward the lamp and opened the book.

"Is Robert coming to visit?" Fran finally asked, her head still turned.

"He'll probably bring us supper tonight."

"Robert thinks I'm a virgin, in more than the usual sense — a 'pure soul' of sorts. That's how I appear around him because he brings out the best, but it's not who I am."

Martha froze, not prepared for Fran's candor. In light of their discussion of Hemingway, Ida, and Vera, perhaps Fran's declaration she wasn't a virgin meant she, too, was violated. Surely not by Jake! No woman, weak from illness, would send a tender farewell kiss to such a man. Martha held her breath, not prepared to answer, not knowing what would come next, afraid to hear it, but eager, nonetheless.

Fran turned toward her, and in the lamp's light Martha saw her swollen eyes. Fran made no attempt to hide the tears.

"You and Louise know I'm not a virgin in any sense. You've seen the scars. I thought the wounds were healed. But they opened a year ago, when Vera stopped me in the drugstore."

A vivid picture of the desperate girl appealing for rescue sprang to Martha's mind.

"I didn't catch her last name, when she grabbed my arm. And I didn't recognize her; she was a small child when I last saw her. But I thought she said something about Oklahoma, or implied it. I notified Sheriff Burleigh immediately. When he reported he sent 'Vera' home, I assumed he found the girl from the drugstore. I put Oklahoma behind me, again."

Months ago, when Martha sat in the back seat of Burleigh's Buick with Ida, she desperately wanted these details, but now Martha was satisfied that whatever role Fran played in Vera and Ida's lives, she played it with integrity. Of grave importance now was the reappearance of "Jake."

But Fran continued with her foiled attempts to help Vera. "I had several girls by that name in my primary classes in Oklahoma. If I hadn't been so determined to stay away from my past, I would have been in touch with folks and known which Vera disappeared. I can't explain the letter that was supposed to inform me of Ida's visit, except I never received it. Again, if I hadn't cut all ties, notification about Ida's arrival might have reached me from several sources."

Jake must have something to do with Vera. Why else would Fran go on at length about the girls after so recently seeing him?

"As it happens, Ida's wounds are much more serious than mine."

Martha dared not interrupt for fear of stopping Fran's disclosures, but why wasn't she saying anything about Jake?

"I've been in touch with Vera. Ida's had the baby and is doing better. They're leaving for Oklahoma soon. I've wanted to visit them, but I don't see how that'll be possible before they leave."

Martha weighed whether to redirect Fran to the conversation about her Oklahoma past, hoping Jake would figure in the story, but it would be odd not to discuss the Olmstead girls.

"A girl or boy?" asked Martha.

"A girl. But they're not taking her with them."

"I don't understand."

"They're leaving her for adoption, at the suggestion of the doctors at the hospital, who think it's best if they take nothing that reminds Ida of Maher."

"What do you think? As time passes, might Ida regret giving up her child?"

"I have no idea. Probably the doctors don't, either. It's just their best guess."

Martha saw an opening to take the conversation back to Jake and the scars, and she took it.

"Fran, I don't say this to hurt you, but you have a better guess than the doctors. From your experience with your wounds, which you've tried to keep hidden, even from yourself, you know no one ever really leaves their past. Isn't giving up the baby similar to hiding one's scars? Eventually…"

Awkwardly done, but she brought the topic back to Fran's disfigurement.

"You speak of 'leaving,' Martha. I do know that when injuries are fresh, sometimes a person has to leave in order to heal. One can't anticipate what will happen years ahead; one only tries to survive the moment."

In different words, Fran expressed Art's sentiment when he talked about his father's disappearance and the speculation that the Ogawas' trek to California put distance between themselves and their grief. Fran's scars spoke of significant harm, and she herself said she never fully recovered. If Martha pressed further, she might damage Fran in ways she couldn't foresee, just as Burleigh forcing the girls to identify Maher had pushed Ida to the breaking point. Ida's incontinence in the car taught Martha that suffering could result in a sort of shell shock, as it did for soldiers.

Fran had only begun her recovery from the flu. If Martha were to pursue the subject of "Jake" in her weakened condition and cause a relapse, Martha would look heartless, particularly in Papa's eyes. Papa entrusted Fran to her, and if anything were to happen while Fran was in Martha's care, particularly if Martha were the cause… Well, she might also hurt Papa in ways she couldn't foresee. She had already hurt her brother; she couldn't have Papa turning his back on her, too.

Fran's laugh broke the somber mood. "Right now, I'd like a hot bath. I want to be presentable for Robert's visit. Do you think I can manage it?"

"No, you'll need help."

"Well, I don't have anything more to hide from you. Will you assist me?'

"Of course."

But Fran hid much more than she disclosed. Martha hoped Louise was correct and that Fran would reveal her past in her own time. If she didn't, for Papa's sake, Martha had to devise a way for her to divulge it.

Lovebirds

Just before Papa was due, Fran called from her chair in the living room. "I don't look haggard, do I? I don't want to frighten him."

"No, you don't look haggard. You look…"

Martha started to say "tired" and "weak" but that didn't capture Fran's frail beauty — pale skin, green eyes, the auburn hair, all set against the satin luster of the burgundy robe.

"You look as delicate as a rare, tropical bird."

"Oh, my. Does your family know you're a poet?"

In spite of herself, Martha laughed. "You'll have to ask them."

The doorbell rang, and Fran took a deep breath, smoothed her hair, and seemed to relax.

Immediately, though, she panicked. "I forgot my lipstick!"

Fran's students wouldn't recognize her for the lack of sophistication. She could be one of them. This Fran couldn't manage duplicity.

"Lipstick would only detract from your natural beauty tonight."

Martha chuckled as she walked to the door, but by the time she reached her destination, the thought that Fran was stringing along two beaus sobered her.

Through the windowpane she saw her father, head turned to the side, moisten his fingers with spit and run them over his untamable eyebrows. He wet his fingers again and passed them through his thick, wavy hair.

Martha couldn't resist. She opened the door and asked, "Are you ready?"

Papa frowned and answered quite seriously, "Not really. I haven't seen her for several days. Do I look presentable?"

Martha's impulse was to take him in her arms as she would Anna and warn him of the dangers ahead. Instead, she said, "You're the second most handsome man to Art in the county. You don't have a thing to worry about."

That last sentence was regrettable. She hadn't intended to be misleading.

Robert handed her the basket of food from the Sage and drifted across the floor to Fran, who slowly rose to greet him. Martha averted her eyes from their tender kiss, and she hurried into Fran's alcove-sized kitchen to warm the food. All that was lacking from the scene was a record on Fran's phonograph playing "I Only Have

Eyes for You." Martha arranged things on the small table, and the lovebirds conversed quietly, their heads almost touching.

"Please, come and eat, you two. Fran, I don't know how much longer you'll feel like staying up, and you need food to regain your strength."

Evidently they heard her because they rose in unison and glided across the living room, but neither looked her way, nor did they answer. Martha waited impatiently. She was sure she and Art were never that dreamy when they were courting, and the obvious pleasure Papa and Fran took in each other's company was all the more painful to watch with Jake and the scars hovering in the background.

Over their last cup of coffee, they talked about Christmas gifts. Papa thought Earl's plan to surprise Josie with a Corona Zephyr typewriter much too extravagant.

"Robert, overly generous gifts might be how he expresses his love. Otherwise, he's not very demonstrative. By the way, I have gifts for Vera and Ida I'll not be able to deliver before they leave the State Hospital. It's a huge favor to ask, but can you?"

Papa reached across the table and took Fran's hand. "Oh darling, I can't do what you ask. I'm so sorry."

Martha looked at him with alarm when she heard the despair in his voice.

"We've so much to do on the farms before Alex leaves," he said, "and the defense committee chairmen are meeting Saturday to work on plans for our first blackout. We have to be ready in a week. You know I would if I could."

Fran's response was nearly as dramatic. "Robert, if I had known how it would inconvenience you, I wouldn't have asked. I apologize for putting you in this position. Please, don't worry about it."

Martha broke into the overwrought scene. "Fran, ever since you mentioned that the girls are leaving, I've been thinking I'd like to say goodbye. May I take them your gifts?"

In unison, Papa and Fran cried, "Oh, would you?"

They laughed in delight at their synchronicity.

It was the last straw for Martha. She stood and announced, "I'm doing dishes. The drive's no problem, now that we have Max's Truck."

Her statement had no impact.

Martha splashed around in the dishwater, but rigorous washing brought no clarity about Fran's intent with regard to Jake and Papa. The unabashed tenderness embarrassed Martha, and not even the noise of plates clattering in the sink drove them back to the living room.

Maxine

Martha welcomed the Saturday drive to Pueblo in spite of the heavy military traffic. Her last trip was over seven months ago, when she and Art visited the Denver Home, and ten days had passed since her outing with Anna.

The weather was ideal — sunny and warm — for the tasks ahead, which included picking up gifts for others in the family who surreptitiously made known their requests for items not available in Greenwood.

Anna, primed to be awed by the decorations in the big stores, chattered non-stop.

"When Papa was sick and I stayed at Auntie Josie's, I found another friend. Her name's Harriet. I went to Harriet's house and we had a tea party, just like the tea party Auntie Josie's having for her friends today. Harriet's mama fixed us real tea and baked tiny, tiny cookies for the little tea plates. Real cookies! Because they were so tiny we could have as many as we wanted. I ate a thousand!"

Another winsome example of Anna's counting idiosyncrasies, but Martha was amazed Addie Lambert Moulton, Harriet's mother and Josie's next-door neighbor, would go to all that effort for Anna. Even though Addie finally caught and married Martha's sometimes high school beau, Walter Moulton, Addie still harbored resentment.

Walter had relentlessly pursued Martha, well after she lost interest. Walter either married Addie out of spite, the wedding coming shortly after Martha and Art announced their engagement, out of necessity, or both. Walter and Addie married at the end of May; Harriet was born mid-January. Addie always made a lot of Harriet coming early, but anyone who could count knew a big, healthy baby like Harriet was conceived well before the ceremony.

Truth be told, Martha couldn't abide Addie, from the time they met in high school when Otto Lambert and Papa first campaigned together for the office of county commissioner from their respective districts. The girls' animosity only intensified when the Lamberts moved to Eagle View.

Addie had all Elsie's forcefulness but none of her mother's heart and repudiated everything Otto and Elsie believed. She rarely visited the Lambert farm. What a shame that Harriet was denied her grandparents' influence. It was unlikely Anna and Harriet would remain friends.

Anna babbled for the next five miles, describing the children's tea party in great detail, before introducing a new topic. "And I have another friend, Elena's cousin. Her name's Maxine. Maxine's my favorite friend. Harriet always makes us play her games, but she's older, and Maxine and I don't know her rules. Once, when Maxine and I were swinging on Auntie Josie's porch, Harriet visited. She didn't want Maxine to sit by me, and she pushed Maxine off the swing. Maxine cried."

In the wake of Anna's preoccupation with friends and her subsequent disappearance with Tip, Elena had proposed that one of her little cousins, Maxine, come over from time to time to play. Martha paid closer attention, suspecting the outcome for Maxine wouldn't be good.

"What happened then, honey?"

"Elena was sitting on the step and told Harriet not to play so rough; all three of us could share the swing. Harriet ran and told her mama, and her mama came over and told Auntie Josie she didn't want any Mexican telling Harriet what to do and Harriet couldn't play with me if Maxine was there."

The outcome was worse than Martha anticipated. Certainly the insult to Maxine, only a child, was inexcusable, but to deny Elena her authority over the children? Why hadn't Josie, or Elena, reported this to her?

Before Martha formulated a comment, Anna asked, "Mama, what's a Mexican?"

Martha was pleased to hear Anna and Maxine were getting on well. She began there. "I'm happy you and Maxine are friends. Elena and Maxine are both Mexicans, which simply means that long ago their grandparents lived here when the part of Greenwood County south of the river was still the country of Mexico. Grandpa came here from the country of Canada, which is to the north. He's Canadian and American, and they're Mexican and American."

A long silence ensued while Martha waited for Anna to react. Perhaps Anna accepted the answer and was ready for another subject, but she asked, "Why can I play with Mexicans and Harriet can't?"

Why, indeed? Mama and Papa had never objected to Martha playing with the children of stoop laborers. Luis Marquez and Alex were friends before they started school. José's accidental death cemented a bond of sorts between the families, but they never invited one another into their homes for social occasions. As a youngster, she enjoyed the tortillas and beans Aneda Marquez, Elena's mother, handed out in the fields at dinner, but the adults never shared meals.

Martha couldn't imagine Art praising the cooking of the Mexican women as he did that of the Japanese wives when he, Papa, and Alex combined wheat for their husbands. Really, though, he wouldn't be eating a meal prepared by Mexican wives. In Greenwood County, Mexicans were field hands and sheepherders. White men combining for a Mexican farmer wouldn't happen.

Anna, growing impatient for her answer, repeated her question. "Mama, do you know why Harriet can't play with Mexicans?"

Honesty seemed the only possible response, so Martha said, "Not exactly, honey, because Harriet's mama and I see a lot of things differently. Let me think about it some more."

Anna let out a long sigh, took off her doll's bonnet, and started fiddling with its hair, apparently despairing of ever getting an answer. But Martha wasn't ready to drop such an important question, if for no other reason than to reassert Elena's authority.

Before she answered, she needed to sort out why, as a child, she hadn't known a prohibition against playing with Spanish children but did sense an invisible wall between families. Perhaps it was the Spanish language. Josie often said that Marguerite succeeded in school because the Marquez family stopped speaking Spanish at home when she started first grade.

Not many Spanish families spoke English, the reason for the Spanish-American PTA and the Spanish church. Martha considered the separate PTA meetings a sign the teachers went more than halfway toward passing through the wall erected by language, along with some separate classes for the youngest Spanish-speaking children.

Then again, there wasn't a Japanese PTA, and most of those parents didn't speak English, at least, not well. Teachers didn't make an effort to scale that wall. Jimmie Ichikawa was at least as smart as Marguerite, and their family spoke Japanese at home. Mr. Mitsuye was an exception because he both spoke and read English… Martha frowned.

"Mama, are you thinking too hard?"

"Yes, Anna. You've asked a very difficult question. I figured if I thought hard enough, I would find the answer, but I can't. I don't know why Harriet can't play with Maxine. When he was growing up, Uncle Alex played with Luis all the time, and they're still friends. There's no reason you shouldn't play with Maxine."

"And Elena is Uncle Alex's best friend."

No higher commendation of Elena was needed. Martha was making this too difficult. Probably Addie Moulton didn't want Harriet to play with Maxine because Addie was mean and would assert her daughter's interests over those of any perceived rival, Mexican or not.

The Administrator

They crossed every gift off the list, including Earl's *Berlin Diary* that Anna insisted on holding in her lap as though it were the most precious. With stomachs full of a delicious dinner and shared banana split, they arrived at the State Hospital. Anna surveyed the extensive and well-kept grounds and declared it to be a "lovely park."

Because of Anna, the administrator called Vera and Ida to his office. He said if Martha and Anna wandered the grounds to find the girls, they might come upon unexpected surprises. "Surprises" wasn't the best choice of words because Anna was disappointed to miss them. While they waited, the administrator advised Martha not to bring up the subject of the baby unless Ida did.

Vera and Ida had both put on weight and looked like normal, attractive girls. Vera actually smiled from time to time, and Ida spoke up almost as often as Vera. They were thoroughly pleasant company.

They were sad to hear Fran had been sick and very disappointed to miss her before they left, but they were pleased she sent gifts. They decided to wait until Christmas in Oklahoma to open them. However, they unwrapped the barrettes from Martha and Anna and allowed Anna to put them in their hair. Anna arranged them quite attractively, and the administrator produced a mirror for the girls to admire her effort.

Martha much preferred to remember them this way than as the emaciated waifs of summer. After goodbye hugs and kisses, the girls left.

"As you can imagine," the administrator said to Martha, "I've heard so much about you from Vera and Ida. They think of you as their savior. You do seem to be a capable woman. I'd like to talk over something, if you have time."

A "capable" woman? An odd comment from a man she'd just met.

"We're leaving Pueblo much later than I planned, and I'm worried about the congestion on the roads, but I can spare another minute."

Noticing Anna's fascination with the brass paperweight on his desk, he let her hold it.

"You, and Miss Reeve, might be interested to know the girls aren't leaving for Oklahoma, not just yet. The psychiatrist decided Ida isn't strong enough. We haven't told them yet. A return to

Oklahoma might be out of the question, anyway. They were going to live with the widow who gave Ida lodging, but her children are objecting. They evidently disagreed about Ida being there, even before her ill-advised trip."

That might explain why the letter never reached Fran, if Ida had given it to one of the widow's unsympathetic family members to mail.

The girls would be horribly disappointed.

"So the girls' future is still undetermined? Why haven't you informed them? They're so excited to celebrate Christmas back home."

"We'll tell them Monday that, with the declaration of war, it's difficult to arrange transportation, which is true enough. Besides, Vera's shown interest in agriculture and seems to have an aptitude for it. She can work on the hospital farm, which, as you probably know, is extensive."

"But why keep your decision from them?"

"We only reached a conclusion in the last few days, when we realized how contentious the Oklahoma home setting is. We're not sure how to broach the subject with Ida. She's been working so hard toward the objective of being well enough to leave by Christmas."

"Why aren't you enlisting Vera's help? Given the circumstances, she was surprisingly capable when I first met her."

"Yes. That's a helpful suggestion."

Martha was taken aback by the administrator's dismissive attitude and that the doctors hadn't thought of enlisting Vera's help themselves.

"You know Ida's baby will be adopted," he said.

"Yes, I heard."

"I'm worried, with the disruption of war and all, not many couples will be in a position to adopt, perhaps for the duration."

"The duration?"

"The duration of the war. I'm also aware, from Vera and Ida, they were saddened to hear from Miss Reeve that you recently lost a child."

"Yes," Martha answered, uncomfortable with the probing direction of his remarks.

"I wonder if you and your husband would consider adopting the baby."

Of course not. She wanted nothing to do with Maher's progeny and thought the administrator grossly inappropriate to insinuate the baby could replace Carrie. He seemed more concerned with disposing of it and enlisting Vera's labor for the hospital's farm than with Ida's well-being.

"She's a lovely baby, if you'd like to see her."

The paperweight unceremoniously slipped out of Anna's hands and fell to the floor with a loud thud.

"We don't have time," said Martha.

She picked up the weight and, unprepared for its heft, dropped, rather than placed, it on the desk.

"We'll be going now."

The Quandary

When they pulled into the lane hours later, Art emerged from the barn wiping his greasy hands on a rag.

"Welcome back, travelers," he said. "I'd help ya carry in the loot but my hands're too dirty. I been workin' on the Old Truck all afternoon. How was the trip? Any trouble with Max's Truck?"

"Not at all. You're right. It's very comfortable, which I appreciated given how long the drive took with all the military vehicles on the roads. The trip was a success in all ways but one."

"Oh?"

"I'll tell you later."

"Later" was after Art tucked Anna into bed.

"And why did his suggestion upset ya?"

Martha was dumbfounded he wasn't indignant, too. She explained a second time.

"Martha, Maher's child's just a baby. The only way she'd grow up ta be as evil as her father is if she's poorly raised. My father is, was, a drunk, but I'm not. I had Rev. Macgill an' the Mattsons ta guide me. In a way, I'm an orphan, an' good people took me in. The administrator's thinkin' along the same lines, ta help the baby. And he's probably right about the war an' couples not comin' forward. After he met ya an' saw yer a good woman, just like Vera an' Ida said, why wouldn't he ask ya? Yer bein' too hard on 'im."

"Are you saying you'd consider adopting that child?"

"I'm not sayin' any such thing, one way or t'other. I'm only sayin' I see why he asked the question."

She should have told him more about her impressions of the administrator, that, at the very least, he didn't seem qualified for the work. His tactless approach about the baby was no less telling than his refusal to deal with Vera and Ida about their inevitable disappointment they wouldn't be home for Christmas.

When they went to bed, Art fell asleep immediately. Martha tossed and turned. She went into the kitchen, stoked the fire in the coal stove, and warmed some milk.

The wind blew steadily against the walls and carried the coyotes' high-pitched yelps on its low moaning. At intervals, the sorrowful whistles of troop trains punctured the monotonous sounds of wind and animals.

Martha's visceral reaction against adopting Maher's baby didn't subside, but Art's observations stung her conscience. She hadn't needed to see the baby to picture its surroundings; her memories of the children in the cribs at the home in Denver awaiting adoption were still vivid. If her life's mission was rescuing the ill and mistreated, she hadn't saved Mama or Carrie, she nearly lost Anna, and she failed Ida's baby.

Was the administrator's request a test of character, an opportunity to rise above her hatred of Maher and her grief about Carrie, a test she failed? The prospect of raising this child might be a challenge Providence put before her, a chance to redeem other losses. But she couldn't. She just couldn't have Maher's offspring in her home.

Art was of no help, and Papa and Josie would react in much the same way if she conferred with them. Perhaps a talk with Rev. Behm was in order.

She would see him Monday, after working in the morning with Dr. McFarland and delivering the presents they picked up in Pueblo to their respective donors. And she would delay the visit to Edith Giffard no longer.

December 1941

Maurice Giffard

"Martha McLennan! Come in, come in! Is Muriel with you?"

Edith's greeting set Martha's head spinning. She expected a scattered Edith, but the woman had completely lost her bearings. Edith called her by her maiden name and expected Muriel to appear, a nurse hunkered down on a naval base overrun by the enemy on the other side of the world.

"Please, come in. You're letting in cold air."

An accurate enough observation.

Edith took their coats. "What a darling child. Is she yours? I thought your baby died."

Martha took Anna by the hand, unable to guess what would come next.

The living room was strewn with innumerable projects — several easels that displayed incomplete paintings; a loom with a partially woven piece whose pattern was, as yet, uncertain; bolts of material on the sofa and chair. The clutter overwhelmed Martha but charmed Anna. She ran from item to item. Edith followed, laughing and squealing with Anna. Martha couldn't calm them.

Hoping a more confined space would corral both woman and child, Martha said, "Edith, let's go to the kitchen and sit down, shall we?"

It, too, was a mess. In her hurry to clear three chairs, Edith piled all the debris on the table.

"Edith, have you eaten today?"

"Oh, I think so. Perhaps Claude brought something from the café. But maybe that's for supper. Or is it time for dinner?"

"It's past dinnertime. I'm going to check your refrigerator for food."

A bottle of milk and four eggs in a bowl.

"Martha, Claude tells me Muriel's missing. I was hoping you had seen her."

The Giffards were at Carrie's funeral a month ago, before the attack. Martha was sure of it. And Edith had seemed herself. But Martha definitely wasn't herself that day, so she might not have noticed behavior out of the ordinary.

"I haven't seen Muriel or heard from her, Edith. That's why I stopped by, to find out what you know and see how you're doing."

"I'm doing fine, but if none of us has news of Muriel, we should talk to Sheriff Burleigh."

Given Edith's peculiar conduct and the disarray of the house, the bang of the door on the back porch jolted Martha from her chair.

Edith, facing the porch, also leapt up. "It's Maurice! He hasn't been home in ever so long! What a surprise! Isn't it wonderful? You, and now Maurice!"

Martha placed her hand over her heart, as though its weight would calm the pounding. By the time she turned, she had composed herself for a proper greeting.

Maurice had graduated from high school two years ago, in Max Lambert's class. Martha hadn't kept track of Maurice other than to know he was away at college.

Claude Giffard followed Maurice into the kitchen with a basket similar to the one Papa brought from the Sage when he supplied supper at Fran's and said, "Martha, I'm both glad and sorry you're here, to see how things are."

Maurice nodded to Martha but focused on the disorder of the kitchen.

"I haven't seen you in a while, Maurice," Martha said.

He was a handsome young man, only several inches taller than she, with straight black hair and dark-blue eyes. Their perpetual melancholy dominated his expression, even when his mouth smiled.

"Yes," he said. "My job keeps me in Greeley, but with the attack, Dad thought I should be here, because we're all so worried… Please excuse me. I'm a little tired from the bus ride. It took twice as long to get home."

Dark circles under his eyes indicated he was more than a little tired.

"I've just picked him up at the station," said Claude.

Martha introduced Anna to Maurice, and he bent and shook Anna's hand, a much more composed boy than the one who fainted in the Old Truck the day Frank Ogawa died. Neither Maurice nor Alex had been protected from the hardships of life and death, nor had their older sisters, Muriel and Martha.

"Anna, Maurice works and goes to college, as Ken does. He's also home for Christmas vacation. Let's allow Mrs. Giffard time with her husband and son. Claude, may I call on you later?"

"Certainly. Let me walk you to the door."

Before Martha turned, Maurice laid his hand on her arm. "That was a swell thing Mr. Lundgren did, drivin' up to Fort Collins and givin' Ken a ride home."

Martha, taken aback that news of the rescue had reached as far as Maurice in Greeley, mumbled, "It was necessary, and the decent thing to do."

She would let Art know that, in addition to their neighbors who approved of his effort, young people in Ken's circle did, also, a circle whose radius was apparently quite long.

"I saw Max's truck parked out front. Dad said you bought it."

"We bought it the same afternoon Art drove to Fort Collins. Have you heard from Max?"

"I was about to ask what you knew."

"Nothing, only that his truck was for sale."

If Max were in contact with anyone, it would be Maurice. They were the best of friends. No wonder he seemed tired — his sister missing and his best friend disappearing.

"I'll certainly contact you if we learn something," she said.

Claude broke the solemn mood with, "Shall we go?"

On their way through the living room, Claude inclined his head and spoke softly. "I agree with Maurice. Art did the decent thing, but not many of us would have made the sacrifice. And at the defense meeting, well, you were remarkable."

Claude's praise shouldn't have come as a surprise, given how Papa admired him when they were commissioners together, and she welcomed his support of Mr. Miyoshi and the others. She mumbled an embarrassed "thank you."

Claude lowered his voice further and said, "Edith's never been strong. She went through short spells like this each time she gave birth. Of course, when Claudia died… Well, her erratic behavior lasted longer, then."

Claudia died when she and Maurice were seven. Muriel wasn't yet thirteen. Even though Martha and Muriel were acquainted with one another through church, the two weren't chums until Martha started high school in town, a year after Claudia died.

Muriel mourned her little sister's death all through their freshman year, but Martha never gave much thought to its effect on the rest of the Giffards. Even then, Muriel must have been holding the household together. No wonder she always wanted to do her schoolwork in the relative order of the lumberyard.

Claude revealed Edith as another mother crippled by grief and now facing the prospect of losing her oldest daughter, her anchor. To her credit, Edith retained a modicum of coherency.

Claude continued, "Her, uh, difficulties come at a bad time for me, with the longer Christmas hours at the lumberyard. Obviously the news about the fighting in the Philippine Islands is what, uh, unbalanced her this time, that, and the fact we've heard nothing from Muriel since, since the attacks. Now that Maurice's home, I expect she'll improve. He's a good boy. I'm not back until late in the evenings, and Edith spends all that time listening to the radio. I'm sure news of the fighting adds to her distress."

"No doubt."

"Thank you for coming."

Maurice wasn't strong enough medicine to work the cure Claude anticipated. Perhaps Edith's poor housekeeping, even in good times, set a low enough standard that Claude wasn't fully aware of the extent of his wife's confusion. As bad a cook as Edith was, she wouldn't have an empty refrigerator on the day her son came home for Christmas vacation.

Martha hadn't shown loyalty to Muriel by avoiding Edith. Rather, their friendship obliged her to help the Giffard household regain stability, if it was even possible.

Zella Behm

Martha and Anna found Rev. Behm in the sanctuary rearranging the evergreen boughs on the sills of the stained-glass windows. His efforts improved the effect, as had many of his small touches in the short time he'd been at the church.

He scurried over to greet them. "Martha! Anna! Hello!"

The windows refracted shards of light into undulating waves. The throbbing behind Martha's eyes foreshadowed more than a usual headache, but she had to talk about the adoption.

"Rev. Behm, do you have a moment?"

Zella Behm and their daughter entered the sanctuary. Lena Mae sang out, "We're ready for our Christmas cookies and tea, Daddy."

Martha reversed herself. "We can talk another time."

She turned to leave, but he rested his hand on her shoulder.

"Martha, you seem upset. Please, sit down. Zella, would you take Anna and Lena Mae into the nursery to play while Martha and I talk?"

"Certainly. Hello, Martha. It's nice to see you. We haven't had a chance to get acquainted other than a brief moment at the welcome reception."

Lena Mae already betrayed plans for an afternoon treat, but Zella didn't seem impatient. "I know the past few weeks have been difficult for your family, with the influenza, so I was especially grateful you were here yesterday to sing the Negro spiritual, "Nobody Knows the Trouble I've Seen," with Eleanor Moulton. It created the right climate for Henry's reading from the Dunbar poem in his sermon. The music and poem gave me consolation as no theology, philosophy, or political ideal have in these difficult times. When Henry read '… human wants and human needs/And human tears and human cares/ Affect me more than human prayers,' I imagined that, at the moment of the attack, even for the soldiers and sailors who didn't have time to formulate prayers, their terror and their screams opened floodgates of divine compassion that overcame the agony."

"I—I don't know what to say. Your capacity for vivid emotional expression is remarkable."

"I'm being overly dramatic, as usual. We don't even know each other, but music and poetry affect me deeply. Anna, would you like to come with Lena Mae and me?"

Martha wanted Zella to stay so she could give a proper response to the extraordinary compliment, but the feeling of compression in her forehead impaired her concentration. Anna didn't need prodding to accept an invitation to join a new playmate her own age, and the three left the sanctuary.

Rev. Behm motioned Martha to sit. "Please, tell me what brings you in."

She dispensed with small talk. "I had the most unusual request Saturday, and I don't know how to react."

She shortened Vera and Ida's story, but could tell it had considerable impact. When she finished with the administrator's request, he leaned back and was silent for what seemed several minutes. His focus was somewhere in the choir loft, and Martha looked there, too, as though it were the source of an answer. Besides, concentrating on the dark recess of the chancel relieved the pressure in her forehead.

He finally spoke. "Martha, I'd be more comfortable if you called me by my given name, Henry. You, Zella, and I are of the same generation. Would you be at ease doing that?"

Martha wasn't prepared for the question. "Perhaps. Papa called Rev. Macgill 'Mac,' the way most men in the church did, but ministers are like doctors and professors, deserving of their titles. Obviously I hold you in high regard, or I wouldn't be discussing such intimate matters."

After she spoke, Martha did consider the fact she'd called Dr. Claffey "Doc." For some reason she couldn't identify, she still addressed Dr. McFarland formally.

"Thank you for your confidence, but consider this," Rev. Behm said. "What I'm about to say comes out of respect for you and your training. When you call me Reverend and I call you Martha, the inequality seems improper, especially just now, because I want to talk to you as one professional to another."

Martha hadn't anticipated this approach. She valued herself as one with specialized training, but to have him put their conversation on a professional level was unusual. She slowly nodded.

"You said the administrator called you the girls' savior. That's a powerful title, but I suspect many more patients will think of you as their savior in the coming years. If you continue to be involved in every one of their lives, as you would be if you and Art adopt this child, as time passes you'll collect a train of folks who will make unending demands of you. You and I aren't saviors; there's only one Savior. Our human capacities are limited; God's are not."

He paused, as though expecting Martha to answer, but she didn't know what conclusion to reach.

"You can be flattered the administrator asked you," he continued, "but I don't think you should feel an obligation. Perhaps you do need to examine your motives. I, myself, don't believe the sins of the fathers are visited on following generations. The fathers' sins die with them, and their children are free to live their own lives. The baby is innocent. She doesn't carry the taint of Maher."

"That's what Art said, only more forcefully," Martha answered, but she recoiled from the thought of even holding the child. "I understand what you mean about it being impossible to maintain a connection with every patient and family. But times are different now. Under ordinary circumstances, I could assume another couple would adopt the baby, particularly if she's as attractive as the administrator says. But doesn't the war change the situation, if fewer families are in a position to adopt? Don't I have additional responsibility for her?"

"That's hard to say. Remember, adoption is a commitment for life, well beyond the duration of this war. You and Art have to decide."

The throbbing behind Martha's eyes yielded to sharp jabs of pain, and she closed them to shut out the growing brilliance of the afternoon light that diffused through the stained glass and penetrated the entire sanctuary.

"Martha, you don't look well."

Martha stood but was so dizzy she sat back down. Henry drove her home in Max's Truck. Zella and Lena Mae followed in their car with Anna.

Christmas Eve

Martha was as surprised as anyone that her fever broke the next day, given how worn out she was from the past two weeks nursing Art and Fran. The flu didn't hit her nearly as hard as it had them, but she was quite weak. The family moved their annual Christmas Eve celebration of supper and gifts at the Home Place before the midnight church service to the Lundgrens'.

Alex was leaving the day after Christmas. He requested the usual routines for the occasion. Turn off all lights except those on the tree while they sang carols and ate popcorn and fudge. As the youngest in the family, Anna distributed gifts, dressed in the child's Santa Claus costume Mama made years ago.

Anna was thrilled with her book from Robbie, her tea set from Fran, and her blue sweater from Louise. The gift that excited her most was the wind-up train from Alex and Grandpa. She set the five cars going around on their track so many times that everyone begged her to stop the noise.

"Now that we have a moment of quiet," Papa said, "I want to be sure everyone's heard about Wally Thompson."

A chorus of voices answered, "Is he all right? What's happened?"

"Earl, I know you saw it in the papers, but evidently the rest of you didn't. He stayed in Moscow when others in the diplomatic corps left with the government for the temporary capital in Kuibyshev. He headed a skeleton staff as the second secretary and has some interesting stories to tell. In any case, we all know the Reds are hailing the battle of Moscow as the greatest ever fought. That he's safe and the Russians kept the Germans out is hopeful news for a Christmas that otherwise looks very bleak."

Everyone agreed, and fragments of conversation preceded Alex's announcement that he needed to be at church early for a last-minute practice. He asked Art if he'd like to ride in together. Martha assured Art she'd be fine, and he and Anna went to the kitchen to set out carrots, cookies, and milk for the reindeer and Santa before he tucked her into bed.

Martha couldn't hide her disappointment at missing the service that meant more to her than any other: the miracle that the divine infant and virgin mother traversed safely through labor and birth; the celestial chorus proclaiming the hope of common folk in every age — peace on earth; the solace accompanying the candlelight singing of "Silent Night"; the calm, hushed departure of the congregation into the dark streets.

Josie knelt by the sofa and whispered, "I know how much the service means to you. It won't be the same for anyone in the congregation, not to hear you sing 'O Holy Night,' especially since it might be Alex's last Christmas at home for some time."

Josie shouldn't have said anything. Martha couldn't hold back the tears. They dampened the pillowcase. All she could manage was to encircle Josie's neck with her arm and kiss her on the forehead.

"You'll be up and around by New Year's," Josie said.

Of course, but it wasn't just a matter of missing the service. She hadn't mended the breach between her and Alex; Edith Giffard was falling apart; and she wasn't past her revulsion at the thought of touching Maher's daughter, much less of adopting her.

How could the gulf between her deportment and Christmas goodwill be overcome, not to mention the one between peace on earth and the worldwide state of war between nations?

Before Art and Alex left, Alex knelt by her side as Josie had. Martha struggled to push herself up and motioned him to sit by her, which he did without seeming to notice her effort was meant to equalize their relative positions.

He rushed into what sounded like a prepared speech. "Sis, I wanna say goodbye now because I don't think you'll get ta the train station."

He paused to take a breath and Martha restrained herself from reaching for his hand, which might interrupt the speech he seemed determined to deliver. "What ya said after we found Anna hurt a lot. It'll take some time ta get over it, on account a how I sometimes do barge ahead without payin' attention."

To answer immediately could be construed as not giving his admission the weight it deserved or not respecting the significance of the moment. She, too, took a breath in order to indicate she heard and was respectfully considering an appropriate response, one that, in fact, she had rehearsed many times.

"Alex, I know I hurt you, and I'm sorry. I realize I was partly responsible for Anna's disappearance. If I hadn't been in such a sound sleep, I, I…"

How could Alex understand how undone she was after Carrie's death, a young man who had yet to be a father?

"I was so distraught after Carrie died that the threat of losing Anna, too, was more than I could bear. I'd like to say I wasn't myself, when I said what I did, but then I wouldn't be taking the responsibility for hurting you that I should."

She would have gone on but Alex held up his hand. "Sis, you don't have to say more."

Prolonged tender moments weren't typical of either of them. Martha saw the twinkle in his eyes before he stood. "I didn't think big sisters ever made mistakes."

"Sing 'Silent Night' extra pretty, for me. You know how I love the midnight service. Alex, take care of yourself."

He waved as he walked away. The animosity was gone, but so was the easy familiarity she had taken for granted.

February 1942

War Time

"Ouch! Mama, you're hurting my hand."

Martha loosened her grip but hurried Anna up the steps of Josie's front porch. "I'm sorry, honey. I'm thinking about something else, and we're late. On days I work for Dr. McFarland, he starts seeing patients early. I like to be there to help him."

Martha reached out to press the doorbell, but drew her hand back quickly when Anna said, "Mama, it's my job to ring the bell, now that I'm big."

Anna's struggle with her mitten caused more delay.

"Yes, honey. I'm rushing everything, aren't I? War Time means we're all in a dither. Beulah and Ginger haven't gotten used to it either, with Papa milking an hour earlier than usual."

Anna's puzzled look would ordinarily prompt Martha to explain, again, why the war efforts included this change in the clock that caused such disruption for farmers, but she was too preoccupied to make the effort.

Josie opened the door. "Sis, you look distracted."

"Guess I'm not good at hiding my feelings."

"I hope the storm cloud isn't about to break over me!"

Josie's rejoinder had its desired effect. Martha smiled and watched Anna toss Robbie's wayward red ball into his playpen. Robbie flipped from his tummy to his back and squealed his pleasure. But Martha's pleasure was momentary.

"Josie, have you seen the sign in the barbershop window?"

She didn't wait for an answer. "It reads 'Japs shaved free. Not responsible for accidents.'"

Josie limited her response to a regretful shake of the head, so Martha continued, "It should be destroyed. Yes, people are afraid, and it's horrible, the things we hear about the Japanese soldiers, but they don't live in Greenwood. Folks like Jimmie and Mr. Miyoshi regularly pass by that sign. Jimmie's an American citizen, and Mr. Miyoshi's spent more of his life here than in Japan. His wife and child are buried here. His friends are here. His life's work is the farm."

"The sign is dreadful, Martha. As if we're fighting the war on the main streets of our towns."

"Even Mr. Churchill refuses to use the word 'Jap,' saying it's too informal. You'll not hear it pass my lips, either."

Josie sighed, and Martha wandered over to sit in the overstuffed chair, aware that, indeed, the word had just passed her lips several times. At least Anna hadn't heard because she was busy tickling Robbie through the bars of the playpen.

Martha studied the patterns made by the morning sun on the Oriental carpet; the red swirls gleamed against the green and black background. Josie's sighs might indicate sympathy or merely tolerance of Martha's stubborn protection of her Japanese friends.

The outburst drained some of Martha's anger, and she changed the subject. "Usually Elena's here by now. I wonder if something happened to her ride. Or maybe War Time's as disruptive for her family as it is for us."

"She'll be along. We need a few minutes to plan. I'm helping at Eagle View School today because Bess Arnold's ill. Esther Ivarson has all the students until I arrive, both Bess' lower-grade room and her own upper grades. I could be there several days. But I'm also helping Fran with auditions for the senior class play, so I have to rush into town, then back out to your place, which means I'll be late picking up Robbie. Martha, you'll love the play. It's so funny!"

Martha didn't listen closely to Josie's chatter. She was thinking about the sign and Elena's tardiness, and her stomach felt a bit queasy.

"It'll all work out," she said. "I'm glad you're so involved. I should be doing more."

"What do you mean?"

"The sign, for example. I should have walked in and removed it, to make the point the Japanese who see it are as patriotic as we are. Also, we're over two months into a war we're losing, and I'm only contributing at Dr. McFarland's three mornings a week and taking the minutes at the medical committee meetings. For another thing, even though I'm relieved the commissioners finally hired someone as capable as Clara Boehler to be the public health nurse, she has so much to get organized — weekly visits to all the rural schools plus the ones in town, teaching the practical nursing class at the high school, and Red Cross home nursing courses, just for starters. Surely I could help, but I'm twiddling my thumbs, waiting for her to figure out where she needs me."

"Martha, you've been far from inactive the past month, since you recovered from the flu."

The change in Josie's tone from friendly chatter to stern schoolmarm caused Anna to look in the direction of their conversation.

"I've no patience for the way you continually discount farm work," Josie lectured. "The 'Food for Freedom' campaign isn't frivolous. It's as direct a way to fight the war as going into the army. The production goals farmers must meet are just as critical as the ones for tanks and airplanes. Right now the country's only facing sugar rationing, but it could get worse. You're part of an effort to feed our soldiers, Europe and the nation. What can be loftier than that?"

"Josie, I…"

"Don't interrupt. By May you'll have three times the number of hens you did last year. And you don't have Luis Marquez and Alex to help in the fields. Surely you're preparing."

As Louise had said, it was insulting to be treated like a child by a big sister.

"Of course we're preparing, Josie. You're simply ignorant about the discussions between Papa, Art, and Mr. Miyoshi."

Josie had touched on a raw subject. Martha wasn't as confident in the preparations as she sounded. The three men talked about their labor problems at length, but they disagreed about solutions. Make do with local students on weekends and evenings after school? Bring in out-of-state hands such as Japanese aliens from the West Coast? But unknown Japanese wouldn't be received well in Greenwood, as confirmed by the sign in the barbershop window.

Evidently breakfast conversations at the Sage nearly led to blows with some men swearing they would never hire "Japs." Mexicans would fill in for departing sons and daughters. In any case, Art and the others had to make a decision before the growing season started.

"I don't mean to be critical," Josie said in a conciliatory tone, and Anna turned her attention back to Robbie. "I'm only trying to assure you that farmers are very important to the overall effort. I don't understand why you're pushing yourself harder."

Martha relaxed somewhat and said, "All of us are trying to do more, Josie. You yourself just described yours as a very busy day teaching and helping with the school play. Isn't that your way of helping with the war effort, by keeping routines in place for children and families?"

"Thanks, Sis, for saying my work has value, but when I look at you and Art, I question if Earl and I do enough. I see the sacrifice Art makes on the rationing board because it's a thankless job to be one of three people deciding who gets the tires and tubes allocated each month for Greenwood County. It doesn't help that the results of who got what are printed regularly in the paper. Every man who applies thinks his need is greater. All Art has is his reputation for fairness to carry you both through."

Josie's tone had reverted to that of bossy older sister. "Martha, don't you dare think about pulling signs out of store windows. That would undermine Art's efforts in a second. And Papa's too, with his defense education committee and draft board responsibilities, what with the names of the forty or more men the board has certified appearing in the paper every month. Papa and Art have to be calm and judicious. Families' vital interests for their men and livelihoods are at stake. You'd be inciting who knows what in an atmosphere where everyone's on edge. Men missing in the Philippines, and Muriel, too. Two brothers just down the highway killed at Pearl Harbor. And who killed them? Japanese soldiers!"

Martha bristled but argument was pointless. She took the row between them as sign of the overall distress. "Josie, I'm not going to pull signs out of windows, but, at the very least, I'll not wait for Clara to get organized before volunteering to teach one of the home nursing classes. So many housewives are wanting them that there aren't enough registered nurses in the county qualified to meet the demand, in spite of the new ones from the West Coast at Fort Lyon. They're quite overloaded."

Josie, who seemed as ready as Martha to stop arguing, said, "Yes, I want to take the course, as do most of the women I know. What drove it home for me was that you were the only family member we trusted to take care of those stricken with the flu."

Martha had felt that singular burden and appreciated Josie's comment. "We found our point of agreement, Josie, as you do with Earl. If farm families aren't kept healthy, we won't meet those production goals."

"I am sounding like Earl, aren't I? Somewhat overbearing. We're feeling the strain, I suppose. Edith Giffard put it well."

"How's that?" Martha asked, as relieved the focus of the conversation shifted as she was eager to hear news of Edith.

"At the AAUW meeting," Josie answered. "She said she was in a rather nervous state of mind."

"I'm not surprised. When I saw her before Christmas, the day I came down with the flu, I'd say her state of mind was on the point of collapse. But at the President's Birthday Ball she was doing much better. She said Clara's arrival helps considerably. Clara and Muriel grew quite close our last year of nursing school, when Art and I began spending so much time together. Clara visits Edith often, yet another burden for her."

"After Clara's visits, Edith says she has renewed hope that Muriel, too, is still alive."

Martha's eyes filled with tears. "It's very difficult, not having any news of Muriel. Imagining that she's in the thick of battle is another reason I want so desperately to do more."

Josie hurried over, knelt down and rested her hand on Martha's leg.

"Josie, look at us. At loggerheads one moment and affectionate the next."

Evidently Josie was as self-conscious about her demonstrativeness as Martha because she stood and went to the window. Martha reached for a magazine on the small round table next to Josie's chair and accidently knocked off the letters lying beside it.

"You've quite a few correspondents," Martha said and bent to retrieve the pieces of mail.

Three letters were from the Will Rogers Training Field, Oklahoma City. They were, of course, from Alex. Martha had received one letter, even though she wrote every week. Their mutual apologies on Christmas Eve eased the hurt, but she wasn't surprised he corresponded more regularly with Josie.

Feeling lightheaded, Martha steadied herself with a hand on the small table before leaning back into the chair. "You have three letters from Alex. He's written me once, a brief letter, at that, which indicates the wound I inflicted is healing but will take more time."

"You hurt him deeply and kept turning the knife every time you criticized him for being irresponsible."

In spite of Josie's violent image, Martha hadn't permanently scarred Alex in the way Fran's scars spoke of the damage done to her. However, her behavior that desperate, cold night of Anna's disappearance shed light on the motivation for the barbershop sign.

"I want to amend what I said earlier," Martha said.

"How's that?"

"About the sign. I do understand the helplessness and fear that drives folks to lash out and place all the blame with someone else, as though by doing so they've taken protective measures. Now their families will be safe. As important, they don't have to face any fault of their own."

"Perhaps, but…"

"I'm not saying it clearly, I suppose…"

Josie held up her hand for Martha to stop and pointed to the front door.

Walter Moulton

Martha turned in the chair and saw two men outside. One raised his fist to pound on the doorframe.

"It's Walter Moulton and his brother, Edgar," Josie said. "What could they possibly want?"

Both sisters walked to the front door. Josie opened it. "Walter, Edgar, please come in."

Neither man stepped forward.

"Martha Lundgren, knew you'd be here," Walter sneered. "Saw Max's Truck in front. Just as well for what we have to say. It's your brother."

"And our sister," Edgar chimed in.

"Mama's at our house with Eleanor," continued Walter.

Martha had a clear view of Maude Moulton's Ford parked behind Max's Truck.

Walter clenched his fists and continued, "Eleanor's hysterical. Went ta visit Alex. Thought they'd be engaged. He sent 'er home. No proposal. No ring. She cried all the way back on the train from Oklahoma ta Greenwood."

Edgar picked up the story. "I heard Alex say she should visit 'im in camp, that night when he left the goodbye party she threw fer 'im. I call that a proposal because no soldier asks a woman ta visit 'is camp if he don't have marriage in mind, 'specially one he was sweet on all through high school."

Martha interpreted the report about Alex's invitation as a thank you more extravagant than necessary for the elaborate farewell party Eleanor threw for him. However, it seemed Eleanor expected more in the way of thanks than he was prepared to give. More to the point, it was obvious to everyone that Eleanor pursued Alex all through high school, not the other way around, but Eleanor's brothers would never see it that way.

Before either Josie or Martha answered the accusations, a vehicle that looked like Mr. Miyoshi's old Studebaker slid to a stop behind Maude's Ford and distracted all four participants in the Eleanor conversation. The pause gave Martha time to reconsider blurting out that Eleanor was just like her big brother; Walter wouldn't take her "no" for an answer, either.

Elena jumped out of the newly arrived automobile and scampered up the sidewalk. The brothers parted, and she flew through the door.

"Mrs. Lundgren, Mrs. Bates. I am sorry I am late. My cousin Rudy's vehicle would not start. The cold weather."

The interruption gave Josie a moment to gather herself. "Elena, it's all right."

To Walter and Edgar, she spoke rapidly, "I'm sorry about Eleanor's distress. In this climate of so many boys going into the service and leaving their friends at home, some confusion is normal. Eleanor and Alex will sort it out. Please excuse us. My sister and I are late for our appointments."

Josie gripped Martha's arm, shut the door, and guided her away from it. Neither sister dared look back.

Josie asked Elena, who was standing by the playpen and had a clear view of the porch, "Have they gone?"

"They are turning to leave. Was that Mr. Moulton, Harriet's father?"

"Yes, Addie Moulton's husband, and his brother, Edgar," answered Martha.

"And Eleanor is their sister?"

Martha and Josie answered together, "Yes."

"They looked very angry."

"Dangerously angry," responded Josie.

To Martha, Josie said, "I didn't know whether to burst out laughing or slam the door in their faces. What did they hope to accomplish by scolding us, as though we had any influence over Alex and his affections?"

"As I just said, lashing out and blaming someone satisfies folks they've protected the ones they love. I hope their attack on us satisfies them; otherwise, I'm afraid we haven't heard the last of this."

Martha hadn't removed her coat, and Josie gathered hers, hat already on her head. Martha stooped to hug Anna goodbye but hesitated when she saw Elena's worried expression.

"Elena, they'll not bother you or the children. They're angry with Alex, and they think they can hurt him by attacking us. According to them, Eleanor went to visit Alex, expecting he would ask her to marry him. He didn't and sent her home. She's very upset."

It was difficult to tell if Elena believed that the Moulton brothers weren't a threat. Then again, Addie hadn't hesitated to scold Elena over the swing incident. Elena had cause to be concerned about the beehive abuzz next door. Josie could drop her and the children off at the farm on her way to Eagle View.

But Elena's expression hardened, and she answered disdainfully, "They are the hateful men Alex has told me about. The day of the Pearl Harbor, they accused Max Lambert for being a coward because he will not fight in the war. Why? What do they have to do with Max?"

From this first hint of what might have prompted Max to leave, Martha tried to piece together a meaningful sequence of events. If Walter and Edgar confronted Max on December 7, and she and Art bought his truck several days later…

"Mrs. Lundgren?"

"Mrs. Walter Moulton, Addie, is Max's sister, but her husband has no business criticizing Max."

In the two months since the attack, Elsie Lambert hadn't spoken a word about Max's departure, only to say she was glad Art bought Max's Truck.

"It is too bad Eleanor went to all the trouble of going to Alex in Oklahoma because he is coming home on furlough for Saint Valentine's Day," Elena said, "if he receives permission."

More unexpected news.

"How did you come by this information, Elena?" asked Martha.

Elena shrugged. "All of Alex's friends know it."

She joined Anna and Robbie's peek-a-boo game.

Martha raised her eyebrows at Josie, who answered, "I didn't know."

Clara Boehler

They heard more pounding at the door and saw Sheriff Burleigh's large frame silhouetted against the light of the morning sunshine.

"Oh, my," exclaimed Josie. "You don't think they've already called Burleigh with a complaint?"

"He can't have responded this quickly. Besides, what claim could the Moultons have against us?"

Josie invited him in. His body filled the small living room. If Walter and Edgar, younger members of Greenwood's pantheon of outsized football heroes, had accepted Josie's invitation to enter, their physical presence would have been overpowering. Surely the conflict with Max that Elena knew about hadn't moved beyond verbal accusations, but in the event that they returned, Josie definitely should drop off Elena and the children at the farm.

"Josie, Martha."

He touched the brim of his Stetson but didn't remove it.

"I telephoned yer house an' Art said ya was in town. Drove by Doc's office but didn't see yer truck. Martha, have ya heard today from Miss Clara Boehler?"

"No, no I haven't. Why do you ask?"

"Since she come ta Greenwood in January ta start her public health work, the two of ya continued yer friendship."

Did Burleigh monitor everyone so closely?

"She don't have family here, so I thought she might contact ya. I got a call last night from Enoch Gwynn that he hadn't seen her come back from 'er trip out south. He's good at keepin' an eye out fer Miss Boehler, on account a her rentin' the small house out back a his an' how often she's out late."

So Burleigh carried around a mental map of the county's residents, their associates, and their habits? Most folks kept track of their neighbors, but Burleigh's pride in, and the extent of, his cache of information was unsettling.

"We got two search parties lookin', but it's cold an' the snow last night down there's drifted over the roads. We can't break through ta Pinion School where she was headed yesterday."

"Yes, she was to give the children physical examinations. They've had some cases of scarlet fever again this year. The families haven't gotten into town on account of the weather."

Only last week a man was found frozen to death in the same locale in his disabled truck after missing for thirty-six hours. Clara, a public health nurse visiting a rural school, faced life-and-death circumstances as formidable as those suffered by their friend, Muriel, in the Philippine Islands.

"Well, that should a told her somethin'," Burleigh grumbled. "If they can't get inta town, what made 'er think she could get out there? I'll call Hank so as he can get another plow goin'."

With that, he stomped out the door.

"My goodness," said Josie. "What will happen next? Now we're both quite late."

Josie passed Martha on her way to the kitchen to leave by the back door. Martha reached out to stop her. "You should take Elena and the children with you. It isn't safe…"

A sharp cramp elicited a groan and Martha grabbed her abdomen.

"Are you all right?" Josie asked.

"Yes. No. I mean, give me a moment to take off my coat and sit down. Elena, please call Dr. McFarland and tell him I'll be on my way shortly."

She gingerly lowered herself into the chair.

"So many lost and missing — Anna, Muriel, and now Clara…" Martha's voice echoed in her ears.

When she regained consciousness, Josie and Elena supported her shoulders. Her head was between her knees. She should commend them for knowing what to do during her brief fainting spell, but she was too nauseated to say more than "bowl."

Elena held Martha steady, Josie ran into the kitchen, retrieved the large mixing bowl, and had it under Martha's mouth when the vomit came — bits of bacon and eggs that retained enough of their original texture and color for the hovering Anna to exclaim, "Mama, that's your breakfast!"

For Anna's sake, Martha made light of her weakness. "And I'm glad it's gone. My tummy didn't want breakfast today, did it?"

But her fear for Clara Boehler merged with the knot in her stomach and grew into a cramp so intense she cried out.

Josie spoke quickly, in a low, measured voice.

"Elena, get the children's coats. We're taking Mrs. Lundgren to Dr. McFarland."

February 1942

Recovery

When Martha opened her eyes, Art stood by the hospital bed and Clara sat in the chair behind him.

Martha mouthed more than spoke, "What happened?"

"Miscarriage. Ya lost a lot a blood. Ya need ta rest. I didn't know."

He doubled his lanky body and kissed her hair.

She whispered, "I had only begun to suspect."

The next time she opened her eyes, Clara stood by the bed and Art slept in the chair.

Her voice more audible, she said, "I thought I'd lost both you and Muriel."

Clara squeezed her clear-blue eyes tightly shut. She opened them wide, leaned down and kissed Martha's cheek. "You're here, I'm here, and someday soon we'll know Muriel's safe, too."

The grimace had belied the confidence of her words. Yes, the two of them survived; Martha willed herself to accept Clara's assertion about Muriel as equally factual. Clara answered Martha's unspoken questions.

"When the car stalled, I walked the mile back to the schoolhouse and built a fire in the stove. Your uncle Malcolm saw the sparks coming out the stovepipe in the middle of the night and thought the schoolhouse was on fire. He rode his horse through the snow and spent the rest of the night with me. He brought over food from his place this morning."

"I've never known him to spend that much time in another's company," Martha mumbled. Clara didn't hear.

"The sheriff found us this afternoon. The road's plowed, and Hank towed the car in."

Martha noted the darkness. "What time is it?"

"About ten. Can you go back to sleep?"

Martha's eyelids had dropped shut from their own weight.

Cora Jane's voice penetrated a thick veil. "Martha, Martha, here's warm porridge for breakfast."

Cora Jane rolled up the head of the bed and wheeled over the tray. Martha tried to lift her hand to grasp the spoon, but the maneuver was too demanding.

Papa rose from the chair and hurried to her side.

"Seems I get to feed my little girl some porridge. But only if you promise you won't spit it back in my face as you did the first time."

"That couldn't have been me, Papa. I love porridge. Must have been Josie."

The effort to speak wore her out, and Martha wanted only to drift back to sleep.

"No you don't," said Papa. "Just open your mouth. You can keep your eyes closed if it's too much effort, and I'll say when to part those pretty lips. Now."

She might have slept between bites but heard a satisfied Cora Jane say, "Mr. McLennan, you have an excellent bedside manner."

If so, why was he flummoxed by Fran's illness?

Dinner was Josie's chicken soup, fed to her by Cora Jane. Supper was orange jello and more chicken soup. Martha fed herself with

Josie standing by. Clara and Art arrived in time for the bedpan struggle, and Martha slept through the second night.

Departure

The next morning, Martha woke to the sound of Louise's voice. "After breakfast, I'll give your bath."

Cora Jane would appreciate Louise's help. Martha ate and felt strong enough to be useful.

"Sis, Doc says we nearly lost you. He says under no circumstances can you get pregnant again anytime soon. You have to give yourself time to heal."

Martha rankled at Louise's presumption to dispense medical advice second hand, particularly about intimate relations with her husband.

"He's yet to talk to Art and me about it."

"There are measures you can take to prevent pregnancy, you know."

"Louise!"

"I'm just saying…"

Martha patted Louise's hand. She didn't have energy for a row. "Stick with baths, which you do well, and let the doctor give out prescriptions."

"And I do a good job cleaning house. You never thanked me for having both the Home Place and yours in tip-top shape when you got home from taking care of Fran."

"I should have known the boys didn't do it. I certainly miss your efforts at the Home Place after you moved to town. A belated thank you."

"No one notices if I'm around or not," Louise grumbled.

She helped Martha sit up, and the warm rinse water trickled down her spine. Louise caught it with the rough towel before it reached the sheets.

After Cora Jane carried out the soiled linen and Martha slipped on a clean gown, Louise started pacing between bed and door.

"I need to tell you something. I'll be leaving Greenwood in the next week or two. I have a civil service job in Washington, DC. But that's not why I'm leaving. The job simply gives me a destination."

Louise's news hit Martha like an anvil between the eyes. She flinched, but Louise didn't take note. Her pacing and barrage of words continued.

"I'm telling you, and only you, why I'm leaving because, because… Hell, someone has to know the truth."

Martha wanted to revel in the warm bath Louise administered so deftly, not hear her curse, not smell the cigarette smoke on Louise's clothes. She had no desire to carry more secrets. The burden of what to do with Fran's scars and Jake's visits was already too heavy. But in her weakness, Martha kept silent.

Louise plunged into her confession. "I've been…"

Martha waited.

"I'm…"

Again, Martha made no response save that of watching Louise pace.

"Stop looking at me, for God's sake."

Martha shrugged as if to say, where else shall I look if not at the sister who's assaulting me with foul language I don't want to hear?

"Look at the door or something."

Then again, if Martha was eager for Fran to tell her story, a woman to whom she was not related, she should listen to her sister's, a family member to whom she owed loyalty, even if they didn't share a natural affection. Besides, Louise seemed compelled to divulge it, as if extracting the stinger of a bee, as painful to keep as to let go. Martha complied and studied the foot of the hospital bed.

"The only way I can tell you this is not to say the man's name. Don't make me say it, all right?"

Martha wasn't making her say any of it. Louise was spilling these beans. The pacing and the suspense exhausted Martha. She agreed just to get Louise out of the room.

Defiantly, Louise blurted out, "I've been having intimate relations with a married man. And I love him. And he loves me. But I think his wife knows, if not exactly what's going on, she knows his affections lie elsewhere. If anyone finds out it will ruin his family and tear up mine. I won't let that happen. I'll not tell him I'm leaving because he'll try to stop me. Not forcefully, but I know the depth of his sorrow if he learns about my plan, and that will dissuade me. I have to leave without even saying goodbye. Eventually he'll see the wisdom of it. He'll have to, don't you think?"

She burst into tears.

"Louise, come here, come here."

Martha reached out to take Louise's hand, even though she was appalled by the confession, but Louise threw herself on the bed. Martha took Louise into her arms, as she had the night their mother died and they cried themselves to sleep; now, only Louise sobbed.

Martha stroked her hair and used the time to practice a response.

What did you expect, falling in love with a married man? That wouldn't do. Louise's behavior was inexcusable, but instinct said now wasn't the time to judge. The confident, mature Louise was nowhere to be found. Louise didn't need anyone telling her how foolish she was, not to mention how immoral.

That she was glad Louise confided in her? She wasn't glad, and it wasn't a confidence. Martha was defenseless, in a hospital bed. What better time to dump a load of trash?

She would say something true, but comforting. She began, "You're taking steps to right a wrong, difficult steps for you. That's courageous. And the way you've chosen is smart. You'll be far removed from him, and this new position will open professional possibilities for you. You'll be able to start over."

Being told she was courageous and smart worked with Louise. To Martha's dismay, Louise wiped her eyes and nose with the clean sheet. She pushed herself off the bed.

"Thanks, Sis. It helps for someone to know."

And she was out the door.

Martha lay in bed, disgusted with Louise and her story. If it had been Josie, or Muriel, or Clara, sharing a confidence would be part of a larger picture of mutual help and respect. But Louise's objective was to partially relieve herself of the weight of a heavy load, and now Martha shouldered more than she wanted. It was like that with Louise, an unequal give and take.

Had Louise used the soothing bath to soften Martha for the blow she was about to deliver?

No, Louise's confession was spontaneous. Maybe she hadn't intended to tell Martha anything, but the tenderness of the bath softened her, instead. Louise was such a mystery, a member of the family but always slightly apart. Even though Uncle Malcolm chose a life of isolation and Martha saw him infrequently, she felt closer to him than she did to Louise.

Deliberating about Louise irritated her. She had to move. She should call Cora Jane for help, but she pushed herself to a sitting position and dangled her legs over the side of the bed. When the lightheadedness passed, she carefully stood. The feeling of pins pricking the bottoms of her feet subsided, and she walked slowly around the bed.

Movement brought little relief. Ever since Carrie died, ever since Anna got lost, ever since the Pearl Harbor attack, of what use had she been? She wasn't even capable of delivering a healthy baby. Alienation from her brother, neglect of Edith Giffard — the mother of her closest friend missing in the Philippine Islands, an enigma not even the government of the United States seemed capable of solving.

She carried Fran's secrets, and now Louise's, but was powerless. She couldn't protect Papa; she couldn't protect the family from the repercussions of Louise's transgression if it became public. Unlike Burleigh, who paraded his cache of confidences, Martha was obliged to be discreet.

Roosevelt had said that, contrary to the enemy's designs, we aren't stunned, terrified, or confused. She would not succumb, even though the attack was mixed in with grief, illness, family discord, and romantic intrigue, not to mention the hostility Mr. Miyoshi and his friends faced daily.

She would not stand helpless as linchpins of her world dissolved; she would regain physical strength and the moral strength to hold firm. Perhaps her outburst at the defense meeting was ill advised, but it was a source of pride. Even Claude Giffard complimented her.

She would urge Louise to give Papa warning about her plans to leave, even though telling anyone else increased the risk of speculation about her sudden departure. Granted, nowadays Louise could answer, "There's a war on, you know," which excused all sorts of behavior.

Martha agreed with Louise about one thing. In matters of the heart, it was surely impossible to both stop the affair and stay in the vicinity, regardless of the man's identity. The only solution was for her to leave quickly, without fanfare.

A sad way to begin a new life — no parties, no gifts from friends and family. At the very least, Martha would be at the station to say goodbye, and she would tell Josie about Louise's new position, not just yet, but soon.

In a few hours, she'd walk again. Soon she'd be moving at full stride, just as Roosevelt had promised the country would do. She crawled under the sheet and slept.

Recognition

Alex was still home on furlough when Louise left two weeks later. Martha saw to it that they were all at the station, even Uncle Malcolm, to say goodbye. If ever Louise felt she could come home again, this show of family loyalty might encourage it. For the others, Louise's secrecy about her abrupt departure, while odd, fit a pattern. She valued her privacy, and thousands of young women were flocking to the nation's capital for employment. Everyone agreed she should leave Giffard's Lumberyard for a position with more promise.

When Louise found her seat and waved from the window, they started to leave. Anna begged to wait until the train pulled away.

Art and Alex answered in unison, "I'll stay with Anna."

Alex, no longer a boy but a man in uniform, drew a pipe from his pocket, and Art lit a cigarette. "Martha, please go ta the truck an' get out a this cold. Yer still not strong."

Martha started to protest but saw the wisdom of Art's request. She blew a last kiss, and Louise put a single finger to her lips.

Onlookers would think she was blowing a kiss in return, but Martha's nod indicated she knew otherwise. Yes, it's our secret.

Unlike with Fran's plea, which she had never assented to because she couldn't conceive of keeping Jake's visits or Fran's dreadful scars from Papa, she would keep her promise to Louise. No good could come of revealing Louise's motivation to take a job on the other side of the country.

Martha walked away but turned for a last look at her sister, to remember what Louise wore, how she fixed her hair, details she would hold on to until they saw one another again. Art dropped the cigarette, snuffed it out with his foot, and picked up Anna. One of Alex's buddies slapped him on the shoulder, and they began an animated conversation.

When Martha sought Louise's face in the window of the train car, she saw not the smiling, encouraging visage from moments before, but one distorted by anguish. Her palm pressed against the window. Alarmed at the crack in Louise's protective cocoon, Martha followed Louise's line of sight to the end of the platform on the far side of the station.

There stood a man in a topcoat with stooped shoulders, hat in hand, eyes cast down. With seeming effort, he lifted his head. Claude Giffard. He straightened and raised his hand, duplicating Louise's gesture, as though touching her palm with his across the intervening space. He dropped his hand, turned, and resolutely walked away, now hidden behind the station.

Martha's groan must have been audible, and she quickly looked around to check if anyone heard. Surely Louise's lover wasn't Claude Giffard! Martha had imagined a much younger man, perhaps with small children. But someone her father's age? How could Claude carry on with Louise when his daughter, Muriel, a woman older than his mistress, was under attack half a world away?

When she looked back at Louise, she saw a composed sister imitating Anna's silly hand signals, apparently unaware Martha saw the exchange and Claude Giffard's torment. His lover gone, an attractive, vibrant young woman, apparently so deeply in love with him that the separation caused visible agony. Claudia dead and Muriel missing. His wife so scattered and distraught she couldn't maintain a home.

Josie said that at the AAUW meeting Edith Giffard was in a rather nervous state of mind. Louise suspected the wife knew. It was a marvel Edith remained as lucid as she did, with her husband unfaithful and the whereabouts of her eldest daughter unknown.

Nervous and confused. Surely her own behavior wasn't as erratic as Edith's, but there were similarities. Daughters gone missing, the odd "spells" with the unbidden void that almost engulfed her several times after Carrie's death. Disorganized and disrupted routines, projects left incomplete, Edith with her weaving and painting, Martha with her good intentions about relieving Clara's burdens.

However, there were differences. Muriel was still missing; Anna had been found. Claude was unfaithful; Martha had no doubts about Art's fidelity, but they did face the possible effects of the miscarriage on their physical intimacy.

The weight of Louise's indiscretion bore down so heavily Martha could scarcely stand. When she reached the truck, she grabbed the handle to support her shaking legs. If she didn't recover sufficiently before Art and Anna joined her, she would blame her frailty on the miscarriage.

Martha couldn't restore the health of Edith's marriage, but she could guard that of her own. And if she were of more help to Edith, a stronger Edith might regain Claude's affections.

Tug of War

On the drive home, Martha suggested, "Art, I've been worried about Edith Giffard since before Christmas. The strain of not knowing about Muriel is awful, particularly since the fall of Manila."

Art answered, somewhat irritated. "And what would ya a done about it? When would ya a had the time?"

"You're right, of course, but still, I feel negligent. I read in the paper that art museums on the East and West Coasts have sent valuable paintings to Colorado Springs for the duration. What would you think if I drove her to the Fine Arts Museum one day next week, even though we might not see those particular items? It would be a wonderful experience for Anna, especially to go with Edith, who could explain what we'd be seeing."

Art answered with mock gravity, "Was that the same newspaper where Eleanor announced her engagement ta Alex? If so, ya'd better not believe…"

Martha reached over Anna and pinched Art's shoulder. "That's not funny!"

Art chuckled. "I don't see a problem with it, with goin', I mean. If the weather's good an' yer feelin' stronger. It'd be fer only a day, an' once spring comes we won't have time fer any extras, in partic'lar ones that wear out parts an' tires. Just so ya don't ride the clutch or drive fast. Ya tend ta do both, an' those are 'specially bad habits with all the shortages."

"I suppose you're going to tell me not to wear my girdle, either, now that they've stopped producing those!"

Art's rejoinder came fast. "That loss I wouldn't mind."

Martha moved to a less embarrassing topic. "I'm so proud of Alex for going to the Moultons and apologizing about the misunderstanding with Eleanor."

"Don't be so sure that's the end of it. The Moultons have long memories when it comes ta supposed insults. Walt still isn't friendly with me fer takin' ya away from 'im, an' from what I gather, Eleanor's still convinced Alex loves her as much as she loves 'im. He just doesn't know it yet. My feelin' is she thinks she'll still catch 'im, one way or t'other."

Martha snorted. "How can she be so blind? By the way, I never belonged to Walter for you to take me away. What a stupid man."

"Mama, you shouldn't call anyone 'stupid.'"

Art winked at Martha over Anna's head; Martha rolled her eyes.

"Men," she practically hissed, encompassing Walter, Claude, and the men at the barbershop who put up the hateful sign. Her mood darkened when she extended her condemnation to include Maher, whose self-serving cruelty was of a magnitude beyond comprehension.

Art's glance was one big question mark, and it brought her back to a more meaningful scale of comparison.

"Except you. You're different. So much different. And Papa, Mr. Miyoshi, and Dr. McFarland. And Henry Behm. Maybe Uncle Malcolm and Enoch Gwynn."

"Can't tell if I belong ta an exclusive group er not. How long is this list?"

"That's about the end of it, but you're at the top, as long as you don't get too confident."

Art smiled and reached in front of Anna for Martha's hand, which she rested in his. The clasped hands dropped into Anna's lap, who immediately tried to untangle the fingers. The tug of war, accompanied by laughter, stopped only when Art needed his hand to shift gears at the turn onto the county road leading to the farm.

March 1942

Resolution

"Mama, the flag's up on the mailbox! Let's get the letters!" From the dining room window and in the near-darkness, Martha couldn't confirm the flag's position. The blowing snow further obstructed her vision. "Maybe the flag's up; maybe not."

"It is! I know it is!"

"We'd have to bundle up and put on our boots to check. Let's wait for Papa to get the mail before he takes off his overalls."

"Oh, Mama. That's too long."

"Look again, Anna."

They watched the headlights of an automobile that stopped alongside the mailbox. The silhouette of the driver passed in front of the lights and back again. The car drove into the lane.

Anna ran through the house, onto the back porch, and back inside by the time Martha reached the kitchen.

"It's Lena Mae," Anna sang and hopped around the kitchen table.

What could Henry Behm want that merited a drive from town? March snowstorms could be so treacherous. She grabbed the empty coffeepot and headed out to the water pump on the back porch. All the Behms entered, and Martha braced herself against the cold air.

But the frigid blast didn't distract her from noticing the bundle in Zella's arms.

"What do you have there? Take your coats and boots off inside by the kitchen stove. It's too cold out here. I'll be right in."

Henry ushered Zella and Lena Mae inside and came back to the porch, more excited than usual. "Let me help. Let me help."

He reached around Martha, determined to grab the pump handle. "We have news. Wonderful news. We haven't even been home. Drove right through town so we could show you. Hurry, hurry. Oh, here's your mail."

The cold water gushed into the pot and splashed on the mail that made its precarious way from his free hand to Martha's.

"Goodness. I'm sorry. I'm sorry."

Martha smiled at Henry's awkwardness. He was so well intentioned.

"Henry, it's fine. Look, just a few drops, and they're rolling off."

Both looked at the mail, which was more drenched than Martha represented.

"Oh," she said.

He mistook it as dismay. "Please, let me dab it with a tea towel before the water penetrates."

"Really, it's all right. It's a letter from my brother! It's written in pencil so there's no problem with ink running."

It was addressed to her, Art, and Anna. Martha had written after his furlough, encouraged by his willingness to resume some of the old routines of visiting back and forth across the road. She couldn't wait to show Anna. Her first letter with her name on the envelope.

But when Martha entered the warm kitchen, Anna and Lena Mae's excitement overshadowed hers.

"Mama, look at Lena Mae's new sister! She's waking up!"

Zella had laid the bundle on the kitchen table so both girls could better see. Pink arms extended from a brighter pink blanket, and a few vigorous kicks loosened the covering further, but the little one didn't cry. She opened her eyes and seemed to examine her surroundings with interest. The exploration stopped with Martha's face. Martha sat the mail on the shelf and reached toward the infant.

"May I pick her up?"

"Of course, of course." Henry practically danced with excitement.

Martha cradled the baby and laughed. "I think I know why she's awake. She's very wet."

"Goodness me, goodness me. I'll retrieve her bag from the car." And Henry dashed for the door.

Martha looked to Zella for an explanation.

"We drove to Pueblo to pick her up this afternoon. Since Lena Mae's birth, I've miscarried once and not conceived since, and before Lena Mae, well, we lost a son. When you told Henry about the baby and indicated you and Art wouldn't be adopting…"

Yes, Martha remembered the stillborn son. She looked down, expecting to be repulsed by Maher's offspring. The baby studied her face. Martha had the eerie feeling she would accept Martha's reaction, affectionate or not, with equanimity.

Henry re-entered the kitchen.

"She resembles her aunt and mother," said Martha, "with her high cheekbones. Vera and Ida are beautiful girls."

Martha prayed silently that her fondness for the mother's side would displace her revulsion for the father's.

Zella's calm voice intruded on Martha's interior conversation.

"Martha, we'll baptize the baby soon. Will you and Art be godparents? You rescued her once. Will you continue to help us watch over her well-being?"

Startled her prayer was answered with a challenge almost simultaneous with the petition, Martha had no choice but to answer yes, as though Providence intervened on the child's behalf. "I'll have to speak with Art, but it's my intention to say yes."

The baby's head turned away with an expression conveying satisfaction that all was resolved, and the eyes sought out other objects of interest.

"Art should be finished with chores by now," Martha said. "I wonder what's keeping him."

"Miyoshi's truck's parked in front of the barn," Henry offered. "I'll check."

He dashed out so quickly he let in only a small draft of cold air.

"What will you name her?" asked Martha.

"We haven't decided."

Zella's deftness with the diaper change prompted Martha to say, "You've had more practice than one child would suggest."

"I've had training. I started a nursing program in Denver and spent time at Children's Hospital. I thought I would be a missionary, and nursing was the skill I would bring to it. I had dreams to see the world. And I met Henry, who had similar dreams. But, here we are."

Zella's summary seemed to be a statement of fact, not disappointment.

"We've never talked about your training," Martha commented. "I assumed your background was musical. You have such a lovely voice!"

"My music's satisfying, but not the way nursing was. Both bring comfort to folks, but nursing gave more immediate contact. I envy you, that you're able to continue with your profession."

Again, Zella's admissions didn't seem laden with regret, but Martha protested, "And I envy your musical talent! I scold Louise that she should take hers more seriously, develop it, that with a gift like hers she should, I don't know, do something more with it."

Zella looked at Martha intently. "And now she's gone. It's a great loss for the church, for Henry, because he'll have a hard time finding an accompanist with her versatility."

She spoke her next words carefully. "I wish her the best. She came by the house one evening and burst out with her problems before I could get out of the living room. Otherwise, I wouldn't know because Henry keeps confidences, even from me. Henry gave her the name of a classmate who has a church in the capitol area. I hope she'll offer her talent. I believe that's her new neighborhood?"

Martha again had the impression she was free to choose, this time between admitting her knowledge of Louise's transgression, or letting it go. She chose to admit it, and with the admission sealed a bond with Zella much stronger than their shared interests in nursing and music.

"Yes, she had no choice but to leave. I'm glad she talked to Henry and has the name of a church contact there. So he knows that the causes of Edith's near breakdown involve her sense that Claude's been unfaithful, on top of Muriel's unknown whereabouts."

Martha was embarrassed for Louise that Zella and Henry knew about Claude, but her relief that they shouldered some of the burden far outweighed the shame.

"He does. It was good of you to take Edith to the museum. She's come back with renewed energy. I think she'll even finish weaving the blanket, but shouldn't we broach the problem of straightening their house?"

Zella's concern coincided with Martha's, that of tending to Edith.

"Perhaps I make too much of a properly run household," Zella said. "But my mother's situation was similar to Edith's. Initially, nursing school was attractive because it meant leaving the disorder and discord of my home."

Martha would never have guessed Zella had a difficult upbringing.

"It isn't a cure," Zella continued, "but perhaps straightening the clutter will help Edith order her mind and make spending more time at home attractive to Claude."

"The motivation must come from Edith. If we do it, everything will fall apart again. Clara and I've talked at length about what approach to take. But Zella, Clara doesn't know Louise's reason for leaving and her role in Edith's decline, and neither do other members of my family. Nor will they."

Martha glanced into Anna's room to assure herself the girls were engrossed with Anna's paper dolls. They were spreading out the whole lot on the comforter that covered her narrow bed.

Martha overheard Anna say, "I had a baby sister, too. Her name was Carrie. And my uncle Malcolm made that picture for her."

Both girls crawled onto the bed, crushing some of the paper dolls and their multiple outfits in the process, to examine Carrie's snowflake. Never mind mangled paper dolls; Uncle Malcolm's snowflake guaranteed, for the time being, Anna wouldn't forget Carrie.

"Do you know about Edith's younger daughter, Claudia?" Martha asked.

"No, I've not heard that name."

"Maurice's twin, Claudia. She died at the age of seven. Rheumatic fever."

"That explains so much. You and I know how the death of a child knocks a mother flat. Some never regain their balance. And with her other daughter missing…"

"Exactly."

Martha heard the mantle clock on the piano in the living room strike seven.

"They should be inside by now. I'm still getting used to daylight savings time. My natural clock says it's six. I suppose the change is a good idea, but don't you think it helps city folks more? One purpose is to get them home from work before dark in the event of a blackout."

"I hadn't really thought about it."

"Why don't you stay for supper? Elena made delicious chili for dinner today, and I baked cornbread this afternoon. There's plenty. Don't worry that it's spicy. Elena says she puts in one-fourth the pepper her mother uses. Anna has no problem with it."

"I know Henry'll say yes. He's very familiar with Aneda Marquez's food from dinners at the Spanish church. He might even be disappointed Elena's isn't quite the same as her mother's, but I prefer less pepper."

"I'll put it on the stove, and you can stir it while I run out to see what's keeping them."

"Before you go, I have an idea. Henry's worried about Mrs. Marquez. He thinks she's too old for the rigors of fieldwork, although she's probably only in her mid-thirties. She married when she was fifteen."

Mid-thirties sounded about right to have children the ages of Luis, Elena, and Marguerite. Dolores Ruiz, Aneda's niece, had married almost that young, albeit a marriage forced on her.

"And we're worried about Edith," Zella said, "who won't maintain a tidy household, much less get it organized. Surely the Giffards have the money to employ a maid..."

Martha mentally slapped herself. Of course. She and Clara grew up in circumstances where maids were unheard of. Neighbors helped in times of emergency, but Edith's problems were ongoing and friends poking around her house would only add to her distress. Martha and Clara talked about Mrs. DeFries coming in, but Edith wasn't physically ill. Someone like Aneda Marquez could become part of a stable routine.

"A wonderful idea!" Martha said. "Now we have to come up with a strategy for convincing Claude and bringing Edith around. He respects me, but I don't think I should suggest it. I'm too closely associated with Louise. He might listen to Clara."

"Or to Henry. Coming from another man, especially his minister, could make a difference. You talk to Clara; I'll talk to Henry. Between the four of us, we'll devise a way to benefit both Edith and Aneda Marquez."

A Secret Weapon

Nothing prepared Martha for what greeted her when she entered the barn. Henry Behm and Jimmie Ichikawa, stripped to the waist; Art's overalls draped over Ginger's stall. The three shot a basketball at a barrel hoop Art contrived to hang from the loft above the cement floor at end of the barn. Art had moved the wagon and swept away the hay. Mr. Miyoshi watched intently, as did the two cows.

"No, Jimmie, no," Art yelled. "Ya gotta be more forceful at blockin' my shots. Don't matter I'm so much taller. Yer too polite. Act like a mad hornet buzzin' 'round me; distract me. Ya got the speed. Watch out, though. Henry's fast, even with 'is boots on. Stay 'tween 'im an' the basket."

Then he yelled at Mr. Miyoshi, "Come throw the ball for a tip-off."

The three breathless players met Mr. Miyoshi in the center.

Henry and Jimmie were the same size, but Henry jumped higher and tipped the ball to Art. Jimmie pursued Art, overtaking him in spite of Art's long legs — Art's work boots did slow him down. Art was forced to pass the ball to Henry, but Jimmie, who seemed to be everywhere at once, blocked Henry's shot. The ball bounced off the edge of the cement and cleared the top board of Ginger's stall. She backed away, nudging the ball into a pile of manure with her hoof.

The players, breathless and covered with sweat, hands on knees, groaned at the ball's fate. Mr. Miyoshi slapped his thigh and bent double with laughter.

"Art, what's your strategy against that play?" Henry asked.

Only then did they notice Martha. They froze. She had the distinct impression she didn't belong.

Art broke the tension. "Martha, ya can't, ya absolutely can't, tell anyone what ya've just seen."

"What's so top secret about a manure-smeared basketball?"

She was annoyed with all of them. Because she had to put on her boots and coat to come outside. Because they were late for supper. Because they were so serious about an inconsequential game.

Art bit his lip, and Henry hurried to cover his bare chest with his undershirt.

"Well, yeah, in a way it is a secret weapon," Art said. "Not the ball but Jimmie. He's asked me fer special coachin'. Ya might not realize it, but if Greenwood wins their last game they'll go ta the state tournament. I'm surprised ya haven't noticed the hoop up there, or the extra time I spend on the so-called chores. Of course, with Henry here, we been at it longer'n usual."

Henry's confidence on the "court" was as surprising as Jimmie's agile play against both men.

She addressed Henry. "Does anyone know you're athletic?"

"I've always been teased about my awkwardness, so I work very hard at sports. You should see me pitch a softball. I'm really good at that."

Jimmie slipped on his shirt and walked over to Martha. "Mrs. Lundgren, please don't tell anyone. You haven't been to any of the games, so you don't know how the fans from other teams yell horrible things at me. I get so mad I don't concentrate. I'm a good player, but not recently. The coach's lost confidence in me. I thought if Mr. Lundgren helped, I'd get better again."

Art quickly assured him, "Ya've improved a lot, Jimmie. If ya think only 'bout the game, 'bout what each player's doin,' where they are, what yer gonna do, ya won't hear what fans yell. It'll just be noise."

To Martha, he said, somewhat proudly, "So, that's what we're doin.' Testin' Greenwood's secret weapon — Jimmie Ichikawa."

Jimmie slipped into Ginger's stall to retrieve the now-browner basketball. He grabbed handfuls of hay to wipe it off.

"You'll need water," observed Martha. "Get a bucket and take some out of the horse tank outside. The sledgehammer's beside the tank, to break up the ice."

To Art and Henry she said, "Can we go in for supper now? Henry, you're staying for Elena's chili."

They obediently finished clothing themselves. Only Mr. Miyoshi retained the dignity of an adult. The game wasn't child's play for him, and it wouldn't be for Jimmie, either. The honor of all the Japanese families rested on a seventeen-year-old's shoulders, at least for one evening.

She now guarded defense plans for the high school basketball team and a strategy to ameliorate Edith Gifford's plight, but all in the company of co-conspirators.

Largess

Zella finished feeding the baby as everyone trouped into the kitchen. Henry noted with relief that the snow had stopped, and, after Lena Mae and Anna said their Sunday school grace, everyone dug into the chili. The baby chose that moment to be fussy; Martha took her into the living room so Zella could eat.

They all laughed at the baby's extraordinarily big burp, and Martha half listened to the ensuing conversation as she paced around the living room, rocking the infant to sleep. She returned, still hungry, wishing Carrie's bassinette wasn't wrapped and tucked away in the barn loft.

Henry took the child without breaking his flow of words. "Art, what do you think of Miyoshi's plan?"

"It has a chance a completely changin' the attitude toward the Japanese, not only 'round Greenwood."

"You think one game is going to accomplish that much?" Martha asked.

"Granted, a lot rests on sporting events for every town in the Valley," Henry answered, "but we're talking about something else. Miyoshi told us tonight the Japanese Farmers' Association's donating their old school building to the VFW. Evidently the Japanese families haven't used it for several years. The expense of bringing the Buddhist priest down from Denver to teach Japanese to the children wasn't worth it because fewer and fewer of them participated. They'll move the building to town, and it'll become the VFW post headquarters. The Boy Scouts will have use of the second room."

"That's a stunning plan," said Zella, crushing another saltine in the bottom of her bowl to absorb the juice from the chili.

"Mama, please fix mine," begged Lena Mae.

"Mine, too," echoed Anna.

Zella temporarily abandoned the conversation to the cracker project, and Martha took up the slack. "I'm surprised the VFW agreed. You know how cruel Al's been in his criticism of the plan to relocate Japanese from the West Coast to Colorado. He'd leave the Republican Party, as angry as he is at Governor Carr for supporting the relocation, if he had anywhere to go but to the Democrats, and the commissioners have taken a stand against using any of those Japanese for field work."

Art frowned at Martha. Whether it was his meaning or not, Martha shouldn't have criticized Al Ivarson. What she disapproved in Papa, she was guilty of herself. Even worse, the Ivarsons were church members, and she put the Behms in an awkward position if they weren't familiar with the ongoing feud between the McLennans and the Ivarsons, or with the fact that the name of Al Ivarson was synonymous with the VFW.

"I'm sorry about the political comment," she said. "I mean to say Mr. Miyoshi might be walking straight into the lion's den, so to speak, with Al and the VFW. It's a bold and generous offer on the part of the Japanese farmers."

"I think it's part of a bigger picture," Henry said. "The Japanese community's organized and careful to take opportunities to express their loyalty. I'm not being critical to say so. On the contrary. I think it's necessary to use every occasion at their disposal to counteract the general impression they're the enemy, particularly with Roosevelt's order about relocating people of foreign enemy ancestry from those states on the coast that they've set up as military zones, the plan you say Al's so against. Hatred tears up younger Japanese who circulate every day in the larger white community, like Jimmie. Some students at the high school jostle him on the stairs and taunt him. Thankfully, his friends, boys on the football and basketball teams, defend him."

"So he needs not only to prove himself to fans of the opposing teams but also to pull his weight with his friends," Martha said.

"Did you see the letter in the paper from the Japanese boy who's preparing to be a translator for the army, the one at the Presidio?" Henry asked. "He describes how his Japanese parents are prepared to give up their boys for defense of our country. Didn't his family live in the area at one time?"

Art and Martha, who had seen the letter, nodded affirmatively to both questions and Henry continued. "The boy's letter, and the gift of the Japanese school, are gentle reminders that families known to local folks want to be part of the American effort against Imperial Japan."

"I'll bet the students who jostle Jimmie in the hallways are the ones the Japanese farmers fed five and six years ago," Martha said.

"What do you mean?" asked Zella.

"The Japanese children would tell their parents who didn't have enough in their lunches, before we had the WPA school lunch program, and their parents would deliver boxes of food in the middle of the night to those families. They delivered all over Greenwood. Left boxes on back porches. I know who some of the families are because Josie and I helped Mr. Miyoshi make deliveries. I'd like to tell the parents throwing such fits about the Japanese now how the farmers in the association kept their children alive."

The moment the impetuous words escaped her mouth, she wanted to take them back. Her impulses, to tear out the sign in the barbershop window and give what-for to the unappreciative families, were small-minded compared to the thoughtful steps the Japanese families were taking.

"Martha, their generosity is well-known," said Henry. "Parker Hayes told me about the food deliveries, as have several others. Some folks are so inflamed now, though, that throwing that in their faces might make matters worse. You have to be careful when it comes to pride."

Even Henry was joining the chorus of voices urging caution.

In a level voice, Martha asked, "How's that?"

"I'll never forget the looks on the faces of men in the bread lines during those years. More than a few couldn't bring themselves to look me at me when I handed out the food. If they did, their faces were distorted with emotion, or worse, completely blank. Maybe they were filled with self-hate that it had come to begging, or maybe they hated depending on me for food. Maybe both. But if those families you describe knew the Japanese gave them food, it might strengthen their resentment. Mr. Miyoshi and his friends probably sense that. They aren't going to remind anyone of their charity. They're simply continuing it with the schoolhouse."

Henry's obvious preference for Mr. Miyoshi's subtler tactics put Martha in her place, even though he hadn't done it purposefully. The evening showed that her bias against Maher's baby was unfounded, her snipping at Al was as close-minded as Papa's, and her impatience with bigoted folks might cause more problems than it solved. Henry confirmed Art's caution that her outburst at the defense meeting might only stoke the fire of hatred in those afraid of all Oriental faces. She must find methods not destined to backfire.

Jimmie tried so hard with the basketball. Mr. Miyoshi and the other farmers took a risk by offering the schoolhouse to the VFW. She prayed the rewards would equal the largess of their hearts.

Training Camp

After the Behms left, Martha said, "Anna, if we get you right to bed, I have a surprise for a goodnight story. Use your chamber pot because it's too cold to go to the outhouse."

Art tucked Anna in and Martha retrieved the now-dry and somewhat wrinkled letter. "Look for the names on the envelope to see who should open it."

When Anna spotted her name, she sat upright so quickly all the covers came undone. "It's for me!"

"And for me and Papa, 'Mr. and Mrs. Art Lundgren.' You open it."

"Ain't this only 'is second letter since he left after Christmas? I hope it has more ta it than the first."

The three settled in and Art read.

> *Dear Sis, Anna and Art,*
>
> *Guess this is your first real letter from me. I never said thanks for the birthday card and the $5, so, thanks.*
>
> *I think I still owe Art $10. Maybe you should have kept the $5 and subtracted it from my bill! It will take me awhile to pay it back. We are paid $21 a month and have laundry charged against it, but I also get a show and canteen coupon.*
>
> *The Grey Ladies of the Red Cross sent a birthday box of divinity candy. The candy was very good, and I am fixing to write Mrs. Hayes a letter of appreciation, even though it is overdue. I think she heads the Grey Ladies in Greenwood.*
>
> *I have not had guard duty yet but lots of KP and latrine duty.*

"What's that?" Anna asked.

Short explanations followed and Art resumed.

> *A fellow who had guard duty was handed a loaded .45. It went off and just missed his foot.*

Another interruption for a discussion about the loaded .45.

Soon we might carry rifles. I practiced with them on the firing range. They kick about like a shotgun, maybe not so hard as most.

We all had IQ tests and mine is 133.

Art stopped, anticipating the need to define IQ, but Anna was fast asleep.

"Go on," whispered Martha. "I'll finish it with her tomorrow."

A fellow has to have 110 for officers' training. I might get into some school if I can. It would be swell to be a lieutenant. One of the fellows I run with made 152, which means very brilliant because 99–110 is average. So you see, I am quite smart myself!

Martha never had any doubt about Alex's intelligence, and she was happy he had something to brag about.

We are crowded. Too many fellows at the dances, but some are moving out soon. The army slogan is true and no fooling. They are building men out of thousands of boys here.

There are also movies at night and everyone writes letters because they like getting letters. I will try to write more often.

I have nothing to gripe about except that everyone gets a little sore after we go over to the hospital for short arm inspection. We have one each month just before payday. Pardon me if you think I am vulgar.

Love, Alex

Martha chuckled. "And how would you have explained the 'short arm' inspection to Anna? Next time we'll have to censor Alex's letters. He seems in good spirits, but it takes a lot to discourage him… I guess that says something about how hard he took my scolding. That it's taken him this long to write a newsy letter to us."

"Ya gave 'im more'n a scoldin.' I'm glad ya two were friendly when he was here Valentine's Day, an' I agree that him writin's another good sign. He hints he'd like ta hear more from ya."

Of all her impetuous behavior the past months, Martha regretted her outburst at Alex the most. She couldn't imagine his daily routine behind the high points he reported. Probably fairly tedious.

"Ta think," Art said, "that guard boy almost shot his self in the foot. Alex might say the army turns 'em inta men, but they're still just boys, many not much older'n Jimmie. What'll happen ta 'em? Makes me wanna work all the harder fer 'em, here, on the farm an' the rationin' board."

"Yes, I feel the same way."

March 1942

"Send the Jap Back"

Martha held Anna on her lap in the packed gymnasium. She hadn't expected such a crowd, given that last week Clara reported sixteen new scarlet fever cases in the county. She certainly wouldn't have come, were it not for Art's practices with Jimmie.

They sat near the door at the end of the third row on Greenwood's side. Given the raucous crowd, she would have preferred that Art sit with them, but he had to squat on the floor below, in front of the bleachers. The coaches for the two teams replicated Art's crouch in front of their boys and gave earnest last-minute instructions.

Earl and Josie sat in her immediate vicinity, Earl as a staunch supporter of his students and Josie because she loved any athletic competition. Martha couldn't see Fran and Papa, but surely they were somewhere on Greenwood's side.

The Moultons clustered together. Walter and Edgar, Martha's contemporaries, had played on lackluster high school teams. Ellis and Mae Ufford sat several rows higher. Hugh Ufford had been on Alex and Luis's team, which Art said had a decent record three years ago.

She didn't think Julia and Gust Mattson would drive all the way up from Pinion, even though they were still big supporters of high school basketball. Art and Eddie's team had made it to the state tournament. Greenwood last won both basketball and football championships in the twenties when Sheriff Burleigh was captain.

She spotted Elsie and Otto Lambert near the Uffords. Elsie saw her and waved. Martha hadn't visited with her in ever so long. Maybe Elsie made herself scarce on account of the rumors about Max's sudden departure.

Anyway, Max's team wasn't all that good, and that was two years ago. The new coach had brought the boys a long way for them to be contenders tonight.

Latecomers filled in the standing room by Martha and Anna between the bleachers and the door, their view severely limited, but Martha heard no complaints. Children sat on the floor in front of the latecomer crowd, their legs crossed.

The cheering started with an intense shouting match between the competing fans. The children punctuated the rhythms by pounding their fists on the glistening wood, and the crowd in the bleachers joined with stomping feet. The seat under her vibrated.

Anna wrapped her arms around Martha's neck. "I'm scared, Mama. Let's go home."

As much as Martha wanted to see Jimmie play, she didn't want Anna to be frightened. Art so loved the game.

"Let's give away our seat and stand by the door," she said. "When the noise gets loud, we'll step outside. When we want to see the game, we'll peek in. We must hurry because it's about to start."

She slid off the bleacher with Anna in her arms, and someone immediately filled the seat. She wound through the standing crowd and expected Art to join her, but he'd disappeared. The buzzer sounded, and Martha hurried to the door.

Anna, who looked back and saw the length of the court from her mother's shoulder, shouted, "There's Papa. He's with the basketball boys."

If Art had known he was going to participate, he could have warned her.

They reached the double doors leading into the lobby, and folks moved aside, opening a spot on the floor next to the doorjamb, almost under the basket. Local and rival supporters mixed among one another in the lobby behind, pressing to see through the wide-open doorway. In the crush of fans, the ticket takers gave up.

Martha had never seen a game this well attended with this fervor of support, even when Josie's women's team went to the state tournament. Perhaps it was because the schools were traditional rivals; perhaps because, as Art explained, they had equal chances of winning; perhaps basketball was a break from the strain of war.

On account of the noise and her worry about how exposed they were on the floor each time the players stampeded to their end of the court, Martha couldn't explain much to Anna, but from where they sat, they could see Art clearly. She tried to tell Anna to watch her papa, hoping that would give Anna a sense of the play, but she needn't have bothered. Anna focused on Art the entire time.

Rarely, if ever, had Anna seen her papa excitedly order other folks around. Martha doubted the boys heard his shouts or those of the coach, but that didn't stop the two men. Art's face reddened from his exertions.

Martha couldn't remember the first time she saw her own papa in a public role. She would have been very young, but she recognized the feelings of pride and amazement in Anna's expressions.

Her primary concern was to protect Anna if the ball or wayward players hurtled their way. She positioned Anna by the doorjamb and planned to shove her behind it if they were threatened.

She shifted her attention to Josie, unable to discern patterns of play in the fast-moving game. Josie leapt to her feet when the Greenwood players had the ball. She booed when the refs called fouls against them. Josie's behavior was comic, and Martha wondered what the ladies in the Book Review Club would think if they saw the normally mild-mannered Josie in this setting.

At halftime all the Greenwood fans were subdued, including Martha and Anna. Their team was behind four points. A nervous and tired Martha suggested to Anna they leave, thinking they could walk to Josie's and wait until it was over. Anna's loud "No" drew attention. She had to stay for the ending, she said, and the cheerleaders and their ceremonial crossing to the opposing side's fans to lead them in the ritual yells enchanted her.

The second half was louder than the first, if that were possible. Greenwood tied, then drew ahead by a basket, then dropped behind. It seemed the seesaw went on forever. The tension fueled the energy of the crowd; it drained Martha's.

At least two other people shared her discomfort with the number of folks packed in the gymnasium, Howard Burleigh and Cecil Thirkell, the chief of police. Burleigh made his presence known by pushing through the lobby crowd periodically and separating it to form an aisle, for safety reasons, he said. Fans kept the aisle open just as long as it took him to go back outside. Martha suspected his regular appearances also justified a quick check on the score. Otherwise, he seemed to be monitoring the activity outside where alcohol undoubtedly fueled confrontations.

Cecil patrolled the gym by pacing slowly in front of one side, across the back below the stage, and returning down the other side. The message was clear — no battles between opposing fans, other than the one taking place on the court.

If anyone directed hostile comments toward Jimmie, Martha didn't hear them in the pandemonium. She was more concerned with helping Anna cover her ears when the cheers and boos erupted, even more startling to a five-year-old who comprehended little of the activity taking place in front of her.

Martha certainly wouldn't have predicted a tie in the last minute of the game and an outcome dependent on Jimmie's free throws. But that's how it happened.

The crowd, absolutely still, watched Jimmie. He walked to the line and took the ball from the ref, facing Martha and Anna. The sweat poured down his face.

"What's wrong with Jimmie, Mama?" Anna whispered into Martha's ear.

"He's all right," Martha answered softly. "He's standing there because he gets two special shots for a basket. He has to make one of them for Greenwood to win the game. Greenwood fans are afraid he'll miss the basket, and the other folks are afraid he won't. He's bouncing the ball until he's ready."

"Should we cross our fingers, Mama?"

Martha wondered where she got that expression, one Martha would never use. She didn't tolerate superstition, but she nodded a barely discernable affirmative. Now wasn't the time for explanations about the merits of the gesture.

"Mama, cross yours, too."

Martha did, to her surprise.

Jimmie missed the first shot, and Greenwood collectively expelled its breath. So much for the efficacy of crossed-fingers. Folks on both sides had done it. How could the gods choose?

A single voice screamed as Jimmie raised the ball for his second shot.

"Send the Jap back. Send the Jap back."

Several other voices joined the insulting chant, but by then the ball was sailing through the air, and into the basket.

Greenwood fans roared and ran onto the floor. Martha stood and gripped Anna's hand. She felt the pressure from the crowd in the lobby behind as it surged into the gymnasium, but she flattened herself against the doorjamb and used it as a brace. Surely there wasn't room for one more body inside; still, the lobby crowd pressed ahead. Moving toward the outer doors against the flow was impossible. Martha felt Anna clutch her leg and tried to bend in the crush of bodies to pick her up, but the best she could do was protectively encircle Anna's shoulders. Anna's tense body partially relaxed, but she kept her face hidden in Martha's skirt.

Comments alternated between "Can't believe a Jap won the game for us" and "Can't believe a Jap won the game for them."

The pack of bodies reversed direction and everyone shoved to get outside. Martha decided the safest place was where she was. Then a small space opened that allowed her to pick up Anna, who buried her face against Martha's shoulder. Henry Behm had used his slight but deceptively strong physique to open a gap and provide them an escape route. Martha walked out in front of him.

"I have to describe all this to Zella," he shouted above the noise. "But she won't believe it. No one will believe this evening unless they were here. Wasn't Jimmie swell? And to think, I was part of his training!"

Henry drifted by, carried by the current of the crowd. The building emptied quickly, and Art soon joined them.

"Wasn't Jimmie the hero?" he croaked.

At the sound of Art's strange voice, hoarse from shouting, Anna's head snapped off Martha's shoulder. She held her arms out to Art. "Are you hurt, Papa?"

Art took her and answered, "No, punkin. I just been shoutin' so long my throat's tired. Let's go home an' celebrate. Martha, I wouldn't a missed tonight fer anything in the world."

"I have a better idea. Let's go to Henry and Zella's for coffee. Between the two of you, you can recreate the game for Zella. He was worried he couldn't do it justice."

Art considered the proposal and said, "An' I'd enjoy talkin' with someone 'bout it, someone who knows how hard we worked fer this."

"Art, what if Jimmie had missed the free throw?"

"I'd a still been proud. Point is, his playin' kept the game close."

Martha hoped that fact wasn't as lost on the crowd as it was on her. She hadn't tracked Jimmie's participation that closely.

"How'd it happen that you joined the coach?"

"His assistant has the flu. Too sick ta stay. Evidently Jimmie pointed me out ta the coach, who knows me. Asked me ta help. Funny. He used ta play 'gainst me, on that other team."

Art's chuckle came out as a squawk, and he said, "Wonder if his home folks'll ever let him back in town."

Martha's bitter response remained unspoken. The coach had a home there or in Greenwood, regardless of the outcome of one basketball game. Jimmie's welcome was tenuous, at best, in spite of his victory.

Conspiracies

The week after the big game, Martha heard Art call softly from the door of the dimly lit henhouse. What could be so important he couldn't wait until she finished gathering eggs?

"Yer father brought the paper. Ya need ta see this."

When she stepped out, the bright sun blinded her. "Just tell me what's happened."

"It's the Japanese schoolhouse. A picture a Congressman Dies from Texas standin' by a big map a the Pacific."

"What does he have to do with the schoolhouse?"

"Paper says the Greenwood VFW found the map stuck behind the drawer of an old desk. They showed it ta Burleigh, an' Burleigh called the FBI."

"What on earth for? Of course there would be a map in a schoolhouse. And what's Congressman Dies got to do with it?"

"It's complicated. Read it. I'll finish with the eggs."

He thrust the paper into her hand. The picture of the congressman filled the upper half of the front page. Whatever the details, Art mentioned a toxic mix of ingredients — Japanese farmers, Al Ivarson's VFW, Burleigh, the FBI, and Congressman Dies's un-American committee. Dies and Burton Wheeler were the same the kind of Democrat, one from Texas, the other from Montana. Dies's reputation for mindless politics rested on his accusation several years ago that ten-year-old Shirley Temple was a communist sympathizer. The public knew better then, but it would believe this one against a western Japanese Farmers' Association.

"Where's Anna?" she asked to avoid reading the story.

"There, in the sun, by the corner a the barn, buildin' her own barn outta old sticks she found in a box under my tool bench."

"Sticks probably covered in dust and grime. She'll be a mess."

Fuming about a dirty child was far more productive than fuming about remote Congressmen.

Art didn't defend the grime and said, "Are ya gonna read it er not?"

She didn't answer and walked to the stump of the dead cottonwood Art had just removed from the edge of the lane. She sat on it and looked closer at the over-sized picture of a sober gentleman beside a large wall map with visible Japanese writing. The headline read "Japanese War Map Found in Greenwood." How had such a well-intentioned gift turned out so badly?

She didn't need to read far to learn Burleigh's role. Not surprisingly, the VFW followed his December directive up to the tee. They found the map, which shouldn't have made them suspicious but did, contacted Burleigh, who should have known better but didn't, and he called the Denver office of the FBI. Their man came for it, and now it hung on the Congressman's wall. The article said it was a Japanese naval map of the Pacific, "convincing proof of Japan's belligerency before Pearl Harbor."

The embarrassment of the map and the FBI's involvement would have been enough to shame Mr. Miyoshi completely, but for the story to become national news? By implication, it condemned all the Japanese schools, evidence for folks who had viewed them as indoctrination centers for American-born Japanese children. Mr. Miyoshi was surely overcome, particularly given his disavowal of the school at her kitchen table the week after the Pearl Harbor attack. Martha didn't bother to straighten out the twists in the so-called logic of the article.

"Mama, are you crying?"

She hadn't been aware of Anna standing by the stump, or her tears.

"Yes," she freely admitted. No need to hide tears shed on Mr. Miyoshi's behalf.

"Mr. Miyoshi and his friends gave folks in Greenwood a very nice gift, and instead of saying thank you, they're being mean. That upsets me a lot."

Anna stamped her foot. "Me, too."

Martha's anger was about as effective. Nothing she could do would take away Mr. Miyoshi's humiliation.

In the letter Henry recently referred to, the one in the paper from the young Japanese soldier at the Presidio Army Intelligence School, the soldier pled for understanding. He asked that United States citizens not disturb or harm American-born Japanese such as him, or their parents, who cooperated one hundred percent in the willingness of their children to sacrifice their lives to protect the U.S. from enemy attack. She particularly remembered the one hundred percent.

Mr. Miyoshi had given one hundred percent, but there wasn't a picture in the paper of the day the Japanese farmers presented the building. She was there. A lovely ceremony. The only remnant of his generosity was a smirking congressman studying a map "hidden" in the school. And few people would remember the young intelligence officer's letter, but everyone would remember Congressman Dies's so-called proof of Japanese belligerency and its association with the school — one they would assume had been sponsored by parents in collusion with Japan.

That evening she drove down to Mr. Miyoshi's, even after she saw the Ichikawa's car in the lane. Ordinarily, she wouldn't disturb Mr. Miyoshi when he had guests, but it was her turn to apologize.

She walked up the porch steps with the newspaper in hand. Mr. Miyoshi came to the door, took note of the paper, and motioned her inside. Mr. and Mrs. Ichikawa stood and bowed.

"I'm sorry, so sorry about the schoolhouse," she began.

She couldn't bring herself to say more. Mr. Miyoshi didn't speak, but in his expression she saw profound sorrow.

"What will you do now?" she asked.

Mr. Miyoshi gently took the paper from her hand and laid it, still folded over so the offensive picture was concealed, on the table.

"It can't be helped. *Shikata ga nai*. We go on."

"But surely there's something that can be done?"

"Perhaps. Perhaps not. We watch and wait. Please, have some tea."

Some tea? Martha was prepared for the silent companionship of a wake, not for an ordinary cup of tea. But what else did one do while one waited, for who knew how long, for who knew what?

"Thank you."

From her view out Mr. Miyoshi's front window, Martha saw Henry Behm's automobile pull into the lane behind Max's Truck.

"Mr. Miyoshi, Rev. Behm is here."

Mr. Miyoshi answered the knock and ushered Henry and Parker Hayes into the living room.

"Mr. Miyoshi, Mr. Ichikawa," Mr. Hayes said, "I have news for you both that you might want to hear privately."

Martha's cue to leave. "Mr. Miyoshi, I'll have tea another time."

"Please stay," he said. "Because Rev. Behm and Mr. Hayes are both here, this must be very bad news. More than two Japanese families should hear it. Rev. Behm is present, which already means Mr. Hayes's news isn't private."

Parker Hayes shifted uncomfortably from one foot to the other. Mr. Miyoshi was correct. If Henry didn't already know what Parker Hayes was about to say, he would.

"It's up to you and Mr. Ichikawa whether Martha Lundgren stays," said Mr. Hayes.

Mr. Miyoshi had already declared himself. After a brief exchange in Japanese with Mr. Ichikawa, he said, "Please, allow me to serve everyone tea."

It was settled. Martha remained seated. The tea would function the same as Papa's coffee did the day he reprimanded her for treating Alex so harshly. Tea or coffee, the cups gave something normal to hold on to while the foundations slipped.

Mr. Miyoshi disappeared, and they talked about Jimmie's heroics during the basketball game. Henry did most of the talking, still as excited as he was that night. An initially somber Mr. Hayes lightened considerably because his son Charlie, one of the six-foot players, also played a significant role, which Henry generously described.

Mr. Ichikawa seemed to follow much of the conversation, and Mrs. Ichikawa smiled and nodded each time they mentioned her son's name. It was said frequently, so her head bobbed up and down and her face wore a steady grin.

Mr. Hayes had the last word as Mr. Miyoshi served tea. "Jimmie's play during the game was night and day different from the several before it. Everyone marvels at the change. What do you suppose made the difference?"

Martha looked at Henry, who winked back. She turned to Mr. Miyoshi, whose eyes rolled toward the ceiling. None of the co-conspirators offered an opinion.

Parker Hayes dumped a spoonful of sugar into the small cup and grew somber again. "I've asked Rev. Behm to accompany me because he agrees that what I'm about to say is a major blow to the Japanese farmers. He's here for moral support, yours and mine."

What blow could be more staggering than the tempest about the school building donation?

Unlike with the basketball analysis that was conducted in English, Mr. Miyoshi seemed to have decided this conversation required complete understanding on everyone's part, so they all waited while he translated Mr. Hayes's words for Mr. and Mrs. Ichikawa, who leaned forward in their chairs and studied Mr. Hayes's face.

He continued more deliberately. "President Roosevelt has issued another executive order regarding Japanese aliens."

Mr. Miyoshi translated for Mr. and Mrs. Ichikawa, all three, aliens.

"The order says a new, special government office will have plenary authority over all alien property interests."

"Mr. Hayes, what does that mean? How do I translate it?"

Martha suspected that, whatever the specifics, Japanese families no longer had control of their money. Unlike the February order that was already uprooting Japanese families in the West Coast military zone, this order affected inland families, too.

"I'm not sure about the full impact, either," said Mr. Hayes. "The order might determine whether or not you obtain loans to farm this year. It might also mean your bank accounts are frozen, and someone else will have oversight of them."

Mr. Miyoshi translated.

Mr. Hayes said it altogether too nicely. Perhaps he purposefully toned down the import of Roosevelt's order or was taking pains to be accurate, giving only information of which he could be certain. There seemed no limit to the indignities heaped on Mr. Miyoshi.

Mr. Hayes was saying, "However, I'll personally see to it you obtain the money you need. Rev. Behm and I are visiting every Japanese farmer and delivering this message. When there is confusion or this order causes hardship, please come to me."

Mr. Miyoshi translated and Mr. and Mrs. Ichikawa nodded solemnly.

Clearly, Mr. Hayes proposed he cover the costs for the Japanese farmers. His offer moved Martha deeply as an example of Roosevelt's challenge for every man to work longer and harder at the task for which he is best fitted, although Mr. Hayes's was a topsy-turvy effort. His profession was finance, but he was extending his money to Japanese aliens, not one of Earl's "measured responses."

Would there be folks, such as Mr. Hayes, in sufficient numbers to ameliorate the ill-advised actions of a president and of impetuous sheriffs and congressmen? His generosity inspired her to extend herself further, but how?

"Martha, Martha!"

"Yes, Mr. Hayes?"

"The executive order is, of course, public knowledge. My personal offer to the Japanese families is not, nor can it be, public. You must not mention it, not even to Art or your father. Do you understand?"

She nodded affirmatively but agreed only in part. True, Mr. Hayes was taking a business and personal risk, possibly legal risks as well. She had no way to judge. At the very least, if his offer became known, people like Al Ivarson and Howard Burleigh wouldn't sympathize with his decision, and that would undermine the community's trust in him and the bank. She'd heard about how ugly folks were to Governor Carr at the meeting in La Junta over the relocation of Japanese aliens to Colorado, Al being among the nastiest.

A case should be made, though, that Mr. Hayes's sacrifice be widely known, as an example of compassion. If Congressman Dies had his picture on the front page of papers across the country, along with his ridiculous insinuations about Japanese schools and farmers collaborating with the enemy, Parker Hayes deserved publicity for his confidence in those very aliens.

But of greater immediate impact was how crucial it was to maintain silence about all the secrets she held in trust. If she betrayed those about Fran — the scars of uncertain origin and visits from a man whose relationship to Fran was unclear — she risked damaging Papa, and Fran, in ways she couldn't predict. Disclosing anything about Claude Giffard and Louise would destroy Edith.

Art's coaching sessions with Jimmie were playful, on the surface, but, taken with Art's rescue of Ken Himuru, many would fault him for helping yet another Japanese boy. His reputation for fairness and his work on the tire rationing board would be compromised, as would Papa's standing in the community — guilty on account of his association with Art.

Thankfully, she had partners in all but the mystery concerning Fran and "Jake" — Louise with the scars on Fran's body; Zella and

Henry with the Louise affair; Henry, Art, Mr. Miyoshi, and Jimmie with his basketball prowess; Henry, Parker Hayes, and all the Japanese farmers with Mr. Hayes's determination to protect them from the latest executive order. The final collusion was especially fragile, constituted as it was of so many.

But Louise was gone, as a result of her ill-advised involvement with Claude Giffard. Martha now bore both the Jake business and Fran's scars alone. About those secrets, she had no one with whom to plot and plan. Henry was the common thread in the other intrigues, among the many he was surely party to in Greenwood. How did he bear them?

She was tangled in confidences originating in just four lives — Fran's, Louise's, Jimmie's, and now Parker Hayes's. Surely everyone in her circle of acquaintances was similarly guarding at least one other, Max Lambert's whereabouts an example. How could there be trust between folks when this shadow world of intrigue hovered over every exchange?

She shook hands all around, a necessary gesture to seal her promise. Mr. Miyoshi saw her out.

In his small entryway, she asked, "Mr. Miyoshi, how do you know when to wait and watch? How do you determine when to act?"

"Martha, the first question is 'What partner should I wait and act with?' For me, the VFW was not a trustworthy ally. A more difficult question is 'Must I act alone?' Even Parker Hayes did not act alone. He allied with Rev. Behm, and you."

May 1942

Harriet Moulton

Martha swiped away the tear that rolled down six-year-old Harriet's cheek and assured her, "You're a brave girl." She couldn't say the same for Addie, who seemed incapable of consoling her daughter. Martha sat the distraught mother in a chair behind the examining table and sewed up the cut on Harriet's forearm. It took only four stitches.

Addie mumbled, "What if she hit her head on the rake when she fell, instead of her arm? Too awful to imagine."

Martha walked to the drawer where she kept lollipops and chose a green one. "Harriet, you followed my directions so well about sitting quietly, you may have a candy."

Martha wondered if Harriet would welcome the treat as anything special, but she said, "Thank you," accepted the sucker, tore off the wrapper, and popped it in her mouth.

With Harriet momentarily occupied, Martha took Addie's hand and spoke so Harriet could hear. "Your mother and I are going into the hallway for a moment, and I'll tell her how to take care of your cut while it heals."

She shut the door and grasped Addie by both shoulders. "Get ahold of yourself. Harriet fell from the lower branches of the tree and cut her arm. It isn't serious. Children have accidents all the time. Keep to yourself what you imagine could have happened."

Martha felt Addie stiffen. When Addie raised her head, her hostile look caused Martha to drop her hands and turn away.

In a less quarrelsome tone, Martha said, "Bring Harriet back when Dr. McFarland's here for a tetanus antitoxin shot, today, if possible. Listen carefully as I explain how to tend the wound."

Martha was a fine one to give advice about not imagining the worst, a mother who did just that when Anna went missing. But she hadn't droned on and on about Anna being trussed up in the trunk of an automobile. Well, maybe, just before they found her. Still, she hadn't invented other scenarios, such as Anna being shot in the head by a pheasant hunter. She shivered. Thankfully, that one hadn't occurred to her at the time.

She should be more tolerant of Addie's distress. Probably in Addie's limited experience, Harriet's injury was serious, but any latitude she might have given Addie vanished when mother and daughter walked out.

"I hope there won't be an ugly scar from those stitches, Martha," Addie said. "I would've been more confident with Doc."

Martha indulged a nasty thought. If his services had been required, Harriet would be in the hospital for an amputation, not several stitches. Martha immediately regretted her lapse. It wasn't fair to Harriet, who seemed to be a normal child, in spite of Addie and Walter. Martha sat at the reception desk and added Harriet's tumble and stitches to her card.

Oblivious

Sheriff Burleigh staggered through the door. "Where's Doc? I been hurt, bad."

She caught sight of a bloody towel wrapped around his forearm and britches torn at the knee. A gunshot wound? Something equivalent?

"He's out. Let's set you on the examining table. What's happened?"

"Down south at Mattson's. Gust thinks there's cattle rustlers. Was climbin' through a barbed wire fence. Damned fence tripped me up an' caught my arm. Scraped my knee on a rock. Bled like hell. Mrs. Mattson wrapped my arm an' told me ta get ta town."

He went silent and Martha looked up. The color drained from his usually florid face. The dried blood on the towel had pulled a bit when she removed it.

"Lie down, now."

She helped swing his legs onto the table just in time. She turned to grab the smelling salts and thought better of it. Might as well let him stay out while she looked more closely at the cuts on his arm — numerous, but none as serious as Harriet's. They wouldn't require stitches, only cleaning and some tincture of iodine. The knee was just scraped, and she doctored it, too. He'd also have to come back for tetanus antitoxin when Doc returned.

There, she'd called him "Doc." Perhaps she was gaining confidence as his assistant and could address him less formally.

Burleigh started snoring, and she let him sleep while she cleaned the room.

A loud knock at the back door startled him awake. Enoch Gwynn, ambulance driver as well as undertaker, didn't wait to be admitted. He met Martha in the hallway of the house that was Doc's office and home away from home.

"Brought in a man from the dam site. Don't think he's hurt bad, and their emergency doc at the dam was busy with a terrible accident. A cat-skinner run over by one of their huge machines. Didn't take my man to the hospital because I thought Doc would be here. Wednesday morning office hours. Talked to his buddy and him while we drove to town. But now he's groaning and says he's in considerable pain."

Martha walked back to the examining room where she'd left Burleigh and her medical bag.

Burleigh sat on the edge of the table. He held his arm stiffly to the side and avoided looking at it. "What's the damage, Martha?"

"Lots of cuts but none requiring stitches. You'll need to come back when Doc's here for a tetanus antitoxin shot."

"Don't take shots."

"You don't have a choice. Keep talking, Enoch. I can hear you."

Enoch entered the room. "Sorry, Burleigh. Hmmm… Seems you scrapped up your arm."

"Yeah, real bad. Martha says I got lots a cuts."

He spotted the suckers in the jar Martha had used to replenish the drawer and reached in with his beefy fingers, much less deserving than Harriet.

"Sheriff, those…" Martha started to object.

"Thanks, Martha."

He grabbed five or six and stalked out.

Swede

Enoch picked up where he left off. "The man's buddy says the safety belt unfastened whilst he stripped forms on a concrete section. The buddy was working alongside and grabbed his arm but couldn't hold on. Broke his fall, for sure. Otherwise the man could be dead, I suppose. Still, the buddy feels really bad."

"How far did he fall?"

She walked rapidly past Enoch with her medical bag, which forced him to call out his estimate to her disappearing back. "Maybe twelve feet."

The "buddy" knelt beside the man on the stretcher, both men filling the back of Enoch's hearse that played the secondary role of ambulance. Each time the man moaned his friend answered with a quiet stream of encouragement.

"We're in town, at the doc's office."

Another moan.

"You'll be jus' fine. Mr. Enoch's gone inside fer help."

The friend's gentle manner reminded her of Uncle Malcolm.

He seemed startled when she said, "Please step out. I can't examine the patient with you in the way."

Perhaps she had been too abrupt.

"Shouldn't we carry the stretcher into the office?" asked Enoch. "And where's Doc?"

"Doc's on a call. No, don't move him yet."

If Enoch was questioning her judgment, perhaps Addie's jab about preferring Doc's treatment wasn't peculiar to her. Maybe a number of folks doubted Martha's abilities.

She hoisted herself into the back of the vehicle with an assist from the steady arm of the friend. She gave him no more than a cursory look but had the impression she had seen him before.

She called back to Enoch, "We should move him as little as possible until we know the extent of his injuries."

The morning sunlight flooded the back of the hearse. The right pant leg was ripped up to the crotch and Martha could easily see the swollen leg. Probably a broken femur and pressure from bleeding inside. And no reason to think Enoch had thought to check his pupils.

She glanced at the friend and took note of a thick scar that ran along the upper edge of his left cheekbone, from close to his nose just past the outer edge of his eye.

"What's his name?"

"Nelson, I think. We jest call 'im 'Swede.'"

The buddy looked at her directly. He removed his hat. No one but Fran Reeve had eyes that green. His hair was thick, auburn colored, but, unlike Fran's, greying around the temples.

"And I go by the name a Jake, ma'am."

Martha froze. She forced herself to look back at "Swede," a man as tall as Art but outweighing him by more than thirty pounds. Although his body was large enough to spill over the edges and end of it, the stretcher seemed to levitate. She rested her hand on Swede's chest to stabilize herself.

She repeated the name in a whisper. "Jake."

"Pardon, ma'am?"

A groan from Swede moved Martha to action. A quick check of his pupils indicated one was larger than the other.

"Enoch, Swede's seriously injured. We must get him to the hospital, and we need Doc, who's at the colonia by the hay mill, delivering a baby. He's been there since before dawn, according to his note. Jake, take my truck. It's parked out front. The keys are in it. You drove by the colonia on your way into town. It's a cluster of adobe houses by the hay mill, which is located on the north side of the road, by the railroad tracks. You'll travel almost halfway the distance back to the dam site before you see it, past the school and the Country Store. You can't miss Doc's car. It's a large black Ford sedan."

"Ma'am, I ain't driven fer some time. Ya sure ya want me ta take yer truck?"

Jake looked intelligent, and sincere, qualities she readily granted him as ones he shared with Fran, surely his sister.

"How to drive isn't something folks forget. If you haven't understood, your friend's injuries threaten his life. Tell Doc I sent you. Describe Swede's fall and this — the right femur's broken and the thigh already quite swollen; the pupil of the right eye is dilated. Doc'll understand. You must hurry, and that means disregarding the forty-mile wartime speed limit. If anyone stops you, explain what happened and that I, Martha Lundgren, am at the hospital with Enoch Gwynn and your friend. The fact you know my name, and Enoch's, might convince someone you haven't stolen the truck."

But Doc might not come right away. The delivery at the colonia must be complicated or he wouldn't be there; otherwise, the Spanish women would have handled it.

She ran into the office, grabbed the card that instructed patients to return later or go to the hospital in an emergency, and hung it on the front door. Enoch had backed the hearse out of the driveway and waited for her in the street.

Delay

When they turned into the alley behind the hospital, Rudy Ruiz abandoned the garbage can he was emptying into a barrel and ran to help Enoch slide the stretcher out. The two struggled to carry the heavy Swede into the operating room. Martha and Cora Jane followed. Martha described his injuries.

Cora Jane said, "About the leg, if the pressure's dangerous and he has to be operated on right away, what can we do without Doc? About the head, we have to wait for him."

In Cora Jane, Martha finally had a partner who understood the danger to Swede and the limitations of two nurses.

They went through the familiar motions of preparing for surgery, and Cora Jane asked, "Martha, would you cut open the leg without Doc, if he's further delayed?"

"I don't know. Would you?"

"I don't know, either."

"Let's hope it doesn't come to that."

She assumed Cora Jane wouldn't have asked if she weren't entertaining the thought. Assured they were of the same mind, that if Swede's condition got much worse and Doc didn't appear, they would take whatever measures with the leg they thought necessary, Martha changed the subject to take her mind off the prospect.

"Why's Rudy here? Elena said he'd enlisted."

"Failed his physical. Bad teeth."

"Strange Elena didn't mention he'd returned, much less he's the janitor here, although I'm sure Dolores Ruiz, uh, Roybal, is grateful to have her brother back."

"Not so strange Elena didn't say anything. Protecting him, I imagine. Rudy's devastated he didn't pass, but the hospital's the better with him as janitor. Good worker. Quick learner."

Swede moaned and the two women were quiet for a moment, but there was nothing more to be done, until Doc came.

"Martha, I heard nurses were evacuated from Bataan to Corregidor Island. Does anyone know if Muriel's in that group?"

"No, but probably not. They're thought to be army nurses, sixty-eight of them. More likely she's one of the thousands of Americans in concentration camps in Japanese-occupied Manila."

Swede groaned and flung out his right arm, landing a blow against Cora Jane's chest with such force she staggered back against the wall.

"Rudy, come here," yelled Martha, hoping he was still within shouting distance. Enoch crashed through the door first, followed by Rudy.

"Cora Jane, you all right?" Martha called out.

No response.

"Enoch, hold down his arms. Rudy, hand me those scissors so I can cut the sheet into strips to tie him down. What's wrong with Cora Jane?"

She had slid down the wall and was gulping for air. She finally managed, "I'm all right. Just had the wind knocked out. That was a surprise. Thought he was unconscious."

It was fortunate Swede remained quiet because Enoch's physical strength wasn't sufficient if Swede exerted himself again. Everyone helped shred the sheet and relaxed when he was bound.

"What is wrong with his leg?" Rudy said. "It is twice as big as the other one, and it is such a strange color."

Martha answered, "The bone in his thigh is broken and the leg's bleeding inside. The pressure's building, and it must be operated on soon. Everyone but Cora Jane, out. After this episode, we have to prepare him again."

Martha moved up by Swede's head, encouraging, sympathizing, explaining where his friend, Jake, and the doctor were.

"Martha, why are you talking to him? He's unconscious."

"Swede might understand more than we realize. Perhaps the sound of a soothing voice lets him know he's not being ignored, that we're helping, which is better than carrying on a conversation between the two of us as if he's not here, and better than silence."

"Martha, we can't wait any longer."

Doc burst through the doors. "Let's get to it."

Jake

Afterward, Martha went to the waiting area, the alcove she still associated with Frank Ogawa's accident at the canal several years ago, where so many folks congregated and learned of his death. At the time of Carrie's premature birth, her family would have gathered here, too, and, more recently, after her miscarriage. The drab walls and chairs belied the weight of hours folks spent there and the depth of their emotions, expectant, yet filled with dread.

This particular morning Jake sat by the window, alone. He stood as she approached. She heard herself saying the vague words that the loss of blood had weakened his friend, that the extent of the injury to the head was unknown, that all anyone could do now was wait. Doc would be out soon with more information.

Jake nodded. They sat. Martha was comfortable with the silence, given the choices. She wasn't going to leave him alone in the alcove, with his friend in such bad shape. His considerate manner with Swede required equally decent behavior on her part.

And she couldn't very well admit she was an onlooker when Fran slapped him at the pavilion or blew him a kiss from the porch. She knew the potency of emotional rifts between brothers and sisters from her outburst at Alex.

Small talk about how Jake came to be working at the dam didn't seem right, either, given the critical condition of his friend. Besides, Jake seemed content with silence, too.

When Doc appeared, Jake stood with the same respect and deference he had shown her. Doc described Swede's condition in much the way Martha had. Maybe soon she would say "Doc" aloud, to his face.

After Doc excused himself, Martha asked Jake, "Will you be staying at the hospital, or do you need to get back to the dam?"

"Boss'll prob'ly be here soon. Maybe some a th'other men. He called the hospital while ya was in the operatin' room, lookin' fer Swede an' me. They'll be surprised it's so bad. Everyone thought he might a just broke 'is leg. That's not a small thing, but when he came to after he fell, Swede kept insistin' it was nothin'. Even tried ta hop over ta the hearse, although said 'is head was spinnin'. He did, too, with us on each side helpin' 'im."

Martha nodded, wordlessly accepting Jake's summary of events and understanding why Enoch underestimated the severity of the injuries. Swede probably made matters worse by putting on such a brave show.

After a respectful interval she asked, "Do you want something to eat? We can go over to the Sage Café, or I can bring back a sandwich and coffee."

Jake turned toward her and wearily, cautiously, said, "That's very nice a ya, ma'am, but I'll wait fer the men. Left the keys in yer truck. Sheriff did stop me on the way out a town. Followed me ta where Doc was gettin' in his car and escorted us back. Good thing ya told me ta mention yer name an' Mr. Gwynn's. That seemed ta satisfy 'im when he stopped me, fer now."

Martha liked Jake, with his sadness like Uncle Malcolm's. She heard his words as a gentle dismissal and stood to go.

Jake respectfully stood, also. "Ma'am, I thank ya on behalf a Swede an' all the men, that ya trusted me with yer truck. When I found Doc at the hay mill, he said he would a been goin' home fer somethin' ta eat if ya hadn't sent me ta git 'im."

Martha hadn't expected the thank you; Jake's willingness to help and his demeanor had already communicated his gratitude. But it made up for the haughty Addie and oblivious Burleigh.

"I'm grateful for how you pitched in," she said.

She reached out to shake his hand. He seemed startled but took it soon enough.

"Please call me Martha."

She turned when she reached the door. "I pray to the Good Lord your friend recovers, healthy and strong."

Jake bowed his head as though enacting her intent, and she went out the door, careful to shut it softly.

Ruminations

On her way to pick up Elena and the children at Josie's, Martha wondered what Fran had told Jake about Papa and his family, or if she had mentioned Jake to Papa.

Whatever Fran's history with Jake, it was more complicated than Martha's was with her brother. The argument with its conclusive slap behind the dance pavilion last summer conveyed a dogged determination to keep Jake at a distance that Martha hadn't enforced with Alex. The tender exchange between Fran and Jake that night on Fran's porch might not signal sufficient resolution.

Jake's restraint was also curious. He didn't offer a last name. He gave minimal answers and followed instructions without taking initiative beyond what was required, not even to move from the waiting room or accept a sandwich until his boss arrived. And, while an onlooker would accept Jake's gestures of polite behavior toward Martha as the conventional ones expected of a man toward a woman he had just met, she detected a stiff formality that caused her to think he wasn't around women often, as though he was out of practice and had to exaggerate each move in order to execute it correctly.

Most bothersome was the phrase "for now" when he referred to Burleigh being satisfied with his explanation of why he was driving

Max's Truck, as though he expected repercussions. Martha assumed he carried a driver's license, but perhaps he didn't, and that's why Burleigh escorted him to the colonia and back to town. Jake said he hadn't driven for a while, and he wasn't driving the night she saw him get into the car in front of Fran's apartment. The lack of a license and ominous facial scar would pique any officer's curiosity, even one less vigilant than Burleigh.

The scar — a sort of brand connecting him to Fran more emphatically than his green eyes and auburn hair. They couldn't have inflicted the wounds on each other. Jake's basic nature was gentle, as shown by the tenderness with which he treated the injured Swede in the back of the hearse. Jake wouldn't attack Fran, but he would leap to her defense if she were threatened, even faster than he reflexively reacted to Swede's fall.

Burleigh was probably already investigating Jake's background and would stumble onto Fran's part in it. Martha had no choice but to warn her that whatever story she insisted on leaving in her past, it wouldn't stay there much longer.

Martha would tell Fran what she knew. The striking resemblance of their green eyes and auburn hair, and the similar texture and shape of their scars. That she saw Fran slap Jake, and, only months ago, blow him a kiss and whisper his name in her delirium. At least Martha wouldn't have to confront Fran with suspicions about her loyalty to Papa. Those were laid to rest.

She would go to Fran and describe the accident at the dam and Jake's conversation with Burleigh. Fran didn't have to disclose anything to Martha, but she had to be prepared for Burleigh's inevitable snooping.

Martha parked the truck in front of Josie's and saw Anna looking out the living room window. Her enthusiastic wave left no doubt about her relief the window vigil was ended. Martha checked her watch. Twelve forty-five. Much later than usual. Surely Elena had already fed the children, but Robbie would be ready for his nap. She would drive everyone to the farm and come back for the conversation with Fran.

The timing was bad, with Fran completely immersed in the senior play. The first performance would be the next evening, but given the disastrous outcome of Burleigh's zealous pursuit of Dolores Ruiz's assailant and how he misunderstood the map in the Japanese schoolhouse, she dreaded to think what damage he could set in motion for the Reeves. Besides, Fran needed to know she had an ally in Martha.

$$May\ 1942$$

Rudy Ruiz

"Thank you, Elena, for feeding the children," Martha said after loading everyone in the cab of Max's Truck. "We had a medical emergency, and I saw Rudy at the hospital. Miss Collins explained he didn't pass his physical."

Robbie squealed and banged his chubby hands on the dashboard. Elena laughed, and Anna duplicated his drumming efforts, which spurred Robbie on.

Martha almost shouted, "Anna, Elena, I can't concentrate with this ruckus. Please find a quieter game."

Elena intercepted Robbie's next solo by slipping her hands under his. They played a horizontal version of pat a cake, and Anna waited her turn.

The children occupied, Elena said, "I am sorry, Mrs. Lundgren. I did not hear you."

"I saw Rudy at the hospital and learned he didn't pass his physical."

Elena's vitality disappeared, which deflated the children. Robbie leaned back into her chest, and Anna took her book out of Elena's bag. She snuggled against Martha.

"Rudy is unhappy," Elena said. "The rejection upset him almost as much as Dolores's forced marriage to that Joe Roybal. But I am glad Rudy failed his physical so he is here for Dolores. I hope he will not leave, but he talks about working at Remington in Denver after Dolores's baby is born. That could be any day."

Martha expected more about Dolores, but Elena was silent. "And how is Dolores?"

"Joe Roybal is gone, and no one knows where. Uncle Zeke allows us to visit her now and insists she come home because it is too expensive to rent her a room and buy her food. Dolores refuses. She will not forgive Uncle Zeke, so Rudy gives her money and food. That makes Uncle Zeke very angry; it is terrible for Rudy at home."

Zeke, too proud to admit the forced marriage was a horrible idea. Rudy, crushed about his rejection. Father and son with wounded pride. Life under that roof must be wretched.

"My mother and Aunt Pauline talk again about taking her to Santa Fe to their sister after the baby comes."

Surely they were relieved Roybal was gone, and his departure couldn't have been a surprise. He was easily lost in the confusion of war, and Burleigh wouldn't go after him this time, now that the baby had a family name. But Dolores and her baby faced a precarious future. If Dolores's brother, Rudy, was her only source of money, the job as janitor at the hospital didn't pay him enough, and it was only a matter of time before Zeke forced him out of the home.

The rehash of Burleigh's role in the Roybal fiasco made all the more urgent the need to warn Fran about the mischief he was bound to cause if he investigated Jake's background.

"Elena, I'm so sorry about these difficult times for the Ruiz family. By the way, I must run back to town later, but we'll have several hours to work in the garden. I'm at least a week behind my planting.

"As for Rudy, do you think he'd mind if I suggest to Mr. Lundgren that he be our hired hand, until he knows what he's going to do? You know how badly we need the help. Mr. McLennan and I can clean out the bunkhouse at the Home Place for him. Farm wages are higher than they've been in years. With room, and maybe board, I imagine Papa and Art would pay between a dollar fifty and two dollars a day."

"That much? Rudy is not predictable these days, but it is worth a try. He might think he is following in Luis and Alex's footsteps, working for you and Mr. McLennan, and feel less awful he is not a soldier. But I should not ask because he would think that I begged you to hire him. He wants to be a man, responsible for himself."

"I understand. Mr. Lundgren and I'll work on how to approach him."

Another conspiracy, but a benevolent one with a number of potential partners in agreement.

Martha described the morning's events and the causes for her delay. By the time she turned the truck into the lane, Robbie was fast asleep. She mentioned in passing that Doc helped with a delivery at the colonia.

"That must be Dolores's friend," Elena said. "This is her second time. The first baby was born early, like Carrie, and died."

Neither Martha nor Elena moved to get out of the truck.

"Elena, as a friend of Dolores's, she must be only seventeen or eighteen, and this is her second child?"

"Mrs. Lundgren, you know most of us stop school after we are fourteen, or younger. The fathers need us in the fields, but many girls marry. As I often say, this is why my mother and I are very proud of Marguerite."

"Yes, and as I often say, Josie's proud of her, too. I'm not well acquainted with Marguerite, but I know she's an unusual girl."

"Mrs. Lundgren, because you are interested in Dolores and her friend, now might be the time to ask."

But Elena didn't continue. Martha gave her an encouraging glance.

Elena took a deep breath. "My mother and Tia Pauline, I mean, Aunt Pauline, want me to ask you…something. We all talk about how Rudy's teeth keep him from his dream, and that many boys we know fail the physical. Also, life in the colonias is difficult, not just for the mothers and children. There is sickness always, and the children do not have enough food."

"I know their lives are difficult, but I'm sorry to say I've not seen it for myself."

The admission made Martha uncomfortable. Josie had described the unsanitary conditions and the poor construction of the houses because she had visited some of her students in the colonias, but Martha hadn't ever made the effort.

Elena drew another breath.

"Go on, Elena. I'm interested to hear what you have to say."

"We have discussed if I should ask you, and everyone agrees I should."

In Elena's reference to a group decision, Martha heard echoes of her conversation with Mr. Miyoshi about the first question to ask before taking action: With whom does one ally? Elena implied she had a number of collaborators urging her on. Being the object of so much speculation added to Martha's unease.

Elena swallowed before continuing, "Would you please teach a Red Cross home nursing class for the Spanish-American women? They learned about it at the last Spanish PTA meeting. Many have family in the colonias, or they came from there. I, or Marguerite, could translate."

Teaching a class for Spanish-American women hadn't entered Martha's mind all the times she cast about for what she was best suited to do for defense. She was uniquely positioned for it, knowing several of the families as she did, and teaching the course went well beyond the Good Samaritan effort she and Elsie made in Ralph's Market when they rescued a solitary, hungry Mexican boy from the closet. Clara could ask nurses from Fort Lyon to teach the classes demanded by the Women's Club and AAUW members, now that more staff had arrived to help with the increased numbers of patients.

Martha leaned around Anna, who was "reading" her book for the umpteenth time, and patted Elena on the hand. "That's an excellent idea. Let me talk with Miss Boehler. As the public health nurse, she's the one who arranges the classes. But I should warn you there's a great demand for them, and many groups of women are waiting."

Art's tap on the metal door interrupted. "You two gonna sit there all day, er can I have some dinner?"

He stuck his head in the open window and kissed Martha lightly on the cheek.

"Art, sorry we're late. I'm starved, too. Everyone else ate at Josie's."

Dusk

Martha found Fran surrounded by students at the back of the stage in the gymnasium. Her apartment was the better setting for their conversation, but Fran might arrive home late, given the last minute preparations for the play.

"If you're looking for Josie, she's in the costume room," called out a red-faced, breathless Fran.

Martha's interruption could not be more badly timed. "No, I need to speak with you, right away."

Fran extricated herself from the circle of students. "Is it Robert? What's happened?"

"No, it isn't Papa. It's Jake. Where can we talk?"

Fran's confusion was so momentary anyone not watching closely would have missed it. It was replaced by a stoic look so cold Martha flinched, but she maintained her determination.

Fran didn't look away from Martha and called out, "Marguerite, please gather the girls on stage and review the lines in the second act. Charlie Hayes, bring the boys out front on the bleachers and do the same."

Without missing a beat, she lowered her voice and said, "A place of privacy? I can't think of one. We'll go to the English classroom and hope for the best."

She turned and strode away. Martha, doubting they'd have sufficient time alone, lengthened her step in an effort to keep up and began her account of the morning: the accident, Jake's role in it, how she connected Jake's looks and scar with Fran's.

They reached the hallway by the classrooms, and Fran turned to face her. "Everything you say is coincidental. Do you have other reasons to connect me with this man?"

Martha walked past her into the English classroom. Fran had to follow to hear the answer. Neither switched on the light that would call attention to their presence. The dim yellow illumination from the hallway that shone through the windowpane of the door was sufficient, combining as it did with the dusky blue light from the east-facing windows. Fran shut the door.

Martha hadn't anticipated Fran would deny Jake was her brother after being presented with this much evidence. Martha's next words were more direct, insistent.

"Fran, when you were ill with the flu, you called out the name 'Jake' a number of times in your delirium. I saw him on your front porch when I arrived that night. I saw you slap him this summer at the dance pavilion."

Fran's defiant expression would have compelled Martha to stop there, were it not for Martha's conviction Fran had to take control before Burleigh did.

"I know you work hard to keep distance between yourself and whatever happened in Oklahoma, so please believe me when I say I wouldn't bring this information to you were it not for the fact Burleigh stopped Jake on his way to the colonia to get Doc. I let Jake take Max's Truck. I have the impression Jake expects some sort of repercussion from their encounter."

Martha had difficulty reading Fran's expression in the dim light, but Fran made no move to leave. Martha, somewhat encouraged, still didn't believe Fran understood the danger.

"Fran, we both know Burleigh isn't discreet. If he investigates Jake's background, no one can predict what he'll do with the information, and you've taken such pains to put your past behind you."

Martha paused for some indication her words were getting through. Fran might never speak to her again.

"I'm not asking you to disclose your past. It isn't my concern. I'm only alerting you so you can protect yourself, and Jake. Whatever your decision, you must make it soon. You know I would never come to you in the middle of your work if this wasn't urgent."

Martha hesitated again.

"Your first reaction when you saw me was to worry about Papa. You would have dropped everything to go to him. Worry about yourself and Jake with the same resolve. Do you understand?"

Fran leaned against the wall, limp. "All too well. You don't realize, Martha, how this shatters what I've worked for, what I've become."

She laughed softly, bitterly. "And to think it's happened because Jake did what he always does — reaches out to save someone at his peril."

Martha grabbed Fran's hands. Thank the Good Lord Fran wasn't angry with her.

Martha's words were no less fierce because they were whispered. "Whatever happened in the past isn't repeating itself. Your circumstances are different. You're different. Don't succumb to this. You have the love and respect of my family, of your students, of your friends. Go to Burleigh. Tell him Jake's story. Satisfy Burleigh's curiosity. He won't investigate if he's persuaded there's no danger to Greenwood County."

Fran withdrew her hands from Martha's and pushed herself away from the wall. "Even if I go to Burleigh, I only know part of what happened in Oklahoma, but pieces of it keep seeping into my life, through Vera and Ida, through the coincidence of Jake coming to work on the dam. I'm afraid to go to Burleigh, but I'm afraid if I don't…"

"Fran, the night Louise and I bathed you I didn't promise to keep quiet about your scars because I was alarmed they implied something dangerous for Papa. I don't feel that way now. I want to help. I'll not betray your confidence, but you must do something about Burleigh so you're in control of your past, not him."

Fran's sigh came from deep in her chest. "I don't know it's something I can control."

Martha, not convinced Fran had the resolve to act, said, "You must go to Burleigh. I have to leave. Everyone will be looking for you."

Martha turned toward the door, but Fran grabbed her wrist with such force Martha spun to face her.

"Martha, I'll understand if you can't agree to what I'm about to ask, but until I take care of this, will you not tell Robert? That's my responsibility."

"I don't know what I would tell him. It would have been such a mistake to say anything about my suspicions regarding Jake. I'm relieved to know the truth."

"Your suspicions?"

"That he was an old beau rekindling a romance."

Fran laughed softly. "If only that was all there was to it."

What could pose more danger for Papa than an old rival?

Grateful Josie hadn't seen her, Martha hurried down the empty hallway. She had no idea what excuse she would have used for being at the school.

Something horrible had happened to have power over a woman as strong as Fran and to provoke such sorrow in Jake. Martha doubted Fran had other allies — Jake wasn't talking, and Fran made clear Papa wasn't to know.

Order Restored

Martha entered the kitchen and saw Elena on her knees by the washtub on the floor, a firm hand on Robbie splashing in the tub and a nude Anna standing by.

"Elena, what's going on?"

"We worked in the garden," Anna answered. "I'm the dirtiest, so I have to wait until Prince Robbie finishes."

Indeed, Anna's arms and legs were streaked with mud.

"Hand me that towel to wrap around Prince Robbie, please," Elena asked.

Anna hurried to comply.

"All right, it is your turn, Princess Anna."

Anna lifted a muddy leg over the edge of the tub. "Brr, it's too cold, Elena."

She lifted her foot back over the edge and a mud puddle promptly formed.

"Don't move, Anna," directed Martha. "I'll add hot water from the tea kettle and you can step right back in. We don't need the whole garden transported onto the kitchen floor."

Martha added the water and grabbed a dirty tea towel to mop up the puddle.

Anna's answer satisfied Martha's question about the immediate scene, but where was Art? And Elena hadn't even started supper.

"Did you lose track of time on account of daylight savings, Elena? We have to get the children fed so Robbie's ready when Josie comes. She might be here any minute."

Martha rarely scolded Elena because she usually had things in order, but her temper was short. The day had stretched endlessly from one shock to another.

Elena frowned and answered, "Mrs. Lundgren, Mr. Lundgren has gone to the tire meeting. He said he did not need to eat before he left because you and he ate dinner so late. He told me to finish in the garden, that you would be pleased. The children and I had a picnic outside. It is a beautiful evening."

Elena's defense was ironclad. Martha closed her eyes, as though shutting out the visual mess would order the confusion in her head. A year had passed since Martha rushed into the kitchen after her grueling day with Vera and Ida, convinced her daughters were at risk with Elena, only to discover Anna playing checkers, hamburgers frying, and Carrie asleep in the bassinette. Carrie. Carrie. She opened her eyes and felt calmer.

"I should have known there was an explanation for the, for the unusual scene that greeted me. You had everything under control, just as you did the first night you helped us. I'm very tired, but that's no reason to question your judgment. I'll dress Robbie while you help Anna. But I believe he's now 'Prince Robbie.' Anna, will you tell me why he's a prince and you're a princess when I tuck you in tonight?"

Elena's frown disappeared and Anna was obviously tickled Martha noticed her new title. An efficient peace descended on the room, children were dressed, muddy water disposed of, and order restored none too soon, for Earl, not Josie, appeared at the kitchen door to retrieve Prince Robbie with a frown more threatening than Elena's.

"Evening, Martha, Elena. I'm to take you home, Elena. I hope Robbie is fed and ready for bed because Josie called from the school and said she'd be late. So much to do to prepare for the play, and Fran was called away for an emergency. With the first performance tomorrow night, it must have been something important. I had to walk back to the school for the car. I have work waiting for me."

Well, haven't we all, King Earl, Martha was tempted to say. Instead, she nodded to Elena, letting her have the satisfaction of answering Earl's questions about Prince Robbie in the affirmative.

After the three left, Martha proposed to Anna they have a petite tea party, the French adjective befitting a princess, more to give Martha opportunity to get food into her stomach than to serve the princess. The telephone rang as they sat to eat.

"Doc, hello. You sound very tired. Is everything all right?"

He never telephoned her at home.

Doc said Swede died, but rather than making the death sound like a defeat, he thanked her. He said she accurately diagnosed Swede's injuries, took every measure possible to get him help by sending Jake to the colonia and having the patient prepared to undergo the operation. Doc appreciated her efforts, and he passed along the gratitude of all Swede's buddies.

Martha hardly knew how to react. The man died, and Doc thanked her. But the man died.

By the time she ate, tucked Anna in, and heard an obviously enhanced version of the origins of the royal titles, she felt somewhat better. The major contributor to her improved mood was Earl's inadvertent clue that Fran left play practice for an emergency, which must mean she was dealing with Burleigh.

Art's tire rationing board meeting had completely slipped her mind. He'd probably mentioned it at dinner that afternoon, but she was too preoccupied with how she would approach Fran. He'd be coming home hungry and at least as tired as she was. She'd have a sandwich and coffee ready and give him the day's news. Well, most of the day's news.

Resistance

Martha followed through on her good intentions as far as having food on the table, but she was sound asleep on the sofa when Art finally came home and didn't wake until she heard the rattle of dishes in the sink. He was heading toward the bedroom before she completely roused herself.

"How'd the meeting go?" she asked.

"Not well. The tire quota fer the county was cut in half this month, an' the requests doubled. How can ya decide 'tween Al Ivarson an' yer father when ya know both can't get what they need? A nightmare. I don't have the wisdom a Solomon, but somehow we muddled through. Everyone knows it's a hellish job, 'scuse me. It's damned work, regardless a who does it."

"I probably shouldn't know the ins and outs. I'll read the results in the paper along with everyone else. I wanted to stay up to give you some good news, but I fell asleep."

"I'm ready fer good news."

"You know Rudy Ruiz, Luis's cousin. He didn't pass his physical. Bad teeth."

"Doesn't sound like good news."

"Not for him, certainly, and he's the janitor at the hospital until he figures out what to do. I suggested to Elena he might work for you and Papa, if he were approached by one of you. She thinks it would help heal his damaged pride if he thought he was following in Luis's footsteps as our hired hand. Rudy's very downhearted."

"I can imagine. Didn't see it in the paper yet, 'bout him failin' his physical. Don't know why they publish the names a those boys. Adds insult ta injury. Not their fault so many're underweight an', like Rudy, have bad teeth. Just how they was raised. But yer right. Could be good news fer us, ta get a hired hand who's a local boy. Robert an' I'll talk an' decide how ta handle it."

"Cora Jane says he's a good worker, and a fast learner."

"Even better. That all? I'm almost asleep on my feet."

"I mentioned the bunkhouse, maybe board, and between a dollar fifty and two dollars a day."

"Wish ya hadn't."

"Why?"

"Ya should a left negotiatin' details ta Robert an' me. Not that ya misled Elena, but don't go makin' side deals we might not want ta, er can't, keep."

She followed him into the bedroom. Now was the moment to throw in the part about Dolores.

"I understand. Usually I wouldn't mention anything about money, but he's supporting his sister, Dolores, too. Joe Roybal, the so-called husband, skipped town. And Elena's afraid Rudy'll go to Denver, for defense work, it's so intolerable for him at home."

"Why isn't Ruiz helpin' Dolores, his own daughter?"

"Perhaps he's still punishing her for humiliating the family, or she refuses his help, or both."

Clothes off, Art lowered himself onto the bed.

"Wasn't 'er fault. Whole Ruiz story seems more like bad news than good. Any more a this 'good news'?"

"Yes. You mentioned so many boys failing their physicals because they're underweight or have bad teeth and you seem to understand it's particularly true of the Mexican boys. Which leads me to this. Elena asked me to teach a Red Cross home nursing class for the Spanish-American women. She or Marguerite would translate. Not only would I be doing something directly to help with defense, I would…"

"Martha, stop right there. That's not good news, neither. Ya can't take on any more. I had ta feed the chicks this mornin' 'cause ya were in town at Doc's, which I accept, but I gathered the eggs this afternoon because ya had ta go back, for what reason, ya didn't say. I ain't finished plantin' corn on our place an' still have ta help Robert plant 'is. Yer behind gettin' the garden in. We gotta have that garden, what with the increase in food prices. Besides, everyone's plantin' a victory garden. It's not right we farmers can't manage one, 'specially since we always have a garden. Ya raise the best vegetables in the county, 'cept maybe fer Elsie, an' I thought ya enjoyed it. As it was, Elena was out with the children, workin' on it by 'erself. Embarrassin.' Like we can't organize our lives. She might as well be doin' field work, fer all we ask a her."

Martha heard the frustration and exhaustion in his voice that had been in hers when she scolded Elena earlier in the evening. He wasn't finished.

"Today reminds me a several months ago when I was finishin' that early, extra round a diskin' ta turn over the dirt an' expose the hopper eggs ta the freezin' air ta keep their numbers down."

"How's that?"

"Well, seemed every day somethin' came up, ya still bein' weak from the miscarriage an' eager ta get back ta yer work with Doc.

Finally finished our place but only got half a Robert's done 'fore it warmed up an' got wet. Point is, farmin' takes us all workin' together, 'specially now with Alex an' Luis gone, an' yer not so dependable lately."

But Doc thought she was. He called to thank her, even though Swede died. She wanted to assure Art today's demands were unusual, for both of them, but she couldn't betray Fran by telling him why she drove back to town.

She knew Art's complaints and Earl's whining weren't comparable, Earl a man incapable of figuring out how to feed his son and get him ready for bed, but she lumped them together, nonetheless. Earl should trust Josie, that her late night at the school with the play was absolutely necessary, given Fran's emergency, and pitch in.

Art should trust she wasn't frivolous, either, and she didn't ask Elena to finish in the garden; he did. Elena probably would have, anyway. She always gave above and beyond. The Red Cross class would make a world of difference for the Spanish-American women and their families.

"Art, I understand today was hard, and you and Elena carried the brunt of it. But today wasn't normal. We'll figure things out tomorrow."

Given Doc's assurances about her nursing, she was confident she could take on more. Besides, she was obligated, on account of the war.

May 1942

The Levee

Two long rings. Pause. Two long rings. The Lundgren line. "Art, wake up. Someone's calling."

Martha threw off the covers, but her feet tangled in the sheets. Art climbed out his side, closer to the door. Martha checked the alarm, and the green line of the hour hand pointed toward the luminous dot of the four, the longer line of the minute hand at quarter past. No one called that early. The decent thing was to wait until five when most folks got up.

Art stumbled to the telephone, which hung on the wall in the dining room next to the kitchen door. Martha couldn't distinguish his words over the sound of wind and driving rain. She threw on her robe to follow and met him in the center of the living room as he picked his way back along the yellow path cast through the archway by the light above the dining table.

"Otto Lambert," he said. "Been checkin' the creek level through the night, an' it keeps risin'. Asks if I can help build a levee where it makes the turn south 'fore it joins the river. Afraid a flood'll take the hayfield, the corn he's just planted, an' maybe the house. Wants ta know if ya'll help with calls ta Ivarsons,

431

Moultons, Uffords, an' anyone else ya feel like askin'. He's already talked ta yer father."

Art kept moving and Martha followed. By the time he finished talking, both were partly dressed.

Ivarsons and Moultons. Now there was a combination. She couldn't imagine Otto, Papa, and Al Ivarson cooperating on anything, especially under pressure, and with George Moulton thrown into the mix… They needed more help.

"I'll call them and Mr. Miyoshi. Also, Lucy and Min Himuru will want to know, if Elsie hasn't already reached Lucy. And the Ichikawas. Thank the Good Lord they're all within the five-mile travel limit for Japanese. Otherwise they'd have to apply for a permit and might not get there for days. Ridiculous."

Martha rattled on to shake herself awake. "But I understand why Otto called Papa first. He could expect Papa will pitch in. Wonder if he's asking us to call Al and George because he feels awkward about Al, and things must be strained with George and Maude Moulton. You've heard the rumor about the row between Max and their sons, when they found out Max wouldn't enlist. Of course, George shouldn't be blamed for whatever Walter and Edgar did, just as Elsie can't be blamed for how Addie turned out."

Martha couldn't gauge Art's reaction to the news about Max. She hadn't meant to let it slip, even though Alex confirmed it when he was home on furlough.

Art stopped in the midst of buttoning his shirt. "Where'd ya hear this 'bout Max? I'd think somebody would a told me, us buyin' his truck an' all."

"Walter and Edgar came by Josie's the morning I had the miscarriage. They were upset about Alex sending Eleanor home, and Elena mentioned Max's troubles to Josie and me after they left. Alex had told her. With the miscarriage, it faded from my mind."

She omitted how threatening the Moulton brothers were that morning on Josie's porch when they accosted them, Alex's two sisters, for the insult to theirs. But Art should know about the rumor if an argument broke out between Otto Lambert and George Moulton at the levee.

"Well, I'd think it was true, 'cause Alex'd know what was goin' on with Max, an' Elena don't exaggerate. Wonder why everyone's keepin' it so hush-hush."

"Don't know. Maybe we'll find out today. I'll make calls and fix up some food. What will Elsie do with her chickens if the water rises to the house?"

Art was headed into the kitchen and didn't hear.

Holding the Line

By six Martha pulled into the Lambert's lane, a sleepy Anna in tow. Instead of stopping up by the road behind the vehicles parked there, she pulled into the lane, near the porch door. She instructed Anna to wait while she sloshed back and forth through the muddy water. One trip for the platter of scrambled eggs, another for the sausage, a third for the pile of pancakes. Not sufficient for all the men assembled, but with what Elsie had, it was a start, if served with copious amounts of black coffee. On the fourth trip, she retrieved Anna.

"Let me walk, Mama. I'm wearing my galoshes."

"I am, too, Anna, but these puddles are so deep I'd lose you in one of them."

Martha was only half teasing. She lifted Anna from the truck.

"We need an umbrella, Mama."

Martha scarcely heard Anna's muffled voice as she bent into the wind and rain.

They shed galoshes, scarves, and coats on the porch, and Martha was grateful to enter the warm kitchen. Anna's clothes were dry; Martha's weren't.

"Elsie, I was out for only ten minutes. I'm soaked. The men'll be half frozen. Are they making progress?"

"So far they've kept up with the rising water. But the mountain snow melt, and if it's raining upstream the way it is here…"

Maude Moulton pushed the door open with a bang. "Martha, move your truck so I can pull in. Elsie, the lane outside your door is a lake. Here, take these biscuits."

Elsie, who towered over Maude, accepted the biscuits but looked above her head toward Martha, winked, and said, "Maude, you're still bundled up. Why don't you move Martha's truck on your next trip? I'm sure she won't mind."

Maude couldn't immediately counter Elsie's logic and grumbled, "All right. Give me your keys, Martha."

Martha, taken aback by Elsie's boldness and concerned antagonism between the mothers-in-law would undermine everyone's efforts, tried to placate Maude. "Keys're still in the truck, Maude. All you need to do is back up a little for the space you need. I'll move it to the road later."

"I'm capable of figuring out parking arrangements," Maude snapped.

She whirled around, splashing drops of water in an arc onto the red-and-white oilcloth covering the kitchen table. So much for appeasing Maude.

"Maude's going to be more difficult than usual," Martha said. "She's still out of sorts about Eleanor and Alex."

Elsie countered, "She's out of sorts? I hardly think your brother's rebuff of her daughter is on a par with her sons' excesses."

At last, perhaps Elsie would confirm the rumor about Walter and Edgar harassing Max and disclose details.

"Then again, Maude's always out of sorts," Elsie said. "I keep telling Addie that with a mother-in-law like Maude, you have to lay down the line or she'll walk all over you. No need to be unpleasant, just firm. But Addie never listens."

Martha nodded in agreement about Maude's temperament, disappointed Elsie was willing to talk about her daughter but not her son. Besides, the principle about how to handle Maude was more easily expressed than executed.

She changed the subject to test Elsie's opinion about another matter. "I'm glad to see Al Ivarson's truck in the lane, with all the bad feeling between former and current county commissioners. How do you suppose he'll get along with Otto and Papa?"

"They're all three opinionated, but they'll pull together when faced with something that threatens one of their livelihoods. Al's a sincere man, just narrow-minded. Besides, he won't hear a thing they say in this weather."

Throughout the exchange, both women moved quickly to set out stacks of plates, saucers and cups, slide platters into the coal stove's warm oven, and arrange crock bowls on the stovetop to serve as warming dishes.

Elsie, not one to waste an extra pair of hands, said, "Anna, do you know how to count?"

Anna stepped out of the corner where she had retreated with her doll. "Yes, Mrs. Lambert. I count hundreds and hundreds."

"That's quite a lot. I only need you to count twenty."

Elsie's inquiring glance elicited a confirming nod from Martha that Anna was up to the job.

"Set your doll on a chair in the dining room," Elsie said. "The silverware trays are in the top drawer of the bureau. Bring twenty spoons and put them here."

Elsie gestured to a spot by the plates. "Same number of forks and knives. Put the piles next to each other."

Martha stole a glance at Anna to ensure she grasped the details of her task, but Anna had turned and was headed to the dining room. Her posture communicated complete confidence, unencumbered by adult intrigues of attack and counterattack.

Maude re-entered, struggling with a large Dutch oven that presumably protected her widely admired donuts, and kicked the door closed.

"The rain's coming harder," she said, "if you can believe it, and the wind's worse. Five men are heading down the road to the creek with shovels. We'll see those who came earlier any minute. I'll meet them on the porch and help with their gear. Elsie, get piles of towels so they can wipe off the water before it drips all over the food. We don't have enough for all that's showed up. Fry more eggs and bacon. I brought two coffee pots but have to get them before I take off my things."

Neither Elsie nor Martha made modifications to Maude's strategy.

Elsie pulled another dozen eggs out of the refrigerator. "It must be bad, or there wouldn't be so many to help. If the water breeches the bank where they're building the levee, it could head right to the chicken house, then here."

Maude called from the porch, "Martha, take these coffeepots. The first group's coming."

Seven men dragged in. Art and Papa took the towels Martha offered and wiped the mud from their hands and faces. They looked like derelicts, beards showing several days' growth. Must be no one shaved every day anymore, with news about razor blades being rationed. Surely those in town weren't doing the same. She couldn't imagine Parker Hayes presenting himself this way at the bank.

When Martha caught Art's eye, he lowered his head. Elsie saw their wordless exchange from her vantage point at the stove.

"It's bad, isn't it?" she said.

Martha pried the fork from Elsie's hands and took over the task of scrambling eggs.

"You've been up most of the night, I imagine," Martha said. "Get yourself some breakfast."

"Where's Otto?" Elsie asked Art.

She grabbed a donut from Maude's Dutch oven and took off her apron.

"He won't be comin' in, Elsie," Art said. "Leastwise, I wouldn't, if I was 'im. Give us somethin' we can take 'im so he don't collapse.'"

"I'll take it," said Elsie.

She threw some food into one of Maude's baskets, covered it with a towel, and went to the porch to slip on galoshes.

In less than five minutes, the food on the table was half gone, and the men headed out the door. Without being asked, Anna took one of the damp towels, got on her hands and knees, and began wiping up puddles where the men had stood in their wet socks.

"Mama, aren't they wearing their irrigation boots?"

"Yes, honey, but they splash around to shovel dirt for the levee they hope will hold the water in the creek. The water pours over the boot tops, as it would have with your galoshes if you had walked in Elsie's lane."

"They better clean and dry them tonight," Anna said.

"I'm sure they will, but why do you say that, honey?"

"To save them, on account of the war."

"From the mouths of babes," Maude said. "Guess even little ones like Anna know about the scarcity of rubber."

Maude began washing dishes left by the first crew, having already started the second and third pots of coffee, and Martha finished cooking the bacon and eggs. The second crew entered.

Al Ivarson didn't mince words. "Even if the rain stops, the creek'll rise. No place for it ta go. River'll back inta the creek. Don't think the levee'll hold. Fields'll flood. Don't know what Elsie'll do with her chickens. Finally farmers have a chance to make money, and we get too much water."

No wonder Al rankled nerves. Did he always find reason to despair? That attitude must be at the heart of the antagonism between Papa and him, and maybe Otto. Papa and Otto worked on the assumption things could get better. Al hunkered down and prepared for the worst. Good thing he wasn't commissioner during the hard, dry years of the dirt storms. Everyone in the county would have starved. Left up to him, there wouldn't have been school lunches, or canning centers. No…

"How many men are out there digging in the dirt?" Maude asked her husband.

"'Bout thirty, I 'spect," he answered.

"We don't have nearly enough food," Martha said and looked at Maude with alarm. "I'll gather more eggs."

"You best gather 'em all," George said. "Al's right. It'll be a surprise if the levee holds. At least you can save the eggs."

Maude snapped, "Then why are you going to all this effort, if it won't be of any use?"

With a scowl, George handed his wife the empty plate.

"Maude, why're they still holdin' the line on Corregidor? They're sufferin' huge losses, but they don't give up. Otto's lookin' to lose two a his fields if the water breaks through. Elsie, her chickens. Water might even flood the house. They'd be helpin' if we needed it. I'm not ready to quit, not yet."

Martha could hardly hide her surprise at George's eloquence, much less how he stood up to Maude. Judging from Maude's reaction, she was no less astonished. Wordlessly, she gathered the dirty plates from the table.

If any of the men thought about giving up, the way George handled his unpleasant wife and the content of his speech, along with hot coffee and food, prompted them to march to the porch and put on their gear. The porch emptied, and Martha took off her apron. Anna grabbed another towel and resumed her floor-mopping.

"Anna, honey," Martha called through the porch door, "stay with Mrs. Moulton while I gather eggs. You can dry the silverware she's washed and make new piles on the table, where Mrs. Lambert showed you. Remember, twenty in each pile."

"Mama, who's going to milk Ginger and Beulah this morning? Who's going to feed our chicks?" Anna asked.

A quick look at the Lambert's kitchen clock confirmed Martha's sense that it couldn't be much later than seven.

"We'll do our chores when we get home, Anna. The animals can wait."

She looked for her coat, but someone had taken it by mistake. She found one approximately her size and put on her galoshes. Outside, Mae Ufford, Effie Collins, and Lucy Himuru were struggling through the puddles with armloads of food.

"Let me help!" Martha shouted.

"Take these warm biscuits," yelled Effie, "and I'll get the rest."

Her words came out in puffs from her exertion.

Maude met Martha at the porch door and took Effie's baskets. "Thank goodness. Don't know we'd have had enough for even this next bunch, otherwise."

Martha counted seven more men trudging through the mud toward the house.

"The rain's slowed, and the wind's died down," she observed.

When she entered the chicken house, Martha stopped and whistled aloud. "This isn't a house. It's a hotel."

Most of Elsie's layers were at one end, each sitting on a nest arranged on a series of shelves that ran parallel to the wall. The rest picked through the straw and gravel at the other end for every last grain of food, and the chicks chirped in cages that rested on wooden tables in the center. The orderly and clean place housed well-loved poultry.

Martha gently reached under each layer, but didn't come up with more than a dozen eggs. It was too early in the morning, too soon after Elsie gathered them yesterday afternoon. Martha saw empty crates stacked by the door and surmised Elsie had run her eggs into town the day before. She carried the bucket back to the house.

The rain had almost stopped. Martha's neck and shoulders relaxed. The levee might hold. She stood aside to let the third crew exit the porch, and Elsie came up behind her.

"Sorry, I think I grabbed your coat," she said. "Sleeves are way too short. The water level's holding steady, but Otto thinks we'll know in the next hour if there was a deluge upstream. They're building the levee higher, anticipating it. How's the food holding out? The next crew's coming right behind me."

When they walked into the kitchen, Anna was on her hands and knees wiping up mud puddles.

"You're a young one, to manage all that work," Elsie said.

Anna beamed.

The Rescue

The fourth crew was finishing their breakfast when Art opened the kitchen door. "Martha, grab yer bag," he said softly. "Quick. Gotta get back."

Art rightly assumed Martha had her medical bag in Max's Truck, particularly on an outing like today's.

Martha grabbed coat and galoshes and headed for the pickup. Maude must have lost her orientation to the lane earlier, in the half-light and driving rain, and had backed it into the middle of Elsie's flower garden. The tulips were crushed.

Rather than walking to the levee site through the field, Martha chose the route along the road, to the bridge. The footing was more solid, and Maude had said she saw several men go that way.

Still, the rain had washed away most of the gravel, so with each step Martha's galoshes sank several inches into the sticky clay. She moved over to walk along the edge; the new grass and weeds gave some traction.

She hadn't foreseen the trouble she'd have getting down the incline at the bridge and over to where the men were working. The water, not two feet below the bridge's wooden planks, splashed up through the gaps. She'd never known the creek, usually dry, to run that high.

From her vantage point, she saw that the newly constructed levee still held. The muddy mass of water shot away from the levee to the south, but it had no more than a few feet to go before it would breach the makeshift dam, and Al was right about the river backing into the creek. A lake had already formed at their junction. She should have told the women to move as many chickens as they could over to the barn, which was on higher ground.

A group half carried, half dragged bales of hay from the pile in the field to the levee site, which others either stacked against the dirt wall or dismantled and mixed with the mud. One man sat on a bed of bales, cradling another in his arms.

Martha started down the incline, intending to head toward that pair. She slipped and slid for three or four steps before she lost her balance. She plopped on her bottom, but that didn't stop her forward momentum. Sliding on the wet grass and weeds, the best she could do was grab her slip and the skirt of her dress around her knees, hold them with one hand, and steady her bag across her thighs with the other.

Had the vegetation been several inches higher, the slide would have been perfect. As it was, bits of gravel and twigs dug into her legs as she gathered speed. The bag tipped, and she tried to right it with both hands. The wind lifted the abandoned skirt, which covered her face. She steadied the bag but flew blind the remaining several feet.

However, she reached the bottom upright, and four hands reached out to pull her to her feet and retrieve the bag — Al Ivarson's and George Moulton's. Wordlessly, Al carried the bag and George steadied her on the short walk to the bale bed where a young man lay. He was still alive, barely.

"Who is he?" she asked.

"Don't know," George answered. "Pulled him out a the creek. Al thinks he's that boy who won the Junior Rodeo championship last year. If that's 'im, family lives ten miles upstream. He's been in the water awhile. Must've washed away tryin' ta drive cattle up from the creek bed."

She knelt beside the boy and said, "We're here to help you, son."

She thought out loud to no one in particular. "The thickness of the sheepskin jacket seems to have prevented injury from the debris, but it's a wonder the water-soaked weight of it didn't drown him. He must have grabbed hold of something. We have to get off the wet clothes and warm him up. Help me turn him on his side. Is there anything dry we can cover him with?"

Al answered, "What?" and George yelled his version of Martha's words.

They turned him and peeled off the jacket.

The men nearby had no trouble hearing George, and they started taking off wet clothes until they got to a dry layer. The details of Martha's request spread.

Meanwhile, she clipped several inches into his shirt and union suit with her scissors and ripped the cloth to expose his back. The skin was smooth, save for the bow of pubescent acne at the shoulders. The unbroken skin confirmed what Martha suspected from the condition of the sheepskin — no punctures, details she repeated to reassure the boy.

George helped roll him on his back. If the chest was in good shape like the back, his heroic ride through the churning water might not have been in vain. She stripped the shirt and union suit away from his arms and chest and convinced herself he'd be all right if they could get him warm.

But she and George gasped when they saw the livid circle of red, blue, and purple, like a bull's eye, centered over his breastbone. It was at least four inches in diameter. The trickle of bloody saliva on the boy's chin confirmed the damage inside. He hadn't come through unscathed. What a strong will, to survive all he suffered.

Martha used her scissors again to slice through his pants and the bottoms of his union suit. She quickly ran her hands down his arms and legs. No broken bones, and the pupils were of equal size. If they could get him to town, to the hospital, to Doc, there might be a chance, and she reported all the pieces of good news to him.

The clothing, mostly shirts, that came Martha's way were sweaty but still warm. George tore off his mackintosh, they rolled the boy on his side again, George spread the mackintosh on the hay bales, and they turned him back. Martha covered him, head to foot, with the relatively dry shirts, and pulled the mackintosh around him. He resembled a mummy more than a man.

"He surely has broken ribs, at least," she said to George. "And a punctured lung. We must get him to the hospital."

But they'd have to carry him along the impassible road to the trucks, and that would take several men and time, draining precious assets from the work at the levee.

"Watch out!"

"Use your shovels to push it away from the bank!"

"That tree's gonna snag on it an' break through!"

"The levee's breeched!"

George, Al, Art, and Papa each grabbed a corner of the mackintosh and used it as a stretcher. No one could run in the mud. They moved at a fast walk as the water rose around their ankles, then up to their knees. Martha saw her bag float away, along with shovels, coats, and a wheelbarrow. Ellis Ufford took her by the arm and half lifted her through the muck.

Mr. Miyoshi shot by them in an attempt to capture her bag. She tried to scream at him not to bother, but she had no breath.

When the water reached her waist, Ellis shouted, "Lift your feet. Swim! I'll steer you through the water."

Martha lost sight of Mr. Miyoshi and the bag, but the stretcher-bearers moved ahead of her. She didn't take her eyes off the mackintosh bundle. The four progressed rapidly when they could float the boy's weight on his waterproof mattress.

They reached the house, and Martha found her footing, but the water still rose.

Otto half swam, half ran, yelling, "Elsie, get everyone out. The water's gonna flood the house. Head to higher ground, by the barn."

Art and his troop carried the mackintosh stretcher to the bed of a truck parked up near the road. Martha tried to hurry through the water that was only ankle high at the upper end of the lane, but the muddy ground sucked at her galoshes.

She reached the truck, and Art helped shove her over the tailgate into the bed. She crawled to the boy and felt for his pulse. Nothing. She waited several seconds and felt again. Nothing. She pulled a sweaty shirt she had tucked around the chest up and over the head as a sign of respect, thought better of it, spread the shirt back over the angry bruise, took off her jacket, and used it to cover the face.

To Art, who still stood at the back of the truck, she said, "We need to call Enoch for the hearse. Is Anna safe?"

"Sure feel bad the boy didn't make it. Otto's phone prob'ly isn't workin'. Don't even know we could get inta the house ta call. I'll look fer Anna. You stay here, with the boy."

"And find Mr. Miyoshi. He went after my black bag."

Even if Martha wanted to leave, she didn't have any choice but to sit by the body because her legs and arms felt as heavy as the tree trunks that had floated past her in the field. She examined her cuts from the slide down the embankment and determined none were critical. They just stung and oozed blood. She scooted away from the body and leaned against the side of the truck bed.

Defeat

The breeze drove the remaining wisps of clouds across the sky, and the morning sun heated the metal of the truck. She rested her arms on the warm edge and laid her head on them. In the half hour or more she sat there, her clothes began to dry.

She heard a constant stream of shouts down by the house but couldn't see clearly through the trees and vehicles. Surely Anna was in safe hands, or Art would have come back to tell her. From time to time she heard his voice rise above the rest, but couldn't determine what role he played in the general uproar.

When he returned, she felt stronger. She pushed herself to a standing position.

"Miyoshi's banged up," he said, "but he's okay. Got whacked by a branch or somethin'. Ichikawa pulled him out a the water."

"He should never have gone after the bag."

"Maybe, but there's not much he won't do fer ya, Martha. Ya know that."

Martha bit her lip to stop the tears. Yes, she supposed she knew, but hadn't thought what it meant. That he would go to such lengths for a bag…

"What's happening, now?" she asked and lifted one leg over the tailgate.

She was pleased she could crawl down from the truck herself, but Art had to steady her once she reached the ground. In the privacy behind the truck, he wrapped his arms around her.

"I'm proud a ya," he said, and caressed her hair, curling a tendril by her ear around his finger. "Ya might not think we saw ya slide down that bumpy slope, but by the time ya reached the bottom, every man was watchin' ya, not because yer skirt was flutterin' 'round yer head, but on account a yer determination ta get ta that boy."

Under other circumstances, Art would have meant his description to be taken as a lighthearted attempt to cover her embarrassment, but he was serious. And she felt oddly serene. She couldn't change anything about her unusual flight. To think, her sacrifice of modesty had won her the respect of the men.

He held her tighter. "We figure it was his horse broke the levee."

Martha pulled away. "What do you mean?"

"A dead horse, saddle an' all, washed up 'gainst it. The force a the water drove its head right inta the soft dirt, and a tree trunk caught on the horse. Their weight tore open the levee, but a surge a water musta come shortly after, ta fill the field the way it did, so maybe the levee would a been breached, anyway."

"He might have lived, Art. He might have lived if we could have taken him out of the field with less jostling. If we had gotten him to the hospital, to Doc."

She cried quietly into his shoulder.

"Martha, he might a, but maybe it was the same as with Frank Ogawa. When Doc Claffey said there was nothin' anyone could a done. Ya tried. We all tried."

He not only repeated Doc Claffey when Frank died, he repeated Elizabeth DeFries when Mama went.

Martha had believed Doc about Frank, because she wanted to excuse herself from failing to stop Art and Alex at the mailbox, for not getting into the truck with Frank. She wanted to believe that even if she had examined Frank on the way into town, there was nothing she could have done to change the outcome.

But after Carrie's birth, with the questionable use of forceps and Doc's insistence Carrie be put in the home, she knew Doc Claffey was fallible. He could have been wrong about Frank, too.

However, she never believed Mrs. DeFries when Mama died. Martha sat for too many days and nights by Mama's bed, listening to her moans, knowing she was in pain. Mrs. DeFries and Doc Claffey told her time and again the pain was simply a sign that Bright's disease had taken over. They said Martha's constant attention relieved the suffering, and she should be satisfied with that.

And Swede. He died, even though Doc McFarland had arrived in time to save the leg. Doc said the blow to his head was the problem. Something they couldn't do anything about.

But was it ever true, that nothing else could be done, or was it the excuse folks used for their failure in the face of death? Still, maybe Art was right about the boy, that they were working against insurmountable odds. Who could anticipate and buttress the levee against the combined force of a dead horse and a tree trunk? Who would ever know whether, if the levee had held for just another twenty minutes, long enough to carry the boy out and to safety in circumstances not so rough, he would have died anyway?

And Carrie. What if she hadn't been so quick to agree with Doc McFarland that she could handle Carrie at home? If she had insisted he put Carrie in the hospital when she came down with influenza, she might still be with them.

Art was saying, "Ta answer yer question 'bout what's happenin', Effie Collins has offered ta take Anna ta their place. Effie thinks ya should stay with Elsie, an' I agree. Anna'll be thrilled ta spend an afternoon at their Country Store helpin' out with the cash register an' all. The Collins's automobile's parked up on the road, so Effie an' Pete can drive away. The water's not risin', but it hasn't budged from the house, yet. The chicken house, they're sayin' that's worse."

"How will you get home?"

"Effie an' Pete'll drop me off so as I can do our chores, an' Robert's. Wish he'd get rid a that durned cow a his. A single man don't need all that milk."

How did one avoid choosing the course of action that led to death? Did anyone have the capability and foresight to beat the odds? Perhaps not and one simply repeated Mr. Miyoshi's philosophy: it can't be helped. *Shikata ga nai.* Go on with life.

"Martha, ya listenin'?"

"Yes."

But surely one could change the course of events. Providence provided multiple choices at every moment.

"Robert's already gone with Al. Al thought ta park his truck up by the road, too. Robert'll bring his team a mules ta pull out the trucks in the lane. Al's bringin' his horses. Robert'll call Enoch from the

Home Place ta come get the body. Good thing you women fixed all that food, or no one would have the gumption ta keep goin.'"

In spite of her preoccupation with death, or perhaps because of it, Martha didn't miss that in the space of time it took Art to tell her the plans, "the boy" had become "the body."

If the boy was who Al thought, how had he managed to survive the pummeling from the water and debris for ten miles to arrive in the Lamberts' field alive? They failed to honor his valiant struggle.

She turned her face up to Art. "Kiss me."

Puzzled, he leaned down and complied.

"Again," she said, and circled her arms around his neck.

He waited until she released him.

"What is it?" he whispered.

"Life and death? Struggle and defeat? I don't know. This is the second boy water's killed in three years."

Anna's voice rang out from the lane. "Mama, Papa, I'm going with Mrs. Collins to their store!"

She ran over and hugged their legs but withdrew in disgust. "Mama, your legs are bloody!"

Martha looked down. Some of the cuts still oozed into the cloth of her dress, but most of the blood in the fabric had washed out in the cold water on the escape through the field.

"It's okay, honey. I got some scratches when I slid down the hill to help at the levee. I'd better wash them and put on Mercurochrome, hadn't I?"

"We need ta get goin', Anna," said Art.

Anna made no move to leave. "Do you want me to stay and hold your hand, Mama? The medicine'll sting!"

Martha picked up Anna, careful to shield her from seeing the body in the truck bed. "All I need are big hugs and kisses."

Anna immediately provided the necessary salve with kisses all over Martha's face.

"Yes, that's just what I needed," Martha said with a hearty laugh. "You go on with Mrs. Collins and Papa. Mrs. Lambert will help me with the medicine."

As Effie passed the truck, she stared at the boy. "What a shame. What a shame. Who's going to stay with him until Enoch comes?"

Martha didn't have an answer. It was disrespectful to leave him unattended in the back of a truck with a jacket pulled over his head, but she couldn't delay getting her cuts washed and Mercurochrome on them. Who knew what impurities floodwaters harbored? Even hangnails could lead to the amputation of a finger. Her nurse's sense of obligation told her not to leave the patient; surely that didn't include a dead one, but abandoning him wasn't right.

Effie, Art, and Anna walked on, and Martha headed down the lane. Everyone was occupied but Maude, who stood by Max's Truck contritely looking at the mangled flower garden. She would probably claim the water had risen high enough to float the vehicle into the garden if anyone pointed out its unfortunate position.

However, the floodwaters would have ruined the garden in any event. What did Maude's deception matter? Maybe Martha could take advantage of her remorse.

When she drew to within five feet, Martha said, "Maude, did you hear about the unfortunate young man whom we pulled from the creek?"

Maude whirled and faced Martha. "Yes, of course. Everyone's talking about him."

"Please stay with the body until Enoch arrives. I have to tend the cuts on my legs."

Martha shamelessly lifted the skirt of her dress and showed Maude the worst of the gashes before Maude could object.

"Um… Well, if it's absolutely necessary."

Maybe Elsie was correct; a firm hand prevailed, particularly if Maude was caught in a moment of weakness.

The Aftermath

Every truck bed near the house contained something — Elsie's kitchen table with a few remaining items from of the gargantuan breakfast resting on top, sofa, chairs, books and papers, pots and pans, dishes, jars of canned fruit and vegetables from the cellar, rolled-up carpets, even an iron bed frame and mattress, which was in the back of the Old Truck.

Probably Elsie's father's bed. He lived with them for years before his death, and his room was on the first floor. She passed her hand over the side of the mattress that rested against the edge of the truck. It seemed dry. The men must have gone straight into the house after the dash across the field and removed the items that would suffer damage.

Martha spotted Anna's doll lying on a dining room chair in back of another pickup. She retrieved it and put it on the seat in Max's Truck, next to her black bag, which someone had stowed away. She grabbed the Mercurochrome and slipped it into a pocket.

The men whose trucks were parked in the lane lolled about, waiting for the teams of mules and horses. The water was draining from under the running boards, and soon they would carry everything back and store it upstairs, or the animals wouldn't be able to dislodge the vehicles.

It took a moment to identify the abnormality in the men's behavior. None of them were having a smoke. She smiled at the thought of soggy, crushed packs of cigarettes stowed away in pants and jackets.

She stepped onto the porch and into several inches of water.

"Elsie? Elsie?" No one answered.

Outside she saw Elsie picking her way carefully through the standing water as she walked toward the chicken house. Martha hurried toward her.

"Martha, thank goodness you're still here. I have to tend my chickens, but I'm afraid to go in alone, afraid of what I'll see."

Why, oh why hadn't any of them thought to carry as many chickens as they could to the barn? One of those diverging pathways, a missed chance to challenge insurmountable odds. Perhaps Mr. Miyoshi's philosophy of *shikata ga nai* wasn't helpful. Sometimes one fought "it can't be helped" instead of simply enduring, as the boy had fought the flood waters.

Come to think of it, Mr. Miyoshi didn't hesitate to abandon his philosophy and chase after her medical bag. That was an "it can't be helped" occasion if ever there was one.

Martha took Elsie's hand. "Where's Otto?"

"The barn. Had to milk the cow. Guess it's dry. Maybe that's where we'll sleep tonight."

"I know you're trying to bring humor to the situation, Elsie, but won't you stay with us?"

"Thank you, Martha, but your father's already asked. We'll be out of the house several nights, and he has room. Normally, mothers and fathers would stay with one of their children, but the last thing I need is Addie complaining and Harriet whining. I'd ask Addie to help with the cleanup, but, honestly, Martha, she and Harriet are more trouble than I want to take on. I know that's a terrible thing to say about my own daughter and granddaughter, but it's the honest truth. I can't imagine either of them pitching in the way you and Anna did. Wasn't Anna sweet the way she mopped the floor after each crew?"

It was awkward to accept Elsie's praise after she had criticized her own family, so Martha remained silent. She almost asked where Max was that they couldn't stay with him but thought better of it. If Elsie wanted anyone to know his whereabouts, she would say.

Elsie bitterly added, "A lot of good that mopping did, and the men struggling to build the levee. Why did we go to the effort, Martha, only to be defeated?"

Elsie's question about challenging the inevitable led Martha to a version of George's speech to Maude and her own conclusions about *shikata ga nai.*

"Because we didn't know that would be the outcome. Our efforts could have made a difference. If we had done nothing, the damage would surely be worse."

Martha also disagreed with Elsie about Addie, but it wasn't her place to speak out. She couldn't fathom Addie being so self-absorbed she wouldn't assist her parents. If it came to that, Martha and other neighbor women would pitch in and put the house to rights. Unlike with Edith Giffard, her mind addled by frantic worry about Muriel and the battle for the Philippine Islands, subterfuge wasn't necessary to get help into Elsie's home.

Thank the Good Lord Claude Giffard had been receptive to Henry Behm when he suggested Elena's mother, Aneda Marquez, help Edith with her housework. With Claude on board, Edith readily agreed. Aneda transformed the place, but it was too soon to tell if the new order would have a beneficial effect on Edith's mind.

But Elsie was the one to be concerned about today. Martha dropped Elsie's hand and put her arm around Elsie's waist to brace both of them for what waited in the chicken house. Closer to the creek, the water was almost up to their knees.

Elsie pulled the door open, and two dead chickens floated out.

"I can't look, Martha. Will you?"

What had been a hotel was a graveyard. Hundreds of bodies floated on the water, along with a brooder and other bits of debris Martha couldn't identify in the dim light. Elsie, who was taller and stronger, helped her push the door shut.

"Elsie, before people leave, tell them to take as many of the larger chickens as they want. If they dress and cook or can them right away, the meat'll still be good. Even then, you'll have a lot of dead ones to dispose of. I can't tell how many survived."

Elsie covered her mouth with her hands and sobbed. Soon the sobs were accompanied by words. "For how many hours have I nursed them? Five hundred chickens, five hundred, most of them lost! Lost!"

The final "lost" came out as a wail. Martha stroked Elsie's arm, concerned by how Elsie's grief, her sleepless night, and the physical strain of the past hours had worn through her usual dignified resolve. The one donut Elsie plucked from Maude's Dutch oven was scarcely enough fortification.

But surely lost chickens weren't pushing Elsie to near hysteria. Over the last five years, ever since Otto and Elsie had moved to Eagle View, she had been the bedrock for nearly every neighbor woman. Granted, it hadn't been an ordinary morning. Still, it seemed odd for Martha, young enough to be her daughter, to console her. Martha put her arms around Elsie and caressed her back.

Finally, Martha interrupted the sobbing. "Elsie, some of the layers might still be on their nests. And the chicks' cages might have been high enough, on the tables. Your job isn't done. You can carry what's alive to the barn, but come with me, first. I can't go inside the chicken house because I have to tend to these cuts on my legs. I need your help cleaning them and putting on Mercurochrome. And maybe we can find you another donut."

In case Elsie didn't understand that Martha wasn't avoiding a gruesome job, that she simply couldn't accompany Elsie into a contaminated tomb, Martha emphasized, "I shouldn't be wading through the chicken house with these open wounds. After we do my legs, I'll stay with the body in the truck, and Maude can help you."

Elsie removed her hands from her face and stared at Martha.

"What body, Martha? Did someone die helping us?"

"No, no, Elsie! A boy washed down the creek. We don't even know who he is. We're taking care of it. Let's get you something to eat, and then you can save your chickens."

Bedtime

When Art and Martha put Anna to bed, the sky hadn't yet made the transition from indigo to black. They turned in shortly after.

"My cuts are so sore, I don't even want the sheets touching them."

"Yer too tired fer them ta bother ya fer long. Turn over, an' I'll rub yer back."

Martha's next words sounded remote, even to her, smothered as they were in the pillow.

"They're saying these are the worst floods since twenty-one. Himurus lost part of a hayfield down by the river, but Elsie and Maude saved about thirty of the layers. And all the chicks. Is it true a tornado touched down to the east this morning?"

"Yep. There's a story goin' 'round it picked up a basket a clothes sprinkled fer ironin' an' set it down a half-mile away, undisturbed. Destroyed the house, though. Killed one a the children."

"Oh, no… What a horrible way to lose a child."

In less than a minute, Martha was asleep.

May 1942

Games

From where she stood at the kitchen sink, Martha saw Anna load her wagon with the Christmas doll and spinning top, her favorite toys save for "Uncle Alex's train." Anna hauled the wagon back and forth over the bumpy ground between the cement cellar and the bench swing that hung between the two big cottonwoods by the porch, all the while maintaining a lively dialogue with the doll.

Anna was too rough with her toys. When these wore out, replacements would be hard to find, if at all. She would have to make do, just as Martha made do without a washing machine, even though they had the money for one. Seemed everything was going out of production — not just washing machines and toys, but vacuum cleaners, refrigerators, lawnmowers, all sorts of kitchen housewares…

She took dirty clothes to the Greenwood Laundromat or over to the Home Place, washed them, and brought them back to hang on the line. She wouldn't dream of asking Josie to use her machine. Imagine Earl's consternation if it was subjected to extra wear and tear. Those who had it, whatever "it" was, knew to take care of it.

Martha pulled the roast and vegetables out of the oven before looking out the window again to see if any of the expected guests had arrived. Anna still transported the toys. Martha couldn't determine the objective of Anna's game, but her doll remained the co-conspirator.

Then the doll did, or said, something horribly wrong, an offense that inflamed Anna's temper. She threw the doll with such force it bounced off one of the trees holding up the swing. Martha's impulse was to run out and snatch the doll to protect it from further damage, but she held back, intent on deciphering the reason for Anna's brutality.

Guests

Josie called out a greeting that broke the spell of Anna's fantasy. Anna scampered to her, out of Martha's view. Elena appeared with Robbie, and Marguerite and Josie followed, arm in arm, Anna trailing behind.

Marguerite, still Josie's star pupil, would work in one of California's airplane factories next year instead of going to college, a bitter disappointment for Josie. Today, Josie was helping at Eagle View School with sugar rationing registration, and Marguerite would translate for the Spanish-speaking families.

Martha turned to put plates on the table, and by the time the new arrivals stepped onto the porch, Art's voice was part of the mix. Six folks fit comfortably in the kitchen with space for Anna's old high chair, Robbie's place.

"You'll need to move out to the dining room," said Josie as she entered. "Papa and Uncle Malcolm drove in behind us. I'll help."

"Papa and Uncle Malcolm? Why's he here? It's not a holiday."

"Holiday or not, they're coming."

Martha looked ruefully at the roast she planned to use for leftovers. Given the expanding number of guests, there wouldn't be enough supper for Art and Anna, and she didn't have time to prepare something else. She planned to arrive for the performance of the Women's Chorus at the banquet even earlier than Zella, as director, had suggested. Martha had to run through her solo, and her costume took ever so much time to get right.

The Women's Club members who planned the annual banquet for the senior girls insisted every detail be perfect, as though their reputations depended on the opinions of eighteen-year-olds. Or perhaps it was simply competition among members. Every year Martha vowed not to participate in the chorus portion of the program, but she always did and was irritated with herself for it.

"Set another place," called Art, who was washing up in the basin by the porch pump. "Here comes Clara."

What on earth? The busy Clara never came by mid-day. Neither she nor Doc could meet all the demands placed on them by their regular work, let alone the additional tasks of defense planning in the absence of the health department. Martha only saw Clara for snatches of conversation at church or the Giffards'.

After greetings all around, they took their seats and Marguerite asked, "Where's our cousin, Rudy? Didn't he start working for you this week, Mr. Lundgren?"

Art pushed Clara's chair in for her. "Brings 'is own food. Weather's been nice since the floods last week, so I ain't thought ta invite 'im in. Guess I shoulda, knowin' you an' Elena would be here."

"He'll be eating with me, once he moves into the bunkhouse," said Papa.

They settled into their chairs, and Elena said, "He's never worked for a farmer who ate with him."

"Is that so?" prompted Martha, hoping to hear Elena's observations concerning the absence of shared meals between white families and Mexicans.

"I do not know of other farmers who invite their Spanish-American hired hands in for dinner, the way you, Mr. McLennan, and Alex sometimes invited our father and brother. They expect to eat their tortillas and beans in the field."

"I remember dinner in the fields with your mother and father," Martha commented, "when you and Marguerite were just starting to walk. Alex and Luis would play. Do you suppose Rudy prefers it that way?"

"I suppose he has not thought about it," Elena said. "He would not know anything different."

Surrender

"May I offer the grace?" Clara interrupted.

"Sure," said Art, looking somewhat off balance, perhaps on account of speculations about Rudy Ruiz's dining habits.

"Heavenly Father," she began, "we don't understand this war and the cruel ways mankind behaves. We're dismayed, no, distressed, by the surrender at Corregidor."

Martha glanced at Art and Papa and saw the shock that she felt. None of them had heard about the surrender. Roosevelt had spoken of a "phase of serious losses," but the surrender drove home the possibility of defeat at the hands of the Japanese in the Pacific.

Everyone looked at Clara, who continued, eyes shut tight, head bowed, hands clasped together and resting on the table in front of her, tears running down her face.

"Give the Japanese soldiers compassion to deal fairly with their enemies, give our troops and nurses strength to face defeat and hardship, give us all resolve to carry on the fight for freedom. Amen."

Clara's emotions were so raw she took several moments to compose herself before she opened her eyes.

Martha spoke first. "Clara, this is the first we've heard about surrender. Do you have other news?"

"I'm, I'm so sorry. I assumed I was the last to know. Things look very bleak in the Pacific. General Wainwright surrendered. The Japanese are winning every battle. But what's upset me most…"

Clara stopped. Her shoulders heaved with suppressed sobs. Uncle Malcolm, seated next to her, reacted first. He scooted his chair closer and put his arm around her, as he would an inconsolable child. Everyone waited until Clara calmed herself.

She smiled at him weakly. "Thank you, Malcolm. What's upset me most, even though I suppose this isn't significant in the grand scheme of war, is the situation with the nurses. A few from Corregidor made it to Australia, but the other group evacuated with them hasn't, including a navy nurse. The rest of the army nurses must still be on Corregidor with the soldiers. Imagine! They've been in the middle of this horrid battle the whole time!"

Martha pressed, "Clara, do they give the name of the navy nurse who didn't make it to Australia?"

"No!" Clara gulped for air but continued, "The point is, no one knows if the navy nurses at Canocao, Muriel's group, were sent to prison camps with other Americans in Manila. The Japanese won't provide prisoner lists. No one knows anything!"

Clara started to tremble as though taken with a violent chill. She continued to speak, although in a ragged whisper.

"I was headed to Eagle View School, but I couldn't go on, not without talking to someone…"

Martha hurried around the table. She had never seen Clara in this state, even when they faced the gore of nurse's training together. Clara was obviously at the end of her rope, doing too much, taking on more responsibility than one woman could bear. The news pushed her over the edge, just as the flood and death of her chickens had pushed Elsie, just as Anna's disappearance had pushed Martha.

Buoyed by her performance at the Lamberts only days ago, Martha knelt by Clara's chair and encouraged her as she had Elsie.

"Clara, you were right to stop for dinner, to be with companions. We're all tempted to think the worst about Muriel and what she might be going through, but you said it yourself. We don't know anything. Don't you see? If we imagine Muriel in distress, we're as good as defeated. We've allowed the enemy to incapacitate us. We cannot, we cannot let our fears carry us away."

The admonition sounded hollow, her version of George Moulton's speech to Maude and the men, to hold the line against the flood at the levee as the men on Corregidor were holding out against the Japanese. But the Americans hadn't held. The levee hadn't held. She hadn't held after Carrie died.

What pulled her out? No one thing. No one person. A combination of Henry's visit; Julia Mattson's Thanksgiving confession about her memorial packet for her dead son, Oscar; everyday demands from Art, Anna, and the farm; the crisis of getting Ken home from college; so many sick with the flu and needing attention at Christmas; working with Doc...

Martha rested her hand on Clara's thigh.

"You've suffered a terrible shock; we all have. Do you need to lie down? Or do you need to eat and listen to us talk about the news you've brought? Or should we talk about normal, everyday things? That might bring you back from the horrors you're imagining."

Martha, everyone, should have been prepared for surrender; still, she was devastated. For her part, she wanted the reassurance of everyday conversation and dinner.

She doubted Clara heard much of what she said, but the familiarity of Martha's voice and her hand caressing Clara's thigh, Uncle Malcolm's arm still around Clara's shoulder, perhaps the smell of roast and potatoes, summoned her back to the safety of an intact world where hungry people sat around a table.

The sobbing subsided, but Clara continued to tremble. Josie brought Martha's shawl from the bedroom, and Uncle Malcolm helped wrap it around Clara's shoulders.

In a voice that sounded more like herself, Clara said, "I should try to eat this delicious roast and be thankful for all of you. I forgot to ask God's blessing for the food, didn't I?"

In his calm baritone voice, Papa said, "You just did, ask God's blessing, that is. I vote with Clara. Let's eat."

Martha resumed her place and kept a careful eye on her friend.

Demands

For several minutes, everyone occupied themselves with passing food and savoring it.

Papa restarted the conversation. "You might be wondering why Malcolm's here. He's thinking about moving in with me for the summer and helping out. With Rudy Ruiz and Malcolm, I think Art, Miyoshi, and I'll finish our planting and produce good crops this year. We might be able to take advantage of the wartime prices, after all."

No one reacted, which left the impression they weren't pleased with Papa's news about Uncle Malcolm, who apparently didn't notice. He continued his methodical chewing, carefully keeping each food category separate from the others on his plate.

Martha couldn't think what to say. Within the space of thirty minutes, her world shook on its axis a second time. The news about Uncle Malcolm wasn't at all equivalent to Corregidor, but its immediacy and unexpectedness had an impact. Uncle Malcolm always lived out south. Uncle Malcolm was a recluse — a remote, benign figure she had been raised to respect, never judge, and never bother.

He was about to enter the orbit of the McLennan clan's daily life with all its demands and folks crossing his path. Surely he presented more problems than he would solve.

Papa tried to smooth over the awkward moment, attributing the silence to other factors. "Guess I shouldn't have switched to talk about farming as though we're glad to be making money due to such awful circumstances, so soon after the shock of hearing about the surrender."

"Mrs. Lundgren?" Elena's voice barely registered in Martha's awareness. "Mrs. Lundgren!"

"Yes, Elena. What is it?"

"Mrs. Lundgren, this is wonderful news! With Rudy's help, and now with Mr. Malcolm's, you will have time to teach the Spanish-American women the Red Cross course."

Innocently enough, Elena's spontaneous reaction established the announcement about Uncle Malcolm as something positive.

Clara chimed in. "Oh, Martha. Would you? I met with the women again after the last Spanish PTA. They've waited so patiently. I hate to put them off any longer."

"But Clara," protested Josie, "you told me the Women's Club request was next on your list. I had hoped Martha would teach our course, if you weren't available. With all the talk about her heroics during the flood, the women are especially eager to have her. We've heard the nurse from Fort Lyon would be a poor choice for us, such a stickler for detail. Very strict, and doesn't give much information beyond what's in the book."

Martha listened for Clara's response with interest, relishing Josie's indirect compliment.

Clara answered, assuming her characteristic, professional tone, but in Martha's experience, an emotional injury such as the one Clara suffered took more time to heal than the space of one dinner. "Oh, this is the first I've heard any complaints about Lola, rather, Miss Crane. I'll look into it. But Josie, I meant the Women's Club was next on the list of American women's groups. The Spanish women asked me several months ago."

"Miss Boehler," Marguerite said, "the Spanish women are also Americans. Their sons, our cousins, are fighting, were fighting, on the Philippine Islands, an American territory, in the American army, along with the Filipino soldiers. Our brother, Luis, enlisted with Alex. Our mother and aunt are Spanish-Americans, but no less American because they speak Spanish. They were born in Colorado.

Clara's face reddened. Josie looked at Marguerite with raised eyebrows, a sign she wasn't at all pleased that Marguerite presumed to correct Clara or about the implicit challenge to her plans for the Women's Club class.

Although Marguerite's point was gently stated, no one seemed to know how to react. But of course Marguerite was correct; many of the women were Americans who happened to speak Spanish.

Art cleared his throat. Martha assumed he would say she and he had talked and she was simply too busy to teach a Red Cross class, regardless of who the students might be.

"Maybe I can give an opinion," he said. "Martha an' I talked 'bout 'er teachin' the class fer the Mex'can, uh, the Spanish-American women, 'fore we knew Rudy would work fer us, an', obviously 'fore this welcome news 'bout ya, Malcolm. Decided she couldn't spare the time, but now things're changed. Wouldn't ya say so, Martha?"

Martha slowly nodded. He seemed to be saying the decision was up to her, if she felt she could handle the additional work of a class. However, she could tell from the thin line Josie was making with her lips that she would push the interests of the Women's Club.

Martha still basked in the glow of Josie's compliment that women like Fran, Mrs. Parker Hayes, Zella Behm, and many of the teachers in the county asked for her to be their instructor. Her! A farm wife! She was elated by the welcome to their group as a woman from whom they wanted to learn. But how could she break the news to Elena that she didn't have time for both the Women's Club and the Spanish-Americans?

Her only response to Art was a nod, and she excused herself to bring in dessert — the peaches she'd canned last year and a pitcher of fresh cream. She'd finally be doing the one activity that connected her to the defense effort more closely than any other. Every locale was losing doctors and nurses to the war, which meant mothers, aunts, and grandmothers had more responsibility for the health of their families. The Corregidor surrender would have an impact on the Women's Club members similar to the way it affected her; they would be chomping at the bit to play a greater role in the country's defense. The Red Cross class offered a tangible means.

Elena cleared the empty platter and vegetable bowl and followed her into the kitchen. Martha returned with the peaches, and Elena brought over dessert dishes from the bureau. Quiet conversations buzzed in the background while Martha served.

Discussion stopped as they relished the dessert until Clara said, "Mr. McLennan, with all our talk about classes for the women's groups, I should mention I know you're wanting to schedule the required first aid courses for the defense committees. Perhaps I can come by in the next day or two. I'll be teaching them, but I'm so busy the best I can do is propose a schedule and ask you to see that the defense workers fit themselves into the times I'm offering."

"Clara, I'm certain everyone will agree that's the best way to get it done."

Josie stood and said, rather formally, "Marguerite and I have to go. Thank you for dinner, Martha, Art. I'll be back to pick up Robbie and Elena in time for you to prepare for tonight, Martha. Marguerite and I need to ready ourselves for the banquet, also. Clara, you'll be letting me know about the class for the Women's Club?"

Clara looked toward Martha, evidently expecting her to say she would teach it, but Martha reconsidered. She didn't need Josie reminding her of the need to be early for the banquet. Other members of the Women's Club would be just as haughty. She stood and started clearing dishes.

Absent Martha's answer, Clara said, "Of course."

Carrie's Snowflake

Josie turned at the door and addressed Martha, but instead of pressing the issue about the class, she asked, "What was going on with Anna when we drove in? She threw her doll at the tree and said, 'You no good, why baby.' Not only rough behavior for Anna, but odd phrasing."

All eyes turned toward Anna. "No, it's not like that, Auntie Josie. It's 'why bee bee.' When Roger's angry, that's what he calls everyone."

"Who's Roger?" asked Papa.

"Hank Philson's youngest boy, at church," answered Martha. "What does it mean, Anna?"

Anna shrugged her shoulders.

"I think I know," Marguerite answered. "The expression might not be a series of words but of letters: Y-B-B. It is an abbreviation for the expression you have heard too many times. 'Yellow-Bellied,' with the final 'B' standing for a word I am not comfortable saying. It is another name used for Japs, uh, Japanese."

"Well, I regret I asked," Josie said, "but thank you for translating, Marguerite. Clara, I hope you'll be feeling better by tonight for the banquet."

With that, Josie and Marguerite left.

"Anna," Martha said, more upset over the brutality that accompanied the Y-B-B name than the vulgar words themselves, "we'll talk about this name and hurting people, and dolls, after everyone leaves."

"That's a discussion I'd like to hear," Papa only half teased, and he and Uncle Malcolm stood. "But we have to head out, too."

Everyone commented on the tasty dinner; Uncle Malcolm was the only guest to take his bowl and spoon into the kitchen. Art followed along behind with his, Anna accompanying him.

When Martha entered the kitchen she heard Anna say, "Uncle Malcolm, come into my bedroom and see Carrie's snowflake. Mama wanted it in the dining room, but after I got lost, she let me hang it on my wall."

Anna reinforced her invitation by grabbing hold of Uncle Malcolm's hand, his first genuine welcome. He smiled down and readily accompanied her.

"Art, I have to arrive in town earlier than planned," Martha said. "With news about the surrender and nothing more about the nurses, Edith's going to be more upset about Muriel than Clara was. I need to visit her before the banquet."

"Bring Anna ta me in the field when ya leave. That way yer sister an' Marguerite can swing by fer Robbie an' Elena an' go right on. Sounds like they're anxious ta get ta this party, too."

"Yes, most of the town women'll be there. The ones who still have time for such things."

Martha reconsidered her tone, given that the Women's Club coveted her services. "I shouldn't be flippant about the banquet for the senior girls. I know it's important to continue with normal routines, but it seems indulgent, and I'm annoyed by the solo I've been asked to sing."

"Do I know it?"

"Yes. It's from that silly minstrel show the Women's Chorus put on last year, the story of the Southern belle and all the darkies on the plantation who sing about her wedding. I'm to do one of the songs tonight, for the humor of it, I suppose, given how serious everything is these days, but it's so inconsequential, especially now, given the surrender."

Martha hummed a few bars. Uncle Malcolm slipped behind Art and hurried to catch up with Papa.

"I recognize it," Art said. "Guess the club women thought it would tickle the high school girls, although with the rash a weddin's on account a all the boys goin' ta war, I don't think they need encouragement."

Martha didn't laugh at his humor, so he persisted. He took her in his arms and whirled her around the kitchen.

"I suppose you'll be wearin' the blackface that takes days ta wash off."

They circled the table again and he stopped. "What am I doin'? We've surrendered at Corregidor an' I'm dancin' with my wife. Makes no sense."

"I'm not sure what we're doing, either, but it feels nice. Maybe you're relieved Uncle Malcolm's come to help?"

"I don't know. Might be hard ta get him goin' on our routines. He's not that active down at his place, ya know."

"I was wondering about that, too."

"I think I'm whirlin' ya 'round 'cause I felt bad 'bout not lettin' ya teach the class. And now that I hear how important it is ta so many women, well, it's a relief not ta be standin' in yer way. Why'd ya hesitate ta tell Clara you'd teach the Spanish women?"

She made no move to extricate herself from his arms. "Because it's so flattering the Women's Club members want me to be their instructor. But Elena asked first. I don't know what to do."

"I don't see yer problem. Yer always criticizin' the women's clubs, 'specially that one. And I'd a thought you'd have some loyalty ta Elena, fer all she does."

Elena, having put Robbie in for his nap, reappeared, and Anna emerged from her bedroom.

"Papa, dance with me, too! Dance with me!"

"One spin 'round the table, then I gotta go. Yer mama's gonna bring ya out ta me when she leaves."

They finished their turn around the kitchen, and Anna followed Art out the door.

Martha called, "Anna, stay in the yard where I can see you. Elena and I'll finish the dishes; then I want to talk to you."

"No Mexicans or Dogs"

"Mrs. Lundgren, will you teach the Spanish-American women?" Elena asked.

"I don't know. Miss Boehler will decide."

Which wasn't quite true. Clara would do what Martha preferred, but Martha hadn't made her choice. She would be ill at ease in front of a whole group of Spanish women waiting for translation of her words, but Art's comment about abandoning Elena made her out to be a weasel. She wouldn't feel as uncomfortable in front of the Women's Club, but Josie's presumption that the club had precedence made it less inviting.

"If Robbie takes a short nap, will you drive with me to the colonia before you start in the garden?" Elena asked. "I want you to see the houses after all the rain. Whether or not you teach the class, you might have some ideas about how the mothers can keep their children healthy."

Elena's unquestioning acceptance that Clara would make the decision pricked Martha's conscience. "Yes, I should visit the colonia. I keep meaning to do it."

Off-handedly she changed the subject to the first one that came to mind.

"If you'll give me some ideas about this Y-B-B matter. Did you see how viciously Anna threw her doll against the tree, after she called it that name?"

"No, I must have been lifting Robbie out of the car."

"I'm more worried about how violent she was than the name she used."

Elena stopped wiping the counter. "I do not think you can separate them."

"What do you mean?"

"Physical blows are violent, but the names people call one another are violent, too. Do you remember the sign in the Sage Café, before the Misses Jennings bought it?"

"Something to the effect of 'No Mexicans Allowed'?"

"Not quite. It read 'No Mexicans or Dogs Allowed' and did terrible things to the children called Mexicans who passed by that sign week after week."

Martha couldn't begin to measure the impact of such a sign on the younger Elena. Martha had walked by often without giving it as much thought as she gave the overall distasteful décor of the window. It included an odd collection of dead rabbits and pheasants standing in an arrangement of sand and dried plants. She presumed the then-owner-now-police-chief Cecil Thirkell shot the wild game and paid the taxidermist to prepare them so he could display a hunting prowess that spoke to his ability to put food on the table, and, by extension, on the menu at the restaurant. But because he never cleaned the window, the display made eating there a disgusting prospect. Martha simply hadn't reacted to what distressed Elena, the "No Mexicans or Dogs" sign that was removed sometime when Martha was away at nursing school.

"You feel less than yourself every time you see it," Elena continued, "until you have trouble finding yourself at all. Do you know that Luis attended every dance when he was in high school but never went inside? Not even Alex knew he was there and listening to the music under the windows outside. We know how to make ourselves disappear. My cousin Rudy is used to disappearing, too, which is why I am not surprised he brings his own food and eats in the field."

Martha was fairly certain Alex would never have expected Luis to attend the dances, much less imagine he lurked beneath the windows. Luis was the only Mexican boy in their class. With whom would he have danced?

As the police chief, probably Cecil Thirkell's dislike for Mexicans hadn't diminished. She didn't share his feelings but wouldn't be acting that different if she chose the prestige of the Women's Club over Elena's group, even though Elena had asked first.

For her part, Elena gave Martha the benefit of the doubt and talked to her as though Martha was capable of being on her side, of understanding what her people felt.

Elena signed. "I was so relieved the day that sign went into the trash. I walked down the alley, just to check that it was in the barrel to be burned."

She had effectively made her point about the destructive impact of degrading names, the sign in the barrel reminiscent of the sign in the barbershop window about shaving ears off "Japs" for free.

Robbie's wail signaled the nap had, indeed, been short.

Martha welcomed the escape from the conversation and the stifling air in the kitchen, so she said, "Elena, get Robbie and let's run over to the colonia. I'll take out the dishpan, dump the water in the garden, and talk with Anna. Maybe we'll still have time to weed before I have to leave for the banquet."

"Y-B-B"

The conversation with Elena impressed upon Martha the need to talk frankly with Anna about smashing the doll against the tree and calling it that ugly name. "Yellow-Bellied-Bastard." Another humiliation for the Japanese. Unconscionable. And even children said it.

She walked over to the swing where Anna rested on her elbows and tummy and ran her feet back and forth in the dirt to make the swing move. The doll and top seemed to be enjoying a peaceful ride, for the moment.

"May I sit with your toys?" asked Martha.

"Yes, we're lonesome. And I can sit on your lap, and you can make the swing go."

"Is your doll resting? From what I saw out the kitchen window before dinner, she's been busy today."

Anna settled into Martha's lap, and Martha pushed gently against the ground with her feet.

"She was naughty. Push harder, Mama. We need to go faster."

"What naughty thing did she do?"

"She wouldn't help load the wagon, so I yelled at her and threw her away."

"How did you know what name to call her, when she was naughty?"

"It's what Roger said when he drew the picture."

"What picture?"

"The picture of the Japs with their guns and airplanes. He drew the picture and cut it up. When he cut it up, he said, 'Take that, you why bee bees.'"

Martha cringed. How could she even begin to explain to Anna everything that upset her about this report? The war and adult fears had completely infiltrated children's play!

"Anna, I don't want you to call people, or dolls, 'Japs' and 'why bee bees.'"

Anna turned her head to survey her mother's face. "Why not?"

"It's a way of being mean that hurts someone's feelings, as when you reminded me not to call anyone 'stupid'. But the words 'Jap' and 'why bee bees' are much worse, which you and Roger seem to know. Shouting, hitting, and injury come with those words. You might have broken your doll by throwing her at the tree."

"I don't like that Harriet hit me."

"Nor do I. When did she hit you?"

Harriet was becoming the bane of Anna's existence the way Addie was of Martha's.

"When we were at Mrs. Lambert's and you were cleaning the mud out of her house."

Before Martha answered, Anna moved the topic forward. "And I don't like that Papa spanked me when I got lost, or when I crossed the road."

Anna remembered both spankings. But their intent was to impress her about the dangers.

"And do you remember why he spanked you?"

"Because I might be hit by a vehicle, or a rattlesnake might bite me."

"And when you were lost it was because you walked away from the house without telling us where you and Tip wanted to go, so we couldn't find you. You must talk to us first about your plans."

Elena came out of the house with Robbie, ready to visit the colonia.

Martha's conclusion was, simply, "Anna, I'm glad you told me these things. We're going to take a ride with Elena, so go potty."

She might have added she didn't like spanking, either, that it was a decision not taken lightly. She didn't hesitate to use forceful means to control a stubborn horse but knew to moderate herself with a gentle one. With a sensitive and headstrong child like Anna, finding the balance was tricky. Art would be just as surprised when Martha told him Anna still nursed her injured pride about the spankings.

What did it mean for a child that perceptive to witness a grown woman, Clara, come undone at the dinner table and overhear discussion of attack and surrender? Roger Philson's vicious disposal of his "Y-B-B" picture, Harriet hitting Anna, which must have reminded her of the spankings — all evidence for Anna that she lived in a violent world as dangerous for her as for grownups. No wonder she invited the gentle creator of Carrie's snowflake to appreciate its delicacy anew.

May 1942

The Colonia

Within fifteen minutes of leaving home, Martha turned off a gravel road and eased Max's Truck into ruts that ran through a hayfield. She took a chance that the pickup wouldn't get stuck in dirt softened by recent rains. The ruts led to a cluster of seven adobe houses and a courtyard of packed earth that separated the four houses on the south from the three on the north. Goats, chickens, and children meandered around the courtyard. When Martha stopped short of the compound, Elena confirmed she should park in the hayfield.

Elena carried Robbie, and Martha took Anna by the hand. She followed Elena to the middle house on the north side. On the way, Martha saw two privies, one for the south row and one for the north, much too close to the homes for proper hygiene. Someone had planted a large garden behind the far house on the south side.

Elena called out, "*Buenas dias*," and a soft voice answered from the interior.

Martha understood enough Spanish to know that Elena announced herself and her visitors and asked if they could enter. The response was *"Si."*

They stepped over the worn wooden beam that served as a threshold into an interior smelling of damp wood and earth. Martha saw pinpoints of light in the roof. The rain must have leaked in horribly. A kerosene lamp and some candles in tin holders sat on the handmade wooden table in the center of a packed-dirt floor. Four chairs, similarly built, stood at the table and two more against one wall. A bench of the same style was pushed against the opposite wall. Several sheepskins lay scattered about. Through a low doorway, Martha saw a young woman nursing an infant and seated on a narrow bed covered with a wool blanket. Another sheepskin lay at her feet.

She joined them in the larger room where Elena introduced her as Mercedes Suarez, Dolores's friend and the girl whose difficult delivery Doc had assisted the day Swede died. Mercedes seemed thrilled to learn that Martha worked with Doc McFarland, who, she believed, saved her life and that of her baby, Emeline. Her family was from Texas, and they worked sometimes in Colorado, sometimes in Nebraska.

While they sat at the table, a boy Anna's age, who was standing in the group of children bunched together outside the open door, entered and took her hand. A girl about the same age walked to Elena and said something in Spanish.

"Lilia says Miguel is inviting Anna to play," Elena explained. "I think it is fine for Anna to go with him, even though none of the children speak English. They have other ways of talking. Lilia will occupy Robbie in here while we talk. We will not be long."

"Do you want to play with Miguel and his friends?" Martha asked Anna, thinking no one could resist Miguel's inviting smile.

"Yes," answered Anna, looking intrigued with her unfamiliar surroundings and ready to explore.

"Usually children work in the fields with their parents," Elena said. "Maybe they are here today because Mercedes is still recovering and can look after them. If so, it is a nice holiday for them."

While Elena explained to Mercedes that Martha wanted to gather information about life in the colonia for her nursing class, Martha examined her surroundings more closely.

A potbelly stove rested on a bed of bricks in one corner, and several bags of beans sat on a shelf near it, as well as a can of coffee. A lower shelf served as a counter, and a flour sack curtain nailed to it created a concealed storage space. Strings of dried peppers dangled from a wooden peg on the wall, and articles of clothing were draped over other pegs. Some boots and shoes were neatly lined up against the wall. If each clothing peg represented an individual, Martha counted four adults and at least as many children who shared the home.

Elena and Mercedes carried on a lengthy conversation, but when Elena translated, Martha learned the gist of it in quick order. They stored potatoes and apples by burying them in the dirt outside, at the back of the houses. Some years ago, a family from New Mexico built two outdoor adobe ovens called *hornos*, structures Martha had noted that looked like oversized, conical beehives, one behind the southern four houses and the other behind the northern three. A large tank behind Mercedes's home held drinking water.

Mercedes's husband had the task of filling it from the pump over at the hay mill. He hated lugging the heavy cans. The tank always seemed empty, and when he cleaned it he usually found crickets at the bottom, occasionally a dead mouse. Several barrels containing water for washing stood outside, near the houses, full from the recent storms.

Each family contracted with the landowner for a certain number of acres and was allowed to live in one of the adobe homes. During the spring planting and fall harvest, school-age children worked in the fields or the families would fall short of their quotas. Mercedes continued to talk, but Elena stopped translating, which seemed to annoy Mercedes.

Finally, Elena relented and, with downcast eyes, explained, "She wants me to tell you that for Dolores to complete the eighth grade, for me, the tenth, and for Marguerite and Luis to graduate from high school is unheard of. She is very proud of us, but many of the parents think it is a mistake, certainly unnecessary, for girls, especially, to continue in school. They are needed in the fields. I am embarrassed to translate this compliment."

What Martha was seeing and hearing wasn't a surprise, but her ignorance of the details unsettled her. Descriptions of the poor living conditions in the colonias appeared in the newspaper from time to time, and her own experience told her that Mexican children attended the lower grades in the rural schools but disappeared in the upper grades. However, observing Mercedes nurse her baby under the hole-pocked roof and walking across the packed-dirt floor was a different matter.

"The families are poor," Elena said, "do not have enough food, and are often sick. One of the older women keeps a box of herbs and roots under her bed, and many of the medicines work for things like upset stomachs and headaches."

Elena paused and conferred with Mercedes. They seemed to reach agreement. "Mrs. Lundgren, Mercedes allows me to tell you this story. Some of the illnesses are serious and there is no medicine for them. Two years ago, when her sister was sick and could not get well, the public nurse, Miss Swanson, drove her to the Denver Children's Hospital. The family could not leave the fields to visit. Her mother was too ill to travel, so Mercedes's sister died there, alone. She is buried in Denver; they do not know where. Her mother died soon afterward."

Martha tried to absorb the impact of Elena's story, but she was chagrinned that these families lived in her neighborhood, not more than ten miles away, and she knew next to nothing about their lives. She wondered if Papa and Art were better informed. Surely Josie and Clara knew the particulars through their contact with the families as teacher and nurse, but they rarely discussed the colonia, certainly not with these specifics.

Elena was saying, "My family is not this poor, and neither are the women who will be in the Red Cross class, but many grew up in these circumstances and have relatives who still live like this. They want the class to help them with their own children and also their nieces and nephews."

Elena had apparently reached the summation of her argument and Martha should honor it somehow, but Lilia had disappeared with Robbie. Martha had no trouble believing Elena about the dangers. Surely the incurable illness Elena just described was tuberculosis.

To what other hazards was she exposing Robbie and Anna? And Robbie wasn't even her child. She conjured visions of Earl's cataleptic fit if he knew where they were.

"Elena, I must find Robbie and Anna."

They followed the sounds of delighted squeals to the further edge of the colonia where all the children, including Anna, played a game of chase on bales of straw, but Martha couldn't locate Robbie.

"Where's Robbie, Elena? Where is Robbie?" she nearly screamed.

Elena, who was walking slightly ahead, said, "He is here, Mrs. Lundgren, in the middle, in the square hole the children made with the bales. It is like a playpen for him."

Martha drew close enough to see it was better than a playpen. He was in the middle of all the fun.

Lilia stood Robbie in the center of the small square, and each time he plopped down on his bottom, he scooted to the bale where the older children congregated and pulled himself up. The game seemed to consist of the children running from the top of the bale Robbie chose to another while trying to maintain their balance on the slippery straw. Lilia jumped again into the center, repositioned Robbie, and he scooted to the bale where the others crowded together. In effect, he was "it" in a game of tag.

"Elena, I hate to break up the fun, but I have so much to do before I leave for the program tonight. We must go, now."

Elena turned from her enjoyment of the children to look at Martha. Her smile vanished. "Yes, Mrs. Lundgren. I will gather the eggs this afternoon and weed in the garden, if that will help, and I can fix the supper for Anna and Mr. Lundgren. Thank you for coming to the colonia."

Martha didn't want to leave Elena, or Mercedes, for that matter, with the impression she was an unappreciative guest, but the visit was an ordeal. The squalid living conditions shocked her, and she was angry that the white family who owned the colonia and farm on which it was situated wasn't more concerned for the health of the workers, not to mention their humanity.

"Elena, please don't worry about getting it all done. We'll do it together. It was important I visit the colonia."

Her discomfort wasn't Elena's or Mercedes's fault. She made an attempt to respond to their hospitality. "Mercedes, *muchas gracias.* Elena, thank you for being so persistent about getting me here today."

She moved toward Mercedes to caress Emeline's head as a goodbye gesture, and, in the bright sunlight, could see the yellow tinge of jaundice in the skin on her face. Martha would persuade Doc to visit his tiny patient, the one whose life he had already saved once.

She retrieved Anna, and Lilia boosted Robbie up to Elena. The chickens perched warily on a higher tier of bales, above the children's boisterous play.

The group walked back through the courtyard, children tagging along, and Martha caught sight of a figure reminiscent of a fairy-tale witch, a shrunken woman no taller than a ten-year-old in a long black dress with a black scarf thrown over her head. She withdrew from the doorway into the dark interior, and Martha didn't call her to Elena's attention. On the drive home, though, Martha described her.

"She must be the grandmother, the one with the box of medicines," Elena speculated. "We were rude not to say hello."

The diminutive woman frightened Martha, who was preoccupied with making a quick escape, not with the sensibilities of a shadowy crone.

Chaos

Aneda Marquez opened the Giffards' door to a hot and breathless Martha. She hadn't wanted to roll down the windows of Max's Truck more than a crack because the swirling air would have messed what arrangement there was to her hair, but the heat of the late afternoon sun had streamed in, and her dress stuck to her back, wet with perspiration.

"Mrs. Lundgren, come in."

Aneda's calm, friendly manner was so like Elena's that it seemed Martha hadn't left Elena behind, even though their physical resemblance wasn't strong. Of Aneda's two daughters, Marguerite resembled her more. Both were Martha's height, taller than Elena, and quite attractive. Not that Elena wasn't pretty, but Aneda and Marguerite were striking in the way of women whose thick, dark hair and black eyes compliment a flashing smile and smooth brown skin.

"Mrs. Giffard is having a bad day. She is trying to prepare for the party tonight, but she cannot choose her dress. Perhaps you should see."

Aneda led Martha to the bedroom, and every surface was covered with an article of clothing. Over the afternoon, Edith had emptied her closet and started on the dresser drawers, slowly, methodically looking for just the right jewelry, gloves, and slip that would complement the as-yet-to-be-selected dress. Perhaps there was some rationale to finding a favorite necklace that would lead back to a suitable outfit, but the lack of success with the dress predicted a similar fate for the jewelry.

"Hello, Edith," said Martha softly, not wanting to startle her.

Edith turned, barefoot and robed in a navy-blue slip, with strands of necklaces draped over her fingers.

"Martha, what a delight you've come. I'm having a devil of a time deciding what to wear tonight for the banquet."

At least she recognized Martha and knew she was preparing for a banquet, all good signs. Martha's objective was to move her away from the chaos. "Edith, let's bring the orange dress and the blue one into the living room, and you choose between the two."

Martha had no reason to select those particular outfits other than they were the easiest to grab. She extricated the necklaces from Edith's fingers, as she would untangle Anna from a mess.

"Once you choose your dress, I'll come back for the appropriate jewelry."

To Martha's relief, Edith followed her into the living room. She tried on the orange dress, which was several sizes too large. Martha had overlooked Edith's weight loss, something that must have happened gradually over the winter. Edith didn't seem to notice that the dress hung in lumpy folds.

"Let's try the blue one, Edith."

The blue dress was baggy but fit better. No matter. The goal was to get Edith into something, anything.

"I prefer the blue one, Edith. How about you?"

Edith picked at the sleeves absent-mindedly. Seemingly agreeing with the selection, she moved to another topic. "They've surrendered in the Philippine Islands. You know Muriel has been working there, in Manila."

"I know, Edith," answered Martha, unnerved that Edith seemed not to remember how many times the two of them discussed Muriel's situation.

"She hasn't written for the longest time."

"Yes, mail isn't getting out of there, with all the fighting."

Martha waited, unable to anticipate how, or if, Edith would follow the thread of conversation.

"Claude says we mustn't worry, until we have something to worry about, but don't you think the surrender gives us cause?"

Edith's was a plaintive, uncertain question. Martha composed a truthful answer, of the opinion that honesty would be more assuring than hedging, which might increase Edith's anxiety. "Yes, I think the surrender changes things. We can assume Muriel and the other nurses are in prison camps, as are the nurses who were on Wake Island and Guam."

Until she spoke the words, Martha wasn't aware she had such definite ideas about Muriel's whereabouts, or that she even believed Muriel was alive. Her confident voice reassured even herself.

"With the other Americans?" Edith asked. "If so, she's safe."

Hundreds, maybe thousands, of Americans must be incarcerated in the Japanese camps. How would an army in the midst of fighting a war attend to the needs of so many civilians? Even if Muriel were in a camp, surely there wasn't adequate food, shelter, or sanitation. Martha doubted Muriel, or any of them, was safe, but she wouldn't quibble about it.

"Yes, she's with other Americans."

"Well, we can't do anything about it today. Weren't you going to get my jewelry, Martha? I want the silver necklace and matching earrings, please."

Edith sank onto the sofa, but her ability to switch so quickly from such a muddled state about the dresses to the decisive one about jewelry, and to assume the role of wardrobe director, upset Martha's equilibrium. Being with Edith was like keeping up with a hummingbird flitting from here to there in the space of a breath.

Martha re-entered the bedroom and saw a neat pile of dresses on the bed. Aneda had already hung up many of them. Usually order descended into chaos much more quickly than it reestablished itself, so Martha gave Aneda a great deal of credit for managing the situation, another way Elena resembled her mother in temperament.

"She's lost weight," Martha said after she handed over the orange dress and pulled the door shut behind her.

"Yes, she only pecks at her food."

The doorbell rang, and Martha said, regretfully, "I'll get the door," wanting to extract more information from Aneda about Edith's current habits.

"Please finish in here, Aneda. If she still has choices, I'm afraid she'll start taking dresses out all over again."

It was Clara who had rung, and Martha joined her on the porch to describe Edith's afternoon.

"Martha, I'm not surprised. Edith's deteriorating. She's losing weight. Have you seen the scratches on her arms? I think she's doing it to herself. Should we advise Claude she be hospitalized?"

Martha knew Clara's was a medical assessment, not a moral judgment. Still, she came to Edith's defense, not able to imagine Edith in a facility with the likes of Vera and Ida, who had suffered so dreadfully. However, Doc had said the number of patients at the State Hospital had increased dramatically since the Pearl Harbor attack, primarily housewives and ordinary working folk.

"Let's watch her tonight at the banquet," Martha said. "Perhaps being around the other women, some diversion…"

"We'd never forgive ourselves if…"

"Clara, you're surely not comparing Edith to the Murray woman whose two sons are missing in the Battle of Bataan."

"The Murray woman did try to take her own life."

"I haven't entertained the possibility Edith would reach such a state."

But Edith also faced the horror of losing two children, the seven-year-old Claudia to rheumatic fever and now Muriel to fighting in the Pacific.

"We can see Edith's getting worse, physically," Clara said, "and we can guess that, with the surrender and all the confusion, we won't hear anything soon about Muriel. I don't know that Edith can continue at this level of agitation."

"But surely the Japanese will provide prisoner lists."

Even if that were to happen, it might take months. Why couldn't Martha accept Clara's appraisal of Edith's condition without throwing up objections? Clara wasn't exaggerating, and she didn't even know about probable lingering effects of Claude's dalliance with Louise.

Martha was giving too much weight to Edith's signs of health and too little to those of her decline, just as Enoch failed to see the severity of Swede's injuries. Of course, Enoch wasn't medically trained and judged only Swede's exterior — a strong, coherent man able to move himself to the hearse with minimal help.

But it was inexcusable for her, a nurse, to ignore symptoms. Perhaps she did because she felt so awful about Louise's involvement, and Clara was doing her a favor by opening her eyes to the possibility that Edith had reached the point where not hospitalizing her had life-and-death consequences.

"What do you think Muriel would have us do?" Martha asked.

"Martha, who's at the door?" Edith called from the entryway.

She was outside before Martha could answer.

"Oh, it's you, Clara," Edith said. "Muriel will be so sorry to have missed you."

"Believe me, I'm sorry, too," Clara said, giving Martha a see-what-I-mean look. "Martha has to hurry to the banquet for rehearsal. I'll help you finish getting ready."

The Banquet

Martha rushed into the ladies' room at the hotel with her costume and makeup in her overnight case. Eleanor Moulton, who was to sing the concluding duet with Martha, stood in front of the mirror touching up her lipstick.

"You're late," Eleanor chided. "We've already run through the numbers."

Martha hated to have missed the rehearsal and said, "Eleanor, do you mind practicing our duet while I change?"

"Don't you think it rather strange to sing 'God Will Take Care of You' in the ladies' room while you apply blackface?"

"Yes, so let's sing softly. But I'd feel worse not to have warmed up at all."

During the time it took Martha to dress and apply the blackface, they rehearsed their duet and two of the chorus numbers.

When several women entered, Eleanor said, "This is ridiculous. I'm leaving."

Martha tucked her overnight case into a corner and walked down the short hallway to the banquet room. The scene impressed even her as one who downplayed fancy decorations. On each lace-covered table sat a centerpiece of red and white sweet peas and blue bachelor's buttons flanked by red, white, and blue candles. At the door, two other members of the chorus, also dressed in blackface and colorful long skirts, pinned a corsage of red and white sweet peas on each girl's formal dress. A glance around the room confirmed that the attendees wore red, white, or blue suits and dresses. Martha supposed Josie mentioned the patriotic wear for the evening, but she hadn't paid attention because she would be in costume. Thank goodness Edith had agreed to wear the blue dress, or perhaps she had remembered the patriotic theme.

Someone called, "Martha, take your place. The line of girls waiting for their corsages is getting too long."

Another point she forgot. All those in blackface were supposed to be "butlers" for the evening, replicating the Negro boys who served in the House and Senate restaurants. However, she doubted women in blackface lent the hoped-for dignity. Congress wouldn't think of having colored girls as butlers.

When everyone had entered the room, Martha took her seat next to Clara and picked up her program. The design on the front was a striking, stylized version of the American flag, reminiscent of the one that hung over the gift table at the Macgills' farewell.

"Clara, did Edith design this?"

"Of course. Confusing, isn't it? She still produces these lovely pieces, but in so many ways she's falling apart."

Martha opened the program booklet but took the opportunity to ask the question she'd intended to before Edith interrupted them on the porch.

"Clara, are you feeling better?"

"I made a fool of myself at dinner, didn't I?"

"Not at all. Your reaction to news of the surrender was quite appropriate, especially given your busy schedule. You're under a lot of strain."

"I hope you're not comparing me to Edith! I'd rather not talk about my nervous state in such a public setting."

"I understand."

Martha busied herself with the interior of the program. She wouldn't make the same mistake with Clara she had at the Macgills' farewell last fall when she roped Josie into that intimate conversation while guests milled about.

The menu listed in the program carried out the Southern theme by complementing the Negro songs the Women's Chorus would sing: mint julep, baked ham with raisin sauce, candied yams, succotash, butter pecan ice cream…

The Women's Club didn't do anything halfway. How could Martha presume to teach a course for them? They'd expect the same diligence in her preparation, and she had neither the time nor the imagination.

After the meal, each committee gave a short annual report. There seemed to be an unspoken competition over the numbers of boxes sent to soldiers, sailors, and marines since the first of the year and the amount of defense stamps and bonds purchased in lieu of refreshments at club meetings.

In her remarks for her committee, Maude Moulton emphasized they should no longer send food in the boxes. She mentioned razors and toothpaste, along with cigarettes, tobacco, and Kodak film, although she realized how the boys would miss homemade cookies and fudge.

The recognition of the senior girls went quickly. Each gave a sketch about her future plans. Martha thought any dispassionate observer would admit Marguerite was the most ravishing in her red formal, and the best spoken.

Marguerite sat down, and Clara's whispered question seemed an impolite interruption, given her reticence to carry on their earlier conversation. "You know why she isn't going to college, don't you, in spite of never missing the honor roll?"

"She said she's going to California."

"Only because the high school counselor told her it was unheard of to give scholarships to Mexican students."

Probably unheard of because she would be the first. But that was no reason to withhold it. Josie surely hadn't known Marguerite was refused, or she would have done something.

Clara continued their whispered conversation in spite of the disapproving looks of the women at their table, especially those of Maude and Addie, her daughter-in-law.

"And the red formal is Edith's. She insisted Marguerite wear it, over Aneda's protests. Edith made the necessary alterations, but look at the blue dress she's wearing. Hangs on her like a sack. She can be so aware, yet oblivious."

Martha nodded in silent agreement. So Edith had known of the red-white-and-blue dress code to insist on the red formal for Marguerite. Martha smiled at Maude and Addie, whose severe frowns of reprobation so distorted their faces they were distracting in their own right. Then, again, smiling behind her blackface must look absurd, especially given the formal setting.

Mrs. Hayes, the club president, called Zella Behm and the Women's Chorus forward, and Martha tied the bandana around her hair, relieved to escape Maude and Addie's censure. How unfortunate that Elsie Lambert had seemingly lost the affections of her daughter to the much less likable mother-in-law. But the practical, outspoken Elsie would never be invited to join the Women's Club, a membership Addie undoubtedly prized.

The performance of the Women's Chorus delighted the audience, especially Martha's frivolous darkie song about the wedding preparations of the plantation owner's daughter. For a contrasting mood, Zella had suggested Martha follow the wedding piece with the spiritual "Go Down, Moses," a song the audience knew and could join on the refrain. Martha sang it a cappella.

The selection was more prescient than either Zella or Martha imagined when they planned the program weeks earlier. No one could have predicted the surrender at Corregidor would be widely known that night.

When Martha and all the other women sang the line in the refrain, "Tell all Pharaohs to/Let my people go!" her mind filled with images of prisoners in camps around the world, men like Elena's cousins and women like Muriel, local boys gone missing whose families had been waiting months for news of their whereabouts, the suffering of those in the occupied countries in Europe. Martha poured her soul into each verse, and the women and girls in the audience responded in kind each time they sang the refrain.

When the song was finished, Eleanor stepped quickly to Martha's side for their concluding duet, one chosen as a benediction for the senior girls: "God Will Take Care of You." Coming as it did on the heels of "Let my people go!" it also became a prayer for the protection of all servicemen and nurses, particularly as she and Eleanor sang:

No matter what may be the test,
God will take care of you;
Lean, weary one, upon His Breast,
God will take care of you.

Martha slipped her hand around Eleanor's waist. Eleanor had such a sweet soprano voice, and Martha momentarily regretted that Alex had rejected her romantic overtures. But Maude would have been his mother-in-law. Martha slowly removed her hand.

When all the women spontaneously joined in the last refrain, Martha took pleasure in the thought they were of a similar mind about the work and worry facing them:

God will take care of you,
Through every day, o'er all the way;
He will take care of you,
God will take care of you.

The room went silent. She heard quiet, but unmistakable, sobs. A group gathered around Edith. Clara hurried over, and Martha slipped out of her place in front of the chorus.

Those hovering around Edith separated to let them through. Josie held her. "What shall we do?"

"Martha, help me take her home," Clara said. "We'll have to call Mrs. DeFries to spend the night. Claude won't want to handle her alone. He can drive you back for the truck."

Confession

They reached the house and helped a more composed Edith through the door. Claude rose from where he sat by the radio, after he placed his glass of, presumably, whiskey, on the floor by the chair.

Edith walked unsteadily toward him and put her arms around his neck. He seemed startled but assented to the embrace.

"Oh, Claude, I made a fool of myself at the banquet. I melted into tears and couldn't stop crying."

She faced Martha and held out one of her hands. Martha took it.

"Don't you know it's your fault, Martha?"

Edith's was as much a question as a gently playful statement. She lifted Martha's hand to her cheek. "Those songs, how can I explain it? They were reminders that many, many people are suffering unspeakable things. I don't know that God disposes of their suffering so much as He helps them endure it until better days, but it's a complicated thought for an artist like me. We'll leave theology to Rev. Behm. I'm very, very tired. Claude, please drive Martha back to the hotel for Max's Truck, who is, we must remember, another missing child."

Still holding Martha's hand, Edith reached for Clara's. "At least I have the two of you, Clara and Martha. Maybe someday Muriel will be here, too. Clara, help me to bed."

Clara and Edith walked toward the bedroom. Claude moved to turn off the radio.

Martha felt as tired as Edith looked. She numbly turned toward the door and saw her reflection in the mirror by the coatrack.

Blackface with a bandana tied around her hair. Maybe no one was herself anymore.

Claude started talking as soon as he turned on the automobile's engine. "I think you saw me at the station the day Louise left. I'm assuming you know there was, there was something, between us. I need to know if she's all right, if she's happy. I'll not write her or pursue her in any way. I just need to know."

How could Claude ask about Louise immediately after seeing his wife in such an awful state?

"Louise is fine," she answered coldly. "In her letters she describes a lively scene, and I imagine she's in the thick of it."

Claude's deep sigh communicated loss, regret, relief — a constellation of feelings.

"Martha, I know you don't respect me, and I don't blame you. But I loved your sister, which I don't say to excuse what I did. I choose the past tense of 'love' purposefully. I won't be unfaithful to Edith again. How can I help her?"

Martha's exhaustion circumvented pretense and subtlety. "None of us knows what to do, Claude. The two of you should visit Doc first thing in the morning, but if she senses your uncompromised love, that might help. You, alone, should have a conversation with Rev. Behm, who is also aware of you and Louise."

June 1942

The Proposal

She grasped the receiver between flour-covered fingers. "Hello, Fran!"

Martha hadn't made an overture toward easing the strain between them since the schoolroom showdown, having already overstepped her bounds. "Yes, I'm planning to work in the garden today, before it gets hot."

The receiver began to slip from her shoulder. In her effort to catch it, she coated it with flour. "A marvelous idea! The work goes much faster when shared… Yes, I agree. We'll weed at our place first and Papa's second. We should stop by noon, before it gets really hot. With a garden, you never finish, anyway."

Martha's enthusiasm wasn't forced. Surely gardening was Fran's pretense to convey the outcome of her talk with Burleigh.

She put the pie dough in the refrigerator, and she and Anna cleaned up the kitchen. After she grabbed their sunbonnets, they gathered gardening tools from the barn. Fran drove Papa's Chrysler into the lane. The temporary loan had apparently become permanent.

"Good morning, Martha, Anna. I stopped by Robert's to collect the implements I need. It's already getting hot. How do the men survive all day out in this sun?"

Perhaps Fran's chattiness came from nerves. She only revealed select aspects of herself, so Martha exercised caution when it came to reading her moods.

"Where are my implements, Mama?"

"Ah, we didn't get your tools, did we?" Martha answered, uncertain that Anna knew the meaning of "implements."

"Let's see if they're in the house. Fran, will you please pour three tall glasses of iced tea? We'll put the tray in the shade near the front door. The ice'll melt, but it's so inconvenient to traipse into the house all muddy from gardening just for tea."

A search through kitchen drawers yielded Anna's bent tablespoon, scratched spatula, and tin cup for digging in the dirt. Satisfied everyone had what she needed, they trooped out, around the front of the house and to the north side of the grassy section of the yard. In the early spring, Martha had persuaded Art to plow under yet another strip of the lawn and expand the garden's length all the way to the irrigation ditch by the county road.

Fran surveyed the expanse and groaned, "I had no idea you had such a large victory garden."

Martha didn't want to discourage the volunteer labor before they had begun. "We'll stop here at ten-thirty. We don't want to cheat Papa. Besides, his cucumbers are always better than mine, and maybe he'll be more generous if he knows Anna and I contributed our share of work!"

Fran gave Anna a quick hug. "I doubt he'll deny Anna her cucumbers. I suggest we start out by the road, in the full sun, while it's cooler, and work our way back toward the shade as the day heats up."

Martha agreed and they started walking. Anna ambled along behind, and Martha was tempted to describe her visit to the colonia. Today little Miguel and Lilia might be laboring in the fields, and girls like Dolores and Mercedes. It was a wonder any survived the heat, cold, and contaminated water. But pressed by the size of the garden and time limit, for the first half hour the women weeded purposefully through the young sweet corn and beans.

Anna eventually arrived at her destination — the puddles near the ditch from last night's showers.

"Honey, stop!" Martha called out, and hurried over. She dragged the toe of her shoe in the dirt alongside the puddles and parallel to the irrigation ditch.

"You absolutely cannot pass this line."

"But Mama, the puddles are shrinking. I can refill them by dipping my cup into the ditch water."

"Anna, absolutely means not at all, under any circumstance, even if the puddles disappear. If you can't think of another game when they evaporate, come to me or Auntie Fran."

When the crew of two women reached the squash, Anna joined them, covered in puddle-project mud. From her lower vantage point close to the ground, she squealed, "Mama, look at the bugs!"

Fran and Martha grunted, not so much in disgust as annoyance at the delay the infestation presented.

"I'll get a bucket and pour in a little kerosene for them," Martha said. "A tedious job, picking off these squash bugs and their eggs. We have to let the weeds go for now."

Anna's interest in bugs soon waned, and she wandered into the strawberries, which proved much more rewarding.

The Assault

Perhaps it was the women's proximity, or the monotony of the work, but Fran started talking.

"I've been married, once. When I was eighteen. A dashing fellow who came through our town, played the guitar, sang in the bar."

Martha suspected a prior romance, but with a guitar-playing drifter? She blurted out, "Bar? I wouldn't have thought…"

"You assume Oklahoma's sober?"

Her outburst concerned Fran's association with a drifter, not liquor, but she didn't object.

Fran plunged ahead. "Oklahoma wasn't any more sober in 1926, during Prohibition, than it claims to be now, but I suppose it depended on the town. Our sheriff made a lot of money off liquor, and other, um, activities. With all his faults, Burleigh's honest. I have some respect for that."

Martha didn't take issue about the impulsive and crude, but principled, sheriff.

"Anyway, my husband, an Easterner who said he came out for the oil boom but never got past the bars, swept me off my feet. I was too young to understand what the drinking meant. Not much entertainment for young men in our town. Tulsa was too far a drive on a regular basis. He was older, Jake's age, and took up with Jake and his friends. They all drank, except Jake. I suppose he did too, but he wasn't a drunk."

Other than an occasional "hm," Martha didn't respond. From Fran's halting pace, she surmised the sordid story had never been told. Martha's intrusion into Fran's life meant she owed it to Fran to listen, however much the story diminished Fran. So far, the outcome promised to be the same as if Jake had been a rekindled romance: Fran was a dangerous woman Papa must avoid.

Fran barely paused for breath and to move forward in the row before she continued. "Sometimes the men'd all come over to our place, such as it was. I'd call it a shack. Our folks were terribly upset

I married him, but they were struggling sharecroppers on a farm some distance away. I had lived in town since starting high school. With a teacher. Did her cleaning and cooking. A nice person. Very disappointed in me. Thought I would go to teacher's college. So did I. But I got married. At least I finished high school. If he had arrived a year earlier, I would have married him then and not even graduated."

Martha listened so intently that when the stray cat brushed against her legs, she let out a startled cry.

Fran jerked to attention. "What?"

The cat brushed against her, and the two women laughed nervously, sharing their discomfort about being so engrossed in Fran's humiliating story that a cat would cause such alarm.

"You need a cat," she said. "If not that one, some kind of cat. I've seen several mice this morning. Why don't you put out food and maybe it'll hang around?"

"Maybe," answered Martha, relieved to talk about something as mundane as cats and mice. She encouraged the diversion by asking, "How many strawberries should we let Anna eat before we decide she's going to be sick?"

"Let's sidetrack her. Can she carry the tea over to us?"

"Anna, honey," Martha called. "Please go to the front door and get your tea. When you've finished, bring ours."

"I'm so hot," Fran said. "When I perspire, my scars itch."

"Should we stop?"

"No, no. This has to be done. It's such a relief to talk openly. About scars. About my husband and that he was a drunk. I've never said these things aloud."

On her part, Martha was more repulsed by Fran's story than by the disgusting details Louise divulged about the Claude Giffard affair when Martha was captive in the hospital bed after her miscarriage. For one thing, Martha didn't hold Louise in high regard as she did Fran, so Fran's fall was all the more shocking. And Louise's confession was relatively straightforward, as was the solution. Leave. Martha, not knowing the conclusion of Fran's indiscretions, dreaded to hear the outcome.

They continued in silence for several minutes before Fran resumed. "I got pregnant right away."

Martha stole a sideways glance to take stock of Fran's facial expression, but it was as blank as her voice was flat. Fran's recitation sounded remote and implausible, as though the events comprised another woman's story. Questions stacked up in Martha's mind, but she kept her mouth shut.

"One night, my, um, 'husband,' came home with Jake and a friend, drunk as usual. Perhaps the friend's name was John; I forget. I heard them in time to stand and wrap myself in the sheet. I had stripped because of the heat. Jake and John helped him into bed, then John yanked off the sheet, and, as I turned, slapped me on my bare bottom with an obscenity and a comment that, even pregnant-fat, I was the most beautiful woman in the state."

Martha stopped dropping bugs in the kerosene and remained motionless, kneeling in soil so damp it was almost muddy. The only connection she had to the depravity Fran described was through Vera and Ida. Martha didn't know if she could listen to more.

"Martha, I can't imagine how lewd this sounds to you, but I have to be accurate so you'll understand why I pushed Jake out of my life, why I fled Oklahoma and why I'm so desperate to put it behind me. Only with all the repugnant details will you appreciate how far I've come and why the prospect of a fall's so terrifying."

Martha, not trusting herself with words, reached into Fran's row and lightly touched her arm, a neutral contact that possibly conveyed consolation and encouragement to continue. Martha herself didn't know what the touch meant. Perhaps she was simply reassuring herself that the Fran next to her was the flesh-and-blood woman she knew, not the fallen one taking shape in her imagination.

Fran apparently took it as reassurance for she dove back into the story. "I never would have thought a drunk could move so fast. Before anyone reacted, my husband grabbed the whiskey bottle by the bed, knocked over the kerosene lamp, broke the bottle over the iron frame and went after John. I know this sounds like badly written drama, but I think that's what happened. The slashes on John's throat and chest started bleeding before Jake and I responded, even though we moved fast. I went toward John, but Jake screamed for me to run. Before I could react, my husband cut me across the chest with the bottle and grabbed my arm. I wrenched free, but as I turned, he swiped my back with it. By then, Jake had reached us, and my husband faced him. Before Jake smashed the lamp over his head, he cut Jake across the face."

Martha, kneeling in the mud and picturing the violent scene, almost retched: a friend, evidently murdered; a naked, pregnant woman brutally attacked.

Just then Anna shrieked, "Let go! Let go!"

Still living in the terrifying world of Fran's story, neither woman moved. They watched Anna run through the strawberries and throw one full glass of tea at the cat and then the other.

Martha pushed herself up, hurdled over the intervening rows, ran through the strawberries, and picked up a sobbing Anna.

"Baby bunny. There." Anna wailed.

The bunny, collapsed on the grass, stopped twitching as Anna spoke. The cat crept closer, intent on retrieving its prey. Anna tore herself from Martha's arms and took off after the cat, which leapt from its crouched position and ran.

"Bad cat! Bad cat!" Anna screamed and sobbed.

She chased after it, and Martha after her. The cat, the black streaks in its calico hair iridescent in the sunshine, soared over the ditch and vanished into the weeds along the road. Anna stood helplessly on her side of the water. She allowed Martha to embrace and lift her.

Martha, cooing and shushing, made her way back toward Fran, who knelt in the grass by the slain bunny. When they reached the site of the slaughter, Anna's sobs were intermittent gasps, and she squirmed out of Martha's arms.

"I hate that cat. I hate it," Anna said with such virulence that both women shuddered. She knelt beside Fran and ran her index finger along the bunny's side.

"The fur's soft and warm," Anna said.

Fran lightly touched the body and whispered, "There's so little blood, as though the poor thing's asleep, except for its odd position."

"We'll give it a proper burial," Martha said. "Anna, come to me."

Martha also knelt, and Anna leaned against her thighs. Martha cuddled her, and they stared at the corpse.

"Anna, the cat isn't bad. We want cats because they catch mice and bunnies. The cats guard our food; otherwise the mice and bunnies eat it. I know the cat seems mean, but it doesn't intend to be. That's how it does its job. You'll remember that Papa shot a lot of rabbits last year because they eat the plants in the field."

"What shall we bury her in, Mama?"

Martha, with no idea how her speech struck Anna, was at a loss.

"I have a box of cigars in the Chrysler for Robert," answered Fran. "He'll appreciate them even if they aren't in a box. Probably has an old one he can use. I'll get it."

Dénouement

The heat, squash bugs, and burial delayed the weeding project, but none of it drained the women as Fran's story had. They sat on the cement step by the front door, drinking their fresh glasses of tea and watching Anna decorate the grave. Fran resumed as if there had been no interlude.

"I collapsed, so I didn't know everything that happened. I wasn't fully aware for several days and was told I lost the baby and Jake was in jail, charged with murdering both his friends."

"Jake, murder? How can that be?"

"Evidently Jake panicked. Before the volunteer fire department arrived, summoned by the landlord because the kerosene lamp started a small blaze, Jake pulled me out, then tried to arrange the bodies so it looked like they killed each other."

Martha nodded. An onlooker would think they were talking about some neutral subject, but the grisly details made her sick.

"They extinguished the fire, and, because the damage wasn't extensive, they could tell the bodies had been dragged through the blood and assumed Jake intentionally set the fire to cover his crime. In the hospital they asked me to confirm Jake's account of events, but at the time, I couldn't. Whether I was unable to remember or refused to, I don't know, but I came to believe my brother was a murderer. I realize now that belief was planted in my mind by the sheriff and the forcefulness of his interpretation about the dragged bodies."

Martha longed for Fran's recitation to end.

Fran sipped her tea and said, "I distorted all of it, for what reason? To convince myself the marriage wasn't a mistake and my husband not a murderer, all evidence to the contrary? Don't you see, Martha, how I compounded my guilt by letting my brother go to prison for defending me? A brother whom I knew to be good but persuaded myself to be at fault?"

Martha opened her mouth to answer but had nothing to say. Fran's tale was so perverse it sounded made-up, but who would imagine such a story?

Fran continued as though she hadn't expected an answer. "They sent me to a Tulsa hospital, and I didn't contact my family. Afterward, I went to teacher's college, taught for several years in another part of the state, moved to Colorado and never allowed myself to remember the 'episode.'"

Martha was ready to speak, possibly to rob the nightmare of its power, and took advantage of Fran's pause to ask, "Your family didn't try to find you?"

"I haven't fully described the poverty of my childhood, another fact I hide. And how uneducated my parents were. They were in no position to look for me, and Jake was in jail. He couldn't help them."

Fran's story lay all jumbled in Martha's mind. She latched onto one manageable detail. "I can understand a poor, rural family not visiting a sick daughter in a distant hospital. I heard a similar story, just recently."

She almost said, "at the colonia," but stopped herself before completing the unseemly connection.

Fran continued as though Martha hadn't commented. "For all Jake knew, I died. I didn't hear from him until last summer, when you saw us arguing at the dance pavilion."

"Are you remembering the details because Jake has told you? But if Jake was in prison for murdering two people, why was he released?"

"The landlord, Mr. Wickard, whose house was located on the same property, heard the commotion. He reached the doorway when my husband swiped the broken bottle across Jake's face, saw the position of John's body, and surmised my husband had also assaulted him. Wickard saw Jake smash the lamp over my husband's head and left to summon the firemen and ambulance. He didn't see Jake move the bodies, but he could confirm part of Jake's account. If I had remembered what happened, three people in agreement might have convinced them about the truth of Jake's version, that he attacked my husband to defend me and John, assuming both of us were still alive, and himself."

It was a good thing they sat on the cement step sipping iced tea. If she continued to follow Fran's chronicle of violence in the glaring sun, it would overcome her.

"Martha, what I'm telling you is disjointed because I heard some of it from Jake and other parts from Sheriff Burleigh, after I went to him that night you urged me to. My visit didn't stop him from investigating Jake. I seemed to have encouraged it."

"Fran, I'm sorry I forced you. I had no idea…"

"Of course not. In your family these events would be unthinkable. But perhaps now you understand why I acted that way at the school. You shoved me into a corner. You, the daughter of the man I fiercely love, and I don't apologize for that, came too close to the truth of a past I desperately hid. You thought you were urging me to gain control before Burleigh uncovered it. Not at all. I had to control it before you did!"

Martha bit her lip and tasted tears running from her sinuses into the back of her mouth.

"Fran, I didn't mean to do harm. I…"

"Let me finish. Unknown to me, my husband came from a family that was relatively well off. They hired a lawyer from Tulsa. Jake had no one, unless you count Wickard. The lawyer easily discredited Wickard based on the sheriff's insistence Jake had moved the bodies to cover his crime. The sheriff had a financial interest, shall we say, in being persuasive due to the money he was promised by my husband's family if their dead son was exonerated. Jake said our mother and father were at the trial, but they were poor, ignorant sharecroppers. Who will ever know what they understood? I can only hope they maintained their faith in Jake."

"But why was Jake eventually released?"

"Wickard, bless him, had seen enough over the months to know Jake took care of us all and knew how my husband mistreated me. He was so upset that my husband's family bought the sheriff's testimony that he never gave up on Jake, and Jake never gave up on himself. I don't know all the details, but between Wickard and Jake they sorted it out. Took years. Burleigh actually got the story from Wickard, who said he eventually compiled enough evidence about the sheriff's corruption to have him tried. Wickard is now the sheriff, and that's how Burleigh came to speak with him, when Burleigh started tracking down Jake."

"Wickard sounds like a good man with qualities similar to Parker Hayes, but I'm upset Burleigh probed into Jake's past in spite of your protestations."

"Don't you see, Martha, that's just what tantalizes a man like Burleigh to sniff out something, because when I talked to him about Jake, the only evidence I could present forcefully for Jake's character was his claim of innocence, a claim even I had refused to listen to, at first, at the pavilion. However, by Christmas I was willing to believe Jake because of his persistence and the fact that he had, indeed, been released from prison. As it turns out, Burleigh's doggedness verified Jake's account. Now Burleigh is Jake's champion. Admires Jake for his determination to get himself cleared, and for protecting me that night."

"How did Jake find you?"

"He thought I'd died. You've seen the scars. It's a miracle I survived. He came to work on the dam and saw me in town one day. I took my maiden name after my husband's death, so it wasn't difficult for him to confirm who I was."

"But last summer, when you slapped him at the dance pavilion…"

"Yes, you've told me repeatedly how you saw that."

Fran seemed more ashamed about the slap than the rest of the coarse tale.

"Martha, for fifteen years I've been pushing against my past. When I saw Jake, naturally I didn't give him a chance to explain. I thought I would lose everything — Robert, my reputation, my position at the school. Folks would find out I married a drunk and that my brother was a murderer. As you can imagine from my muddled account, it's taken a number of conversations with Jake and Burleigh to put together the story."

"And after Jake's story was confirmed, it's been worse for you."

Fran studied Martha's face. "How did you know?"

"I just assumed, because if I were in your place, I'd feel such remorse…"

"Yes."

Fran traced a pattern in the condensed water on her glass and didn't speak for some moments. When she did, the words came slowly.

"'Remorse' doesn't begin to capture how I feel about abandoning Jake and my parents. I betrayed them, but 'betrayal' doesn't come close, either. How differently it would have turned out had I made other decisions: my refusal to appear at the trial and verify Jake's account; my hasty marriage that set it all in motion. My parents were good people, but they died with their son in jail and their daughter dead, at least, dead to them. Jake and I were all they had of any value. Actually, we don't know if they're dead. Jake's tried to find them, but folks said they left for California after the trial. No one heard from them again."

Martha, plagued by the belief her missteps in Mama's care had led to her death and sharing Fran's regret for attacking the integrity of well-intentioned brothers, ached to know what strength and resolve Fran drew on, to throw off her burdensome past and accomplish all she had. Moreover, what was the source of Fran's courage that she could reveal such repugnant events?

"Why did you tell me, Fran?"

"You deserve to know. You took great risk in coming to me at the school to alert me about Jake. And unbeknownst to both you and me at the time, you did us a great service by forcing all of it into the open. But it's been very rough, and it took weeks to assemble the various pieces of the story, as I said. Only in the past few days did I come to the realization I had to tell you the whole of it."

"What will you do now?"

They sat silently for several minutes.

"What's to be done, Martha? I thought I was running from the poverty of my childhood and the scandal that my brother was a murderer. Instead, I've been running to escape the poverty of my character."

"The poverty of your character?"

Fran sat the glass on the cement step between them. She reached toward Martha's hand. Martha offered it. Fran's hand was damp and cool from holding the iced tea.

"I was a headstrong young woman and married rashly. I ignored the appeal to testify on my brother's behalf and, were it not for the persistence and integrity of Wickard, would have completely ruined Jake. I lived under the illusion that all my schooling and hard work earned me the right to be part of the life of a man like Robert. But I'm a fraud with an unredeemable past."

Fran's conclusions appalled Martha.

"Fran, Jake has sought you out. And Papa's hopelessly in love with you."

Fran murmured, "I've avoided the conversation I must have with him…"

"But you told me your story, Fran. What have you learned from my reaction?"

While the details were horrifying, Fran had won Martha's sympathy through the telling. Now that Fran was confronted with a past at odds with the one she thought to be true, Fran faulted herself in error. She was nearly mortally wounded, and only eighteen, perhaps nineteen. She reached her hopeless conclusions because she was looking at the circumstances from the perspective of a mature woman with the benefit of wisdom gained over time.

Martha couldn't predict Papa's reaction but was certain he, too, knew Fran hid something. Learning the details, while shocking, would eventually be reassuring — that Fran's hesitancy to marry was on account of reservations she had about herself, not him.

"Look at me, Fran. I ask again, what have you learned from my reaction?"

Fran turned toward her but kept her eyes on the empty glass.

"That telling you was a test," she whispered, "and practice for when I tell Robert. I learned I can speak the truth. He deserves no less."

"Fran, practice one more time before you tell Papa by repeating your story to Rev. Behm. You said Jake never gave up on himself. In your way, you never gave up on yourself, either. Don't give up now. Henry can give you a more dispassionate reaction than I can. He's seasoned in handling difficult…"

Martha would have said more, but Anna called out from the edge of the garden. "Mama, Papa's coming home. Is it time for dinner?"

"No, honey, it's early yet."

The Old Truck sped across the county road from the Home Place without stopping and careened into the lane. Martha and Fran ran toward it.

The Accident

"Grab Anna," Art yelled. "It's Robert. No time ta get yer bag."

He started the Y-turn in the lane without pausing. Fran ran to swoop up Anna, whose child's legs had carried her only halfway from the bunny grave to the lane. Martha climbed into the back of the truck when Art stopped; Fran lifted Anna to Martha and vaulted in as the truck started to roll. Fran landed with a thud.

"You all right?" Martha shouted.

"Yes, don't worry about me."

Martha secured Anna between her legs and the women grabbed the sides with both hands.

Art raced past the Home Place and straight into the barn. Mr. Miyoshi, shirtless, knelt by Robert, who lay on his back near the combine.

"Anna, do not move from this truck," Martha said. "Do not move."

Her feet hit the ground. Fran sprinted ahead.

Art jumped from the truck cab and, with his long strides, caught up to Martha.

"Repairin' combine," he said. "Left sleeve caught. Pulled arm in. Wrapped Miyoshi's shirt 'round it."

Martha reached Papa, ripped a strip of cloth from the bottom of her housedress, and started talking. "Papa, it's Martha. And Art, Mr. Miyoshi, and Fran are here to help. I'm tying a tourniquet around your upper arm. We'll lift you into the back of the Old Truck and take you to the hospital. Your left arm's…"

She wanted to say "badly cut" but "mangled" came out, instead. Papa didn't respond.

"Mr. Miyoshi, after I tie the tourniquet, help me move his arm across his chest."

She worked the strip of cloth under and around his upper arm. She secured it and slid her fingers under Papa's hand and lower arm that were wrapped in Mr. Miyoshi's shirt. She waited for him to maneuver his hands under the mid and upper arm. Together, they lifted and rested it on Papa's chest. Through the blood-soaked shirt, his skin felt like pulp.

"Art, get Anna into the cab, turn the truck around and let down the tailgate so we can slide him in. Fran, you'll carry his head and encourage him when we're ready. I'll take his feet."

She moved to Papa's right side. "Fran, turn him toward me so Mr. Miyoshi can place his arms underneath Papa's back from that side."

When Art returned, they rolled Papa toward Mr. Miyoshi, who pressed his shoulders and chest against the upper part of the injured arm so it didn't flop off the chest. Fran and Martha helped hold it in place, and Art grasped Mr. Miyoshi's exposed hands and wrists. Fran and Martha allowed Papa's body to shift back to its original position. Now Papa's back rested on Art and Mr. Miyoshi's clasped arms.

"We must lift together, slowly, steadily," Martha said. "On three. One, two, three."

Papa was a stout man, and, although the lifting was successful, the height differential between Art and Mr. Miyoshi meant Art had to stoop so low he had trouble gaining leverage. They all struggled with the imbalance, but Fran got Robert's head onto the truck bed, crawled in and held the head again, and Art and Mr. Miyoshi slid most of the torso in. The men let go of their grip. They climbed in and repeated the routine of establishing the cradle hold below his waist. Martha strained to hold Papa at the knees, and they eased him in the rest of the way.

During the drive to town, Martha silently repeated one prayer: "Please, dear God, let Doc be there; please let Doc be there; please…"

Art pulled into the alley and drove to the hospital's back door.

Martha hopped out. "Wait for the stretcher."

The hallway was cool, empty. Martha ran to the reception desk in front. A young man whom she didn't recognize quickly lifted his feet off the desktop and closed his book.

"Where's Cora Jane? Where's Dr. McFarland?"

He stared. Martha looked down at her chest and arms, coated with Papa's blood, and at the jagged rip around the bottom of her dress.

She heard herself scream. "Where are they? Get the stretcher!"

Only when she reached toward his shoulder with a bloody hand to shake him into action did the young man stir himself. "Doc's at the office. Miss Collins is in the toilet."

Martha composed herself. "Please get the stretcher and help the injured man in the truck that's parked by the back door."

"I can't carry someone in the stretcher by myself, ma'am."

Martha shouted, "This is an emergency. Move! Call Dr. McFarland, now. I'll get the stretcher."

Cora Jane appeared and rested her hand on Martha's shoulder. "I'll call Dr. McFarland, Martha. What shall I tell him?"

Martha sobbed, "Papa. Arm mangled repairing combine. Out back."

"Eugene, get the stretcher," Cora Jane said. "There'll be help to carry him into the operating room."

Eugene ambled off in response to the unbloodied Cora Jane.

Loss

The family gathered in the all-too-familiar hospital alcove. Earl and Josie, who brought clean clothes for Martha and Fran, came with Elena.

She took Robbie and Anna over to the Sage Café. Martha saw Alex's truck pull up in front and, for a moment, accepted the unlikely prospect he would actually walk in the door before she realized it was Uncle Malcolm.

Mr. Miyoshi took Alex's truck home and bathed and changed. He brought Art another shirt and pair of pants neatly wrapped in brown paper and tied with twine.

Even though the tidy parcel was for Art, Martha reached for it. She wanted to touch it, hold it, reassure herself that, in spite of her father's mangled left arm and the turmoil in Fran's life, order and civility prevailed. For an instant, while the package rested in Mr. Miyoshi's hands, Martha and Art's fingers overlapped on top of it. Martha quickly withdrew her hand.

"Obviously, this is for you, Art," she said. "Thank you, Mr. Miyoshi."

After Art reappeared from cleaning up, Doc came into the alcove with a colleague. "I've asked Dr. Lund from Fort Lyon to help me. He has experience with war wounds, which Robert's arm and hand resemble. He's brought a nurse to assist. You already know the hand is nearly crushed, and the lacerations on the arm are numerous and deep. I didn't feel qualified to make a determination about amputating the hand and part of the lower arm, and repairing the rest of the arm will take a while, even with the two of us working on it."

For the second time that day, Martha tasted salty tears sliding into the back of her mouth. Fran's complexion paled, and Josie buried her head in Earl's shoulder. Mr. Miyoshi stood up, as though he could better comprehend what his friend faced if he were in an upright position. Uncle Malcolm wiped tears from his cheeks.

Martha spoke for the group. "Thank you, Dr. Lund. We know how busy you all are at Fort Lyon. Doc, we're sure you'll do everything possible to minimize the damage. What have you decided?"

"We'll amputate and do our best with the lacerations. Dr. Lund and I think you saved his life with the tourniquet. Otherwise, the blood loss… The repair will take some time. You might want to get something to eat."

The doctors turned and walked down the hallway.

Fran involuntarily wailed, "Oh, Robert!"

June 1942

The Barn

Martha woke before dawn the next morning, but Art had already left the house. She walked to the barn and passed under the single bulb dangling from a rafter. Art crouched on the milking stool in the golden light reflecting off the kernels of corn in the full bin, his left knee resting against Beulah's black-and-white haunch and his right pressing against her stomach. The calico sat nearby. Tip seemed to have reached a truce with it and lay behind the milking stool until she saw Martha. She rose and leaned against Martha's leg, who obliged by stroking behind her ears.

"I know what's going on," Martha said softly so as not to startle Beulah, a temperamental cow if ever there was one. "You're bribing the calico with squirts of warm milk so he'll patrol for mice. He'll be good, judging from his performance yesterday with the bunny. I should tell you about it, and lots of things we haven't had time to talk over."

"I'm thinkin' 'bout Robert an' the farms," Art mumbled into Beulah's flank. "Malcolm, Miyoshi, Rudy, an' me could pick up most a the slack if this was temp'rary, but, from what I saw, Robert'll be real slow ta mend, an' then, well, we don't know what he'll be like. Malcolm an' Rudy can't carry the weight Alex an' Luis did. They're good help, Rudy more than Malcolm, but they're jus' learnin'."

"I don't know what to expect about Papa, either. Losing a hand is more than a physical thing. It could really throw him, or, as bull-headed as he is, he might adjust quickly. I think we'd best try to involve him again right away. Even if he can't do the work, include him in all your decisions. How about visiting him each morning to plan the day, as you usually…?"

The cat brushed against Martha's leg. She cringed. Tip moved back to her place behind the stool where the straw on the dirt floor offered the softest bed.

"What were ya sayin'?" asked Art, without turning his head.

"The cat. He sneaks up on me. What do you think about including Papa?"

"Course. Wouldn't think a keepin' 'im outta things. Why're ya so skittish 'bout the cat? By the way, Anna told me the bunny story. She's tryin' ta convince herself the cat was 'Doin' her job.' Actually, she said 'Doin' his job,' but this cat's gonna have babies. Mrs. Calico an' me have regular mornin' an' evenin' routines when I'm milkin', which is why she's hangin' 'round."

"Babies? I'm not fond of cats, but they'll be playmates for Anna. As soon as she wakes up, we'll go to town."

"Isn't this yer mornin' ta do nursin'? Doc is sure understandin', lettin' ya come an' go."

"He's wonderful. He told me to forget it this morning, but Art, he was so thorough yesterday, I want to go in for several hours to help him after I check on Papa. Josie will sit with Papa when Fran goes home to rest."

"What's happened 'tween the two a ya?"

"Between Fran and me?"

"Yeah." Art shifted on his stool.

"Art, I see why milking isn't your favorite chore. Let me take over so you can stretch those long legs."

"Don't believe I've ever seen ya milk."

In her best imitation of a mysterious, smoky voice, Martha replied, "There's a lot you haven't seen me do, mister."

She lowered herself onto the stool and took Beulah's teats in her hands. Beulah looked around, the rope tying her head to the ring on the wall constraining her movement, but other than a swish of her tail to displace several flies, the jittery Holstein didn't object.

"Ya must be feelin' better 'bout yer father, ta joke around."

"I'm thankful he's alive," Martha said without hesitation.

She had no idea where the playfulness originated. Certainly out of gratitude, but also relief that Papa couldn't wish for a better partner than Fran right now. More than anyone, Fran knew the perils of the recovery that lay ahead, and she wouldn't abandon him, now that his need was so obvious. She had too much to prove, mostly to herself.

Alternating streams of milk hit the sides of the metal pail, and she varied the tempo and pitch by how fast she squeezed and where she aimed. She matched the rhythms of the pings to the tune of "Swing Low, Sweet Chariot" and started humming it.

She interrupted herself with, "It's soothing to milk."

"If ya'd like, I'd be happy ta let ya do it every day," said Art from where he squatted, scratching Tip's stomach. "Want ta take over the cultivatin', too, an' I'll weed the garden?"

"As long as you do the cooking and canning, along with the cleaning, washing, ironing, and mending, but, seriously, we need to think of ways Elena, Fran, and I can pitch in, until we sort it all out. I know you and Papa don't approve of women doing heavy field work, but these are extraordinary times."

The streams of milk shrunk to drops, then to nothing. Martha fingered Beulah's shriveled teats one last time and stood.

"Stop! Art yelped. "Sometimes she…"

And he swooped the pail away from the udder. Beulah, with the grace of a well-practiced ballerina, lifted her hoof and would have tipped over the milk had it still been in place.

"Why didn't you warn me?"

"Sorry, but it's natural fer me ta grab the bucket 'fore I stand up. That's what I'm sayin' 'bout Malcolm an' Rudy. They're willin', an' we try ta explain things, but so much is routine ya don't think 'bout explainin' every last detail. Would be worse with even more fingers in the pie, so ta speak. Then ya got spilled milk, an' irrigation water not set right, an' a broken combine that leads ta an amputation. Here we have a chance ta grow more crops than we have in years with all the rain, an' at good prices. Mostly, we have an obligation, with the war."

Art looked tired. "But yer right. We should be thankful he's alive."

Martha took the bucket from him. He'd change his tune about women working in the fields once everything piled up.

"I'll take it to the porch and strain it," she said. "This'll be for Josie, even though she prefers Ginger's milk. She skims it for the cream, and she and Earl want fresh milk for Robbie."

When she reached the barn door, she turned and said more confidently than she felt, "Art, we'll figure it out."

His answer was lost in Ginger's flank and the streams of milk pinging against the sides of the pail.

Martha spoke louder, not concerned about disturbing the more reliable Guernsey. The aptly named Ginger chewed her cud with a single-mindedness that excluded the outside world.

"I don't know when I'll be back. Depends on what kind of night Papa's had. Your breakfast'll be on the stove."

Art turned his head. "I'll try ta see 'im, but only if Rudy an' me make good time this mornin'. Want ta finish repairin' the combine. Hope we can put together the spare parts we need 'cause we won't find any fer sale in town. We could grab a hamburger together at the Sage fer dinner. Don't wait on me, though."

Not until she reached the porch did she wonder what Art meant by his question about her and Fran. What difference had he observed during yesterday's tumultuous afternoon and evening? They had always behaved cordially toward one another in public, even after Martha intruded on Fran's past at the high school.

The Hospital

Martha packed Anna's breakfast and woke her at six forty-five. When they arrived at Josie's, Elena was already there. Martha and Josie walked into the hospital room by seven thirty, but Fran and Papa both slept, Fran in a chair drawn next to the bed with her upper body resting on the white sheets. Her arms were crossed under her head, next to Papa's injured side, and her auburn hair spilled over the dressing. Martha assumed her sleep came from exhaustion, his from morphine. She and Josie backed out the door.

"I'll ask Cora Jane how the night went," said Martha, "then go to Doc's office."

"He's surely worn out by the long hours with Papa and will appreciate your help. Will you thank him again?"

A search for Cora Jane turned up a nurse Martha didn't know. "Hello. I'm Martha Lundgren. Where's Cora Jane?"

She sounded more blunt than she intended, but the woman didn't take offense and answered with a broad smile. "I know who you are, and your quick thinking yesterday with your father has made you even more famous than your efforts to save the boy from the flood. That's partly my fault. Last night, at the Red Cross course I'm teaching, I used you and Mr. McLennan as examples of how a correctly applied tourniquet can save a life. I'm Lola Crane."

Josie joined them and Lola extended her hand. "I was with Dr. Lund yesterday for your father's amputation. I arrived with the attendants and psychiatric patients evacuated from California to Fort Lyon several months ago."

Martha and Josie, as was their habit since childhood, signaled by touching fingertips they were thinking along similar lines. They scrutinized Lola in light of the criticisms circulating about the Red Cross instructor from the Fort, the supposed stickler for detail Josie found objectionable as a teacher for the Women's Club.

If the instructor was Lola, Martha disagreed with the rumors. Lola was impeccably groomed and attractive — petite, with blond hair tied at the back of her neck in a tight bun. Quite a contrast to the tall, awkward Cora Jane.

Surely Martha could persuade Josie that the Women's Club members would enjoy and benefit from Lola, who resembled them in sophistication and appearance. Martha was more suited to teaching the course for the Spanish-American women on account of her growing sympathies for their circumstances.

Josie introduced herself.

Formalities out of the way, Lola said, "Cora Jane's off today. I've been volunteering from time to time since I learned she's sometimes at the hospital days on end without a break. Local doctors and nurses carry heavy loads, now that the military's trying to recruit a thousand nurses every month."

Lola's comment increased Martha's respect for her. Given her demanding schedule with psychiatric patients at Fort Lyon and the Red Cross class, only a nurse with a sense of duty would willingly pitch in to help a town nurse like Cora Jane.

"Do you know what the night was like for Papa and Fran?" asked Josie.

"Difficult. The shock wore off sufficiently for him to be in a lot of pain before they got enough morphine into him. Fran was a trooper, though. Not put off at all. She should get some rest, but I have the impression no one can pry her away."

"Martha, go on," Josie said. "Lola can call Doc's office if you need to come back. I'll stay in the alcove until they wake."

The Station

Later, Doc asked, "Martha, have you ever watched the hoopla when a troop train pulls in?"

"I didn't even see Alex's departure on account of having the flu. But it was before dawn, and evidently few were there to say goodbye to the boys."

"We're done here. It's still early, and a train's scheduled within the hour. I recommend it as a diversion for you, and Anna would enjoy it."

"I'm sure it's a sight to see, but I do want to get to the hospital for Papa."

"He's probably still sleeping. Troop trains are something to behold, with all the girls rushing to the tracks, promising the boys they'll write, rounds of farewells, all that. Don't know if any keep their promises. Must happen in every town, and I'm sure the boys enjoy each stop."

When Martha went by Josie's for Anna and presented the plan to Elena, she wasn't enthused, either. "Marguerite meets the trains. She has asked me, but I do not like it the way she does."

Surely the Spanish soldier boys would enjoy chatting with Elena as much as they did Marguerite. In her quiet way, Elena was winsome enough, and she never indicated she had a beau.

"Still, it must be worthwhile for Doc to urge me to take Anna. We could remain in Max's Truck and simply observe."

"But Mrs. Lundgren, the soldiers will want to meet Anna. So many leave younger brothers and sisters behind. I could stay in the truck with Robbie."

"Perhaps, but I don't want to spend much time with it. After, we'll stop at the Sage, eat with Mr. Lundgren, and get right to the hospital."

However, there were so many cars parked at the station she had to drive to the back of the gravel lot and ease into a narrow space behind a large truck from the sugar beet factory.

"Since we're here, we might as well stay. Quickly, Anna."

She got out but Anna knelt on the seat of the truck, her eyes fixed straight ahead. She pointed and whispered, "Mama, look!"

Martha turned and found herself face to face with an Indian woman dressed in a white blouse and long dark skirt, her black hair pulled back in a great knot. She carried a small bundle wrapped in cloth and wore more silver bracelets on each arm than Martha could count before she passed by. She accepted the hand of a man from the sugar beet company and climbed onto the bed of the truck. She was followed by another woman in similar dress and a man with his long hair also rolled into a knot at the back of his head, then another man, and another. The men wore silver-and-turquoise jewelry and carried small bundles, too.

Martha stared. She had never seen Indians, unless Greenwood County's state representative qualified, but she wasn't in the habit of thinking of him as an Indian, even though an ancestor down his line was. However, Art once traveled with Al Ivarson to New Mexico to help buy sheep from the Navajo, and, from his description and pictures Dr. Salisbury showed the Missionary Society of the Ganado Mission, she concluded these were Navajo.

One of the men looked at her with an amused expression. In clear English, he said, "Good morning."

His greeting and dignified carriage encouraged a response, so before he climbed onto the truck, Martha called out, "Why are you here?"

"Not enough workers for the beets, ma'am. The war, you know."

The first truck pulled away, and at least twenty more Indians walked by and crawled into the second that was parked on the other side.

"Mama, Elena, aren't they beautiful?" Anna said, mesmerized, as were the two women.

Martha had never anticipated such a sight in Greenwood. The train whistle snapped her out of her trance. "Yes, honey. That was a special treat. Do you still want to see the soldiers?"

"I do! Let's go! There's lots of people," Anna observed from her vantage point in the cab.

Martha and Anna, hand in hand, worked their way to the front, next to the track. As they did, voices belonging to senior girls who had attended the banquet called out, "Hello Mrs. Lundgren." One was Marguerite.

"You look especially pretty today, Marguerite."

Marguerite's brown complexion shone with a lively pink undertone. Martha's compliment evidently made her blush. All the girls were dressed up for the occasion.

"Elena thought you might be here. She stayed in Max's Truck with Robbie."

"I am glad you still refer to it as Max's Truck. He was a nice boy."

The train's metal wheels screeched on the tracks. Marguerite had said "was." It couldn't be that Max was dead! All of Greenwood would know.

It was bedlam. Anna snuggled closer. The train stopped with a final shriek.

The first soldier's boots appeared on the stairs. Martha had pictured the boys talking to the girls from the open space between the cars or waving from the windows rather than disembarking.

The cheering stopped. At first, Martha thought the girls, too, were surprised the soldiers were coming off the train. Then she looked up. The soldier was colored.

He paused before stepping down, seemingly to gauge the situation. His foot landed on the brick walkway by the side of the train, and he said, "Afternoon, ma'am. You brought your daughter to wish us well? Is your husband in the service?"

 Martha stepped back. "No. Yes. I mean I brought my daughter, but my husband's not in the service. My brother is."

Martha tried to cover her confusion, but she wasn't successful. A Negro soldier. And so well spoken. Just a wisp of a Southern accent.

"Sarg, can ya move on? We wanna stretch our legs, too."

The girls stepped aside, and the Negroes filled the space. No one spoke until Marguerite came forward.

"We come to the station to wish our fighting men good luck," she said to the boys closest to her. "My cousins were, are, in the New Mexico National Guard, on Bataan. I've brought some candy."

Slowly, one by one, each girl stepped forward and offered her small package to the nearest soldier. They and their hostesses gathered in small groups. Polite, careful, conversations.

"That went better than usual," mumbled the one they called "Sarg," who remained near the stairs.

Anna raised her face to him and said, "Mister, please pick me up. I want to say 'good luck,' too."

Sarg looked to Martha for guidance. She hesitated, even though she didn't mean to.

"Ma'am, if you don't want me to touch her…"

But Anna held up her arms expectantly, and Martha, seeing no reason to object, nodded her assent. He lifted Anna.

When she reached her perch, she rubbed her finger against his cheek.

"Your blackface doesn't rub off," she said, puzzled.

"I don't understand," Sarg responded and looked at Martha.

Martha, mortified, explained, "You're the first colored man she's seen. I've sung in several local minstrel shows and worn blackface, so she thinks…"

A grimace passed quickly over Sarg's face. "I see. What sorts of songs do you sing?"

Martha couldn't bring herself to tell him about the little play with its silly songs sung by the darkies on the plantation. "The Women's Chorus performs 'Go Down Moses' and other spirituals. In fact, just recently we sang it at the senior banquet attended by many of these girls."

Sarg began the chorus in a soft voice. He stopped himself and said, "Let's give your daughter, and the girls, something to remember from the time they talked to soldiers in a Negro regiment from Alabama. Will you join me?"

He started the first verse quietly, before Martha gathered her nerve. Not that she was self-conscious; the source of her uncertainty lay in singing with the Negro sergeant. Would he render the song in an unusual way, one with which she wasn't familiar? However, Sarg's voice was strong, confident, and he gave her a smile. Perhaps encouragement, perhaps a challenge. His version was familiar enough, so she joined him on the chorus, her voice still unsure. As he increased his volume, so did she, and her voice stabilized, although her alto was weak against his baritone. The quiet talk stopped.

When they finished, the crowd gave them sustained applause before resuming subdued conversations.

Sarg handed Anna back to Martha. "Ma'am, you have a very nice voice, but next time you sing spirituals, please don't do it in blackface."

Martha wanted to learn more about him before he boarded, so, rather than questioning him about blackface, she asked, "Is your voice professionally trained?"

"I was a member of the Fisk Jubilee Singers, and I'm leaving a son in Alabama about your daughter's age."

He lifted his head and addressed the crowd, "Come on, troops. Time to go."

Sarg nodded as though bowing his farewell.

Martha had the presence of mind to say, "Thank you for your service to our country," but he pulled himself up the stairs and didn't seem to hear.

Anna put her hands on either side of Martha's head and turned it, as she had in front of the Give-A-Doll window.

She looked directly into Martha's eyes and asked, "Mama, when he sings, he breathes very big. Why don't you breathe big like that?"

"Because he's had singing lessons, and I haven't. But now I see how a professional does it, and I'll take deeper breaths that produce a stronger sound."

Dorothy Thompson

They pulled in front of the Sage, and Martha spotted the Old Truck parked around the corner.

"Anna, Papa's already here. Elena, let's hurry."

They entered the cramped café. Several of the counter stools were empty, and Art was taking a seat at the only free table.

Alice brought the high chair for Robbie, and their party settled. They gave her their orders, and she walked behind the counter to shout them to Ruth through the serving window. Alice started setting glasses of iced tea on the table but stepped aside to allow Al Ivarson and George DeFries by.

The men took places at the counter and continued their loud, animated conversation. One could never tell if the volume signaled disagreement or simply the effort required on account of Al's poor hearing.

Al yelled, "I didn't even want 'em in the state, but now that they're comin', thanks to our traitor of a Republican governor, we gotta set down the law. No leavin' the camp. They definitely can't come into town. Or use the park. No workin' on any farm."

George shouted back, "That's not up to us. Government wants them to work, but it's not 4-H camp. They're to be guarded with machine gun turrets and barbed wire. Still, they'll have passes…"

Martha couldn't imagine the newly arrived Indians would be held under guard!

Al slammed his hand on the counter. "If they're a threat in California, they're a threat here. The *Post* says every one of 'em's either an actual or potential enemy. We gotta keep Colorado American. Besides, who's gonna hire 'em?"

Alice broke in to take the men's order. They studied the menu, even though their selection probably never varied.

Martha quietly asked Art, "What camp?'

"Ya know, the internment camp fer the aliens, the Japanese from the West Coast."

"I thought it was to be located over in the San Luis Valley."

"Nope. Government's buyin' up land here. Startin' ta build as soon as they take care a the last hold-out. Army engineers already set up headquarters. There'll be thousands a people. Huge camp. East a the dam site."

Alice sat Martha's food in front of her and leaned over to say, "Ruth and I were so sorry to hear about your father from Elena yesterday. If you or the family needs anything, you don't have to walk over from the hospital. Telephone and we'll bring food to you."

She patted Martha's shoulder and walked on. Martha gulped back tears of gratitude and didn't delay starting on her hamburger. She urged Anna and Elena to do the same.

Al's contemptuous words interrupted. "During his time, my pa knew the only good Injun's a dead un. Same way with these here Japs, just a bunch a yella-bellied, sneakin' skunks."

Martha took offense at the "dead Injun" comment, particularly given Anna's recent enchantment with those who had to come to help with the beets, but when Al coupled it with the offensive "yella-bellied" epitaph, she slid back her chair and got to her feet. She walked over to Al, fists clenched. Had she been a man, she would have punched him in the face.

However, taking a breath as deep as the Negro sergeant's, she said, loudly and firmly, "So you're going to kill the Indians who've come to work in the beet fields? Al, there are children and women in the café. Clean up your language."

To George DeFries, she said, "Don't encourage these rants."

Martha walked back to the table and sat. When she picked up her spoon to eat her applesauce, only Art saw that her hand trembled.

He rested his on it and said, "Wish you hadn't a done that. I was 'bout ta go over an' ask him ta stop, but ya beat me to it. Isn't right fer ya ta tell 'im ta respect women an' children with me sittin' right here. Was my place."

To save Art's feelings, Martha said, "I'm sorry. I acted in haste. I should've known you'd do something. It's just that at the train station, before we…"

How could she explain to Art the dignity and grace of the Indians Anna saw, only to hear them degraded? And the yellow-bellied business was an unspeakable offense, shouted as it was in front of Anna, so recently made aware she was never to use such foul language.

Art said, "Still, ya prob'ly made more an impression than if one a us men was ta say it. Made every man here ashamed they didn't do somethin'."

"Thanks for backing me up, but it would make an even greater impression if everyone objected to this preposterous camp. I agree with Governor Carr that Japanese in the United States share only their race with those in Japan, not their loyalties. He insists their dignity be maintained, but the camp doesn't accomplish that. We might as well confine Jimmie Ichikawa, or one of us."

"The camp causes another problem," Elena said. "The Spanish-Americans are afraid that with all the Japs, um, the Japanese, coming, there will not be farm work for us."

Martha was irritated Elena presumed to take part in the conversation between her and Art. However, Art handled it gracefully. "Well, isn't this somethin'? We're worried 'bout not havin' help, 'specially with Robert's accident, and yer worried there'll be too much."

The talk had gone on long enough. Martha's concern was Papa. She abruptly changed the subject. "Art, have you been to the hospital yet?"

"Nope. Wanted ta go together so it would be more a family visit. Didn't want to seem like I was checkin' up on 'im, seein' how soon he would work again. Have ya talked it over with Anna?"

Martha looked down at her plate. "I'm ashamed to say, no. I could have explained on the way into town this morning, but I was rushing her to eat before we got to Josie's. Then I left the office early, and we went by the train station… I haven't even thought about how to tell her."

What could be more important than telling Anna about Papa's lost hand? When Doc suggested she take Anna by the station to see the soldiers, she had no idea it would be so dramatic. The arrival of Indians and Negroes would never have happened before the war. She hadn't wanted to add another strange experience to Anna's day by talking about her grandfather's hand, or lack of it.

But it was war. Folks didn't have the luxury to mull over anything. She shouldn't have protected Anna from knowing the severity of Papa's injuries. Horrible accidents happen, and you see Indians and a Negro regiment at the train station. You adapt. Look at the Japanese in Colorado and on the West Coast. Money seized, homes lost, families uprooted. Papa's accident was simply another adjustment. *Shikata ga nai.* It can't be helped. Life goes on.

To herself, Martha recited Dorothy Thompson's bracing advice from the editorial she'd cut out of the paper only last week. Martha had slipped the clipping into the side of the mirror on her dresser.

"In favorable moments, we must not relax; in distressful moments we must pull ourselves together. At no time must our efforts be affected by our moods."

Martha began, neglecting to tell Art she intended to have the conversation then and there. "Anna, we're going to see Grandpa in the hospital, but the nurse might not let you in his room today because he needs to sleep. There are big cuts on his arm, and his hand was hurt so badly that Dr. McFarland called another doctor to help him. Neither of them could fix it, so Grandpa doesn't have his left hand anymore."

Martha almost gagged at the thought of saying "amputation" and defining it for her five-year-old, and she certainly didn't want to attribute such violence to Doc in a conversation over dinner. "When someone is injured as seriously as Grandpa, they're very tired. Sleeping is good for Grandpa because when he sleeps his body will work extra hard to make itself well."

Anna, not one to be excluded from seeing her grandpa, said, "If he's sleeping, I'll peek in the door and blow him a kiss. He stands at my door and blows me kisses when I'm asleep. He told me he does."

Art squeezed Martha's hand. Martha knew he meant it as approval of her explanation of the gory mess, but it reminded her that Papa would no longer blow kisses, at least, not with his left hand. For that matter, how would he milk the cow? Trivial concerns but they brought tears. More to the point, would he learn to compensate in the hundreds of ways necessary to earn his livelihood?

In lieu of Martha's failure to respond to Anna's proposal, Elena said, "The nurse will tell us if you can."

Papa's Room

Fran was walking in when they parked in front of the hospital. She waited at the door, seeming to have grown old overnight. No longer a vivacious teacher but a tired, worried farmwoman. Martha took her hand, and they entered together.

Fran bent to whisper in Martha's ear, "I came back from freshening up, talked with Doc, and couldn't bear to stay in the room. Went out for some air. Robert's not doing well. Doc says the injuries are such a shock to his body, and the morphine makes him look like a dead man. It's awful, Martha, just awful."

Doc hadn't given Martha any indication Papa's condition was life threatening that morning, as Fran was implying. Fran's worries were surely overdrawn.

Lola Crane and Doc stopped their conversation behind the reception desk when the group entered. He walked over to them. "Robert's taken an unexpected turn. We're working through possibilities."

Art moved to Martha's side and put his arm around her shoulders.

"Martha, even though the patient is your father, would you come with us and give a professional opinion?" Doc asked.

Art gave Martha's shoulders a quick squeeze and dropped his arm. They both knew she would oblige. It was much easier to see Papa through her nursing eyes and draw up a dispassionate checklist of possible causes for his decline than, as his daughter, to watch him suffer.

"May I go to Grandpa's door and blow him a kiss?" Anna asked.

Martha and Art drew breaths to say no, but Doc answered, "Yes, and please tell him in a big voice what you're doing."

"I'll breathe like Sarg and say it very loud, the way Mama scolded Mr. Ivarson for using naughty words in the café."

"Who's Sarg?" Art asked.

"I'll explain later. Doc, what do you think is happening?"

"We don't know. It might not be any single thing, and if one of the factors is his will to live, hearing Anna's voice might be medicinal. She won't be close enough for his appearance to frighten her."

The kiss announced and delivered, Art lips touched Martha's hair and he said softly, "What I meant this mornin' 'bout you an' Fran, you did again, when you walked in together, talkin' everything over. Ya've not acted that comfortable with 'er before. It's nice ta see, 'specially now that Robert needs ya both."

All but Martha, Doc, and Lola left. Martha walked to Papa's bedside. He seemed lifeless.

"Could it be he's had too much morphine?" she asked.

"We monitor it closely," Lola answered. "I gave him some when I came on duty this morning and another dose about an hour ago. Cora Jane stayed with him through the night and left record of what she administered."

"Cora Jane stayed with him all night?" Doc asked. "She didn't have any sleep?"

"Her words to me this morning were 'I haven't slept a wink.' She's quite fond of your family, Martha, so she kept a close watch, but I suppose you know of her regard."

"She's certainly seen a lot of us this past year," Martha answered, but her thoughts raced.

"You seem so thorough and precise, Lola. You wouldn't have given him morphine first thing this morning if you hadn't checked Cora Jane's notes. May I see them? And is there a way to measure the morphine on hand against what was there yesterday, before we brought Papa in? If Cora Jane was so tired…"

"Of course," answered Doc. "I'll look over the supply while you check the notes. Miss Crane, please stay here with Mr. McLennan. Has his breathing been shallow like this all morning?"

"Not that I've noticed, but I was hesitant to wake him and Miss Reeve, so, although I peeked in frequently, I neglected to check him closely."

Martha corrected her. "Lola, please don't say 'neglect.' Given the circumstances and their need for sleep, you reached a conclusion and acted accordingly. You didn't 'neglect' Papa."

All Martha saw in Cora Jane's notes were variations on ways to describe Papa's pain. There was no mention of a morning dose of morphine, so, if the notes were accurate, Lola hadn't inadvertently doubled it.

On his return, Doc confirmed that the amount remaining was consistent with Cora Jane and Lola's reports.

"I still think morphine is the problem," said Martha, "but I haven't seen this reaction."

"May I call Dr. Lund?" asked Lola. "His experience with wounds and morphine in the Great War might be of help."

"By all means," said Doc.

Doc McFarland accepted — no, he sought — advice, not only from other doctors but also from his nurses. Doc Claffey barged ahead, as if no one else knew the answers. Martha much preferred Doc McFarland. Carrie's delivery and life might have been so different if he had been in Greenwood…

When she returned from telephoning him, Lola reported, "Dr. Lund said some patients do over-react to morphine. He won't be able to leave for several hours; otherwise, he'd come into town right away. He did confirm the shallow breathing might indicate such a sensitivity."

Papa stirred himself and groaned. Then he began to gag. Martha grabbed the enamel pan off his bedside tray, and Lola and Doc held up his shoulders and head. He retched, again and again. The intervals between the subsequent dry heaves eventually lengthened, intervals Papa filled with moans.

"Awful, awful," were the first words they heard distinctly.

"He's talking; that's a good sign," Doc said.

"My hand?" Papa asked.

"I don't know how aware he is, or what to say," Martha mumbled. With someone else, she would have been more decisive.

"I'll talk to him," said Doc.

The dammed-up tears overflowed and ran down Martha's cheeks. She stepped to the window, shaken that her nursing demeanor insufficiently shielded her from the emotion. So much for Miss Thompson's editorial decree about not letting moods affect efforts.

For the next ten minutes, Robert rested quietly. When the moaning began, it was louder and accompanied by sharper cries of pain.

"Help me! Crows clawing my arm! What's wrong with my hand?"

He reached across with his good arm to slap at the phantom crows, and Martha and Doc grabbed it.

"Miss Crane," Doc hissed, "get something to restrain him."

Sharply, loudly, he said, "Robert, this is Angus McFarland. Your arm was mangled in your combine. Hand crushed. Had to amputate. Your hand's gone."

They tied down the good arm and to Martha and Lola, Doc said, "It's as though he's only now coming out of the ether. We'll have to explain this to him until he indicates he grasps it."

"Fran should be here," Martha said, "not me. She'll be better at helping him come to terms with it."

"You think she can to stand seeing him in such agony?" questioned Lola.

Robert moaned and asked about his hand again. Martha answered, expanding on Doc's script.

"Papa, this is Martha. Your sleeve caught in the combine and pulled in your arm. Mr. Miyoshi wrapped his shirt around it to stop the bleeding. He, Fran, Art, and I brought you to the hospital. Dr. McFarland amputated your hand and stitched up the cuts."

Papa looked at the bandaged arm without the hand. He closed his eyes and groaned.

The tedious repetitions underscored for Martha how difficult it would have been for Fran to reconstruct the events from that terrible night she nearly died. No wonder she remained confused for years, given how the sheriff purposefully misled her.

"Lola, we need Fran. She has to be here from the start of his recovery."

Lola opened the door, and Fran was standing right outside.

"You've heard? You know what to do?" asked Martha.

Fran nodded, her face pale, her eyes fixed on Robert. "No more morphine, right?"

"No more morphine," answered Martha. "Give him accurate information every time he asks, even if you repeat yourself. You, of all people, know the importance of accuracy in this circumstance. It will seem cruel, but he needs to know."

"Thank you, Martha, for insisting I be here. I'll try to live up to your expectations…"

"I have no doubt you will," interrupted Martha, anxious to resurrect the confident Fran that Papa needed and to stop her from disclosing even the slightest hint about her past. Lola and Doc shouldn't be party to a story meant only for Papa.

The Presidio

If Martha had expected anyone in the hospital alcove, it wouldn't have been Al Ivarson. Surely he wasn't going to upbraid her for scolding him in the café, but Clara Boehler was also waiting. Al wouldn't make a scene in front of Clara, at least not a big one. Both stood as she approached.

"I heard about the accident," said Clara. "How's he doing?"

"Better. He reacted badly to the morphine. It'll be hard without it, but not as awful as with it. Are you here about Papa?" she shouted at Al, hoping to corral him into admitting to a mission of mercy instead of recrimination.

"Don't know anyone else hospitalized at the moment," he snapped. "I'll say this one time: Robert's a worthy opponent. He'll fight this, just like he's always scrappin' with me. I came to tell him that, but you tell 'im for me when he's in shape to hear it. And you're a chop off the same block, but that's not a bad thing."

Al grabbed his hat off the chair and stomped away.

Martha felt like crying and laughing, all at once. Elsie Lambert was right in that Al was an opinionated cuss, but sincere.

"What an obnoxious man," Clara said. "Will you give your father his message?"

"You bet. But I'll save it for when Papa's spirits really need a lift. Believe it or not, Al lifted mine."

Clara shrugged and said, "I hate, I really do hate, to come to you at a time like this, but it's Edith."

"What's wrong?"

"Have you heard about the nurses from the Philippine Islands who are recovering at the Presidio?"

"No!" Martha clutched at Clara's arm. "Is it Muriel? Did she make it?"

"No, they're army nurses, like the ones evacuated to Australia. But folks from all around the country are calling and writing them, even traveling to California to visit them. And I mean everyone and anyone who has someone missing from Manila, Corregidor, and Bataan, not just families of nurses but of soldiers, too. The Red Cross had to assign someone to help sort through all the mail."

"And what does this have to do with Edith?"

"She's insisting on going."

"Going?"

"To San Francisco. She's determined to talk to the nurses. To find out if any of them knows Muriel's whereabouts. Claude can't dissuade her. She's packing to leave tomorrow. She certainly can't travel alone, but I don't know who can go with her. If she's that determined, nothing will stop her short of putting her in the State Hospital."

"Goodness, I obviously can't go, even if Papa…"

Martha's voice trailed off as she imagined the prospect of a train trip to California and conversation with women who had been in the midst of battle.

"But Clara, wouldn't you love to make such a trip and talk to them, learn what it's like to test yourself in the unrelenting theater of war?"

"With what your father's going through, how can you say such a thing? One man, a mangled arm. Imagine piles of entire mangled bodies! An unending procession in field hospitals with artillery shells falling all around. I'd be emotionally shattered, which I'm sure is why the Red Cross is shielding those nurses and handling the correspondence and calls. They're probably physically shattered, too."

Both women were quiet, Martha struggling to express for herself the guilty exhilaration she felt in a crisis, the surge of energy that came from taking charge and giving succor. But if the crises were constant and the numbers of wounded endless, as they were on Corregidor, perhaps exhaustion would overtake her, especially if the outcome was death, as it had been for Frank Ogawa, for Swede, for the boy in Lamberts' field. Perhaps for Max.

With Mama it was different. Martha wasn't yet a nurse when Mama was sick, and Martha didn't know how to help.

But with Carrie, shouldn't she have done something different? No, Carrie was too fragile and couldn't fight off the illness. If that episode hadn't taken her, something else would. Martha's first admission of it. And wasn't that what Mrs. DeFries kept telling her about Mama? The Bright's disease was going to take her, regardless?

It wouldn't end that way with Papa. She wouldn't let it.

Clara broke into Martha's thoughts. "I can't go with Edith, not with all my responsibilities."

Martha forced her attention to the problem at hand.

"I've three Red Cross classes and a nutrition course," Clara said. "I'm working on an education program on tuberculosis with the Spanish PTA and the American Legion Auxiliary, and the sugar beet company wants the Navajos they brought in to be part of it. I'm busier this summer than I was with the schools."

"Clara, are you careful to get your rest?"

"Probably as careful as you are."

Martha didn't answer, although she thought a better approach to the problem of tuberculosis for the Navajos and Mexicans was to badger the farmers and the sugar beet company for better housing.

She returned to the subject of Edith. "But a trip like that, seeing those nurses, might be the best medicine for Edith."

"Or the worst, depending on what they say to her, or if they even see her."

"Clara, I think it's worth the risk. And even if she doesn't see them, she'll have taken action to help her daughter. Making the effort might be useful in itself. Is Aneda capable of managing it?"

"No. The train trip alone would overwhelm them both."

But Marguerite handled the awkwardness with the Negro regiment without hesitation. "Marguerite could do it."

"She's so young!"

"No younger than the boys we're sending to war. Is Claude in a position to cover the expense?"

"Money isn't a problem for the Giffards. If Claude's convinced there's wisdom in it, he'll pay, particularly if it keeps her out of the State Hospital."

July 1942

A Standoff

While Papa slept, Martha started reading Fran's copy of *Hold Autumn in Your Hand*. She became so absorbed by the story of the East Texas sharecropper that she forgot the discomfort of the straight-backed hospital chair.

Papa's voice came as an unwelcome distraction. "Sis, what're we going to do about all this?"

"All this?"

"The whole business."

The whole business might or might not include Fran's past, so she said, "Papa, are you asking how you're going to farm with one hand?"

"You're not one to mince words, so neither will I. I'm asking about farming and Fran."

"What about Fran?"

"You and she seem to have grown close in the two weeks since my accident, so I want your opinion. Will she throw out this broken-down old man?"

If he had heard even a scrap of Fran's story, he would know she wouldn't describe his condition as "broken" any more than he would hers. They were damaged, but not broken.

"Papa, don't talk like that. None of us think of you as 'broken' because of the accident. And certainly not 'old,' least of all Fran."

Fran came in with a Sage Café basket. "This is a fine 'how-do-you-do.' I return from my errand, and I'm the subject of conversation. Glad I'm back to defend myself. By the way, did you know Alice and Ruth Jennings are giving a ten-percent discount on food at the Sage if you buy War Savings Stamps with your order? So, here's your contribution to the one billion dollars for war bonds this month. They'll help collect cooking fat, too, if you bring it to them in coffee cans."

Perhaps Fran's insistent chatter covered a fear that Martha had revealed something of her story. But only Fran could tell it with convincing force. And only Papa could persuade Fran of his love, which would likely strengthen if he knew about her suffering. On his part, if Papa would confess his dread that his amputation made him less of a man in her eyes…

"I'm glad you're here to defend yourself, too," Martha said. "And Papa, have a frank discussion with Fran before you leave the hospital so you know where you stand."

Papa looked away.

"Thanks for the sandwich, Fran. I'll eat it on the way to Josie's and leave you two to talk."

But she wasn't going to let Fran off that easily. "By the way, I find Perry's *Hold Autumn in Your Hand* instructive. Even a sharecropper living in wretched poverty can be a worthy example of valiant struggles against all odds. Is the hardship it depicts in East Texas all that different from what growing up was like for you in Oklahoma, Fran?"

The ruse was obvious, so Martha didn't wait for an answer. Fran was reading the popular book aloud to Papa, and the dreadfully unfortunate Sam Tucker could be a mirror for them both. If Papa saw his reflection in Sam, he would realize he could surmount his much less trying circumstances. As for Fran, her hardscrabble childhood and cruel husband spurred her determination as Sam's struggles did his. Hers was far from a poverty of character, as she insisted on putting it.

Martha leaned over to kiss Papa on the forehead and mumbled, "Please ask her your question about 'all this.' Each of us carries injuries into a marriage that separate or bind us."

To both she said, "I'll not be coming back till after supper, on my way to the Red Cross class with the Spanish-American women at their café, and I've heard rumors about a charivari tonight for Hugh and Eleanor. I'll meet up with Art and Anna there, after the class."

"So you accepted Elena and Marguerite's request and refused Josie?" said Papa. "I applaud your choice. Anyone can teach the Women's Club matrons, but not everyone can understand the hardships the Mexican women face."

"Why didn't you say something sooner, Papa? It would have helped with my decision."

"I try not to take sides when it comes to you and Josie."

As she was trying with him and Fran.

Fran walked her to the door and said in a voice so soft Martha strained to hear, "I know you're pushing me to tell him. But is he strong enough, or am I, for that matter?"

"What are you two whispering about?" Robert asked.

After what she hoped was an imperceptible pause, Martha answered, "Bacon drippings. I asked how taking bacon drippings to Alice and Ruth will help with the war effort."

"What's the answer?"

"Something about glycerin and bombs," replied Fran, without hesitation.

Martha raised her eyebrows, impressed with Fran's quick wit, and both women stifled giggles.

The Gathering Storm

Even though she had parked in shade and left the windows down for a breeze to move through, the heat in Max's Truck was stifling. She gained speed, but the blowing air felt like a blast from the steel furnaces in Pueblo.

The longer Papa stayed in the hospital, the more he acted like an invalid. Doc should send him home. Although Uncle Malcolm or Art, usually with Mr. Miyoshi, came by every morning to talk over their work for the day, Papa listened but didn't offer opinions.

Not that Papa's injuries weren't serious. Initially, everyone harbored the fear they were life threatening. The Red Cross brought Alex home, all the way from Camp Young in California. Martha speculated that Mrs. Parker Hayes, the chairman of the local group, initiated the request and used her influence to press for his furlough. Now in the air corps, Alex regaled them with stories, and the more ribald versions that he saved for the men prompted chuckles between them for hours afterward. Even Papa brightened when Alex came in his room.

But the story that captured all of Greenwood was Hugh Ufford and Eleanor Moulton's marriage before a Kansas judge. The newlyweds came home that evening to an extravagant dinner at the Moultons', so it wasn't meant to be a secret. It was just sudden. Alex gladly attended to celebrate his friend's good fortune and left for camp the next day.

Martha assumed Maude invited Alex out of spite to make the point that Eleanor landed on her feet, no thanks to him, but social slights were wasted on her carefree, big-hearted brother. Had it been her, she wouldn't have attended to spare herself the indignity.

Alex confided that no one knew Hugh fell for Eleanor in high school, but Hugh's friendship with Alex and his assumption Eleanor and Alex would someday marry kept him from revealing his lovelorn misery. Hugh wasted no time courting her after Alex sent Eleanor home brokenhearted.

Martha had absolute confidence in the integrity of Hugh's feelings. Eleanor's, she doubted. She probably latched onto Hugh because she was still distraught about Alex. Hugh would return to camp next week before being sent somewhere in the Pacific, and Eleanor would go back to Denver and her work as a welder at Lowry Field. It was right for her to have left Greenwood and her memories of Alex, but gossip was the "khaki-wacky" Eleanor used her recent time at the Aviation Institute's welding and riveting classes to shop for a man. Eleanor had better settle down, now that she'd accomplished her mission to replace Alex. Hugh deserved a faithful wife.

Resolution of the Eleanor problem could mean the Moultons wouldn't be so prickly toward the McLennans, but the more serious rift between the Moultons and the Lamberts festered on account of the rumor that Eleanor's older brothers, Edgar and Walter, had attacked Max for refusing to enlist. Not even Alex knew Max's whereabouts, or if he was alive.

When Martha got out of Max's Truck at Josie's, a gust of wind blew through the leaves. Air that cool must be coming off a hailstorm somewhere, but Josie's house obstructed Martha's view to the west. The weather would come from that direction, so if they hurried they might beat the storm on the drive east to the farm.

The view from the bridge over the river disclosed a bank of dark clouds stacking up along the western horizon, and the wind blew harder. They turned into the lane as the first quarter-sized drops of water smacked against the windshield. Martha parked by the swing, and they scurried onto the porch. The wind and rain hit with such force Martha thought it might as well as be hail for all the damage it would do. She prayed Art found shelter in time.

Desolation

Martha sat Anna on the sofa, next to an inside wall, and she rushed from window to window pulling down the new dark-green blackout shades to prevent glass from shattering into the house. Still no evidence of hail, just torrents of rain and flashes of lightning. Elena held on to Robbie in Anna's more secluded bedroom to protect him from flying shards. The storm scared Anna, so Martha joined her. Anna tucked her head between Martha's back and the sofa and whimpered with every clap of thunder.

It passed in less than twenty minutes and left all the windows intact. The four emerged from the porch and saw no damage other than one large tree limb in the yard and smaller branches and leaves scattered among puddles in the lane. The smell of freshly mown hay filled the air, hay probably not cut by human hand but stripped and flattened by hail.

Martha pulled on her galoshes. "I'll check the garden. We might as well take advantage of the puddles and let the children play."

"Yes, how lucky to have wading pools just outside the door."

Elena removed her shoes and anklets and set to work taking off Anna's and Robbie's, then stripped Robbie down to his diaper and Anna to her panties. Anna romped toward the largest pool; Robbie plopped down in the first one and contented himself with hitting the water. The first splashes to strike his face startled him, but the next ones elicited squeals that drew Anna back to his puddle. She sat next to him and joined the fun.

Martha laughed. "They'll empty that one soon enough."

She slogged through the water that nearly covered the grass to survey the garden. Art would know what plants were too beaten down to recover, but many looked as though they would revive.

Reassured, Martha walked back to the lane and saw Art and Uncle Malcolm driving in from the fields to the east. Thank the Good Lord they had the Old Truck for protection during the storm.

Martha shouted, "What's the damage?"

"Not much. Only heavy rain, but we're drivin' over ta the Home Place ta see what went on there. Wanna come?"

Martha climbed in and waved to Elena, "We'll be back shortly."

No signs of hail around the house of her childhood, but Martha spotted several open windows.

"There'll be a mess inside," groaned Uncle Malcolm. "I shoulda closed 'em, but it was so danged hot."

They drove up the road leading to the cornfields and saw Rudy walking toward them.

When they reached him, he explained, "Left the tractor in the field. Thought it would get stuck if I tried to drive it out."

To their expressions of concern, he answered, "I curled up against the tractor tire, and it protected me."

"Someone got hit," observed Art. "Or we wouldn't be smellin' fresh-cut hay. Climb in the back, Rudy."

They returned to the McLennan lane, but before they headed toward the road, Rowdy made his dash from under the porch to nip at the tires. Rudy yelled at Art to stop and lowered the tailgate. To Martha's astonishment, Rowdy jumped in and snuggled next to the boy.

"What's the matter with Rowdy?" she asked.

Uncle Malcolm answered, "Doggondest thing. Since Robert's been in the hospital, Rowdy's latched onto 'im. Guess even a creature as fierce as Rowdy needs a buddy."

They met Mr. Miyoshi in his truck at the road. "Everything all right?"

"Yeah, an' at yer place?" Art said.

"Just lots of water."

They breathed a collective sigh of relief but couldn't shake the foreboding that someone hadn't escaped. While they talked, Ellis Ufford's truck approached from the south. Everyone waited. Ellis and Hugh climbed out and walked over to the two vehicles. Ellis's head was down, which Martha interpreted as prelude to bad news. She had yet to congratulate Hugh on his marriage, but now wasn't the time.

"Art, Miyoshi," Ellis addressed the drivers of the two trucks. "Hail hit to the south. Lamberts, possibly Ivarsons. Don't know how far east it went."

"How bad?" asked Art.

"Bad," answered Ellis. "No details yet. At least Otto got all his wheat in last week."

"We'll check on 'em. You go by Ivarsons'," said Art.

"Drop me at home first," proposed Martha. "I'll collect Elena and the children and follow in Max's Truck."

"I'll check Himuru and Ichikawa," Mr. Miyoshi added.

He was right to point out they neglected to mention the Japanese farmers who were also in the path of the storm.

Elena and Martha dried and dressed the children, drove down the county road, and crossed the highway. Water rushed alongside, but the barrow pit contained it. Martha didn't see hail until she reached Otto's north wheat field. A giant hand seemed to have drawn an east-west line across the landscape to guide the storm's path.

To the south of the line, hail alongside the road deepened until it reached the running boards.

"Mama, look at the snow!" yelled a delighted Anna.

"Honey, it's hail — little balls of ice."

When she stepped out of the truck next to Elsie and Otto's house, Martha scooped up a handful of the stones that floated in a puddle. Some were the size of a fifty-cent piece, or larger. Hail that size, and the force of the wind…

The house was empty. Art, Uncle Malcolm, and Rudy must be searching for Elsie and Otto in the fields. Martha, Elena, and the children waited in Max's Truck. When Robbie, tired from his exertions in the puddles, fell asleep on Elena's lap, Martha and Anna walked through Elsie's garden. The hail pummeled everything — tomatoes, beans, cantaloupe, cabbage, the remaining, unharvested peas… The leaves on the sweet corn, stripped.

Martha couldn't bear to look any longer and parked Anna on the front porch swing while she walked to the chicken house. She poked her head in — layers on their nests, some of the young fryers Elsie bought after the flood milling about.

Martha walked through, into the chicken yard, and the scene nauseated her. All but a few of those animals dead, the carcasses surrounded by ice. Maybe a several hundred of them. They survived flood one month only to perish in hail the next. It must have come down like bullets. Martha started gathering the limp bodies by their legs and stacking them by the fence. She couldn't imagine Elsie had it in her to bury more chickens.

Martha was so engrossed in her grisly collection she didn't notice Art's return until she heard the horn honk. Art sat in the driver's seat of Otto's truck, Otto beside him. Elsie rested her head on Otto's shoulder. Martha walked to the driver's window, and Anna ran over from her perch on the swing. Art stared straight ahead; his face was pale.

Someone must have died in the field. She picked up Anna.

"Half the calves dead," Art said. "A couple a the cows. Hide ripped by the hail on the ones still alive. Gruesome sight. Ya can imagine what happened ta the corn that survived the flood last month. Won't be much that'll come out of it. Prob'ly the same at Al an' Freda Ivarsons'. But the two fields of Otto's hay're in the stack, so wasn't much damage there."

Numbed by the extent of this second disaster to hit the Lamberts, Martha stood still. Uncle Malcolm and Rudy drove up beside them in the Old Truck. With a large white handkerchief, Uncle Malcolm wiped his eyes and blew his nose.

"If hail did this much damage ta Otto's cattle," he said, "imagine what happened ta the ewes an' lambs over at Ivarsons'. And the crops… Most everything gone, 'cept the grasshoppers, I suppose."

Perhaps he meant the grasshopper remark to be a humorous attempt in the face of disaster, or maybe he was simply resigned that in twenty minutes one storm canceled months of coaxing crops to grow while the less visible forces working for their destruction remained hearty. She reached in the open window and patted his shoulder.

She forced herself to walk around the Lambert truck and opened the passenger-side door where Elsie sat. Her hands rested on her lap, and she seemed unaware of Martha, who gathered Elsie's hands in hers and waited.

Finally, Otto cleared his throat. "Art, Martha, thanks for comin'. Don't think we could've taken seein' all those…all of it, alone."

Art responded with a low-pitched "Hmm…."

Elsie's warm tears dribbled onto Martha's hands.

Otto cleared his throat to continue, as though words could wrap the magnitude of the devastation into a manageable package. He reached for Elsie's hand, and Martha quickly removed hers.

"Elsie," he said, "guess it's our year to be the biblical Job. I'm close to breakin' on account of all this disaster, but I'm not entirely broken, leastwise, not yet. We got the wheat harvested, and most of the hay stacked."

"I'm broken," whispered Elsie.

Otto didn't hear and opened his mouth to continue, but Elsie spoke again, this time loudly, bitterly, "Where's God in all this, Otto? Where is God?"

Withdrawing his rough, chapped hand from Elsie's, Otto shifted his upper body to look directly at her and turned her face toward his.

"You mean, is God directin' these storms at us, or failin' to protect us from 'em? They're storms, Elsie. Just storms. They go where the wind takes 'em. As for God, He helps me. God keeps me strong. Without Him, don't know I'd go on."

"I'm not talking only about wind and hail, Otto," Elsie said. "He's taken our son, and our daughter, too. Our daughter for not tolerating our beliefs and our son for taking them too much to heart."

Otto sighed and fell back against the truck's seat. "Elsie, God isn't punishin' us; God is love. What Addie and Max do is between them and their Maker, not us."

Art climbed out, motioned to Martha, and they joined Uncle Malcolm and Rudy. He was right to give Otto and Elsie privacy in their grief, but Otto hadn't listened. Elsie was unraveling, and telling a mother "God is love," which might do for a Sunday sermon, wasn't going to pull her away from the brink. Martha frantically rehearsed ways she could help Elsie, and they all fell short of the power of Julia Mattson's Thanksgiving dinner story about Oscar, her dead son.

Did Elsie imply Max was lost to her as Oscar was to Julia or as Muriel perhaps was to Edith? It could be that he was dead, or was Elsie simply hinting that Max decided not to register for the selective service when they lowered the age to eighteen? If so, he was in prison. That's what happened to pacifist boys who chose, on principle, not to register.

And Addie must have chaffed all her life at the simplicity of her home and wardrobe. Quick to anger, envious of well-off families, and one to promote her self-interest, Addie wasn't temperamentally a Quaker. But Max was kind to a fault, a puppy dog who accepted and loved everyone, if Walter and Edgar hadn't scared those qualities out of him. If he was alive, surely Max wasn't lost to Elsie.

Lucy Hart Himuru

By early evening, Martha and Elena were bumping over the railroad tracks in Max's Truck on their way to the Red Cross class at the Spanish café. Martha hadn't been inside the café, just as she hadn't visited the Spanish church, but she knew its location.

Elena assumed she needed direction. Martha only half paid attention, bone weary. She relived the scene at the Lamberts and barely heard when Elena started giving her information about women who would be in the class.

They had tackled the chickens first, to remove death from nearest the house. Mr. Miyoshi, Min Himuru, and the Ichikawas helped dig a pit before they left for the cleanup at the Himuru and Ichikawa farms. Martha began the task of throwing in chickens and covering them with lime. From time to time she went to the house for a break.

Lucy Himuru stayed in the kitchen with Elsie and proved to be the medicine Elsie needed, with soothing "there there" and "what misfortune you've had" statements applied liberally. While Lucy cooed and fussed, she busied herself with boiling water for Martha, who took it outside and used it to immerse several of the dead fryers so she could pluck the feathers. Lucy prepared the naked carcasses for supper. Eventually, Elsie moved from the kitchen rocker and wandered into the ruined garden. Lucy kept track of Elsie from the window and said she seemed to be coming back to herself.

When Otto returned with the salve after conferring with Phil Ferguson, the veterinarian, Martha's responsibility shifted to helping Otto with the injured cattle. Eventually they corralled five or so cows, several of the steers, and the few surviving calves in a corner of Otto's small pasture with Rowdy's help. At Rudy's direction, Papa's imposing dog didn't let the animals out of formation and provided enough distraction for Martha and Otto to complete the job of spreading globs of foul-smelling ointment on gouges in the animals' skin.

Art and other neighbors were still digging a trench for the dead calves when she and Elena left with the children. It fell to Uncle Malcolm and Rudy to shoot and butcher one of the more badly injured steers.

Martha escaped her reverie from time to time to insert "I see" into Elena's description of the Spanish women. Elena's intricate knowledge included ages of their children, their various connections to each other, and the like. When satisfied that she wasn't missing anything significant, Martha retreated into her thoughts.

They dropped Anna and Robbie off with Josie, and Elena waited in Max's Truck while Martha ran into Papa's hospital room. Finally, tidbits of good news in an otherwise grim day. Doc said Papa could go home the end of the week, and she had interrupted a subdued conversation between Fran and Papa. Perhaps they had begun the difficult work of disclosure because they were so absorbed with each other that news of the hail damage barely made an impression, nor did Martha's description of Rowdy's unlikely conversion from watchdog to farmhand.

The storm, chicken and cow corpses, Max's disappearance and possible death, Papa's imminent return — all of it lay strewn about in

Martha's mind, alongside the topics she was to introduce in the home nursing class.

"Mrs. Lundgren, Mrs. Lundgren?"

"Yes?"

"I asked what you think about the Himurus' change of name."

Elena made no sense. Martha repeated the words, "Change of name?"

"Yes, I heard Mrs. Himuru tell Mrs. Lambert this afternoon they decided to change their name from Himuru to Hart. Hart was Mrs. Himuru's name before she married Mr. Himuru. Mr. and Mrs. Himuru, I mean Hart, have been considering it since the problem Ken had getting home from his college after the Pearl Harbor attack. I think it is a good idea because Lily and Ken look as much like some Mexicans as they do Japanese, so they will not have all the problems of being Japanese. What do you think?"

"I, I don't know what to think, Elena. This is the first I've heard of it."

The news was extraordinary and Elena's summary deceptively simple. Elena was right that Lily's and Ken's features could pass them off as Mexican, but their Japanese heritage was the dominant part of who they were, wasn't it? The name change shifted Martha's perception, though, to emphasize the white half contributed by Lucy. What nationality was the name Hart? Probably English. So now Ken and Lily were English, not Japanese, and would perhaps take on the appearance of Mexicans?

Ken's and Lily's faces floated in and out of Martha's vision and with each passing took on a different aspect. Martha blinked her eyes hard, hoping to recapture the Ken and Lily she knew. But that was beside the point. The name change was a matter of practical concern and shouldn't disorient her so.

Martha chose what she hoped was a straightforward response. "It's very clever of them to emphasize the Hart side of the family in these difficult times for children with a father of Japanese nationality. It'll be helpful, but I wonder if a change of name will change how they think of themselves."

"Mrs. Lundgren, when women marry they change their names, and everyone calls them Mrs. This and Mrs. That as a sign of respect. Does that change how they think of themselves?"

"Yes, but that change is one every girl grows up to expect. It primarily means new sets of responsibilities."

From childhood, she knew she would lose the McLennan name. She, and her children, might become something other than Scottish. She and Anna were Swedish Lundgrens, but because Art wasn't connected with his Swedish ancestry, neither was she. It never occurred to her to join the local Swedish Ladies Aid Society, nor did he ask for Swedish cooking or traditional observances. She doubted if he even knew any, given the difficulties of his childhood.

So her answer was accurate. Only a change of responsibilities, even though all married women were known by their husbands' names: not Martha McLennan Lundgren but Mrs. Arthur Lundgren.

However, Lucy's movement from Hart to Himuru and back to Hart was of a different magnitude, even though it could fit in with how Min and Lucy managed their family. Lucy encouraged her children to embrace Min's ancestry. On his part, Min joined the church. They moved between companionship with Japanese and white families. Would that change, and would Lucy and the children lose their connection to the Japanese culture? Min would be a Hart, too. For him, a Japanese man, wasn't the change cataclysmic?

"Mrs. Lundgren, you missed the turn!" Elena chided.

Martha drove to the end of the gravel street and circled back. She turned right and parked in front of Andy's Café, avoiding two large puddles that would take days to drain. Streets weren't paved south of the tracks. There weren't sidewalks or sewers. They must have a terrible problem with mosquitoes after rains like today's.

"Maybe the change from McLennan to Lundgren was not such a large one for you," Elena said, "but for some women who marry, a change of name is a very big step."

"Perhaps," Martha conceded, but Lucy was too matter-of-fact. The change was simply a question of protecting her family. She was solidly herself regardless of name.

Martha took Lucy's stability as her inspiration. She was a registered nurse and could teach the Red Cross home nursing class blindfolded, even if she was tired and hungry and hadn't listened to Elena's description of the students.

July 1942

Andy's Café

Instead of the twenty women Martha had anticipated, several families gathered around a birthday cake. A girl played the piano in the corner, and the young man standing by her raised a violin to his chin. Although Martha wasn't familiar with the tune, their lively playing made her pause.

She remained at the doorway when the song finished, arms full of Red Cross manuals, unsettled by the incongruity between the birthday party and her expectations. Elena greeted the families, addressing some in Spanish, some in English. She motioned for Martha to join her.

Martha pasted on a sociable smile, regretting that she hadn't paid attention when Elena tried to prepare her for the evening. Had she presumed she would meet women seated on sheepskins scattered about on a dirt floor, shrouded in black with heads draped in shawls, resembling the grandmother who lurked in the shadows of the adobe doorway at the colonia?

Someone relieved her of the books and explained that three of the women taking the home nursing class were sisters. The party was for one of their children, and the others would arrive shortly. She invited Elena and Martha to join them.

Elena readily accepted, briefly described the devastating afternoon hailstorm and its outcome, and indicated neither of them had eaten. There followed great consternation, not only about the lack of supper but because some of the party guests knew field workers who might have been in the path of the storm.

Lost in a sea of Spanish and English, Martha gratefully accepted black coffee, a bowl of rice and beans, and the plate of steaming tortillas Ernestine Armijo set before her.

Andrés emerged from the kitchen wiping his face on a tea towel and extended his hand. "Welcome to Andy's, Mrs. Lundgren."

Martha shook hands, muttered, "Thank you," and retreated into silence.

She realized she'd failed to make the proper response when Elena answered, "Mr. and Mrs. Armijo, thank you for letting the Red Cross use your café. I am happy you will be part of the class, Mrs. Armijo."

Martha turned to her meal and idly listened to the swirling conversations. She did make out the general topic, which consisted of dramatic stories about working in fields under life-threatening circumstances — cowering under lightning flashes, collapsing in the summer's heat, digging beets out of frozen soil in December with frostbitten fingers.

La Llorona

The violinist spoke up, and the general talk faded. He was describing his work on the construction of, as he called it, the "Jap Camp," and did so in English, apparently taking into account Martha's limited Spanish. Only then did she appreciate that she, along with the birthday child, was a guest of honor.

All present seemed thoroughly familiar with the camp and its purpose, and none were happy about it. Most of the comments involved a sense of threat, that the "Japs" confined there would take hundreds of jobs from Spanish-American field workers up and down the Valley.

He continued above the grumbling and said that several evenings ago, at dusk, his friends had urged him to walk across a field near the camp to a certain head gate where it was rumored La Llorona appeared. He didn't believe in such a creature and ridiculed the others for their superstitions. They countered, if there was nothing to the folktale, was he afraid to go with them? Accompanying them became a matter of honor.

Elena interrupted to ask Martha if she knew about La Llorona. "No" was the simple answer.

The whole group took it upon themselves to explain, everyone speaking at once, some in Spanish, some in English, until Elena said, "Let Guillermo explain. It is his story."

The violinist soberly accepted his task. "All of us know La Llorona. Mothers and fathers use her to frighten their children so they will not wander away from home because she might snatch them. She is a horrible creature, with the face of a horse."

"No!" someone interrupted. "Her face is gone. Her face is a hole."

Martha shivered, even as she tried to resist her childish fear of the developing ghost story.

Several people speaking in Spanish added versions of La Llorona's dreadful countenance. They were barely audible, as though their descriptions might summon the creature.

"However she looks," Guillermo resumed, "she is fearful. She appears at dusk and wails for her lost children."

Her lost children? Yes, mothers grieving even one lost child are fearsome sights, which is why they learn to mourn privately.

An eager voice interrupted when Guillermo paused for breath. "She killed her children in a river. Then she killed herself."

Martha shifted uncomfortably in her chair. Surely La Llorona didn't throw them into raging waters and watch trees and bodies of dead animals pummel them to death, as had happened to the unknown young cowboy during the flood. Or were La Llorona's children drawn down, down toward all that was buried in the muddy depths, their bodies tangled in debris, where they writhed and twisted to free themselves until their necks broke, as Frank Ogawa's had in the canal?

"But you have not given the reason," chimed in another. "She was a Mexican peasant girl who loved a rich Spaniard, and he made the children with her. Then he married a wealthy woman and left them."

"No, La Llorona is Cortez's mistress, and he left her with their children," offered another.

Martha braced herself. She pasted what she imagined was the face of Maher the abductor onto that of the mythical Spaniard's — or perhaps it was the face of Fran's dissolute husband. No matter. It was the same face in all cases: men who destroy young women for pleasure.

The woman who championed the peasant girl version said, "After the Spaniard's wedding, La Llorona took revenge by killing his children and herself."

Perhaps La Llorona was terrifying because she'd done the inconceivable. Surely no woman would kill her child to avenge herself against a man like Maher. Vera and Ida had preserved their children, and Fran had only lost hers on account of her husband's violence.

"When she approached heaven," the woman continued, "El Señor stopped her and asked about her children. She refused to answer. Of course, El Señor knew their fate and told her she would never rest until she found them."

Guillermo reclaimed his story. "She wanders the ditch banks, canals, and rivers after sunset looking for them. That is who my friends say appeared at the head gate by the Jap Camp."

A general murmuring on the part of his audience encouraged him to continue. His words tumbled over themselves. "We came near the place, and we heard wailing. My skin tingled, and I wanted to stop. But my friends laughed and called me coward."

Guillermo cleared his throat before continuing. "They said, 'Guillermo, you claim there is no La Llorona. The howling is just the wind.' They taunted me with these and other words. We walked on, and the wailing became louder. We saw mist rising in the gray light, and it took the shape of a woman wrapped in a shawl. I turned and ran. So did my friends."

Guillermo's story was done, but not comments from his listeners, who outshouted one another in a yet more boisterous brew of English and Spanish.

"Yes, the story of La Llorona, the weeping woman, is true, and she is a danger to be respected."

"No, this is a tale told by foolish boys to explain strange sounds."

"He was frightened and imagined he saw the shape of a woman in the mist."

Martha believed that Guillermo and his friends had convinced themselves they saw and heard something, and that they were as horrified as she was when she imagined the void that sucked up everything behind her in her kitchen the day Anna disappeared. How else to put words to the dread and despair felt in the face of suffering, abandonment, and death than to describe such anguish as a void, Julia Mattson's word, or as a crazed woman named La Llorona?

War advanced ever closer. Families clung together in the warmth of their homes, behind blackout shades. Mexican boys, soon to be in uniform themselves and wandering through an open field at dusk after a day's work on a camp for Japanese families dislocated from the West Coast, were susceptible to the menacing tale meant for children who strayed from home. Two hundred of them were missing on Bataan and Corregidor from one small New Mexican town, Elena's cousins among them. And all those in the service drowned in ships at Pearl Harbor. Pilots whose planes disappeared into the ocean in the Battles of the Coral Sea and Midway and in the attacks on Dutch Harbor, Alaska…

The tips of Martha's fingers remembered the feel of the young cowboy's unbroken skin in the Lambert's flooded field, and she pictured the Old Truck passing her by with the injured Frank Ogawa lying in the back. La Llorona most certainly collected children who wandered into danger.

She shuddered, and La Llorona took on the appearance of the shrouded crone standing in the doorway at the colonia. Martha sought her arsenal of assurances: the words from "God Will Take Care of You"; Roosevelt's declaration after Pearl Harbor that we are not stunned, terrified, or confused; Dorothy Thompson's editorial tucked into the edge of her dresser mirror — at no time must our efforts be affected by our moods.

Señora Morales

The birthday crowd dissipated. She stirred herself and engaged in the routine task of helping Elena arrange chairs for the class.

Women dribbled in by twos and threes until eighteen were present. Martha checked her watch and saw, to her consternation, they were starting forty-five minutes late. She walked around the room and introduced herself, and the act of conversing with her students drew her back from the chill of La Llorona's purgatory to the warmth of female chatter.

Martha decided to begin. "The hailstorm and its damage might have delayed the other two members of the class. I've met each of you, but I'll need help remembering your names. When you ask a question, will you please introduce yourself again?"

She paused, and Elena immediately inserted her translation. Those who hadn't nodded their assent to Martha's request indicated their agreement with Elena's Spanish version. Martha would have to stop for Elena much more frequently than she had imagined. It would take forever to cover the material, and the clatter from Andrés washing the party dishes didn't help.

"Elena will now hand out your books. Please turn to…"

The tardy students entered the room — the old crone from the colonia and Marguerite, who assisted her. They walked to the front, where Elena had placed their books on the two empty chairs. Could the elderly woman even read? If so, probably not English. Martha hadn't thought to talk with Elena about the absurdity of books for barely literate women. Hopefully most of them had the equivalent of a fourth-grade education, the level required of boys in the service, since the army used training manuals.

She had sense enough to wait until the newcomers sat down. She started to speak, but Elena quickly intervened. "Mrs. Lundgren, please come to the grandmother so I may introduce you."

Elena was evidently determined to correct her mistake of not acquainting Martha with the woman and her box of healing remedies during their visit at the colonia. Martha heard the respect in Elena's voice, but she also sensed anxiety. Its source could well be Martha's social missteps, which had piled up by the dozens since she'd entered the café, or concern that the grandmother would disapprove of the class, or both.

Elena had said that she knew how to disappear. Martha longed to do the same, but she made herself walk to the grandmother, mostly for Elena and Marguerite's sake. The two sisters had worked diligently to make the class happen; Martha wouldn't disappoint them.

She needed Elena's wisdom, as well as the support of her physical strength, so she took Elena's hand. Elena looked confused but accepted the gesture.

"Señora Morales, Señora Lundgren. Señora Lundgren, Señora Morales."

Elena placed Martha's hand in the old woman's. Martha felt the warmth of her rough skin, and her black eyes recalled Elena's the day of Carrie's delivery, when Doc Claffey inserted the forceps and Elena screamed. That day, Martha had fallen unconscious into the bottomless pools of fear and compassion in Elena's eyes. She saw similar depths in the grandmother's.

Her image of La Llorona as resembling Señora Morales was accurate, but only in part. Señora Morales knew betrayal, pain, and loss, but she also knew kindness, generosity, and sacrifice.

Martha understood what she needed to do. "Elena, please tell Señora Morales I'm honored to have her in the class. I look forward to learning how she treats the various illnesses and injuries we'll discuss, as I hope she'll want to learn from me."

The tension in Elena's demeanor dissolved, and Martha relaxed. This wasn't going to be the typical Red Cross home nursing class, and, while she expected some of the women would pass the test and obtain their certificates, their number wouldn't measure the group's success.

The Charivari

Elena and Marguerite rode home with friends, so Martha drove back across the tracks alone. From the number of vehicles parked in front of Hank's Motor Company, Martha decided the charivari had started and would finish there. She parked Max's Truck by the padlocked gate in front of the empty car lot. A sign in Hank's office window read: "We are 100 Percent American and Do Not Solicit Any Jap Trade."

Hank's sign could just as well be directed at the likes of Mr. Miyoshi and Jimmie as at the West Coast Japanese. His lot was empty because no new cars, trucks, or tires were being produced. He needed all the repair and maintenance business he could muster. As Cecil Thirkell had with his "No Mexicans or Dogs" sign in the old Sage Café window, Hank worked against himself. He also denigrated children and adults alike. Martha hadn't seen to it that the crude sign in the barbershop window disappeared, the one about "Japs" being shaved free and the proprietor not taking responsibility for "accidents." But now that the Japanese relocation camp was about to open, both the barbershop sign and Hank's must be removed.

The charivari parade with its attendant noise rounded the corner. Hugh pushed Eleanor down the center of the street in a gaily decorated wheelbarrow, followed by the good-natured crowd. Anna, one of the few children in the group, along with Harriet Moulton, followed behind Hugh, beating her spoon against the side of her tin cup. Every participant had some means of clanking, banging, or blowing squawks and squeaks.

As soon as Anna spotted Martha, she broke away. Martha laughed when the force of Anna's impact almost knocked her over.

Anna hugged Martha's legs. "Mama, you missed the charivari!"

"But I'm so glad I'm seeing the end of it! What a swell parade!"

Hugh's face must surely ache from having smiled most of a whole week, and Eleanor Moulton, now Mrs. Hugh Ufford, wore the blush of married delight, signs that augured well for their future. Even Addie Lambert Moulton, Eleanor's sister-in-law, looked pleasant, although Martha couldn't fathom why, given the destructive wind and hail that devastated her Home Place that very afternoon. Martha would never drop Addie's maiden name. Perhaps maintaining the memory of the Lambert upbringing, if only in Martha's mind, would dilute the Moulton influence.

Eleanor's brothers, Walter and Edgar, stomped along at the rear of the group, weaving a bit. Apparently not even alcohol had the power to lighten their moods.

Martha only noticed Art had slipped in beside her when he put his arm around her waist. "A nice night an' party after an awful day. It's past Anna's bedtime, but why don't we stop by the dance fer the newlyweds at the inn fer a few minutes so she can see what one's like, 'fore all the drinkin' starts?"

Martha leaned against his chest, savoring the smell of his Old Spice. Long past exhaustion and having missed the parade, she wanted a little fun from the evening. "That's a wonderful idea. Although, judging by Walter and Edgar, the drinking has begun."

Art frowned. "For those two, drinkin's a way a life, with no beginnin' er endin'. Even Malcolm knows ta stay clear, an' he's one a those gentle souls who looks fer the best in everyone."

"I wonder if I didn't fully appreciate Uncle Malcolm's humor this afternoon."

"How's that?"

"I think he made a joke that the hail took everything but the grasshoppers."

"Is that right? Well, Rudy an' me must be a good influence on 'im, for 'im ta joke 'round, 'specially at a time like that. Maybe, though, it's like I always 'spected; yer one a his favorites, an' he was tryin' ta make it easier fer ya."

"It's only taken him twenty-six years to warm up to me, if you're right. You said the same thing recently about Mr. Miyoshi."

"Yer the daughter neither will ever have. As fer Malcolm, it's a shame, what yer family did ta 'im, up in Canada."

Martha looked away from Hugh's grinning face into Art's sober one. "Both he and Papa were treated poorly, but you make it sound as though it was worse for Uncle Malcolm. What are you referring to?"

Art opened his mouth to answer, but Addie passed by. "Well, Martha, I'm surprised you're here, seeing that Eleanor's chosen Hugh over your brother."

What a hateful thing to say. Did Addie really have such a short memory, or did she twist the truth on purpose? Alex had sent Eleanor away from training camp without a proposal. Eleanor had no choice.

Addie lifted her chin and kept moving.

"Art, I'll stop by the dance on one condition — that you keep me away from her."

Walter called out to Hank, "Like your sign. Barbed wire, machine gun turrets, an' military police ain't enough to keep us safe from the Japs in that camp. Every store should have somethin' like it, to let 'em know they're not welcome here."

"Not if I can help it," said Martha. She didn't care who heard.

Art gripped her arm. "Remember what I said 'bout Ed an' Walt. They're drunk most a the time. Too bad. George Moulton's a good man. You can't reason with 'em, Martha. They'll take on a woman as soon as they will a man. I'm tellin' ya. Don't cross 'em, partic'ly since Walt's never got over ya."

Art was always the one to bring up Walter's feelings for her, which she inevitably interpreted as a reproach. Because his words of caution concluded with what sounded like jealousy, she asked in as neutral a manner as possible, "Will they be at the dance?"

"Prob'ly, but we'll be gone. I guarantee they'll stop by a bar first. How da ya suppose George lost his haystack in that fire?"

"Thought it was a lightning strike."

"His own sons, Walt an' Ed, set off fireworks they had from last year, even though George begged 'em ta stop. They rigged up some kinda chute fer the explodin' rocket. Musta been a feed trough. Thought they was infantrymen, I guess. Shot the rocket up the trough; it arched as beautiful as ya could wish an' went straight down inta the stack, which smoldered some before it busted inta flames. Blazed so hot George was afraid it would burn the whole field. Called the fire department."

"How do you know about this?"

"Earl told me. One a his buddies is a volunteer. They're still laughin' 'bout it, but it weren't no laughin' matter."

Bridge Club

"You haven't played since before the attack," said Josie. "Please come next week. We're all working hard and need relaxation. You'll already be in town at Doc's, so Art won't object to additional wear and tear on tires, or the gasoline. To placate all husbands in that regard, we're not meeting but every other month, and it's the right thing to do, of course."

Martha twisted the phone cord. Before the attack. Three weeks after Carrie died.

Josie must have interpreted the silence to mean Martha was considering it. She added enticements. "It'll be so pleasant. I'm setting up pretty little tables in the shade of my back yard and have invited Clara and Zella."

It would be a miserable afternoon with too much gossip and too little satisfaction of bidding and playing a good hand. Relaxation was choir practice on Thursdays and church on Sundays. Certainly folks gossiped at church, but the service gave time to think and make sense of things, to feel part of a larger purpose for mankind beyond war, the inspiration of the music…

Martha assembled her excuses. Yes, everyone was working hard, but she calculated Josie didn't put in the hours she did. She took more time to prepare for and teach the Spanish Red Cross class than Clara or Lola did theirs, and they didn't cope with cumbersome translation. Lola's class for the Fort Lyon wives of the doctors and staff took place there, where they all lived, which meant Lola didn't even drive to town. Granted, Clara taught two of the twenty-six session courses, and Martha just the one.

But none of the bridge club women contended with a large garden and all the canning, mixing the mash for chickens, and gathering and crating eggs, which Josie should appreciate, given the way she always went on about how food could be the decisive factor in war. Papa struggled with his one hand, and they hadn't found more help than Uncle Malcolm and Rudy Ruiz. The burden fell to Art and Mr. Miyoshi. Martha did the morning milking and Jimmie helped Mr. Miyoshi when he could tear himself away from the Ichikawa place, but football practice had already started. With school beginning soon, and harvest, even someone with Jimmie's enthusiasm couldn't handle that much. Martha was more exhausted than when Carrie was alive and required so much attention.

She recited the tiresome list of responsibilities aloud, but Josie objected. "Martha, do you think only farm women are worn out? Town women work hard, too. I'm teaching a literacy class, which I haven't told you about yet. So many boys are refused for service because they can't read at the fourth-grade level, so Bess Arnold and I designed a course. Elena knows about it because several Spanish boys attend, and some of their mothers from your Red Cross class. And Vacation Bible School took ever so much time. But you never pay attention to me. You think my life is a bed of roses because I have hot running water and an electric stove!"

Martha never made a point of her sister's laborsaving equipment, or the fact that Elena helped her enormously with Robbie. What physical work did Josie actually do apart from tending her small garden? However, Martha drew breath to commend Josie for her efforts.

"Martha, let me finish. Yarn's coming into the Red Cross sewing room — next week, actually — for us to knit sweaters and turtlenecks for the soldiers. In addition, I advise the Girl Reserves at the high school and help with their perpetual scrap rubber drives. Do you have any old bathtub stoppers, sock supporters, babies' rubber panties, car mats, or teething rings to contribute? We ask for that, and more, at the door of every house in town. And Earl and I are fixing up our little garage to house a military man who teaches at the aviation training school. There aren't enough places for them. The man's paying board, too, and you know how I hate to cook. Most of the women who'll be coming are just as busy."

By now Josie was shouting into her end of the telephone line, and her fervor struck Martha as funny. She started to laugh.

Josie shot back, "How dare you laugh at me?"

Each woman in the bridge club struggled in her own way. Just think of Edith. Who was Martha to judge them?

"I'm not laughing at you," she said forcefully so Josie would believe her. "I'm laughing because you've made your point about how we're all so frazzled. I give up! I'll come to your party! And thanks for the reminder about collecting rubber. Anna's ball is going flat, my swimming cap has a tear in it, and I still have all the nipples from Carrie's bottles. I'll try to remember to put everything in the mailbox. On the farms, the mailman gathers it. Which reminds me that I must drop Art's used razor blades in the box at City Hall for gun production. Are you collecting Earl's? But we've been talking too long. We need to hang up."

No sooner had Martha put the receiver on the hook than the telephone rang again.

"I hope you don't think I'm being forward," Elsie Lambert said, "but I've come up with an idea. I don't have tomatoes, but I have a cooker. You have tomatoes and goodness knows what. Would you accept my help with canning the crop from your prolific garden? Here I sit, with little to harvest from the few things I replanted after the hail. It would…"

"Elsie, no need to explain."

Elsie's transformation from confident, outspoken woman to timid, apologetic one distressed Martha. No word yet from Max. Short of his return, or some news of him, if canning tomatoes would lead to restoration of the former Elsie, Martha would agree to it.

"It'd be a huge relief to have your help," Martha said. "I don't know what we were thinking when Art plowed under so much grass to enlarge the garden. I got sick of the peas when they came in, and the beans were worse. I can't imagine what I'll do with all the tomatoes."

"Thank you, Martha. I feel so useless."

"There's more to it, Elsie. Papa and Fran have asked me to help harvest his garden, too. They're both trying so hard, but even between the two of them, and with Uncle Malcolm, the garden's too much."

"I'm sorry. I should have offered, but I didn't want to impose."

The operator broke into the call. "Martha, you've been talking for twenty minutes, unusual for someone who answers promptly and keeps calls brief to save time and facilities from the press of additional and longer calls on account of the war volume, but we can't slack off in monitoring ourselves."

Nellie's prolonged scolding served no other purpose than to lengthen Martha's time on the line, but she answered politely. "Thank you. Elsie, why don't you drive over so we can work out plans?"

Anna burst into the house. "Mama, come quick! Uncle Malcolm needs you!"

The receiver on its way to the hook, Martha guessed at Elsie's answer.

The Rattlesnake

Anna disappeared without specifying where Uncle Malcolm had the need, but Martha caught sight of her as she sprinted behind the barn. Perhaps he really was in distress.

Martha rounded the corner, and Anna was surveying a long rattler by the tree. Martha snatched her away before she noticed Uncle Malcolm slumped against the barn.

He gasped, "Fourteen rattles. A big 'un. Struck hand. Sliced head off with shovel. He was goin' after Anna. Get kerosene. Can't drive to town. Sorry, Martha."

Elsie and Uncle Malcolm with their needless apologies.

"Uncle Malcolm, don't be sorry. You probably saved Anna's life!"

Martha doubted the treatment, but the can was nearby, and kerosene would cool the hand.

"Anna, go to the barn and wait in Max's Truck. I'll be right there. Uncle Malcolm, don't move. I'll bring the kerosene before I get the pickup."

They passed Elsie as they turned onto the highway. Martha called out the window and explained. She hoped she heard Elsie say something to the effect that she'd tell the others when they came in for dinner. Moreover, she might prepare the meal.

"What were you doing behind the barn?" Martha asked.

"Movin' the pile a manure away from the wall. When it's stacked like that, manure heats up. Can't let it rest near a frame building or it'll start the wood ta smolder."

Where to throw manure was the least of Art's worries, so he shoveled it there. According to Uncle Malcolm, cobwebs also fueled fires, so he had cleaned them out of their barn and Papa's. His fire-safety efforts weren't confined to barns; he plowed strips around the various fields for firebreaks and placed buckets of sand at strategic locations around the buildings. He didn't need to take measures at Mr. Miyoshi's, who was even more orderly.

Uncle Malcolm's fastidiousness drove Papa crazy. So many other chores needed doing. Their first responsibility was to grow food, for the troops and for the country, but Uncle Malcolm insisted — in his own, mild way — that his efforts averted disaster. Besides, he'd say, wasn't Robert on the defense council? Shouldn't his farms be examples?

In the absence of an opinion from Martha, Uncle Malcolm continued with uncharacteristic chattiness, perhaps a symptom of his anxiety about the snakebite.

"If enemy planes attack munitions plants or airstrips in Colorado, like the one at the aviation trainin' school, they'll have ta drop their excess bombs ta fly away fast. I'm not gonna aid the enemy by burdenin' our volunteers because we aren't prepared."

He moaned and leaned his head back.

"Please don't talk, Uncle Malcolm. Just rest until we find Doc."

She'd heard Uncle Malcolm's arguments from Papa, who claimed his brother worried more than an old woman. Coming directly from Uncle Malcolm, though, his points sounded reasonable. Art stayed neutral in their disagreement, and so would Martha. This was a minor irritation, but Martha sympathized with Uncle Malcolm. Doc labored with one nurse who worked only three mornings a week

— her — and the Red Cross class reinforced how each family could, and must, take responsibility for their own safety. That certainly included precautions against fire.

However, Uncle Malcolm hadn't included rattlesnakes in his calculations. For a time, they were stuck with two one-handed brothers.

Indian Writings

Everyone was amazed at Uncle Malcolm's quick recovery, which they attributed to the kerosene. Doc and Martha thought it had more to do with his quick reaction and the shovel. The snake's fangs had hit at an angle and didn't penetrate very deep. That, and Anna and Martha's speed, meant Doc administered the anti-venom shot soon after the bite.

In any case, in spite of his physical recovery, Uncle Malcolm was in a nervous uproar. No one argued he had faced down death, and the ordeal came on the heels of several months of more socializing than he'd done in years. All he asked for was the next Sunday afternoon. Wouldn't someone drive him out south so he could put things in order at his place, in case the outcome of the next accident was worse, what with all the war turmoil? And he wanted to visit his few cows, now living at his neighbors' place.

Who could deny his modest request? In fact, the prospect of a Sunday afternoon picnic in the cedars while Uncle Malcolm enjoyed a quiet retreat appealed to everyone. They'd barely celebrated most holidays of the past year, what with Carrie, the Pearl Harbor attack and all the influenza at Christmas, farm labor problems, flood and hail. Everyone anticipated Martha's contribution of a sort of Black Cake made from a sugar rationing recipe that called for molasses instead. She hadn't baked one since last Thanksgiving. Even Earl, Josie, and Robbie would join Art, Martha, Anna, Papa, and Fran.

The weather on Sunday afternoon was typical of late August, warm enough to feel like summer but close enough to September for the air to smell of dried grass and weeds. After dinner, they explored the canyons and looked for the Indian writings Art swore he and Eddie Mattson had discovered when they were in high school. The effort paid off.

Martha stood alone at the bottom of the west-facing sandstone cliff after everyone else wandered off. Heat radiated from the rock, and sunshine illuminated the figures. She reached for them, but they were too high above her head. The origins of the drawings were ancient, but their shape and color so immediate she sensed the artist whispering to her across centuries. She shuddered and stepped away. Perhaps those who studied such things could decipher their meanings and weren't overcome by eerie feelings of being addressed by folks long dead.

Earl shattered her mood with his shout. "Here're some real Indian writings. Everyone, come and see!"

By the time Martha joined the group, Art was lifting Anna to touch the rock where the letters AL and EM were inscribed. Art Lundgren and Eddie Mattson.

"Oh, Art," Martha scolded. "You've defaced the rocks."

Art set Anna back on her feet. "We was just boys, Martha. Didn't know better."

Earl came to Art's defense. "I appreciate that the initials don't have the historical value of the Indian writings, but weren't they done in the same spirit? The human impulse to declare, 'We were here!' At least Art and his friend carved the letters far enough from the ancient 'writings' not to spoil them."

The Shed

By the time they hiked out with empty picnic baskets, shadows were spreading up the sides of the canyon walls, and the air down on the trail had cooled considerably.

On the spur of the moment, Martha proposed, "Let's give Uncle Malcolm a little more time. Would everyone follow us to the Maher place? I'd like to visit it, since we're so close."

"Why?" Josie and Fran asked in unison.

"What you described was so horrible," Josie added. "Why would you want to see it again?"

Martha's rescue of the two girls had happened over a year ago, but Guillermo's La Llorona story had minimized the time interval. "I'll never shake the memory, but seeing the house will remind me Ida and Vera have gotten on with their lives. If you all come, you'll help rob my recollections of their power."

Fran countered, bitterly, "You're too optimistic about the girls, Martha. They'll carry the burden of their injuries for a very long time."

She reached for Robert's arm, and everyone involuntarily looked at the stub. "I'm sorry, Robert. I didn't mean to draw attention to the accident. I wasn't even thinking about it. I just wanted the reassurance of touching you. Surely you realize I had something else in mind."

"I know." He took her hand in his right one and rested her palm above the stub. "Both you and Martha have a point. Some folks overcome their injuries and escape their nightmares, but a lot don't, either because the physical or financial loss is too much or the mental damage weighs on them. Just visit out at Fort Lyon a time or two with those veterans and you'll see. Always upsets me so much I vow I'll never go back, but I do. Then again, thank the Good Lord, sometimes recovery is possible. With the help of friends and family."

Martha moved to touch his shoulder, but Earl interrupted.

"Wasn't Maher that scoundrel who kidnapped the two girls?"

"Yes," Fran and Josie answered together a second time.

Martha smiled in appreciation of their companionability. Surely Fran and Papa would announce wedding plans soon.

"I'd be curious to see his setup, to figure out how he got away with it for so long," Earl said.

He always missed the point. His reaction was purely investigative. Historical. Never mind how Maher had crushed Vera's and Ida's spirits––and Earl had ridden right over Papa's eloquence about loss.

However, she tried to give Earl leeway and looked for a point of agreement, as Josie was always advising. "So your interest is more, shall we say, scientific?"

"Now it is, because you found the girls and they're rebuilding their lives. At the time, though, I was scandalized when Josie told me the story. How can a whole county of good folks have someone like that living among them and not know it, not see that something is terribly amiss?"

Ah, the point of agreement. At least initially the girls' predicament had outraged him. The colonia came to mind as another scandalous presence that no one seemed to notice.

"Earl, not everyone in this county is good, but even presumably good folks overlook a great deal. I've been driving by the colonia at the hay mill for years, and I would never have believed folks were living in such squalor if I hadn't seen it myself."

As soon as she spoke, she had second thoughts. Even if she hadn't invited another disagreement with Earl, Josie might take issue. After all, Josie had seen the conditions when she taught at Eagle View and had done nothing.

Art undoubtedly anticipated a lengthy discussion about whether the Spanish-American families were forced to live in undesirable conditions, Martha's position, or were responsible for the squalor, Earl's position, because he quickly pointed out, "If we're gonna go by Maher's, we'd better pack up."

They drove out of the cedars and across the flat land in the soft light of late afternoon, when the sun's rays weave shadows through the prairie grasses and make them look thicker and of deeper hues. The landscape lulled Martha far away from thoughts about difficult brothers-in-law.

When they turned into the lane of the abandoned house, the grinding of the gravel against the tires on Max's Truck, the same sound made by the wheels on Sheriff Burleigh's Buick, thrust her back to that day. She half expected another wary girl with a hoe to walk around the corner.

The house still seemed abandoned, but the screens no longer hung half off the windows. The scraggly, dried weeds and the leprous chips of paint had disappeared. The prairie grasses rolled away from the front in a carpet of innumerable browns and greens. They climbed out of the vehicles, trying to interpret what they saw.

"Doesn't look so bad. Just empty," observed Josie.

"It's changed," said Martha. "But who made the repairs? And why?"

"Where's the shed, where he kept Ida?" asked Fran.

"Around back. I'll show you."

The group stayed together, as though a herd offered better protection against the unknown. When they turned the corner, the lean-to was gone, but not disappeared. Its boards were neatly stacked by the house. The gulf between what they saw and Martha's memory was so great as to convince her she had overstated the horrors Vera and Ida endured. The house was just an empty building on a plot of ground. How did it come to be divested of its malevolence?

"I don't understand," Martha whispered.

"You said he kept one of them locked in the lean-to?" asked Papa.

"Yes."

"I think I know what happened. Malcolm's done the repairs. Probably tore down the shed first. It'd be important to him."

"Why?"

"Surely you know, from his boyhood in Canada."

"Papa, I don't know. I don't know what happened to him in Canada. Just that the two of you were cheated out of your property."

Papa's mouth dropped open, but he composed himself enough to say, "How could you not know? Anna was always bringing it up. She said Malcolm and black Aunt Lottie both came to Colorado as ruined people and even the pure air and searing wind of the high plains couldn't cleanse their sorrows. She said 'pure air and searing wind' often, probably from the years she lived on open prairie in the soddie."

"Papa, you're making me feel strange. I really don't know particulars about Uncle Malcolm. Perhaps when I was younger I didn't pay close attention when you and Mama talked. Or perhaps I didn't understand. After she died, you didn't talk to us about it, and I never thought to ask. And who's black Aunt Lottie?"

Papa let his body down, heavily, on the back stoop. "This is unbelievable. It's always at the front of my mind. How could you not know? I never meant to keep Malcolm's problems a secret from any of you. Josie, you surely remember what I'm talking about. You were older, when Anna died."

"All I know is that your father remarried after your mother's death, and she was a widow with a son older than you and Uncle Malcolm. Also, you said she was mean. As for black Aunt Lottie, the name's familiar, but I haven't heard it for so long I'm not sure I know who she was."

"She was one of the slaves on the tobacco plantation where your grandfather Stone worked. She didn't leave after emancipation. Nowhere to go, so when the Stones came west from North Carolina, she did too. Worked for the family for board and room. However, she died only a year or so after they settled near Greenwood, when Anna wasn't much older than her namesake here."

Papa motioned for his granddaughter to sit on his lap, which she did without hesitation.

"Don't remember where Anna said black Aunt Lottie's buried, but your mama thought of her as part of the family. Lottie spent many more hours in a day with Anna than with her parents. They were always in the fields scraping out a living."

He stopped talking, lost in reminiscing. Josie prodded him to continue. "I can see how slavery left damage that even 'pure air and searing wind,' as Mama said, could never heal, but what about Uncle Malcolm?"

"Josie, you described our stepmother as mean. That's hardly the word. Nothing about Malcolm or me pleased her, ever. I was older, so I could keep my distance. Went out to the barn and took as long as I could with chores. Left for school early and stayed late. Anything to be away from the house. But Malcolm, he was young when they married. Such a handsome little boy. Mischievous, but in a cute way. Alex resembled Malcolm, when they were little. Anyway, she used a switch on him. When he got older she took to locking him in the woodshed for hours on end. That went on for several years, until he outgrew her. Never figured out why she hated us so. You know Malcolm. Not a spiteful bone in his body. Except maybe she thought Papa favored us, that, and her son wouldn't get his share. But then, it turned out just the opposite. She, and her son, got everything when Papa died."

Martha sat down beside him. "This explains so much, Papa, about Uncle Malcolm and why you so firmly protected Alex and Louise's interests when you announced you were thinking of marrying Fran. And you assumed we understood."

She slipped her arm into his. "I can't resist a tease. Knowing these details about Uncle Malcolm and how Alex resembles him explains something else, too."

Papa looked at her suspiciously. "What?"

"Why you've always been so indulgent with Alex, of course!"

Papa drew away. "That's not true! I expect as much from him as I do from you girls. And don't you two even think of rolling your eyes at one another, as you always do."

But he laughed along with the others.

Martha kept her reaction to black Aunt Lottie's story to herself. If she had known about the former slave when she'd encountered the Negro soldier from Alabama at the train station, she wouldn't have been so awkward. A Negro was part of her mother's family and someone Mama was comfortable with, not a caricature like "Festus" in the jokes the newspaper regularly printed, with his absurd and slow-witted punch lines.

How had a character like Festus come to be? Folks like him could have been slaves on plantations, as had black Aunt Lottie. They shouldn't be ridiculed. Although Grandpa and Grandma Stone gave her board and room in exchange for her work, even the pure air and searing wind of the plains couldn't sweep away her memories of captivity, and she must have been desperately lonely.

Everyone started back to the vehicles, with Martha struggling to reconcile the discrepancy between the neat, abandoned house she showed her family and the hellhole where Maher imprisoned Vera and Ida.

Goldenrod

When they left Maher's, Josie and her family headed to town. Art and Martha decided to follow Papa and Fran to pick up Uncle Malcolm. They were to meet him at his friends', who were successful dryland ranchers, and Art was curious to see their place. Martha didn't know them, although she had seen them from a distance in town from time to time when they drove in for supplies.

Art turned off the road and followed Papa's Chrysler along two ruts through a pasture. They bounced along for a half-mile or so. In the glowing light of late afternoon, white-faced Herefords to their right and left grazed on the tall grass.

"Do you think we'll be able to pull Uncle Malcolm back to the farm after he's spent an afternoon in this paradise?" Martha asked.

"He knows too well it ain't no paradise. Just try pullin' a calf in a blizzard on this pasture, when the grass is stubbly an' winter-dead. Or gettin' hay out ta 'em when the temper'ture's below freezin'. Our life is soft compared ta this. It's amazin' how those two women do it. Course they have hired help."

They drove up to the house, and she exclaimed, "Our garden isn't big at all compared to this! Look at the variety of zinnias up by the house. How clever to outline the flower bed with goldenrod."

Martha could have enthused longer about the flowers, and Art, too, seemed moved by the profusion of colors, intensified by the golden light the western sky unleashed on the landscape.

Anna was beside herself. Martha had barely opened the door before Anna scrambled over her lap. Anna's feet landed on the running board, and she scampered toward the garden. "I'm going to dance with the flowers; I'm going to dance with the flowers."

"Dance with me, first," an obviously rested Uncle Malcolm called out from the front porch.

He intercepted Anna, lifted her high in the air, twirled, and set her down, seeming to know it was unwise to impede her progress for more than a few seconds.

Martha felt she was stepping into a movie picture, the scene was so vibrant. The transformation of Maher's house must have intensified her emotions, and the afternoon sun played its part. But as blissful as the ranch appeared, she knew Art was right. Such beauty came at enormous cost — of time, sacrifice, heartbreak, and sweat.

She was prepared to like Uncle Malcolm's friends instantly. She wasn't prepared for them to be as old as they looked. Both had graying hair. Both were dressed in pants. Why not, given the difficulty of their work and the fact that they rarely had visitors? One was tall and thin, with a face browned and toughened by the sun. The other was short and plump, with rosy cheeks, a ready smile, and a broad-brimmed hat in hand, which she jammed down on her head as she walked down the porch steps.

"You must be Martha. We've heard all about your exploits, sliding down the embankment to save that boy. We know his family. Gilchrist. He was James, but they called him Jamie. A handsome young man. Good with horses. Met up with them from time to time at rodeos. Went to the funeral. Of course, there aren't many rodeos this summer, the war and all. They're so grateful someone was with him, you know, when he died."

Martha felt as queasy as she did after a carnival ride, unsettled by the unforeseen conversation about the dead boy alongside the idyllic garden glowing in the sun's rays.

She had been physically intimate with the boy's flesh but had known nothing about him, save for Al Ivarson's speculation that he was a rodeo cowboy. Jamie Gilchrist. No longer just a damaged body washed up on a levee. Uncle Malcolm's friend gave him personality, and Martha grieved his death anew.

She wanted to match the candor of her vivacious hostess, but she had no idea where to begin. Her awkward slide down the embankment? Half running, half swimming when the water breached the levee? She tried to maintain his dignity, but what dignity was there in being wrapped in a mackintosh and dying while bouncing along in a flooded field in the makeshift stretcher? Jamie's body lying in the back of a pickup for hours? The boy had died. She hadn't saved him. And the family was grateful for her companionship?

Jamie Gilchrist. Knowing his name muted some of the absurdity of the horse's body stuck in the dike, but knowing it made his death all the more tragic. How could she explain all that to a woman she'd just met?

The tall one rescued the moment. "Yes, yes, Gladys. Maybe our guests would like some iced tea. And to sit on the porch. And enjoy the sunset."

"Of course. We haven't even introduced ourselves. I'm Gladys; this is Ellen."

They shook hands all around.

Martha gathered herself sufficiently to say to Gladys, "Thank you for telling me his name. I'm so sorry I wasn't able…"

She couldn't say more, and Gladys took Martha's unfinished sentence in an entirely unexpected direction. "Honey, if we apologized for even half the things we're sorry about, we'd never accomplish a thing."

They accepted Ellen's invitation by walking toward the porch.

"Mama, Papa!"

Martha whirled, ready to run in the direction of Anna's excited call. Anna stood surrounded by flowers, enveloped in a cloud of butterflies.

"Art, she'll trample the flowers. We need to get her out."

"No, no," protested Gladys. "That's what flowers are for — butterflies and children."

Indeed, with several butterflies still crowning her head, Anna moved carefully, picking her steps deliberately through the flowerbed.

Uncle Malcolm touched Martha's arm so lightly she thought she might have imagined it, but she turned toward him. "While Ellen's gettin' the tea, will ya come with me ta the barn?"

As they walked, Uncle Malcolm didn't speak. They reached their destination, and he slid open the heavy wooden door. The interior was subdued, no riot of color, just dust motes floating in the beams of now-pink light reflecting off the clouds. They hesitated until their eyes adjusted. Uncle Malcolm led her to a stall at the back where a sleek Guernsey patiently allowed her calf to butt at her udder.

He spoke reverently. "She's the cow Burleigh said ta pick up from that abandoned place last year. Doin' fine. Wanted ya ta see 'er beautiful baby. Born last week."

He laid his forehead against the cow's and stroked her neck on each side with his rough hands, the right one still discolored from the snake bite. Martha ran her fingers along the calf's sturdy back and stopped herself from saying, "If only it were as easy to heal people."

September 1942

Greenwood News

Martha stayed after the bridge party to help Josie tidy up. Anna and Harriet had played contentedly, probably on account of Lena Mae's pleasant company, and the women had talked about matters of substance, not pretentious topics like bringing fur coats out of storage, as Martha had feared they would.

With Edith Giffard there, even Maude and Addie Lambert Moulton had behaved. Most had heard snatches about Edith's trip to San Francisco and the Presidio, but repeating it apparently consoled her. Although none of the nurses evacuated from the Philippine Islands had information about Muriel, she seemed more coherent.

As far as Edith knew, not any of the mothers and fathers who visited the Presidio discovered the whereabouts of their missing children, but they found comfort in talking with one another. Some resigned themselves to wait because they knew war mixes up everything. Many were frantic. Others were angry that the military wasn't better organized. Why didn't they know where anyone was? Twenty-five thousand missing on Bataan alone.

She'd had the privilege to speak with an evacuated nurse in person, perhaps because the daughter Edith sought was also a nurse, but Edith could tell she was schooled on what to say so as not to alarm the families. Even though the reassurances rang false, Edith was encouraged by hearing them from a woman who had been there and returned. She'd apparently decided that would be the outcome for Muriel. Martha was skeptical but didn't fault her for a hopeful conclusion.

Josie and Martha finished taking the card tables down and were stacking them on the back porch when Josie said, "Of all the topics that came up this afternoon, the one I'm surprised no one mentioned was the grand jury."

"Grand jury?"

"You did need to be here this afternoon, to learn about everything that's happening around Greenwood."

"Well, are you going to tell me?"

"On second thought, maybe it didn't come up because it's not widely known. I only heard it from Earl."

"So, you've tantalized me only to let it drop."

"I'm not playing with you. No reason to keep it secret. One, or several, of the commissioners and others are suspected of embezzlement and who knows what. Hank Philson's apparently pocketed thousands from sales and repairs of county vehicles. The county treasurer doctored the books. I'm sure I'm not describing this accurately, but a grand jury will get to the bottom of it."

"And Earl knows because…?"

"Because Al Ivarson's told him. Al's beside himself."

"Al's beside himself? Josie, I'm furious to hear this. The commissioners have been eliminating programs like the Health Unit and school lunches to save money, all the while taking it for themselves! Papa mentioned something about dishonest officials, but I had no idea it involved this many, and so much money."

"Papa always tells you the juicy gossip that I hear weeks later."

"Josie, I…"

"I'm just giving you a bad time. It was a wonderful afternoon, and I don't intend to end it with a row. Let's finish the dishes."

With her hands busy in the warm, sudsy water, Martha said, "I'm so glad Clara could be here. Do you suppose she's sweet on that dentist? Something about the way she played up his sacrifice of time…"

"Yes. I heard a catch in her voice when she said he'd been called to army duty, and then she emphasized that he's staying until ten at night to finish up with his patients in each of the towns he visits up and down the Valley. You'll let me know if there's something to it? Clara deserves a good man, and it's too bad he's leaving, if he's the one."

"And she abruptly changed the subject to request help compiling the list of girls interested in nursing studies as though a dentist's schedule was too emotional to discuss. I understand she wants the list quickly for the representative of the State Nursing Council who's coming to recruit for the armed forces, but it wasn't something she needed to ask everyone. Fran and I can make the list and narrow it down. She can talk to us any time."

"So many changes in one year…"

Camp Amache

"Josie, were you surprised when Bess Arnold said she'll be teaching at the Japanese camp? Another teacher lost to the war, but I'm pleased someone of her caliber will be there."

"No, I wasn't, even though she hadn't told me. I imagine Bess is influenced by her father, as we're influenced by ours. Judge Arnold's very clear that he thinks the camps are unconstitutional, imprisoning

American citizens just because they have Japanese ancestry. I can understand she wants to help. I didn't even know there was such a place as the small hotel near the camp that's been converted for the teachers. Her announcement was brave, because I'll wager more than a few of the club women disapprove of any contact with the camp."

"If you're asked, will you take the fourth grade she was to teach in town?"

"I haven't given full-time teaching a thought, but with men enlisting or being drafted, the board members are probably worried they won't fill the vacancies."

"If you take it, you'll finally have the right to claim you're fully involved in the war effort."

Josie twisted the towel and snapped Martha's bottom with it. "I'll not rehearse all my war efforts for you again! Seriously, Martha, I'm a married woman with a baby. The board will think it's too risqué to hire me. Still, if they're desperate enough…"

Bess's announcement had forced Martha to think very differently about the camp. What had been the site of Guillermo's La Llorona tale became a place where families would live with thousands of children. Bess said they'd named the massive construction site Camp Amache after a Cheyenne Indian princess from the prior century-- peculiar for a detention center for Japanese aliens, as everyone referred to them.

She also said that out of the thirty or so blocks of buildings, half of the plumbing and mess halls remained to be installed, and internees were already arriving. Martha pictured a giant colonia of seven or eight thousand inhabitants, suffering from disease and hunger.

Martha was still thinking about the camp when she drove through downtown, intending to stop at the pharmacy to inquire again if they had scissors or tweezers. The ones in her medical bag had rusted from their adventures in the Lambert's flooded field, and it was so difficult to replace metal items.

She started her left turn onto Main Street, but Sheriff Burleigh's Buick sped toward her from the right and screeched to a stop in front of the radiator. She slammed on the breaks.

He shoved his bulk out and shouted to anyone within hearing distance, "Gotta wait, folks, fer the convoy from the railroad station ta the Jap camp."

Convoy? Still shaking from almost hitting his automobile, Martha stood on the running board for a better view. Anna opened her door, too.

"Stay inside, honey. I don't know what's going to happen."

A truck similar to the one that had transported the Navajos to the beet fields turned right onto Main Street, just missing the Buick, followed by others.

The first carried what seemed to be families — fathers, mothers, children, even grandparents. Through the slats on the side of the truck, Martha could see the suitcases they used as seats. The second truck carried the same configuration of passengers, and the third. Soon a crowd gathered and silently watched the equally silent cargo. The younger children in the trucks peeked shyly from parents' laps; the older children were bolder. Some of the young men returned the stony glare of the town's inhabitants. The adults kept their heads down, looking defeated and ashamed.

The fourth truck approached, and Martha thought she recognized one of the passengers. She cried out, "Mrs. Ogawa, Mrs. Ogawa!"

She jumped off the running board and ran around Burleigh's car. She touched the side of the transport, still calling Mrs. Ogawa's name; a guard stood in the front of the truck bed and raised his gun.

Anna had clear access from her passenger's side door and joined her mother. Burleigh grabbed them both. The transport crept forward.

"Whada ya doin'?" he shouted, more alarmed than hostile.

"Don't you see? That's Mrs. Ogawa. I'm sure of it. She turned her head when I called her name."

"I don't care if it's Vivian Leigh. Yer not ta approach the aliens, and ya can't have yer little girl runnin' loose 'round these trucks."

Not confident his words were sufficient, Burleigh maintained a tight hold on their arms and guided them to the driver's door of Max's Truck.

"Get in. Parade's almost over," he ordered.

Martha was frantic, but she lifted Anna into the cab. "Burleigh, we know them! They don't belong in a camp. They're friends! You have to do something. You're the law. You can get them out."

"This ain't a local matter, Martha. The place they're goin' is a military zone. Even if I could do somethin', I wouldn't. If they are who ya say, we don't know but what they left here ta go ta Los Angeles, or wherever they're comin' back from, an' spy fer the Japs. Hell, what am I sayin'? They are the Japs!"

He shoved Martha in. She almost landed on Anna's lap.

"Go home. I don't want no more trouble. I'm telephonin' from my office in fifteen minutes. Ya'll be there ta answer."

Martha was surely mistaken. It wasn't possible that Mrs. Ogawa would be herded onto a truck bed under guard. Not able to think of an alternate plan, she drove home as instructed to wait for Burleigh's call.

When the telephone rang, she picked up the receiver, confirmed Burleigh was on the line, and said, "Satisfied? I'm home."

She hung up before Burleigh said so much as another word. Her hands trembled.

Anna, who hadn't spoken since Burleigh grabbed her, approached Martha, who sat in a chair pushed against the wall under the telephone. "Mama, why is Sheriff Burleigh angry? He hurt my arm. I thought he liked us. He helped find me in the field."

"Honey, I'm too upset to think. Crawl on my lap. Give me a minute to calm down."

They sat still.

Finally Martha said, "Sheriff Burleigh's just being a…"

She shocked herself that she almost said "son-of-a-bitch," not even the softer "son-of-a-gun." She imagined Burleigh's parentage and thought hers an unjustified criticism, to attribute maternity of a monster like Burleigh to a creature no more culpable than Tip.

And that made her laugh. "Anna, Sheriff Burleigh's just being obstinate, and I'm very upset at him."

"What does 'obstinate' mean?"

"Stubborn. Hard-headed. Won't listen to reason. Then again, he probably thinks I'm unreasonable. We have to tell Mr. Miyoshi that his friends, the Ogawas, have come back."

They drove over to his place and checked the barn. Both his truck and grey coupe were inside, which must mean he was in the house for supper already. But when she opened the door and called inside, no one answered. Thinking he could be in his bathhouse, she debated whether to come back later. She hesitated to interrupt his evening routines with Anna in tow, but the Ogawas' plight demanded it.

They passed the corral, and Old Grey trotted up to the wooden fence. Martha didn't see any sign of Old White, Mr. Miyoshi's other mare. It was possible he had ridden out to the fields to preserve vehicles, tires, and gasoline.

She and Anna entered his garden, walked along the smooth gravel path, and approached the bathhouse. She called out his name several times. Still no answer.

They went back to Max's Truck, and she sat for a moment behind the steering wheel. Mr. Miyoshi could be anywhere — on his place, at theirs, at the Home Place. She could drive to the Himurus', now known as the Harts', and tell them, but they probably hadn't come in for supper, either.

Marguerite Marquez might know something. She and Susie Ogawa were such close friends. Surely the two girls corresponded. But Martha had to fix supper before Art came in from the field, and Marguerite might, or might not, be over at the Home Place helping Fran. That depended on whether Rudy'd had time to fetch her in Papa's truck.

Marguerite. She should be on Clara's list for the nursing recruiter. The school counselor had denied her an education by not allowing her to apply for a scholarship on account of being Spanish-American, but if nurses were in such great demand… She'd make an excellent one — quick to think on her feet, bold, intelligent.

Martha drove slowly up Mr. Miyoshi's lane toward the county road, still hoping he would appear. In her rear-view mirror, instead of Old White, she saw an automobile speed around Mr. Miyoshi's barn. She edged over to the side of the lane to allow it to pass, but it pulled alongside.

"Afternoon, Mrs. Lundgren," Jimmie Ichikawa called out the open window. "Charlie an' me are late for football practice. Mr. Miyoshi's been showin' everyone how to grade and sack onions, when the high school boys an' girls from town come to help with harvest. It's Miss Reeve an' Mr. Bates's idea."

Charlie Hayes leaned over from behind the steering wheel and said, "Hello, Mrs. Lundgren. Sorry, we have to hurry."

Another car stopped behind Charlie. The driver leaned on his horn. Martha yelled to be heard. "Jimmie, wait! I just saw the Ogawas in one of the transports going to the camp. Do you know anything about it?"

His broad smile vanished, and he answered through clenched teeth. His voice dropped an octave. "Don't know anything 'bout the Ogawas, or that camp. Don't wanna know. They must a done somethin' wrong, or they wouldn't be put in there. How often do I have ta say I'm not Japanese? I'm American!"

He motioned to Charlie to drive on. Martha quickly rolled up her window to keep out the clouds of dust generated by the vehicles as they sped past.

Spilled Milk

She and Anna found Art on the milk stool in the barn. Anna lugged the big calico away from Beulah's udder, having determined the cat had enough treats. They cuddled in the straw. Anna stroked the cat, and the cat bathed herself.

Martha described the scene in town to Art and didn't leave out anything, even the gun, to emphasize the Ogawas' predicament and the brutality of their confinement.

Rather than reacting to her shock about seeing Mrs. Ogawa, Art zeroed in on the gun and Burleigh's roughness. "Martha, I swear, an' I've said this before, yer gonna get yerself in big trouble if yer not more careful. It didn't occur ta ya the MP might've shot ya, everyone bein' so nervous 'bout that camp an' the Japanese? He's prob'ly jus' another edgy kid like Alex. How was he ta know ya weren't some crazy woman causin' a ruckus? Or tryin' ta free those folks in the truck? Yer lucky Burleigh got ya an' Anna under control."

Martha was speechless. She struggled to see it from Art's viewpoint and was successful to the point of imagining the explosion of a shot aimed at her. So when the calico howled and Anna screamed, "She scratched me," Martha let out a scream, too.

The commotion was well beyond Beulah's tolerance level. She prematurely lifted her hoof, and Art, distracted, didn't grab the bucket in time. Milk splashed over his work boots, and he let forth with a string of obscenities — a short string, to be sure, but enough to bring both him and Martha to their senses. They directed their attention to Anna.

"Where did she scratch you, honey?" asked Martha.

The spilled milk and her parents' reactions sidetracked Anna, so she had to search for the small red specks of blood on the top of her hand. The cat howled again and writhed on the straw several feet away.

"Oh, she's jus' havin' 'er babies," said a relieved Art. "Martha, why don't ya an' Anna find 'er a box, put some rags in it, an' fix supper. I'll come tell ya when she's finished, an' we'll get 'em all settled. It'll take me that long ta calm Beulah down, finish milkin', an' clean up this mess."

He squatted over the cat, slid his large hands under her body, and carried her securely on her human-made stretcher to a far part of the barn. The calico had already delivered one small bundle that squirmed in the straw.

"Art, don't forget this one, her first kitten."

A search for rags wouldn't be easy, what with all the rag drives and Uncle Malcolm cleaning the dirty ones out of the barn as part of his fire crusade. She'd bequeath the cat several stained tea towels.

They didn't get back to a discussion of the Ogawas until supper.

"Go over ta Miyoshi's tonight," said Art. "He needs ta know. The two a ya can decide what steps ta take. Anna an' I won't expect ya till late."

They started clearing the table, and Martha said, "All I can think about is the Ogawas at the hospital, when Frank died, and how Rev. Macgill walked down the hall behind Doc Claffey, who gave them the news. Art, this is too cruel, to bring them back, under guard, and force them to relive the pain they thought they left behind."

Art had nothing to say, and they washed dishes in silence.

Finally Martha asked, "Did you know Earl and Fran are organizing high school students to help Mr. Miyoshi with the onions?"

"Yep, an' they've got more, as they call 'em, 'teams' ta help other farmers. Not just with onions. It's a good idea, don't ya think? We might get a team fer the corn, come October."

"It's marvelous. One of Earl's infrequent but pleasant surprises. Oh, let me tell you another surprise. Jimmie was leaving Mr. Miyoshi's, and I told him about the Ogawas and the camp. His reaction was so callous. It baffles me because Bennie Ogawa was his best friend. What do you make of it?"

"Don't know. Maybe Miyoshi can explain. Jimmie's young. Could be he don't understand what's goin' on."

Disbelief

By the next afternoon, few folks hadn't heard about the Ogawas, Japanese and white alike. The white families outright didn't believe it. The Japanese families were polite but thought Martha had mistaken someone else for Mrs. Ogawa. Most of them assumed the Ogawas had relocated months ago, before the forced evacuations, just as Mrs. Ichikawa's friend and family had moved from Sacramento to a Colorado farm on the other side of La Veta Pass in the San Luis Valley.

The outcome of that move made even the Greenwood newspaper. The father, a dentist with no farm experience, had stood in front of a team of horses straining to pull a wagon out of the mud. He tugged on the reins to encourage them, and the wagon dislodged with a jolt. He slipped and was crushed under the hooves of one of the horses. Voluntary or forced relocation, equally lethal.

Martha was flabbergasted that her visit to Mr. Miyoshi and some of the Japanese families hadn't started an investigation. As a last resort, she left Anna with Elena and went to discuss it privately with Lucy Hart, most recently Himuru, thinking Lucy, a white woman, could serve as an effective mediator between the administration of the camp and the Ogawas. Whites would trust her, and she knew that Lucy had maintained contact with the Ogawa family.

Over coffee at her kitchen table, Lucy told Martha she'd heard from Susie at Christmas, shortly after the Pearl Harbor attack, but nothing since. Susie had written that the Japanese minister at the church they attended had been held overnight for questioning, and the owner of a large Japanese fish market had disappeared, as had the priest at the Buddhist temple on the corner of the Ogawas' block. If the two men had been arrested, no one knew why, or where they were.

In spite of the mysterious disappearances Susie described in her letter, Lucy doubted such a bizarre thing would happen that the Ogawas would be interned in a location where, only three years before, they'd moved freely.

"Martha, you saw someone who resembled Mrs. Ogawa."

"But the woman turned her head when I called her name!"

The only difference between Lucy Hart and Jimmie Ichikawa with his steadfast refusal to discuss the camp at all was that Lucy extended the courtesy of listening. Meanwhile, there was every reason to think, from Bess Arnold's description of the camp's lack of readiness, the Ogawas were confined in a facility with no plumbing and little access to food.

"Martha, any woman would turn her head if someone approached the truck shouting out a name."

"No, because all the adults in the trucks kept their heads down, as if to hide their faces from public view. When I called out, they shrank further into themselves, all but that woman."

Martha's persistence half convinced Lucy there was some truth to her account, and Lucy agreed to go to the camp if accompanied.

When they tried to picture what a visit to a military zone would entail, both women were stymied, given Martha's experience with the MP and his gun. Martha telephoned Bess for guidance but was told Bess had moved to her new lodgings, and Martha didn't know how to reach her.

Sanctuary

Martha and Lucy drove into town to consult with Henry. The three of them sat in the church sanctuary, and Martha described the scene with Burleigh, the truck, Mrs. Ogawa and the guard. Lucy presented their plan to visit the camp.

While Lucy talked, Martha relived Frank's accident at the canal in '39, something she had done frequently in the past twenty-four hours. At first, she'd relived it as a remote event. Anna was barely two, and Carrie's birth a few years in the future.

But with each recollection, Martha's memory of Art bent over Frank's body in the back of Alex's pickup felt more immediate. That must be why Jamie Gilchrist's death haunted her so — Art's hair dripping over Frank as hers had dripped over Jamie's body in a truck bed.

She could have done more for Frank if she had gotten to the canal before Art, or if she had stood by the mailbox and forced Alex to stop. Then again, she had been of no help to Jamie Gilchrist.

If Frank hadn't died, the Ogawas wouldn't have moved to California, and they would be free. Their movements would be constrained, regardless of where they lived, their cameras and radios confiscated, along with their money, but they wouldn't be in a camp.

"Martha, Martha?" Henry said from the pew in front of her. He pulled a clean handkerchief out of his pocket and offered it. She must be crying. Lucy looked at her anxiously.

"I'm all right," she said and dabbed the tears off her cheeks. "It's just, I was comparing Frank's accident at the canal to the death of the young boy at the Lamberts' in the flood. So tragic, and we didn't save either of them."

The boys were dead, and they weren't even old enough to join the armed services. Children, just children.

Swede, dead. Papa and Uncle Malcolm nearly fatally wounded by farm equipment and snakes.

Surrounded by mayhem. How was anyone to survive? Hundreds of Czechoslovakians murdered on account of the assassination of one Nazi officer. Thousands killed or missing in the Philippine Islands. Millions of Jews slaughtered in Poland and the other captured countries. Families like the Ogawas imprisoned behind barbed wire at a camp, without adequate food and in barracks thrown up in a month's time, fleeing the site of their son's death only to be dragged back in the most inhumane manner.

She groped for the back of the pew in front of her where Henry sat, but the chasm between it and her widened. Somehow, Henry crossed the void. He sat by her. He took her hands in his and spoke sensibly.

"This is what I propose. The superintendent of the camp is speaking at the Lions Club tomorrow. You can imagine how distressing

Camp Amache is for everyone, located as it is under our very noses. I'll approach him with our suspicions that former residents are detained there. I've heard he's compassionate and working against all odds to make the camp livable. We might get results by going through him."

"Do you think they'll release the Ogawas? It's absurd to hold them in such a place."

"It's absurd to hold any of them. I doubt the Ogawas will get special treatment, but at least we'll know if they're in residence and what assistance we might give."

Martha tried to stand, but her knees nearly buckled. Henry took one arm, and Lucy, the other. By the time they reached the door, she had regained enough strength to support herself.

Henry had one more piece of advice. "While I value the Parable of the Good Samaritan and the way you're taking up the Ogawas' cause in that spirit, I believe we're most helpful when we're rested and have some perspective about what's required of us. You seem overwrought."

He never spoke to her in that patronizing manner, even the day Carrie died, when she was truly distraught. Surely she didn't resemble Edith Giffard, who hadn't even been capable of selecting her dress for the banquet.

Relief

There was nothing more to be done than wait for Henry's report. She arrived home in time to fix supper and walked into the kitchen to find Papa, Art, and Mr. Miyoshi at the table.

"Martha, you look tired," Papa said. "Sit down. We have some good news."

She expected Mr. Miyoshi to say they had word from the camp that Martha had, indeed, mistaken another woman for Mrs. Ogawa.

Instead, Papa spoke. "You just missed Art and Miyoshi's new hired hand, but I think you already know him. He'll be staying at Miyoshi's for the time being, if he can stand Miyoshi's cooking."

The three of them laughed; Martha struggled to recalibrate her emotions. As far as she was concerned, the only good news would concern the Ogawas, but finding a hired hand was, indeed, welcome. He'd be around for harvest.

She forced a smile. "You say I already know him? And I'd say he's a lucky man to eat Mr. Miyoshi's cooking."

"Go ahead, Robert. Tell 'er who he is. She'll never guess," said Art.

Martha was in no mood for their playfulness. Papa seemed to sense her irritation but wasn't forthcoming. "I have a better idea. He'll be at the Home Place for supper. Why don't you all come and we'll celebrate? Marguerite's helping Fran with the food, and we'll bring Rudy in early from chores. Give us thirty minutes. Art, don't you spill the beans."

Who could have so mysteriously appeared at just the right time? She couldn't even make an educated guess. Maybe Henry was correct that she was overly disturbed about the Ogawa business. *Our moods must not affect our efforts, after all.* A celebration would be the right corrective.

Anna ran into the kitchen from the dining room. "Did you meet the nice man, Mama? He's going to work for us!"

"Pumpkin, don't say another word," Papa cautioned. "We're going to surprise your mama. She'll see him when you all come for supper. If it's too hard to keep the secret, why don't you come with me right now?"

"Oh, it's way too hard, Grandpa. Let's go!"

When Martha walked into the dining room at the Home Place, Marguerite and Fran were rushing to put everything on the table, just as she, Josie, and Louise used to do. Place settings for ten, two more than for family gatherings before the war. Indeed, it seemed festive.

"I hear they're keeping this a secret from you," Fran said. "Have you guessed yet?"

"I don't have any idea. You seem to have swallowed the Cheshire cat, though."

"I'm forbidden to say a word. Let's get folks to the table."

They trickled in, Rudy and Uncle Malcolm from the porch, where they had washed up from doing chores, Marguerite from the kitchen, Fran and Papa, Art, Anna, and Mr. Miyoshi. Where was the mystery man?

All eyes turned to Martha––actually, to a point behind her. They must have hidden him in one of the bedrooms, but what hired man did they know that well? Martha turned.

With a self-conscious smile, he said, "Evenin', ma'am. They've cut back at the dam. Won't finish construction till after the war, so yer father asked…"

"Jake Reeve, this is wonderful news in so many ways. Welcome, and now you really must call me Martha."

September 1942

Max Lambert

Elsie Lambert walked into the kitchen and produced a letter from the bosom of her dress. In not quite a whisper, she said, "From Max. Came yesterday," and pressed it, damp with her perspiration, into Martha's hands.

"Elsie?"

"Just read it."

Martha sat down and unfolded the pages on the kitchen table. Elsie leaned over her shoulder.

August, 1942

Dear Mama and Papa,

I am sorry I have not written but I did not want to add to your worries because I was upset and moving from place to place. Now I live and work at a swell hostel called Scattergood. Quakers here in Iowa are helping Jews and other folks suffering from Hitler settle in our country. We treat them gentle-like, share the work, and make all decisions together, in the Quaker way. It helps them get back on their feet.

I cannot compare my troubles to theirs, but I was also in bad shape when I arrived. If you remember, the night before I left I had gone to Sister Irene's meeting where she explained to us boys how to be conscientious objectors. If you do not remember, she is from the Fellowship of Reconciliation in Denver.

Afterward, I ran into Walt and Ed. I was excited about Sister Irene's talk and told them I would be a conscientious objector. They called me a coward instead of understanding that I refuse to kill other men. They beat me, my own brothers-in-law! When Sister Irene came out the door, they jumped her, too.

The man who drove her from Denver and another Quaker named Jake, who works at the dam, heard the ruckus and scared them off. The Denver man brought me home, and Jake drove my truck. I did not tell them I knew the drunks who beat me. You were already in bed, which was good because I did not want you to know.

Martha was horrified by the Moulton brothers' misdirected violence toward Max and the innocent woman, but, knowing the outcome was positive, forced an unemotional response.

"Is he referring to Jake Reeve, Fran's brother?"

She didn't need confirmation. After what Jake and Fran went through, naturally he would be drawn to the Quakers, and he was thoroughly familiar with the destructive capabilities of men in drunken rages.

"Yes. A good man."

Martha read aloud so Elsie could follow her progress.

I decided to follow Sister Irene to Denver. Early the next morning I went to the barn to say goodbye to Ole Andy before

Papa came out, and Alex McLennan found me there. I did not know about the Pearl Harbor attack from the day before until Alex told me. Then I understood why my excitement about not fighting made the Moultons so upset.

Alex was asking boys to enlist and came to me first. I said I was a conscientious objector and told him I would not go to war. He did not understand, but he was not angry with me. He saw my black eye but not the other cuts and bruises. I told him only that Walt and Ed had roughed me up a little because they mistook me for a coward.

Elsie rested her hand on Martha's shoulder.

"Elsie, Alex told one person about Walter and Edgar — Elena — and she dropped a hint regarding an altercation to Josie and me, but we didn't know what to make of it. I thought if something serious had happened, you'd tell me."

"After Max disappeared and we knew he hadn't taken his truck because we saw you and Art driving it, Otto and I couldn't put it all together. Jake was scarce at meeting for a while, but when he returned he told us that hooligans beat Max the night of the Pearl Harbor attack and he brought Max home, but he didn't know Max's whereabouts. Otto and I guessed the Moultons were the culprits because they were more standoffish than usual, especially Addie. She doesn't think I understand her, but I know my daughter better than she knows herself. You escaped a bad marriage by choosing Art over Walt. Still, Walt might have been a better man with you."

Martha didn't disabuse Elsie about there being even a remote possibility of choosing between Walter and Art. She wouldn't have married Walter under any circumstance. Life with him would have been so…restricted.

The women read aloud, in unison:

*After Alex left, I put my things in a pillowslip, sold my truck
to Hank Philson for a good amount of money, but not as much
as I thought he would give me, and hitchhiked to Denver, to
Sister Irene.*

Martha shouldn't have been shocked that Hank had cheated Max
on the price after Josie's news about the grand jury investigation,
but how could Hank filch money from a boy in obvious distress,
physically beaten and in haste to make a deal?

"Hank stooped very low to take advantage of Max. You've heard
about him and the grand jury investigation?"

"Oh, yes. Al's fit to be tied. He's come by our place several times
to talk to Otto about the whole sordid business. As a commissioner,
Al sincerely wanted to build on Otto and Robert's groundwork for
the county, just in his way. But let's continue."

*I did not want you to know where I was on account of the
Moultons. Walt and Ed might force it out of you and come for me.*

"Do you think Max exaggerated the danger?" Martha asked,
which she wanted to retract the moment she said it since that was
something Papa had said she was prone to do.

"Yes and no. Max is a gentle boy. I don't know if he'd ever been
in a fight, and the Moulton brothers can be frightening, even when
they're not drunk. But because they attacked Sister Irene, Max might
have been afraid there'd be no limit to their savagery. We ourselves
didn't dare say anything because we couldn't be sure about what had
happened."

*I have had hard times and good, but now I mostly have
good times. I have met other boys who are conscientious*

objectors, and they say it will be rough. Most of us have registered. Some will serve as non-combatants, but I cannot bear the thought of being near the wounded and dying. I will probably be sent to one of the Civilian Public Service camps soon. Roosevelt wants to keep us away from everyone on account of our ideas but says we will do important work in the camps.

Quaker meetings must pay the government for the fellows' room and board, about $35 a month. Many of the meetings also give their boys spending money, maybe $2.50 monthly. I know this is a lot, but do you think our meeting will help me?

A Quaker man here says conscientious objectors are aliens in our own country. I know he is right from what I went through, beaten by my own family, but in camp I will be around men like me.

Love, your son Max

Elsie chuckled.

Martha saw nothing to laugh about, but Elsie said, "Just as any child does, he writes when he needs money. For a mother, that's as good a reason as any."

Edith Giffard would welcome most any reason to hear from Muriel, too. Martha stood and put her arms around Elsie to celebrate that Max was alive, but she didn't believe he would be safe in a camp. Doc Claffey had urged her and Art to put Carrie in the Children's Home so she could be with children "like her," but it wasn't safe for Carrie. Max's camp, and the Ogawas', served the same purpose as the Children's Home — to isolate inconvenient folks, probably why Ida and Vera were still at the State Hospital.

Anna ran into the kitchen and saw Elsie in Martha's arms. "Are you all right, Mrs. Lambert?"

"Oh, I'm feeling very fine today, and your mama's congratulating me because of it."

Anna scampered into her bedroom for her doll, only to disappear onto the back porch where Elena waited.

"Elsie, I've been so worried."

"If you, or anyone, had asked about Max, I would have broken down. That I couldn't allow, but the hailstorm brought me low, very low."

Elsie hadn't broken, but after the beating Max had, evidently overcome by emotions stronger than his hysteria the day Frank Ogawa died. Max had a tender heart, much like Uncle Malcolm, and she was glad like-minded folks were around him for guidance. But that didn't make it right to isolate him or all the Japanese from the West Coast.

In light of Elsie's amazing resolve not to succumb to her troubles, Martha re-evaluated Henry's rebuke in the church sanctuary that she pull herself together about the Ogawas and Camp Amache. He had been altogether too gentle. Dorothy Thompson's editorial admonition about not allowing moods to adversely affect efforts was absolutely correct. An overwrought woman wasn't of use to anyone.

Mrs. Alex McLennan

Martha and Elsie busied themselves with canning, and Henry came by in the late afternoon. He passed Elsie at the kitchen door as she left. "Blazes, it's hot in here. Is it always this way with canning? Judging from the bushel baskets of tomatoes on the porch, you'll be at it again tomorrow."

Martha wiped perspiration from her face and neck with the soiled tea towel. "We've been working all afternoon and haven't made a dent. Today, with every peach, I'm certain two more took its place. But I shouldn't complain. We thought we wouldn't get any. They had a dickens of a time shipping them from the western slope with so many transport trucks allocated for other purposes, probably hauling Japanese-Americans to relocation camps."

Elena's voice came from the porch. "Anna, set your basket there. I will put mine here."

She stepped into the kitchen, massaging the palms of her hands. "Rev. Behm, how nice to see you!"

Henry extended his hand in greeting. "And I'm happy to see you, Elena. Oh, my! What's wrong with your hand?"

Embarrassed, Elena quickly withdrew it. "Nothing, Rev. Behm. The dents are from the wire handles on the bushel basket. It happens when it is too full. I am used to it, and Anna and I did not want to make another trip. She had a full basket, too."

Martha could almost feel the pain from the deep creases in Elena's hands, as she had stubbornly carried heavy baskets for the same reason many times.

Elena's attempt at deflection worked; Henry turned toward Anna and asked, "May I see what you picked?"

Anna was only too proud to show him, and they went to the porch. Martha suspected Henry was looking for an escape from the hot kitchen, which also appealed to her. If he had news of the Ogawas, she would rather hear it outside on the swing.

Elena brought her purse in from the dining room and set it on the edge of the kitchen table. "Mr. Malcolm is waiting outside to take me home, but I must wash up."

Martha stepped onto the porch and helped pump water. She saw the pink runoff in the basin. "Elena, show me your hands."

The wires hadn't only indented Elena's palms. They'd inflicted several cuts.

"I'll put Mercurochrome on those before you leave."

"No, thank you, Mrs. Lundgren. I do not want Mr. Malcolm to wait any longer. He hopes to go to the dance at Eagle View School tonight and has persuaded Mr. Jake to go with him. They say the band is good and people from up and down the Valley will attend."

Quite an adventure for a former recluse and a shy Quaker.

"It won't take a minute, and he'll want me to do it."

Martha retrieved the bottle from the kitchen cabinet and heard Anna and Henry sympathizing over the cuts. Mortified by all the fuss, Elena hurried out to the truck the moment Martha finished applying the medicine.

She saw Elena's purse and yelled for Henry to stop her. Martha snatched it off the table, but it slipped from her hands. The contents scattered. Henry reappeared, and they hastily scooped up everything, save a letter that slid under the table. Martha reached for it first.

She had no interest in Elena's personal business, but the letter landed face up. And because Martha was on her hands and knees and had to slide it out, she noted the USO envelope. She surmised it was from Luis, Elena's brother, but the return address was Alex's and the handwriting unmistakably his. It was addressed to Mrs. Alex McLennan at a post office box.

Martha sat back on her heels and stared at the letter. Henry gently took it and slid it into Elena's purse.

"Do you know about this?" she asked.

"Yes." He didn't offer an explanation and waited for her to say more.

"Henry, please take Elena's purse to her."

Martha's pulse throbbed in her temples. She made her way outside, gulped in the cool air, and flopped down on the swing. She saw Henry hand Elena the purse, speak briefly to her, and Elena slowly emerge from the truck.

Alex had always supported Elena, Martha presumed out of his generous nature, but even Anna had pointed out some time ago that Elena was Alex's best friend. It was just…the thought of Alex marrying a Spanish girl had never entered her mind. There was nothing objectionable about Elena, but…

"Mrs. Lundgren?"

Martha patted the wooden slats as an invitation to sit. She was relieved that Elena didn't apologize. That wouldn't do. Elena had to live with the consequences of her marriage. For a girl who never wanted to call attention to herself, Elena had made a disastrous mistake.

Martha attempted an unbiased tone, almost lighthearted. "Elena, if you persist in addressing me as Mrs. Lundgren, I should call you Mrs. McLennan. That would be rather formal day in and day out, don't you think? I prefer Martha and Elena. After all, Alex has made us sisters-in-law."

A thought not fully formed until the words left her mouth. Even then, she couldn't absorb it. How long had they been married? Was it before or after the curious conversation in Max's Truck on the way to Andy's Café about the Himurus' name change to Hart and the potential for new names for married women to alter how they think of themselves?

"Elena, you must know this is a shock or one of you would have said something."

"Mrs. Lundgren, uh, Martha…"

Elena's immediate implementation of the first-name address jarred Martha's sensibilities.

"Alex and I have talked many times about how we will announce it, but we always thought we would do it together. Will you be telling everyone?"

"No, Elena. This is for you and Alex to communicate, as the two of you decide. I do need to talk to Mr. Lundgren, I mean, Art, just to have someone help me think it through, and perhaps we should continue to address one another in public as we always have or folks will be curious."

She lightly set her hand on Elena's arm. "Uncle Malcolm's waiting. You and I'll have other conversations about this, but I'll tell only Art and wait to hear what you and Alex decide."

Before she followed Martha's cue to leave, Elena said, "I am surprised you are not happy for me, for us. Surely you suspected, after all these months, after seeing how hard I work for your family, for our family."

Before Martha could think what to say, Elena stood and walked back to the truck, proudly — one could say defiantly. Henry came from where he was leaning against the fender and took Elena's place on the swing.

"I'm numb," Martha said. "I'm just numb. I've never dealt with something like this. I like Elena and obviously trust her, even with my only child, but to have her as a member of the family is…"

"I confess. I performed the ceremony. They're very much in love. Of course I would say that; otherwise, I wouldn't have married them. What I mean is, they treat one another tenderly, respectfully."

"She is a sweet girl, always composed."

Except for when Elena had seen Doc Claffey insert the forceps to deliver Carrie and screamed for him to stop, a gesture of compassion that cost Elena her job.

Forcing herself to match Henry's positive evaluation, Martha added, "Elena's a good complement for the devil-may-care Alex. I should be happy for him. For them. Who were the witnesses?"

"Zella and Malcolm."

That Zella would be a witness was logical. The minister's wife could be expected to fill such a role and keep confidence. But Uncle Malcolm?

"Why him?"

"Alex wanted someone from the family. Your father was in the hospital recovering from the amputation, although I doubt Alex would have asked. Malcolm, on the other hand, refrains from judgment. Alex and Elena are very afraid no one will approve, from either family."

"If that's the case, why did they marry?"

"Why do any of us marry?"

Martha dismissed his question with a shrug. "Why did you consent to perform the ceremony, knowing how difficult this will be for them? Knowing the impossible lives their half-breed children will live?"

"Half-breed children? Martha!"

Henry wasn't being fair, or he had no idea how difficult life was for children like Ken and Lily Himuru, now Hart, and she didn't know if she would feel enthusiasm for Alex's children, as she had when Earl placed Robbie in her arms. Martha stirred herself.

"Anna! Where's Anna?"

"I saw Art come in from the field, and she went with him to the barn."

Martha settled back and pushed against the dirt with her feet. For several minutes, she and Henry sat quietly, rocking. The rhythm corresponded with Martha's breathing — in and out, back and forth — and it soothed her.

The Santa Anita Race Track

Finally Henry said, "I should tell you tomorrow what I've learned about the Ogawas. You have enough to think about tonight."

"No, no. Tell me. The wait has worn me down."

"It's not that simple."

"I don't understand."

"They are at the camp, the Ogawas, and his brother and family. I visited them in their barracks rooms. As you can imagine, it's very hot during the day. No shade trees, naturally, with all the construction and the camp's location on the open prairie. Barren outside, and in."

"Pure air and searing wind."

"What?"

"Nothing. Just an expression for the supposed cleansing properties of the Great Plains."

"Each one was allowed a single suitcase."

"So they left the rest of their belongings in California?"

"No, they were told to dispose of it all. They didn't say, but I'm sure they had to sell everything at much less than its value."

As Hank had cheated Max on the sale of his truck.

"So all they have is what they brought in their suitcases?"

"They weren't concerned with possessions. The difficulty was Mr. Ogawa's mother."

"Oh?"

"She had a paralytic stroke several weeks ago."

"Goodness! So she stayed in California?"

"No, they were required to bring her. She would have been lying in the truck when you saw them approach from the train station."

"And where is she now? Do they have medical facilities at the camp?"

"They do, and it will be well staffed and equipped, from what the superintendent says. Many of the residents have excellent credentials. But Mr. Ogawa's mother died two days after they reached the camp."

"Oh, no!"

"They are of the opinion that the grief of losing everything, the stress of the months at the Santa Anita Race Track, and the strain of travel led to the stroke and death."

"Race track?"

"Yes, that's where they were forced to live, in the horses' stalls, after they were evacuated in May and until the camps were ready."

"This is unthinkable!"

"Yes, for them and everyone at the camp."

"Why didn't they contact Mr. Miyoshi when they arrived? Or when Mr. Ogawa's mother died. He would have wanted to know!"

The swing continued its motion for several cycles before Henry said, "With all the disruption, I doubt they're thinking much beyond surviving the moment. I also have the impression they're very ashamed to be back under these circumstances. Martha, when cold weather comes, living there will be even more hellish. That wind you speak of will sweep through the barracks, but at temperatures below zero. I could see blue sky between the walls and roof. Your barn offers your animals more protection."

She saw Art, milk buckets in hand, emerge from the barn and heard him say, "Anna, take the kitty back to its box while I carry the milk into the cellar to mix with the chicken mash. She's too little to be away from her mama."

The barn did offer more protection, and the calico cat and her kittens had an overabundance of food and affection. But next month the kittens would be weaned and romping about, prey for the barn owl. They were outside cats and would have to fend for themselves. Just as Max was learning to survive, just as Elena and Alex must in their encounter with a hostile world.

But obstacles to the Ogawas' survival in their raw circumstances were much more daunting. Two of them already dead, a son and a mother.

From Max to Elena to the Ogawas and back again, thoughts all jumbled. Martha wouldn't be flummoxed in the same way if Alex had married Eleanor Moulton, and she had no respect for the Moultons. However, she had high regard for the Marquez family, and Elena was so much more likable than Eleanor.

But the Ogawas' circumstances demanded immediate attention.

"Henry, will you stay for supper? Elsie fried up bacon before she left, while the stove was still hot, so I'm slicing some tomatoes and we'll have sandwiches, and fresh peaches, of course. Won't take a minute."

"You mean, what I felt when I stepped into the kitchen was 'cool'? That coal stove'll radiate heat all night. How will you sleep?"

"We'll start Anna in our bed and move her to the sofa when we turn in. Cool air moves through the west windows and our bedroom after sunset. We'll eat in the dining room where it's not so hot. Please stay. I need your advice about the Ogawas, as well as Elena and Alex. And you'll be interested to learn what's happened to Max Lambert."

As if summoned by Martha's words, a breeze rustled the leaves on the cottonwood trees that held up the swing.

"Certainly I'll stay, but I have to get back to town right after supper. Martha, you understand, don't you, that discussing these situations might help us come to terms with them, but we won't alter what's been set in motion."

Dread

While they ate, Martha and Henry told Art about the Ogawas and the camp. Each time they paused for Art's reaction, he simply shook his head. Martha wanted more.

Anna, single-mindedly focused on eating, finished and was excused to settle on the floor in front of the radio with the Tinkertoys Uncle Alex had "loaned" her while he was away.

"What are you thinking about the camp, Art?" asked Martha.

"It's not thinkin' I'm doin.'"

"That doesn't make sense."

"What you've told me 'bout the Ogawas, 'bout the camp, fills my head ta overflowin.' I thought the camp was wrong from when I first heard 'bout it but never imagined it would be this bad. I can say better what I feel. Sad. No. Dread. I almost can't breathe for the dark cloud that's settled on the land. It won't lift till that camp's gone, till all those folks get their lives back. We done a terrible thing, a terrible thing."

Art's cloud was as vivid in Martha's mind's eye as La Llorona wailing for her lost children at the head gate by the camp. "How can you say 'we,' Art? We didn't build that camp."

"Not with our own hands, but our gov'ment did. I'm sure President Roosevelt thinks it's a necessary part a fightin' the war, an' the public agrees, but he don't know the Japanese in this country. They're jus' families, Martha, like the Ogawas. An' here we have Jimmie Ichikawa on one side a the fence an' Bennie, a boy he buddied with, on t'other. Don't make no sense."

She still needed to explain about Max, from the same cohort of friends, who was headed to another confinement Roosevelt thought necessary for fighting the war.

"Jimmie an' Bennie, Frank an' Alex. One of 'em already dead, one imprisoned in that camp, an' Alex a soldier. Ta think. Three years ago they was just boys goin' fer a swim in the canal. We ain't got a letter from Alex in a while. Have ya been writin' 'im?"

"Only twice since Papa came home from the hospital. Haven't had time. Josie writes regularly, and also to Louise. Elena helped Anna write Alex a letter about Uncle Malcolm's encounter with the rattler."

Of course she did. Martha had missed every sign when it came to Elena and Alex. Martha wasn't up to telling Art they were married, certainly not with the tenderness Henry would muster.

"Art, we still have a lot to talk about while Henry's here, but why don't I run over to the Country Store for some ice cream? It'll taste so good on the peach slices and cool everyone off. It won't be our favorite, homemade…"

Almost a year ago she, Art, and Carrie snuck spoonfuls of fresh peach ice cream straight out of the canister before Robbie's welcoming party. She forced herself to control her voice and continued. "And I need to clear my head."

"By drivin' over ta the store? Won't it be closed? And we don't want ta keep Henry longer. Plus, it's one a those spur a the moment trips we said we wouldn't make ta save gasoline an' wear on tires."

"I know, but I have to get out of this house after canning all afternoon. I'll be back in twenty minutes. There's a dance tonight at Eagle View. Effie and Pete Collins always stay open when there's a Friday crowd at the school because folks do double purpose with their driving. They'll shop for groceries or a cold soda pop and go to the dance. Elena said even Uncle Malcolm and Jake are going."

"Art, Martha should go. Sometimes a drive straightens out one's thoughts, which I think she'll benefit from, especially tonight. Let's sit out on the swing for a smoke. Twenty minutes won't make a difference for me. Martha, do you want me to tell Art the other news?"

"Yes, I prefer you tell him, Henry."

She splashed cold water on her face from the pump, glanced in the mirror over the basin and straightened her hair, and walked out into the cool air.

"Do ya have money?" Art called from the swing.

"There's change in Max's Truck."

Ambush

Vehicles filled the open area in front of the school on her right, and the overflow spilled into the Country Store lot across the highway, as it had at the Halloween dance last year. Martha slowed and looked for a space in front of the store.

The lights of an automobile speeding around Collins Curve behind her illuminated the cab of Max's Truck. Brakes screeched, and the driver leaned on his horn. She saw an opening, signaled with her left arm straight out the window, and pulled in. The offended driver continued to honk as he passed.

She heard Jimmie Ichikawa call out. "You okay, Mrs. Lundgren? You sure upset that driver."

"He sped around the curve and didn't notice I'd slowed, in spite of not hooding his headlights," Martha replied, a bit shaken. "I'm more upset than he is, but I didn't make as much noise!"

She meant the last part as humor, and they laughed.

"Mr. Miyoshi brought me for a soda pop. We just finished repairin' the onion shed."

He turned to go, but Martha called out, "Jimmie, Rev. Behm went to the camp. The Ogawas are there. Bennie is back."

Jimmie didn't stop and snarled over his shoulder, "I already told you I got nothin' to do with that camp. The second I graduate, I'm joinin' the army to defend my country."

He ran back between the vehicles.

Jimmie should have been sympathetic about Bennie's confinement. Bennie was probably just as frantic to distinguish himself as patriotic, maybe more so, given his predicament. The only difference between the two boys was which side of the barbed wire they inhabited.

Very little light escaped along the edges of the blackout shades drawn over the store windows, and the door was open just a crack. She couldn't distinguish the features of the men scattered throughout the lot. Some sat on the running boards of their vehicles. Others leaned against their trucks. One raised a bottle to his lips, and it wasn't soda pop. She hurried to the front door.

"Martha, how've you been?" Effie asked.

It would take hours to tell her. Evidently she didn't know yet about Max or she would have spoken of it immediately.

"Hot and tired from canning. Came to buy ice cream before Anna goes to bed. Rev. Behm stopped by for supper. They're all waiting. Have to talk another time."

She moved down the narrow aisles to put word into action and snatched the vanilla ice cream from the freezer.

She set it on the counter in front of Effie. "Oh, I forgot my money in the truck because when I was turning in, a driver came up so fast from behind I thought I was a goner."

She wound through the vehicles to Max's Truck parked up by the highway. The lights from a passing car shone on a nearby cluster of men and revealed Walter Moulton handing Edgar a bottle. She opened the door and felt for the loose change in the dashboard pocket. Hearing loud, angry voices coming from the center of the lot, she quickly gathered the coins. She gave the argument wide berth on her walk back.

Effie rang up the sale. At the sound of breaking glass, followed by shouts, both women ran to the door. Men rushed toward the noise.

"They're not from the camp. Let 'em go!" Uncle Malcolm yelled.

Jimmie must have caught someone's attention when he ran over to check on her.

The thud of a body, or something, against a truck, spurred her to move. She sped through the gaps between the parked vehicles and tried to locate the fight as her eyes adjusted to the dark.

"He's a farmer up the road," Jimmie shrieked. "We're not from the camp."

She placed where Jimmie's voice originated and thought she saw a man punch him in the stomach. A blow with that force would cause anyone to collapse, but Jimmie stayed upright. Although the shadows played tricks with her eyes, Martha could just make out that someone was holding him from behind, pinning his arms back.

A voice snarled, "Shut up, ya yella-bellied bastard!"

Uncle Malcolm pled, "No, if you hit 'im again, you'll kill 'im!"

A figure brandished a two-by-four in front of Jimmie. Martha dashed toward the spot, but just before she reached it, she stumbled and nearly fell over a body lying on the ground.

"Mr. Miyoshi!" she screamed.

The board smashed down on her back.

When she came to, her head was cradled in someone's lap. She strained to look up and saw Effie. A spasm seized her entire torso. She would have cried in pain, but her lungs seemed empty of air.

Uncle Malcolm's voice came from the darkness on her right. "She's alive! She's alive!"

She struggled to move, but Effie said, "Stay still, Martha. Enoch's comin' with the ambulance. We've telephoned Art."

"Out a my way!" Burleigh shouted. "You say she saved Miyoshi when that fella over there took after him with the two-by-four?"

A chorus of voices answered in agreement.

"And what's this about a corpse? Damn blackouts. Everyone, turn on your headlights!"

"Here, by Martha," Jake answered. "Saved 'er life when he saw that the fella swingin' the two-by-four was too strong fer me. Put his self 'tween her an' the board when he swung it a third time."

Several men reached down to turn the body. Martha fought nausea and vertigo.

"I'll be damned," Burleigh said. "It's Walt Moulton. I'd say the board caught 'im d'rectly on the head."

The void originated below the parking lot and widened with a speed unmatched by prior advances. No longer silent, its roar devoured the air. Martha grabbed for Effie's skirt, but missed. Effie caught the errant hand just as Martha's feet disappeared into the hole, but the moment Effie adjusted Martha's head against her massive breasts, the expanse collapsed.

"Martha, Enoch's here with the stretcher," she heard Art say. "Doc'll meet us at the hospital. Henry's headed there now, with Anna, Robert, an' Fran. Jimmie an' Miyoshi'll go with ya in the am'blance. They ain't doin' so good, neither."

She felt his lips on her forehead. He didn't seem to know about Walter.

"Ya shouldn't a got mixed up in this. Yer so danged stubborn, but so am I. 'Tween us, we'll get through it."

Art was wrong. Loyalty prompted her dash across the parking lot, not stubbornness. In any case, the threat of death demanded action, as even Walter knew.